THE SAD GHOST CLUB

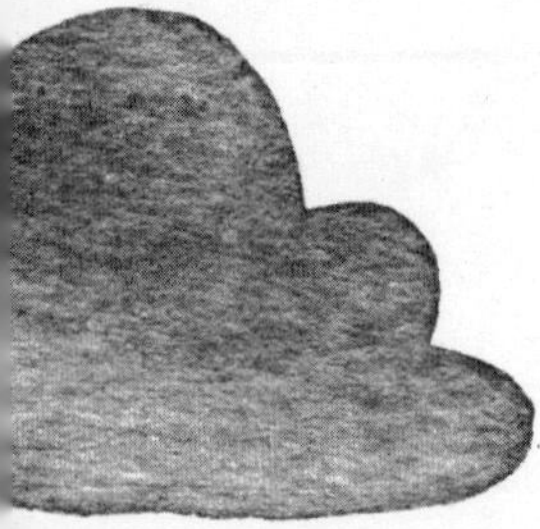
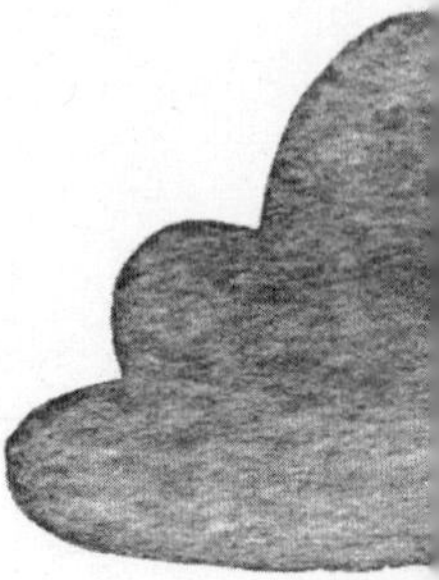
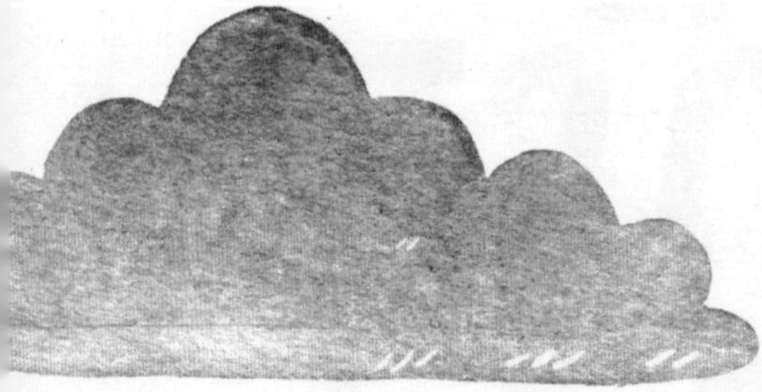
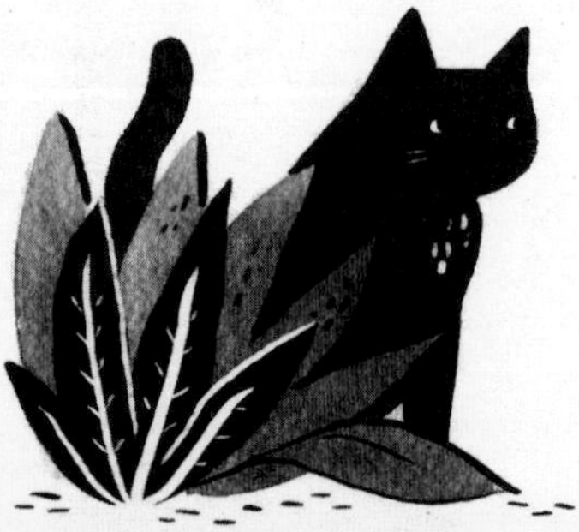

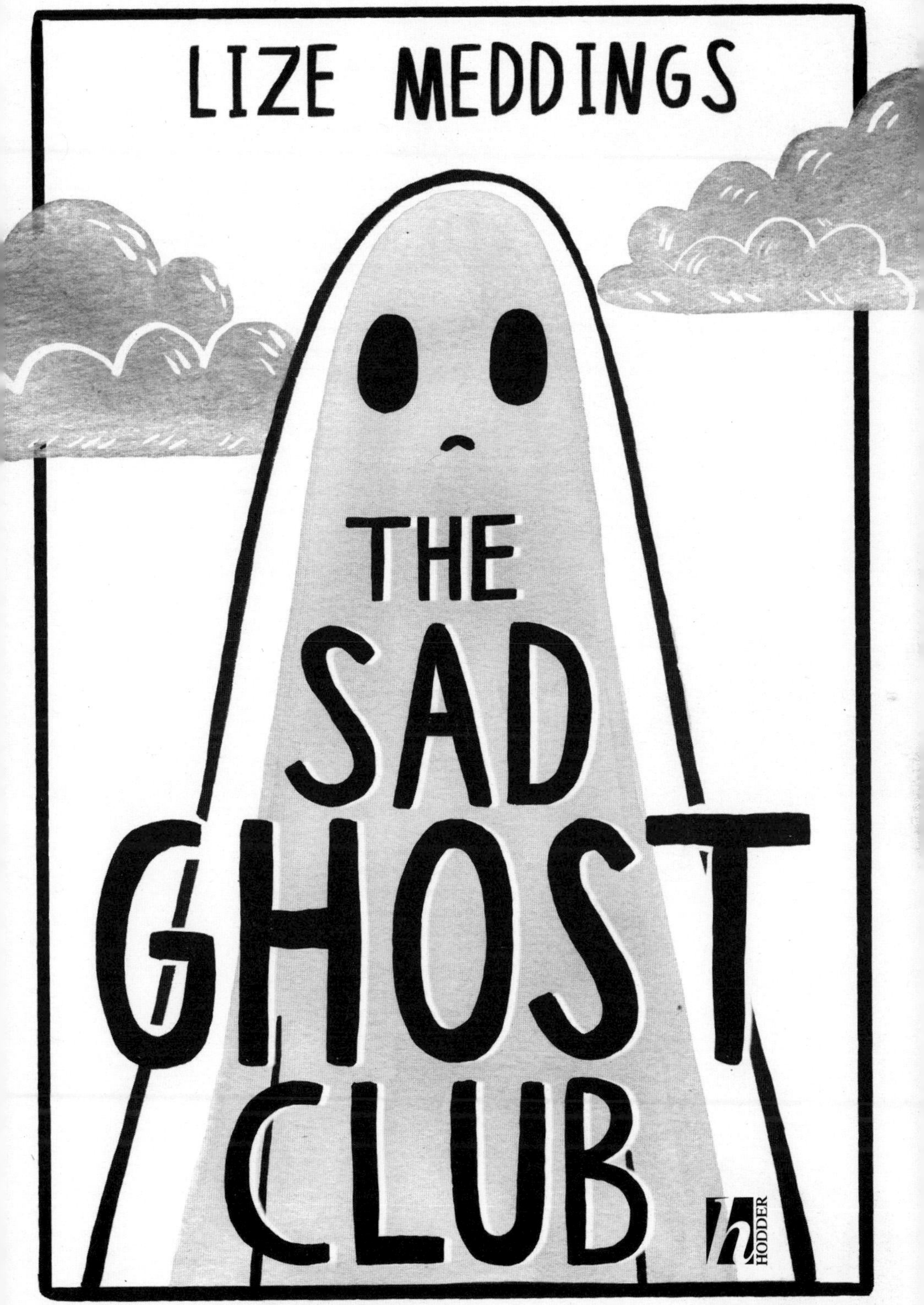
LIZE MEDDINGS
THE SAD GHOST CLUB
HODDER

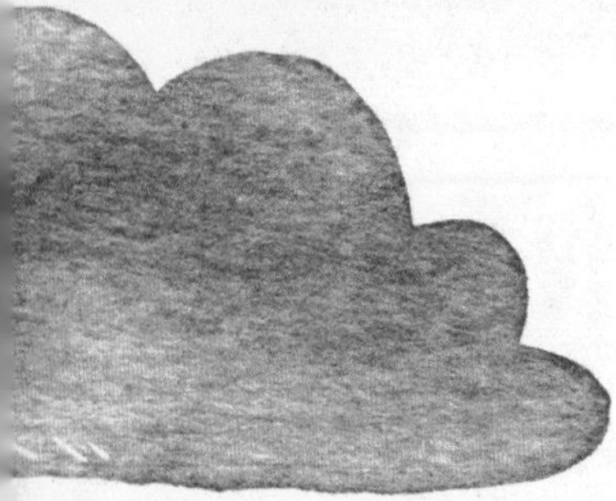

HODDER CHILDREN'S BOOKS

First published in Great Britain in 2021
by Hodder & Stoughton Limited

1 3 5 7 9 10 8 6 4 2

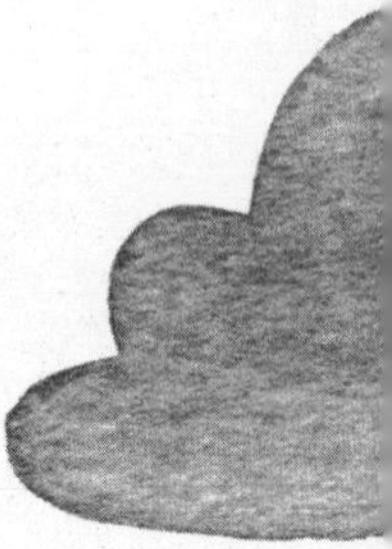

A CIP catalogue record for this book is available from the British Library.

ISBN 978 1 444 95735 8

Printed and bound in Great Britain by Clays Ltd, Elcograf S.p.A.

The paper and board used in this book are made from wood from responsible sources.

FSC www.fsc.org MIX Paper from responsible sources FSC® C104740

Hodder Children's Books
An imprint of
Hachette Children's Group
Part of Hodder & Stoughton
Carmelite House
50 Victoria Embankment
London EC4Y 0DZ

An Hachette UK Company
www.hachette.co.uk
www.hachettechildrens.co.uk

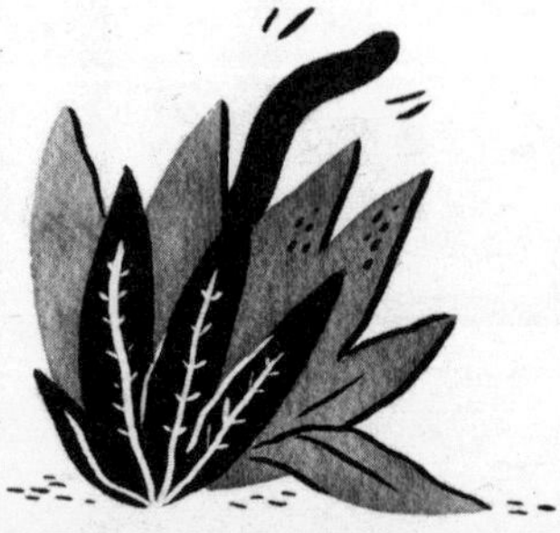

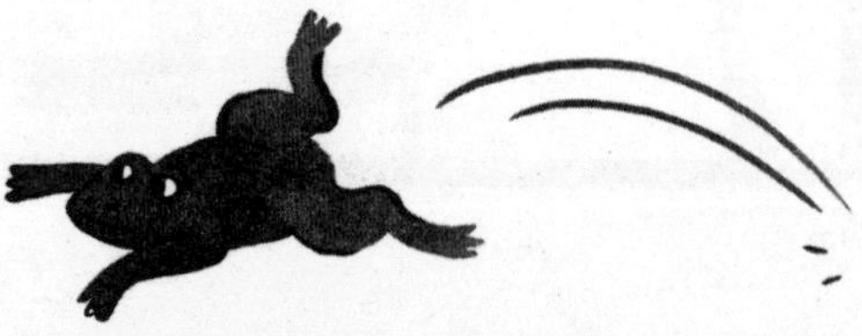

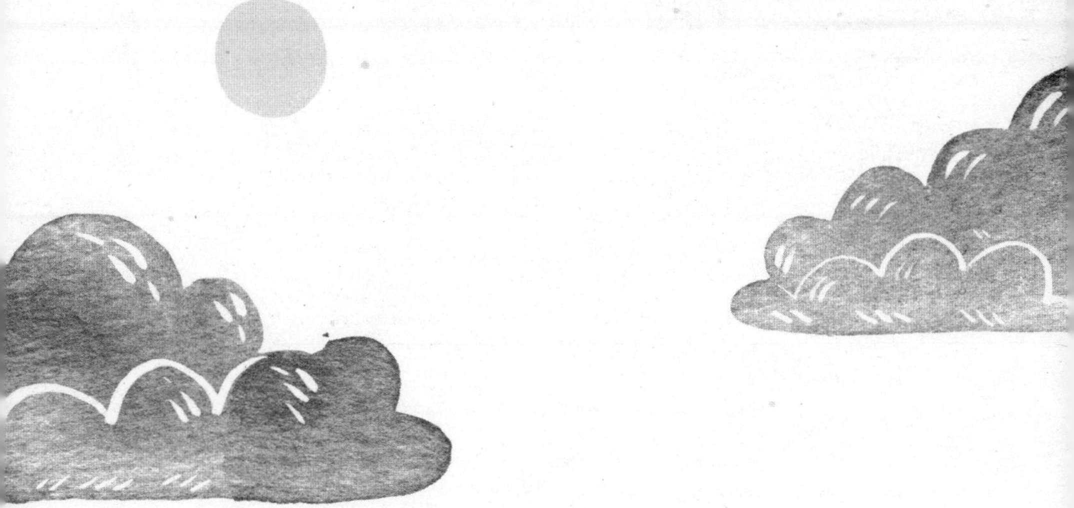

FOR ANYONE WHO'S EVER FELT
LIKE A SAD GHOST.

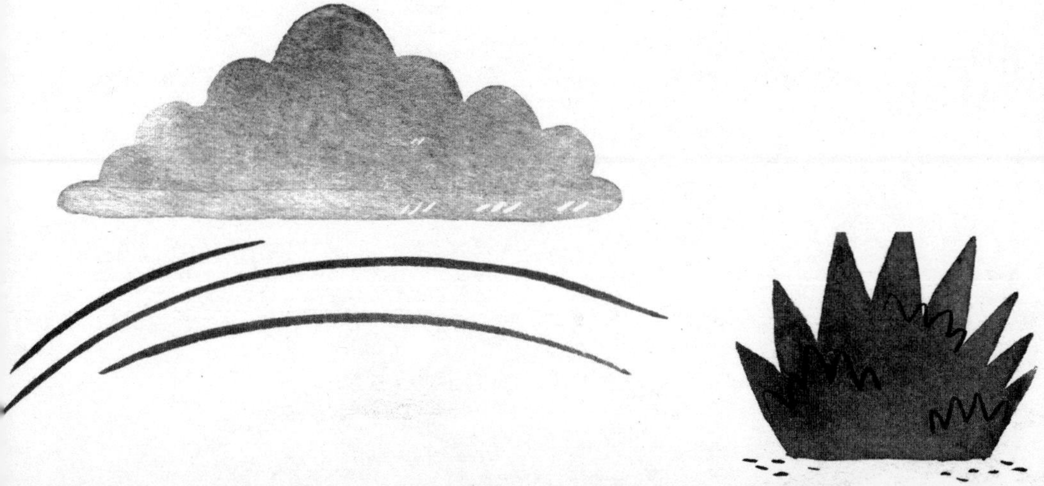

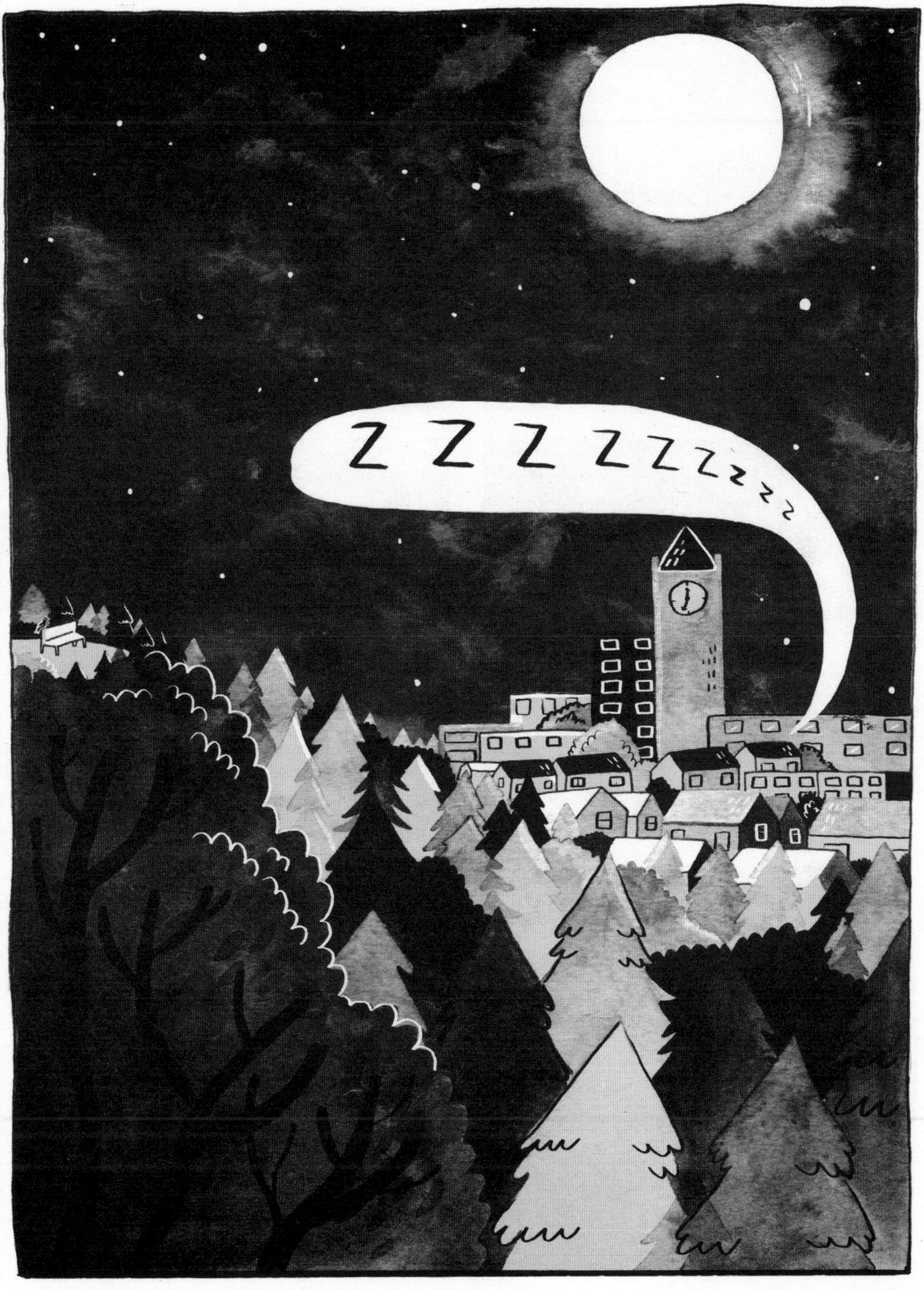
Z Z Z ZZZzzzz

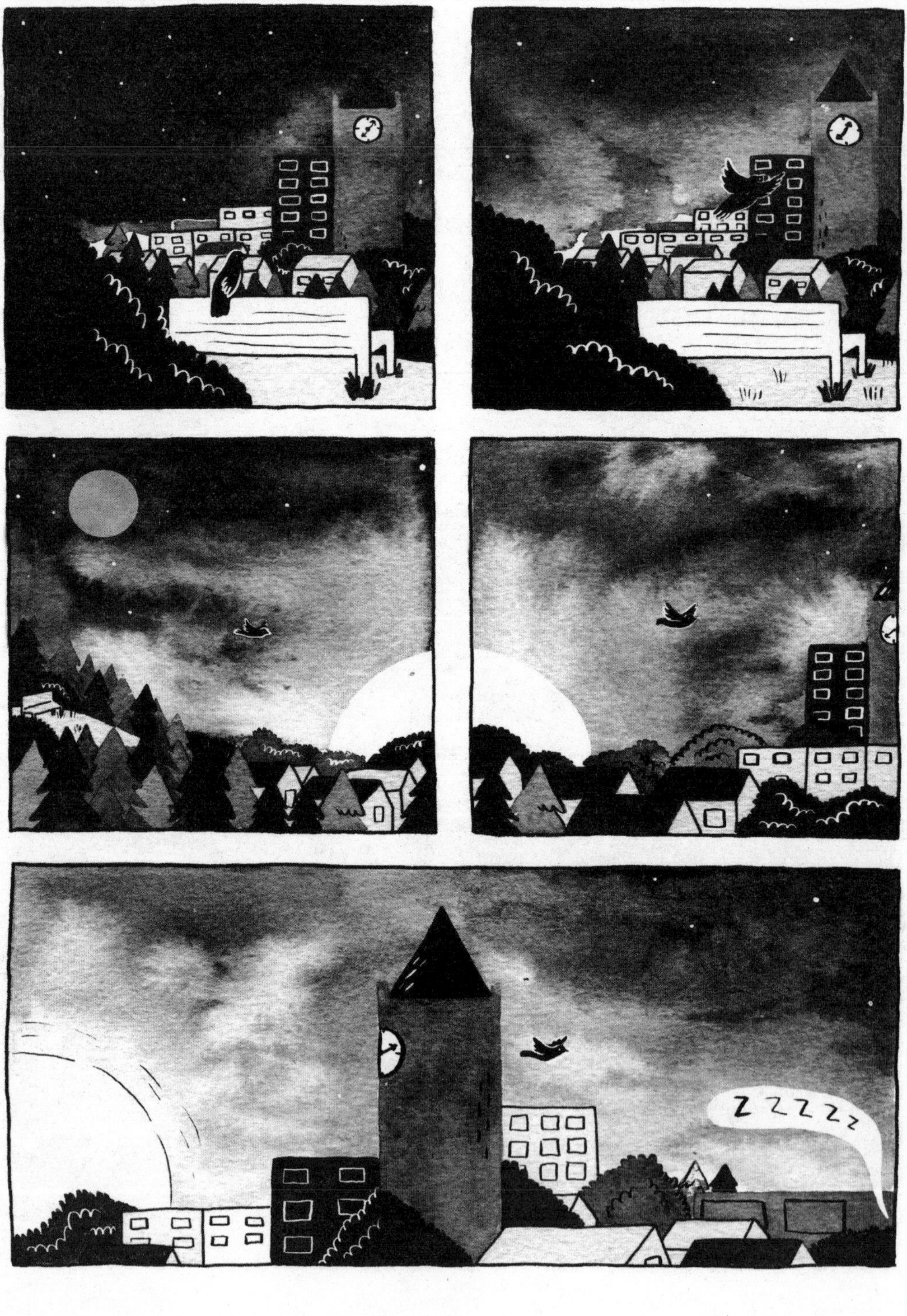
Z Z Z Z Z

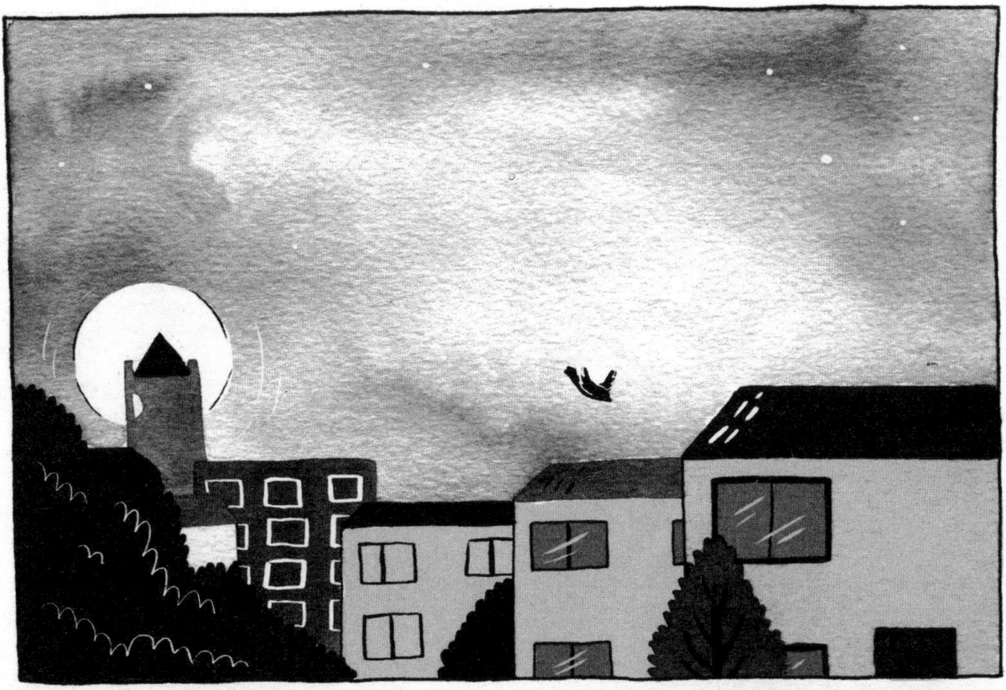

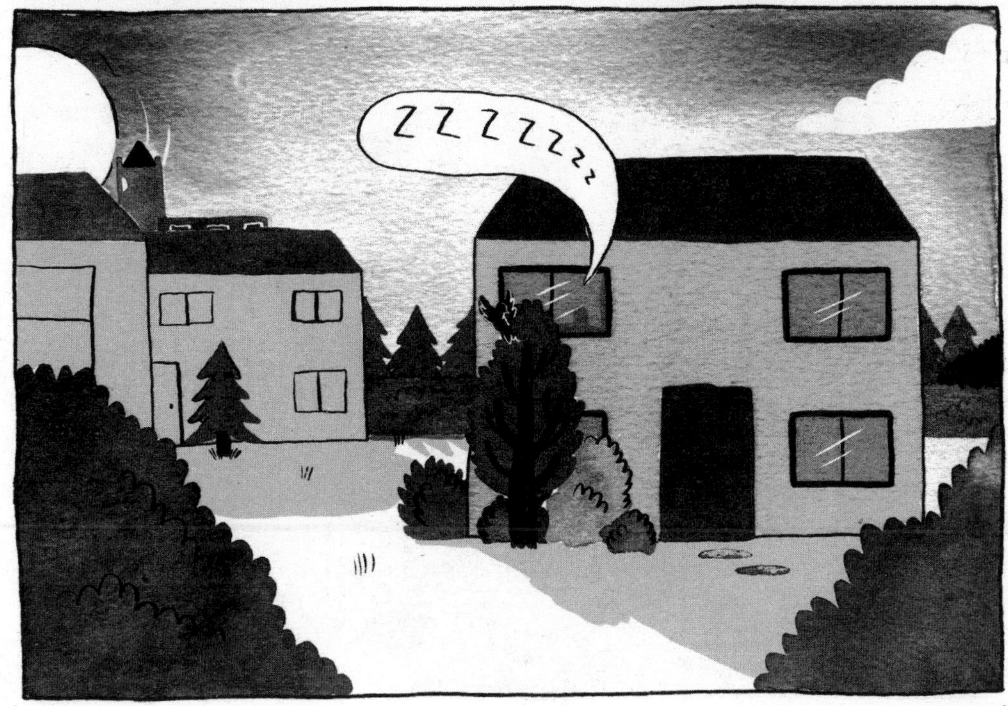
ZZZZZZzz

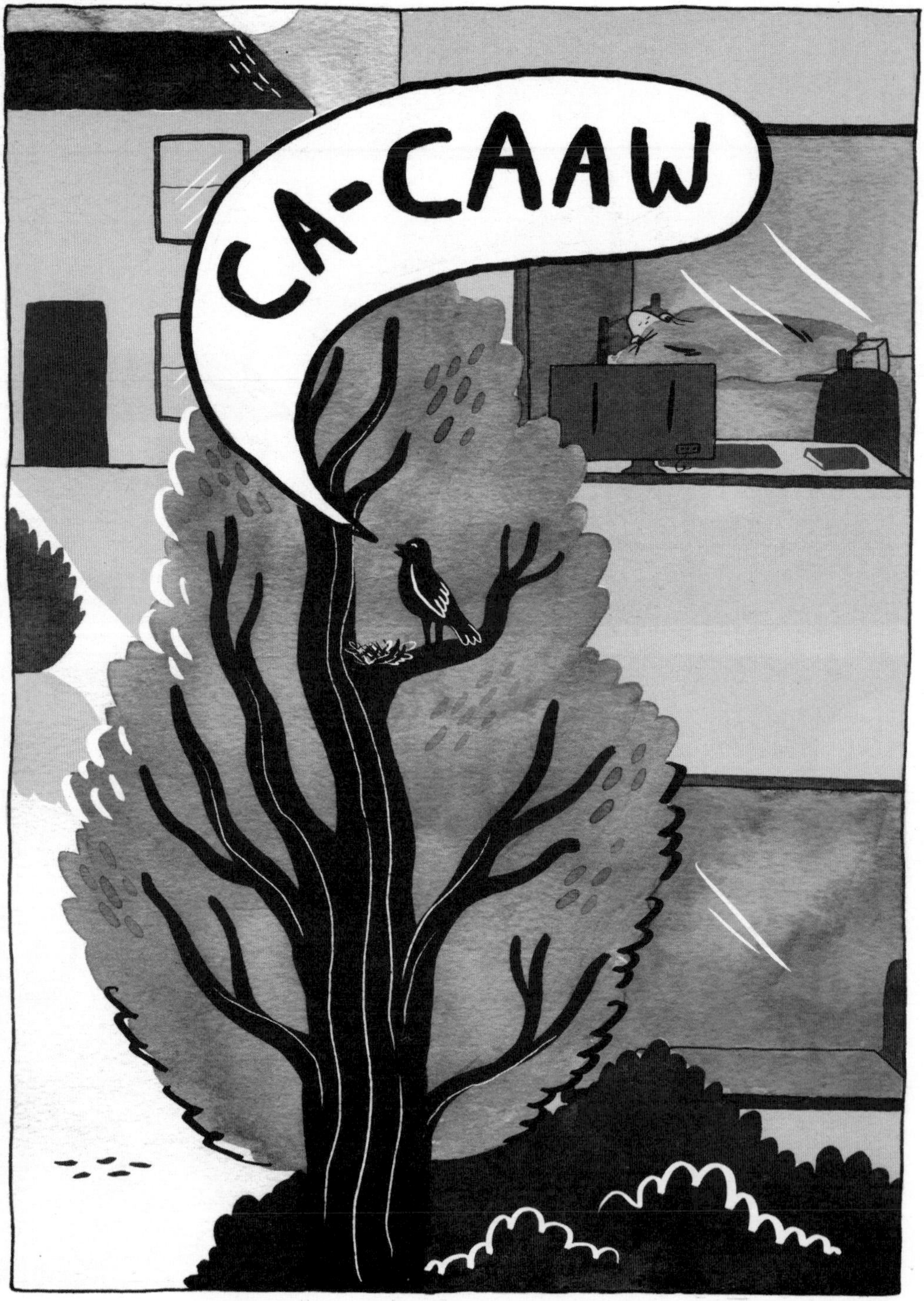
CA-CAAW

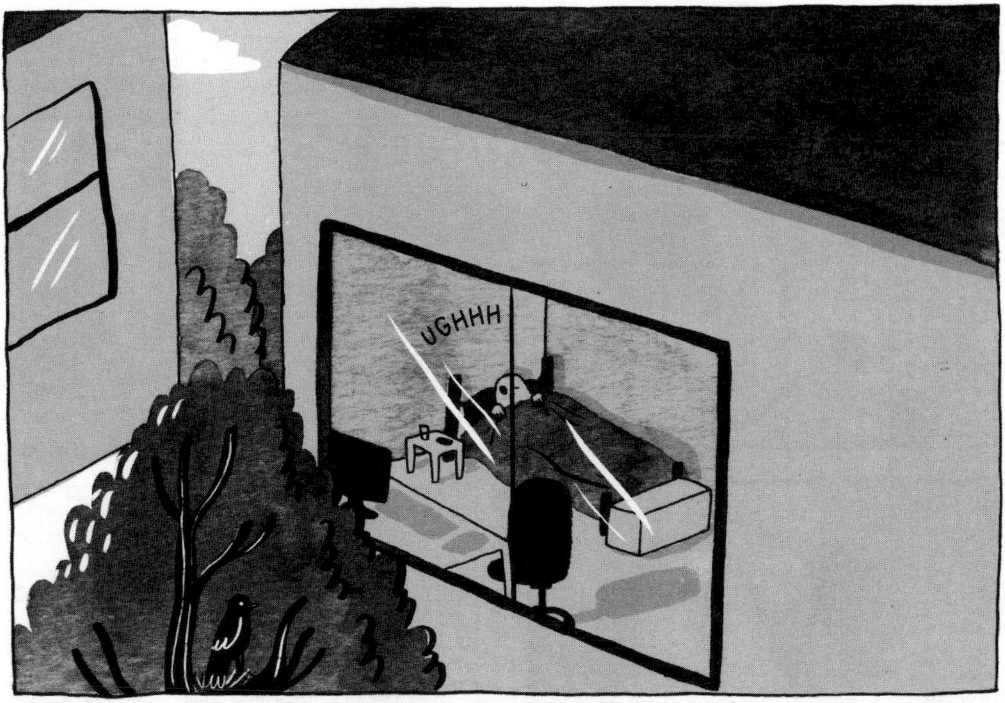
UGHHH

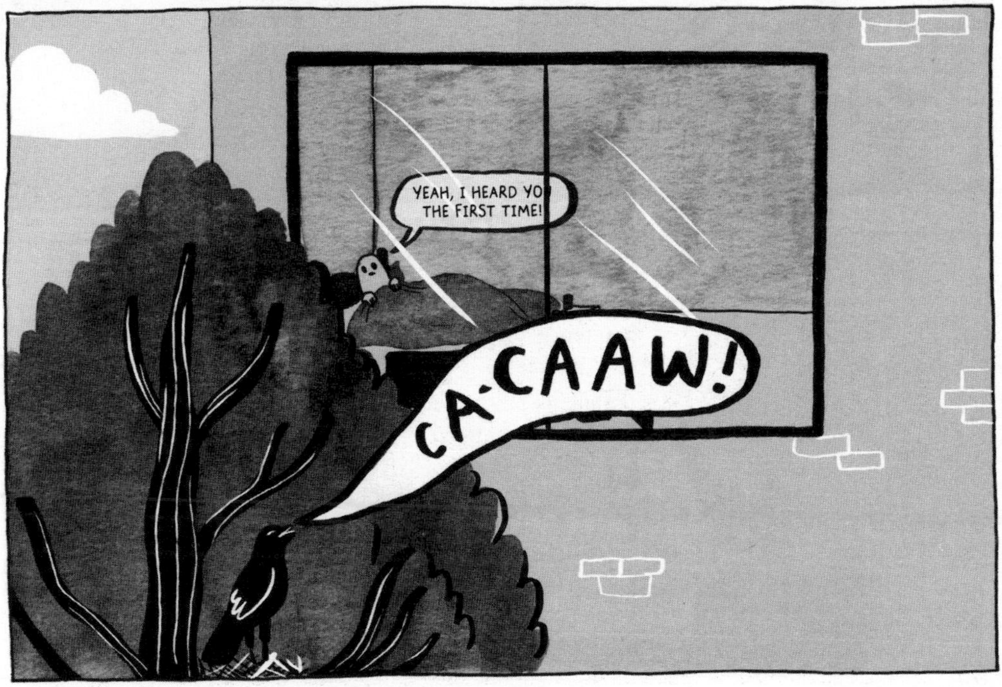
YEAH, I HEARD YOU THE FIRST TIME!
CA-CAAW!

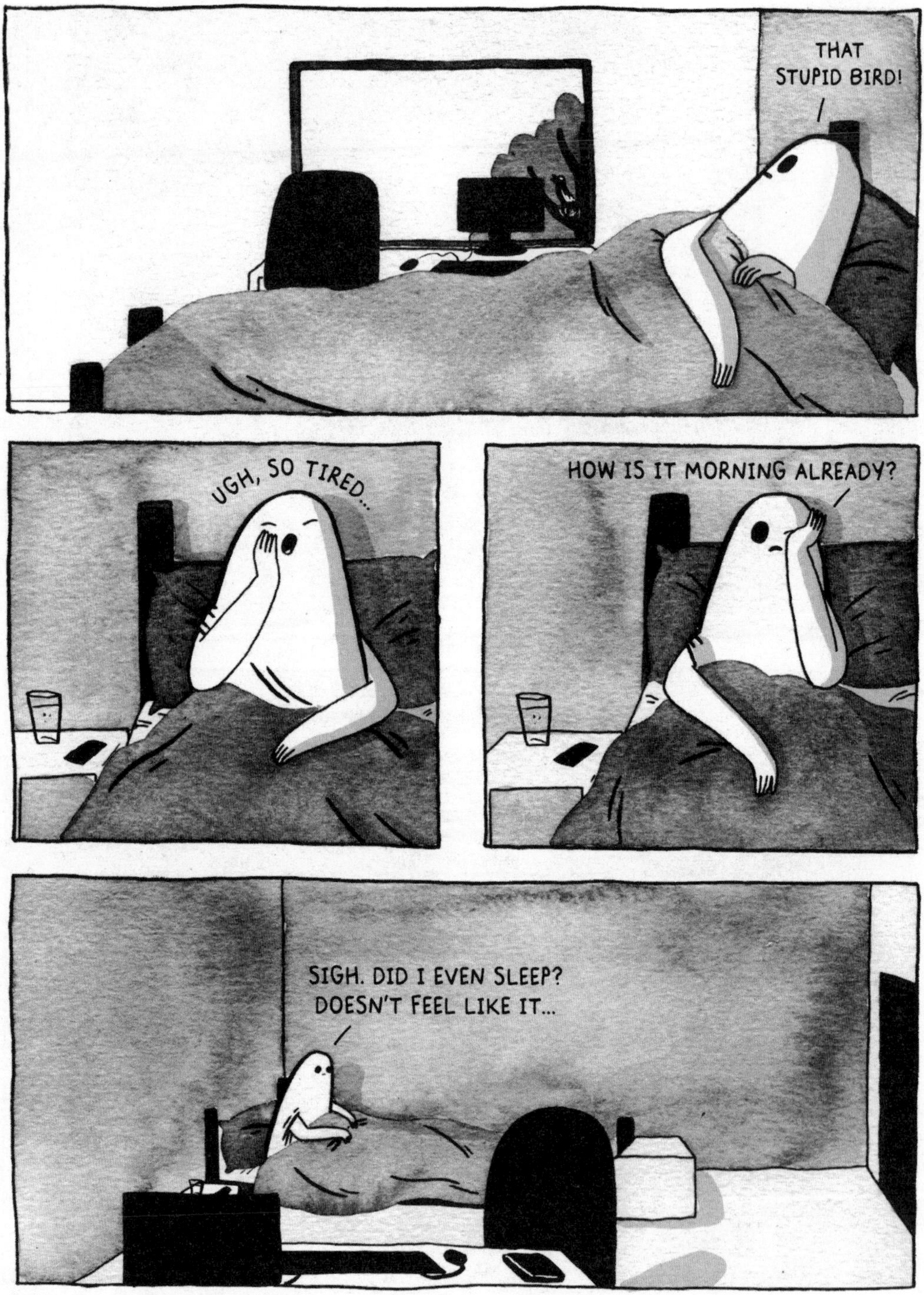
THAT STUPID BIRD!
UGH, SO TIRED...
HOW IS IT MORNING ALREADY?
SIGH. DID I EVEN SLEEP? DOESN'T FEEL LIKE IT...

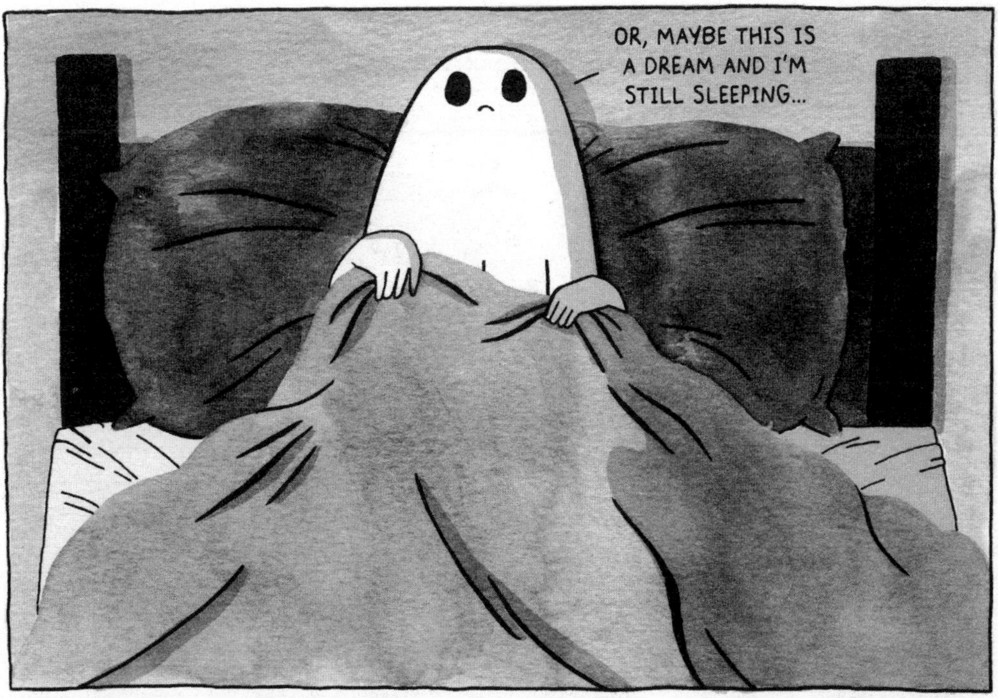
OR, MAYBE THIS IS A DREAM AND I'M STILL SLEEPING...

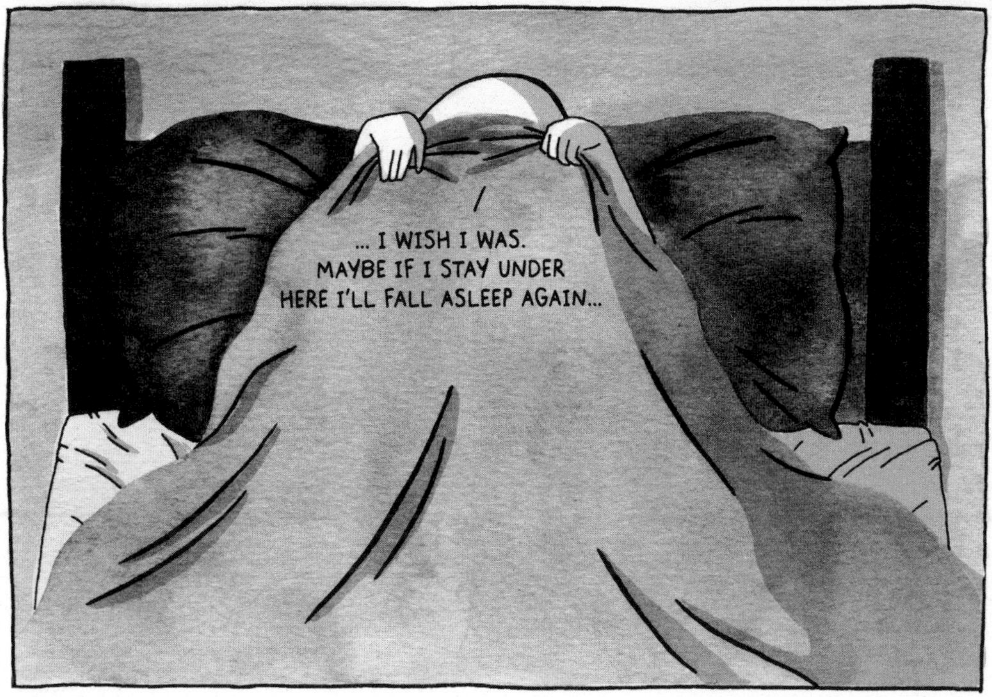
... I WISH I WAS. MAYBE IF I STAY UNDER HERE I'LL FALL ASLEEP AGAIN...

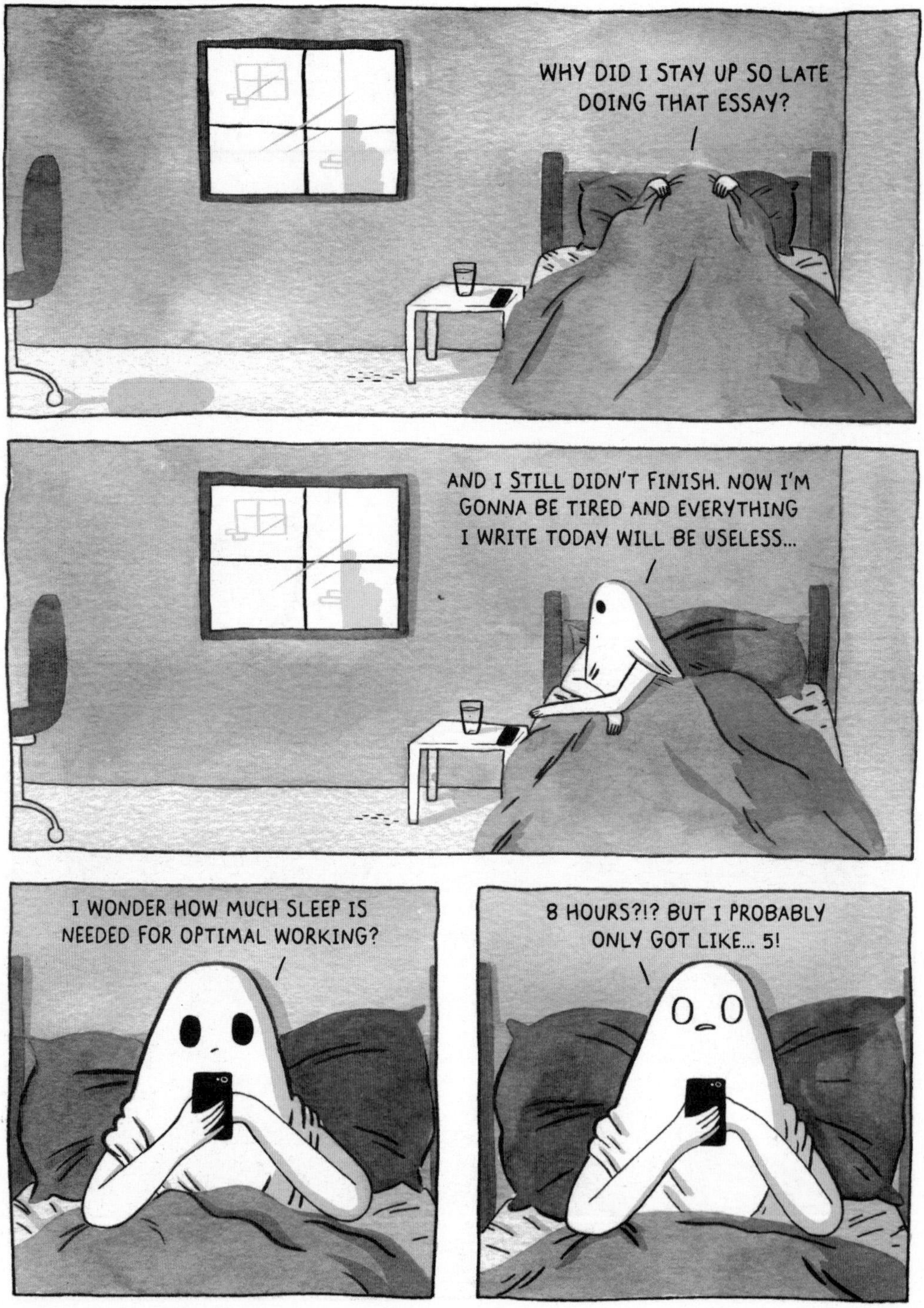
WHY DID I STAY UP SO LATE DOING THAT ESSAY?
AND I STILL DIDN'T FINISH. NOW I'M GONNA BE TIRED AND EVERYTHING I WRITE TODAY WILL BE USELESS...
I WONDER HOW MUCH SLEEP IS NEEDED FOR OPTIMAL WORKING?
8 HOURS?!? BUT I PROBABLY ONLY GOT LIKE... 5!

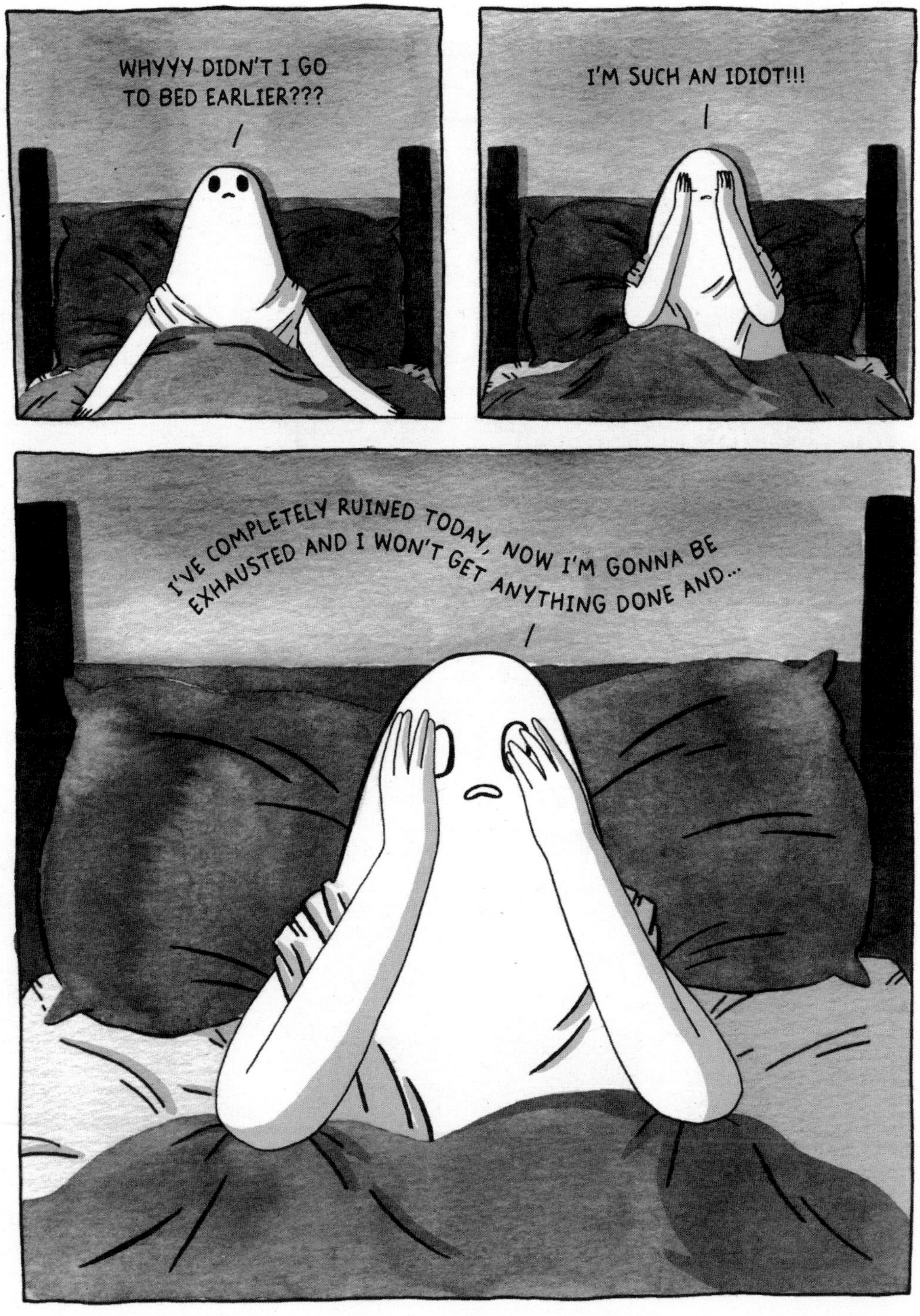
WHYYY DIDN'T I GO TO BED EARLIER???
I'M SUCH AN IDIOT!!!
I'VE COMPLETELY RUINED TODAY, NOW I'M GONNA BE EXHAUSTED AND I WON'T GET ANYTHING DONE AND...

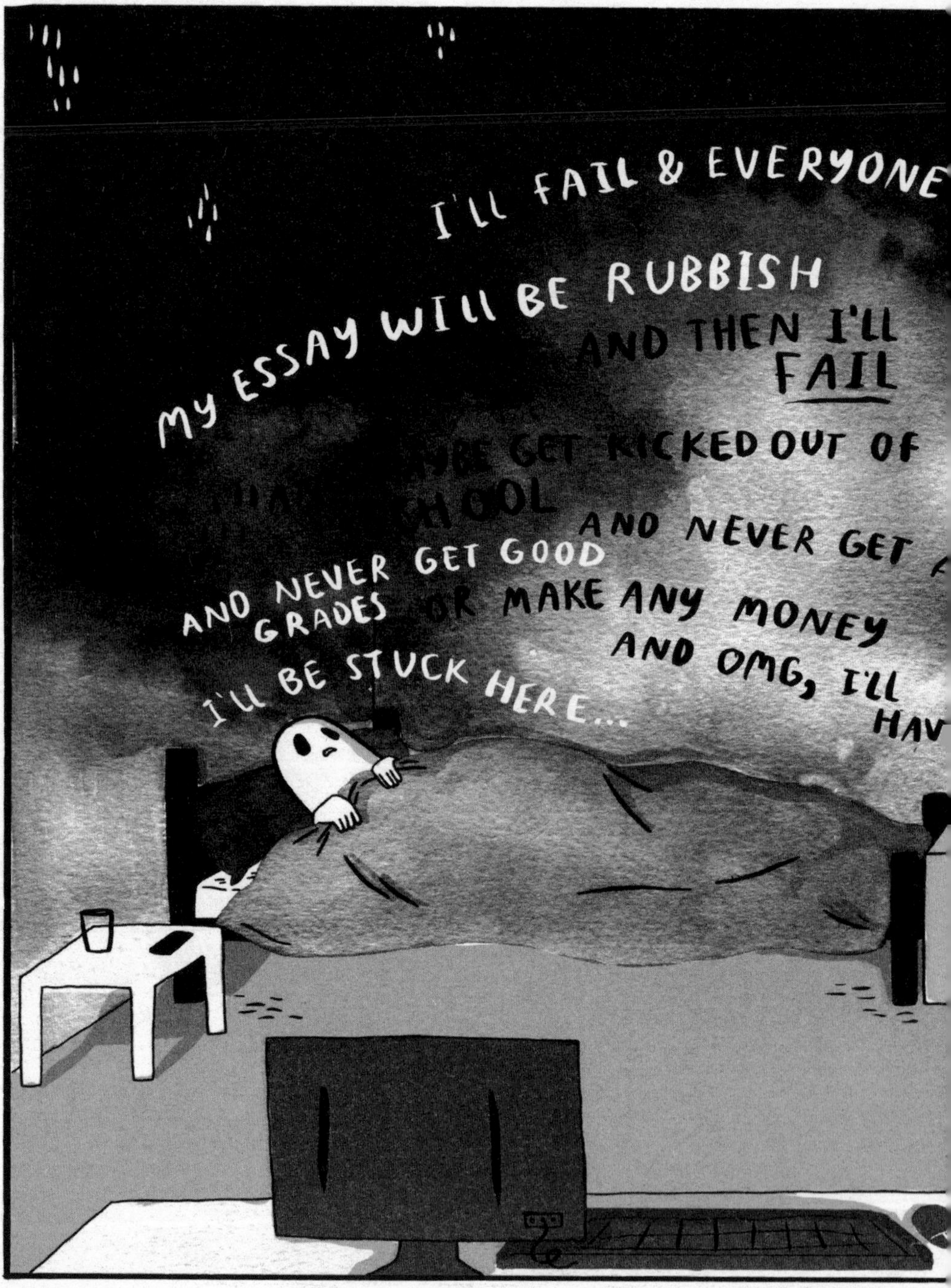
I'LL FAIL & EVERYONE
MY ESSAY WILL BE RUBBISH
AND THEN I'LL FAIL
GET KICKED OUT OF
AND NEVER GET GOOD GRADES
OR MAKE ANY MONEY
AND NEVER GET
AND OMG, I'LL
I'LL BE STUCK HERE...

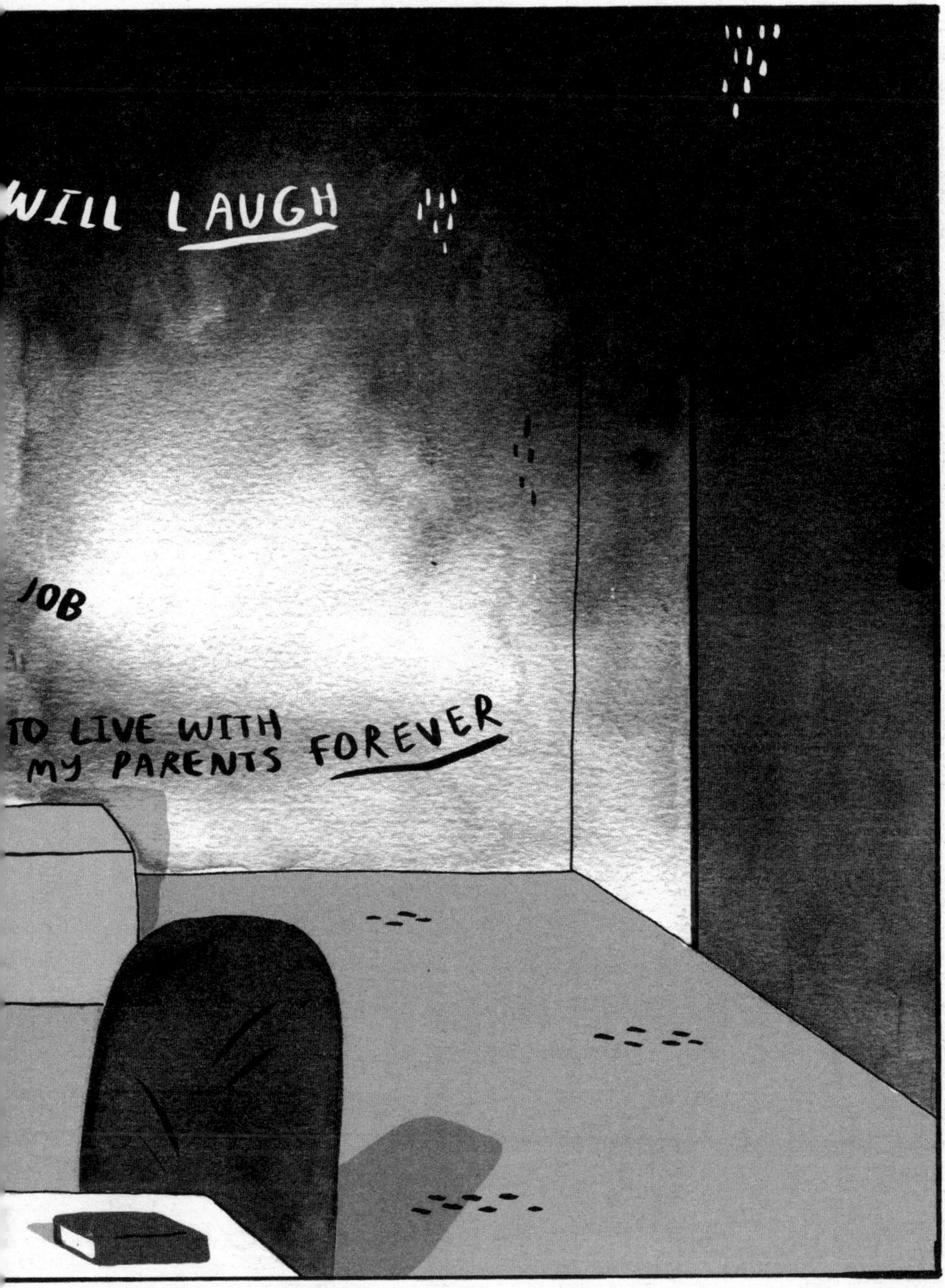
WILL LAUGH
JOB
TO LIVE WITH MY PARENTS FOREVER

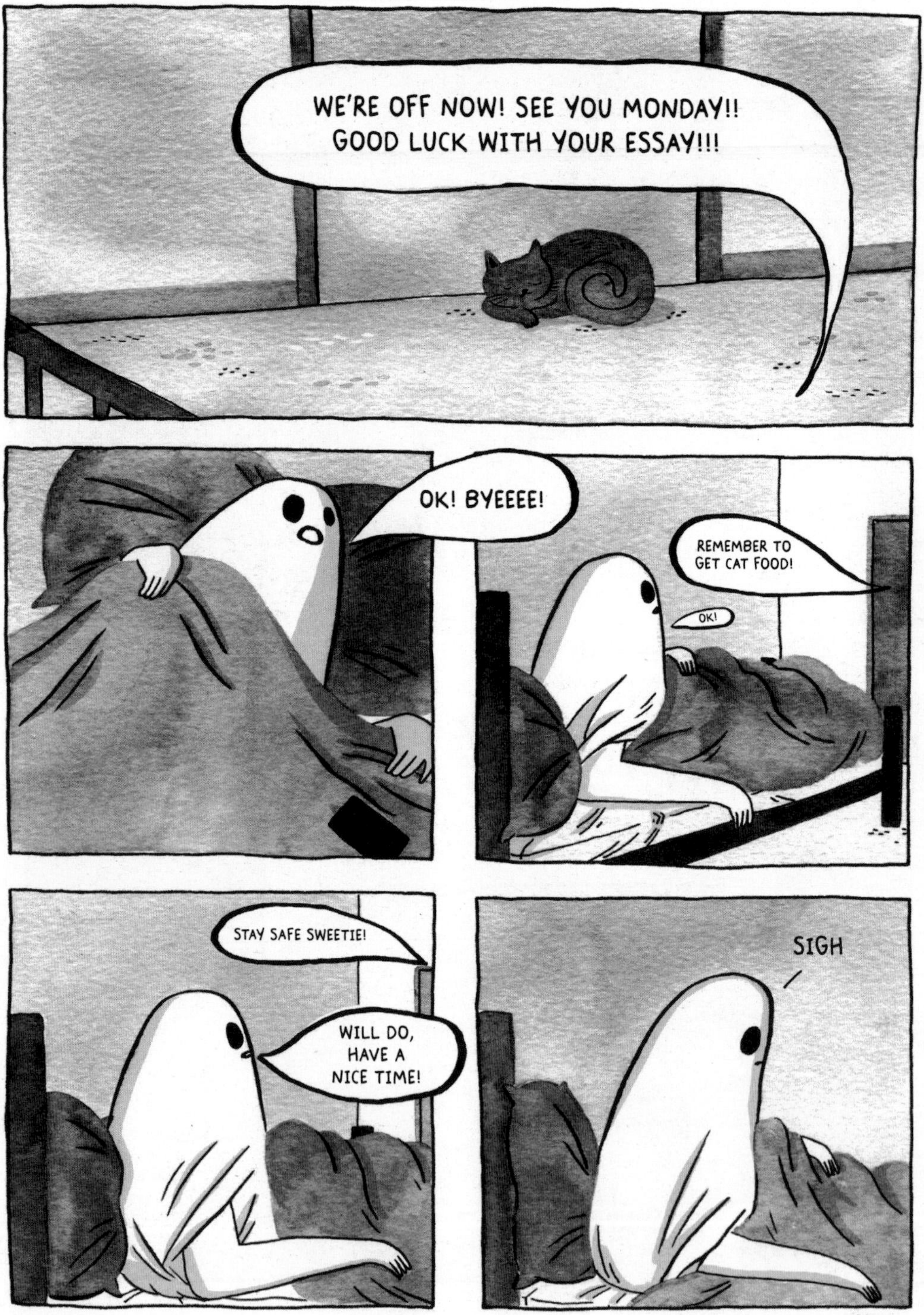
WE'RE OFF NOW! SEE YOU MONDAY!!
GOOD LUCK WITH YOUR ESSAY!!!
OK! BYEEEE!
REMEMBER TO GET CAT FOOD!
OK!
STAY SAFE SWEETIE!
WILL DO, HAVE A NICE TIME!
SIGH

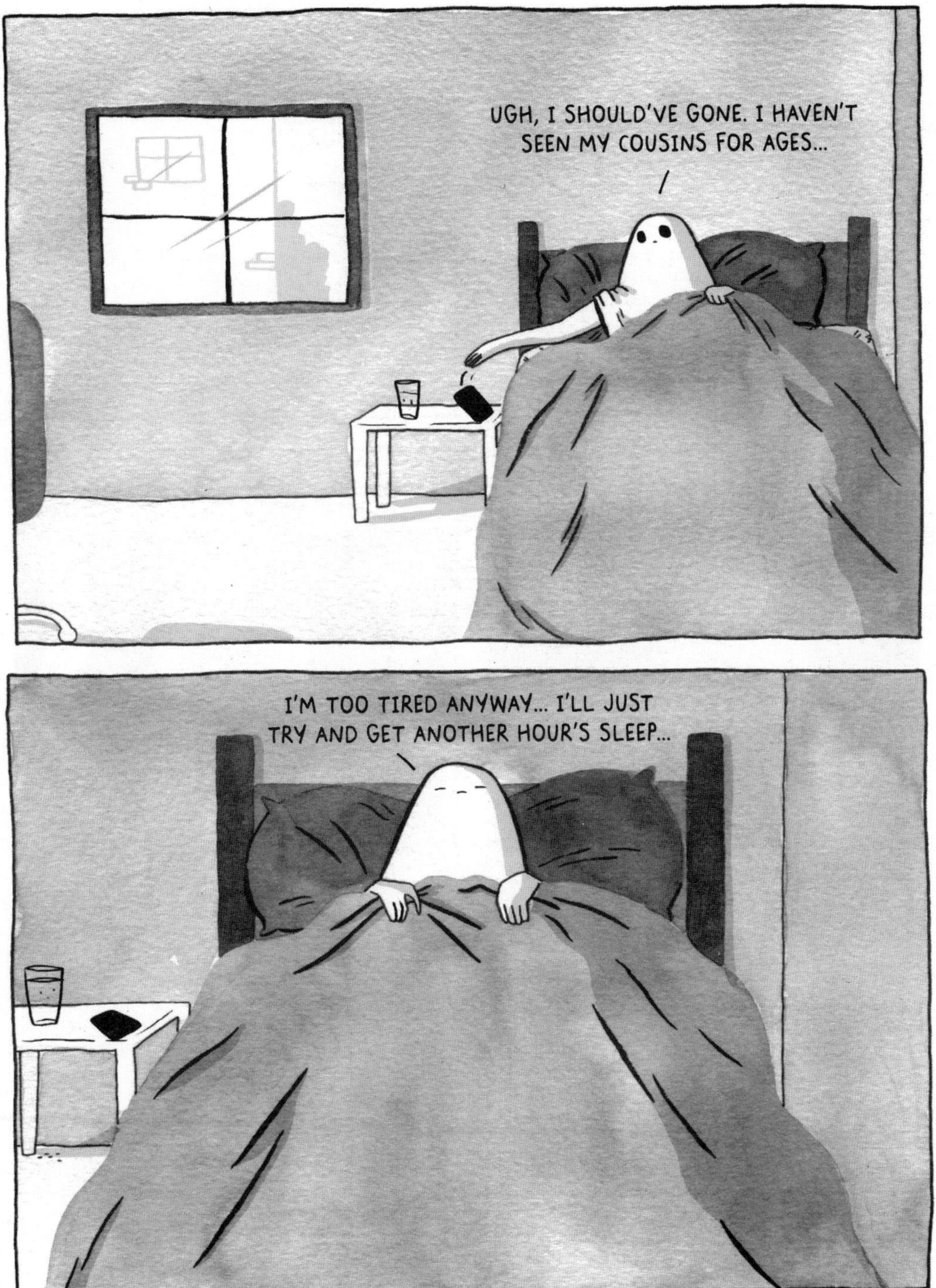
UGH, I SHOULD'VE GONE. I HAVEN'T SEEN MY COUSINS FOR AGES...
I'M TOO TIRED ANYWAY... I'LL JUST TRY AND GET ANOTHER HOUR'S SLEEP...

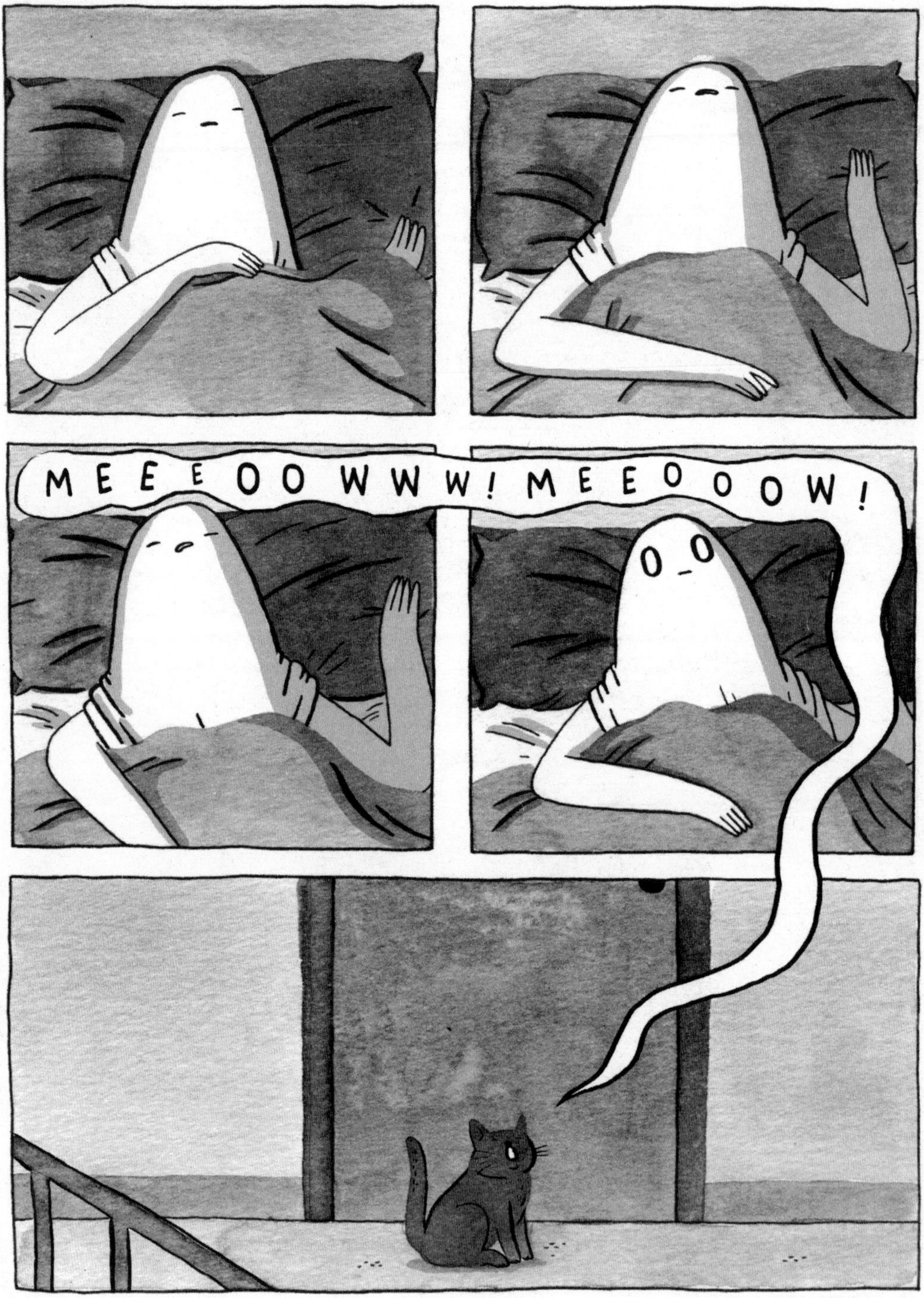
MEEEOO WWW! MEEOOOOW!

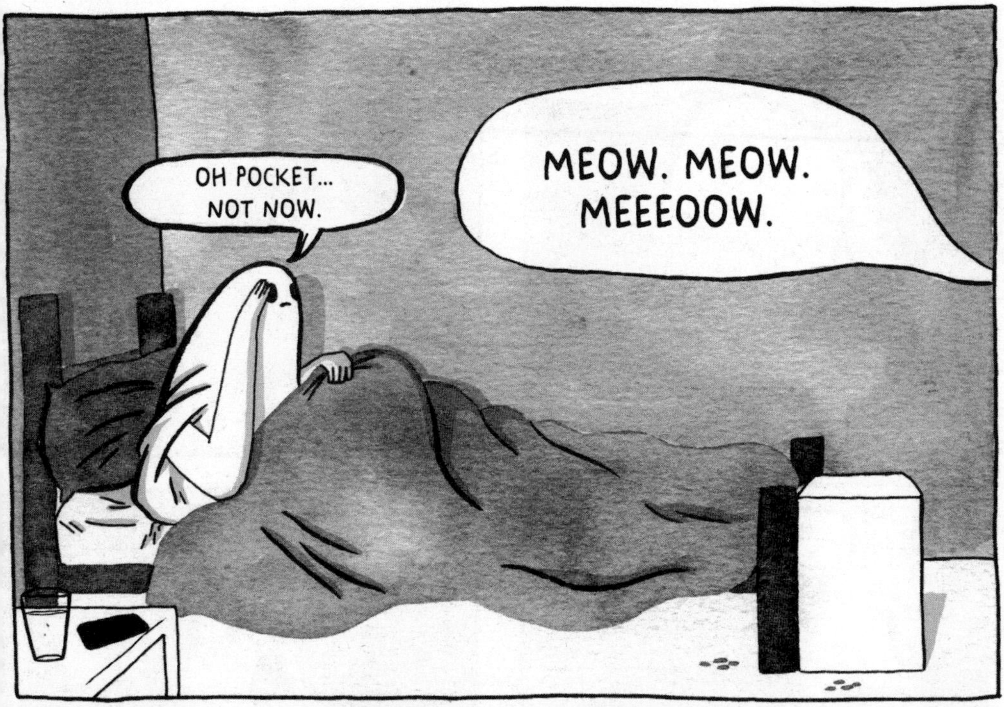
OH POCKET... NOT NOW.
MEOW. MEOW. MEEEOOW.

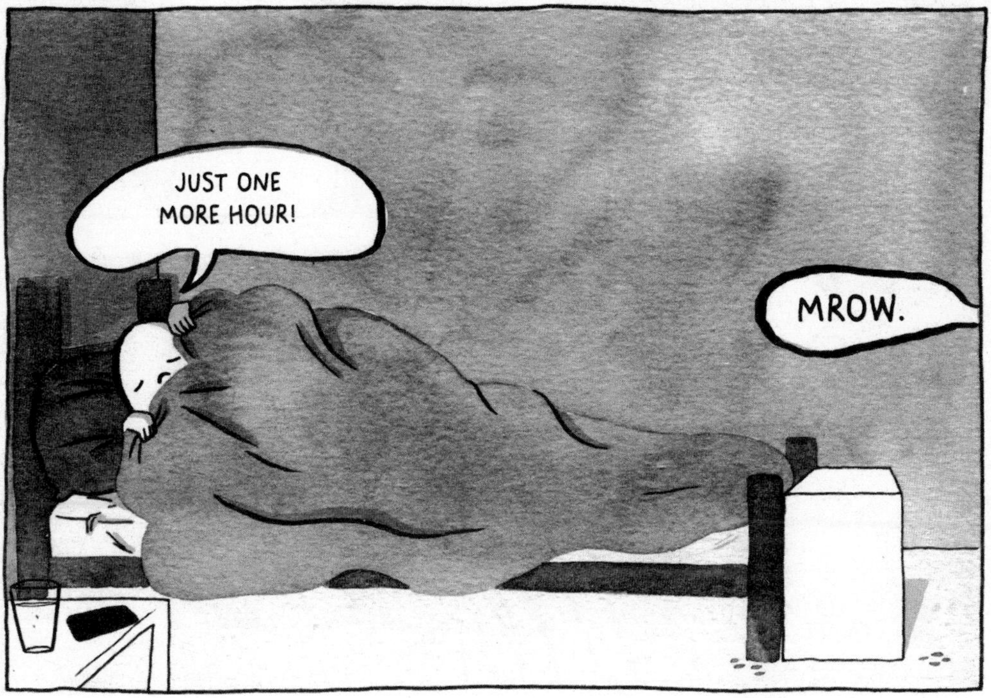
JUST ONE MORE HOUR!
MROW.

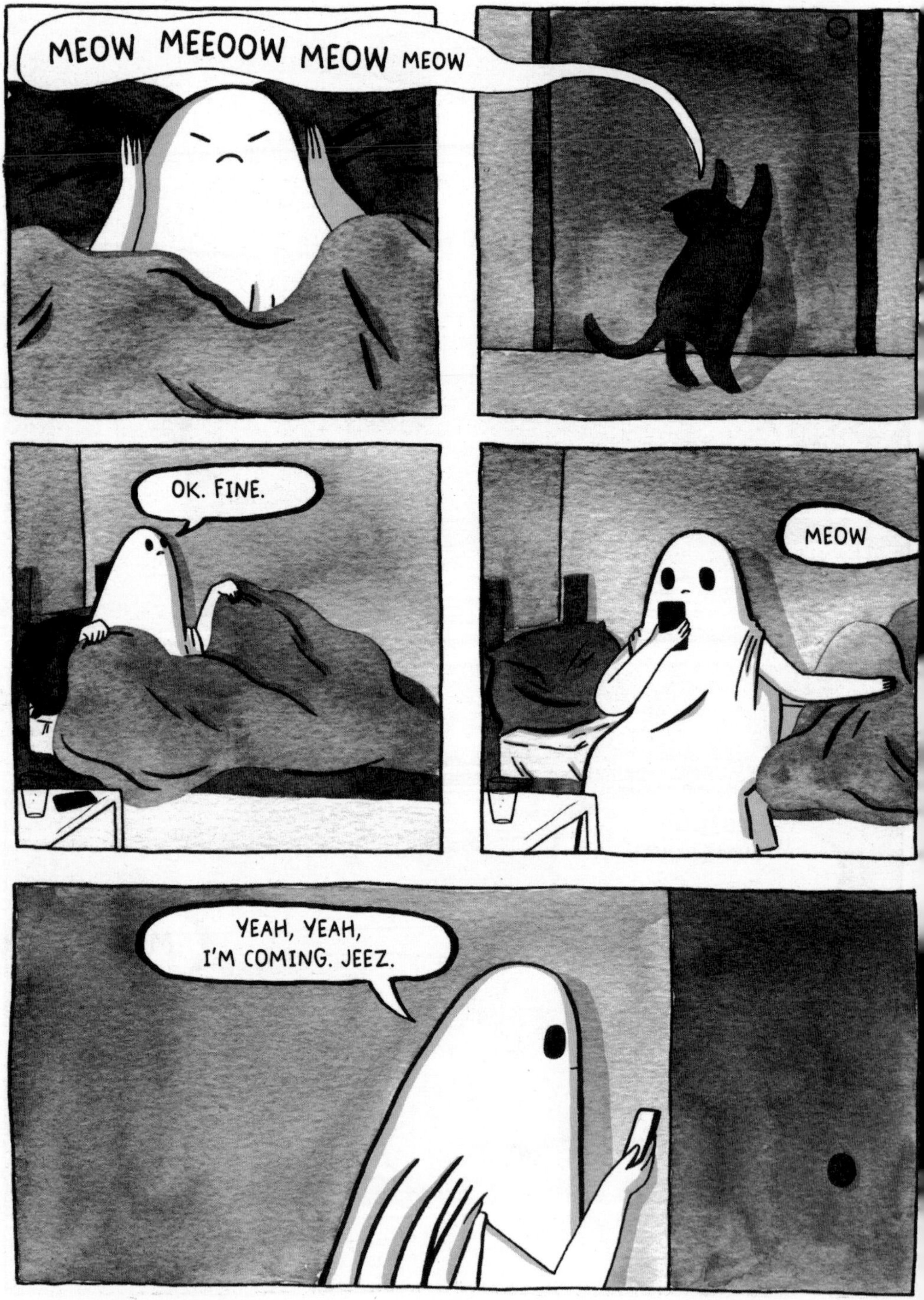
MEOW MEEOOW MEOW MEOW
OK. FINE.
MEOW
YEAH, YEAH,
I'M COMING. JEEZ.

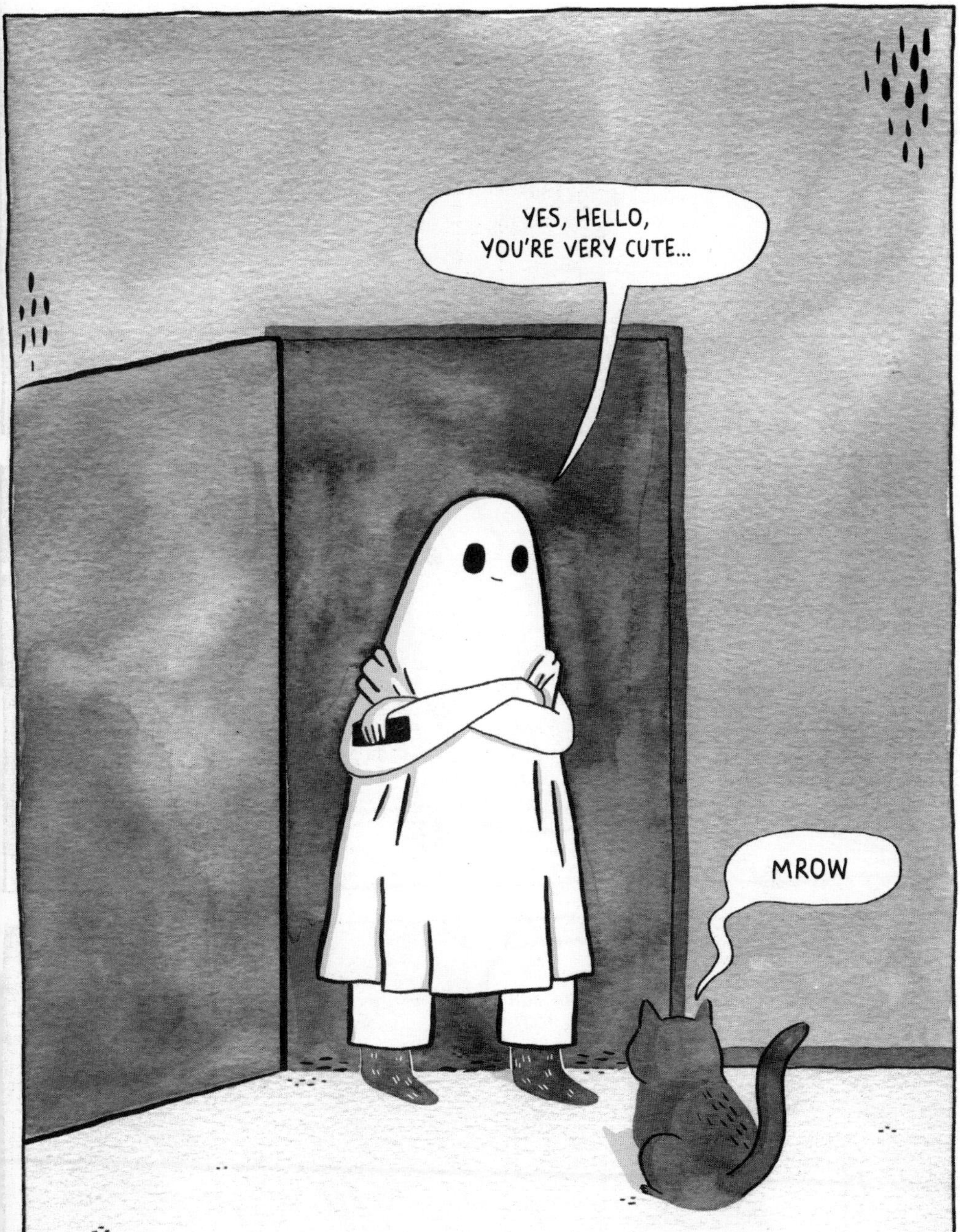
YES, HELLO, YOU'RE VERY CUTE...
MROW

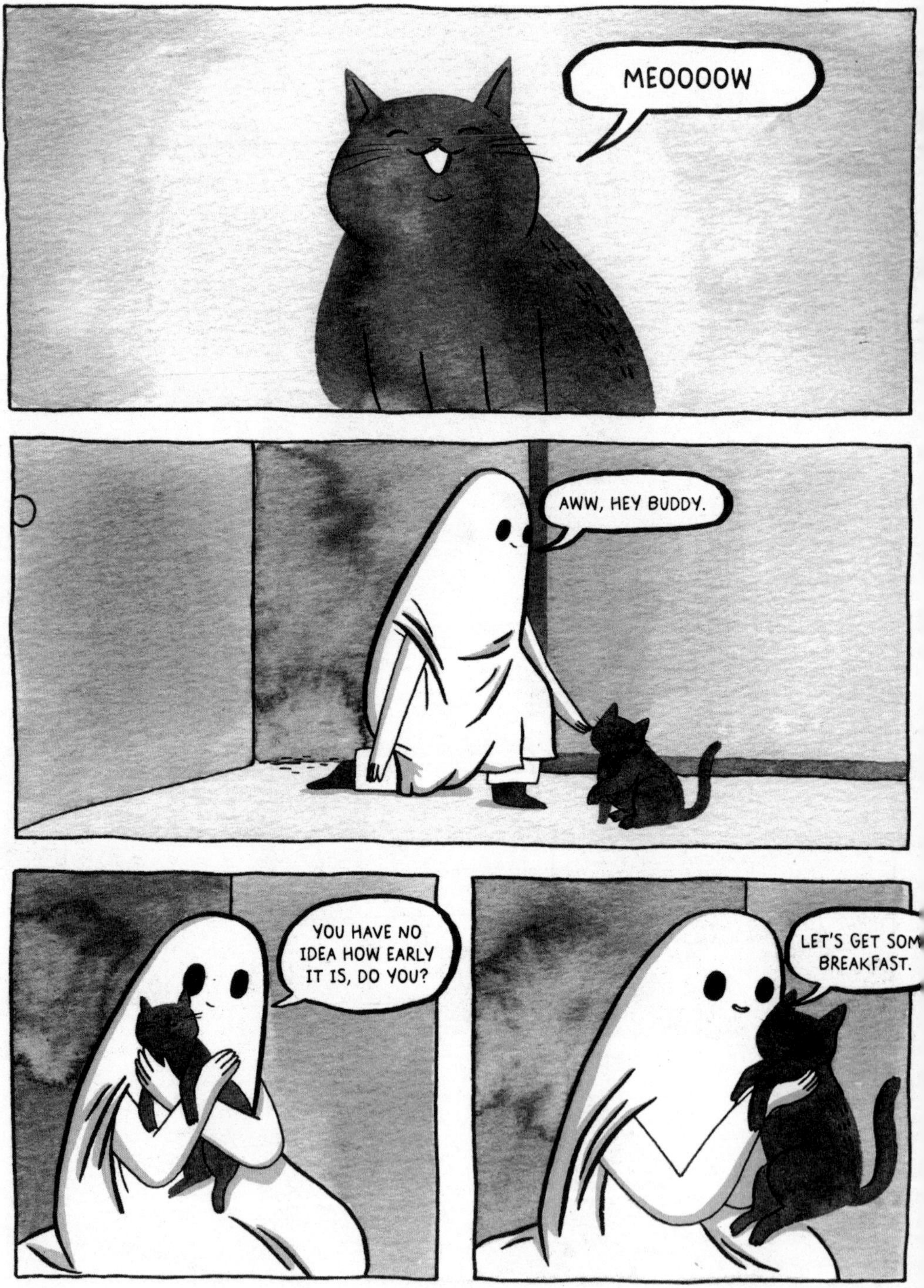
MEOOOOW
AWW, HEY BUDDY.
YOU HAVE NO IDEA HOW EARLY IT IS, DO YOU?
LET'S GET SOM BREAKFAST.

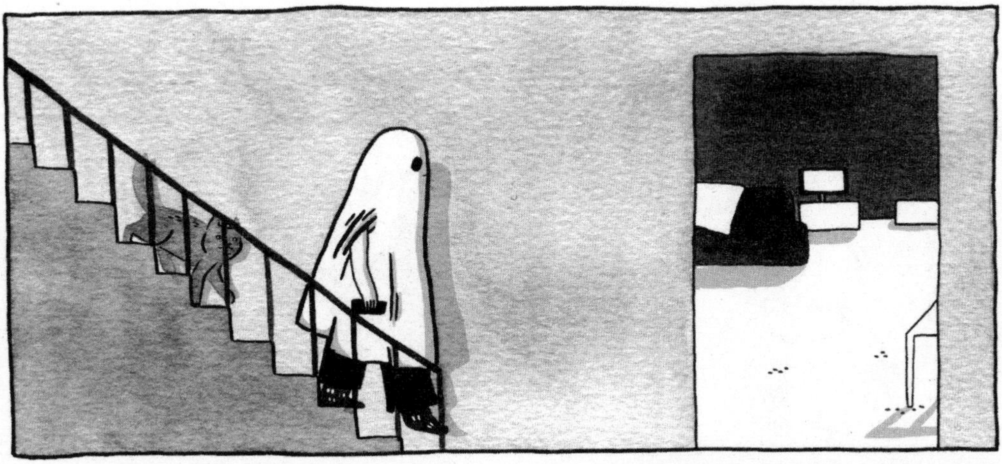

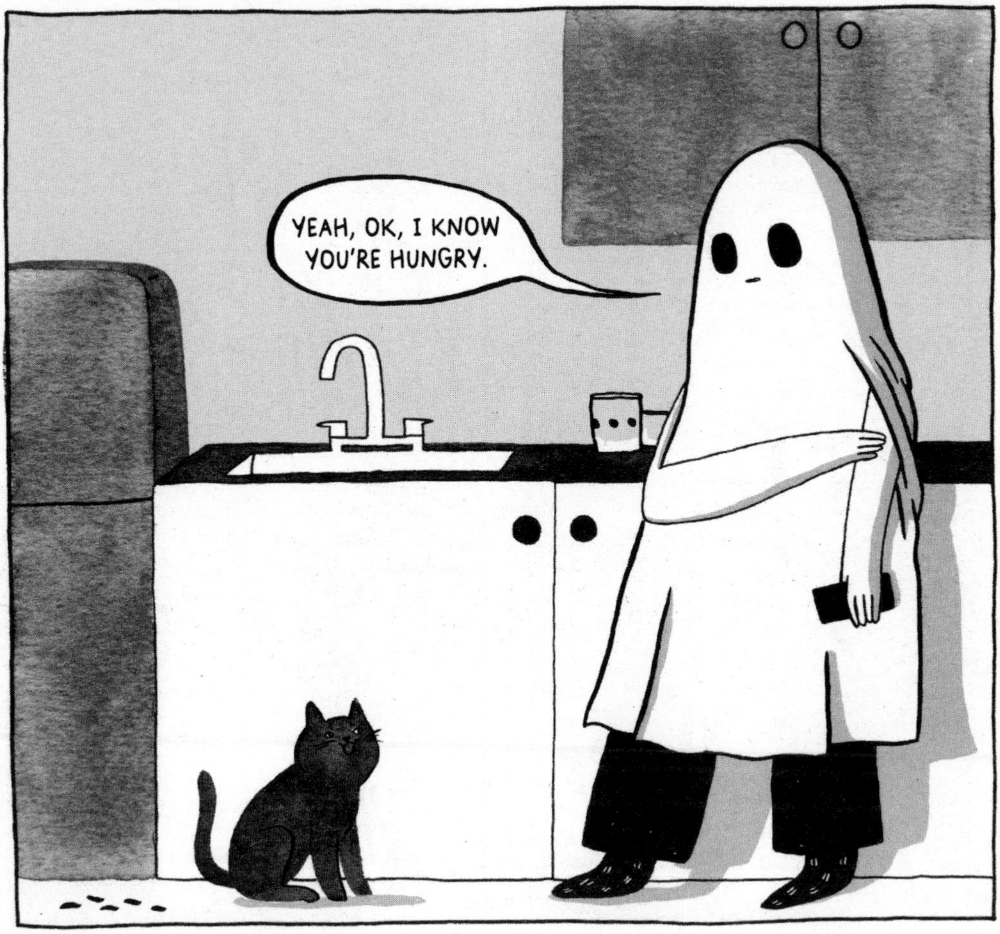
YEAH, OK, I KNOW YOU'RE HUNGRY.

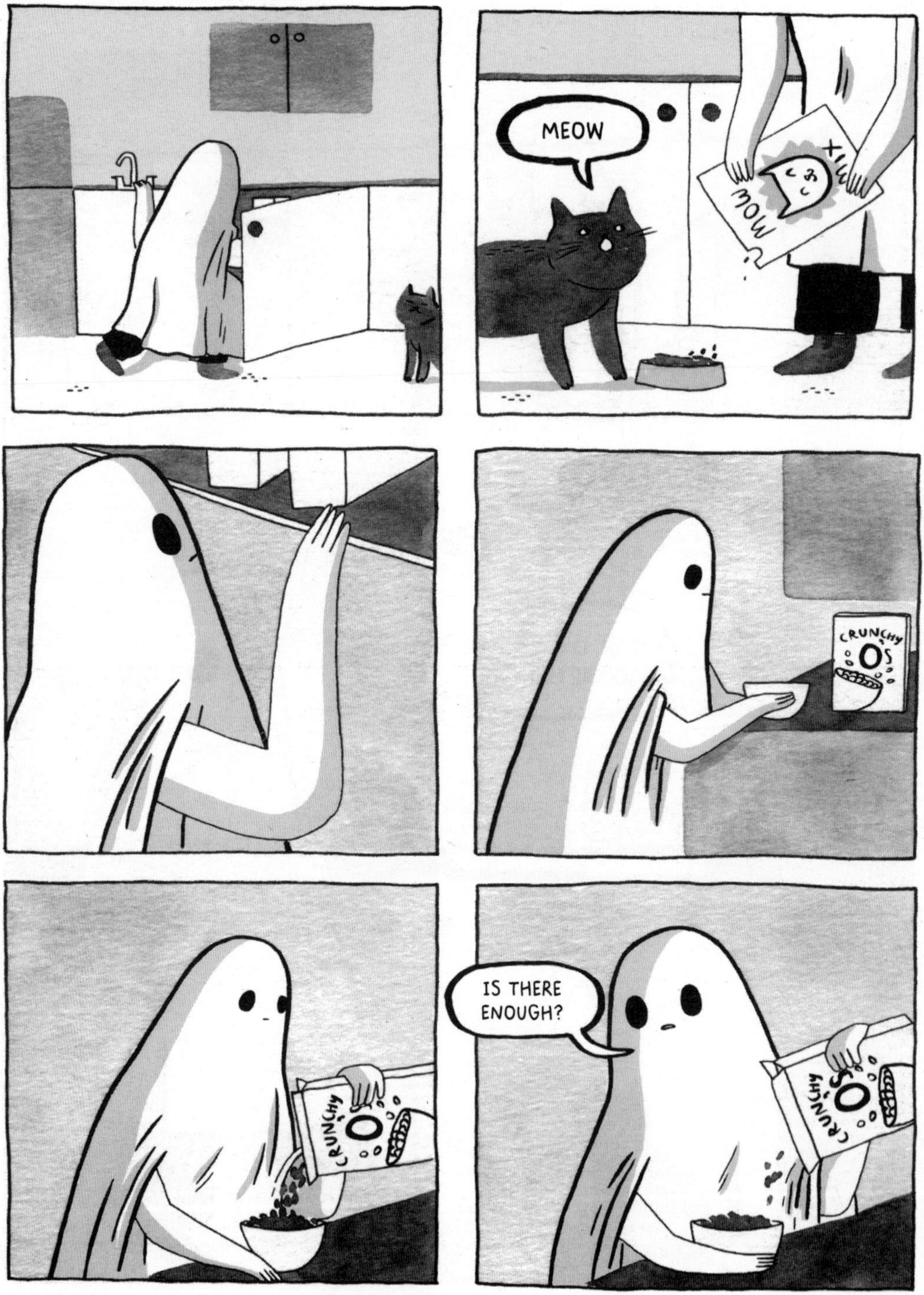
MEOW
CRUNCHY O'S
IS THERE ENOUGH?

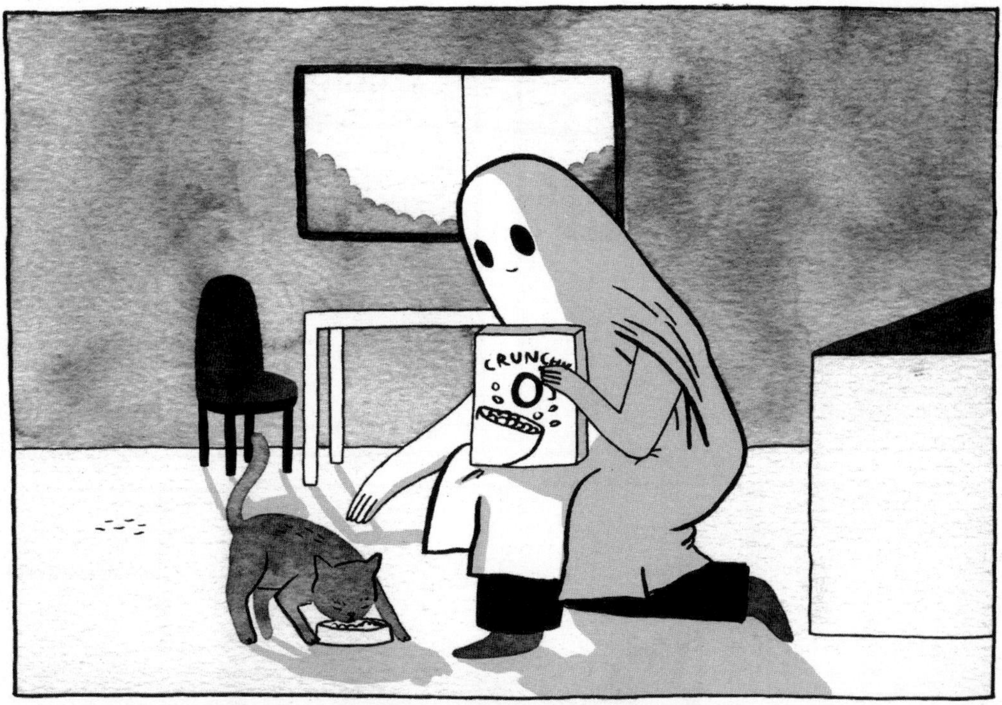
CRUNCH
O

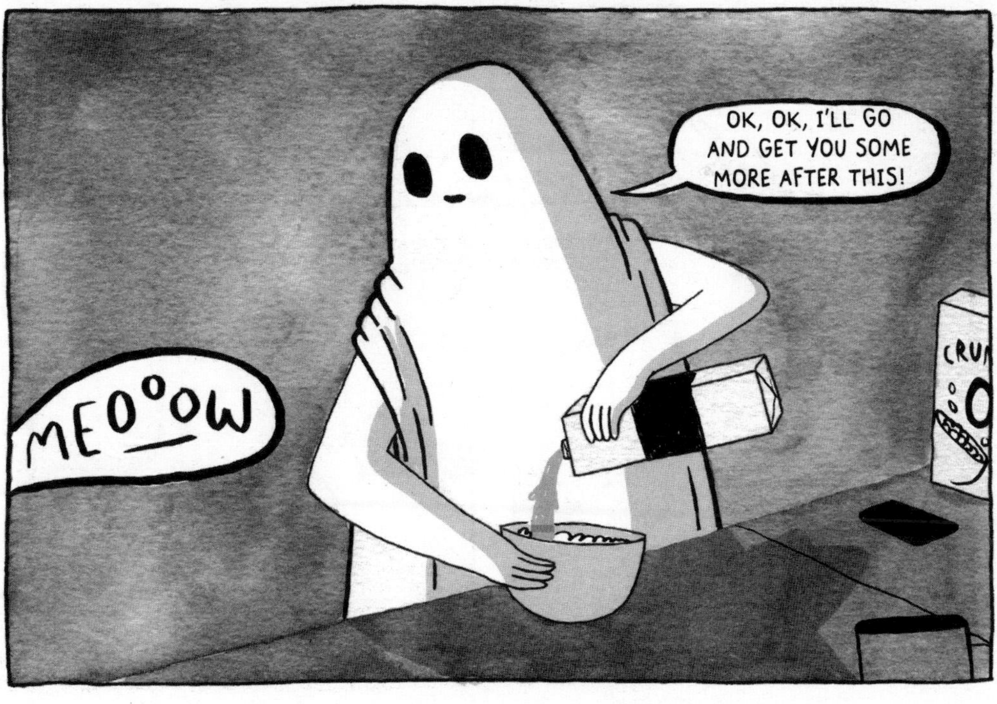
OK, OK, I'LL GO AND GET YOU SOME MORE AFTER THIS!
MEOOOW
CRUN

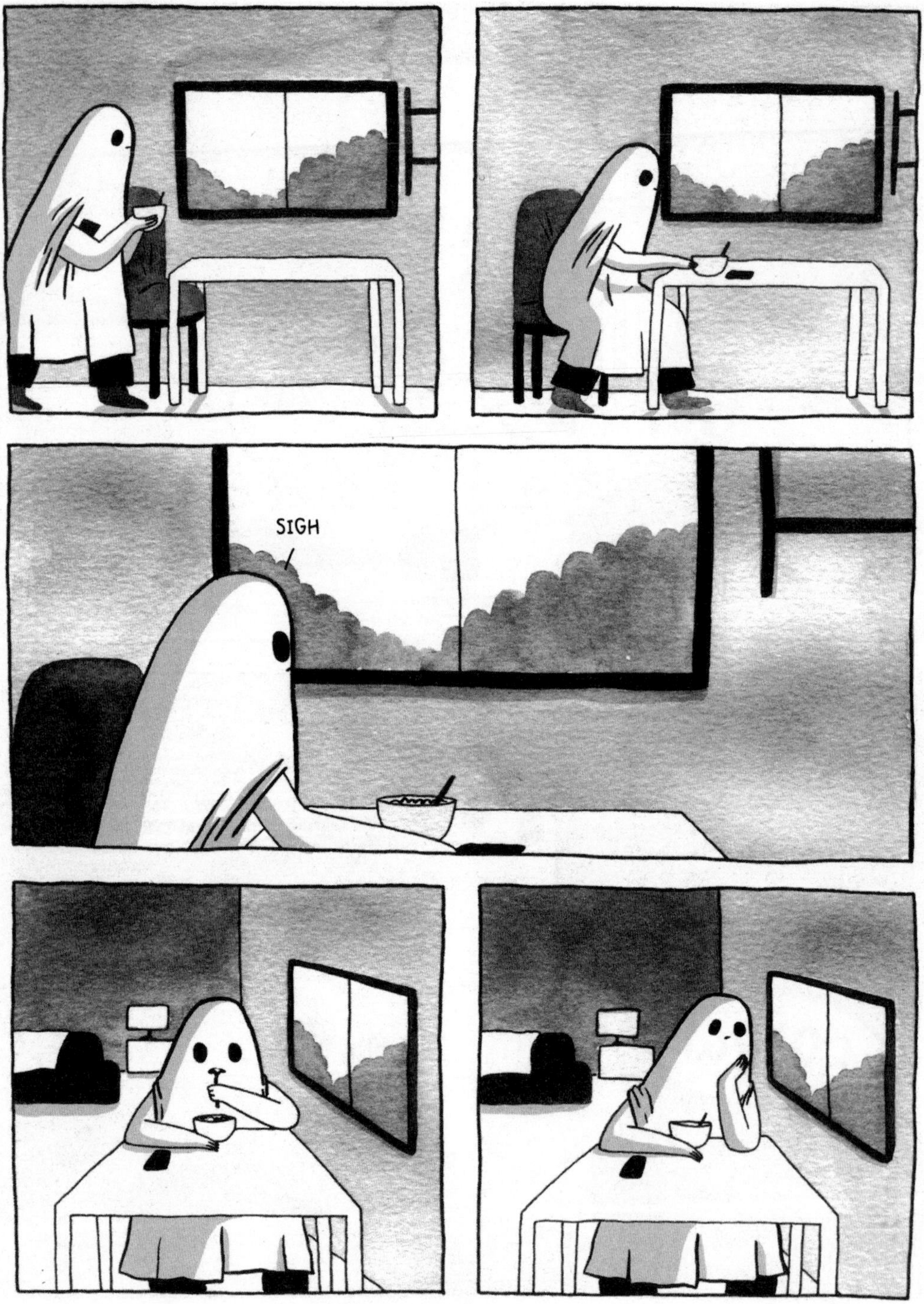
SIGH

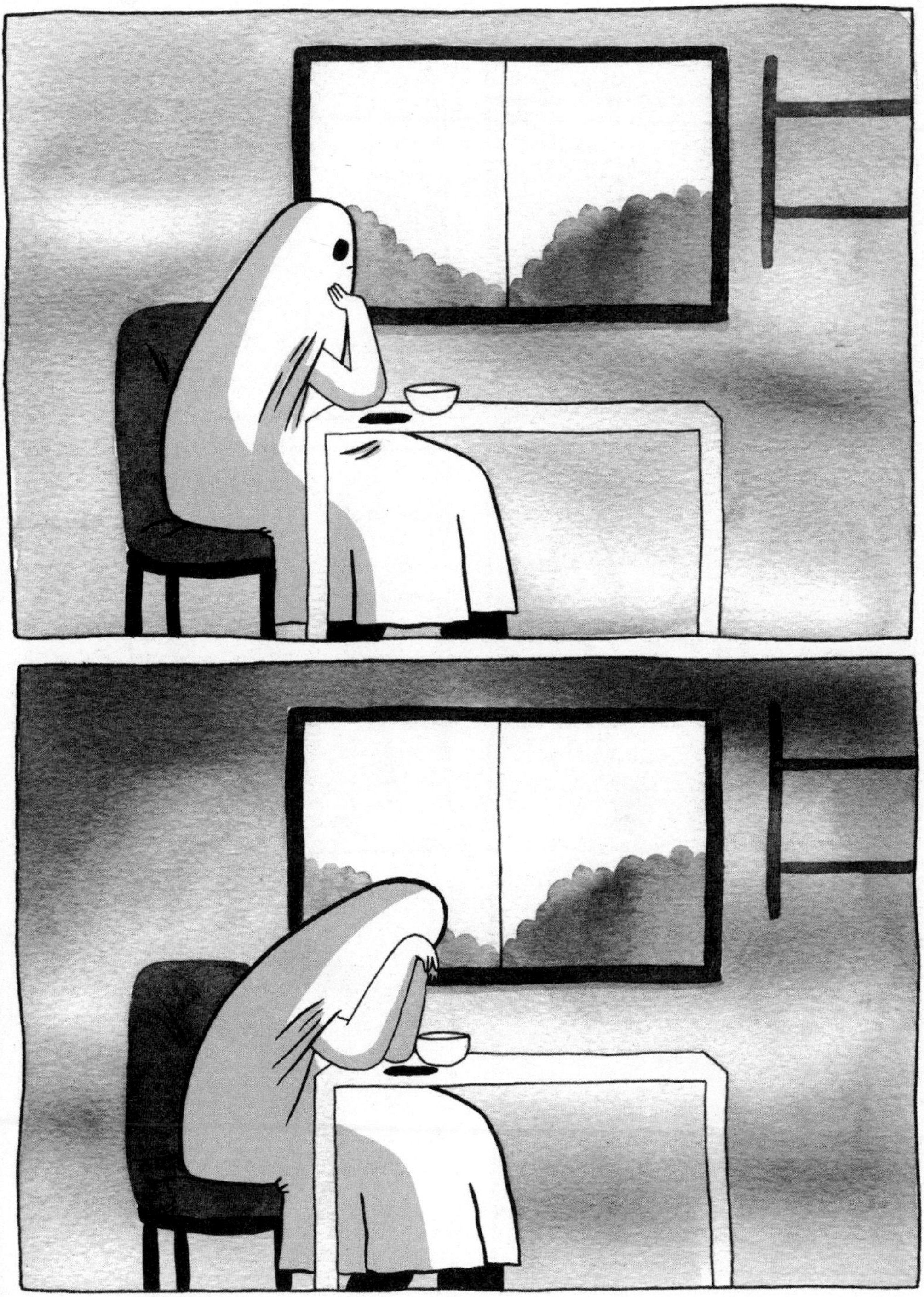

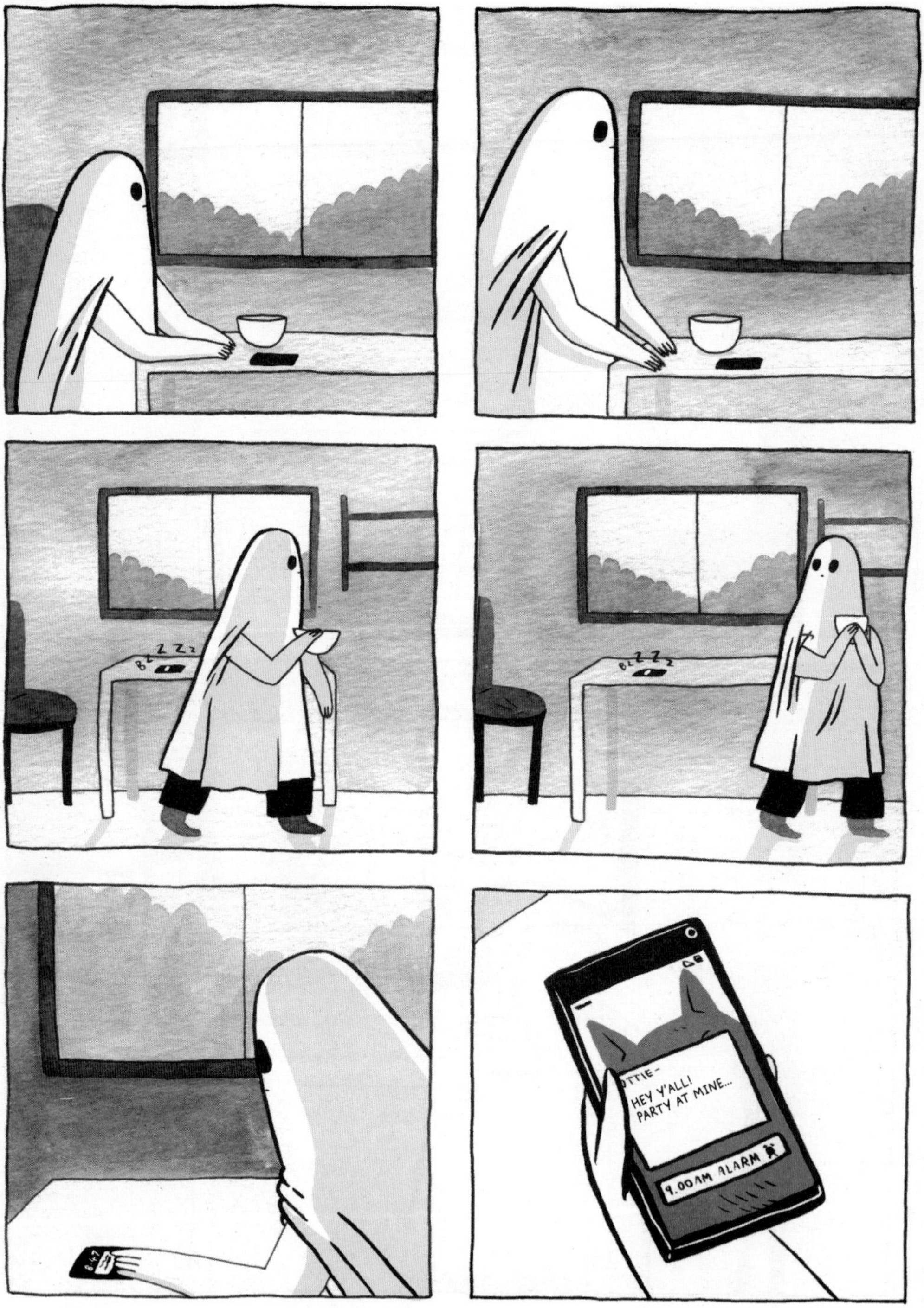
HEY Y'ALL!
PARTY AT MINE...
9.00AM ALARM

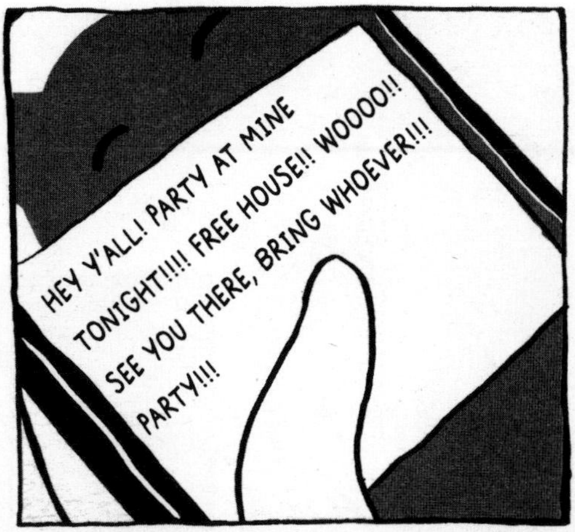
HEY Y'ALL! PARTY AT MINE
TONIGHT!!!! FREE HOUSE!! WOOOO!!
SEE YOU THERE, BRING WHOEVER!!!
PARTY!!!

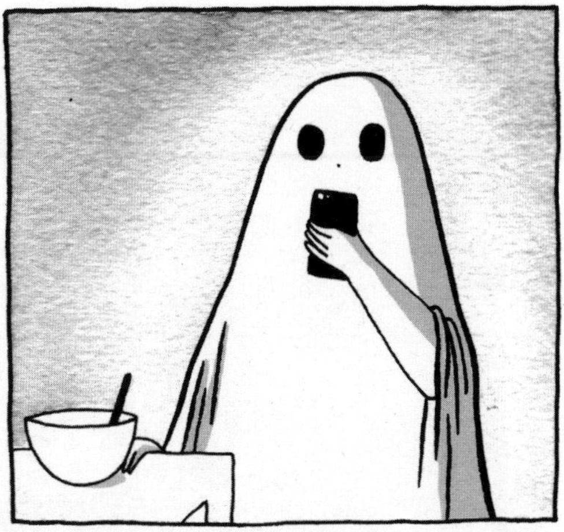

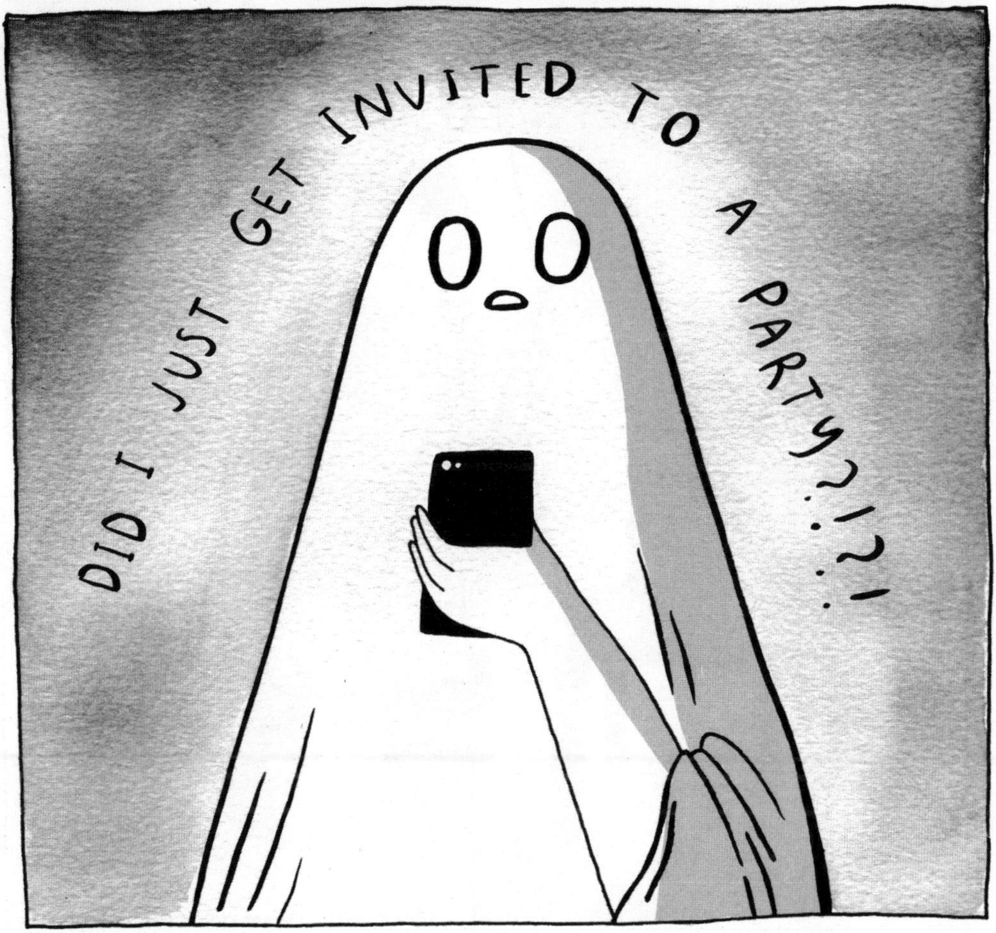
DID I JUST GET INVITED TO A PARTY?!?!?!

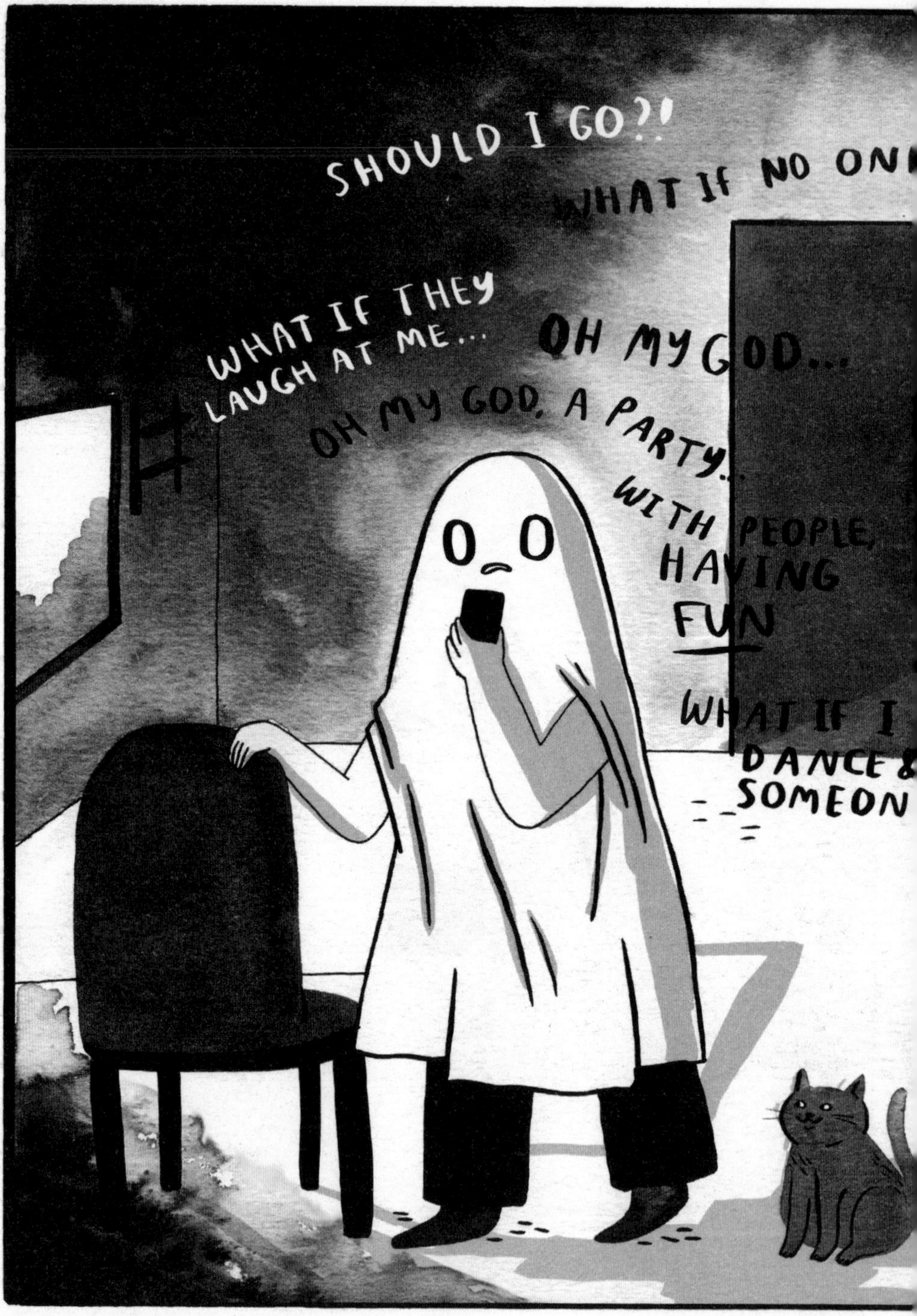
SHOULD I GO?!
WHAT IF NO ONE
WHAT IF THEY LAUGH AT ME...
OH MY GOD...
OH MY GOD, A PARTY...
WITH PEOPLE, HAVING FUN
WHAT IF I DANCE &
SOMEON

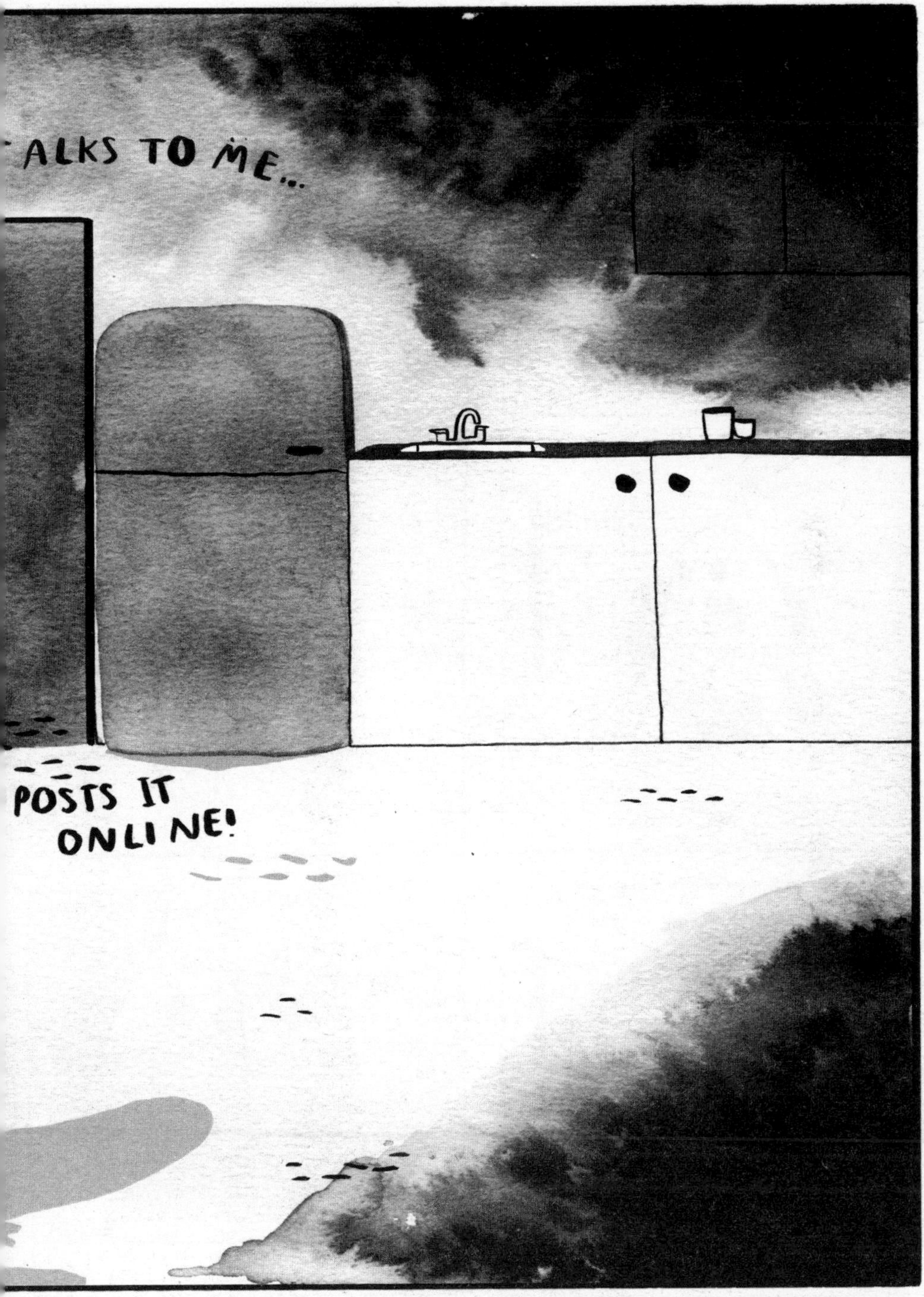
ALKS TO ME...
POSTS IT ONLINE!

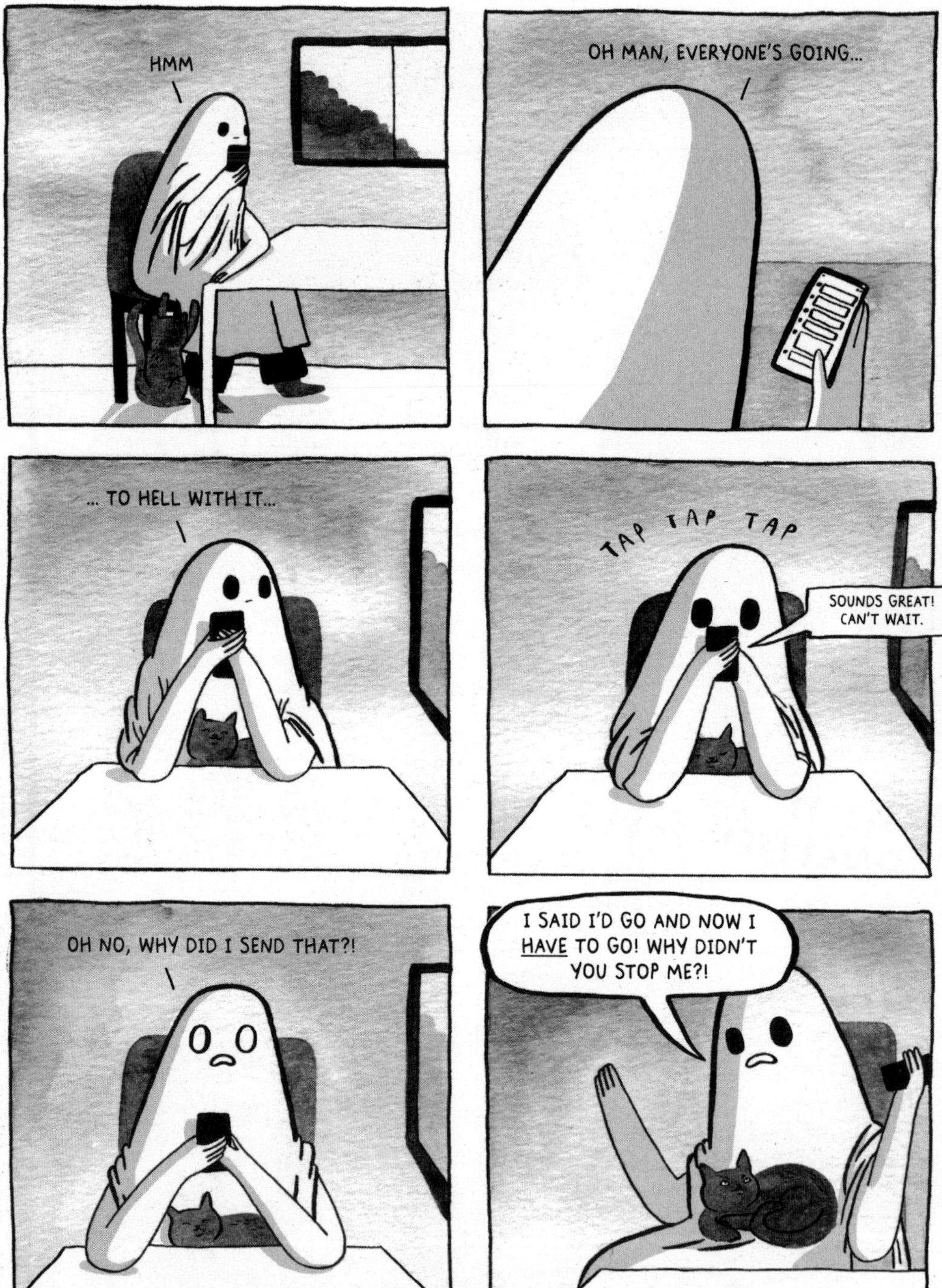
HMM
OH MAN, EVERYONE'S GOING...
... TO HELL WITH IT...
TAP TAP TAP
SOUNDS GREAT! CAN'T WAIT.
OH NO, WHY DID I SEND THAT?!
I SAID I'D GO AND NOW I HAVE TO GO! WHY DIDN'T YOU STOP ME?!

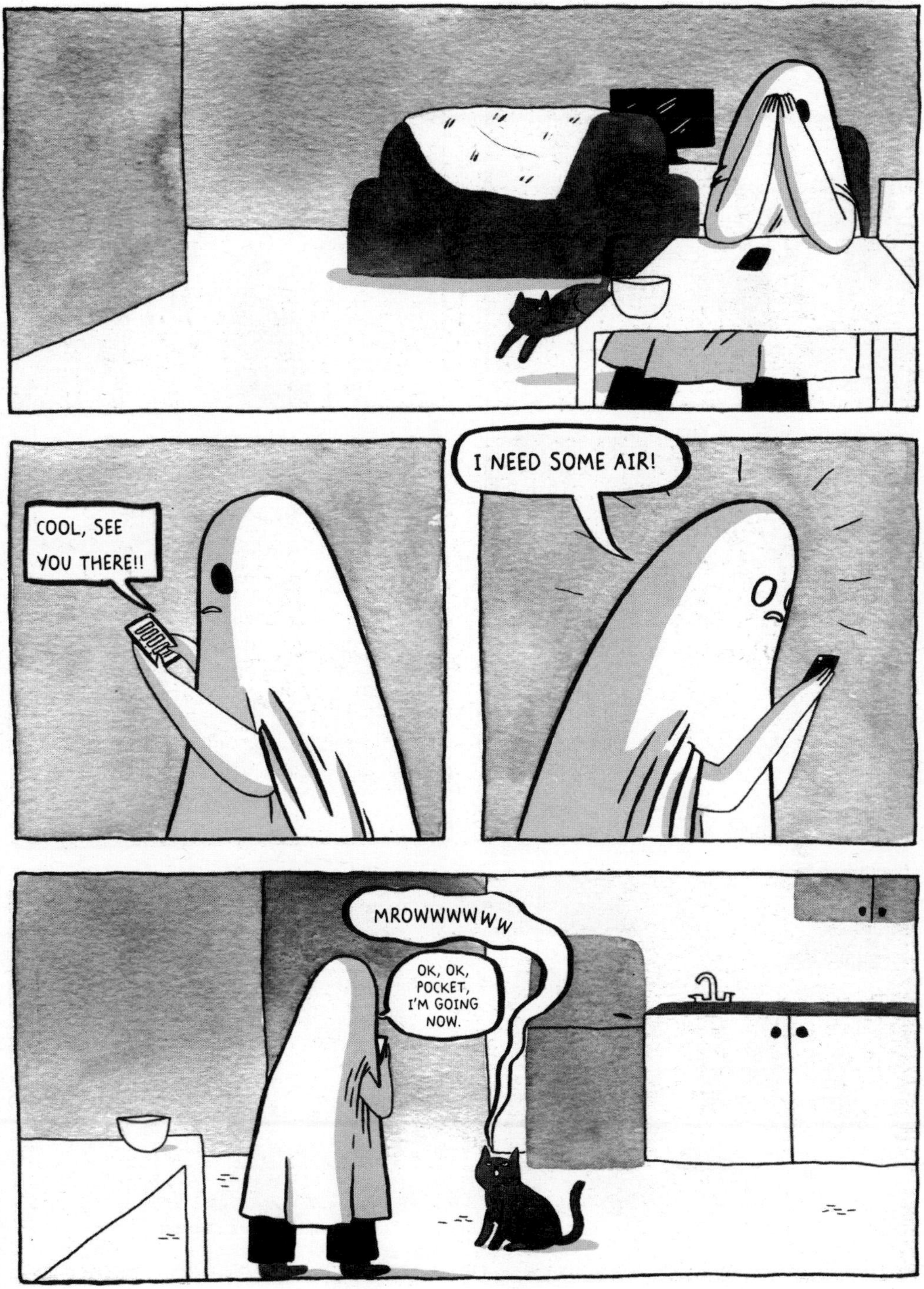
COOL, SEE YOU THERE!!
I NEED SOME AIR!
MROWWWWWWW
OK, OK, POCKET, I'M GOING NOW.

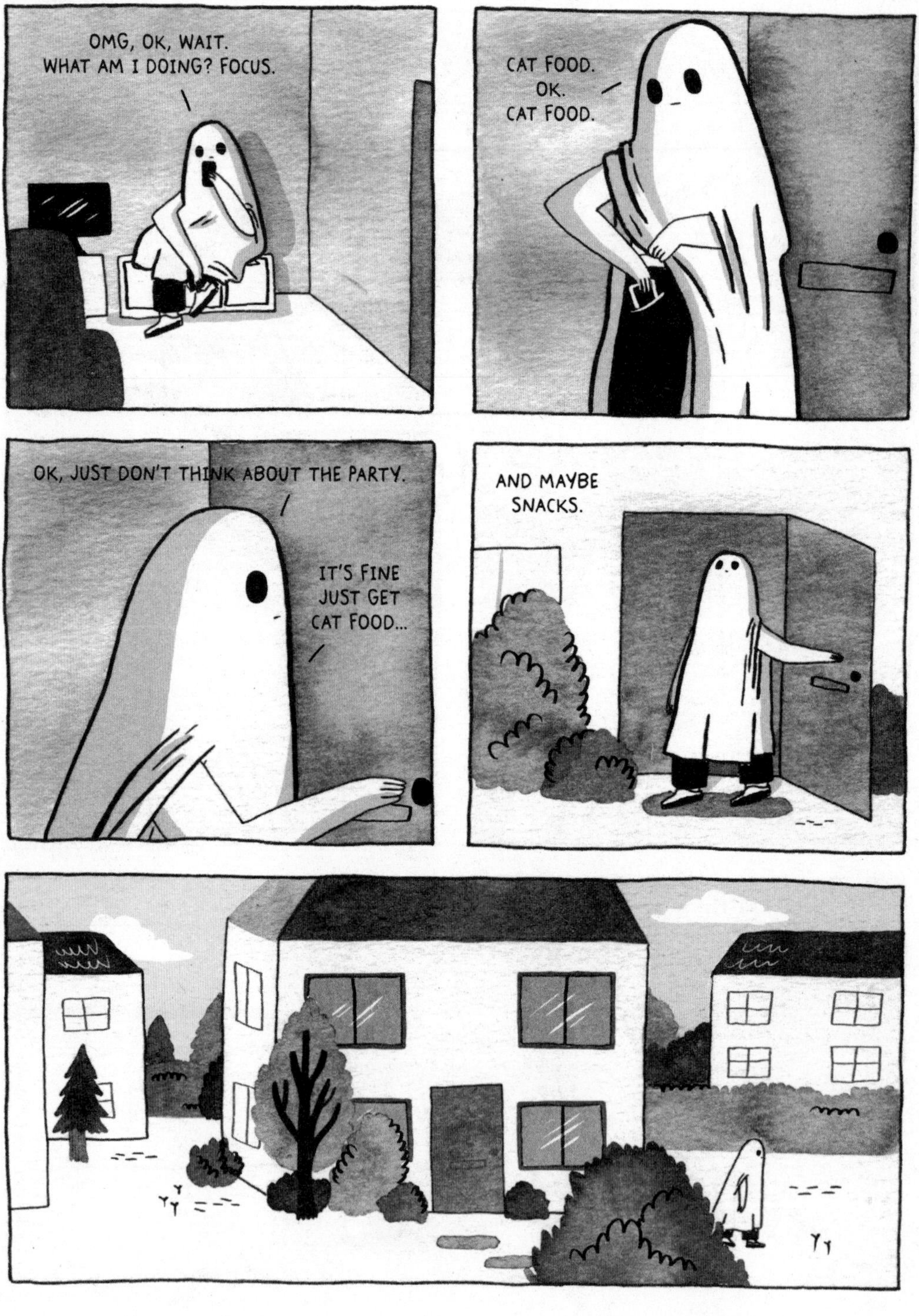
OMG, OK, WAIT.
WHAT AM I DOING? FOCUS.
CAT FOOD.
OK.
CAT FOOD.
OK, JUST DON'T THINK ABOUT THE PARTY.
IT'S FINE
JUST GET
CAT FOOD...
AND MAYBE
SNACKS.

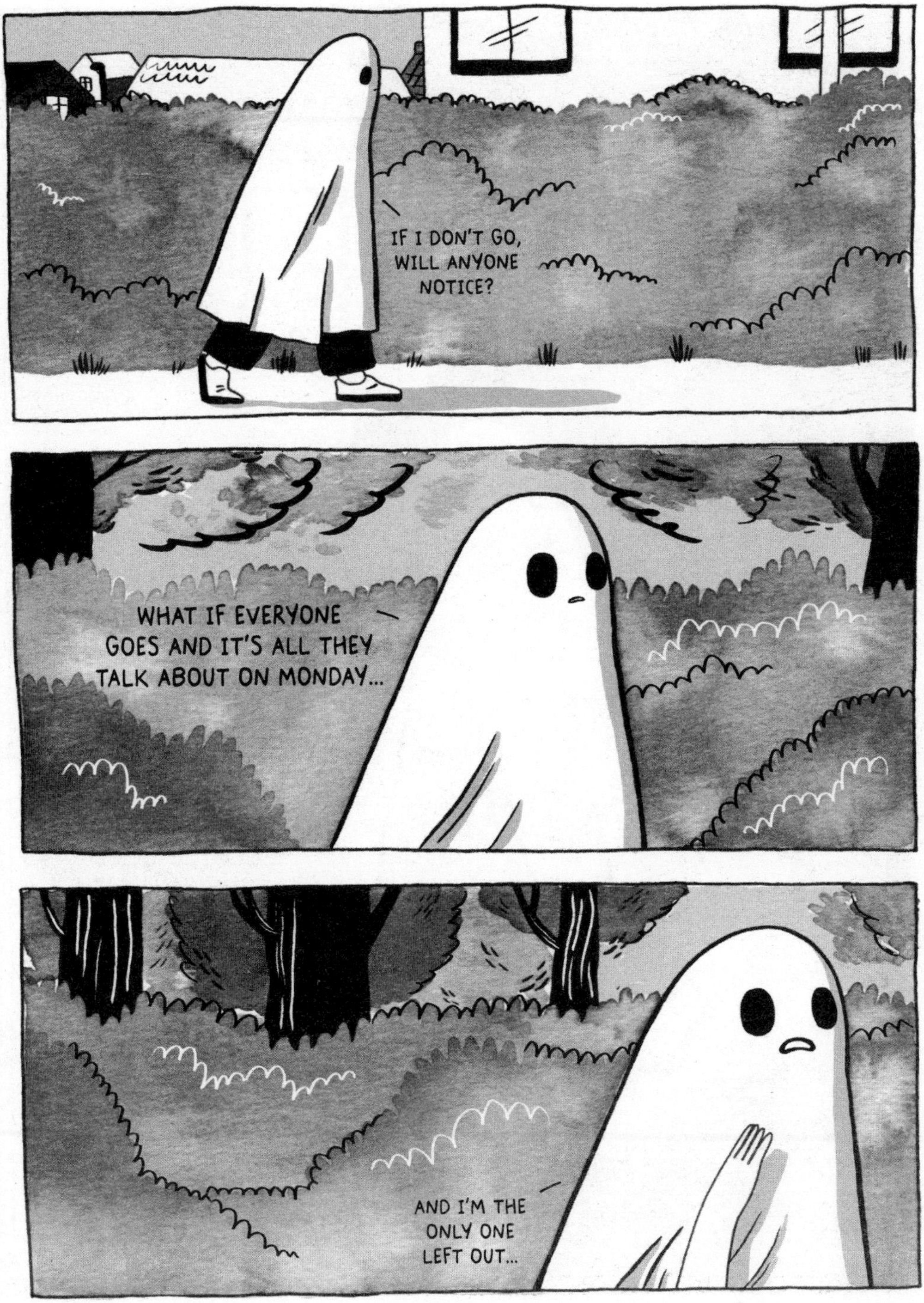
IF I DON'T GO, WILL ANYONE NOTICE?
WHAT IF EVERYONE GOES AND IT'S ALL THEY TALK ABOUT ON MONDAY...
AND I'M THE ONLY ONE LEFT OUT...

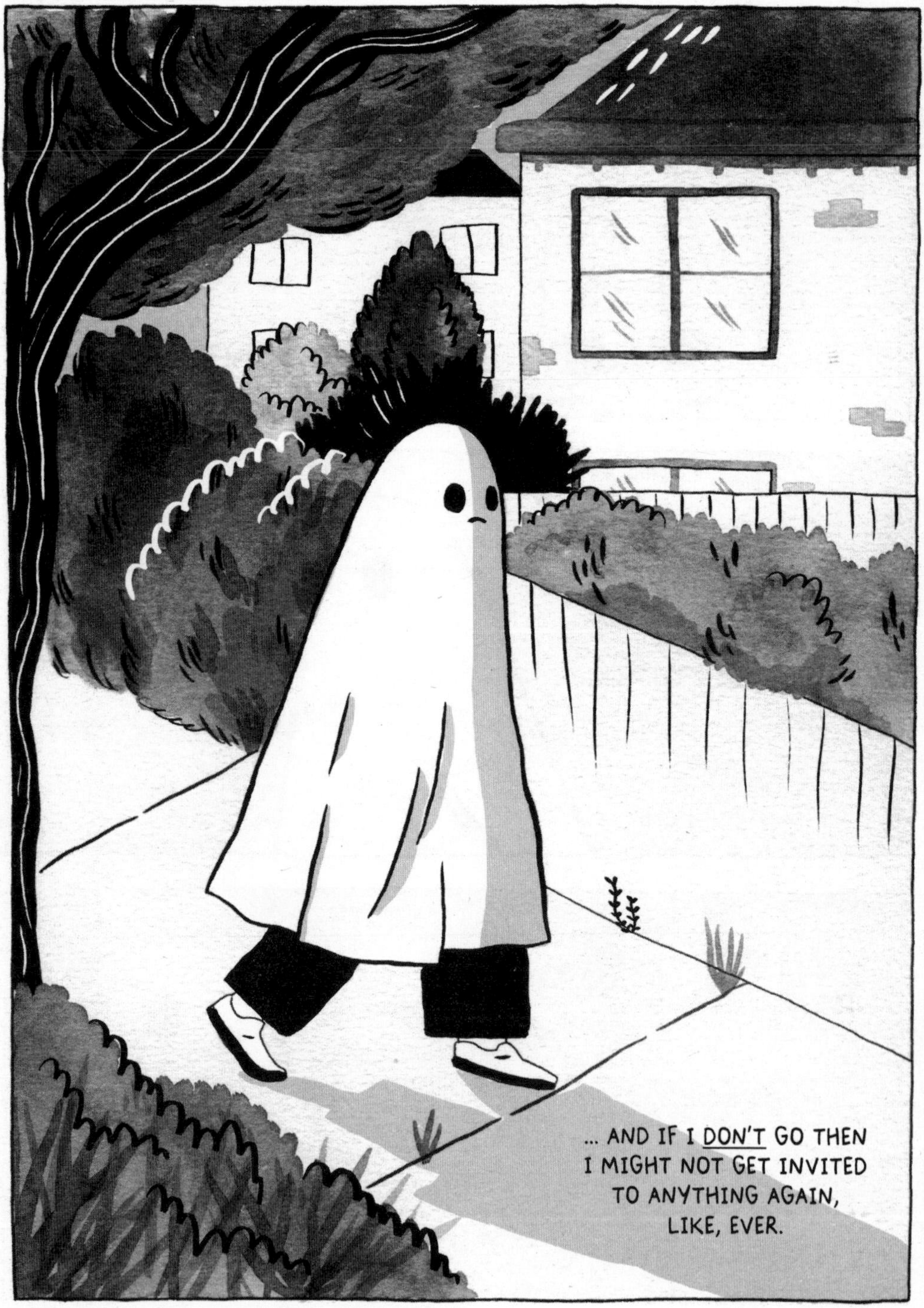
... AND IF I DON'T GO THEN I MIGHT NOT GET INVITED TO ANYTHING AGAIN, LIKE, EVER.

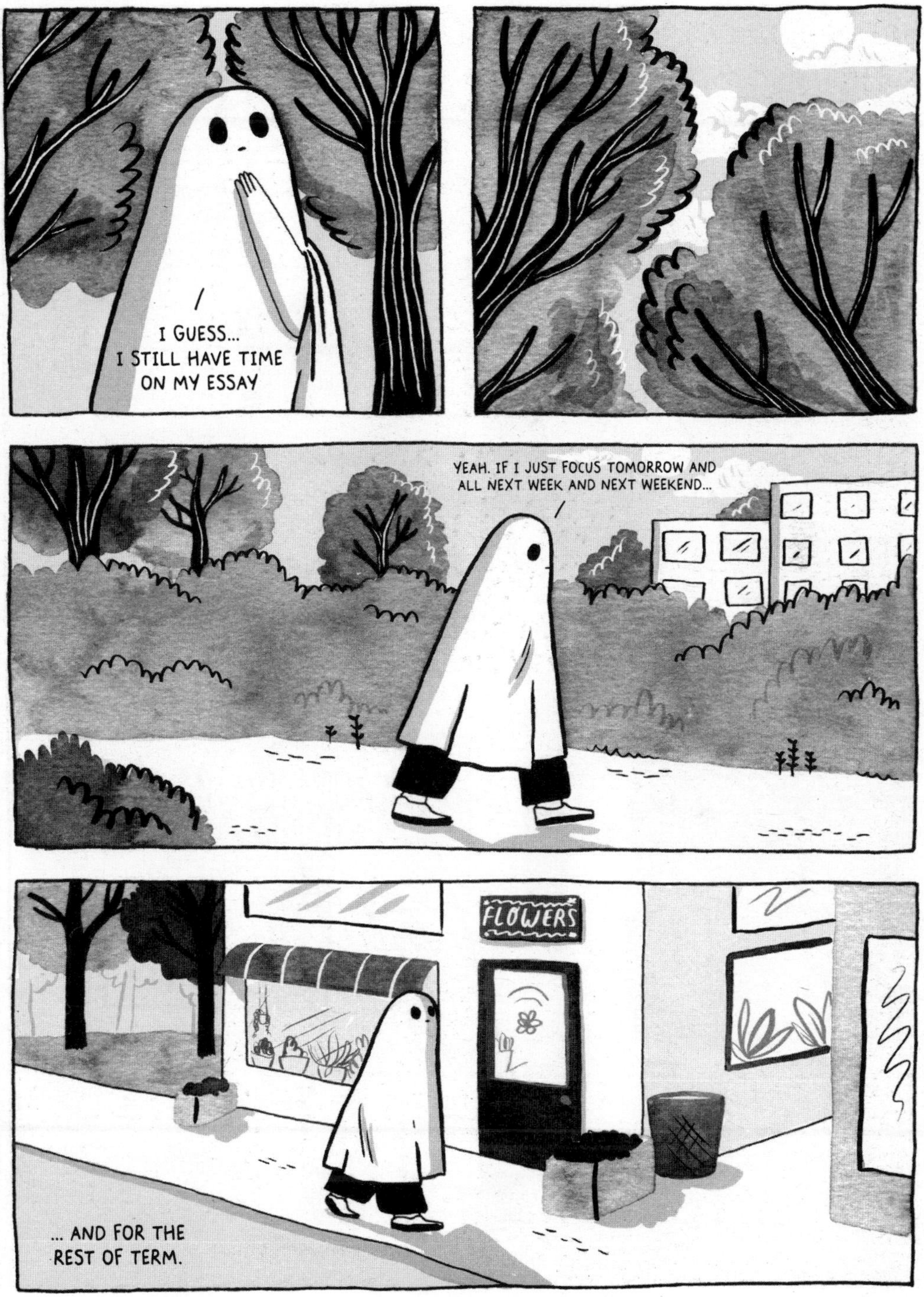
I GUESS...
I STILL HAVE TIME
ON MY ESSAY
YEAH. IF I JUST FOCUS TOMORROW AND
ALL NEXT WEEK AND NEXT WEEKEND...
FLOWERS
... AND FOR THE
REST OF TERM.

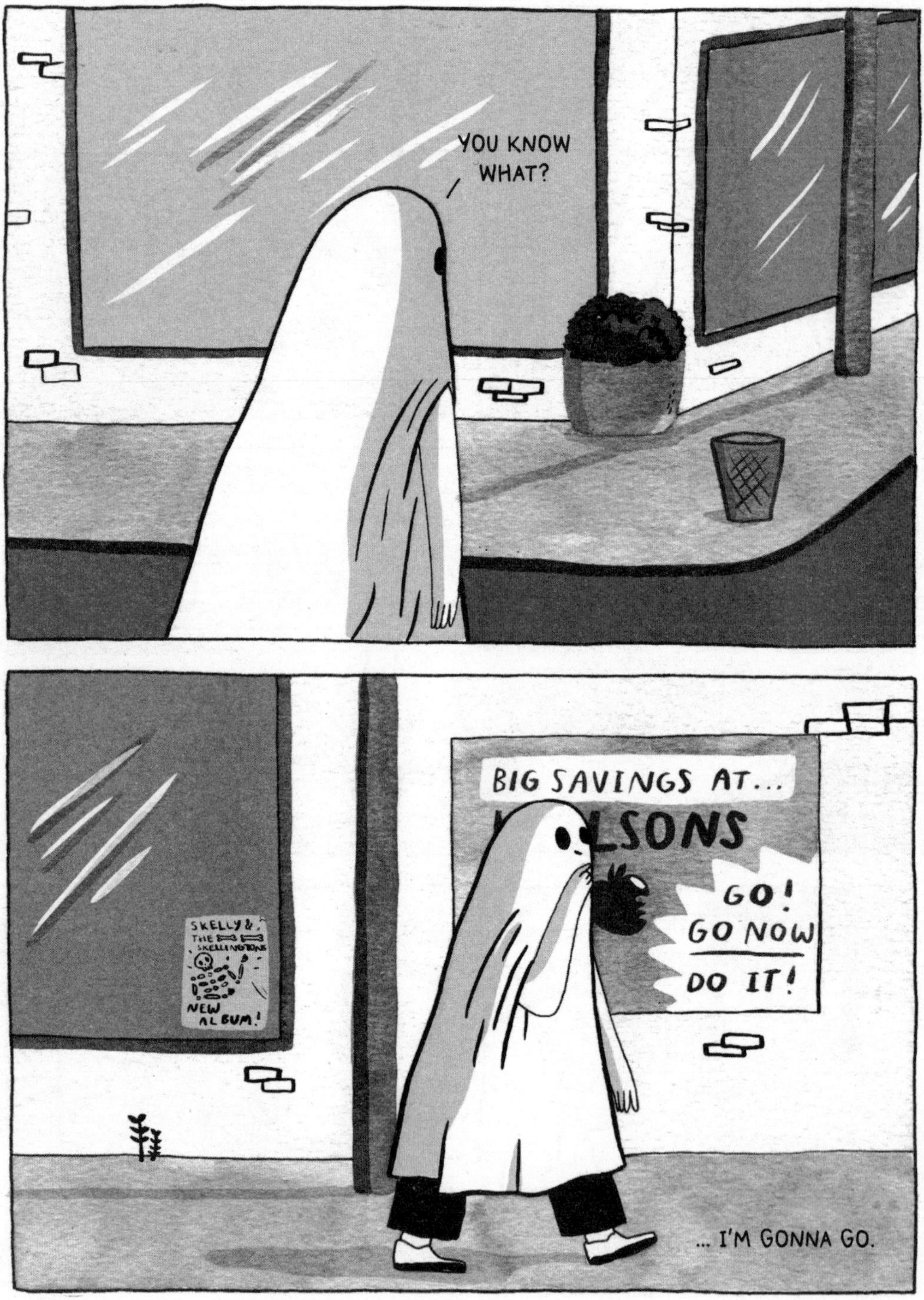
YOU KNOW WHAT?
BIG SAVINGS AT...
GO! GO NOW DO IT!
SKELLY & THE SKELLINGTONS
NEW ALBUM!
... I'M GONNA GO.

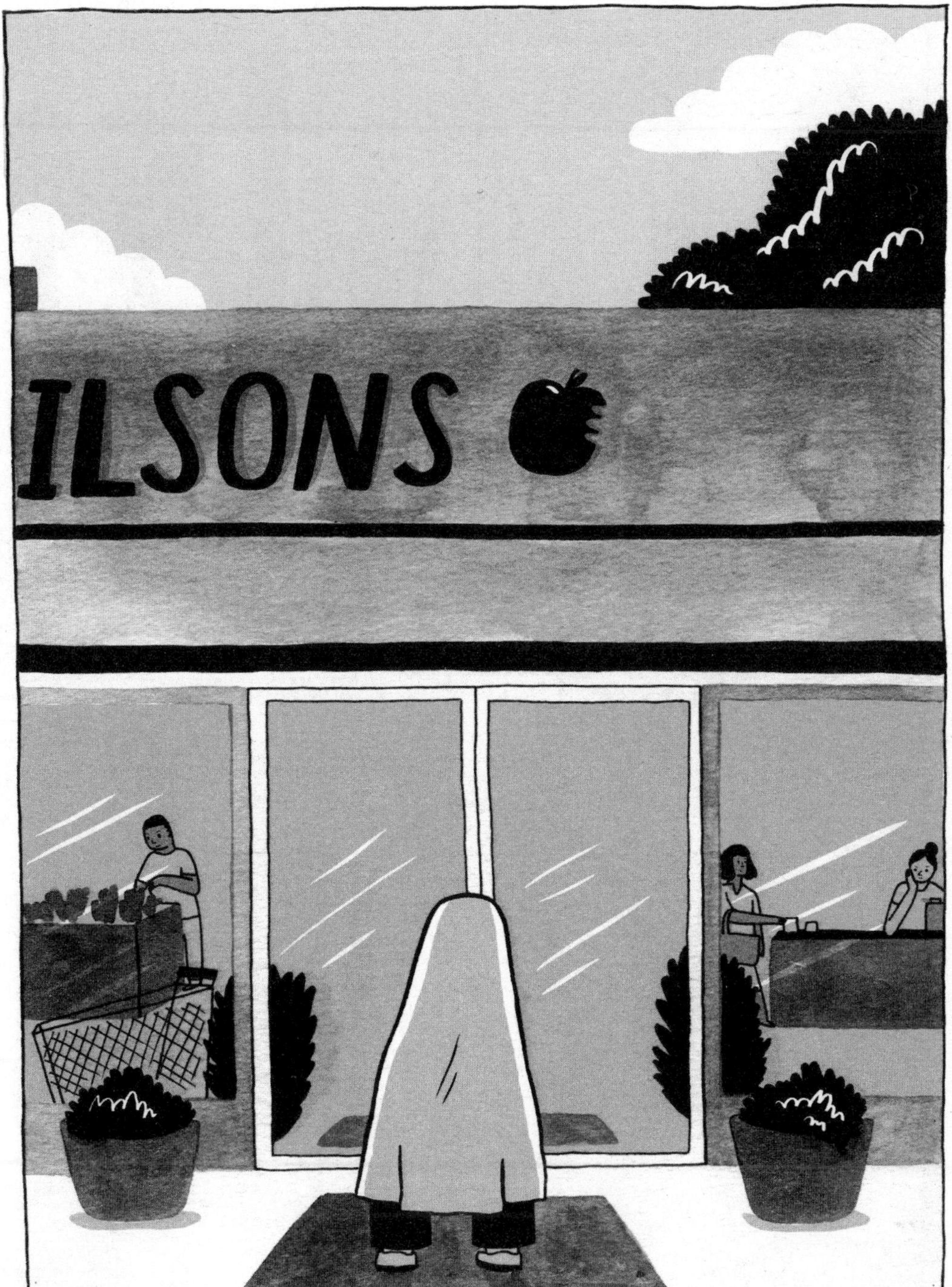
ILSONS

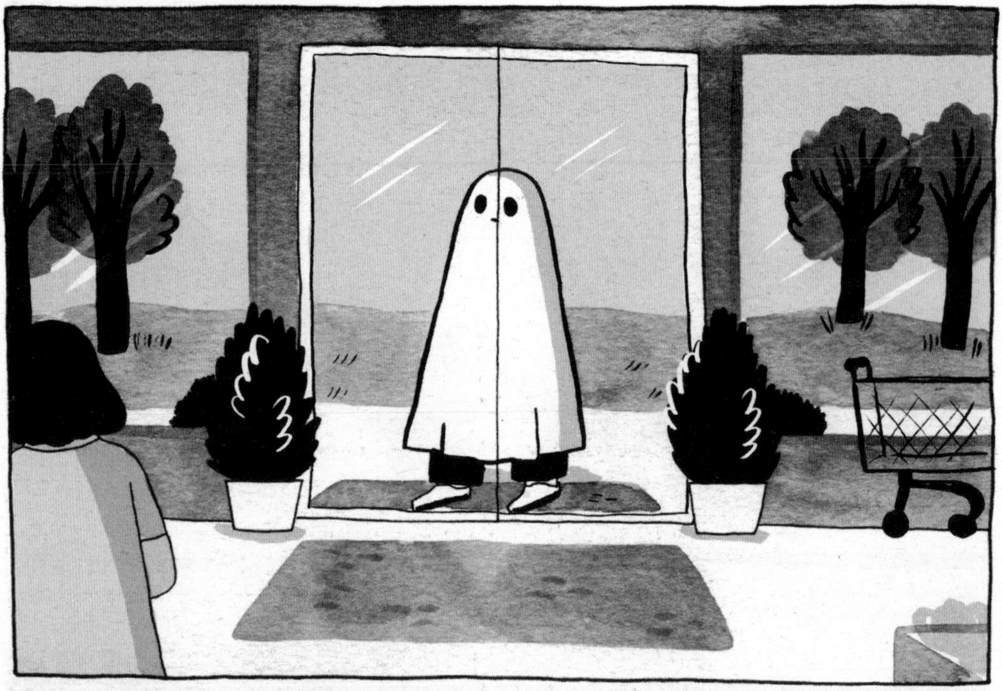

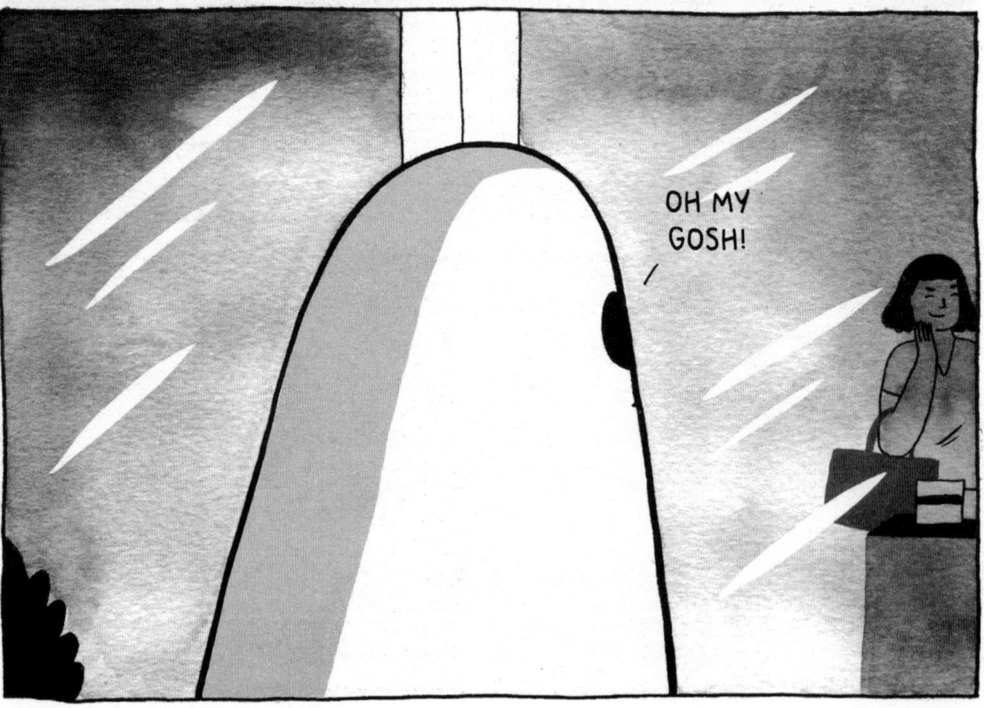
OH MY GOSH!

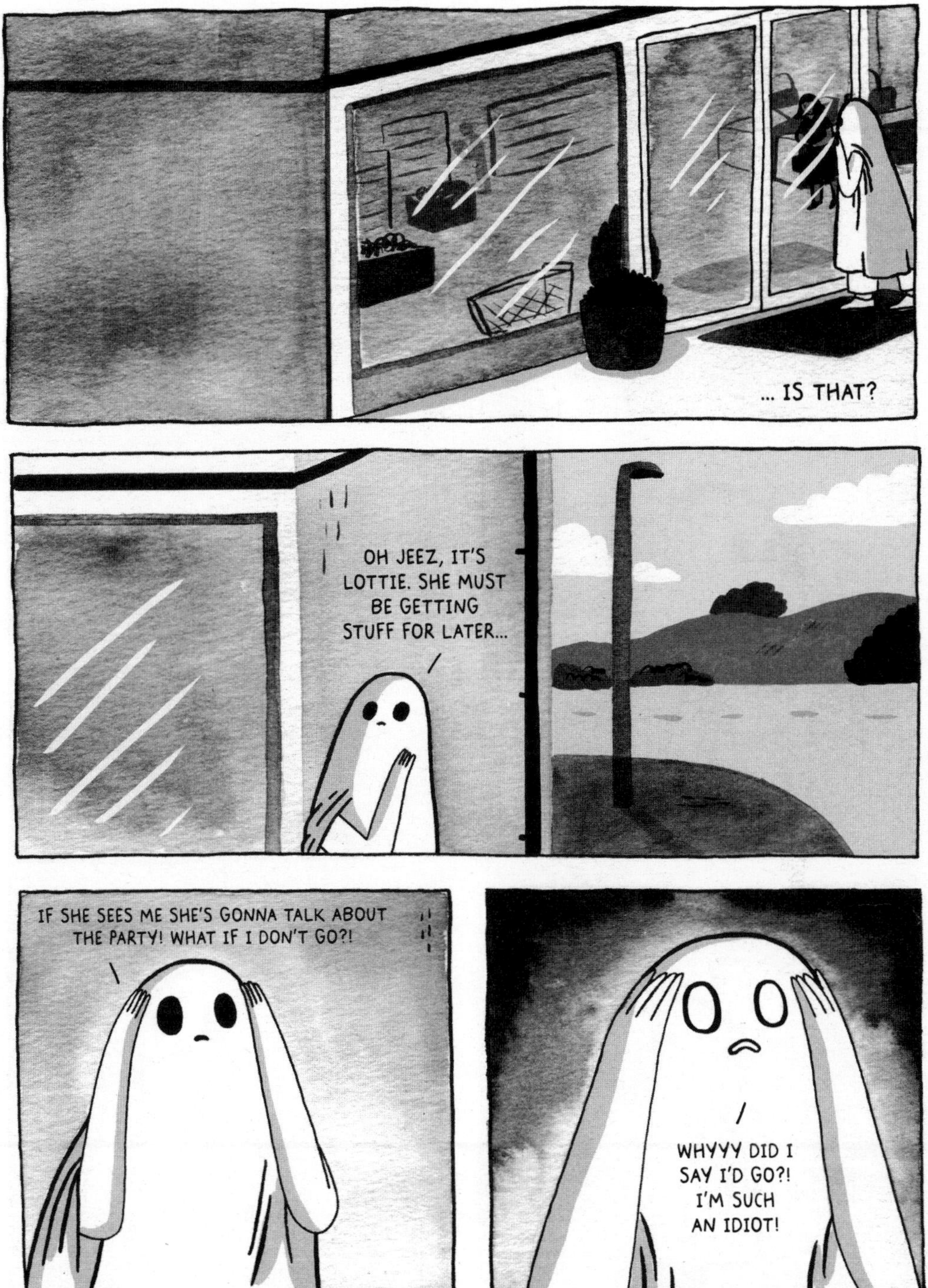
... IS THAT?
OH JEEZ, IT'S LOTTIE. SHE MUST BE GETTING STUFF FOR LATER...
IF SHE SEES ME SHE'S GONNA TALK ABOUT THE PARTY! WHAT IF I DON'T GO?!
WHYYY DID I SAY I'D GO?! I'M SUCH AN IDIOT!

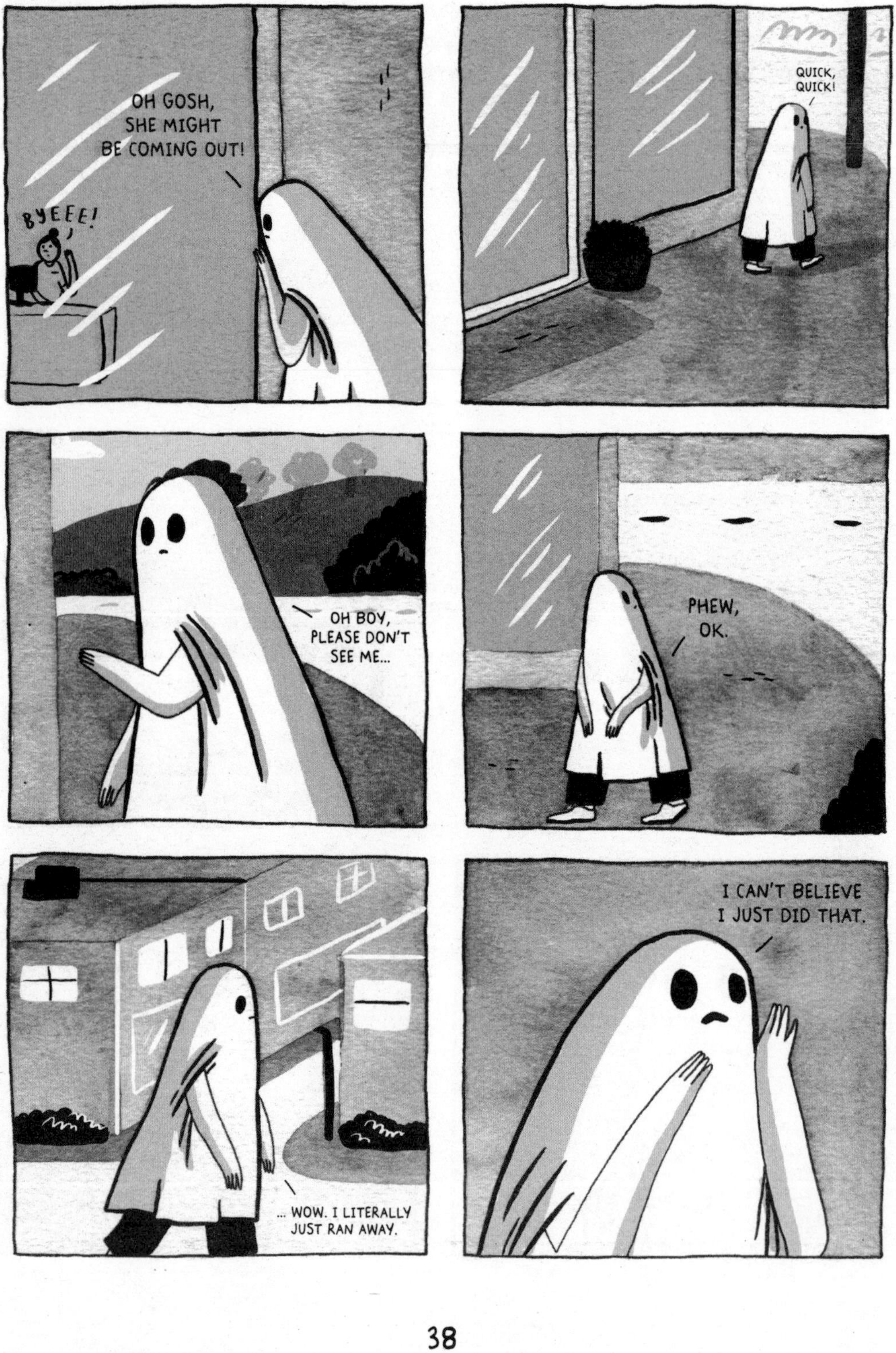
OH GOSH, SHE MIGHT BE COMING OUT!
BYEEE!
QUICK, QUICK!
OH BOY, PLEASE DON'T SEE ME...
PHEW, OK.
... WOW. I LITERALLY JUST RAN AWAY.
I CAN'T BELIEVE I JUST DID THAT.

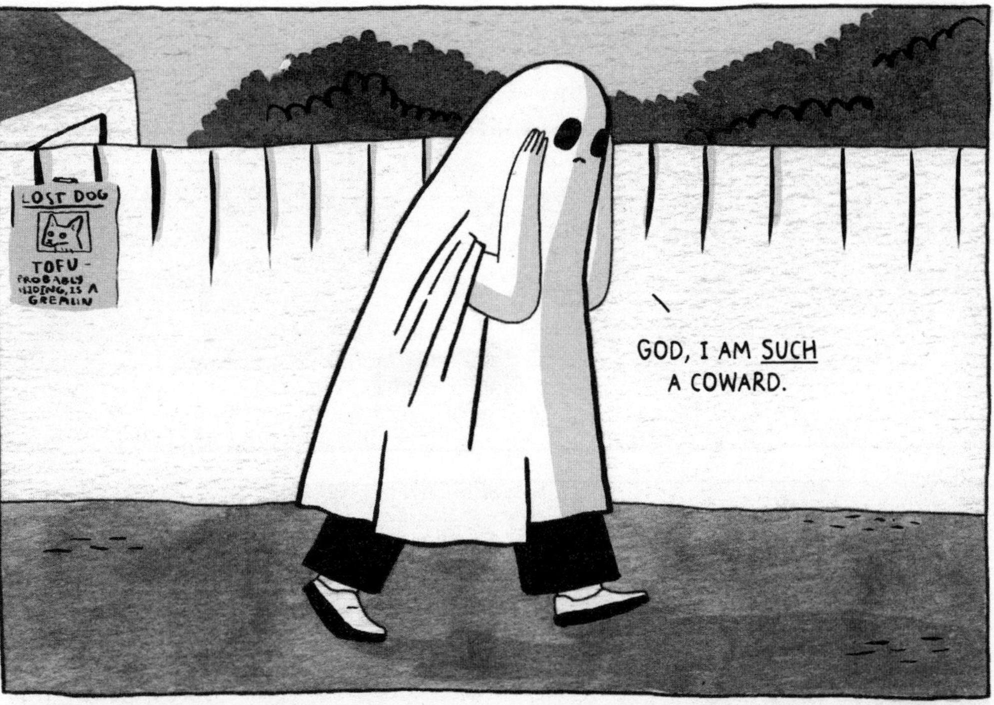
LOST DOG
TOFU - PROBABLY HIDING, IS A GREMLIN
GOD, I AM SUCH A COWARD.

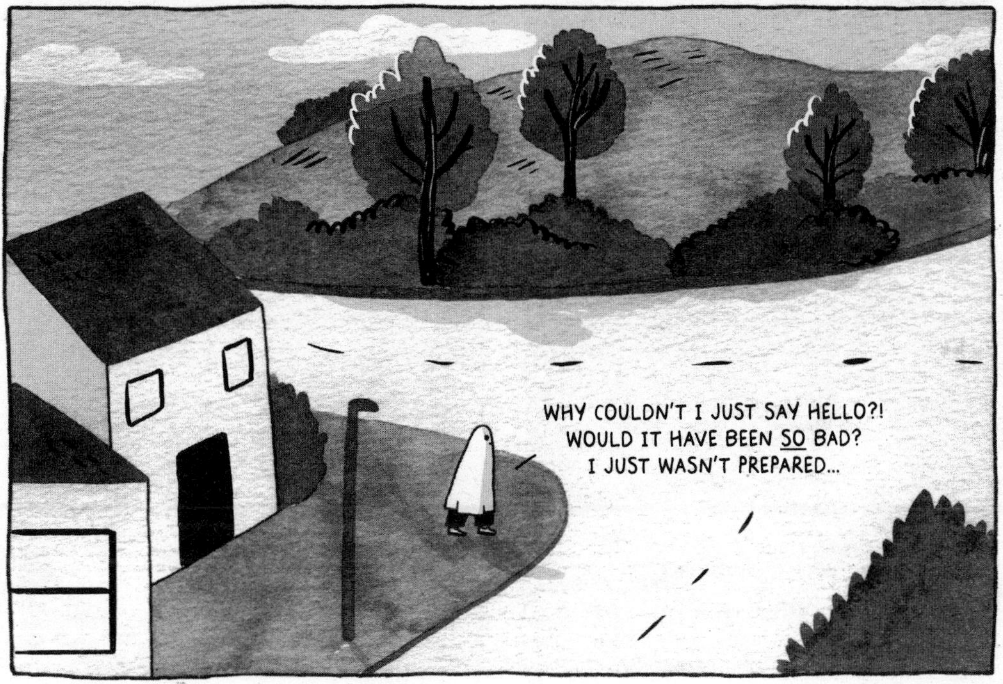
WHY COULDN'T I JUST SAY HELLO?! WOULD IT HAVE BEEN SO BAD? I JUST WASN'T PREPARED...

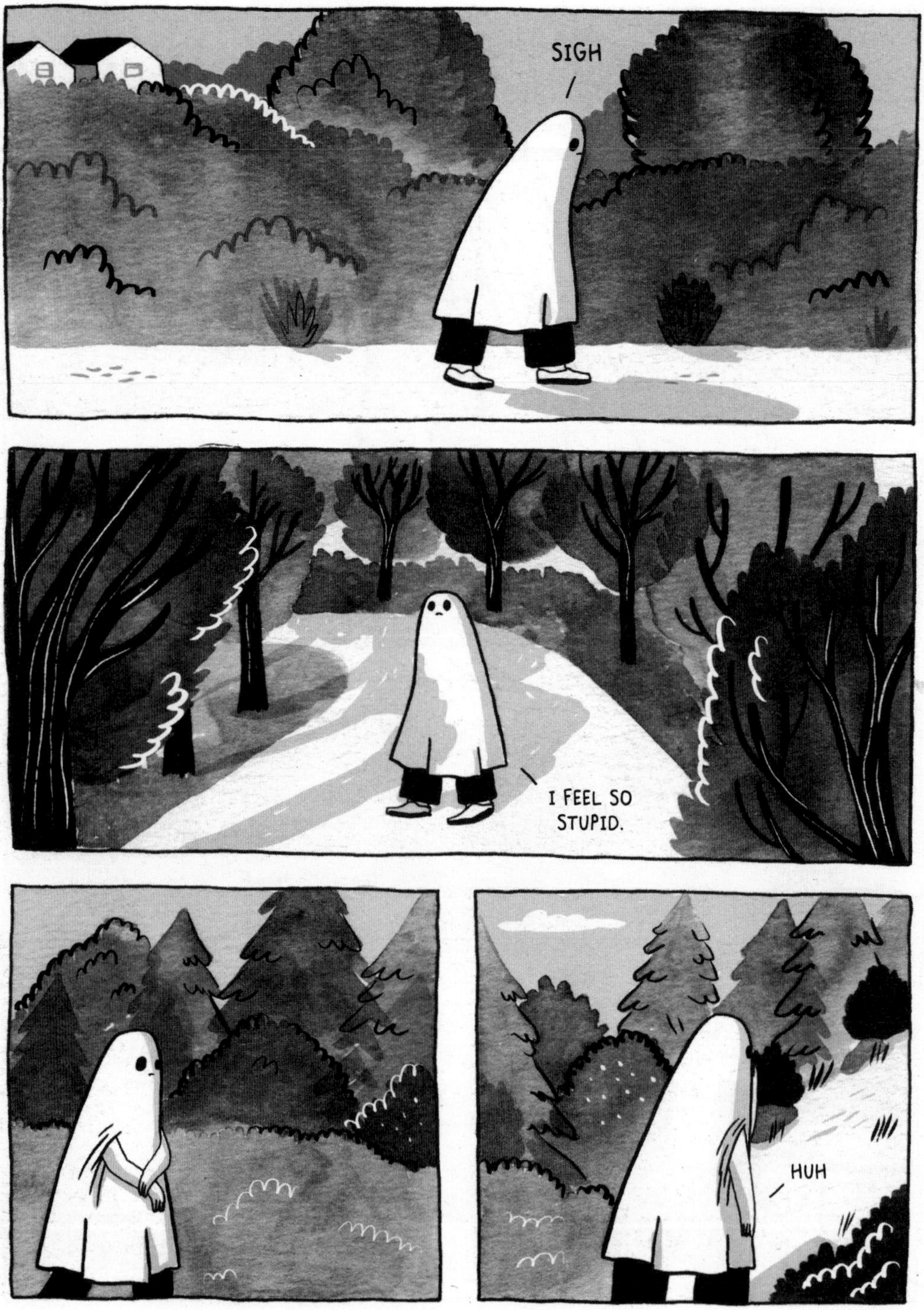
SIGH
I FEEL SO STUPID.
HUH

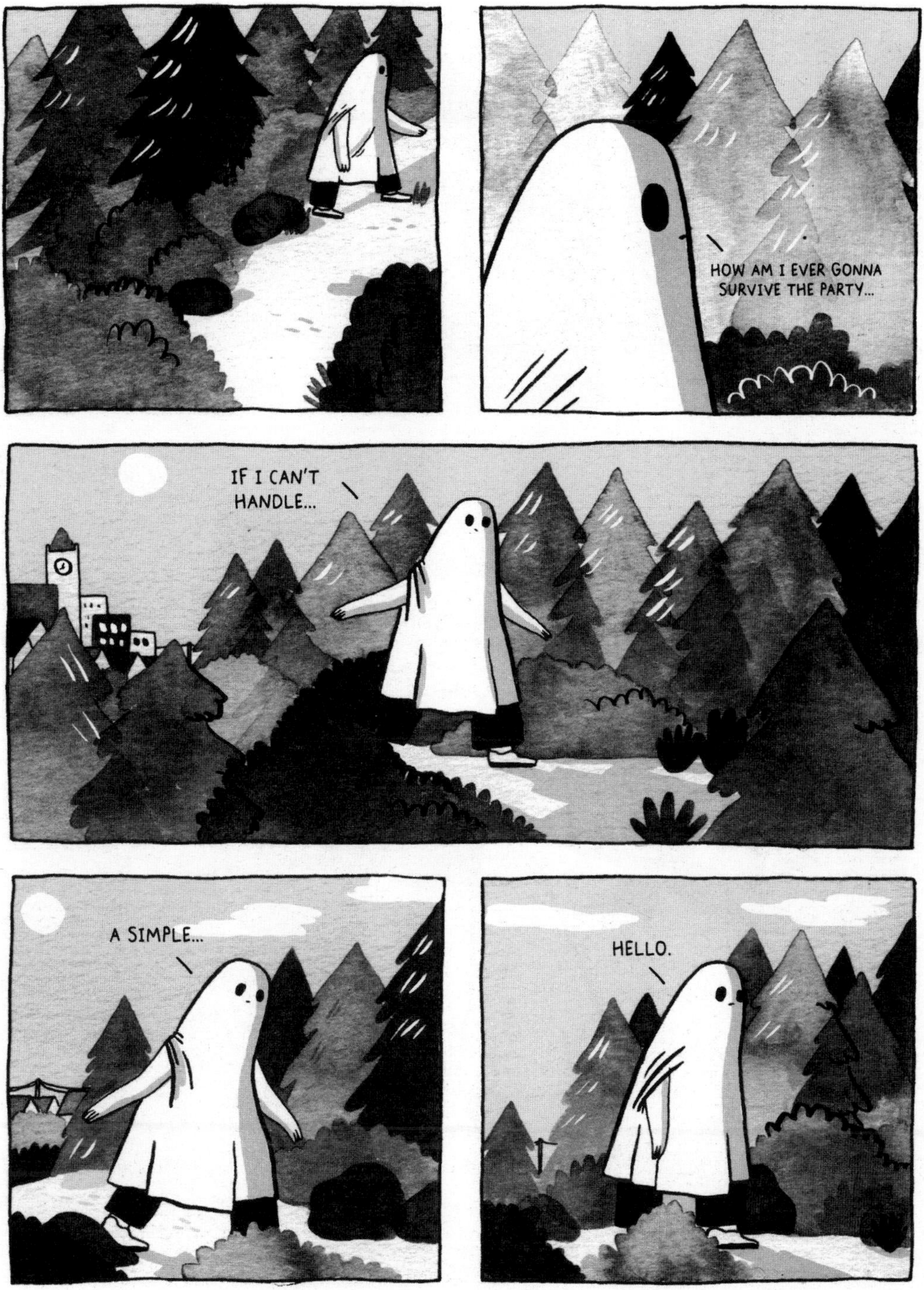
HOW AM I EVER GONNA SURVIVE THE PARTY...
IF I CAN'T HANDLE...
A SIMPLE...
HELLO.

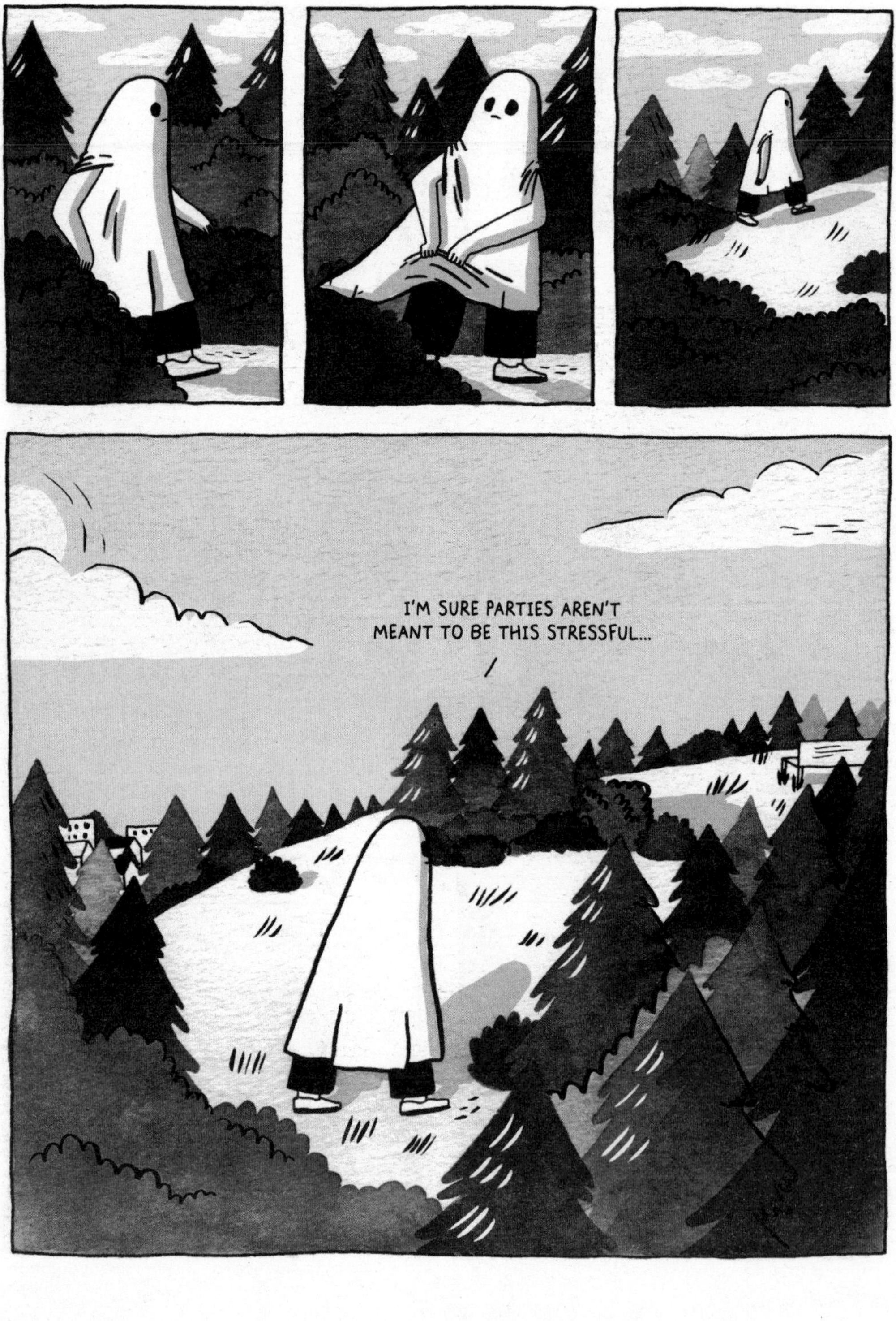
I'M SURE PARTIES AREN'T
MEANT TO BE THIS STRESSFUL...

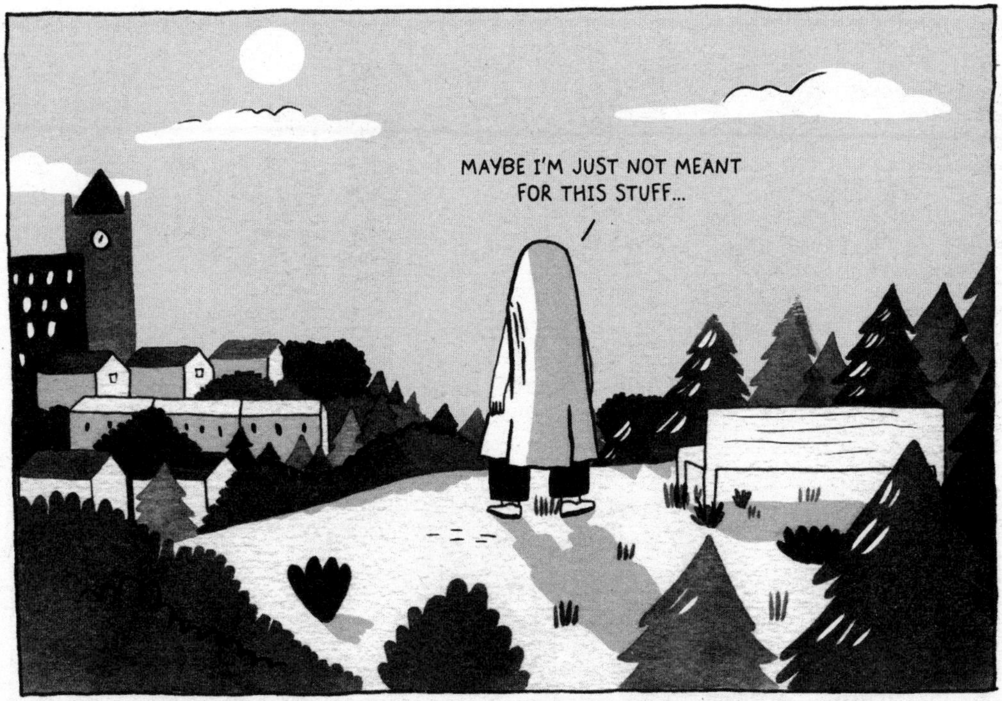
MAYBE I'M JUST NOT MEANT FOR THIS STUFF...

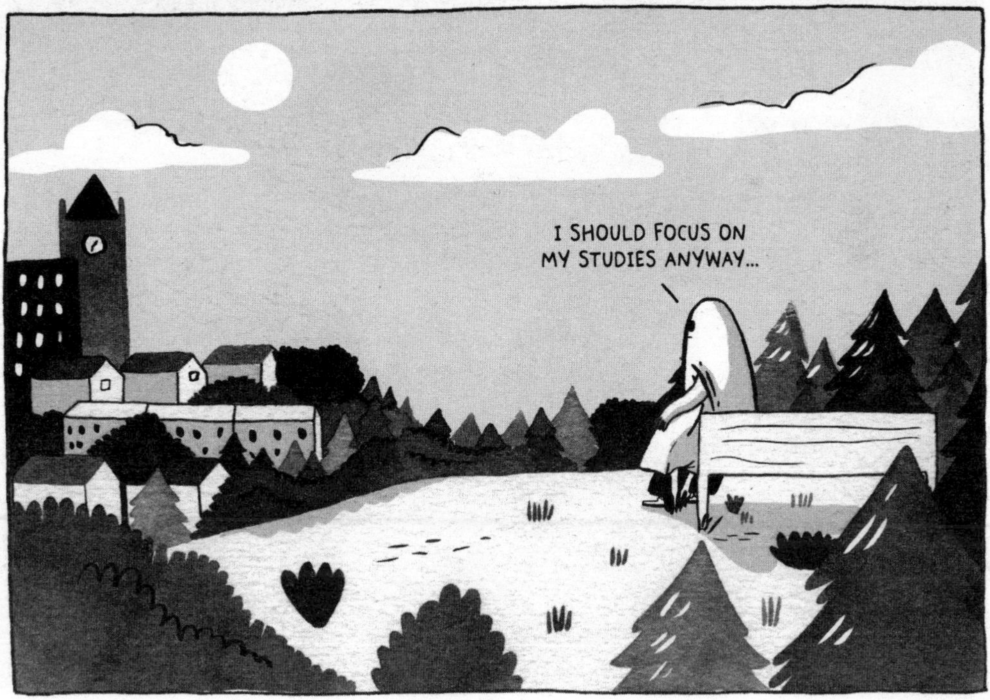
I SHOULD FOCUS ON MY STUDIES ANYWAY...

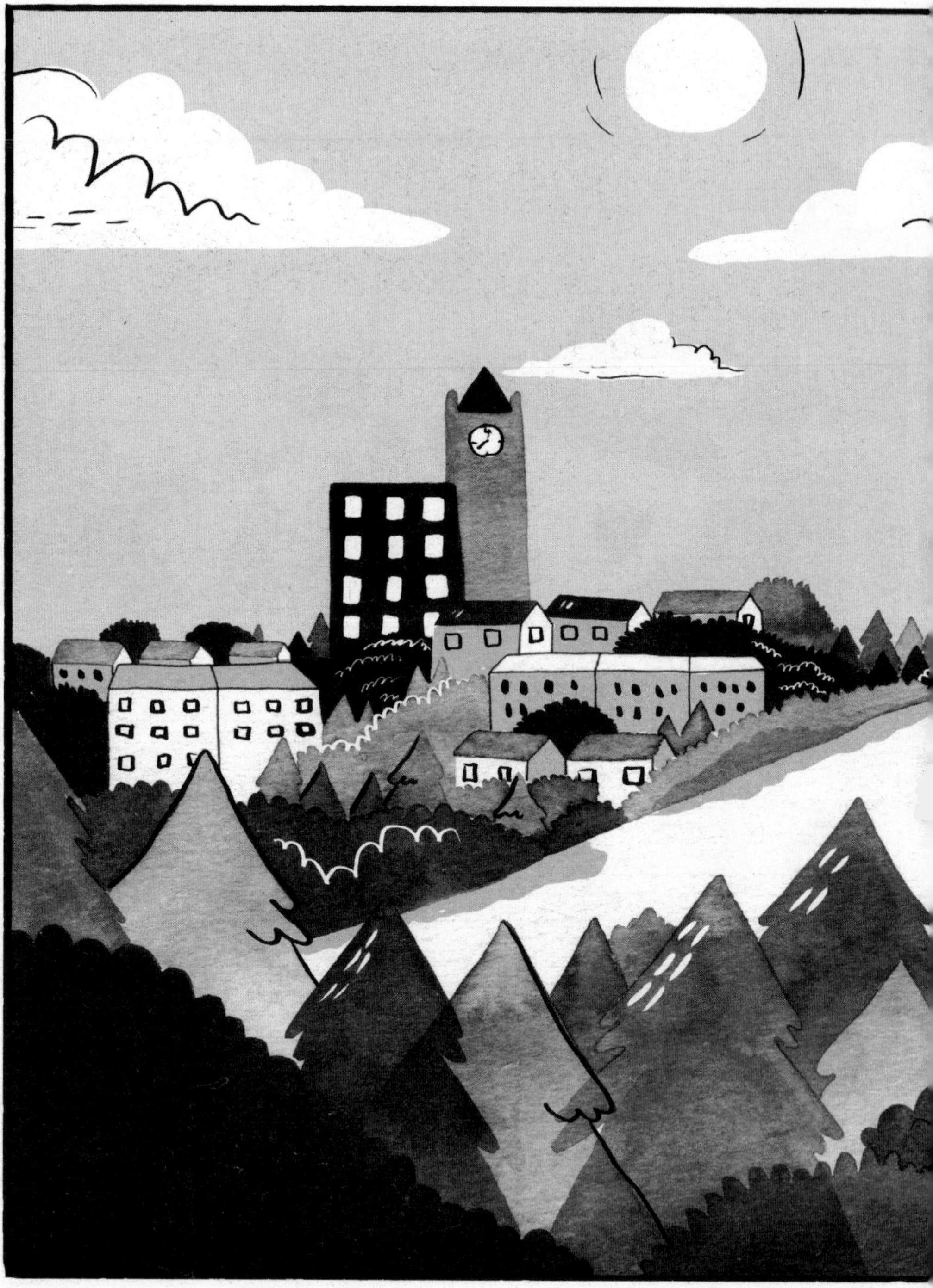

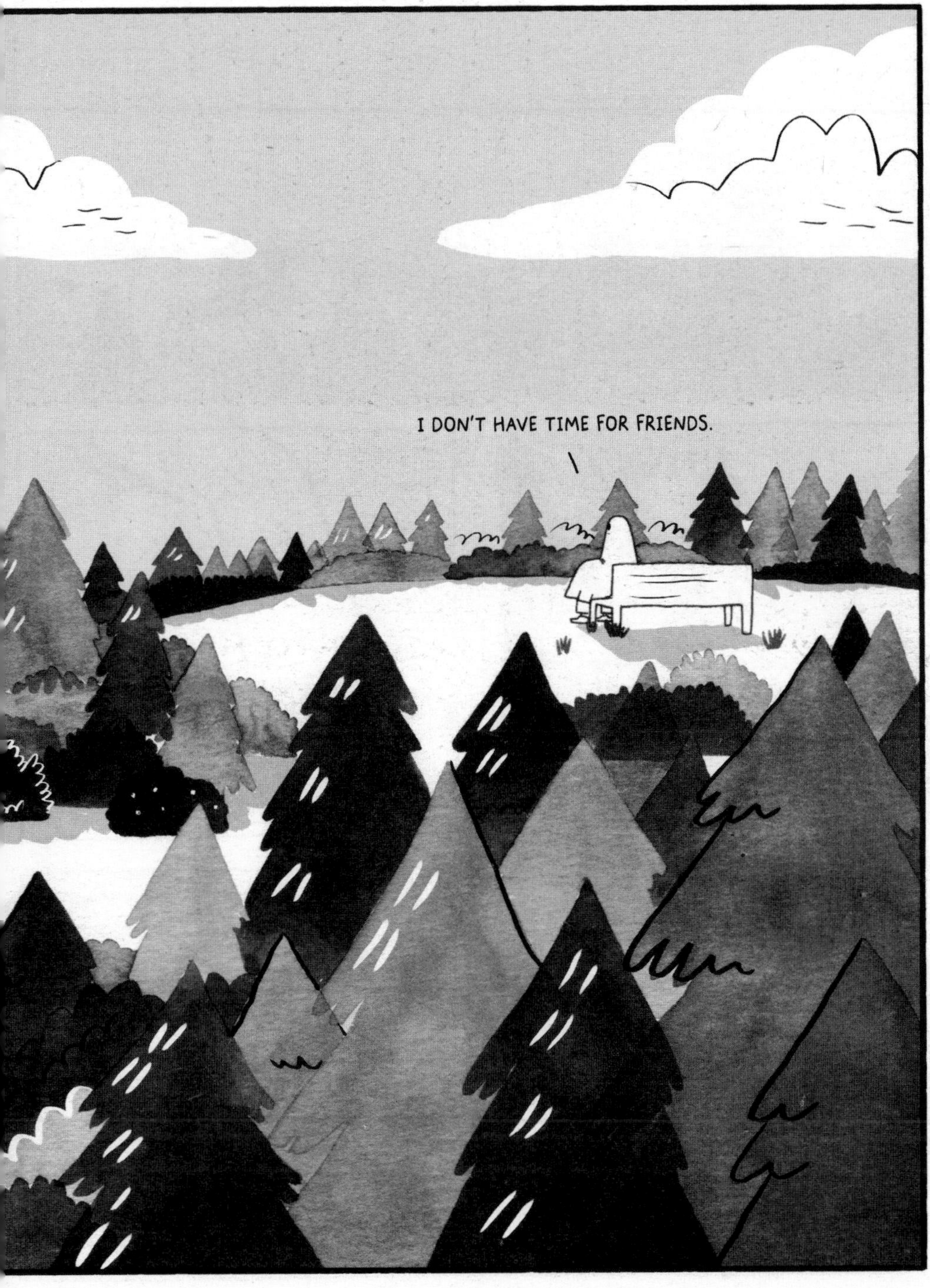
I DON'T HAVE TIME FOR FRIENDS.

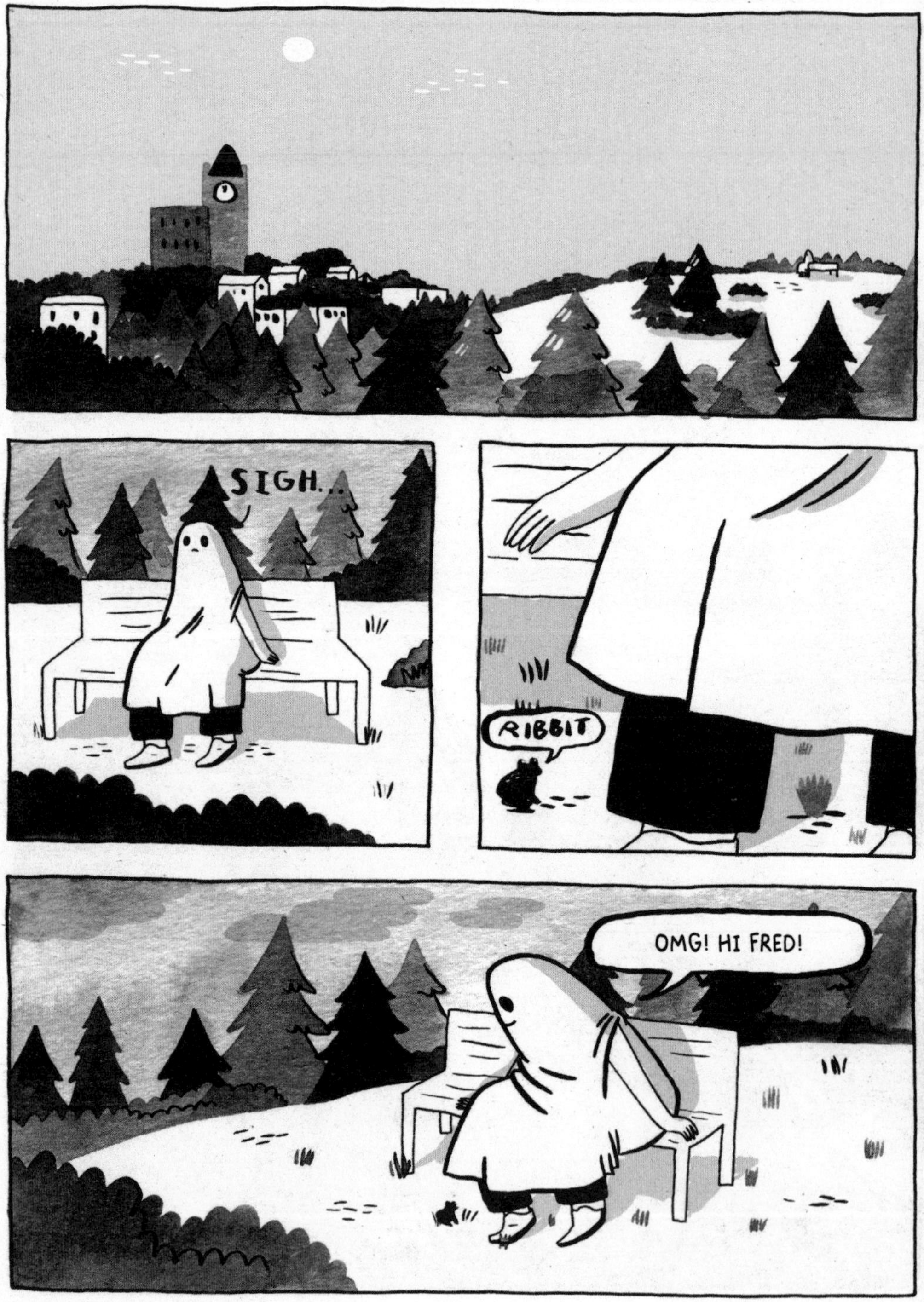
SIGH...
RIBBIT
OMG! HI FRED!

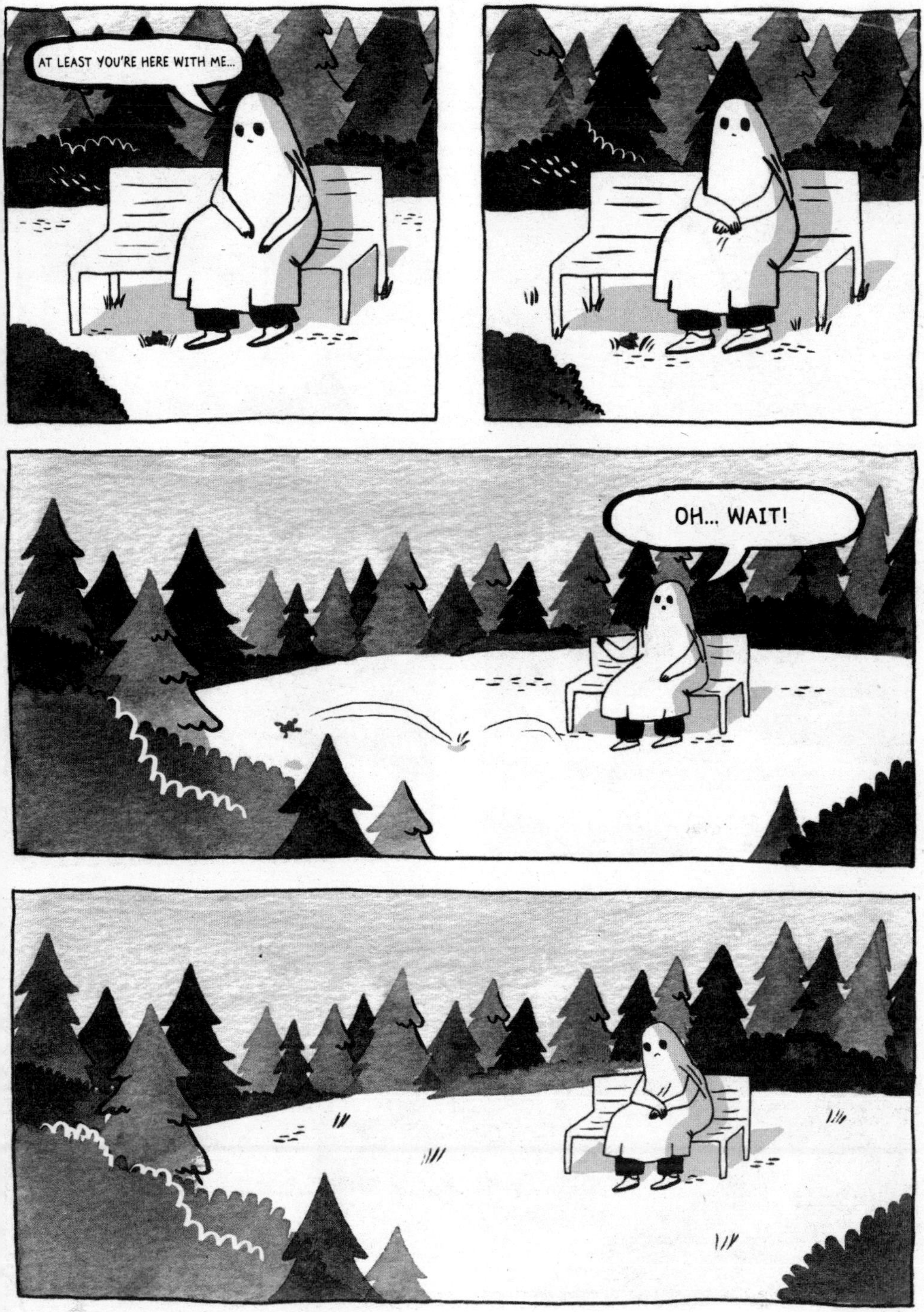
AT LEAST YOU'RE HERE WITH ME...
OH... WAIT!

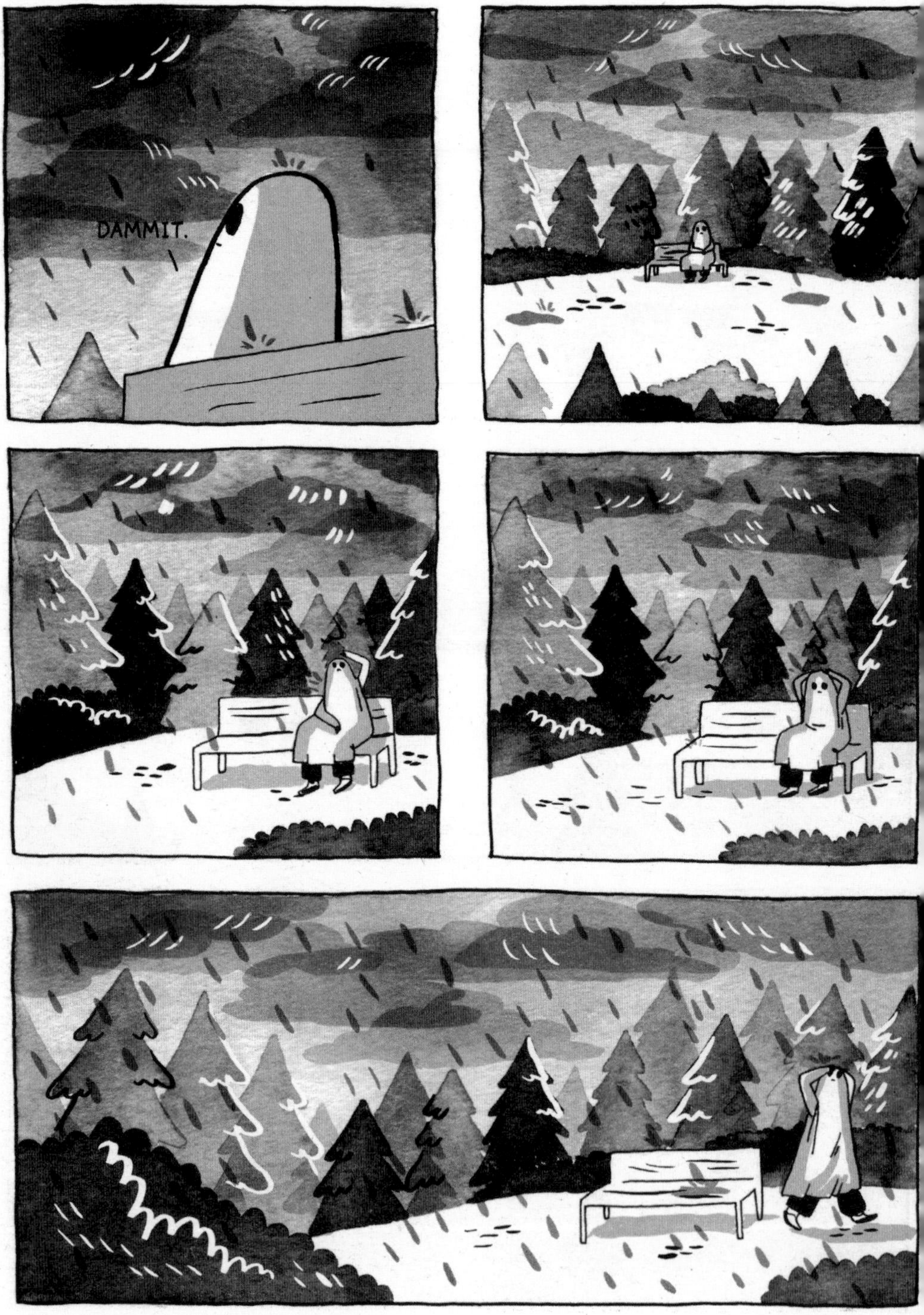
DAMMIT.

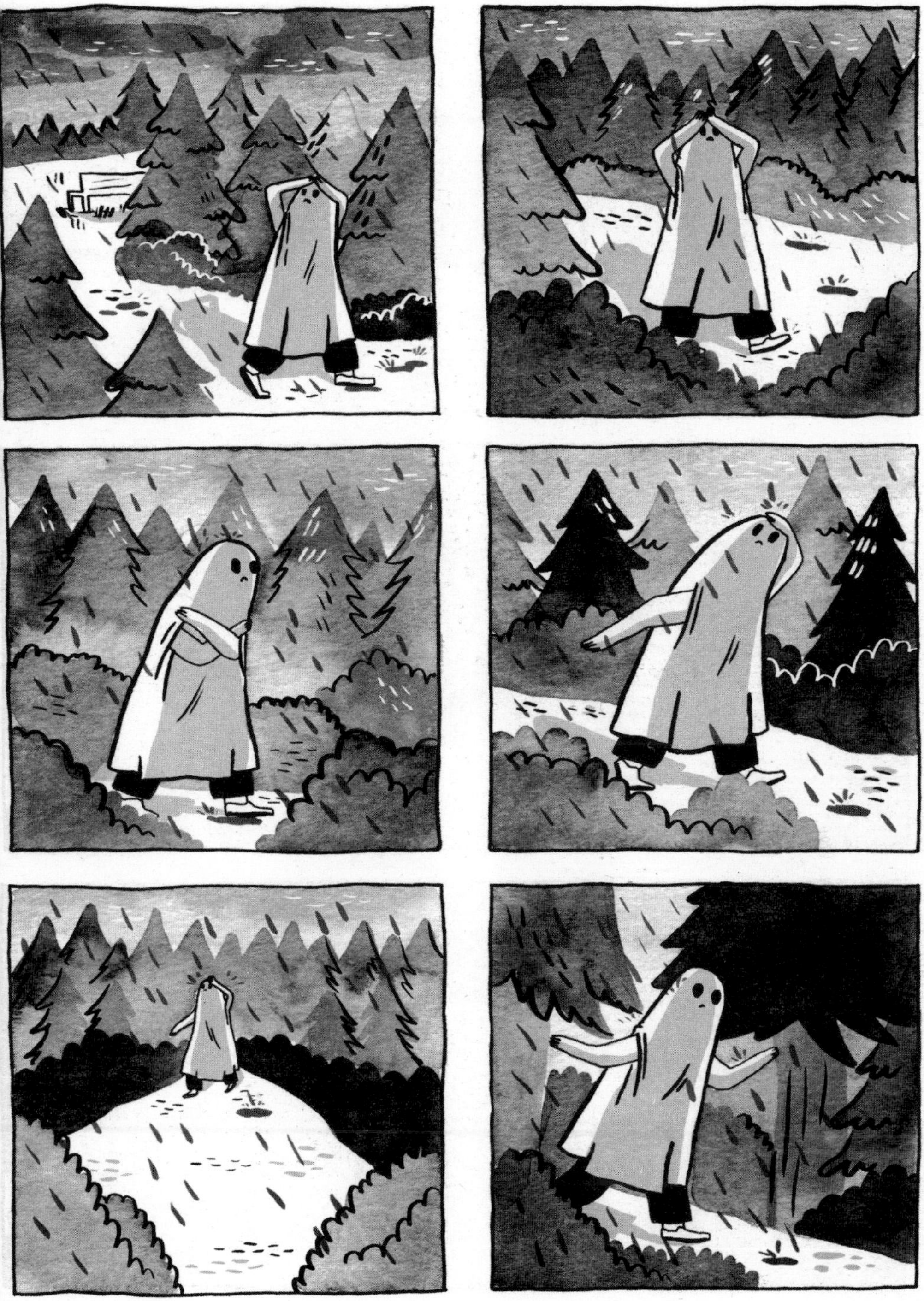

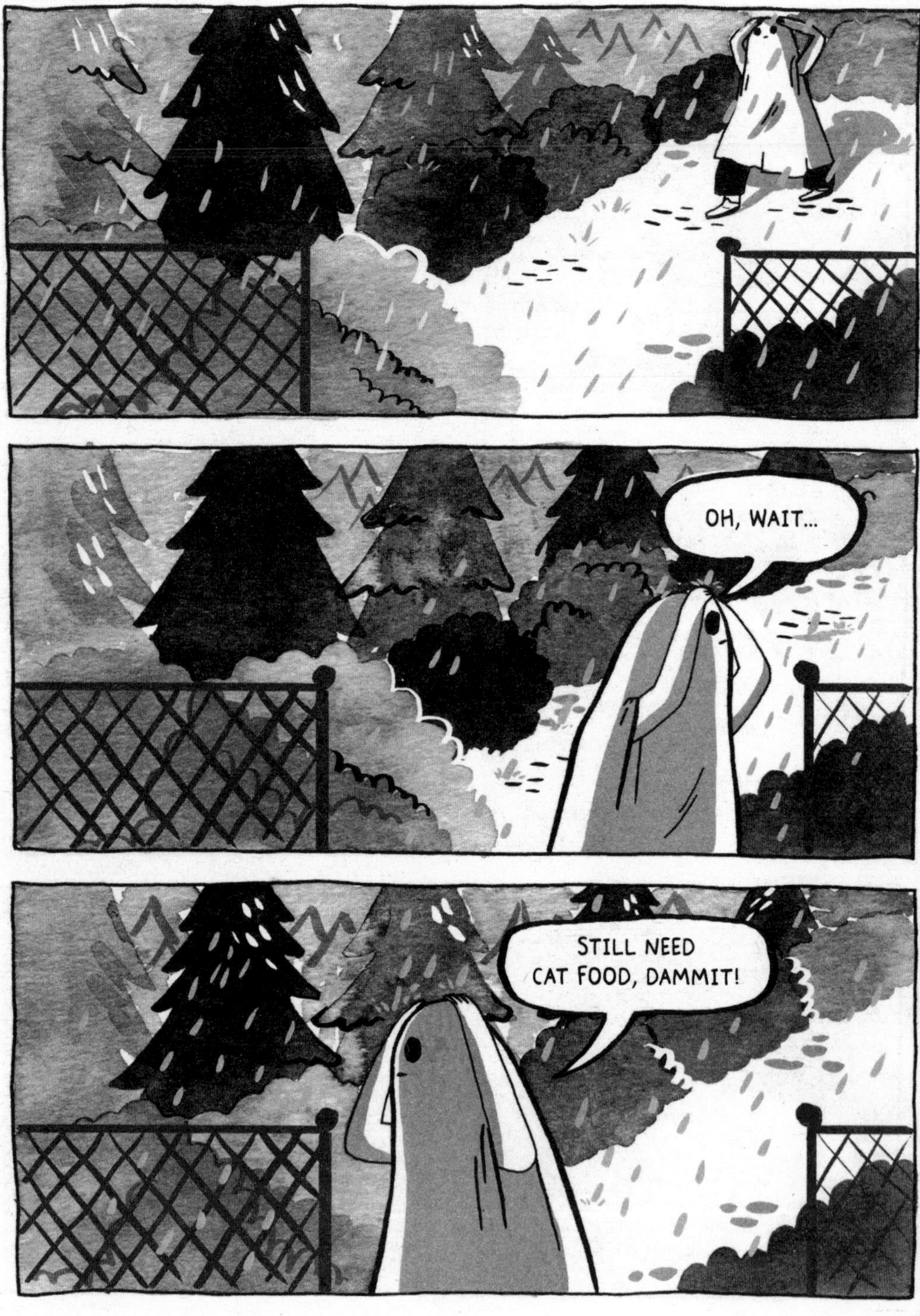
OH, WAIT...
STILL NEED
CAT FOOD, DAMMIT!

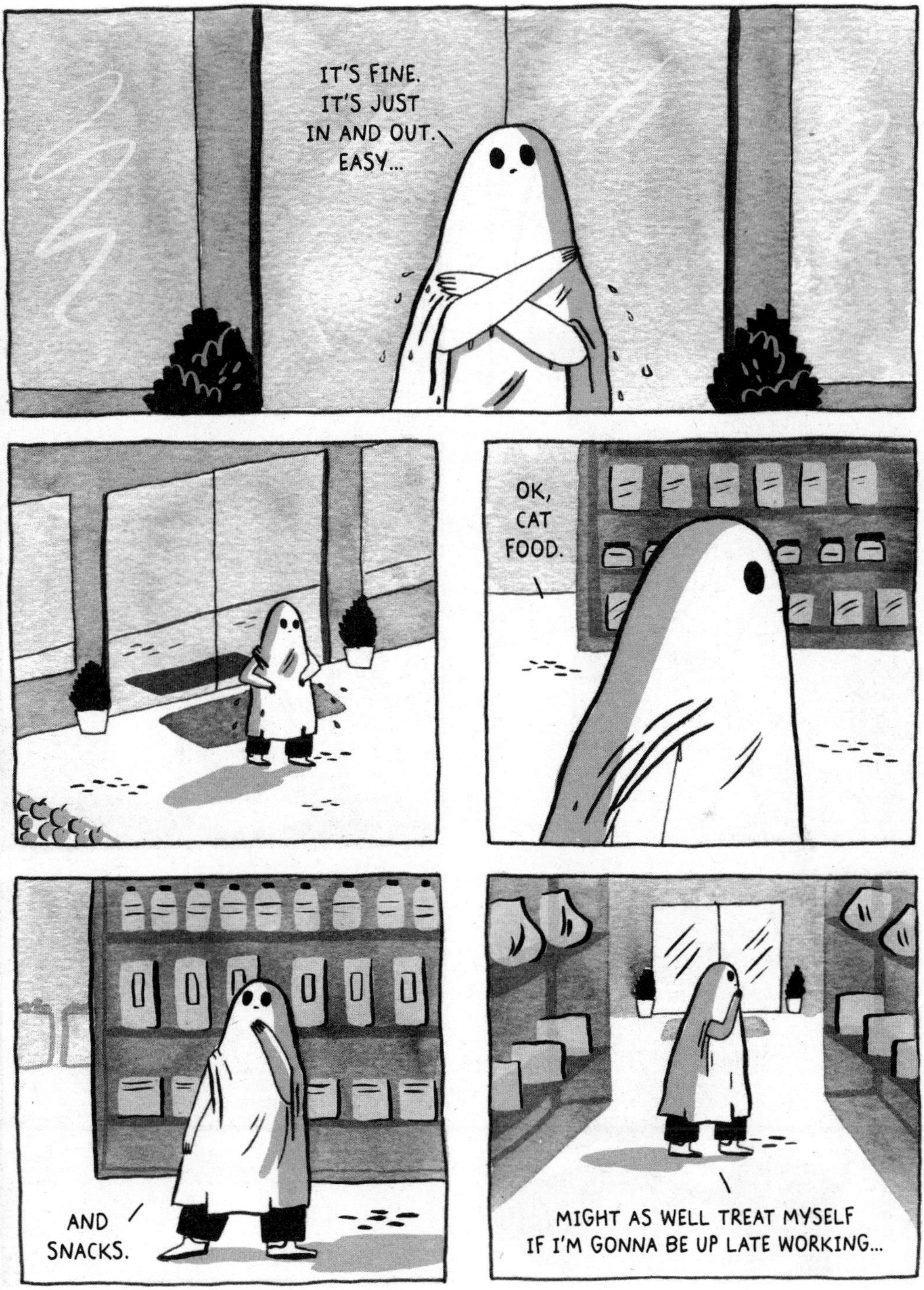
IT'S FINE. IT'S JUST IN AND OUT. EASY...
OK, CAT FOOD.
AND SNACKS.
MIGHT AS WELL TREAT MYSELF IF I'M GONNA BE UP LATE WORKING...

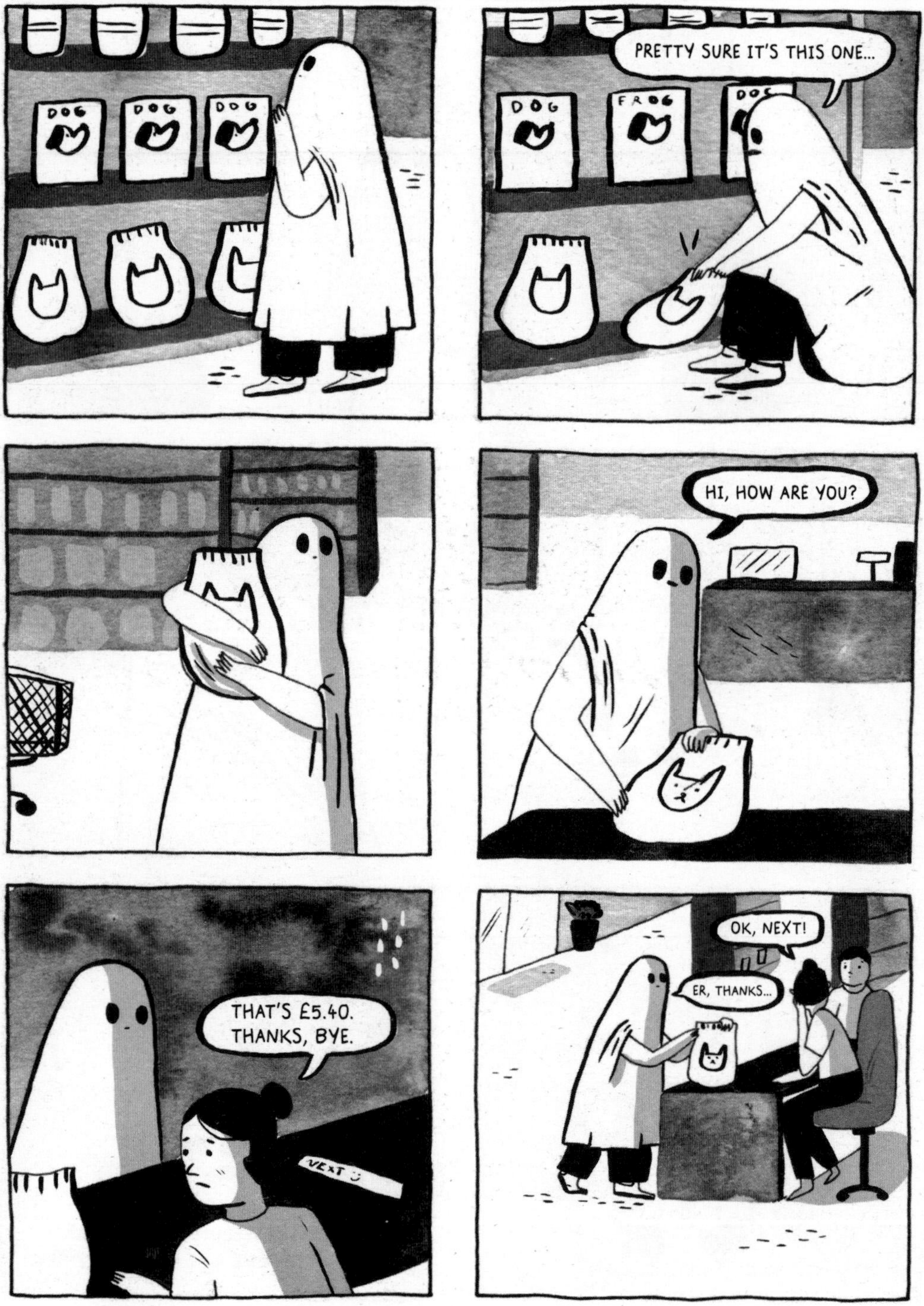
DOG
DOG
DOG
DOG
FROG
PRETTY SURE IT'S THIS ONE...
HI, HOW ARE YOU?
THAT'S £5.40.
THANKS, BYE.
NEXT
OK, NEXT!
ER, THANKS...

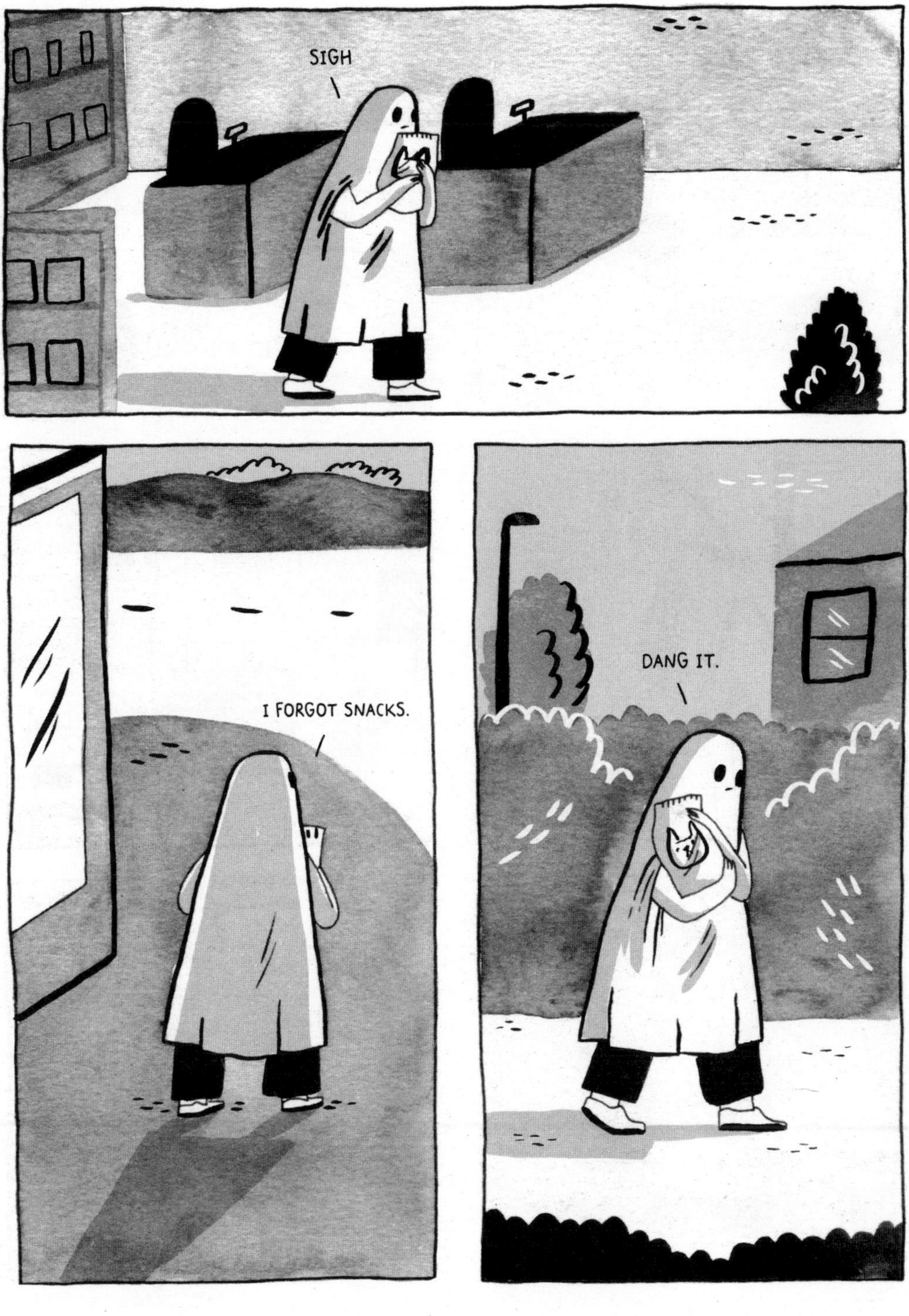
SIGH
I FORGOT SNACKS.
DANG IT.

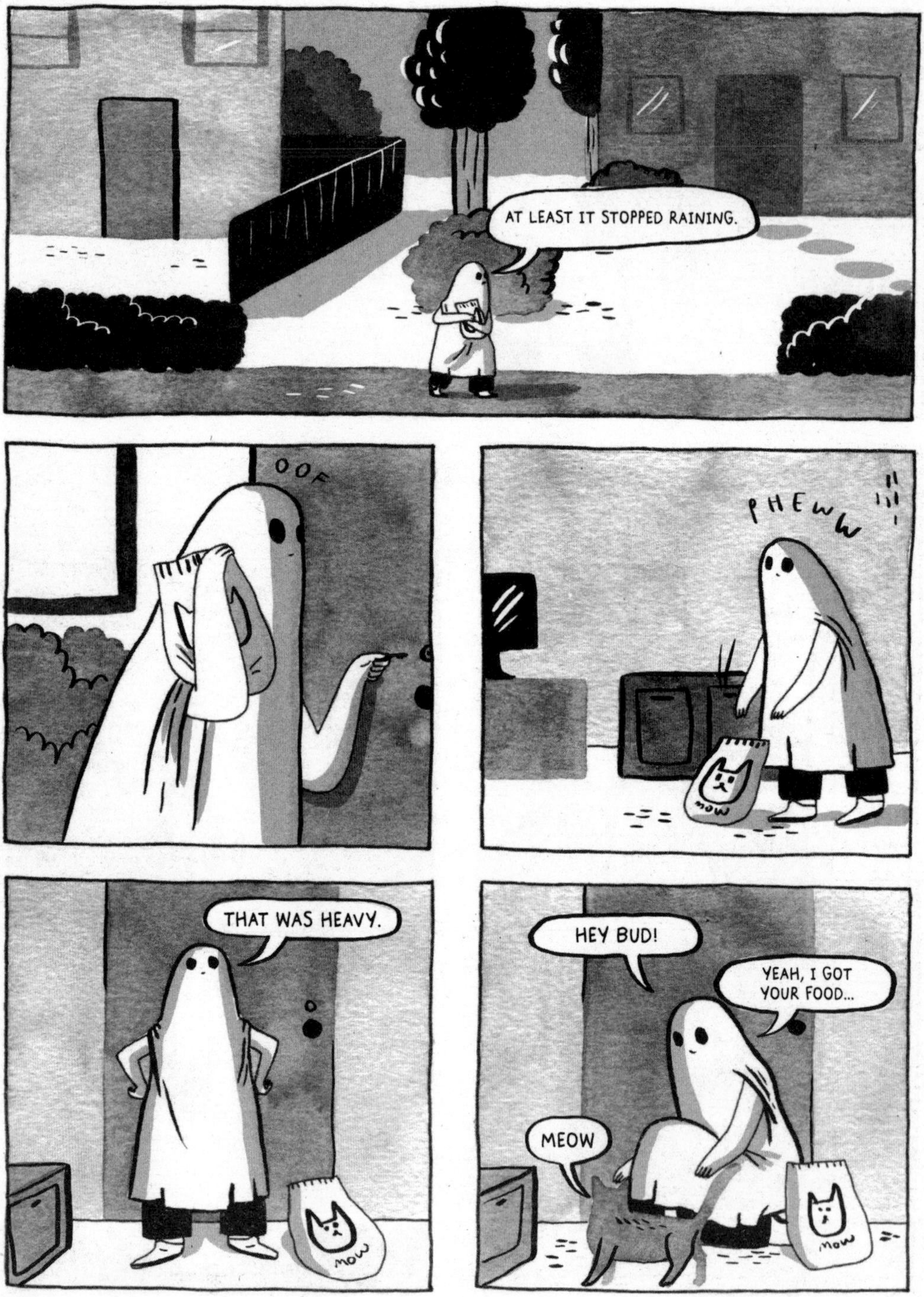
AT LEAST IT STOPPED RAINING.
OOF
PHEWW
THAT WAS HEAVY.
MOW
HEY BUD!
YEAH, I GOT YOUR FOOD...
MEOW
MOW

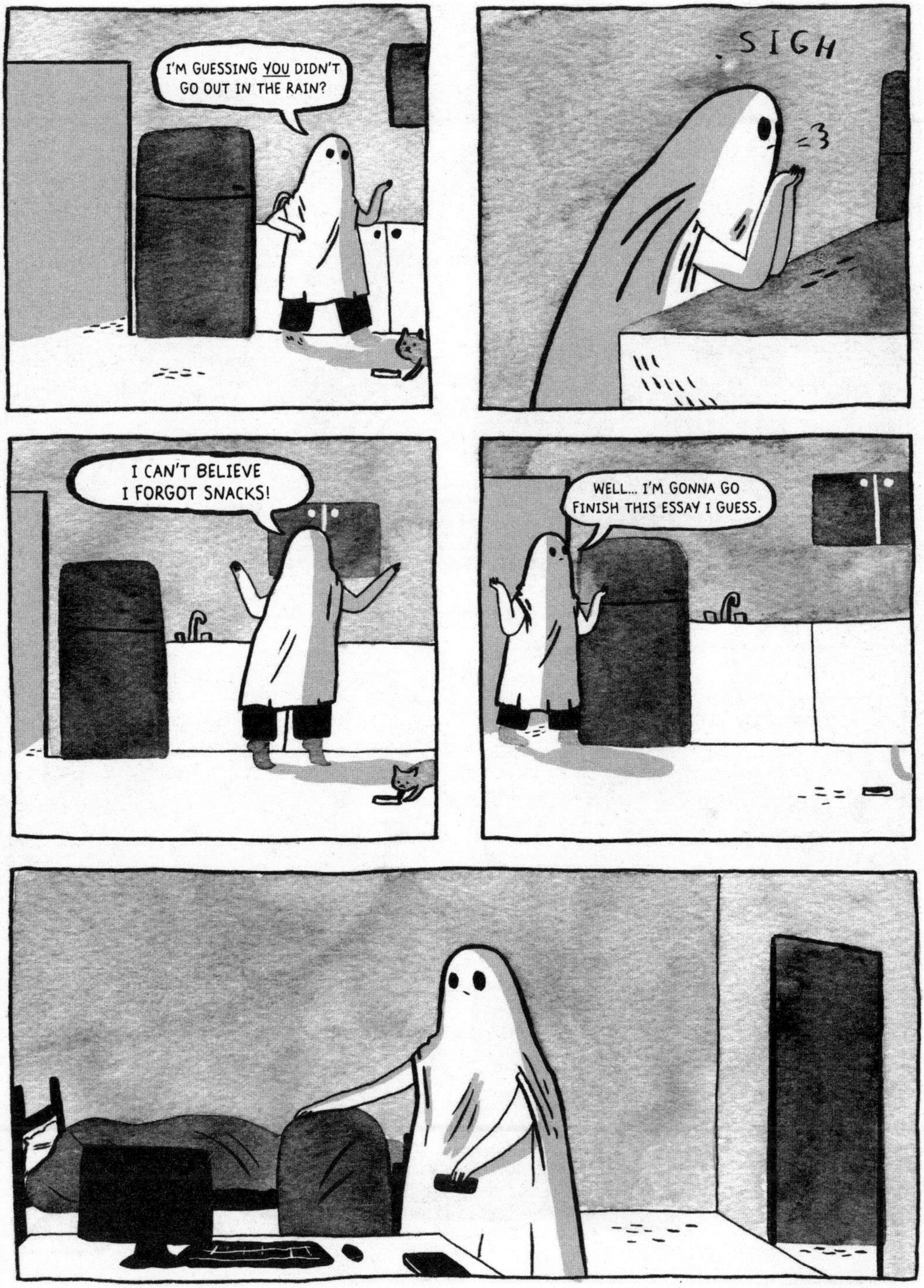
I'M GUESSING YOU DIDN'T GO OUT IN THE RAIN?
SIGH
I CAN'T BELIEVE I FORGOT SNACKS!
WELL... I'M GONNA GO FINISH THIS ESSAY I GUESS.

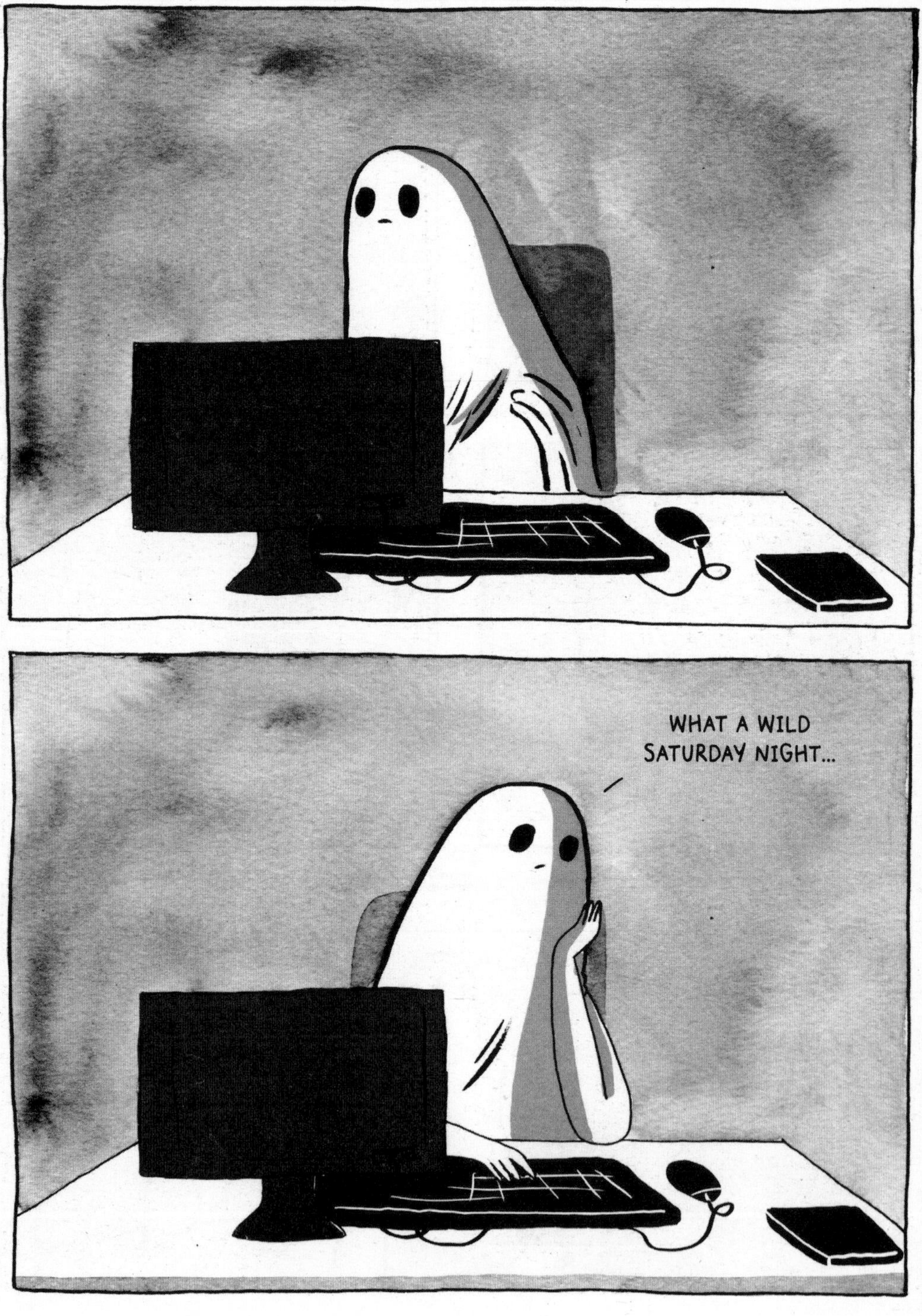
WHAT A WILD SATURDAY NIGHT...

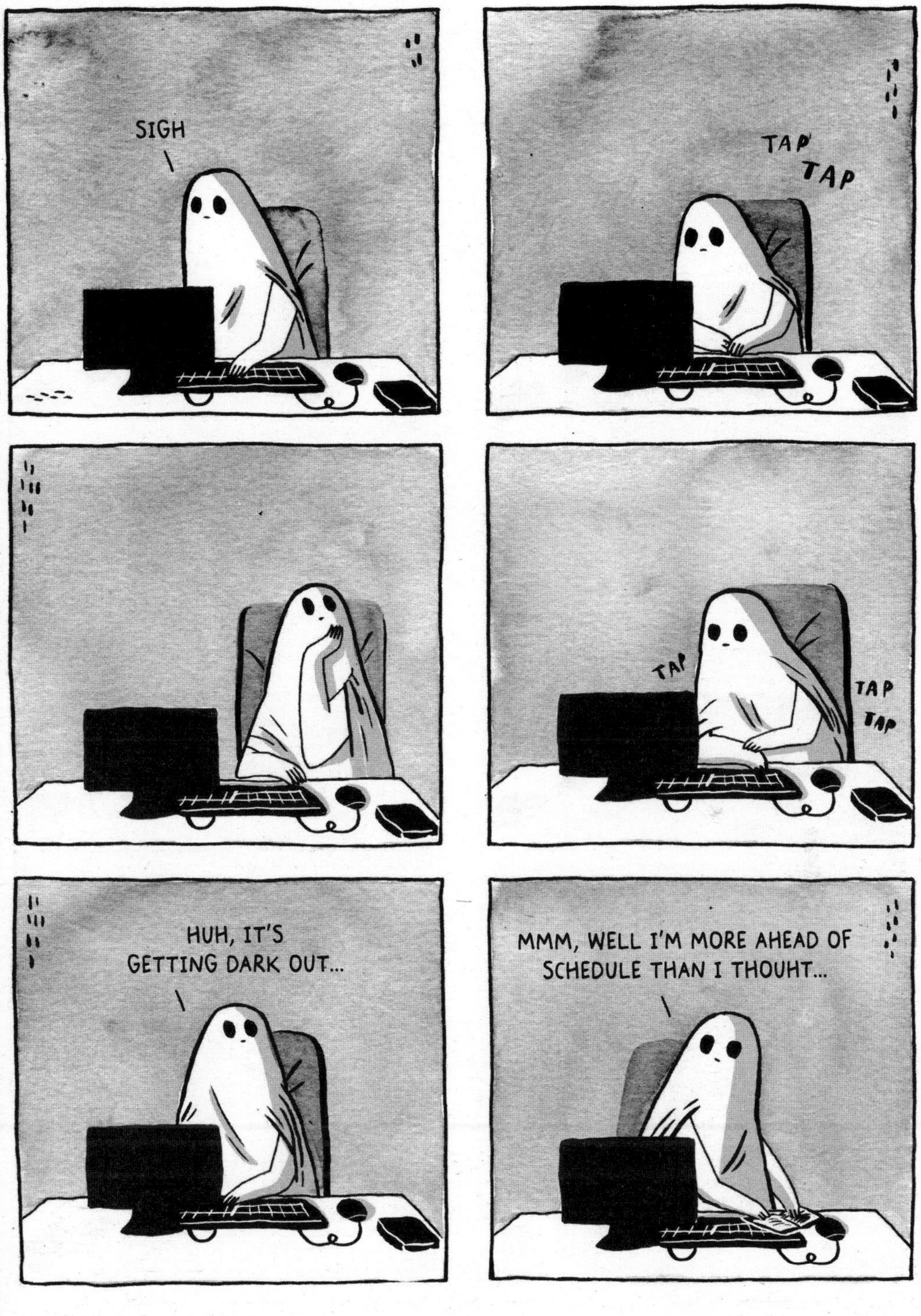
SIGH
TAP TAP
TAP
TAP TAP
HUH, IT'S GETTING DARK OUT...
MMM, WELL I'M MORE AHEAD OF SCHEDULE THAN I THOUHT...

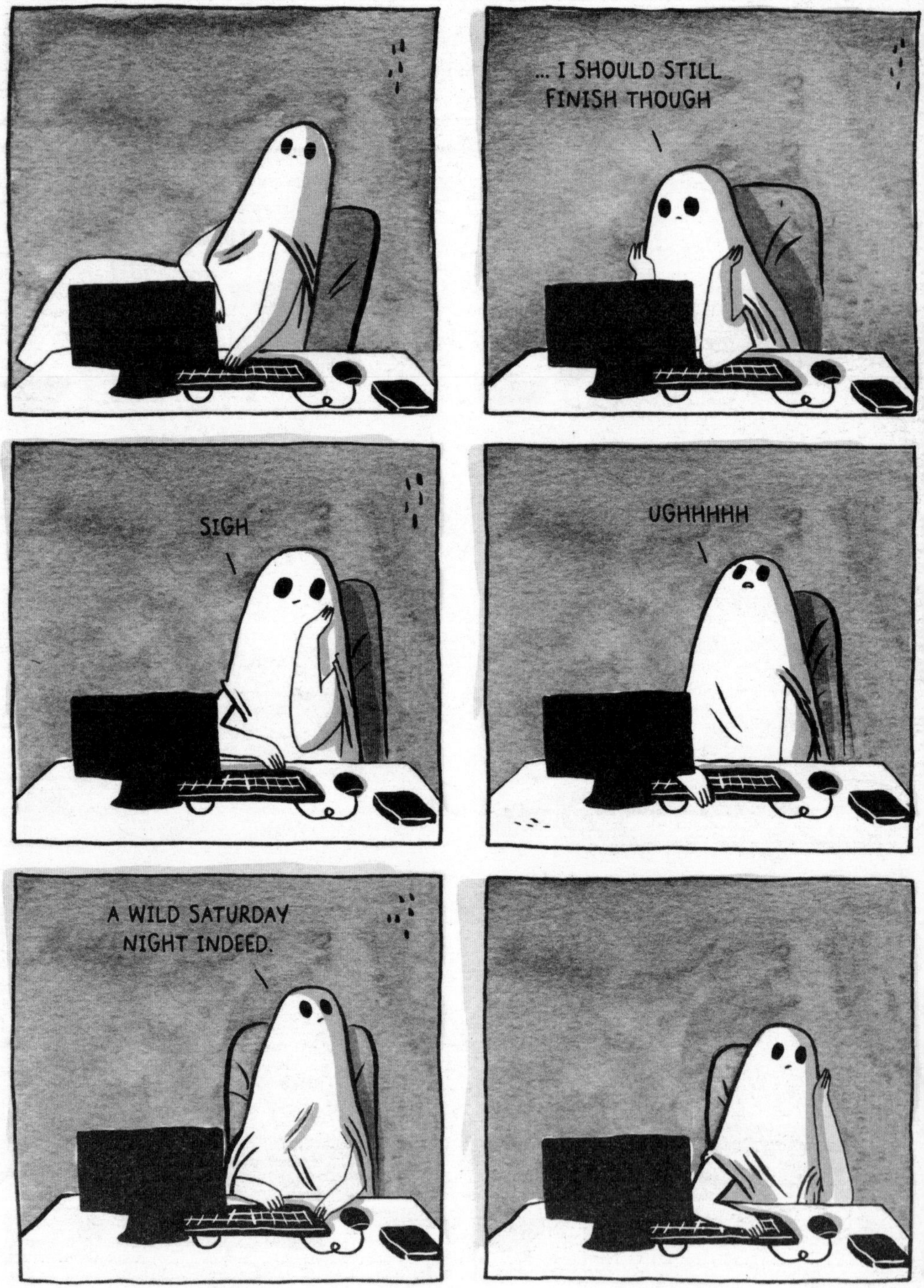
... I SHOULD STILL FINISH THOUGH
SIGH
UGHHHHH
A WILD SATURDAY NIGHT INDEED.

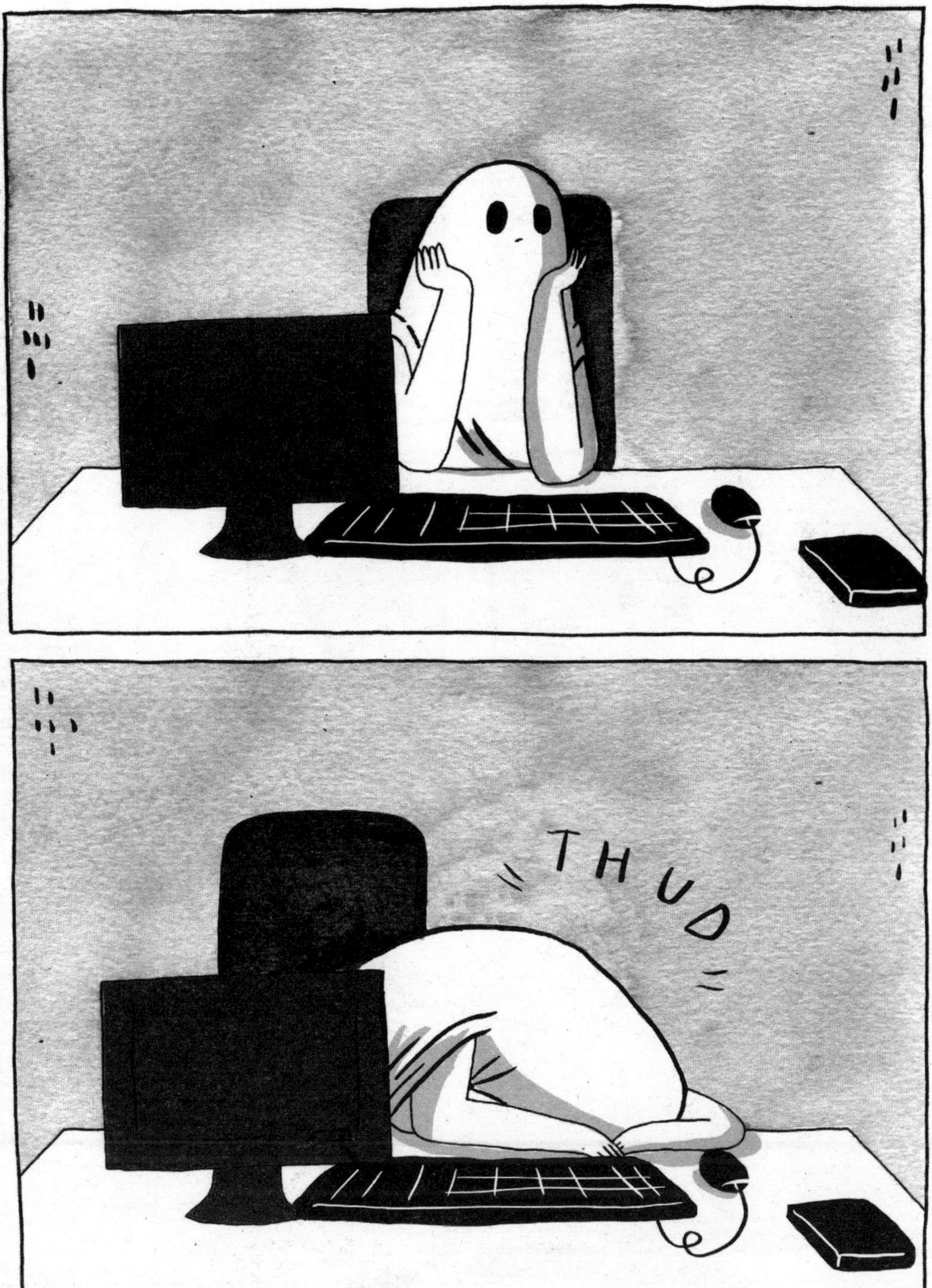
THUD

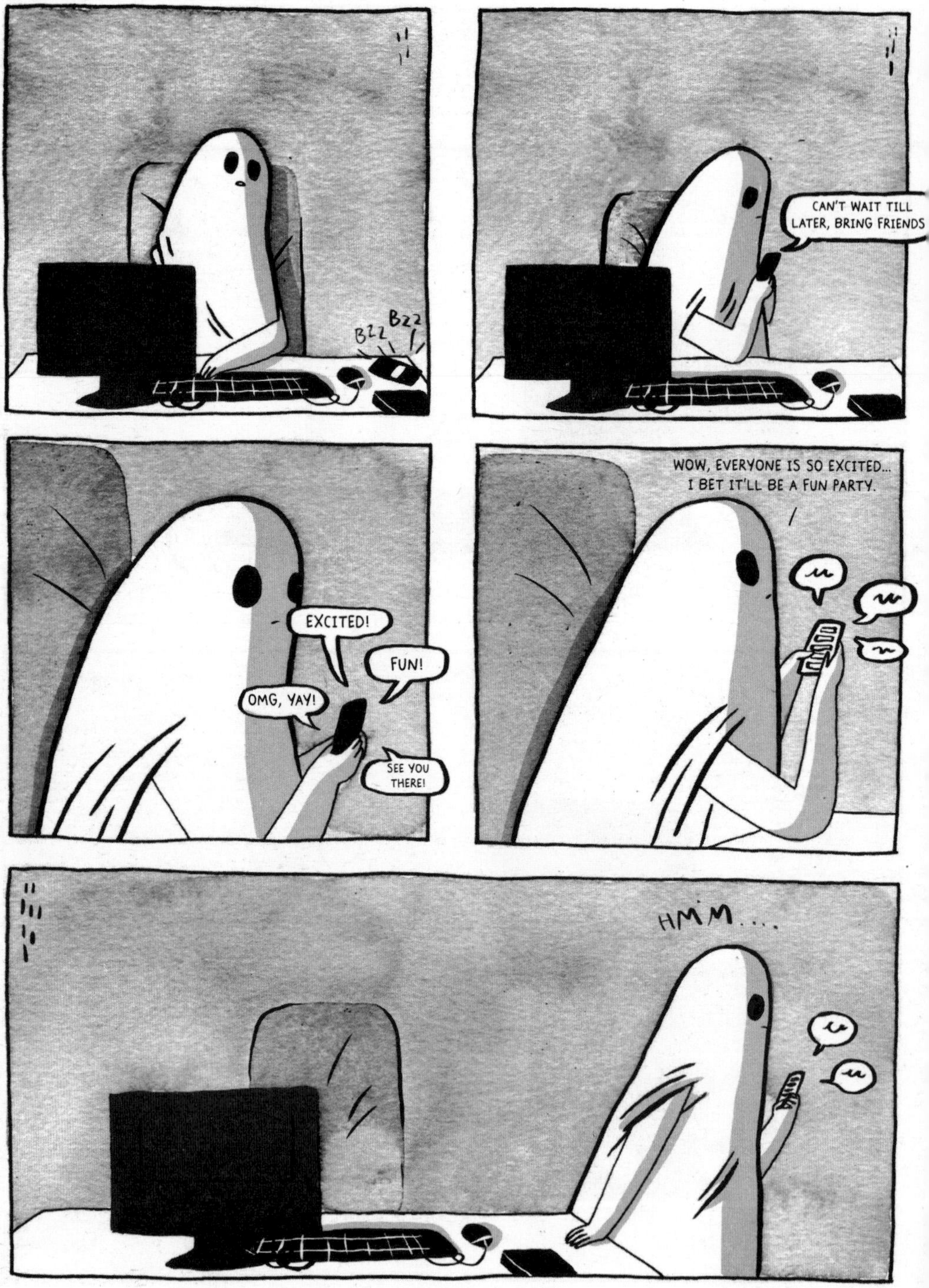
BZZ
BZZ
CAN'T WAIT TILL LATER, BRING FRIENDS
EXCITED!
FUN!
OMG, YAY!
SEE YOU THERE!
WOW, EVERYONE IS SO EXCITED... I BET IT'LL BE A FUN PARTY.
HMM....

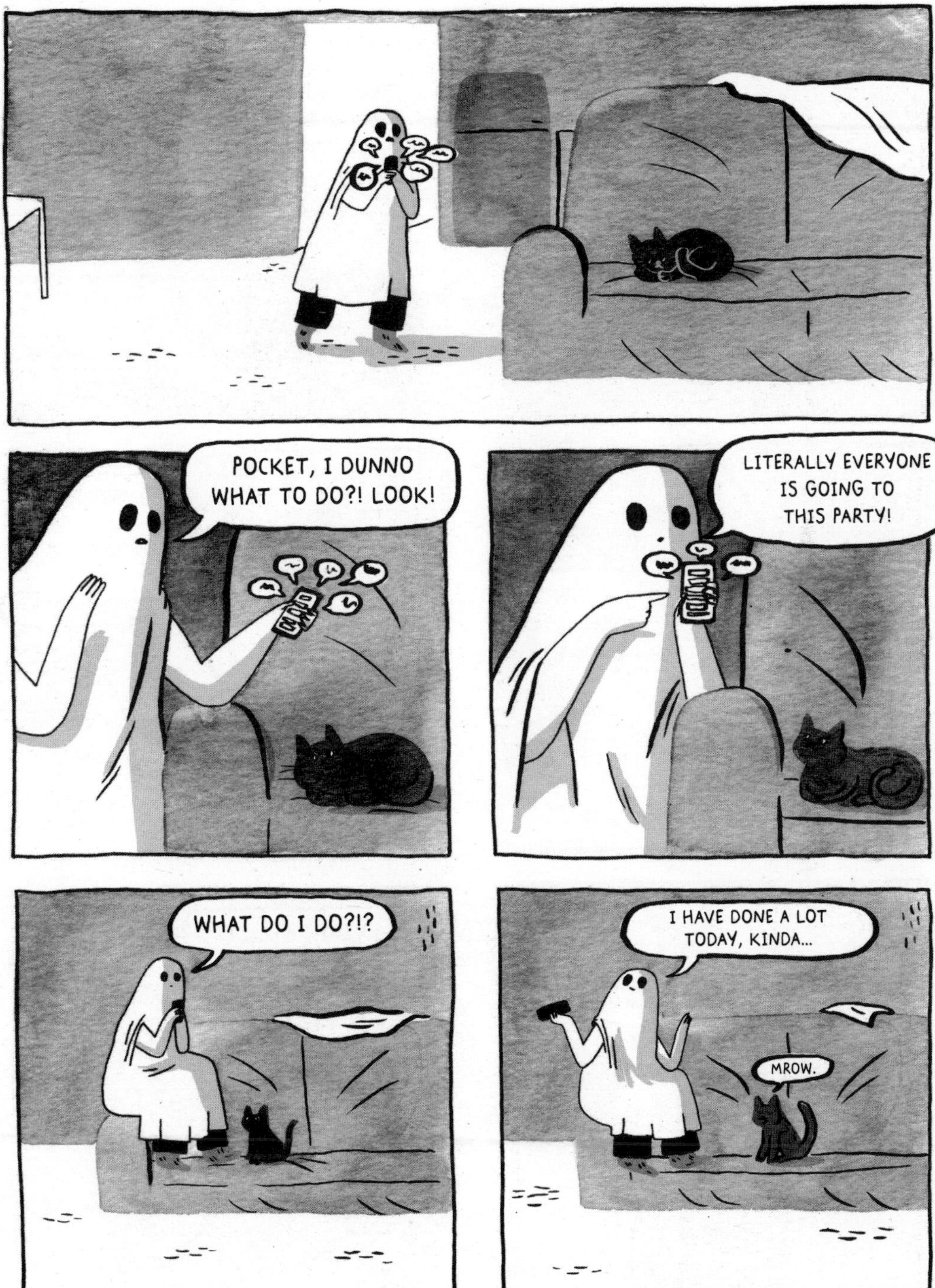
POCKET, I DUNNO WHAT TO DO?! LOOK!
LITERALLY EVERYONE IS GOING TO THIS PARTY!
WHAT DO I DO?!?
I HAVE DONE A LOT TODAY, KINDA...
MROW.

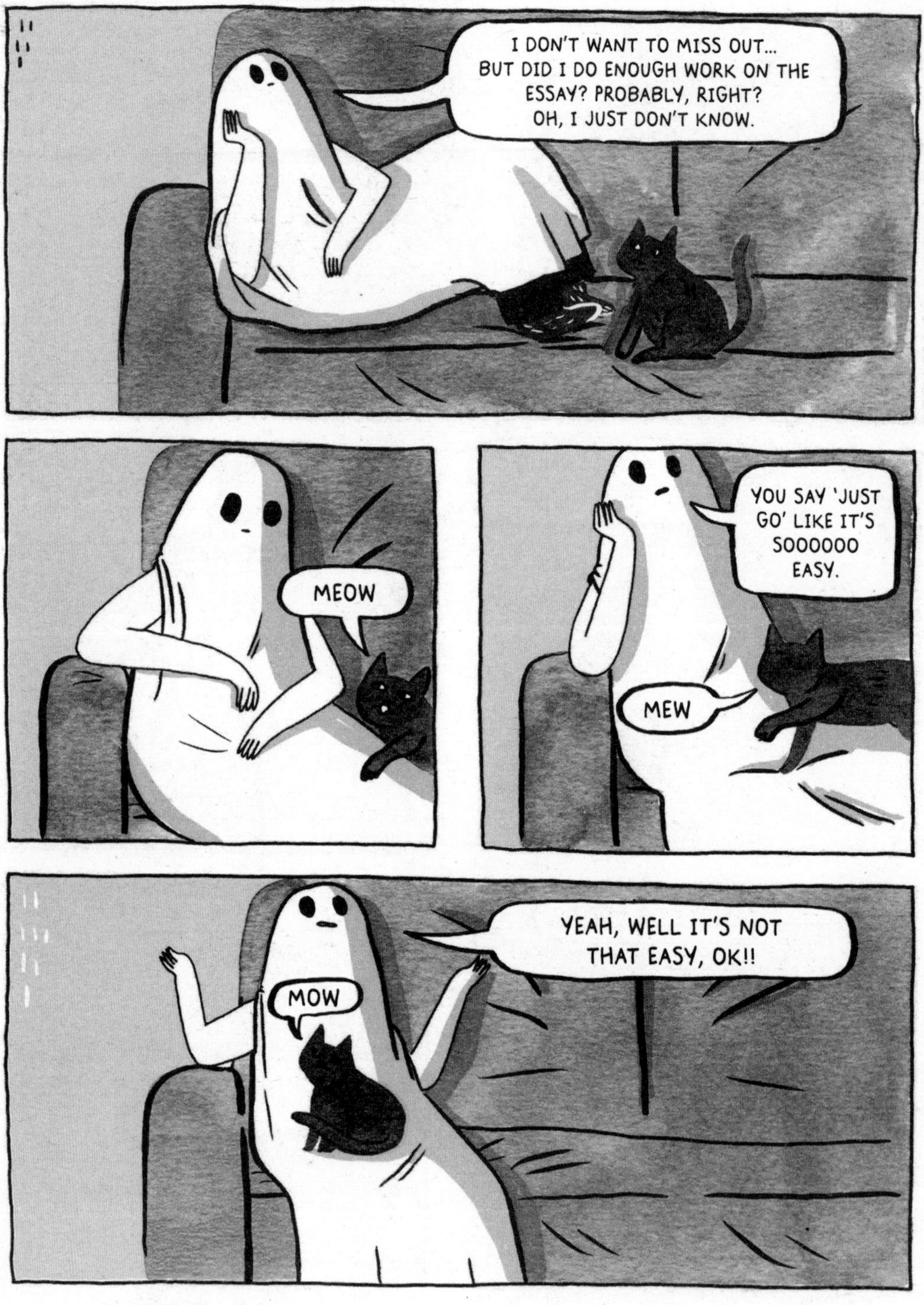
I DON'T WANT TO MISS OUT...
BUT DID I DO ENOUGH WORK ON THE ESSAY? PROBABLY, RIGHT? OH, I JUST DON'T KNOW.
MEOW
YOU SAY 'JUST GO' LIKE IT'S SOOOOOO EASY.
MEW
YEAH, WELL IT'S NOT THAT EASY, OK!!
MOW

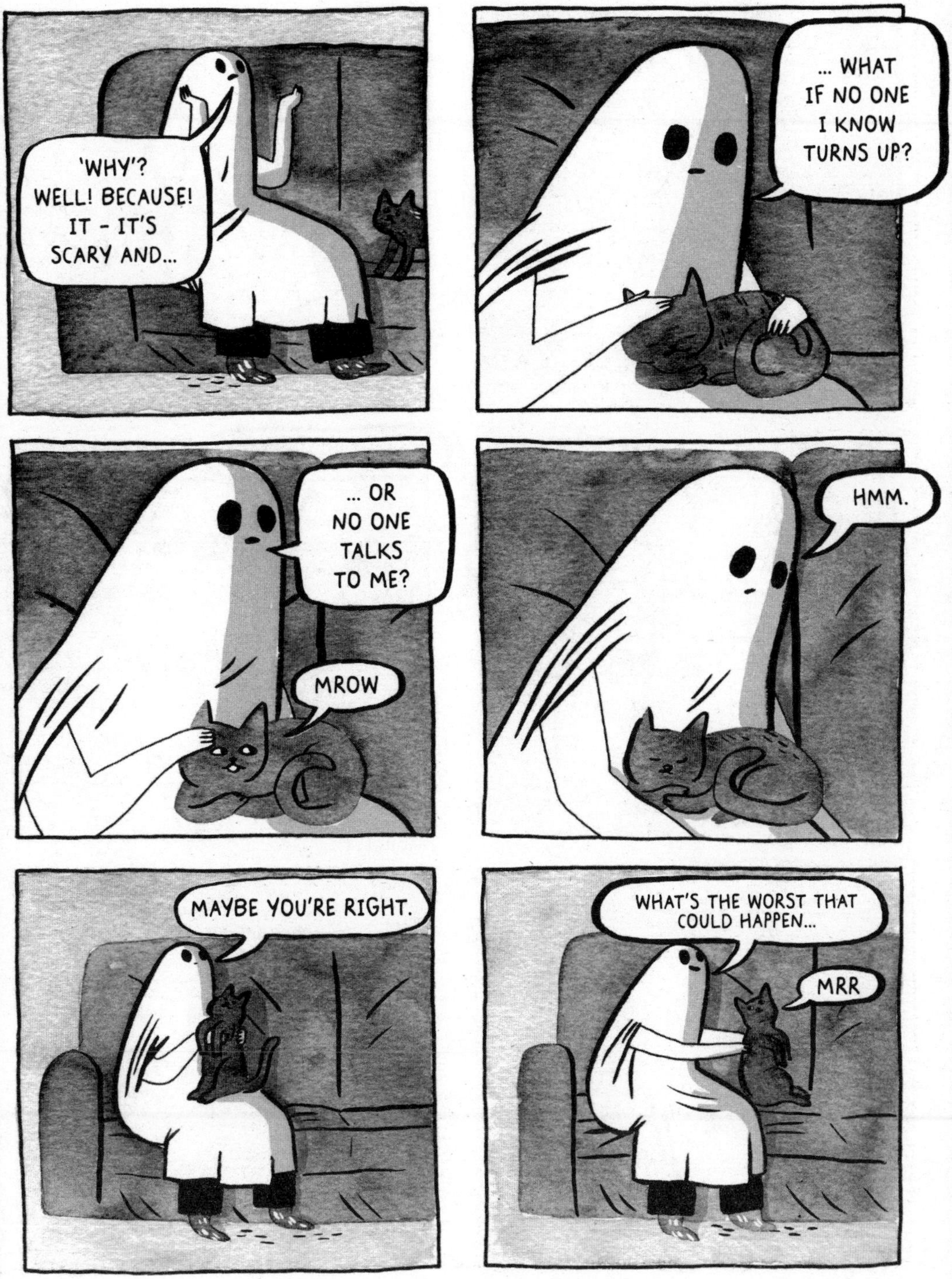
'WHY'? WELL! BECAUSE! IT - IT'S SCARY AND...
... WHAT IF NO ONE I KNOW TURNS UP?
... OR NO ONE TALKS TO ME?
MROW
HMM.
MAYBE YOU'RE RIGHT.
WHAT'S THE WORST THAT COULD HAPPEN...
MRR

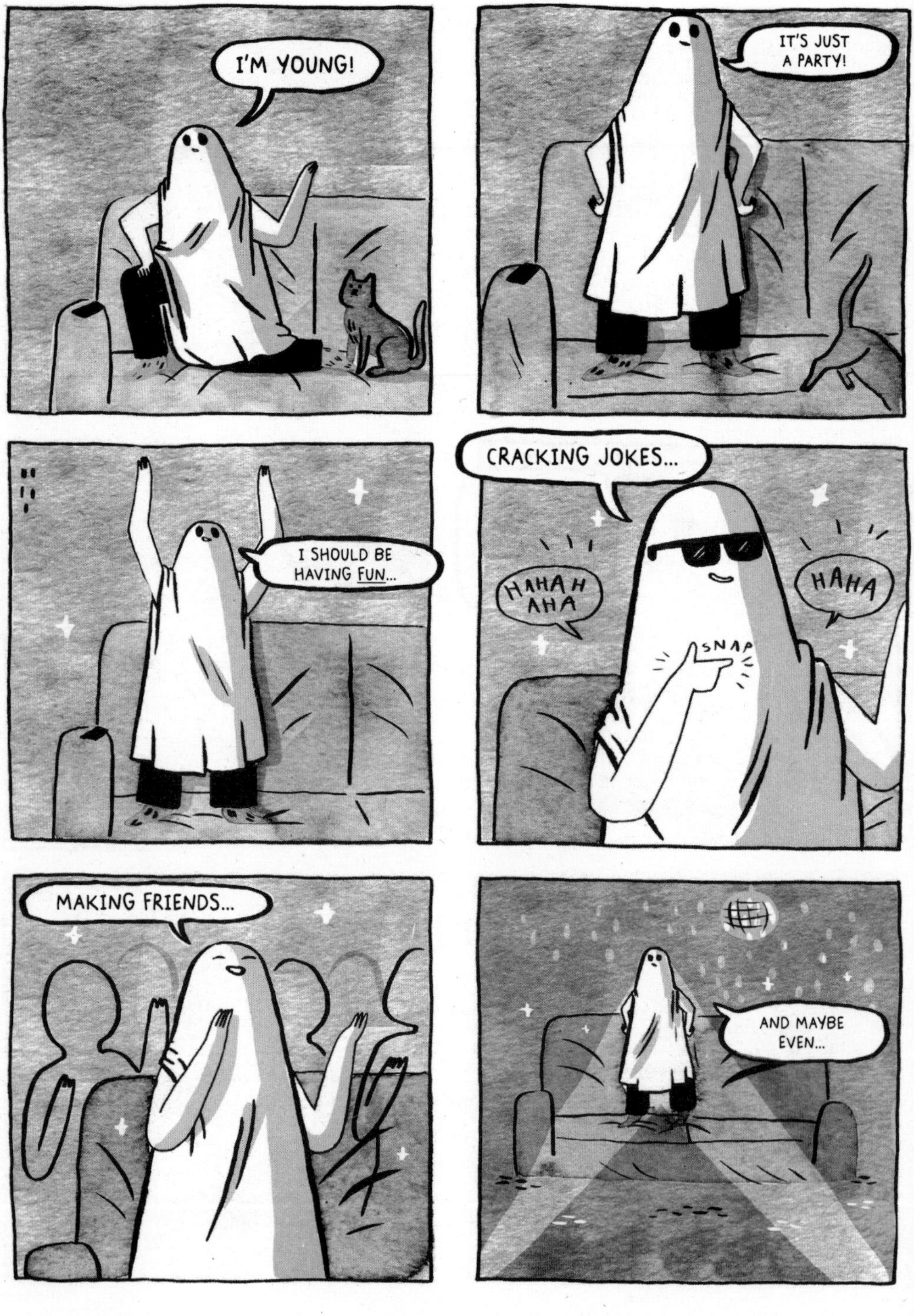
I'M YOUNG!
IT'S JUST A PARTY!
I SHOULD BE HAVING FUN...
CRACKING JOKES...
HAHAH AHA
SNAP
HAHA
MAKING FRIENDS...
AND MAYBE EVEN...

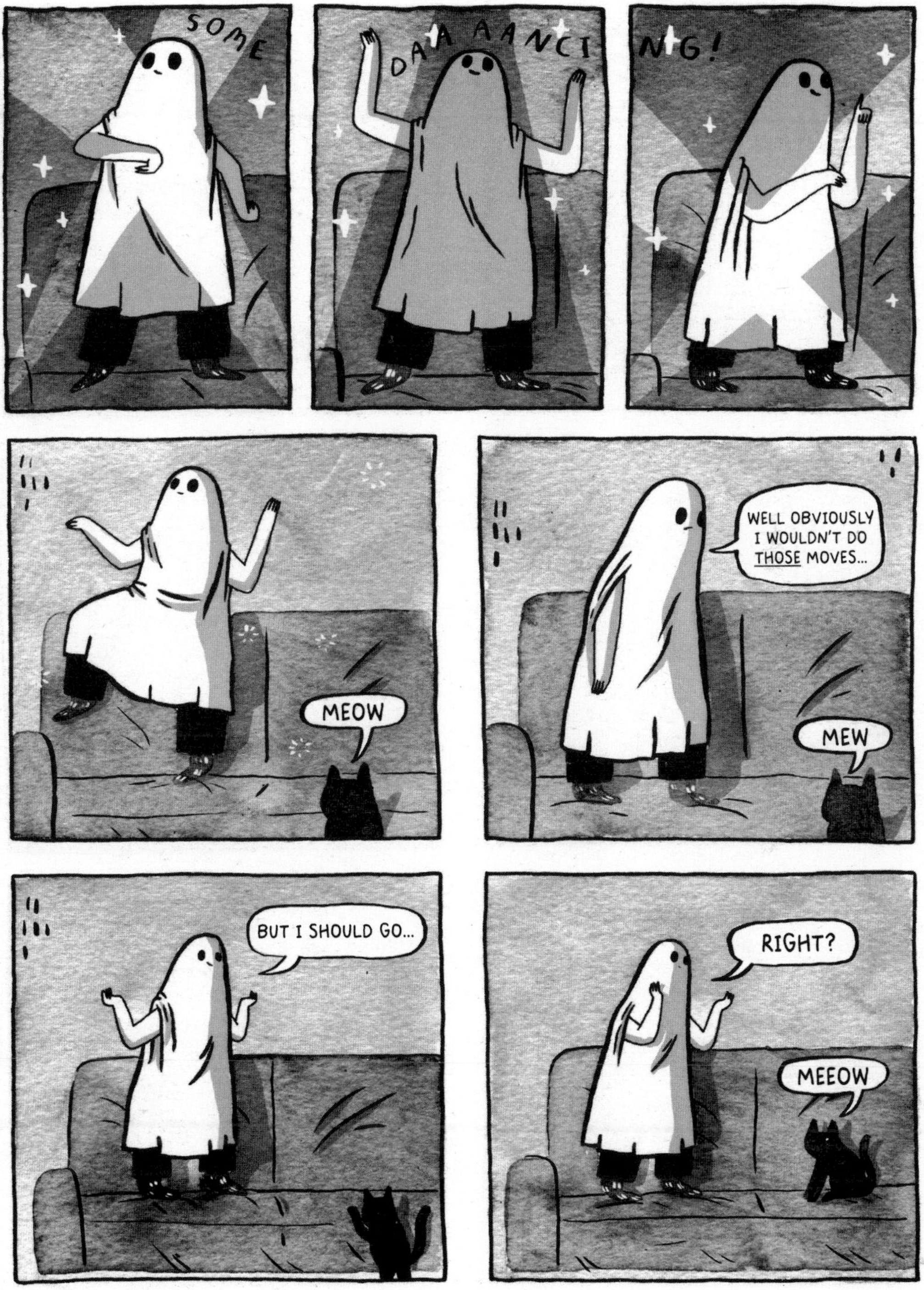
SOME
DAAAAANCI
NG!
MEOW
WELL OBVIOUSLY I WOULDN'T DO THOSE MOVES...
MEW
BUT I SHOULD GO...
RIGHT?
MEEOW

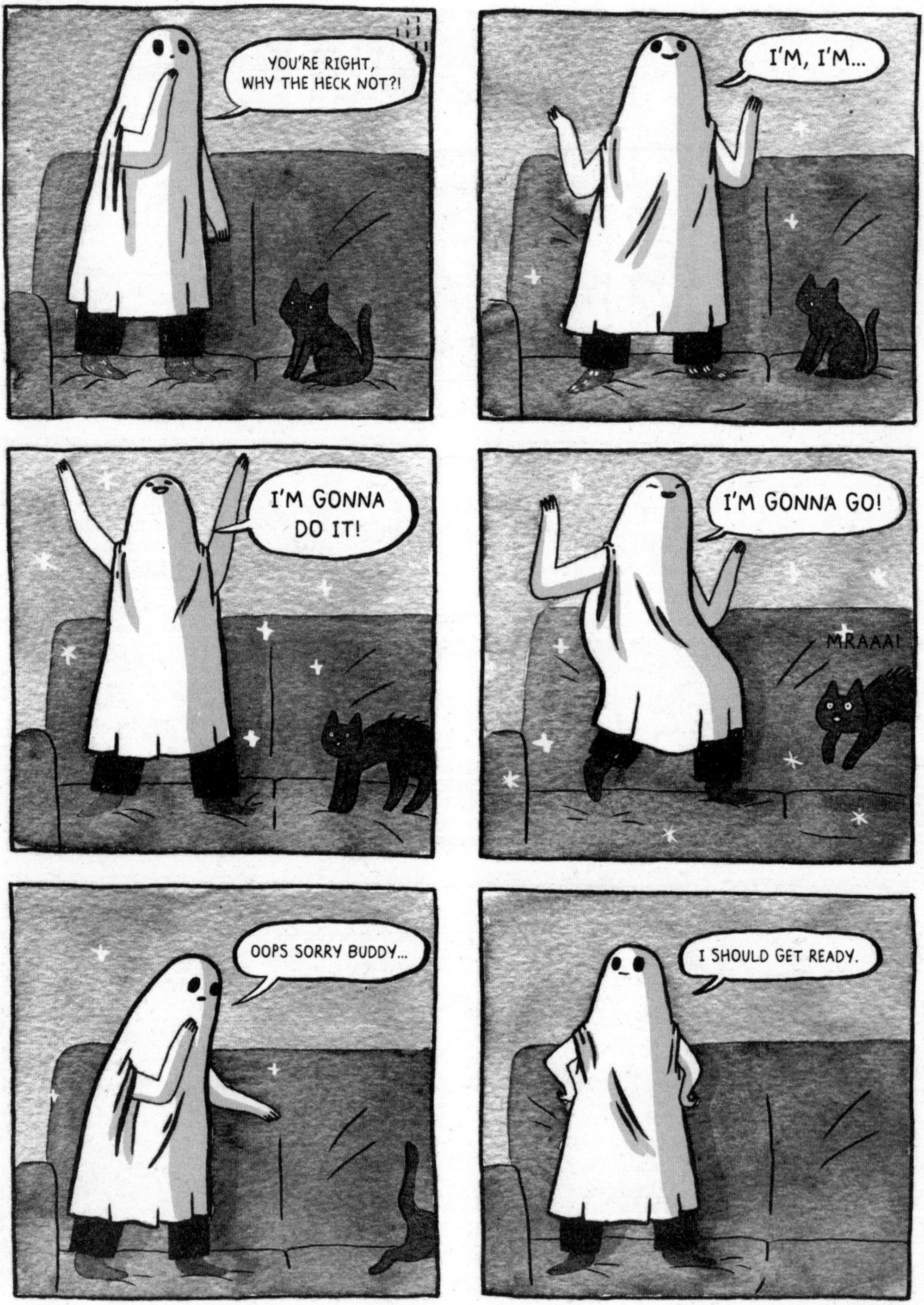
YOU'RE RIGHT, WHY THE HECK NOT?!
I'M, I'M...
I'M GONNA DO IT!
I'M GONNA GO!
MRAAA!
OOPS SORRY BUDDY...
I SHOULD GET READY.

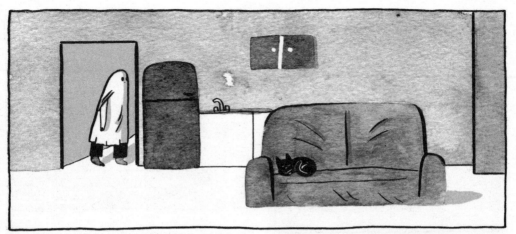

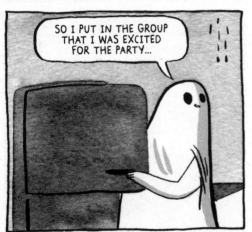

SO I PUT IN THE GROUP THAT I WAS EXCITED FOR THE PARTY...
SAT NIGHT DINNER
STUDY HARD!
LUNCH
... AND CHRIS AND ROBBIE REPLIED LIKE, 'COOL! SEE U THERE!'
ISN'T THAT NICE? 'SEE U THERE...'
CUTE.
OH MY GOSH POCKET, I AM SO EXCITED...

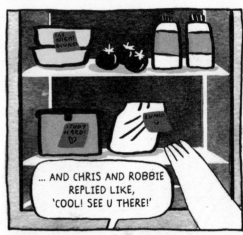

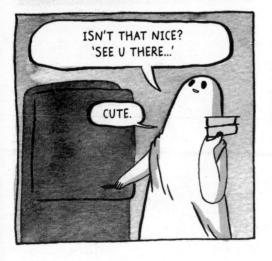

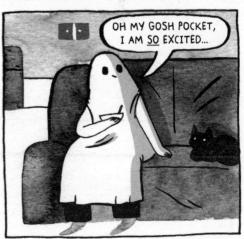

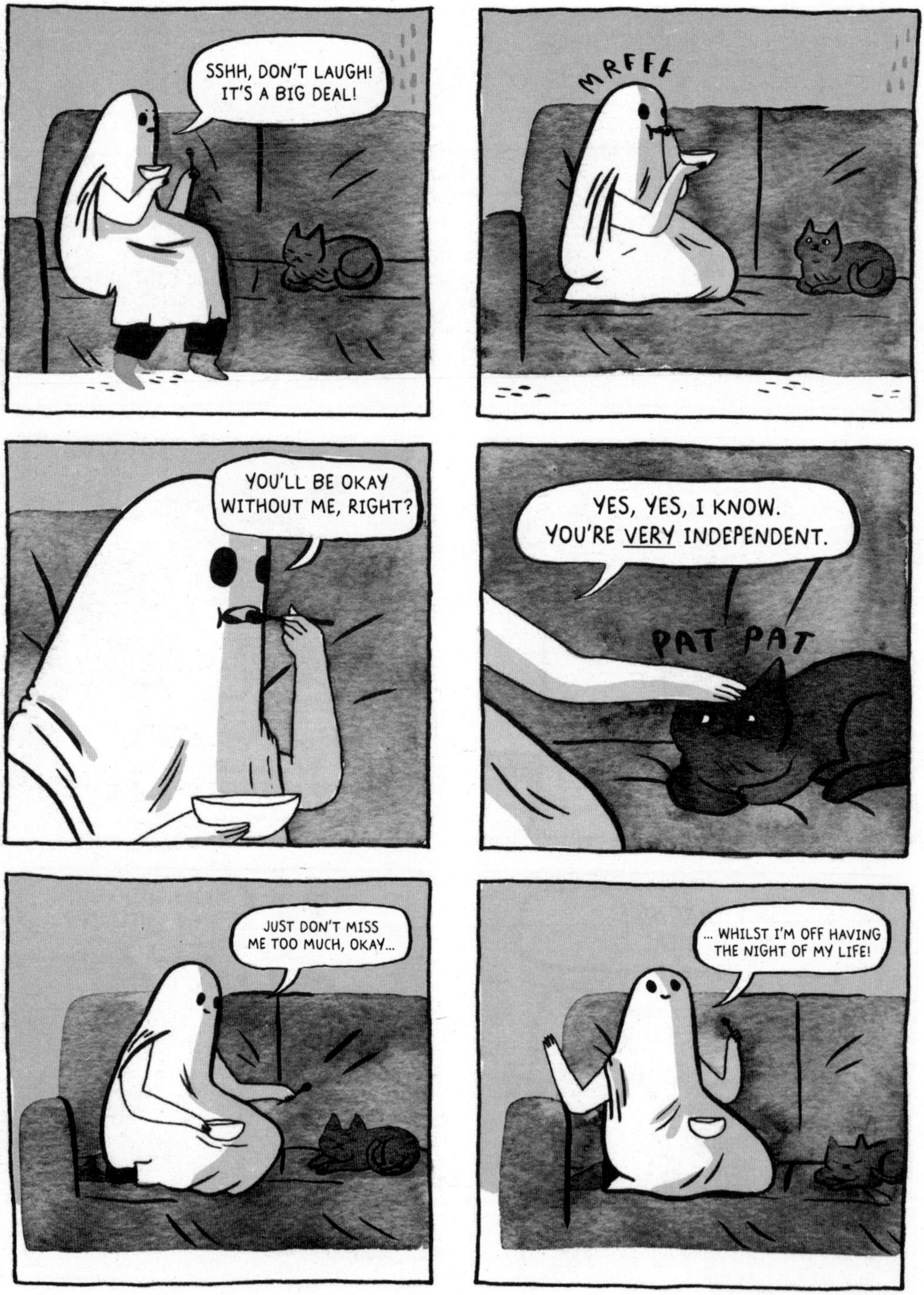
SSHH, DON'T LAUGH!
IT'S A BIG DEAL!
MRFFF
YOU'LL BE OKAY
WITHOUT ME, RIGHT?
YES, YES, I KNOW.
YOU'RE VERY INDEPENDENT.
PAT PAT
JUST DON'T MISS
ME TOO MUCH, OKAY...
... WHILST I'M OFF HAVING
THE NIGHT OF MY LIFE!

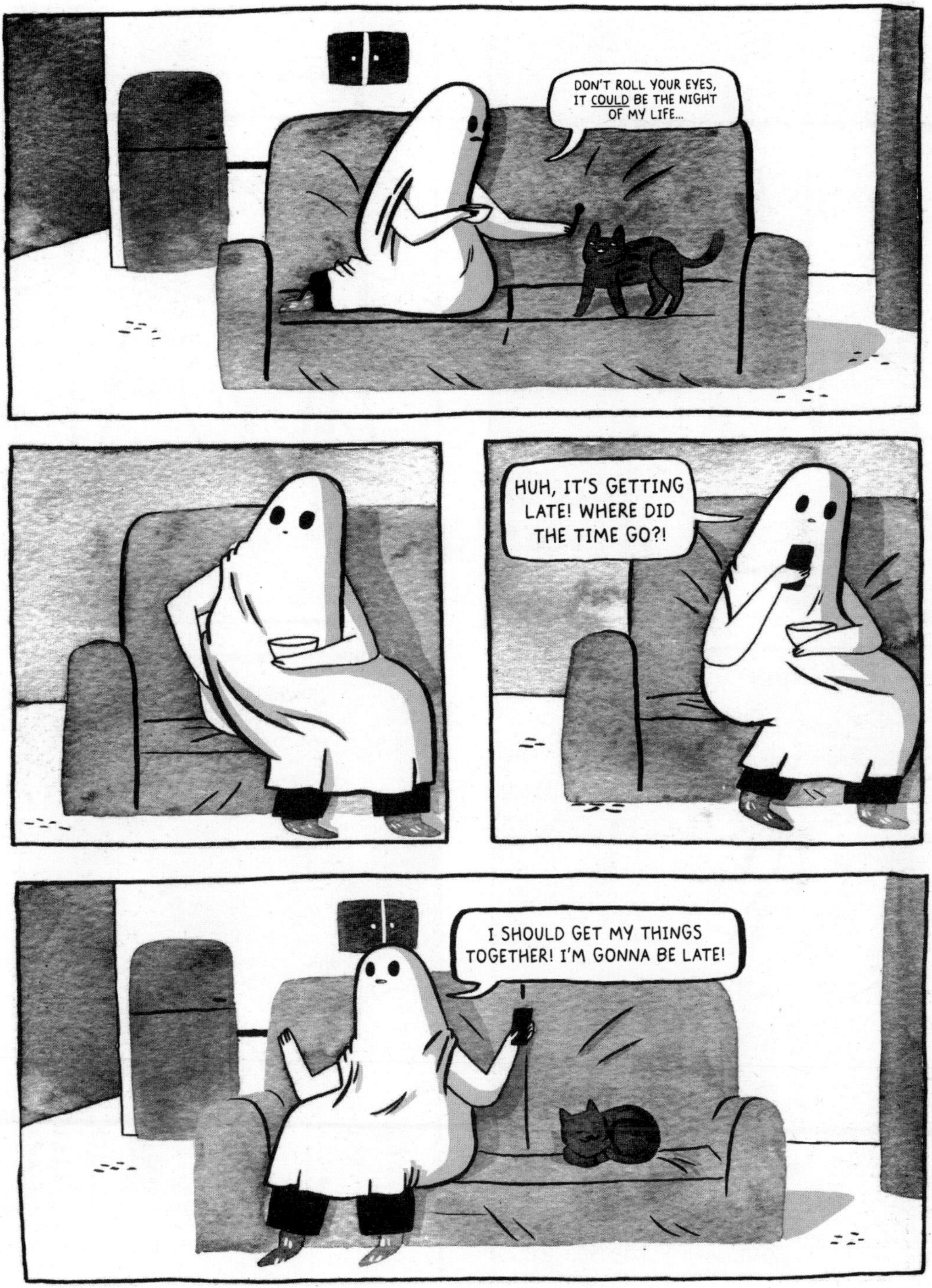
DON'T ROLL YOUR EYES, IT COULD BE THE NIGHT OF MY LIFE...
HUH, IT'S GETTING LATE! WHERE DID THE TIME GO?!
I SHOULD GET MY THINGS TOGETHER! I'M GONNA BE LATE!

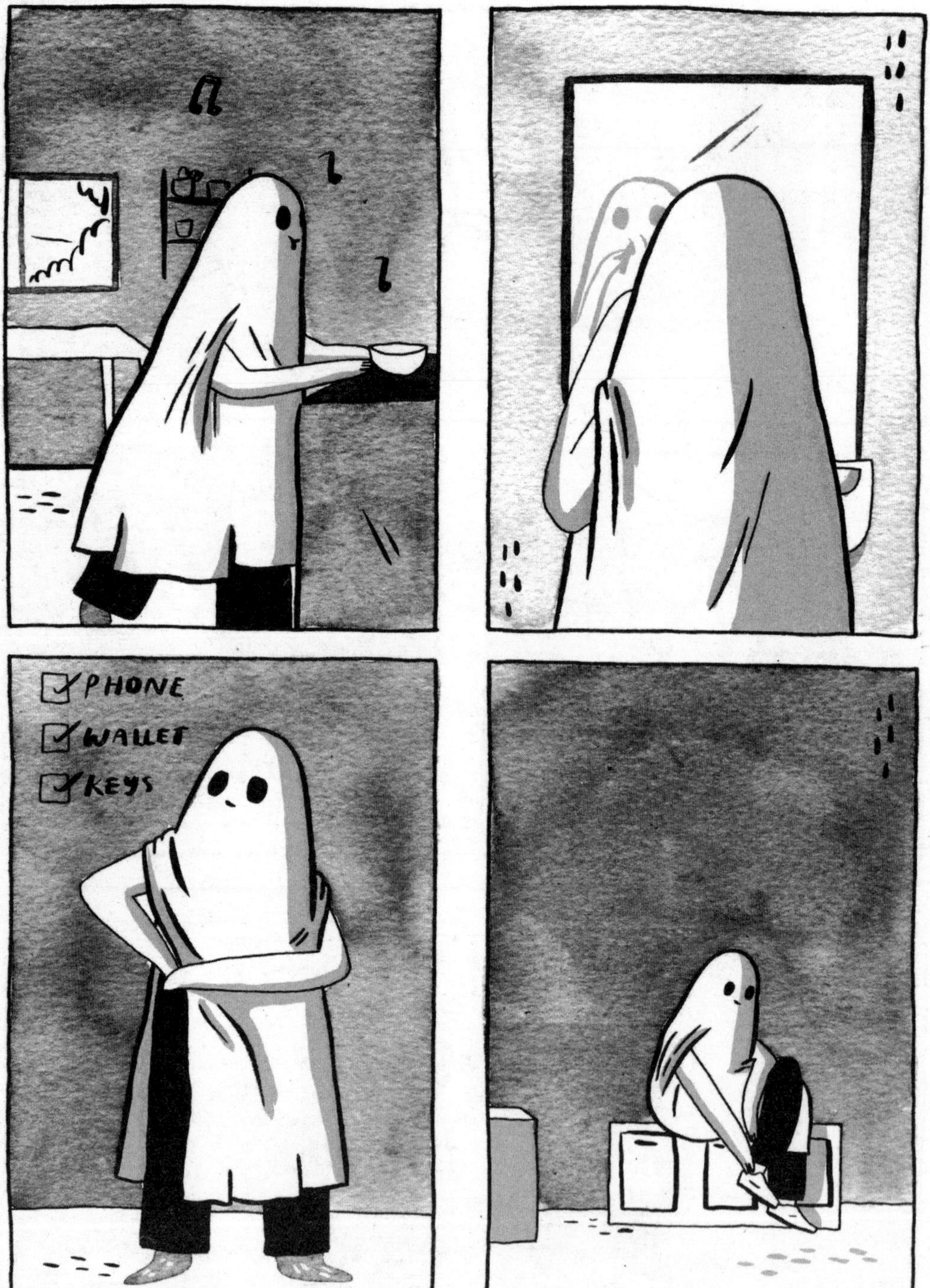
PHONE
WALLET
KEYS

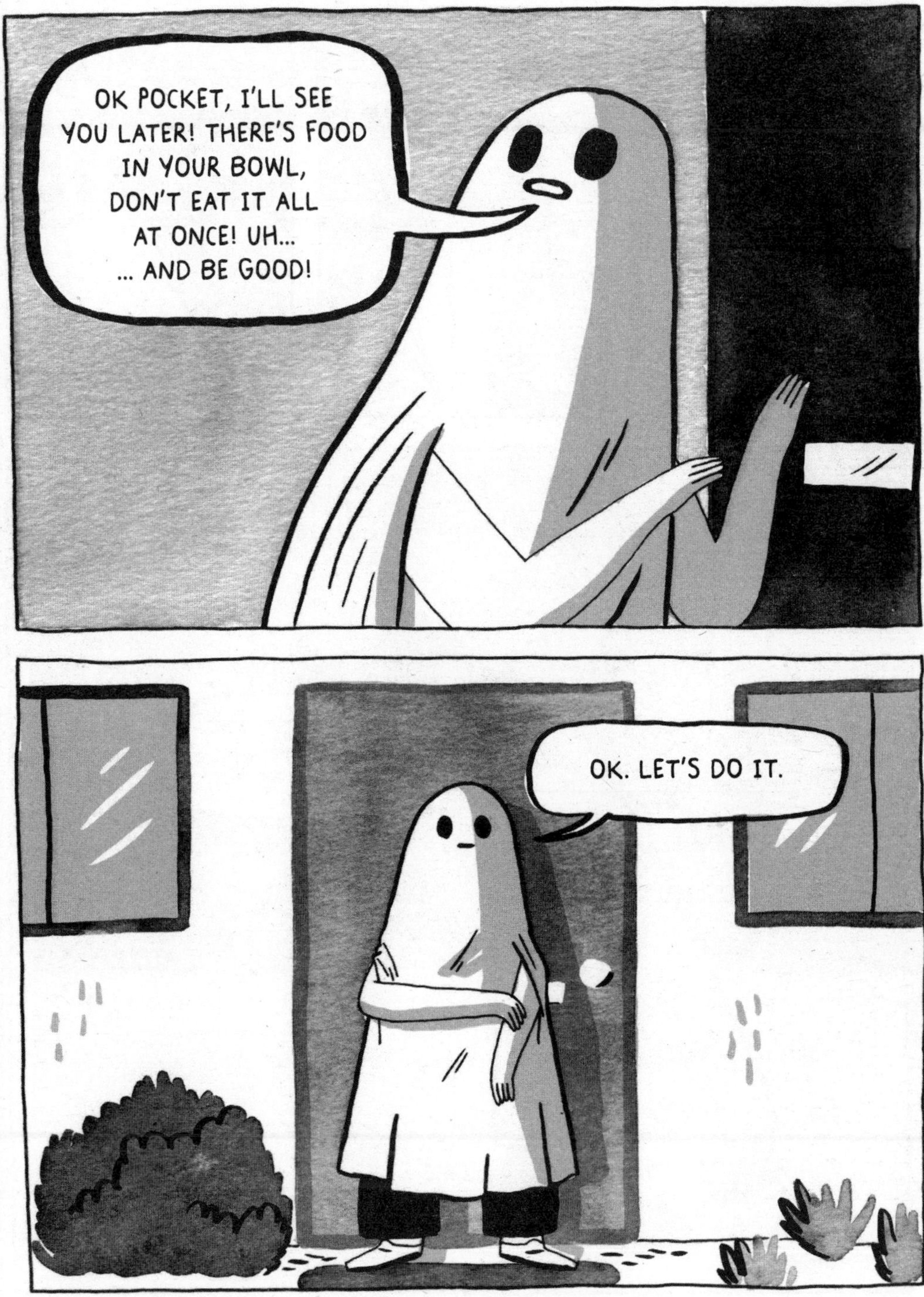
OK POCKET, I'LL SEE YOU LATER! THERE'S FOOD IN YOUR BOWL, DON'T EAT IT ALL AT ONCE! UH... ... AND BE GOOD!
OK. LET'S DO IT.

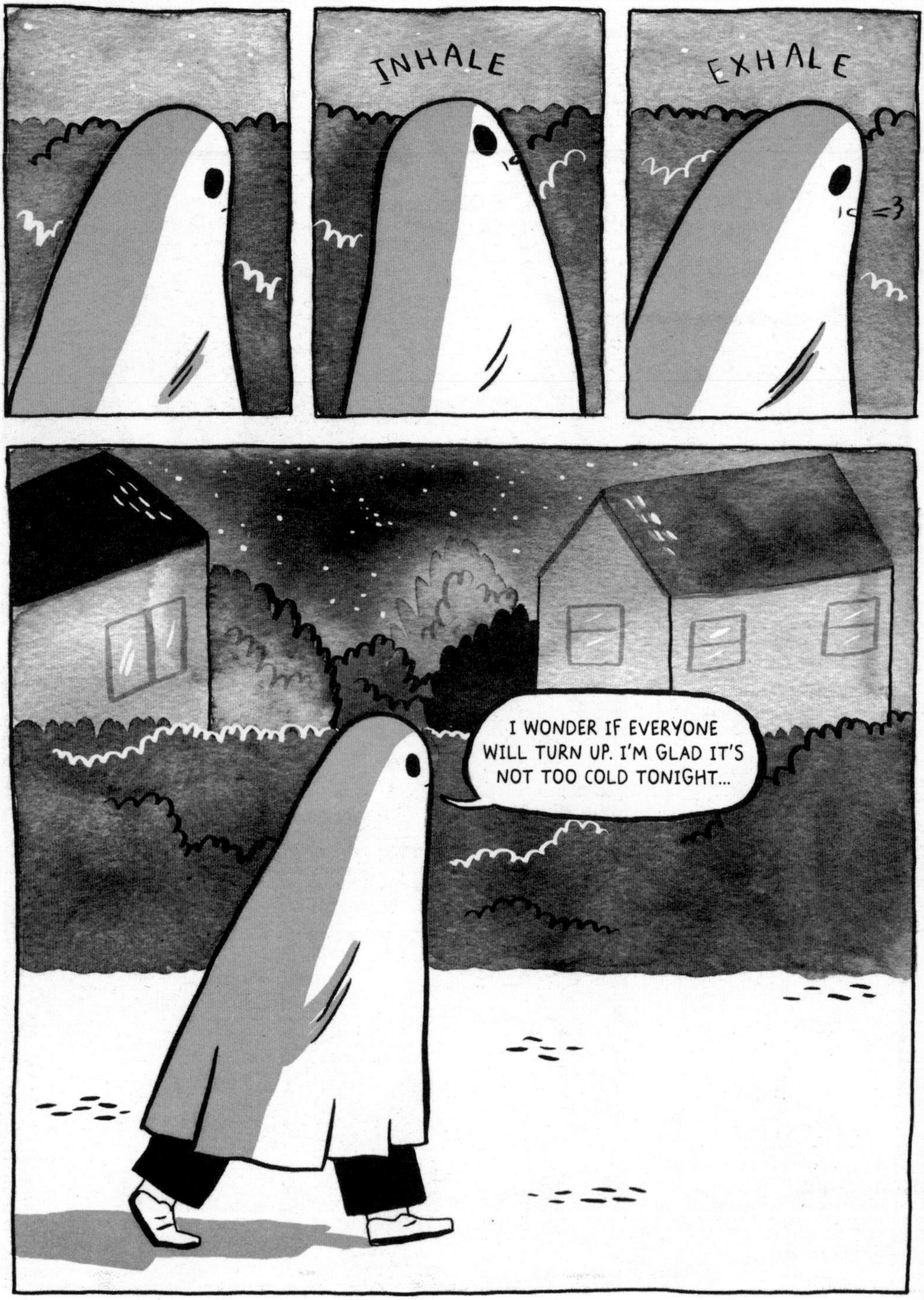
INHALE
EXHALE
I WONDER IF EVERYONE WILL TURN UP. I'M GLAD IT'S NOT TOO COLD TONIGHT...

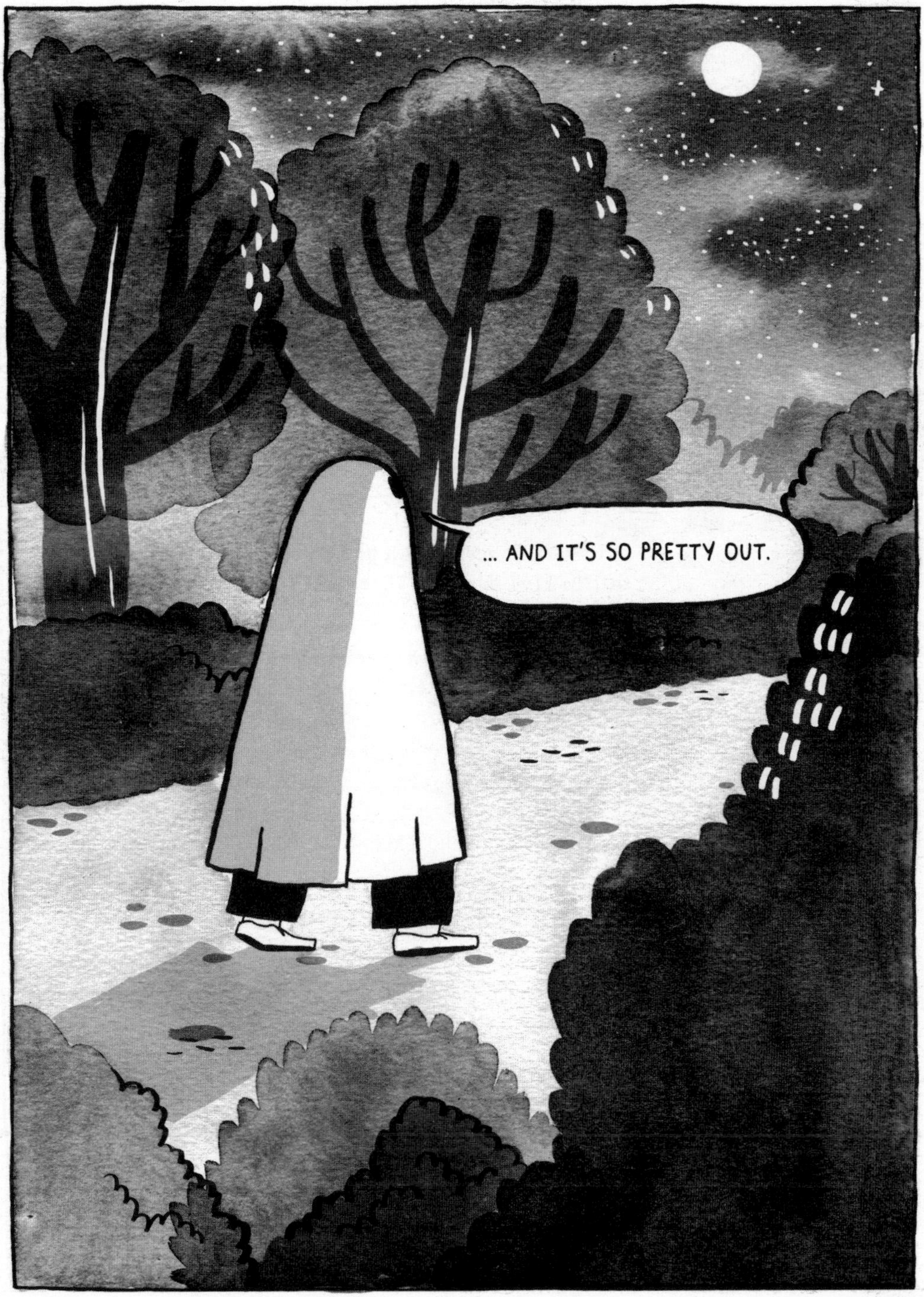
... AND IT'S SO PRETTY OUT.

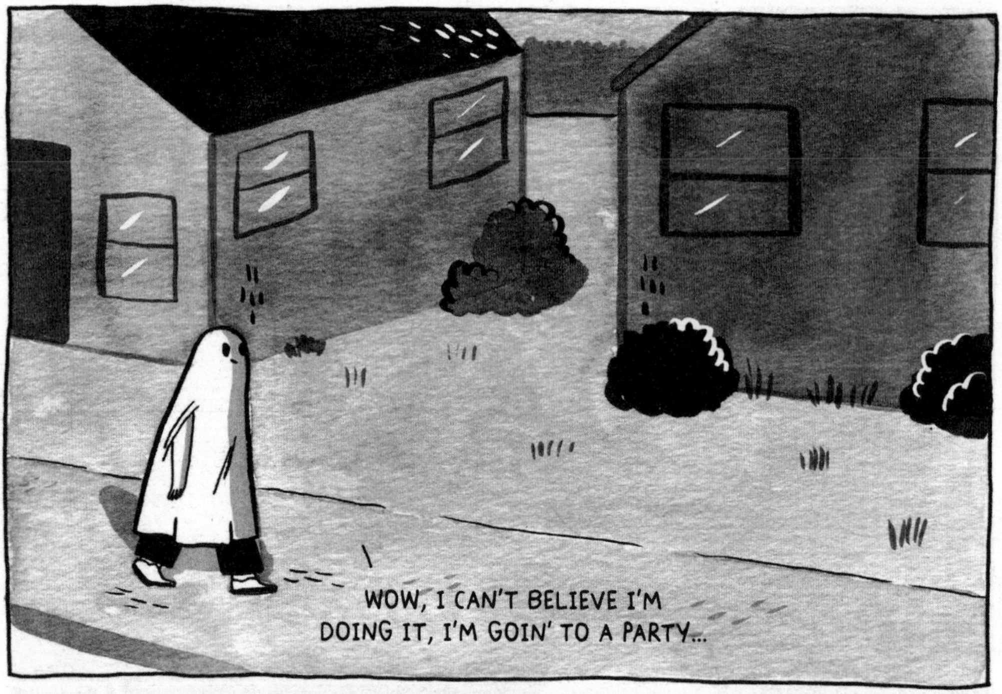
WOW, I CAN'T BELIEVE I'M DOING IT, I'M GOIN' TO A PARTY...

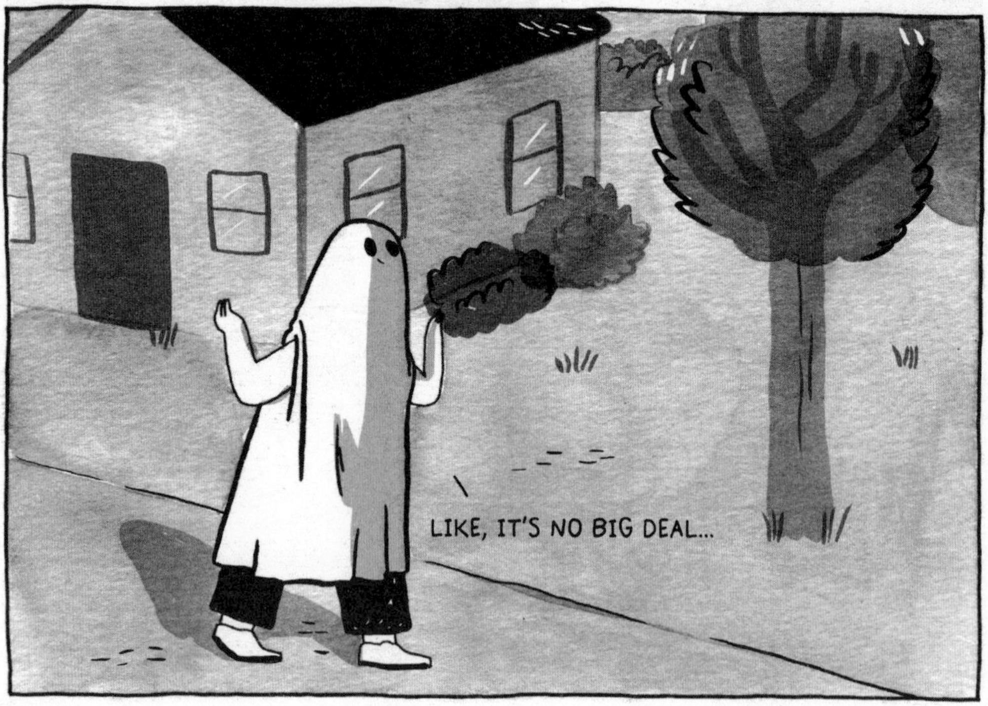
LIKE, IT'S NO BIG DEAL...

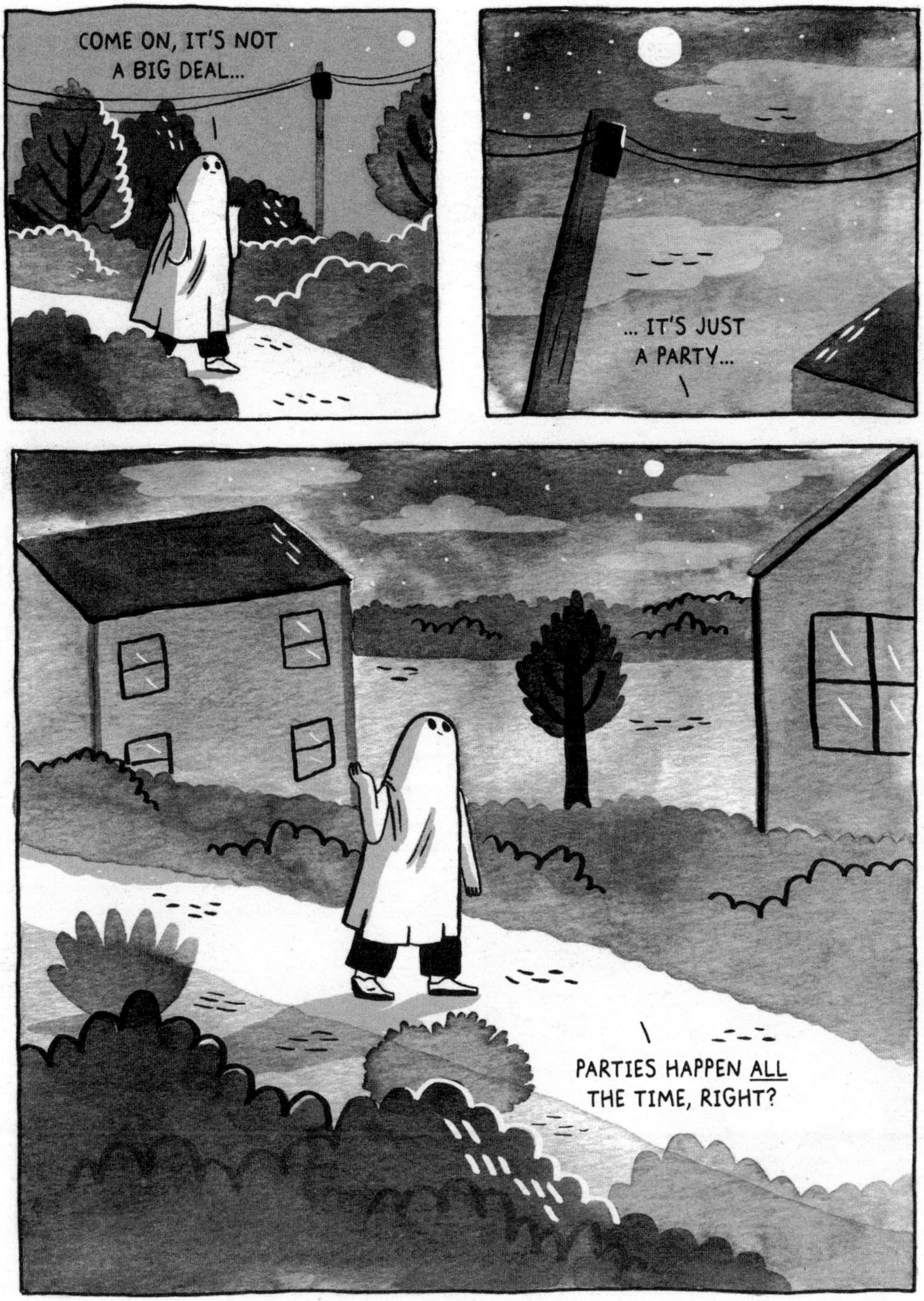
COME ON, IT'S NOT A BIG DEAL...
... IT'S JUST A PARTY...
PARTIES HAPPEN ALL THE TIME, RIGHT?

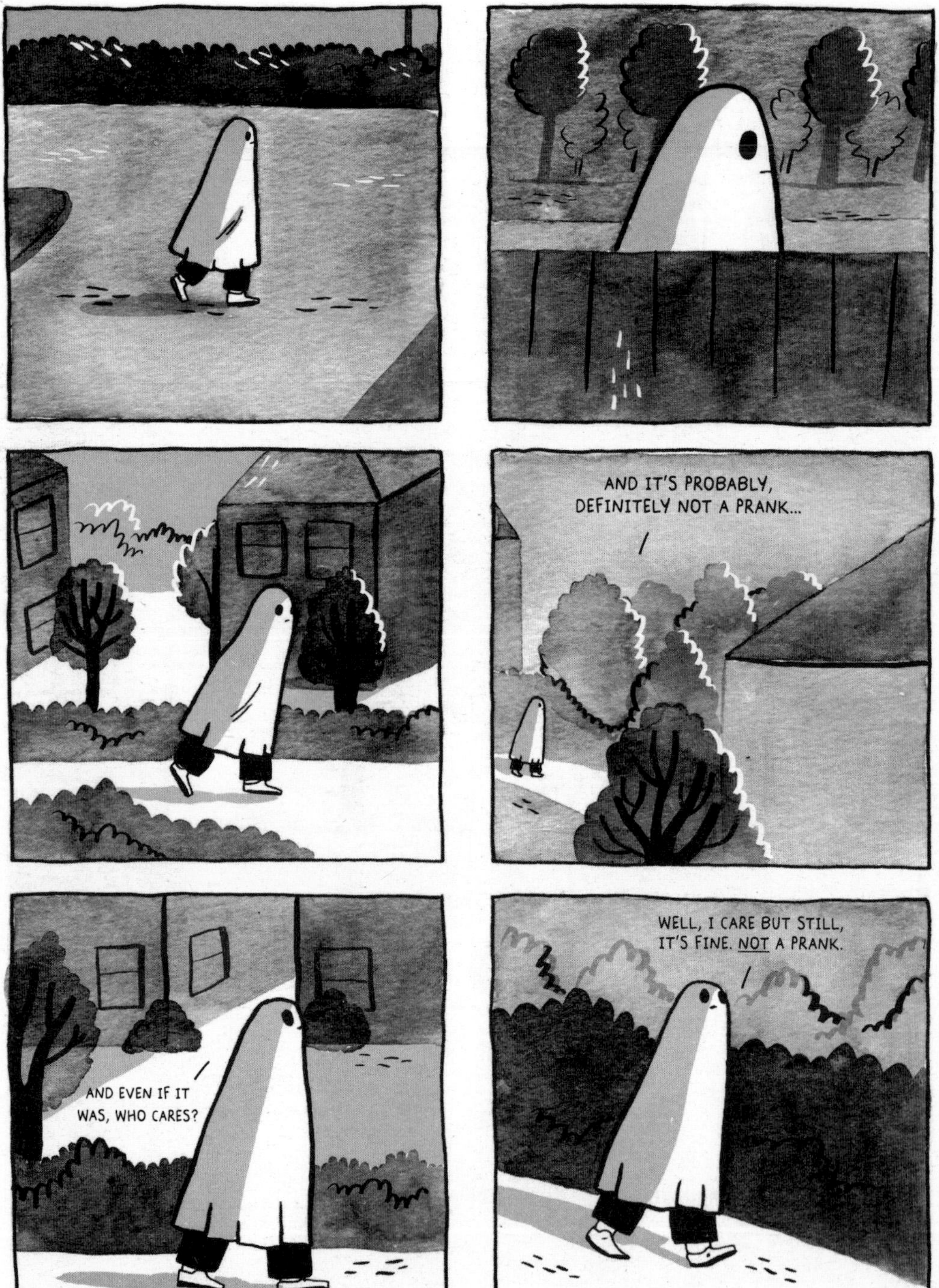
AND IT'S PROBABLY, DEFINITELY NOT A PRANK...
AND EVEN IF IT WAS, WHO CARES?
WELL, I CARE BUT STILL, IT'S FINE. NOT A PRANK.

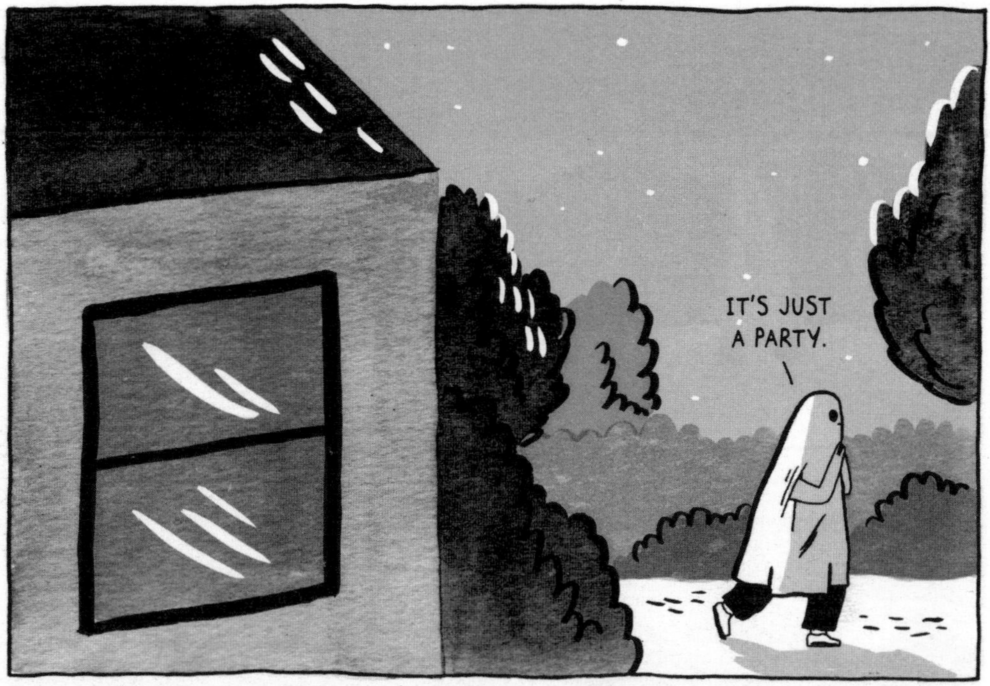
IT'S JUST
A PARTY.

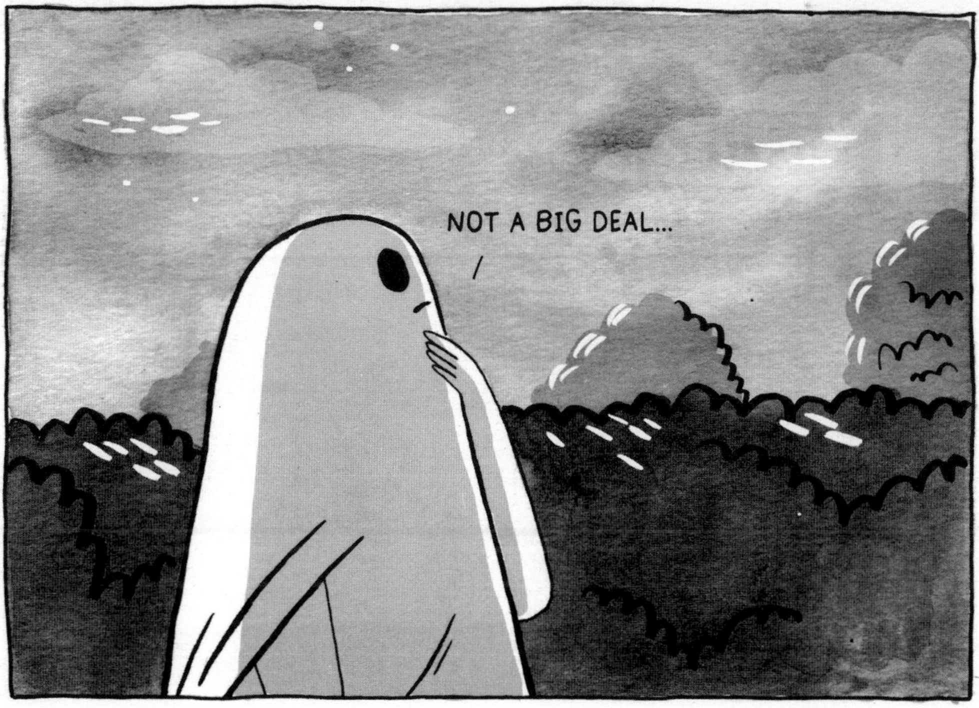
NOT A BIG DEAL...

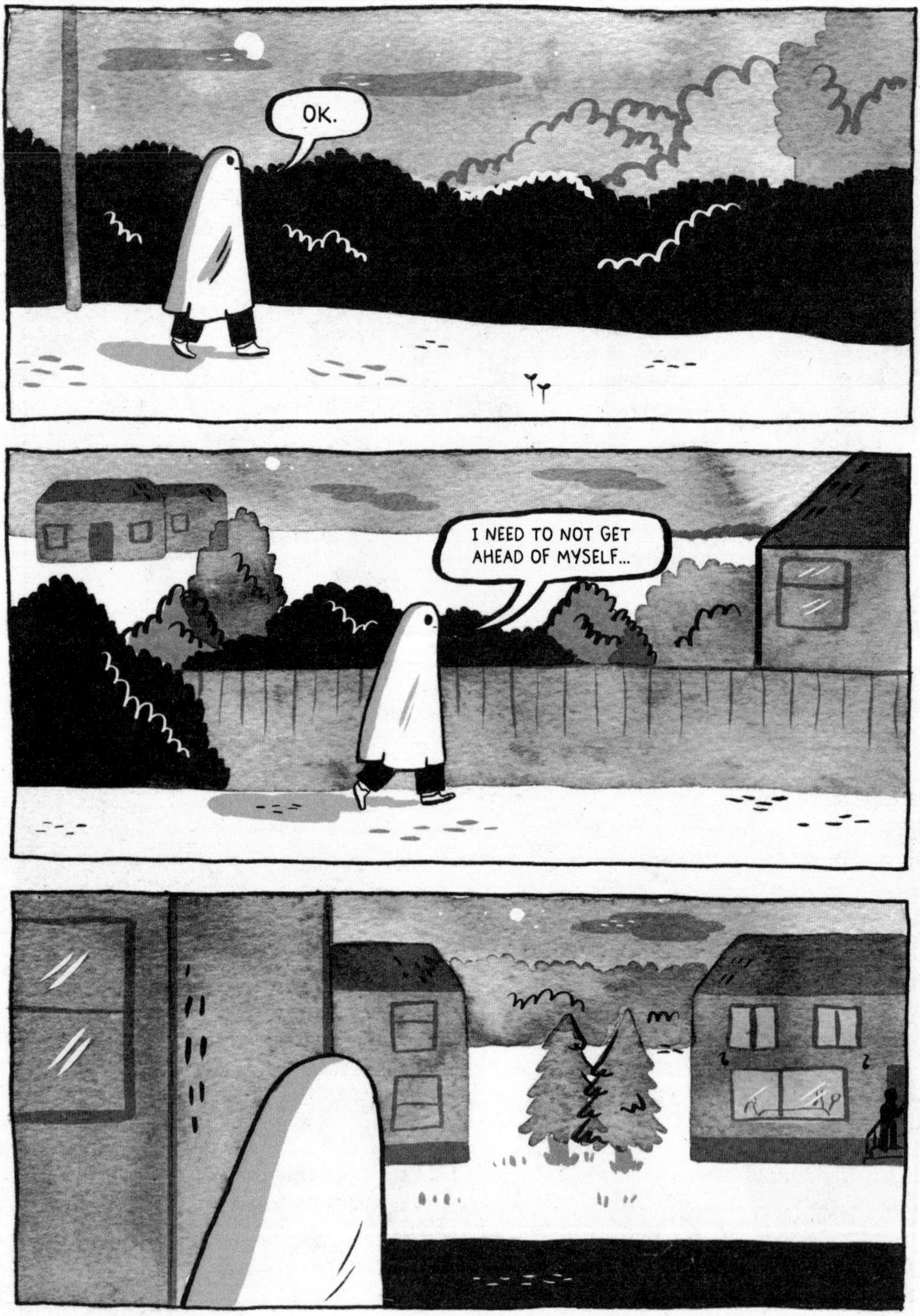
OK.
I NEED TO NOT GET AHEAD OF MYSELF...

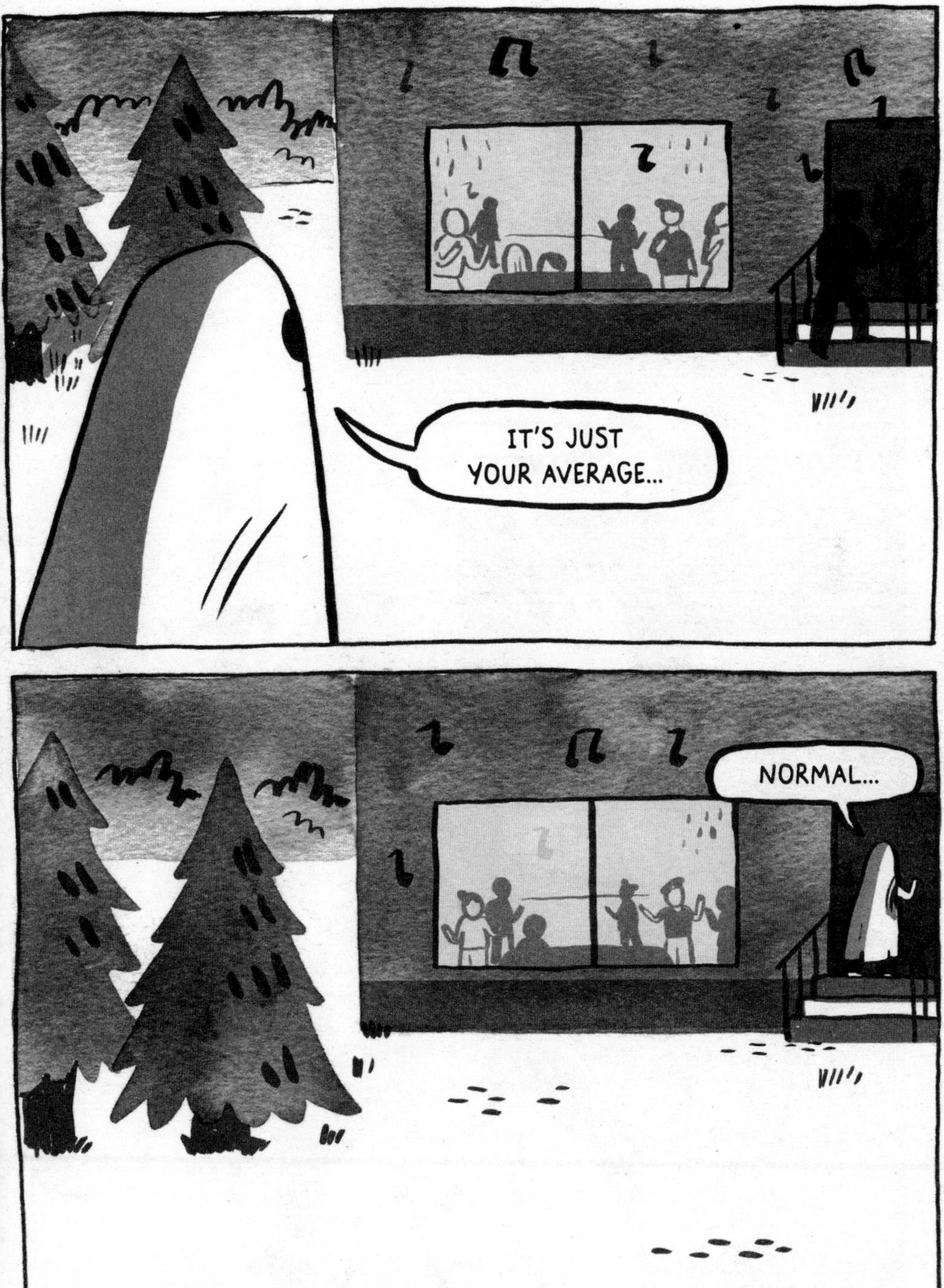
IT'S JUST
YOUR AVERAGE...
NORMAL...

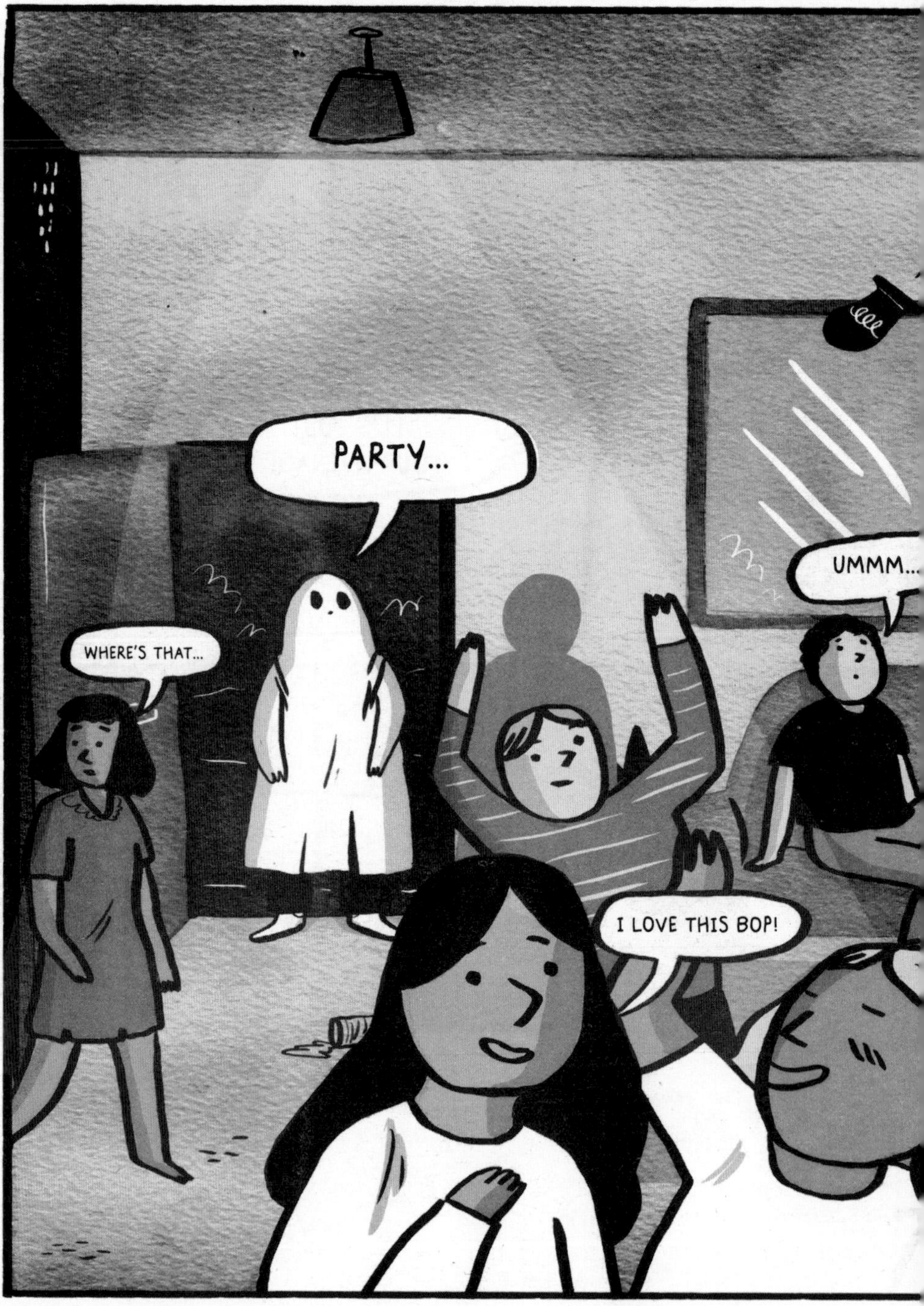
PARTY...
WHERE'S THAT...
UMMM...
I LOVE THIS BOP!

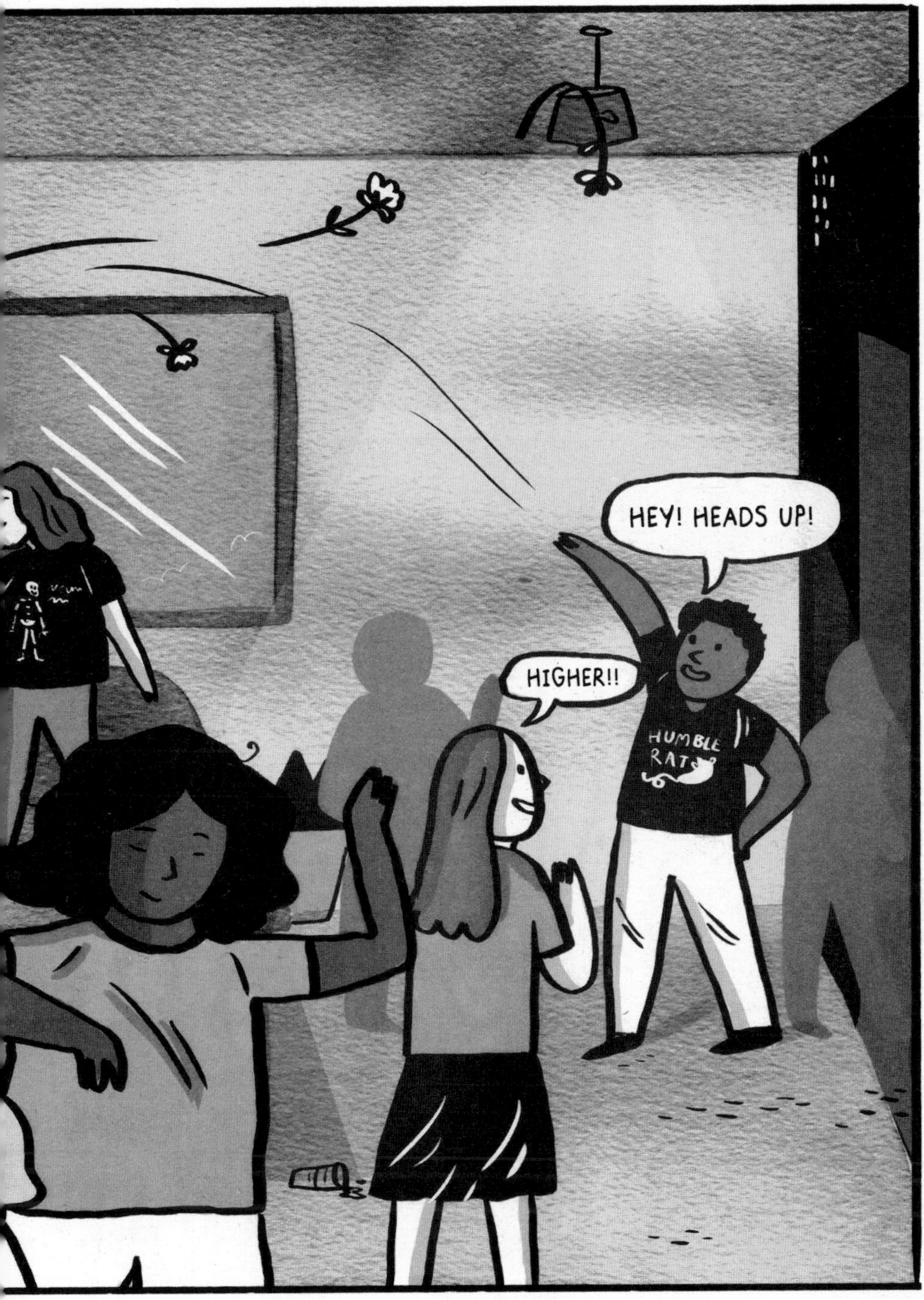
HEY! HEADS UP!
HIGHER!!
HUMBLE RAT

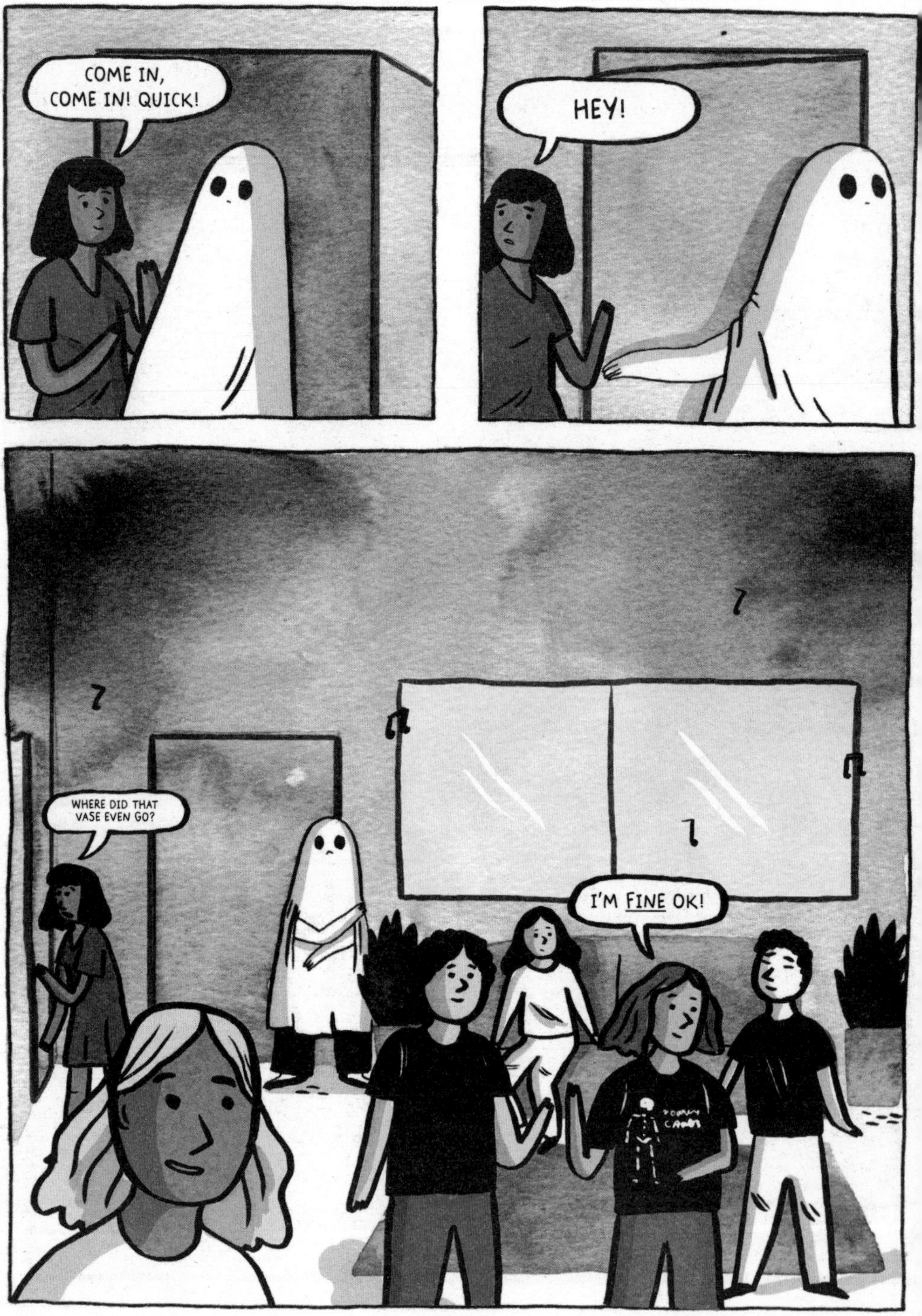
COME IN, COME IN! QUICK!
HEY!
WHERE DID THAT VASE EVEN GO?
I'M FINE OK!

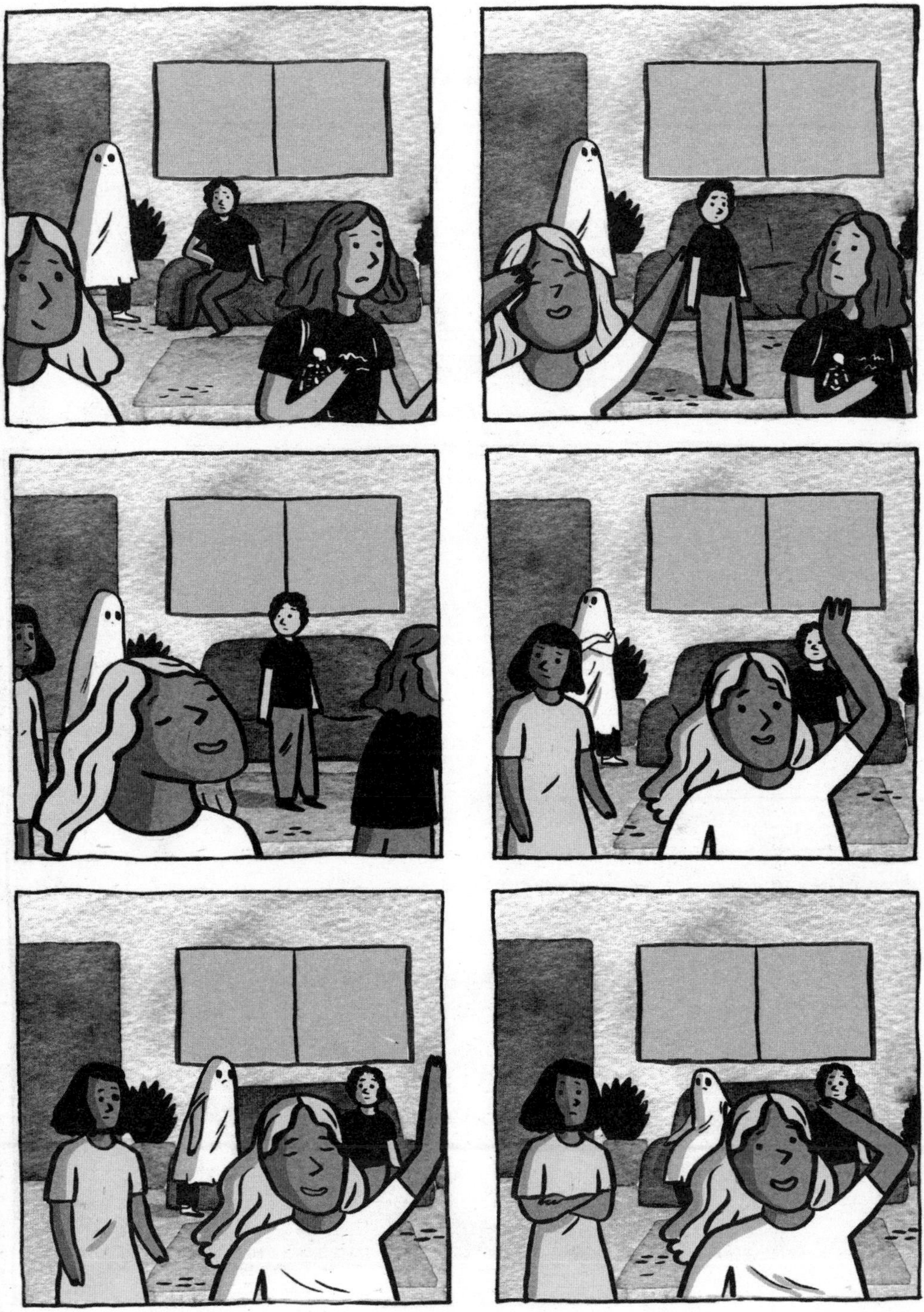

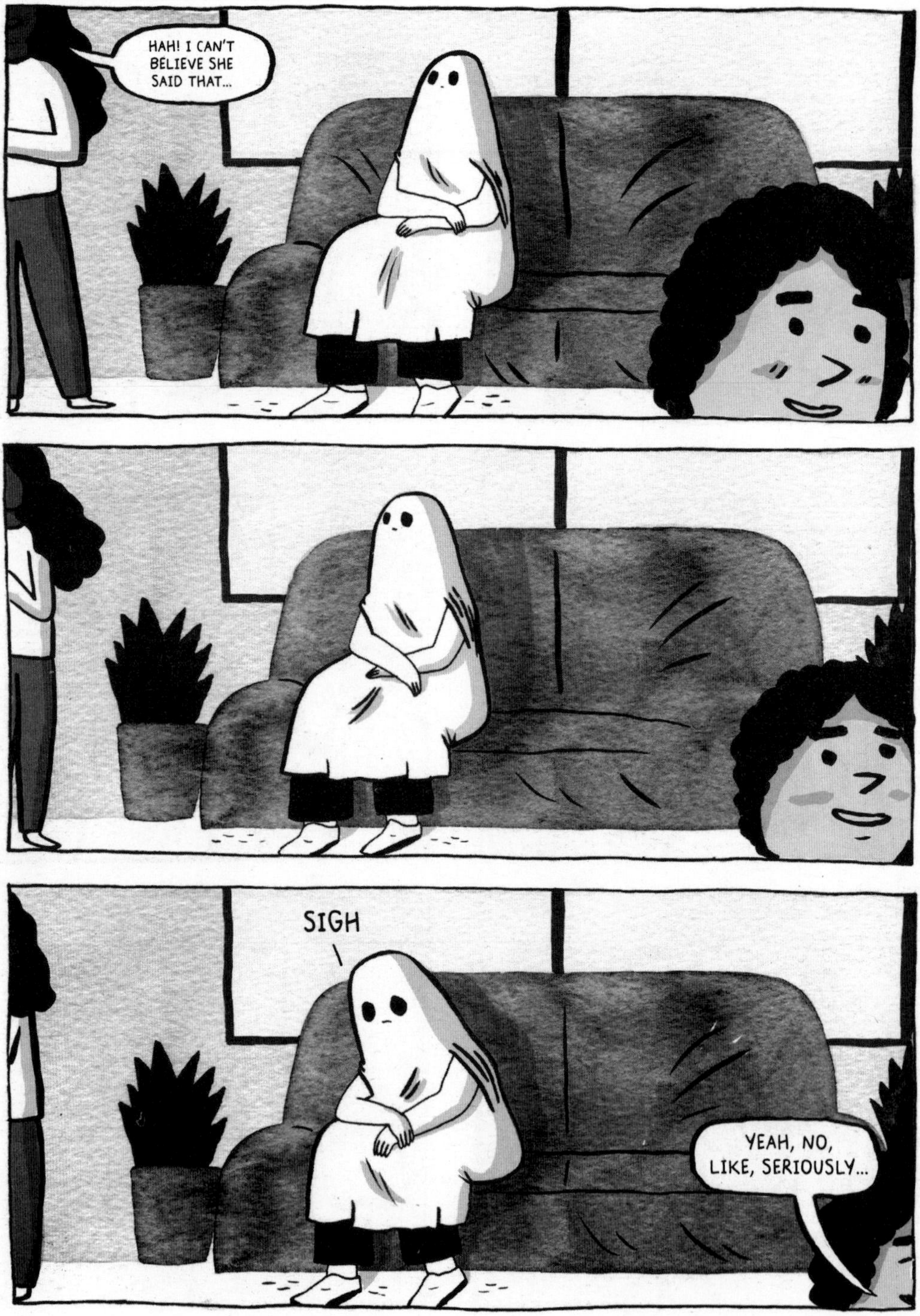
HAH! I CAN'T BELIEVE SHE SAID THAT...
SIGH
YEAH, NO, LIKE, SERIOUSLY...

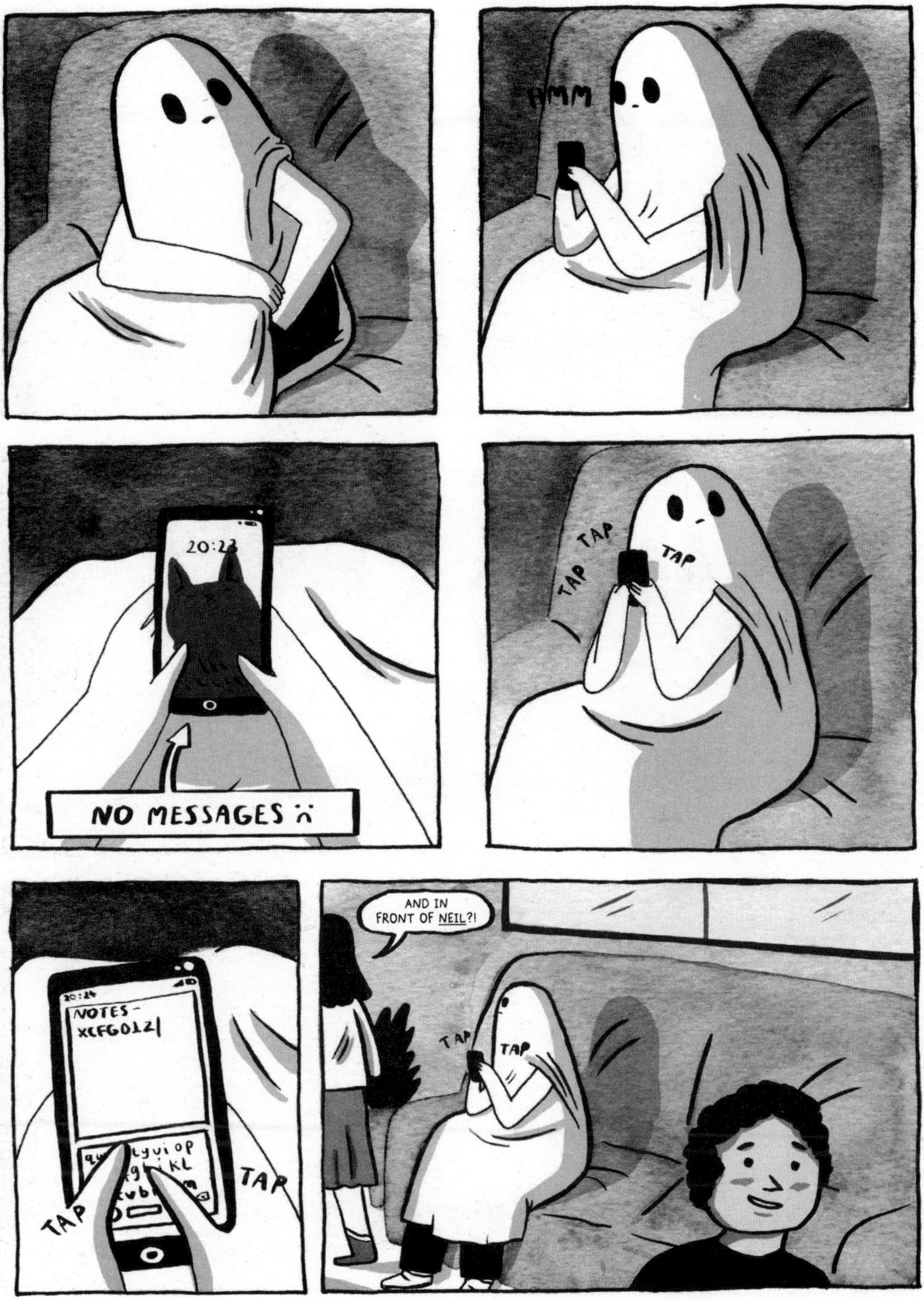
HMM
20:23
NO MESSAGES
TAP TAP
TAP
TAP
NOTES -
XCFGO12
TAP
TAP
AND IN FRONT OF NEIL?!
TAP
TAP

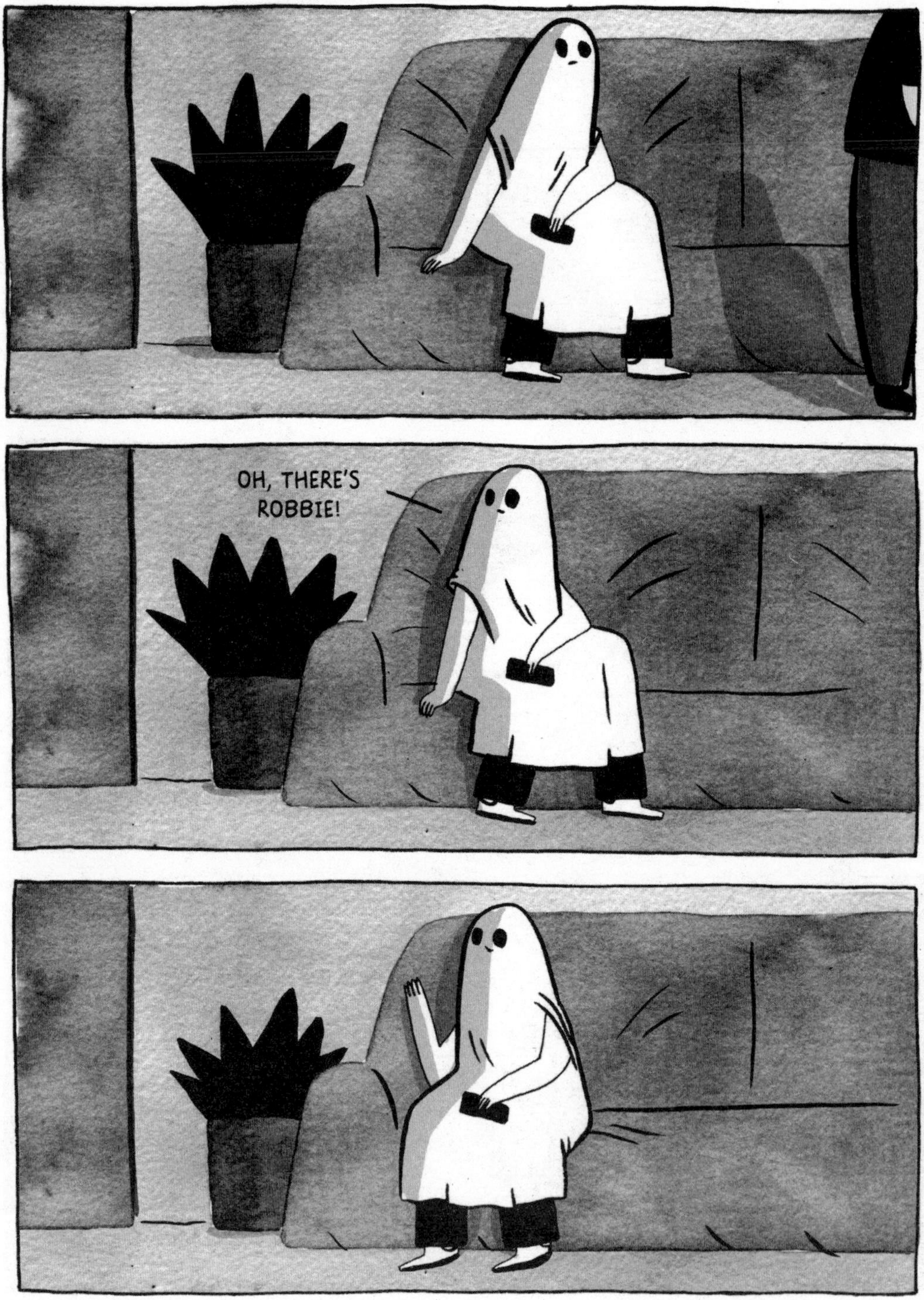
OH, THERE'S ROBBIE!

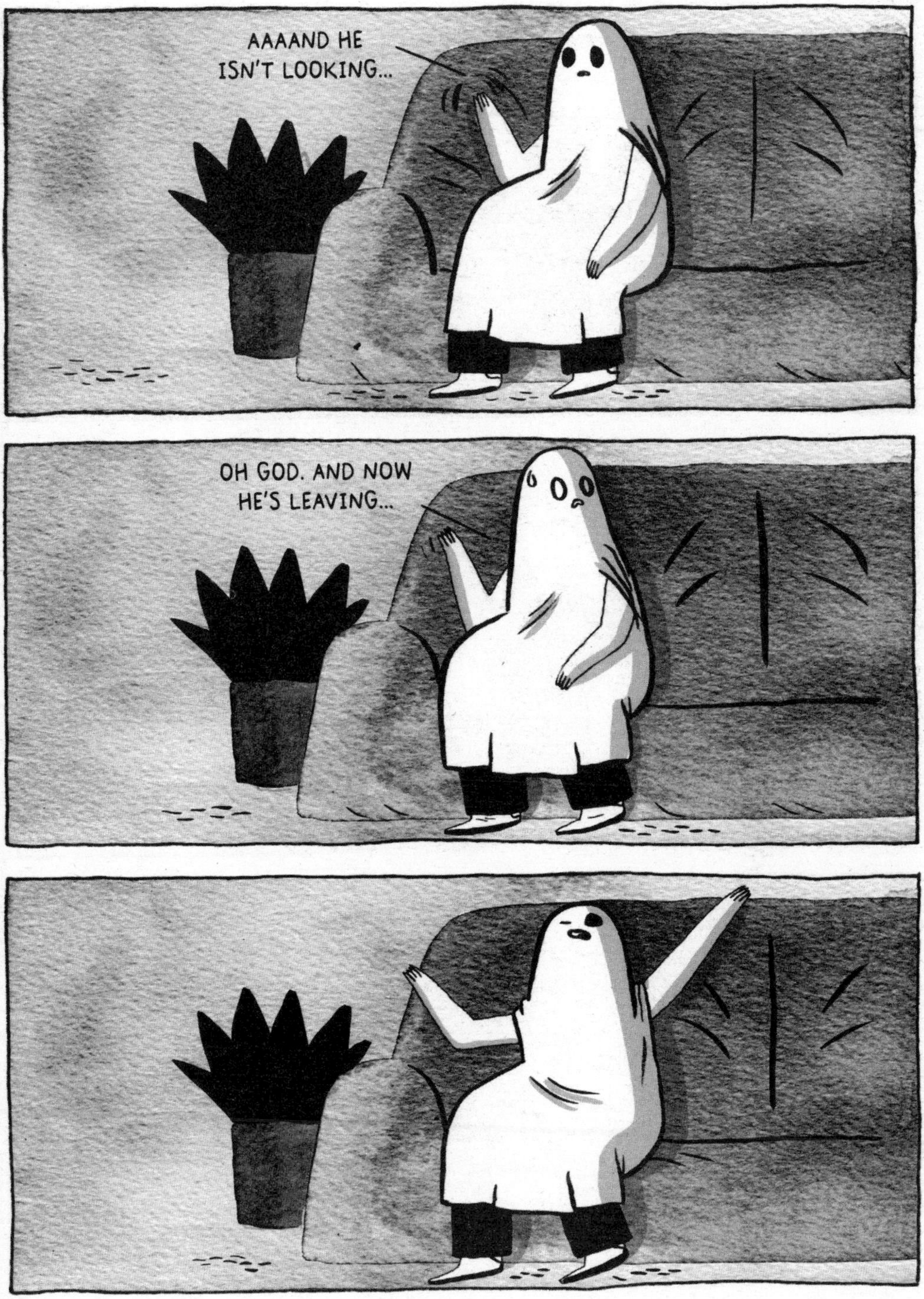
AAAAND HE ISN'T LOOKING...
OH GOD. AND NOW HE'S LEAVING...

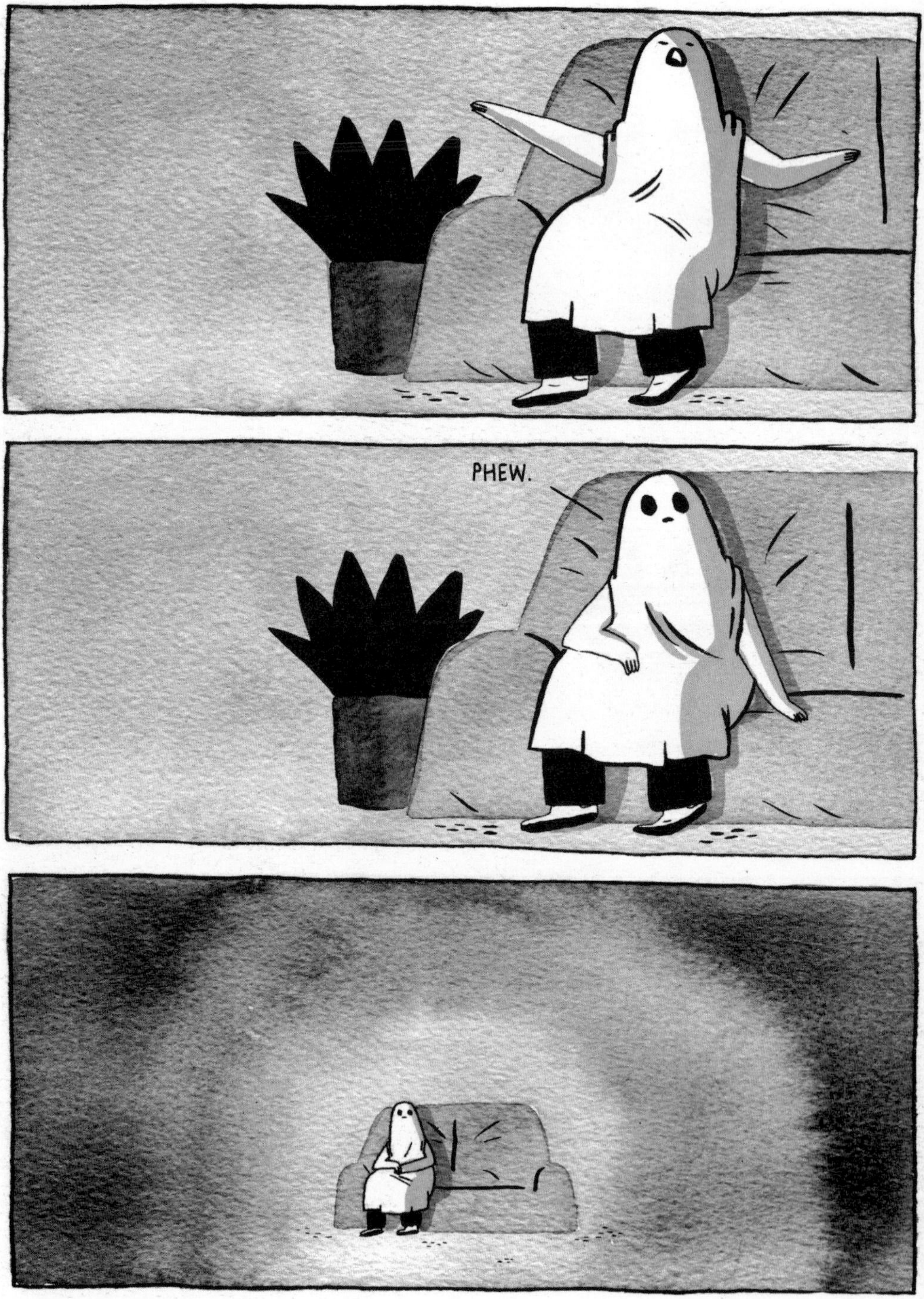
PHEW.

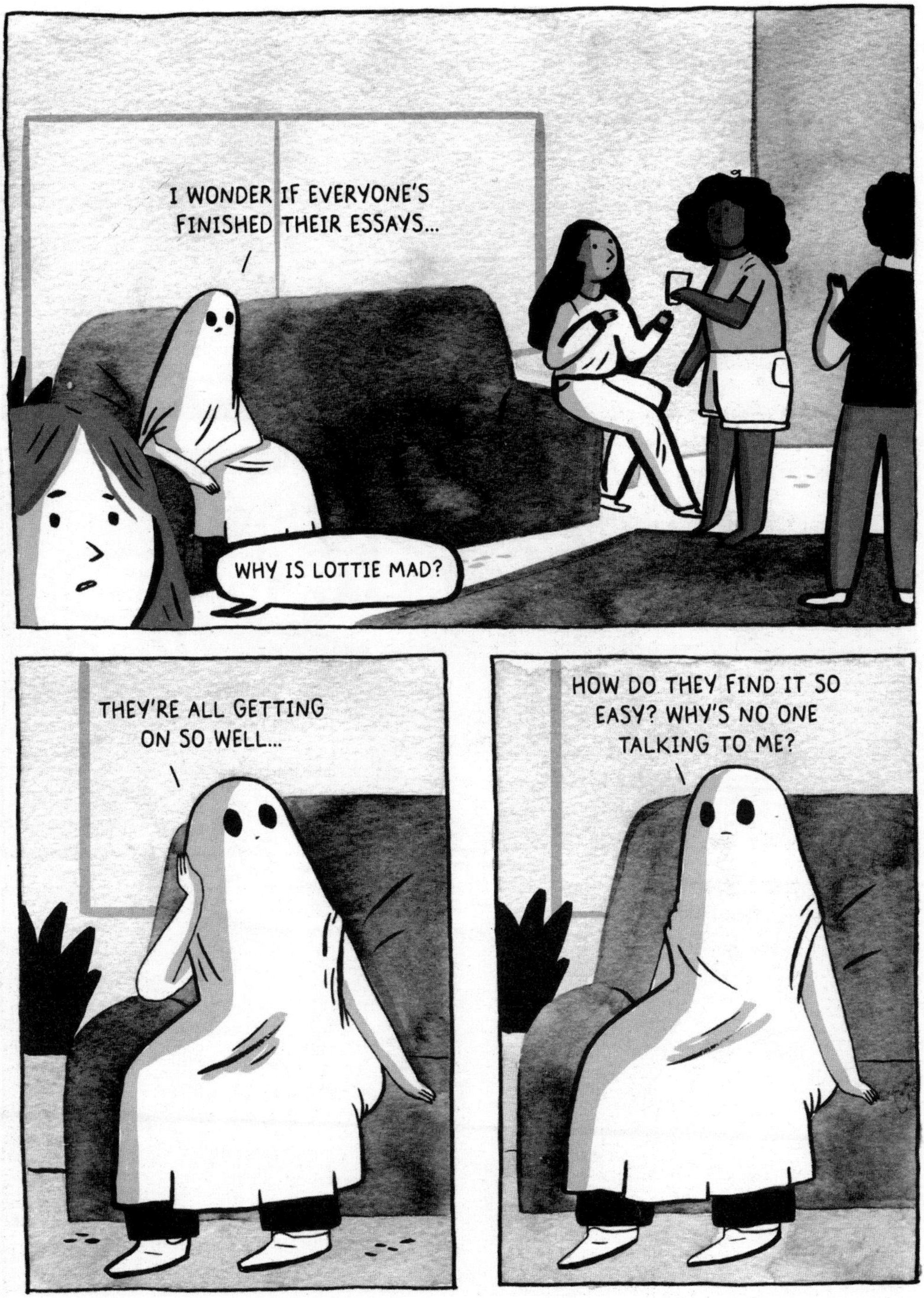
I WONDER IF EVERYONE'S FINISHED THEIR ESSAYS...
WHY IS LOTTIE MAD?
THEY'RE ALL GETTING ON SO WELL...
HOW DO THEY FIND IT SO EASY? WHY'S NO ONE TALKING TO ME?

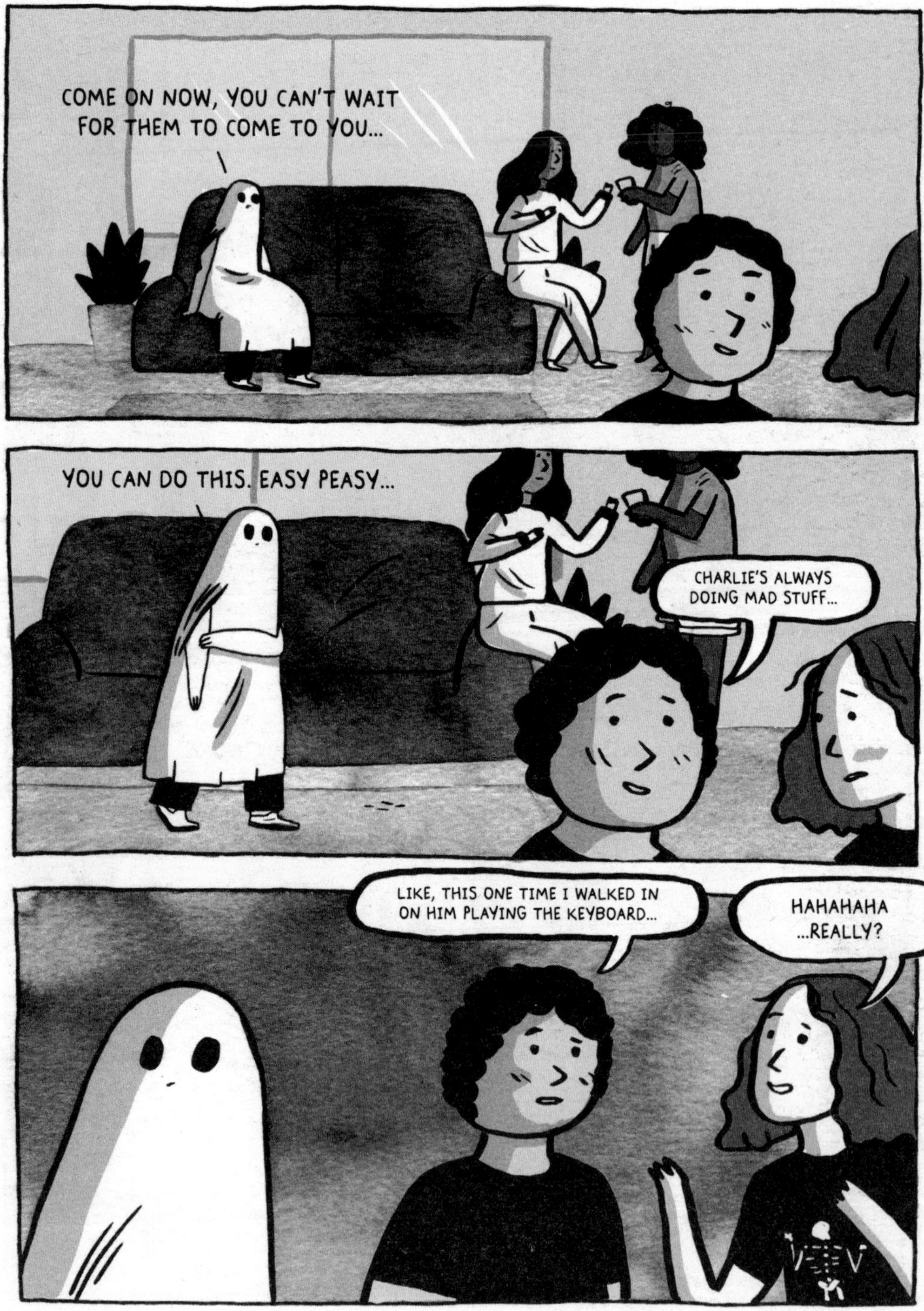
COME ON NOW, YOU CAN'T WAIT FOR THEM TO COME TO YOU...
YOU CAN DO THIS. EASY PEASY...
CHARLIE'S ALWAYS DOING MAD STUFF...
LIKE, THIS ONE TIME I WALKED IN ON HIM PLAYING THE KEYBOARD...
HAHAHAHA ...REALLY?

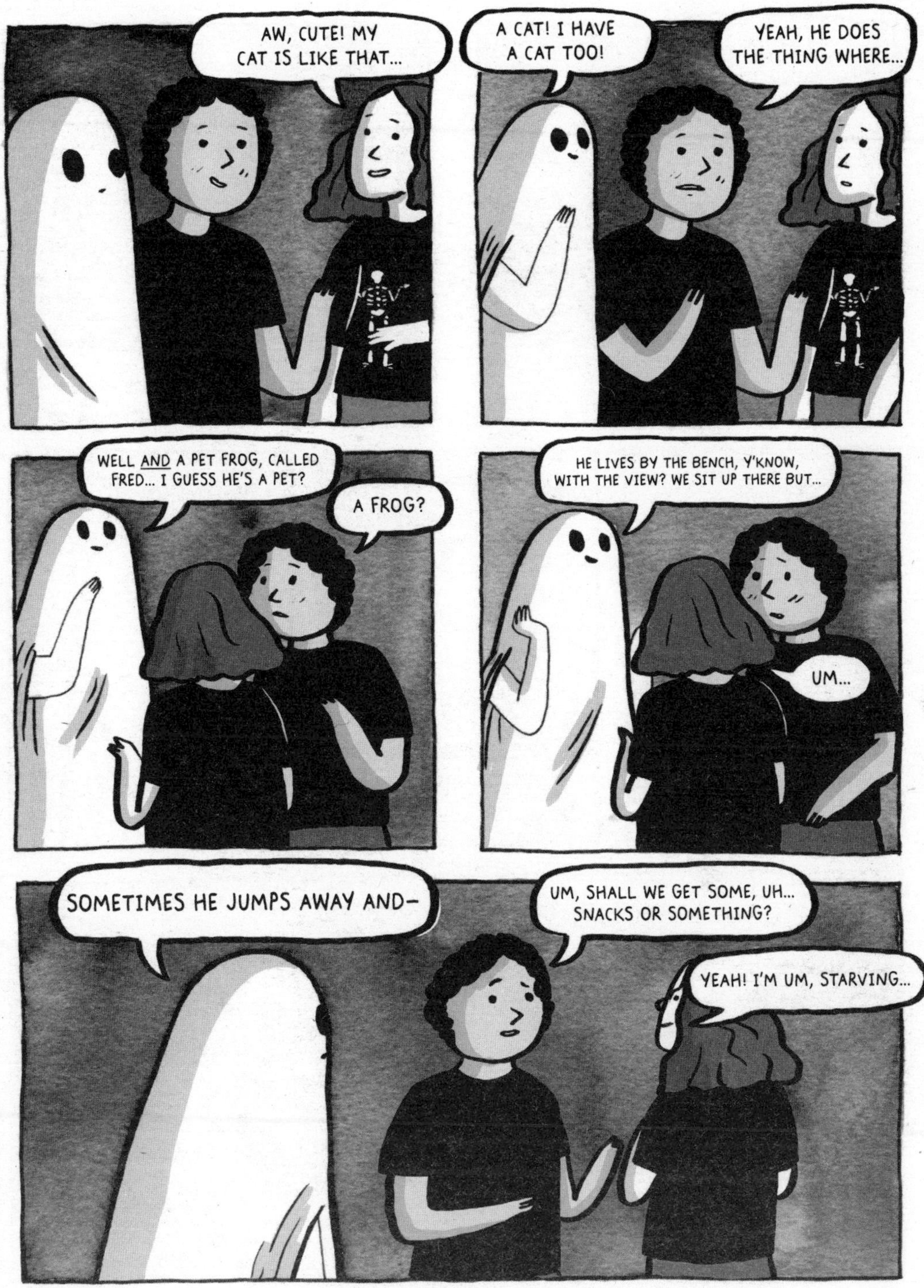
AW, CUTE! MY CAT IS LIKE THAT...
A CAT! I HAVE A CAT TOO!
YEAH, HE DOES THE THING WHERE...
WELL AND A PET FROG, CALLED FRED... I GUESS HE'S A PET?
A FROG?
HE LIVES BY THE BENCH, Y'KNOW, WITH THE VIEW? WE SIT UP THERE BUT...
UM...
SOMETIMES HE JUMPS AWAY AND-
UM, SHALL WE GET SOME, UH... SNACKS OR SOMETHING?
YEAH! I'M UM, STARVING...

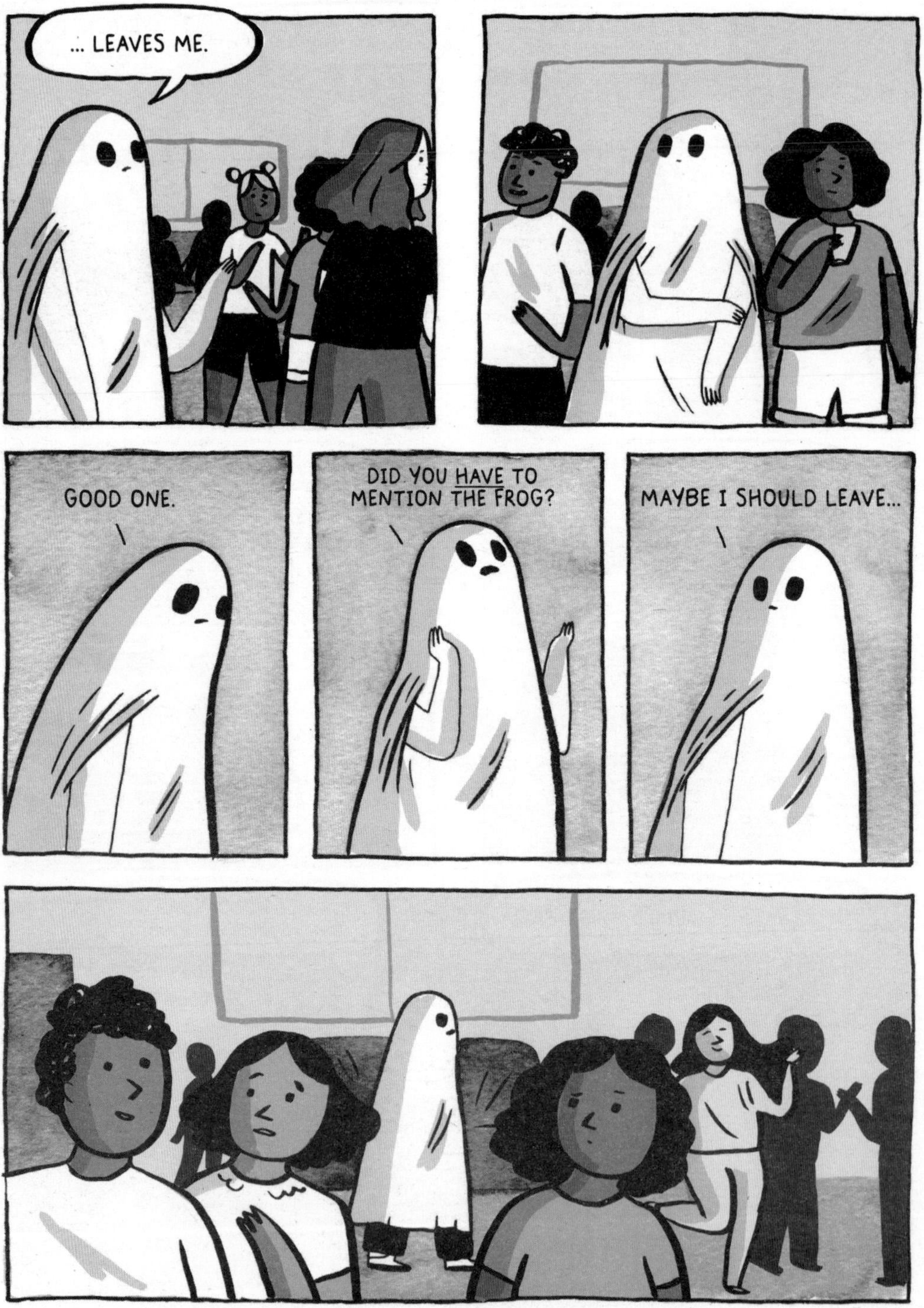

... LEAVES ME.
GOOD ONE.
DID YOU HAVE TO MENTION THE FROG?
MAYBE I SHOULD LEAVE...

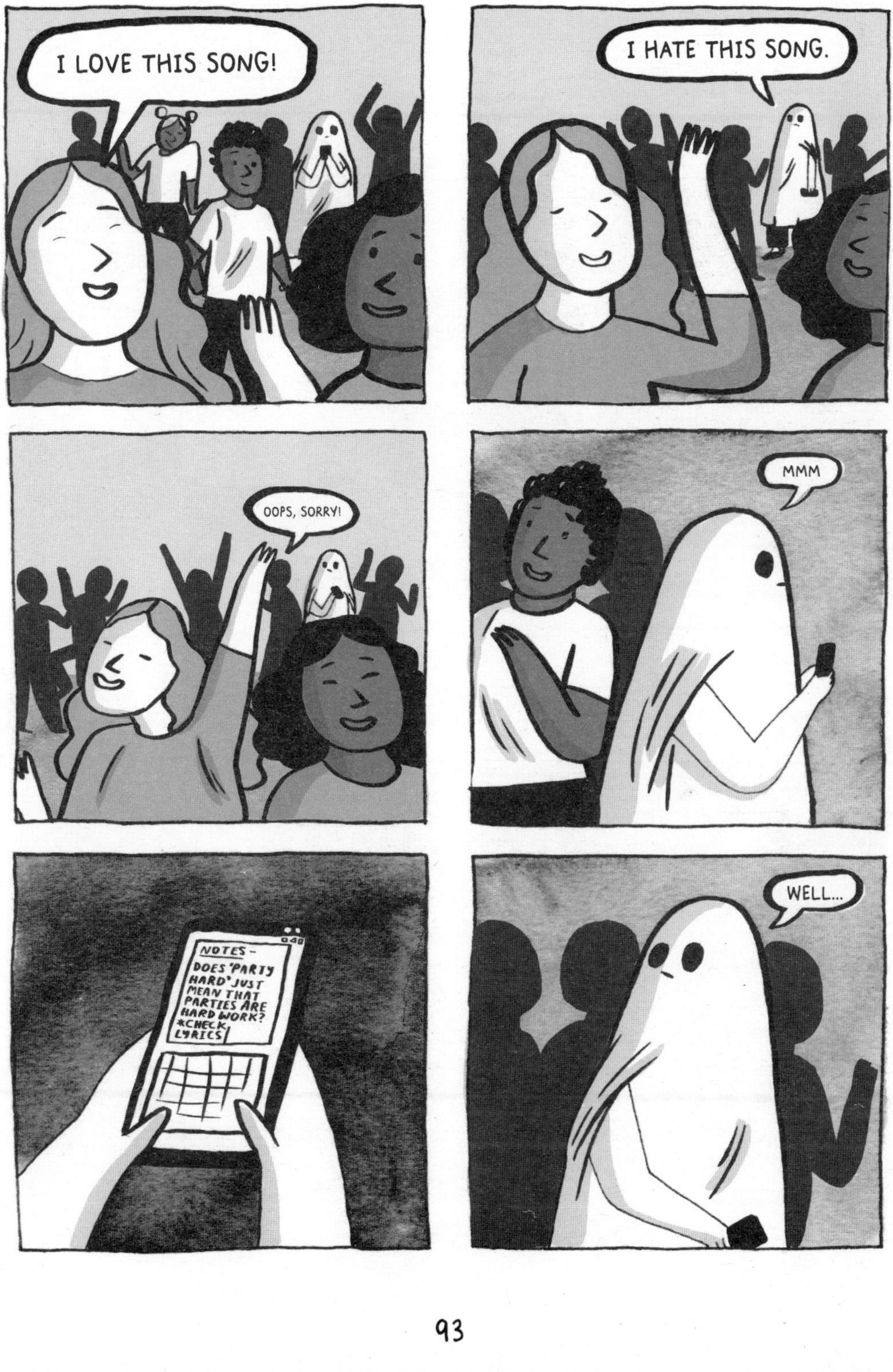

I LOVE THIS SONG!
I HATE THIS SONG.
OOPS, SORRY!
MMM
NOTES -
DOES 'PARTY HARD' JUST MEAN THAT PARTIES ARE HARD WORK? *CHECK LYRICS
WELL...

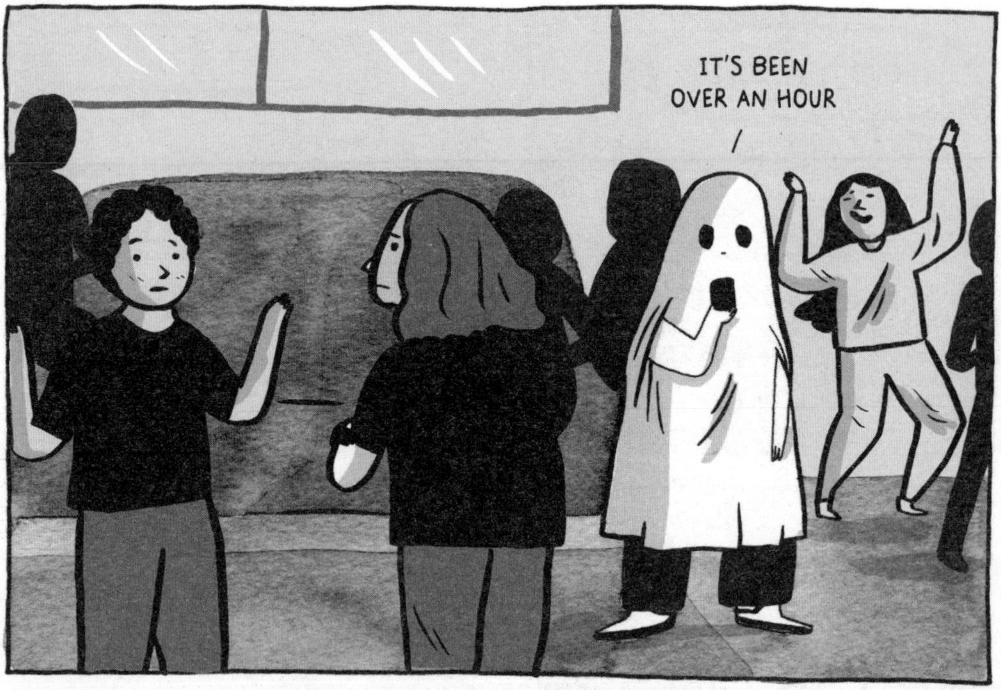
IT'S BEEN
OVER AN HOUR

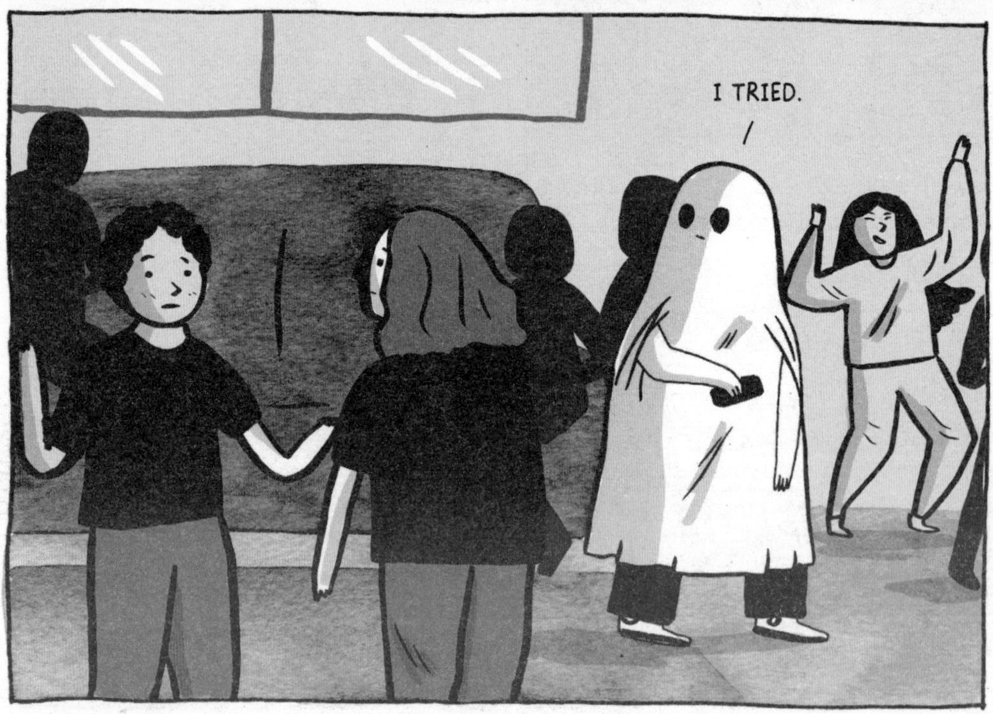
I TRIED.

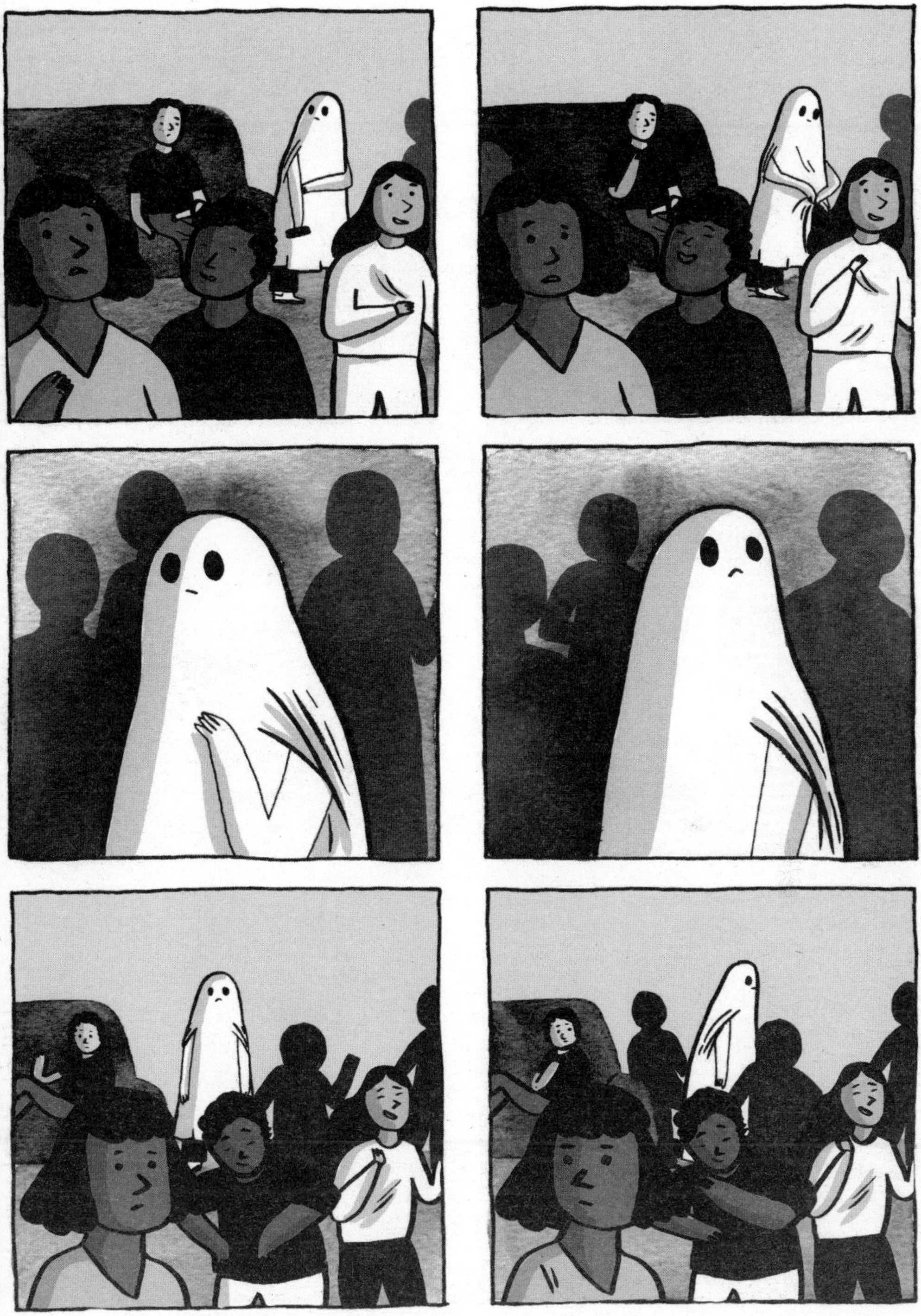

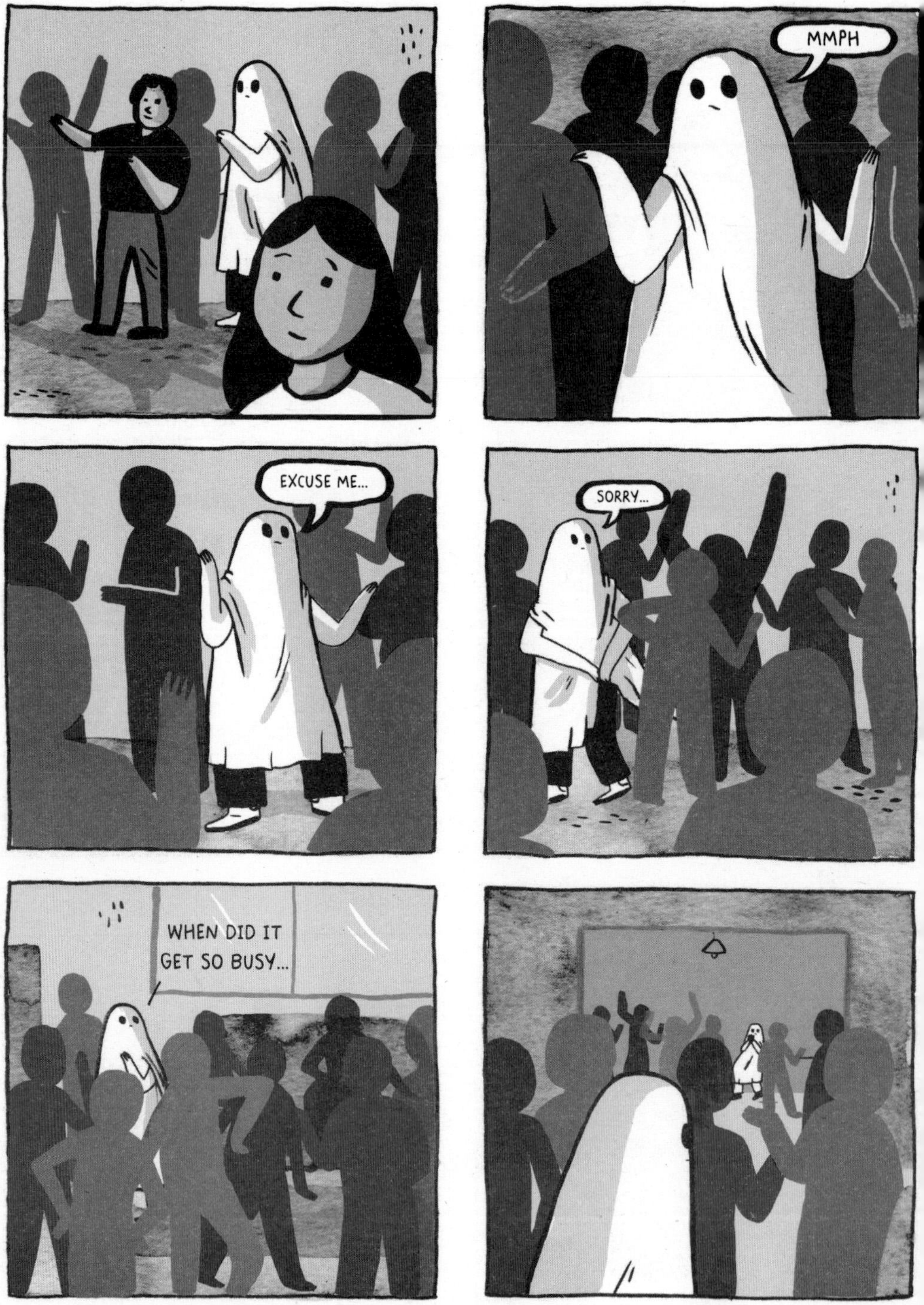
MMPH
EXCUSE ME...
SORRY...
WHEN DID IT GET SO BUSY...

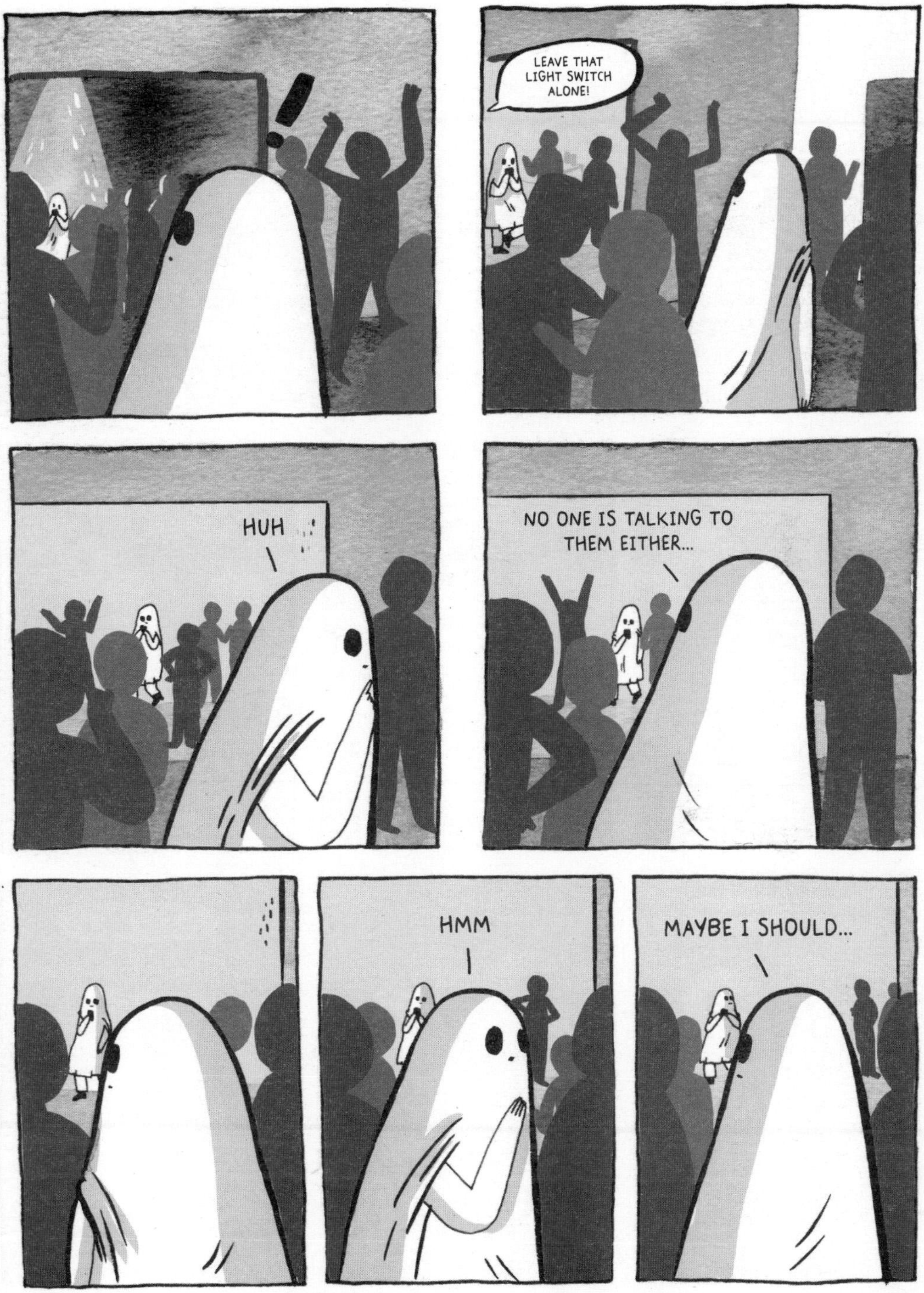
!
LEAVE THAT LIGHT SWITCH ALONE!
HUH
NO ONE IS TALKING TO THEM EITHER...
HMM
MAYBE I SHOULD...

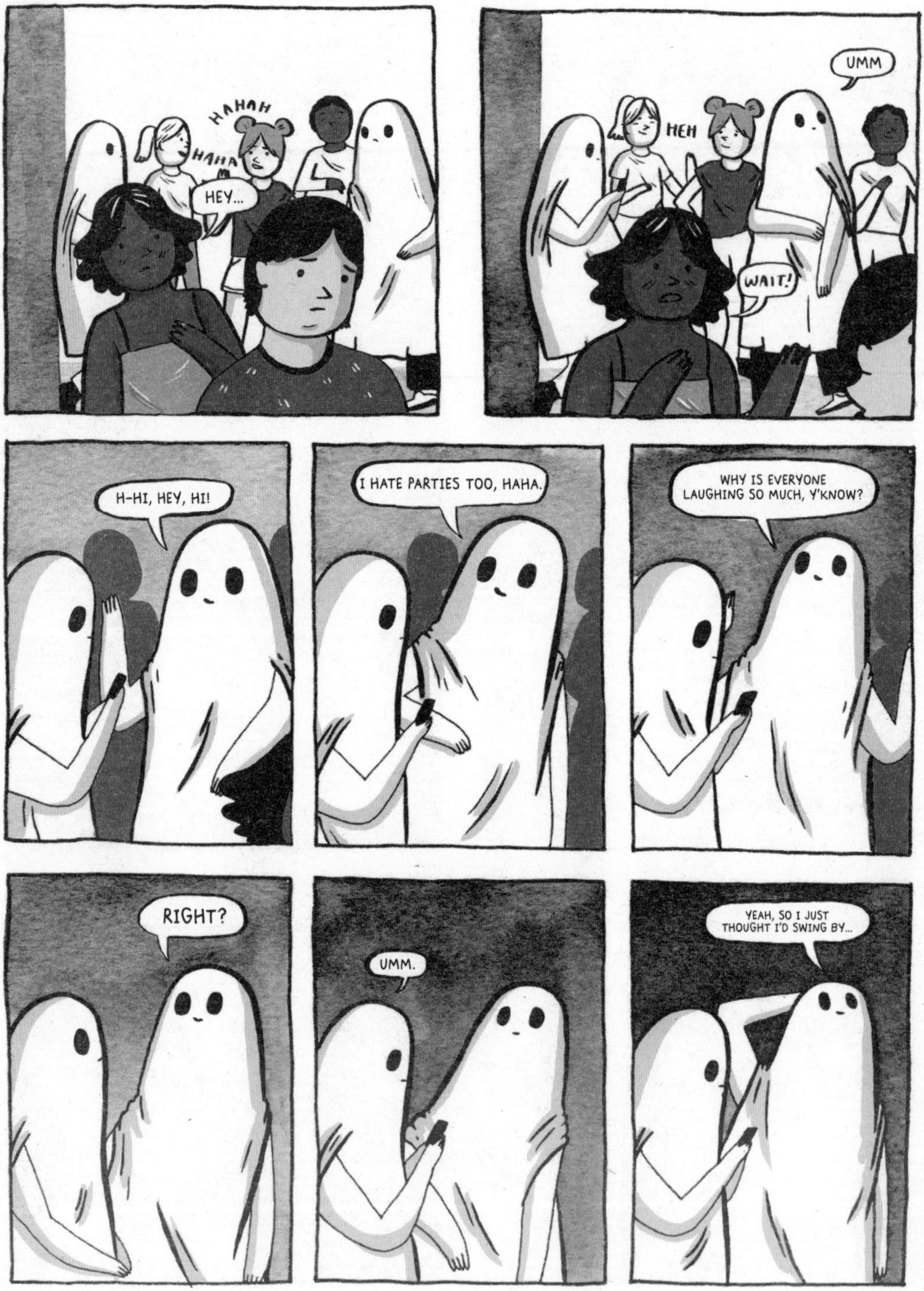
HAHAH
HAHA
HEY...
UMM
HEH
WAIT!
H-HI, HEY, HI!
I HATE PARTIES TOO, HAHA.
WHY IS EVERYONE LAUGHING SO MUCH, Y'KNOW?
RIGHT?
UMM.
YEAH, SO I JUST THOUGHT I'D SWING BY...

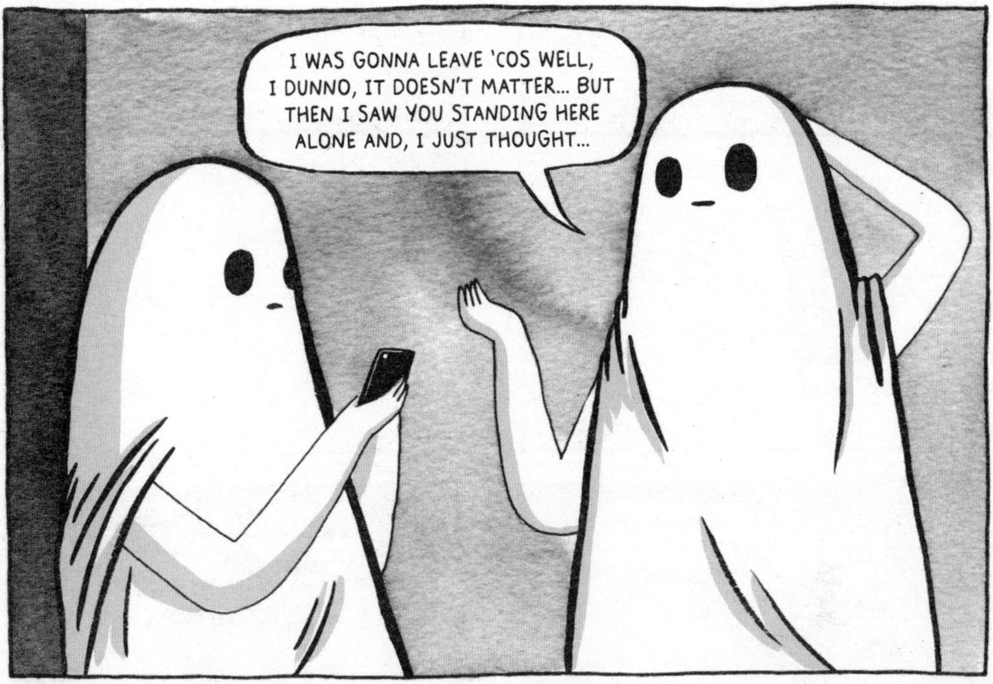
I WAS GONNA LEAVE 'COS WELL, I DUNNO, IT DOESN'T MATTER... BUT THEN I SAW YOU STANDING HERE ALONE AND, I JUST THOUGHT...

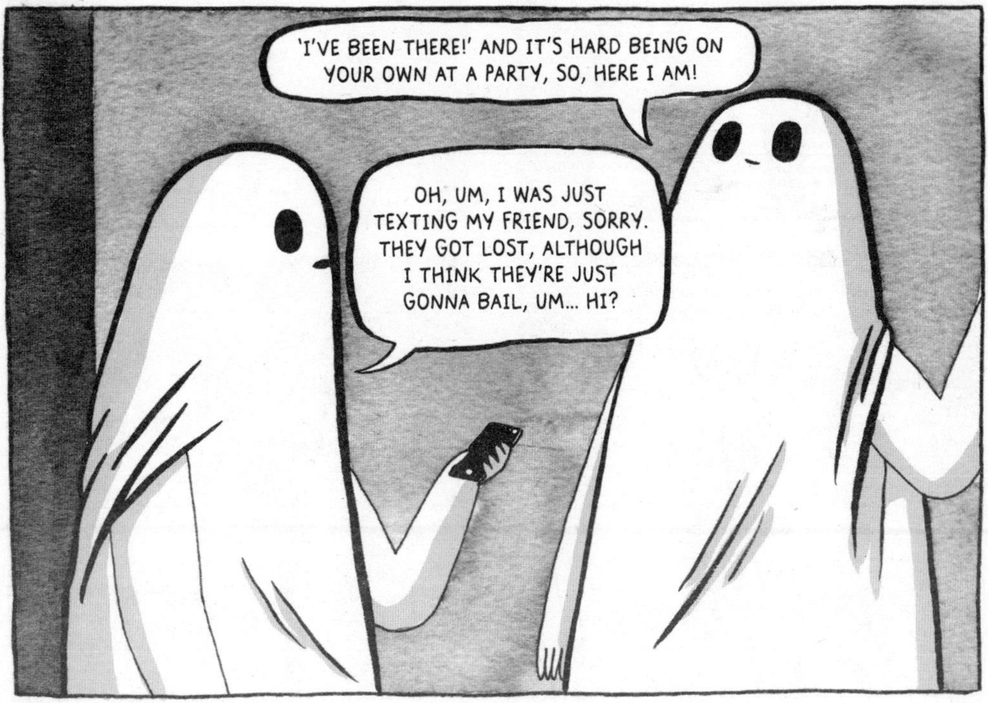
'I'VE BEEN THERE!' AND IT'S HARD BEING ON YOUR OWN AT A PARTY, SO, HERE I AM!
OH, UM, I WAS JUST TEXTING MY FRIEND, SORRY. THEY GOT LOST, ALTHOUGH I THINK THEY'RE JUST GONNA BAIL, UM... HI?

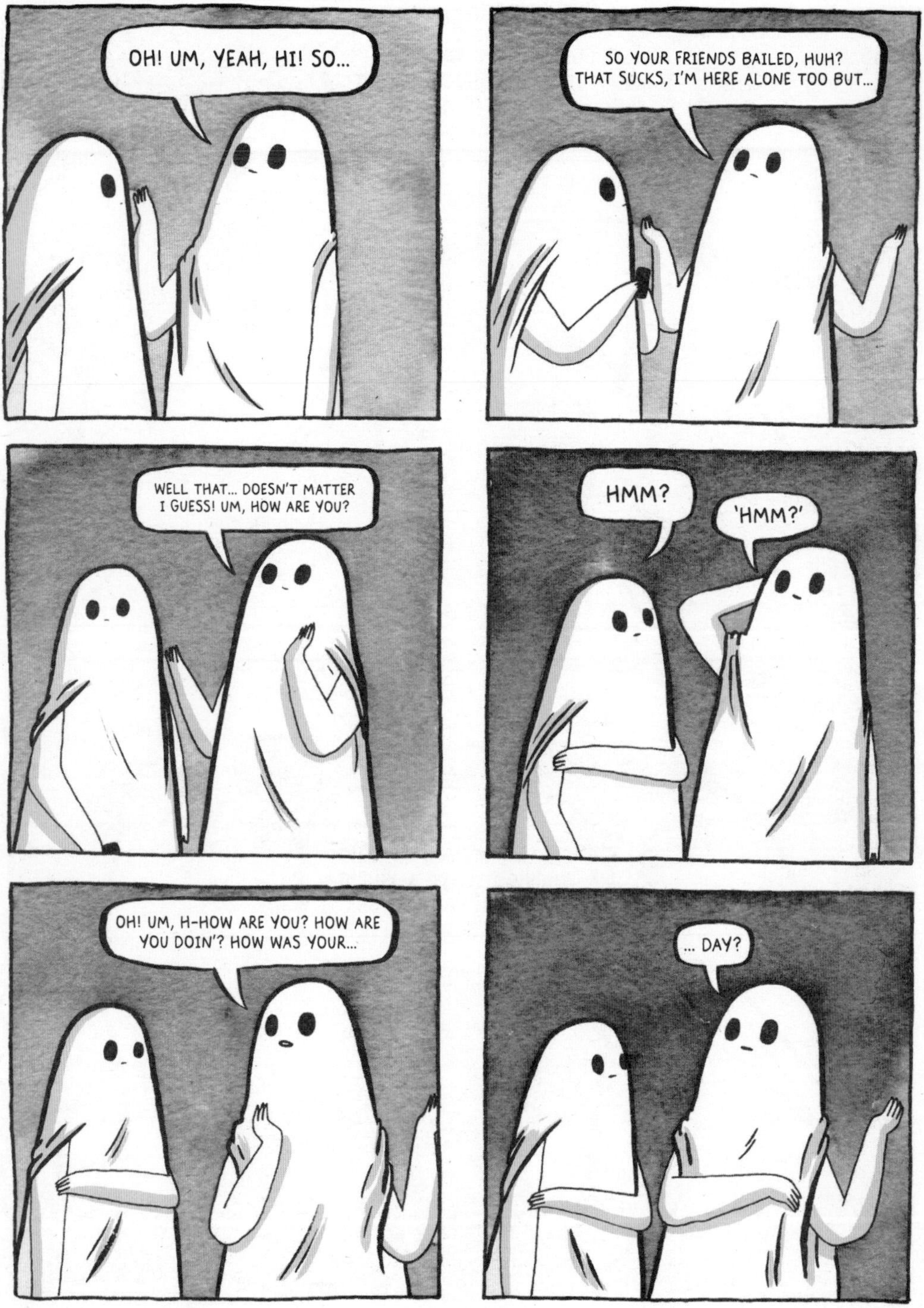
OH! UM, YEAH, HI! SO...
SO YOUR FRIENDS BAILED, HUH? THAT SUCKS, I'M HERE ALONE TOO BUT...
WELL THAT... DOESN'T MATTER I GUESS! UM, HOW ARE YOU?
HMM?
'HMM?'
OH! UM, H-HOW ARE YOU? HOW ARE YOU DOIN'? HOW WAS YOUR...
... DAY?

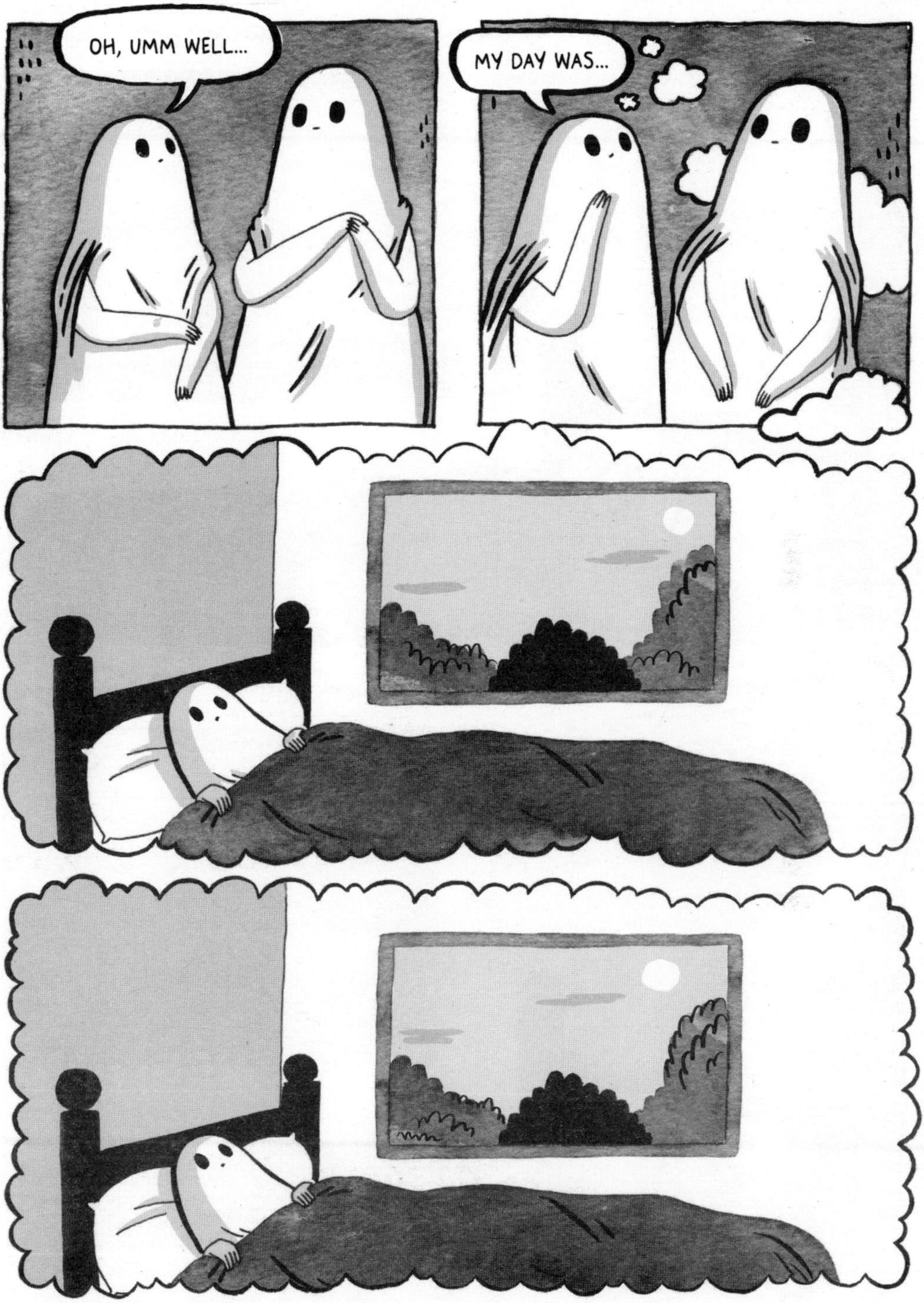
OH, UMM WELL...
MY DAY WAS...

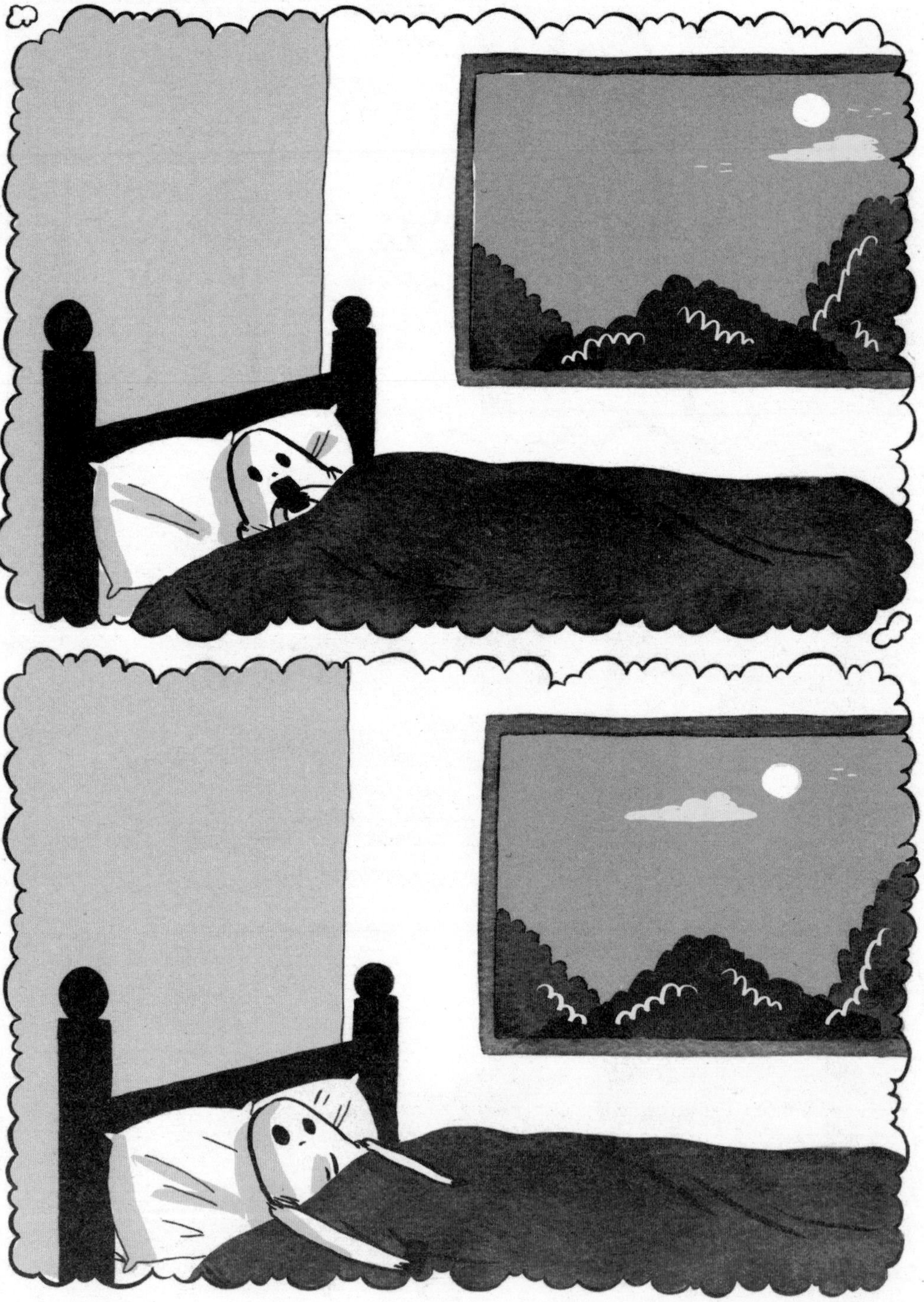

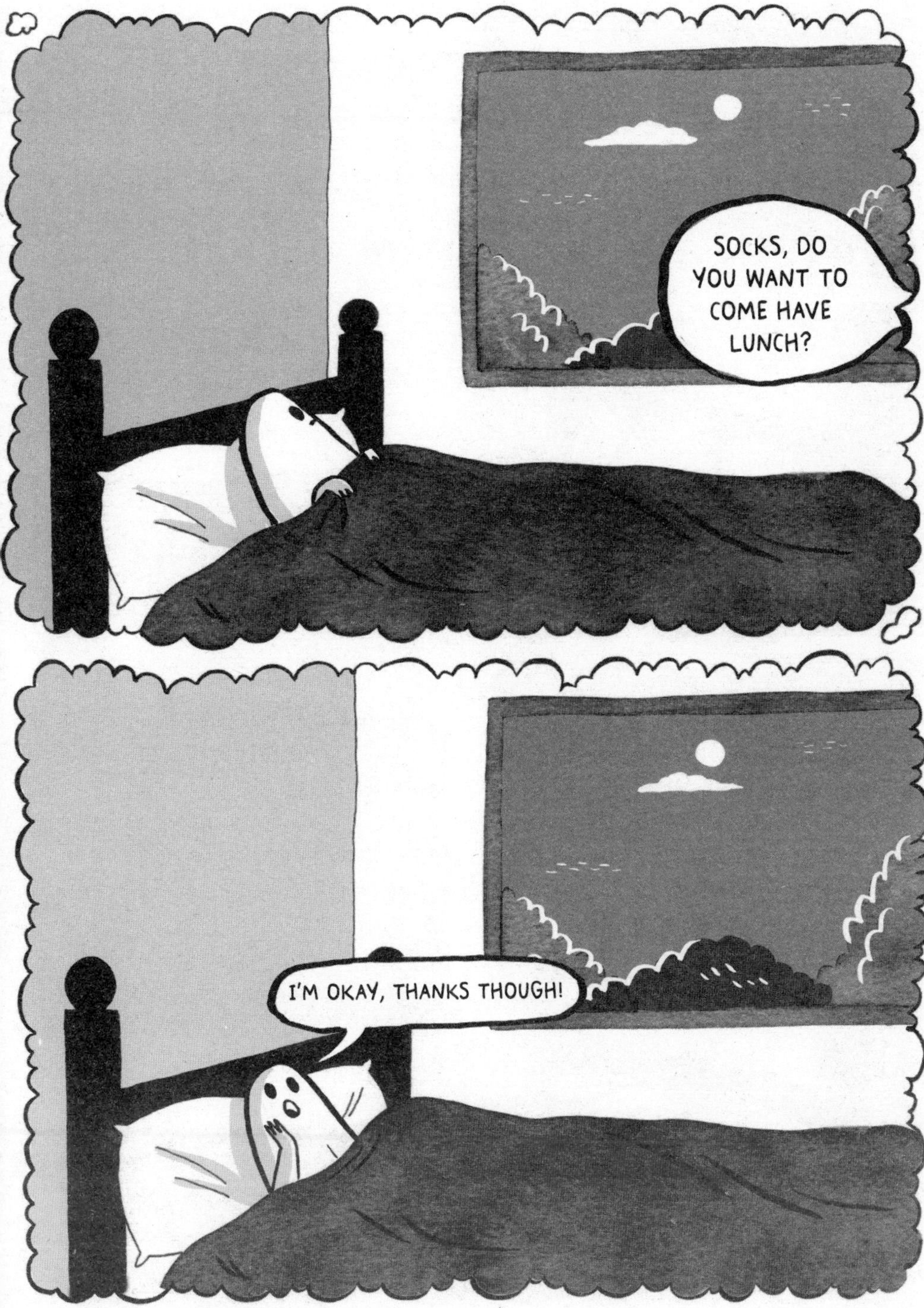
SOCKS, DO YOU WANT TO COME HAVE LUNCH?
I'M OKAY, THANKS THOUGH!

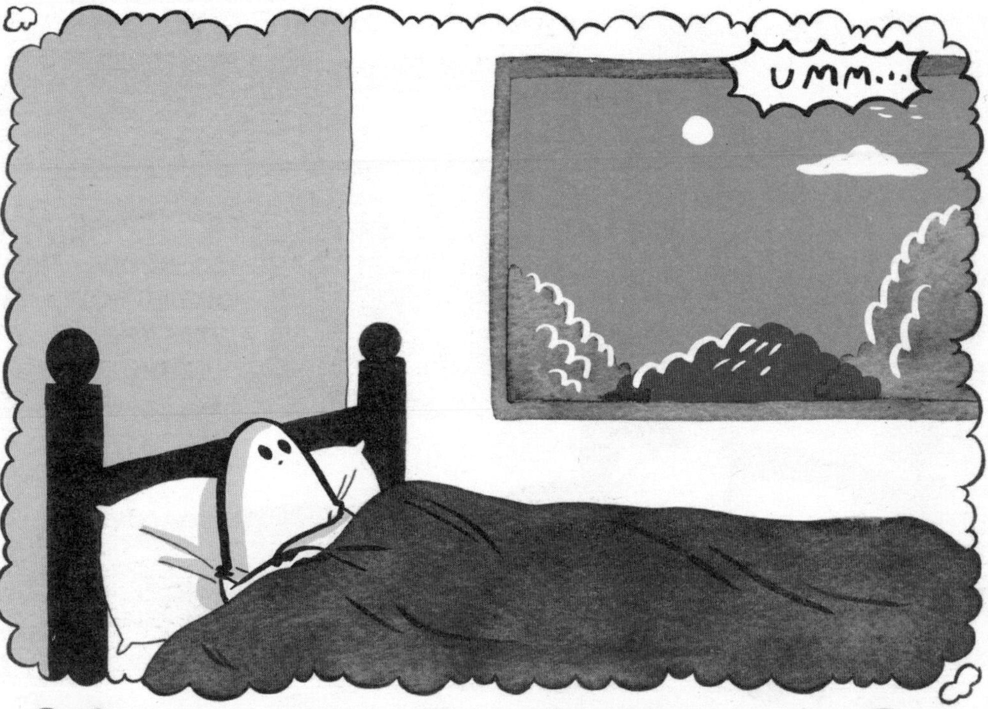
UMM...

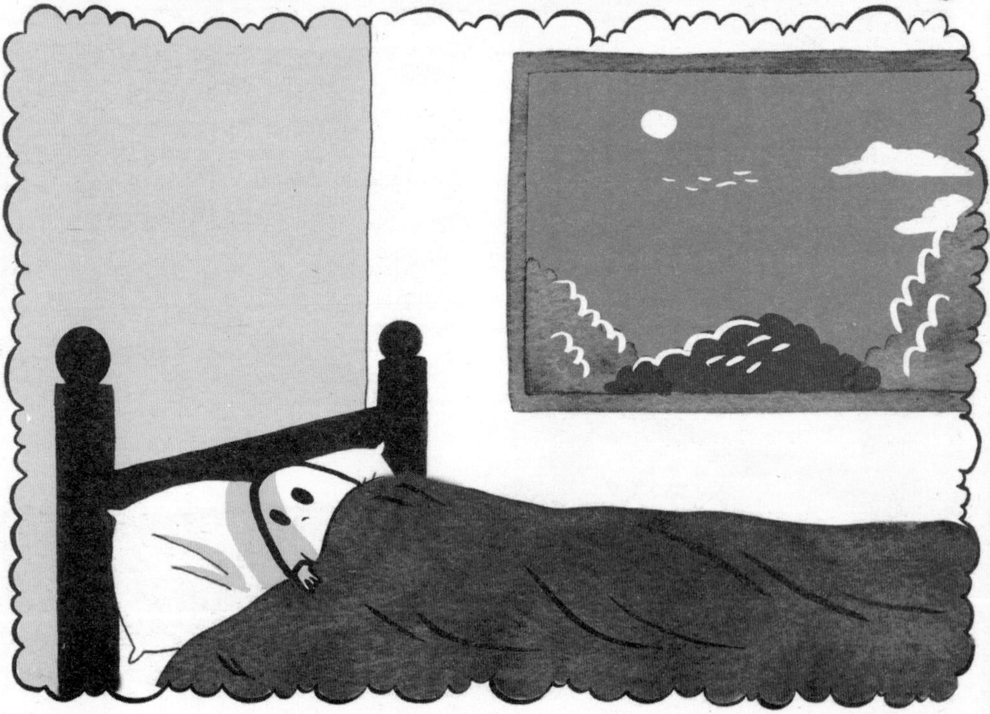

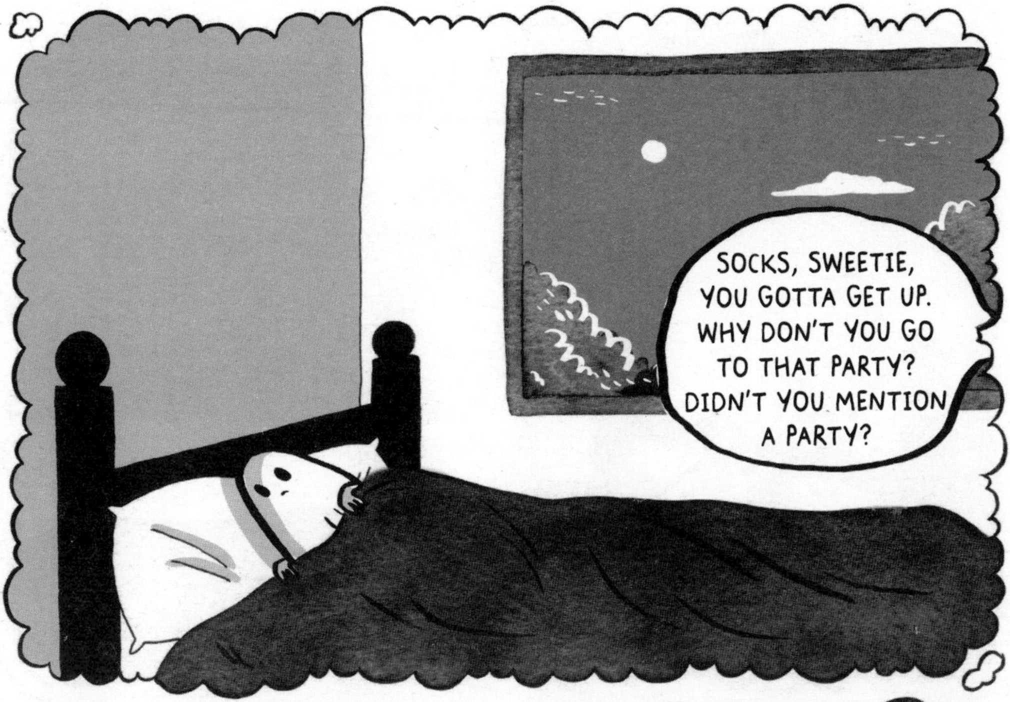
SOCKS, SWEETIE, YOU GOTTA GET UP. WHY DON'T YOU GO TO THAT PARTY? DIDN'T YOU MENTION A PARTY?

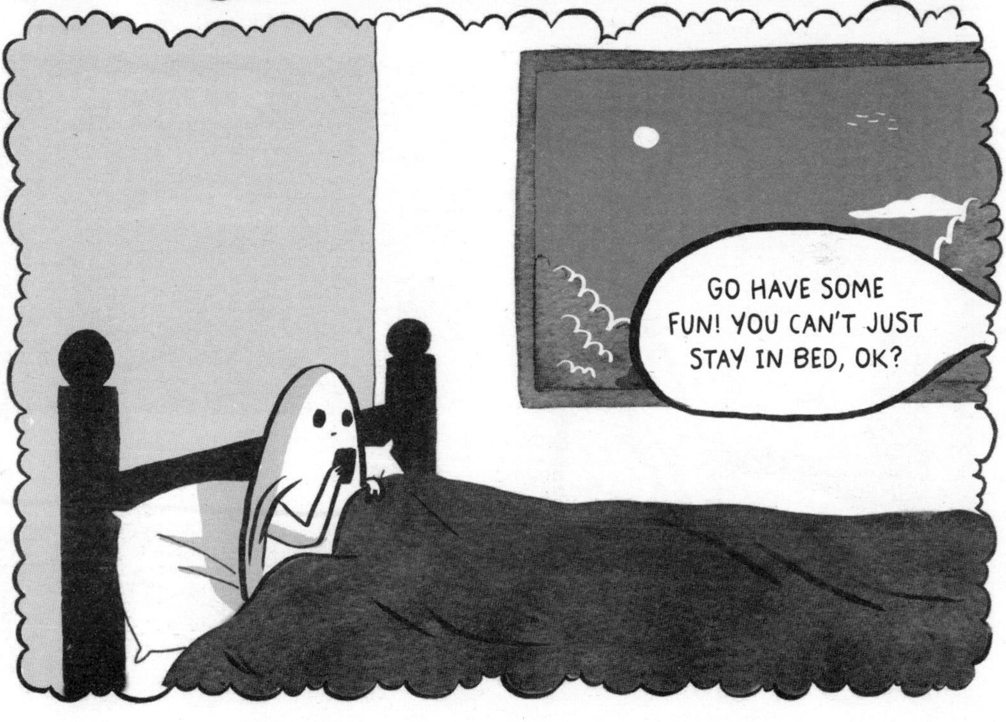
GO HAVE SOME FUN! YOU CAN'T JUST STAY IN BED, OK?

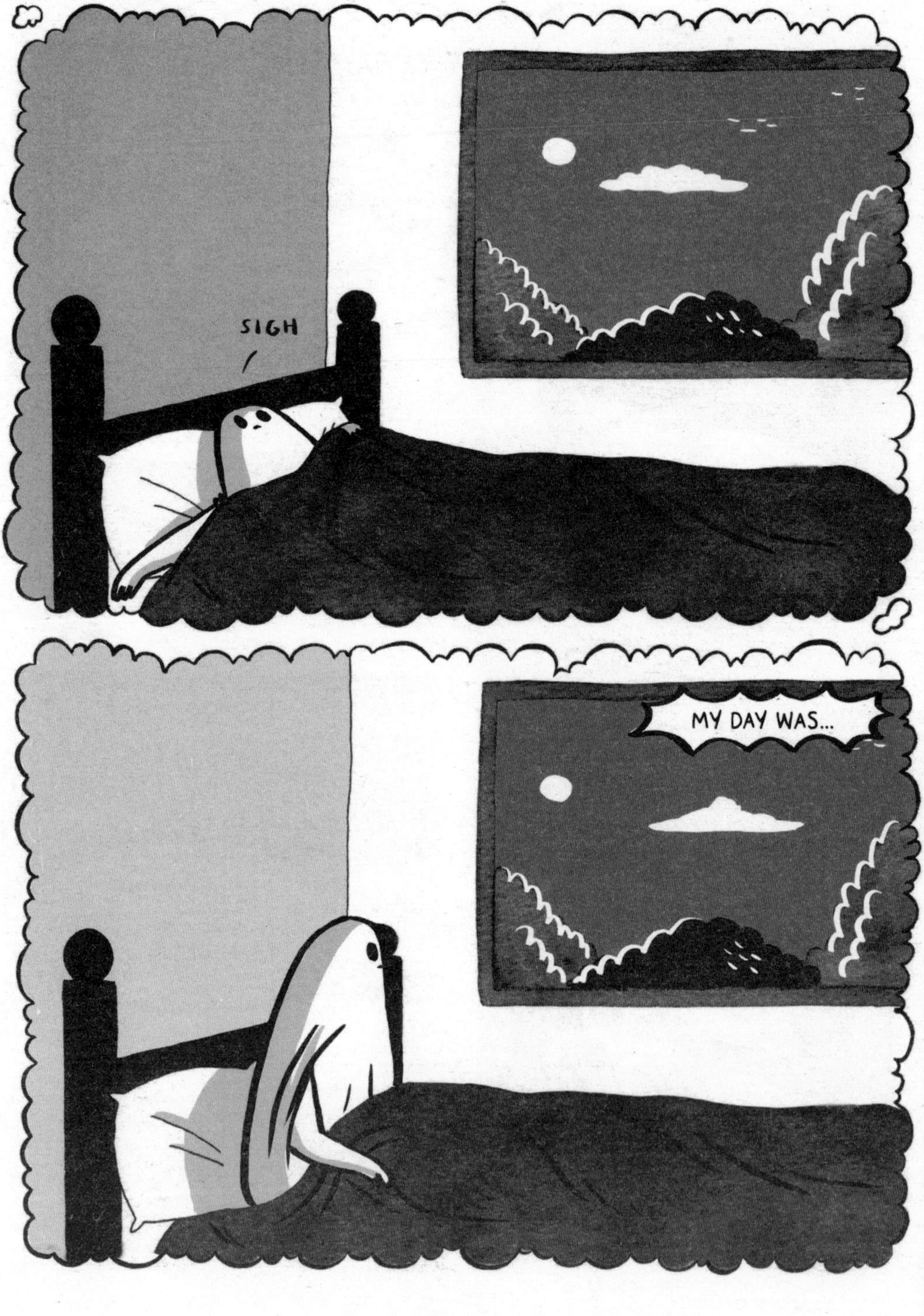
SIGH
MY DAY WAS...

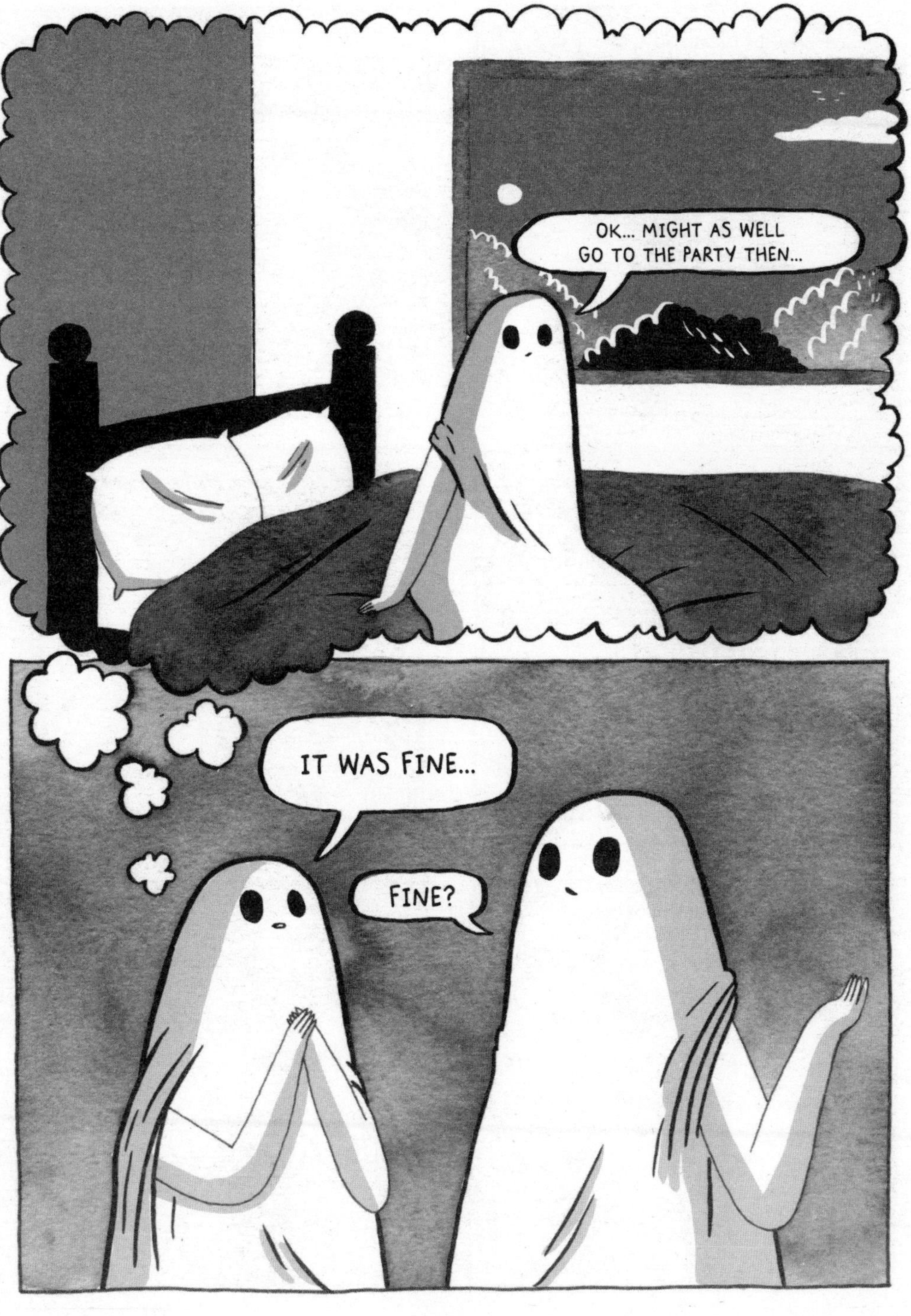
OK... MIGHT AS WELL
GO TO THE PARTY THEN...
IT WAS FINE...
FINE?

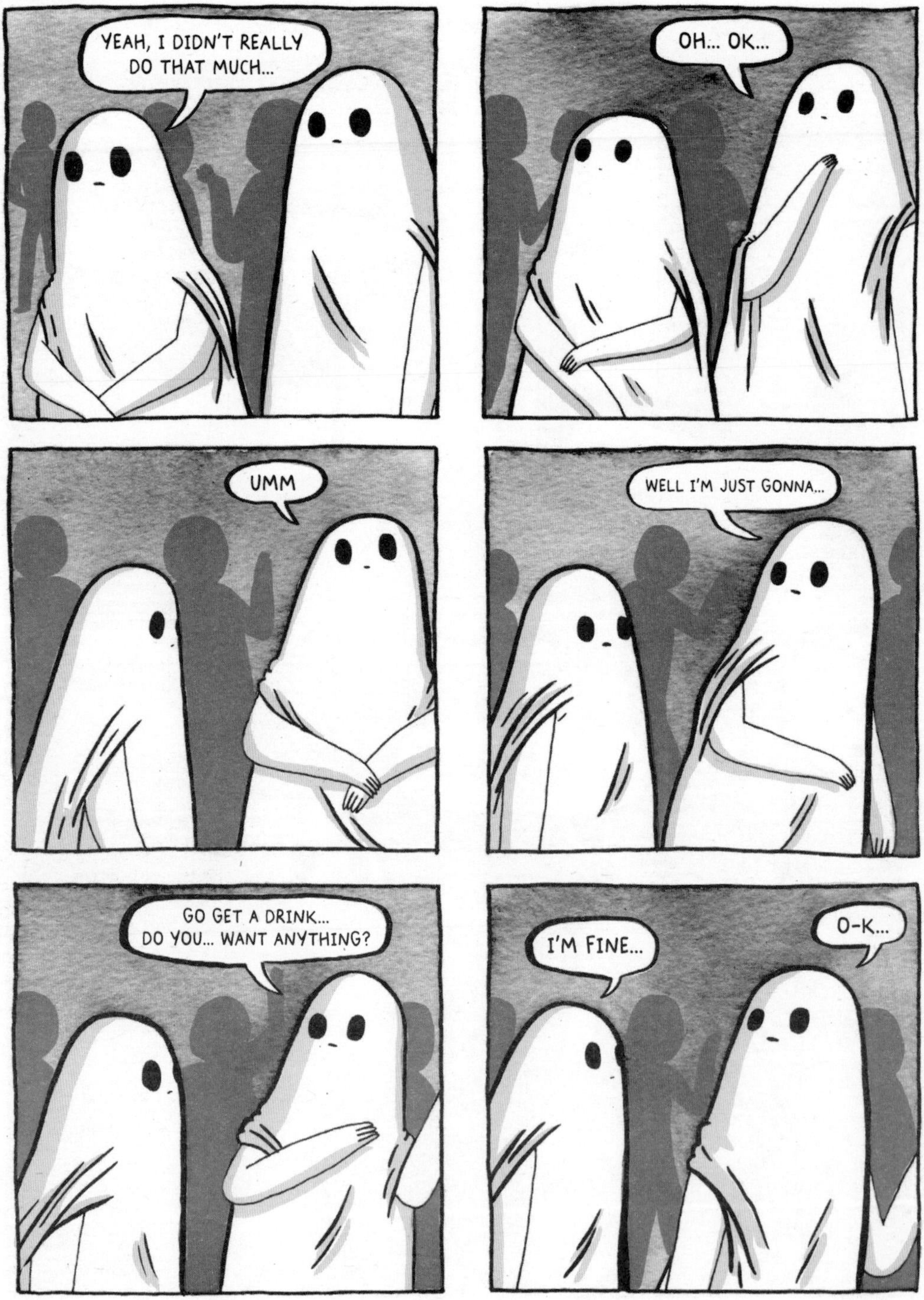
YEAH, I DIDN'T REALLY DO THAT MUCH...
OH... OK...
UMM
WELL I'M JUST GONNA...
GO GET A DRINK... DO YOU... WANT ANYTHING?
I'M FINE...
O-K...

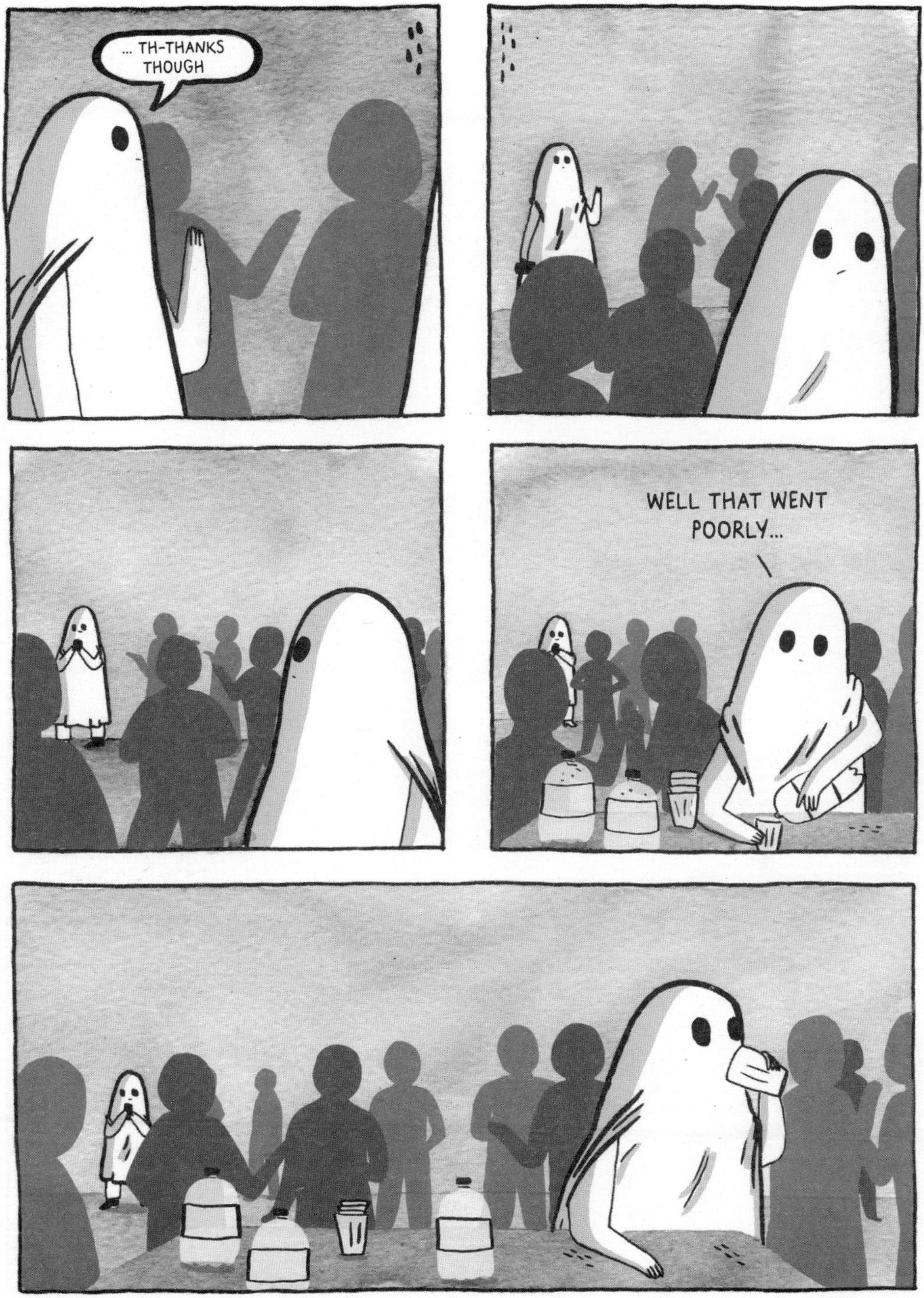
... TH-THANKS THOUGH
WELL THAT WENT POORLY...

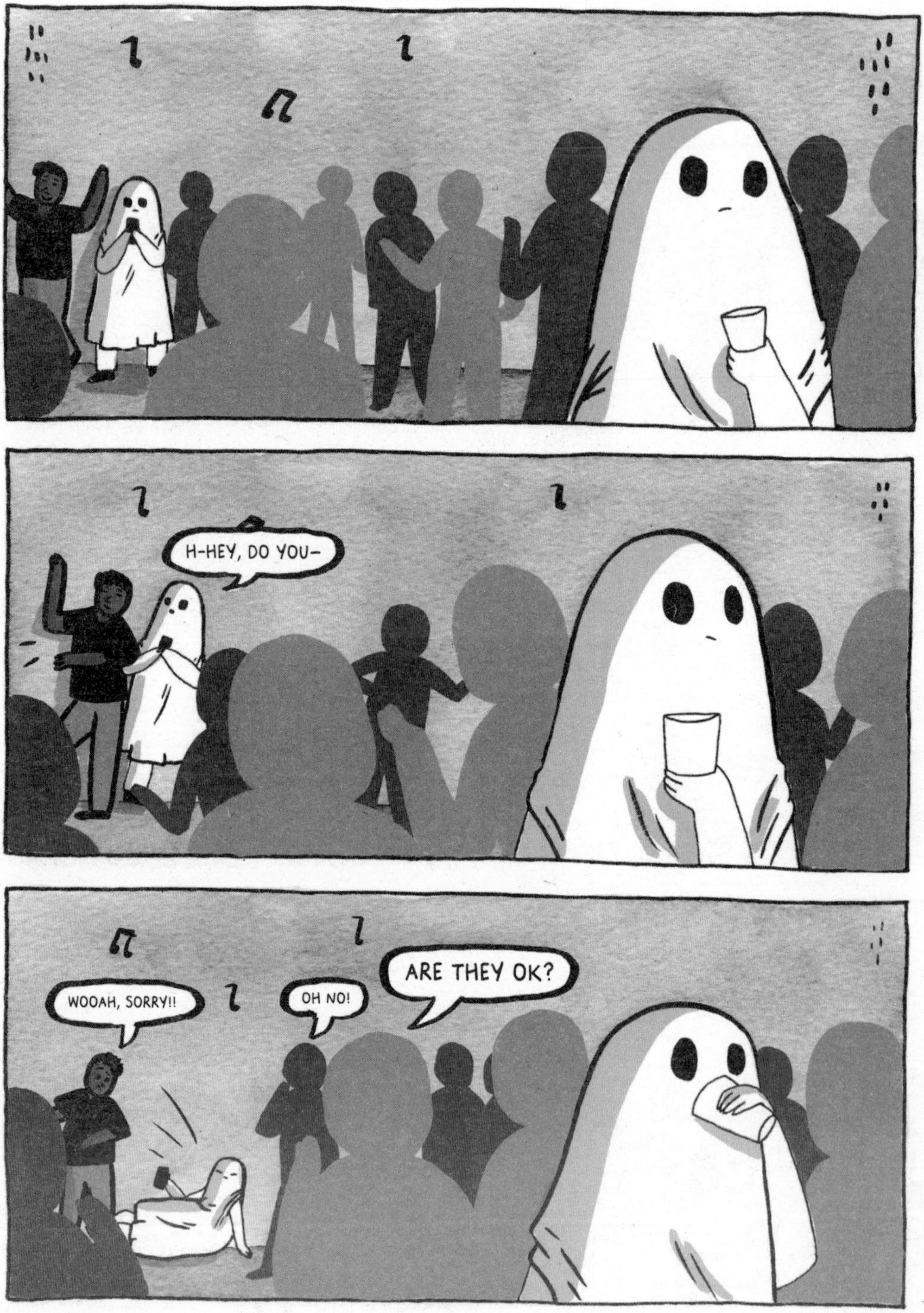
H-HEY, DO YOU-
WOOAH, SORRY!!
OH NO!
ARE THEY OK?

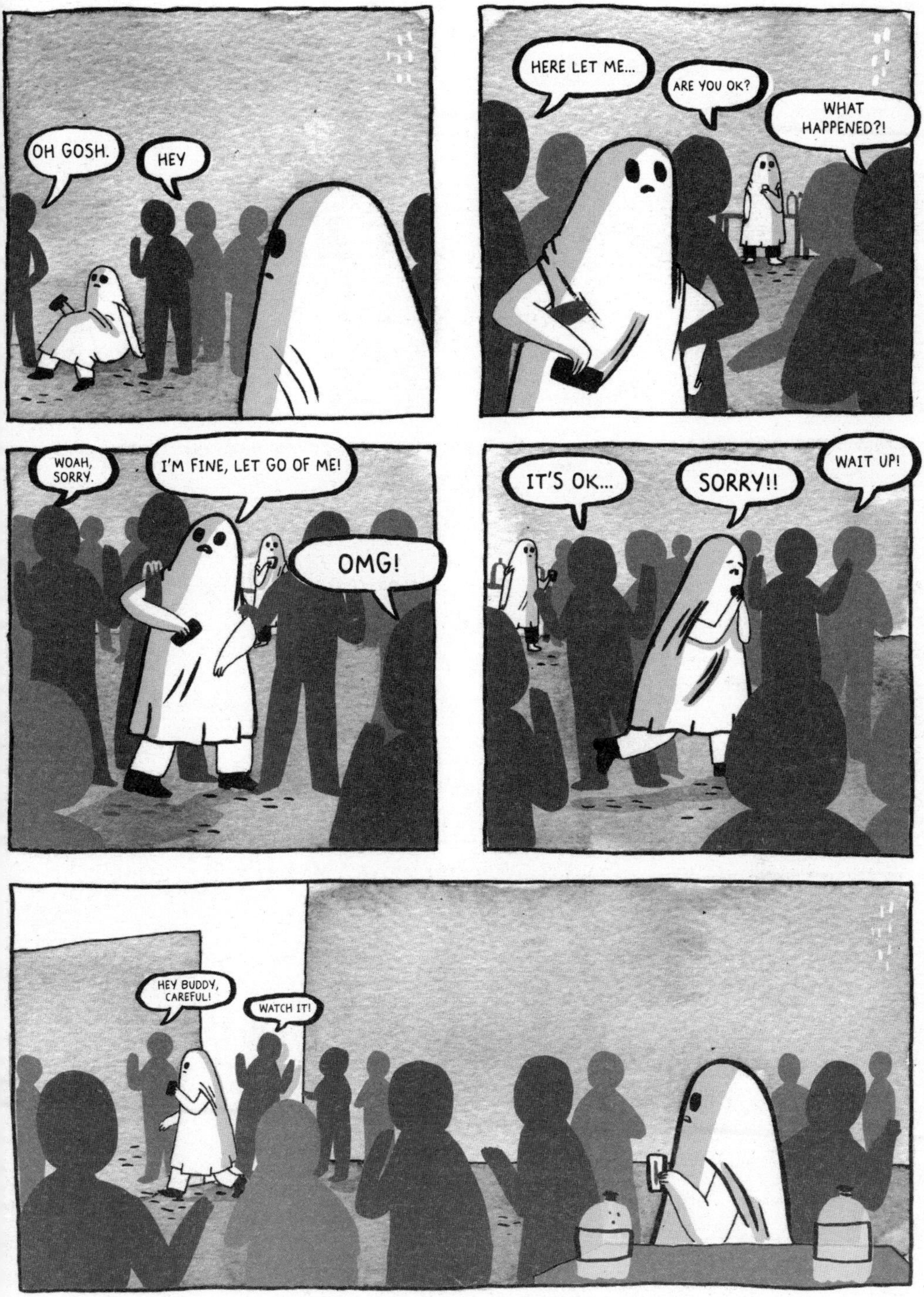
OH GOSH.
HEY
HERE LET ME...
ARE YOU OK?
WHAT HAPPENED?!
WOAH, SORRY.
I'M FINE, LET GO OF ME!
OMG!
IT'S OK...
SORRY!!
WAIT UP!
HEY BUDDY, CAREFUL!
WATCH IT!

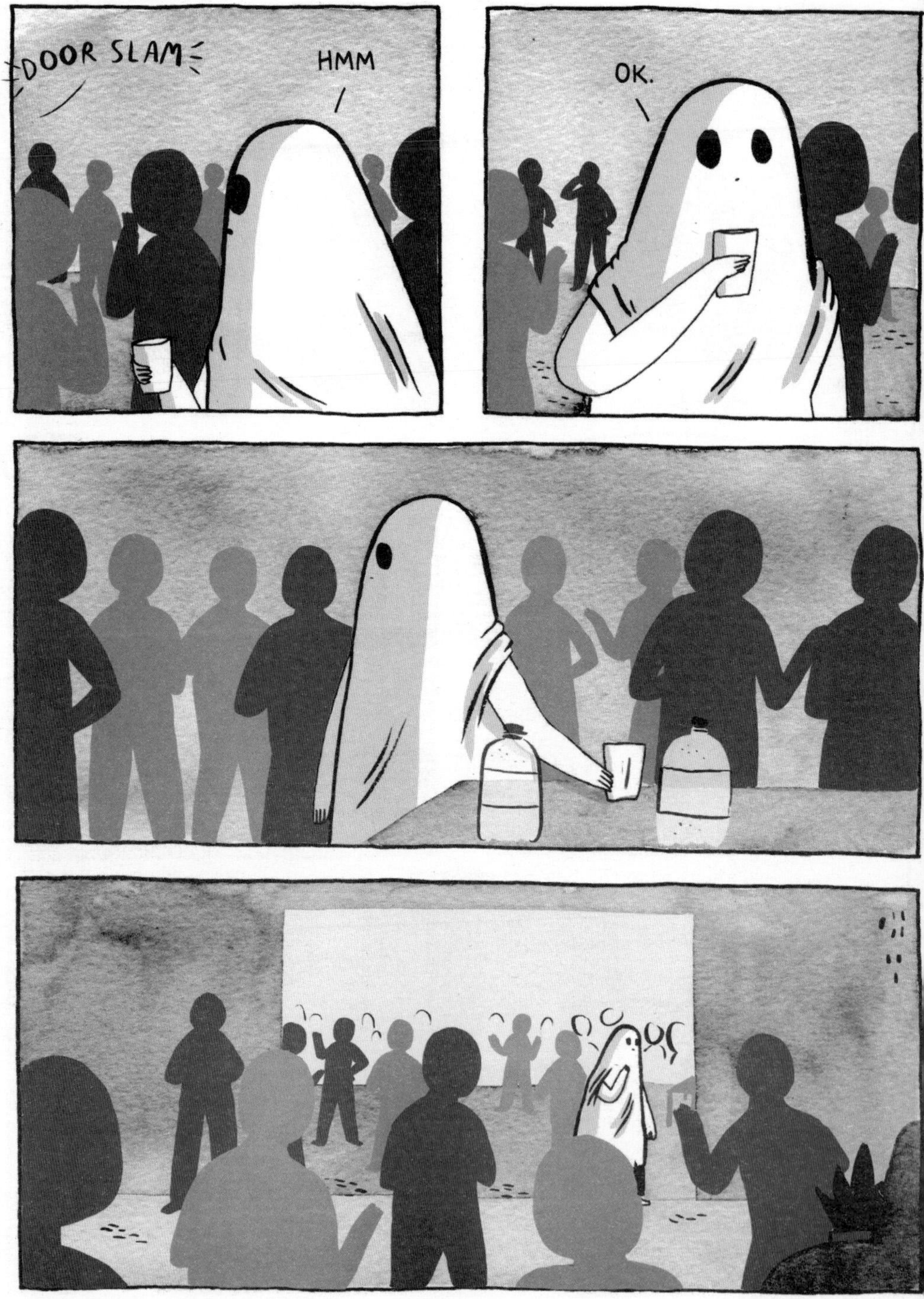
DOOR SLAM
HMM
OK.

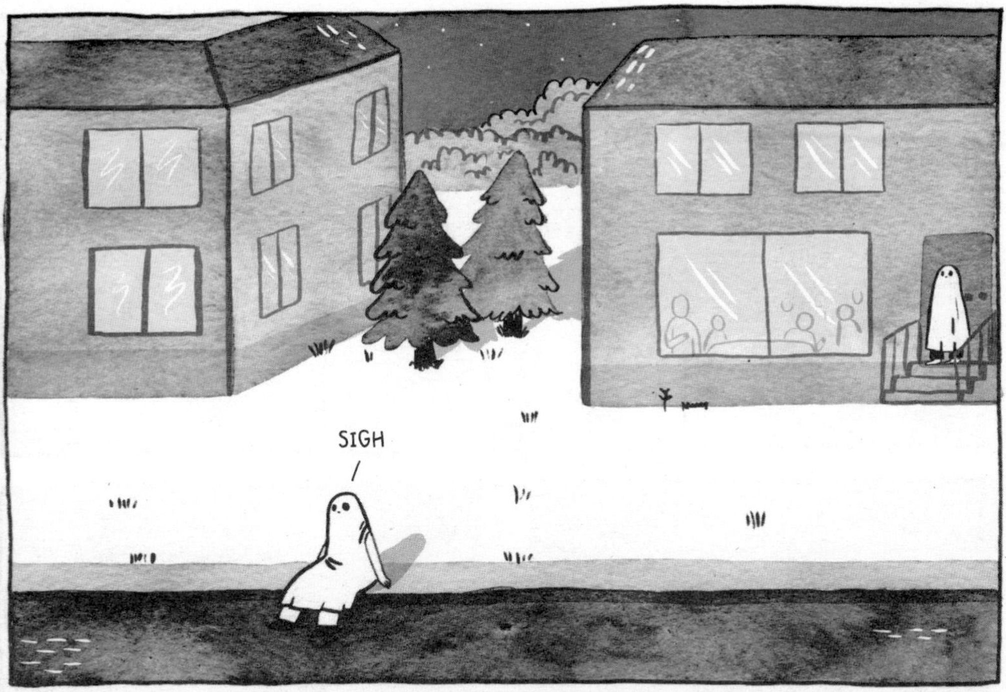
SIGH

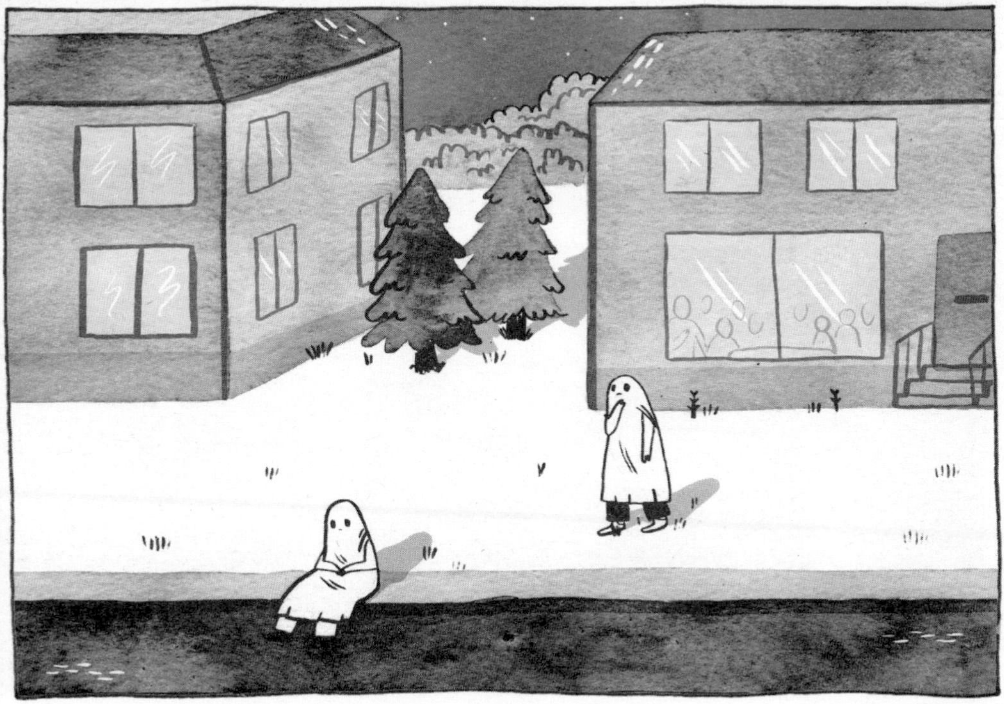

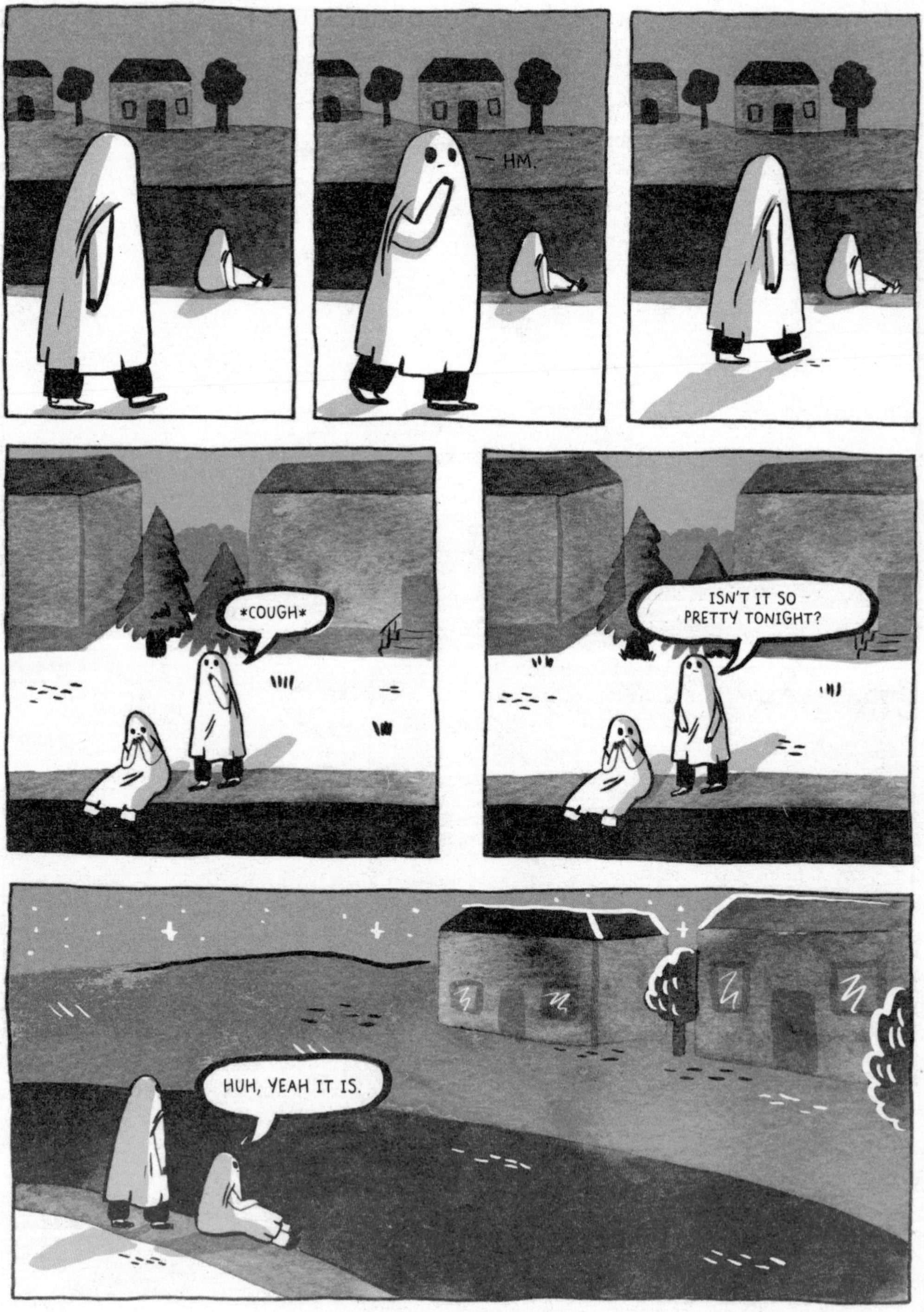
HM.
COUGH
ISN'T IT SO PRETTY TONIGHT?
HUH, YEAH IT IS.

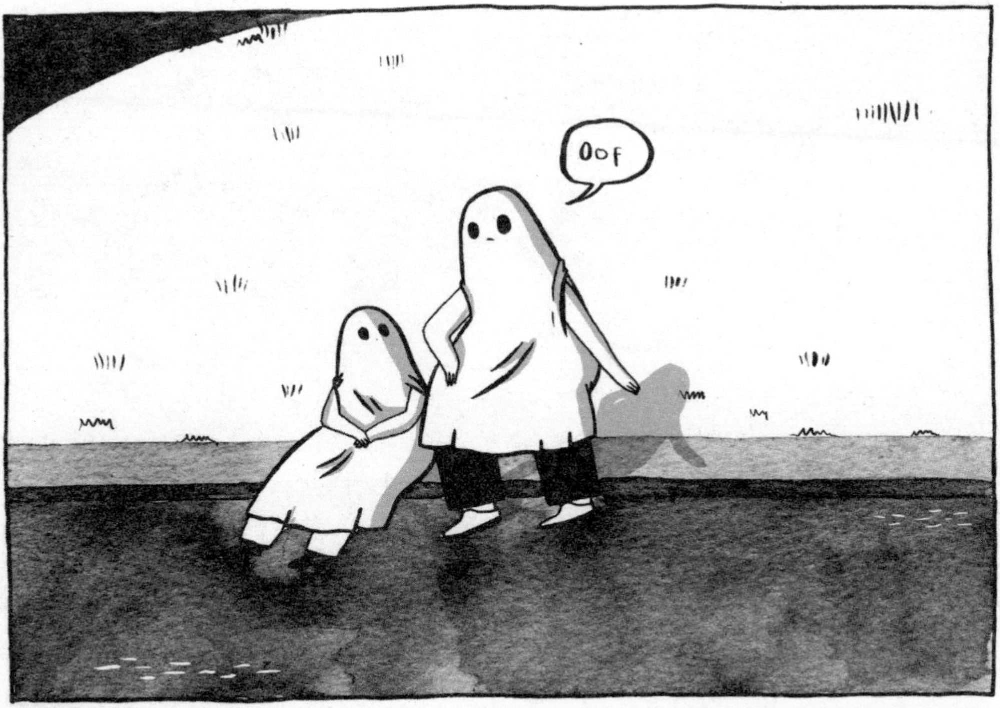
OOF

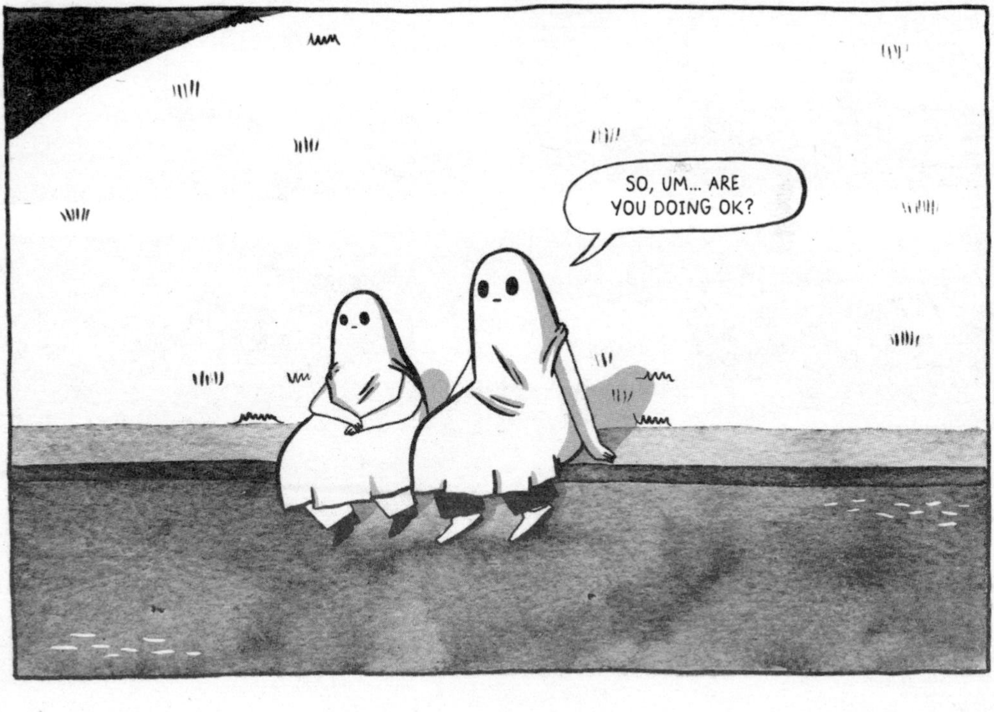
SO, UM... ARE YOU DOING OK?

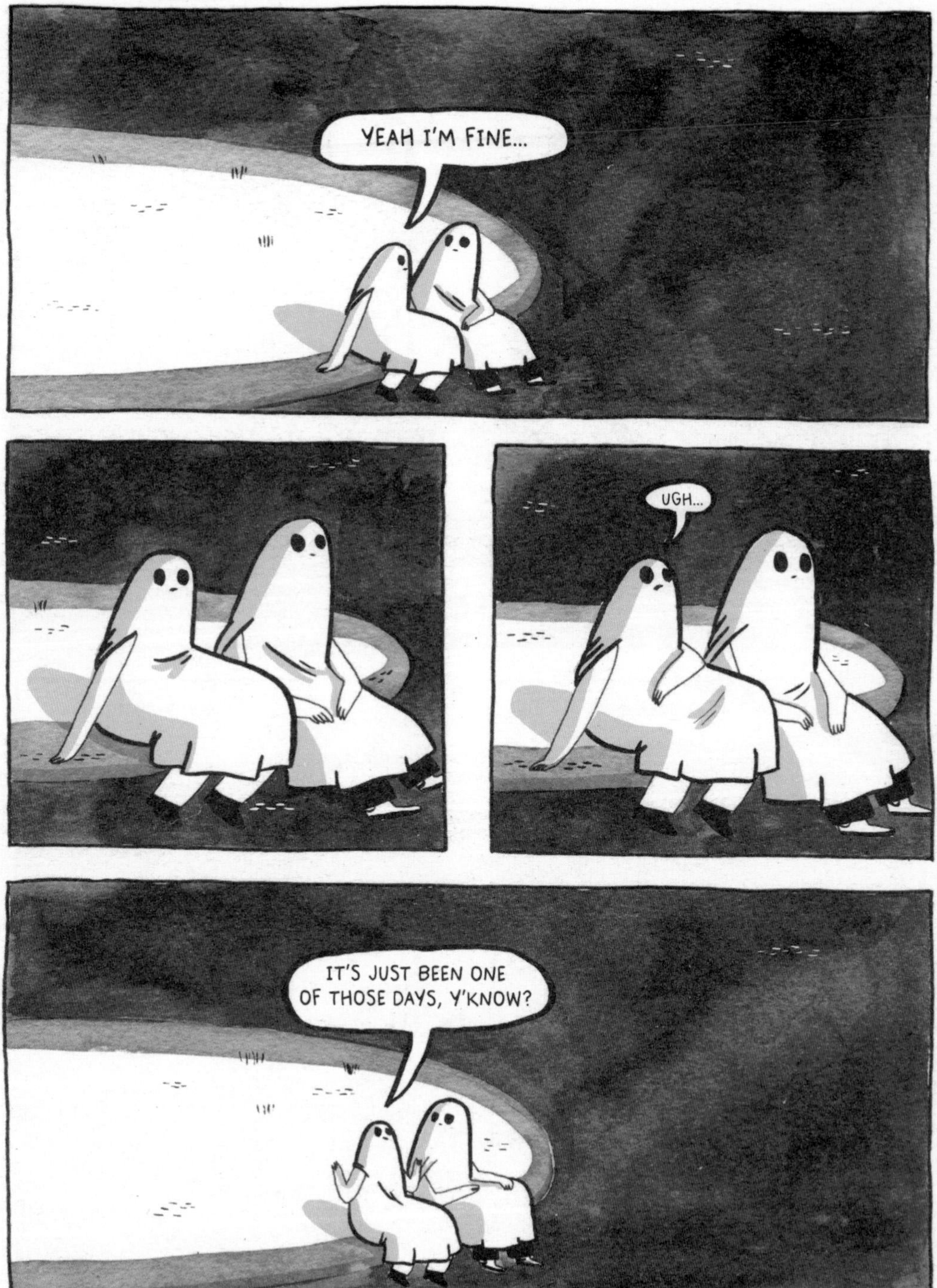
YEAH I'M FINE...
UGH...
IT'S JUST BEEN ONE OF THOSE DAYS, Y'KNOW?

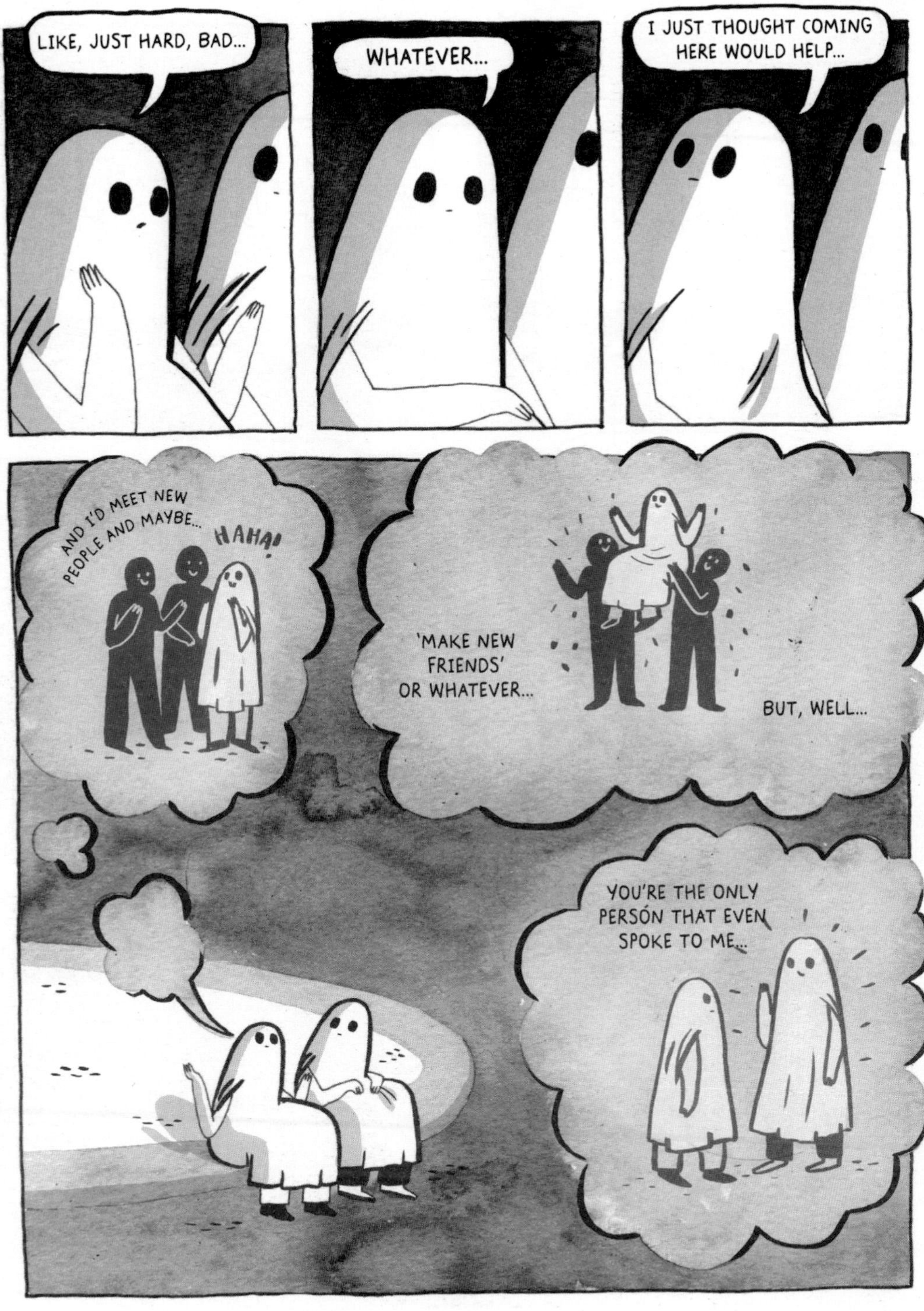
LIKE, JUST HARD, BAD...
WHATEVER...
I JUST THOUGHT COMING HERE WOULD HELP...
AND I'D MEET NEW PEOPLE AND MAYBE...
HAHA!
'MAKE NEW FRIENDS' OR WHATEVER...
BUT, WELL...
YOU'RE THE ONLY PERSÓN THAT EVEN SPOKE TO ME...

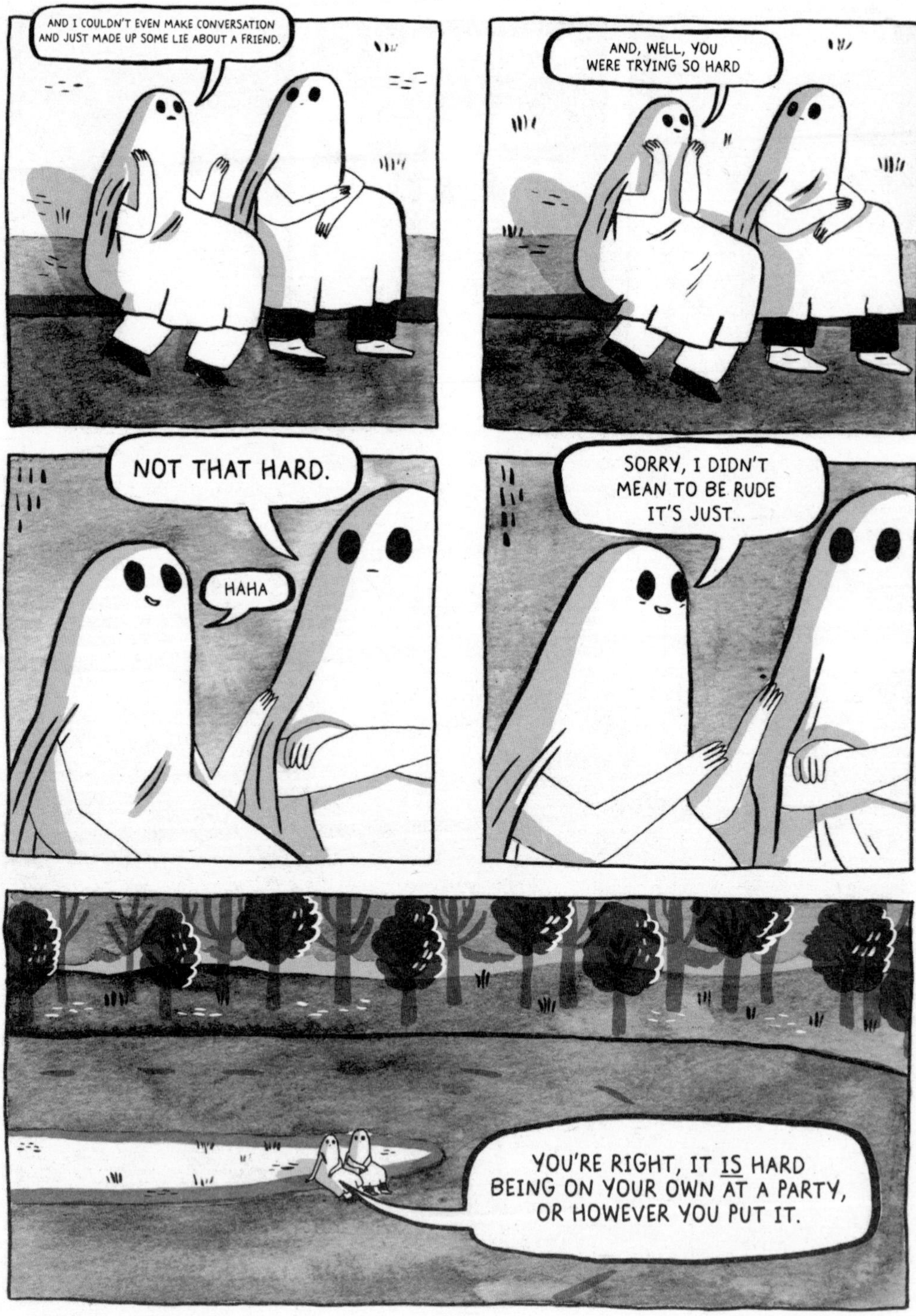
AND I COULDN'T EVEN MAKE CONVERSATION
AND JUST MADE UP SOME LIE ABOUT A FRIEND.
AND, WELL, YOU
WERE TRYING SO HARD
NOT THAT HARD.
HAHA
SORRY, I DIDN'T
MEAN TO BE RUDE
IT'S JUST...
YOU'RE RIGHT, IT IS HARD
BEING ON YOUR OWN AT A PARTY,
OR HOWEVER YOU PUT IT.

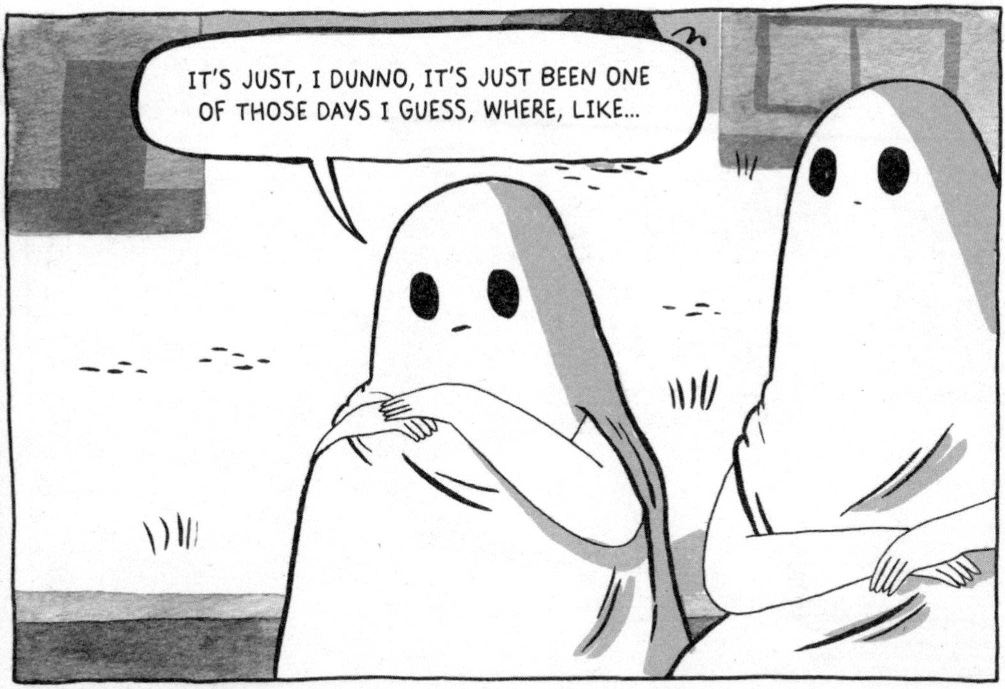
IT'S JUST, I DUNNO, IT'S JUST BEEN ONE OF THOSE DAYS I GUESS, WHERE, LIKE...

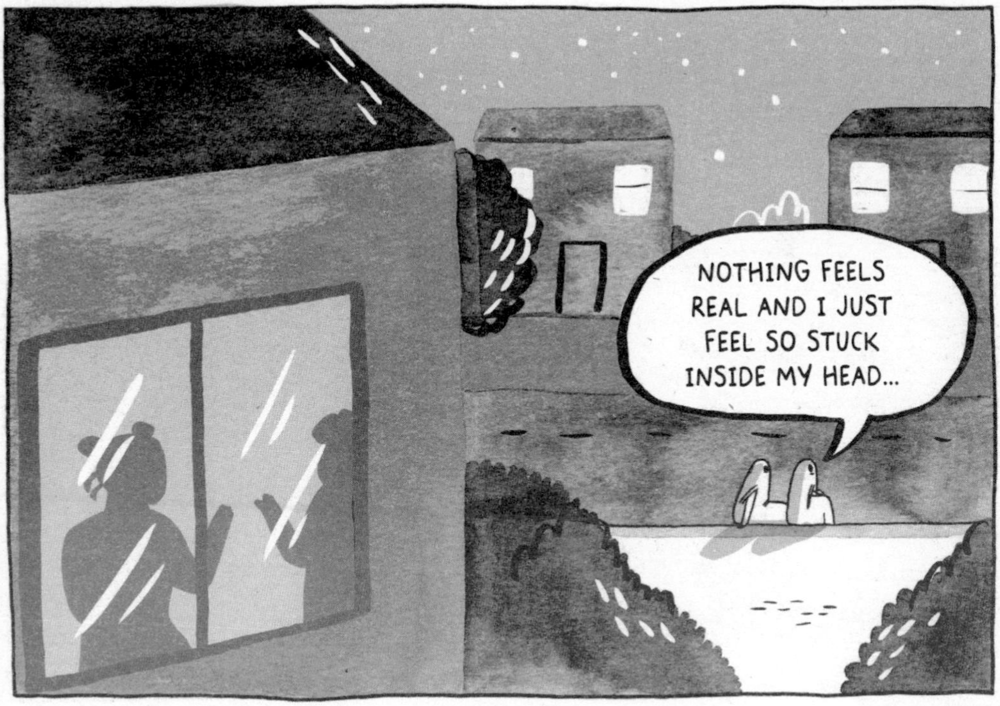
NOTHING FEELS REAL AND I JUST FEEL SO STUCK INSIDE MY HEAD...

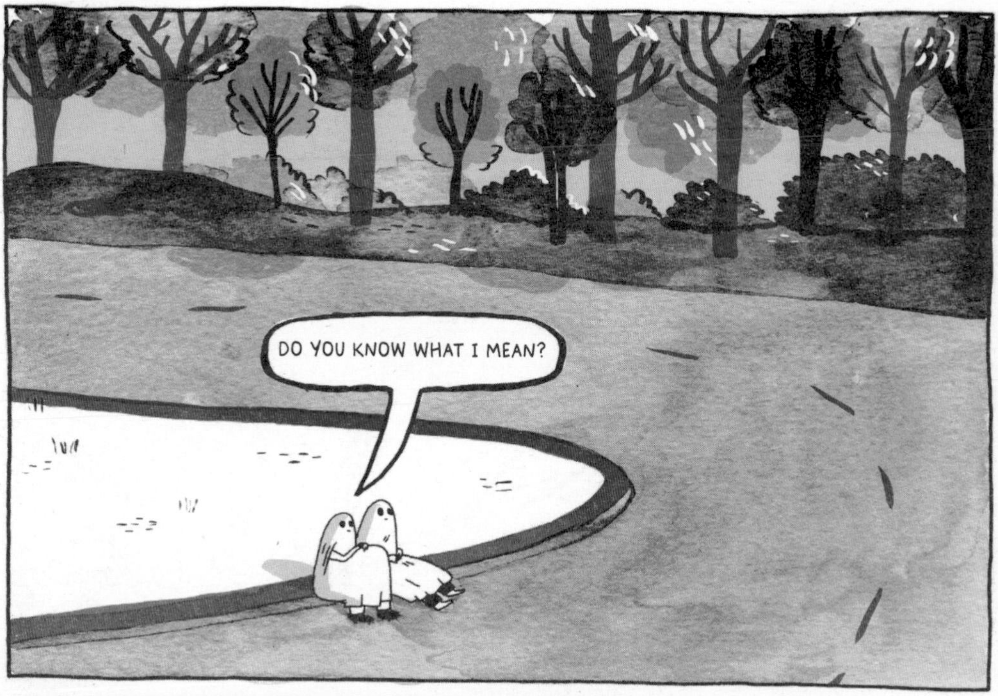
DO YOU KNOW WHAT I MEAN?

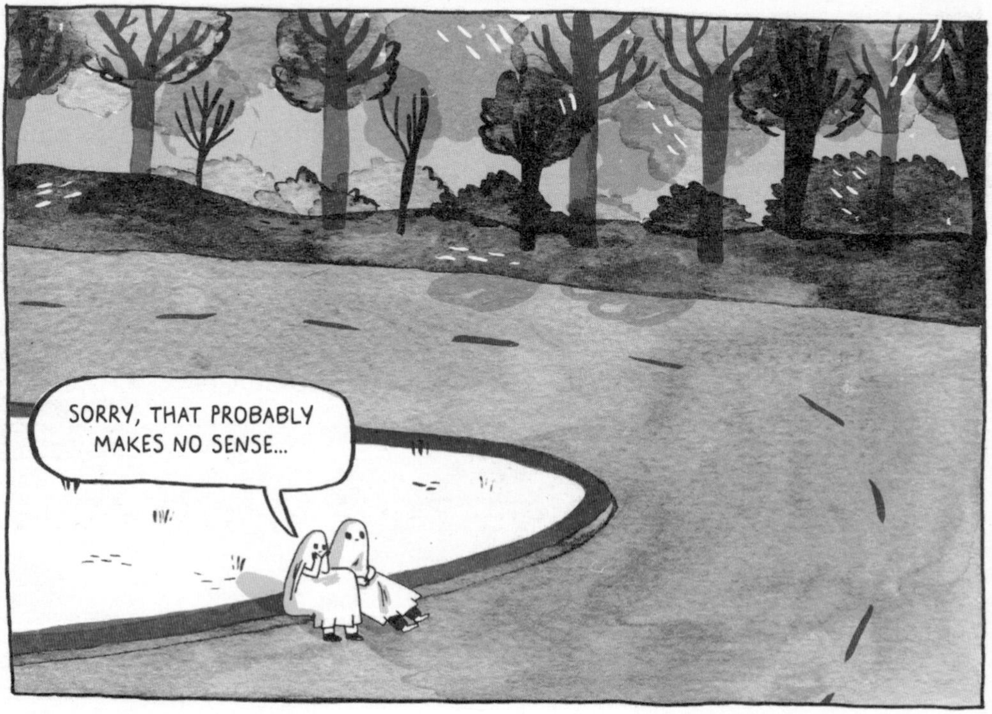
SORRY, THAT PROBABLY MAKES NO SENSE...

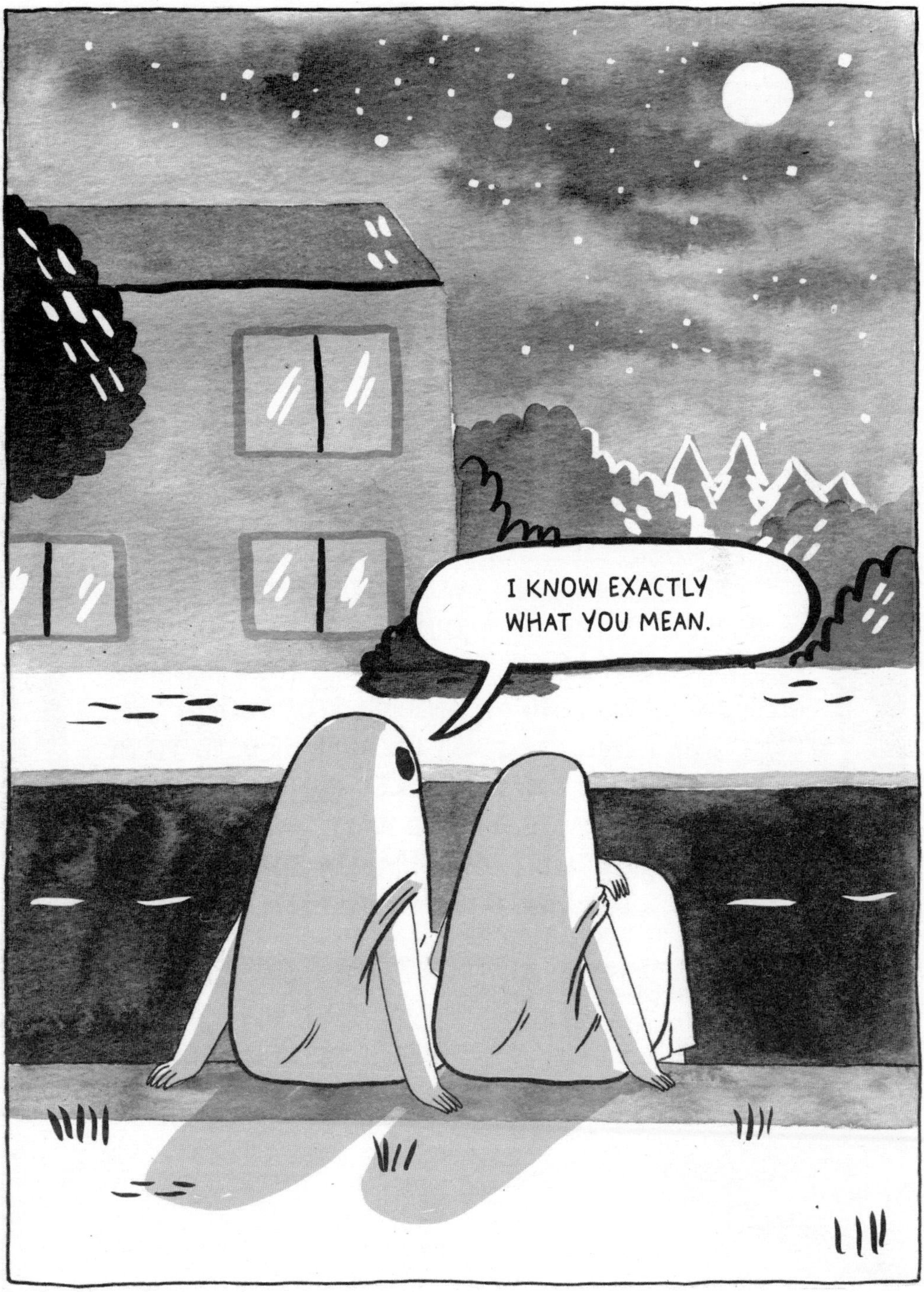
I KNOW EXACTLY WHAT YOU MEAN.

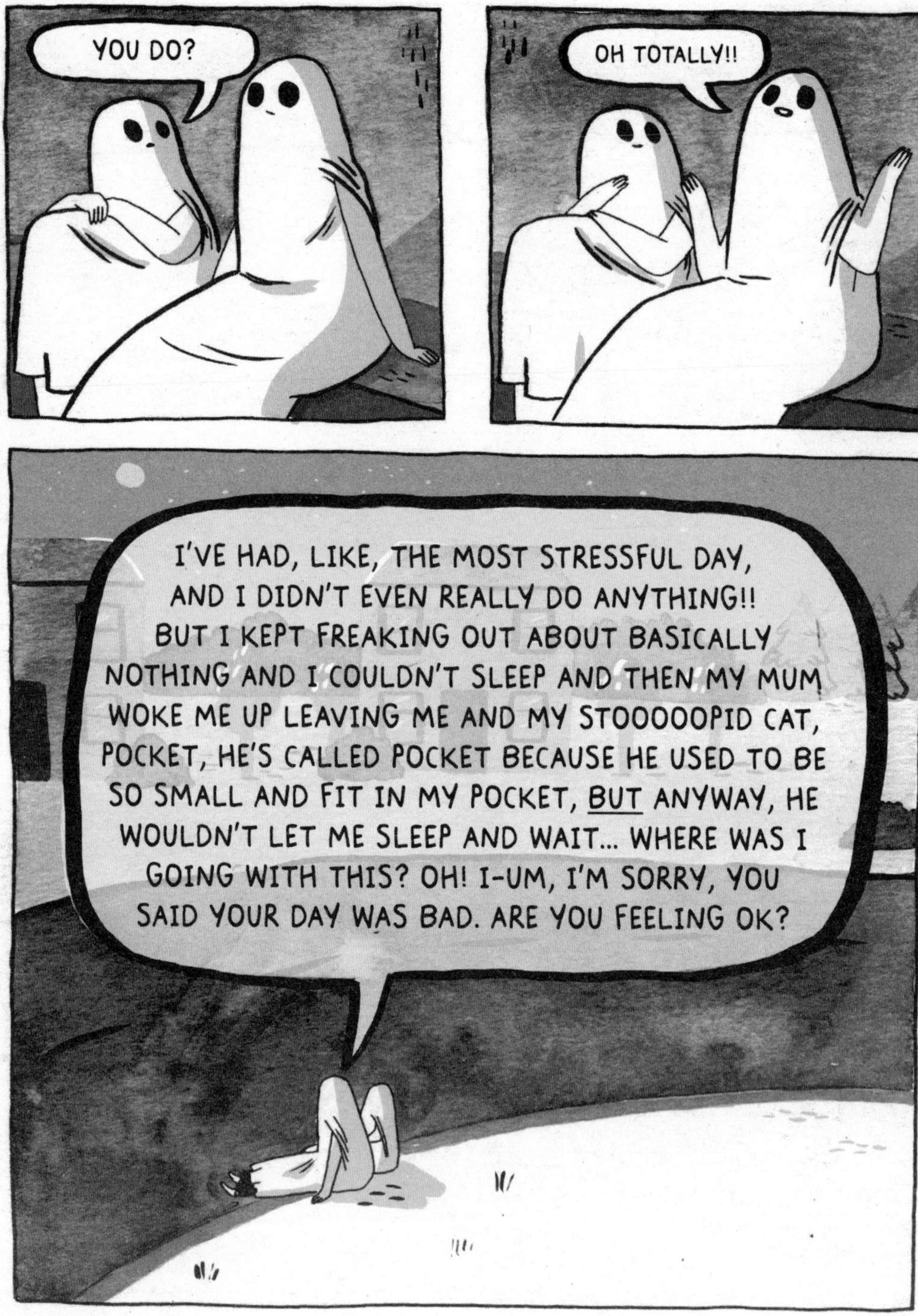
YOU DO?
OH TOTALLY!!
I'VE HAD, LIKE, THE MOST STRESSFUL DAY, AND I DIDN'T EVEN REALLY DO ANYTHING!! BUT I KEPT FREAKING OUT ABOUT BASICALLY NOTHING AND I COULDN'T SLEEP AND THEN MY MUM WOKE ME UP LEAVING ME AND MY STOOOOOPID CAT, POCKET, HE'S CALLED POCKET BECAUSE HE USED TO BE SO SMALL AND FIT IN MY POCKET, BUT ANYWAY, HE WOULDN'T LET ME SLEEP AND WAIT... WHERE WAS I GOING WITH THIS? OH! I-UM, I'M SORRY, YOU SAID YOUR DAY WAS BAD. ARE YOU FEELING OK?

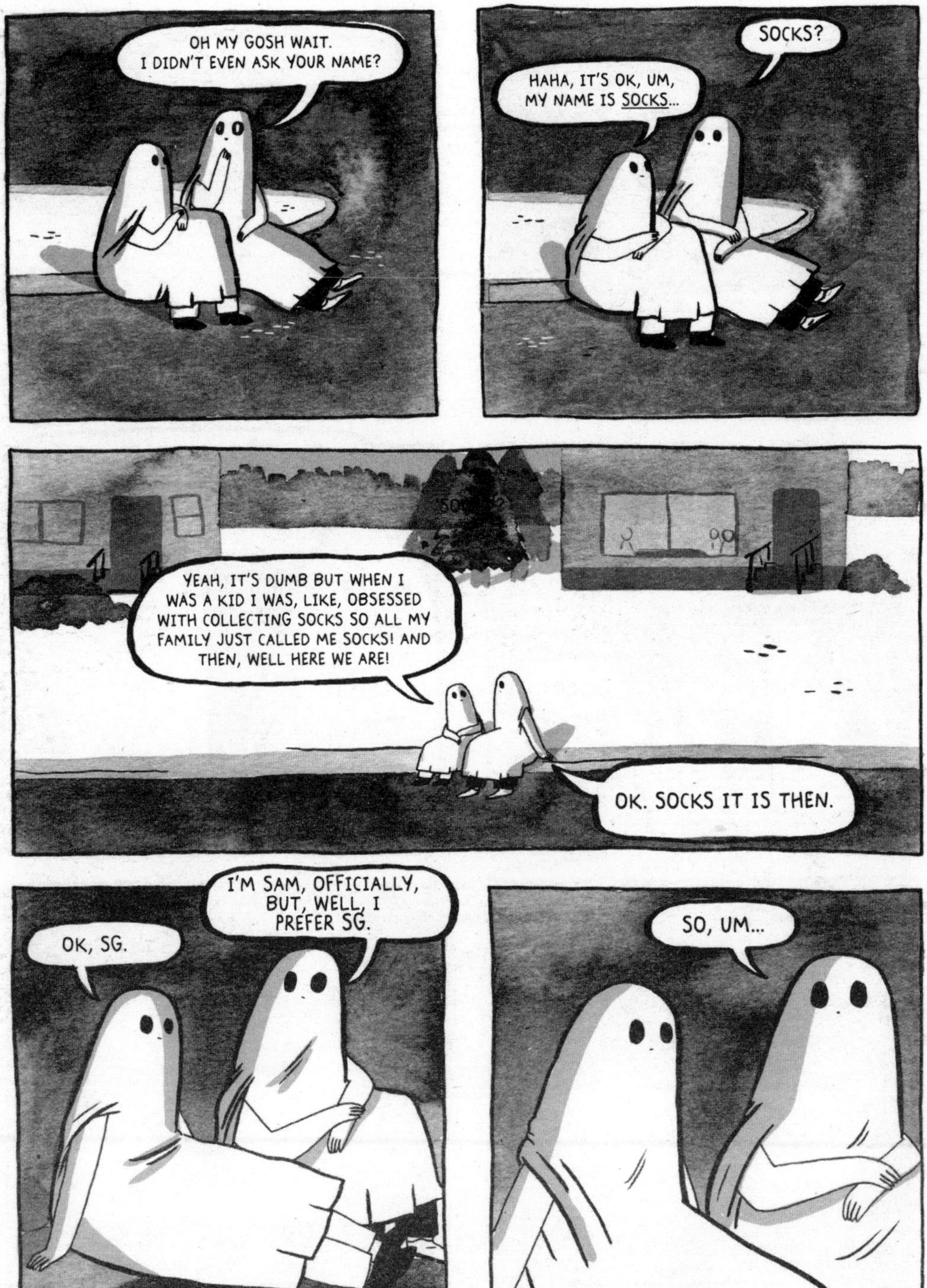
OH MY GOSH WAIT. I DIDN'T EVEN ASK YOUR NAME?
HAHA, IT'S OK, UM, MY NAME IS SOCKS...
SOCKS?
YEAH, IT'S DUMB BUT WHEN I WAS A KID I WAS, LIKE, OBSESSED WITH COLLECTING SOCKS SO ALL MY FAMILY JUST CALLED ME SOCKS! AND THEN, WELL HERE WE ARE!
OK. SOCKS IT IS THEN.
I'M SAM, OFFICIALLY, BUT, WELL, I PREFER SG.
OK, SG.
SO, UM...

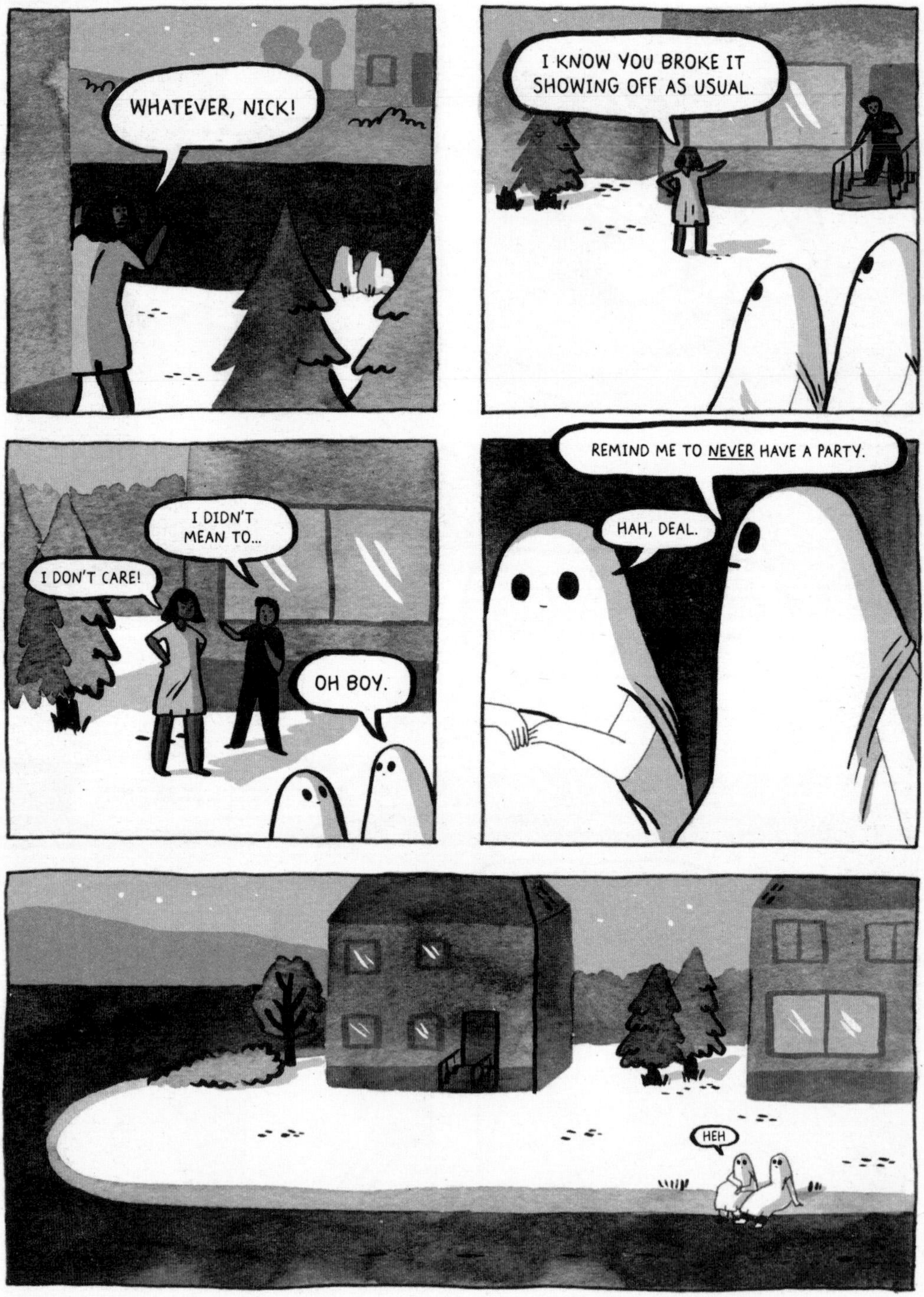
WHATEVER, NICK!
I KNOW YOU BROKE IT SHOWING OFF AS USUAL.
I DON'T CARE!
I DIDN'T MEAN TO...
OH BOY.
REMIND ME TO NEVER HAVE A PARTY.
HAH, DEAL.
HEH

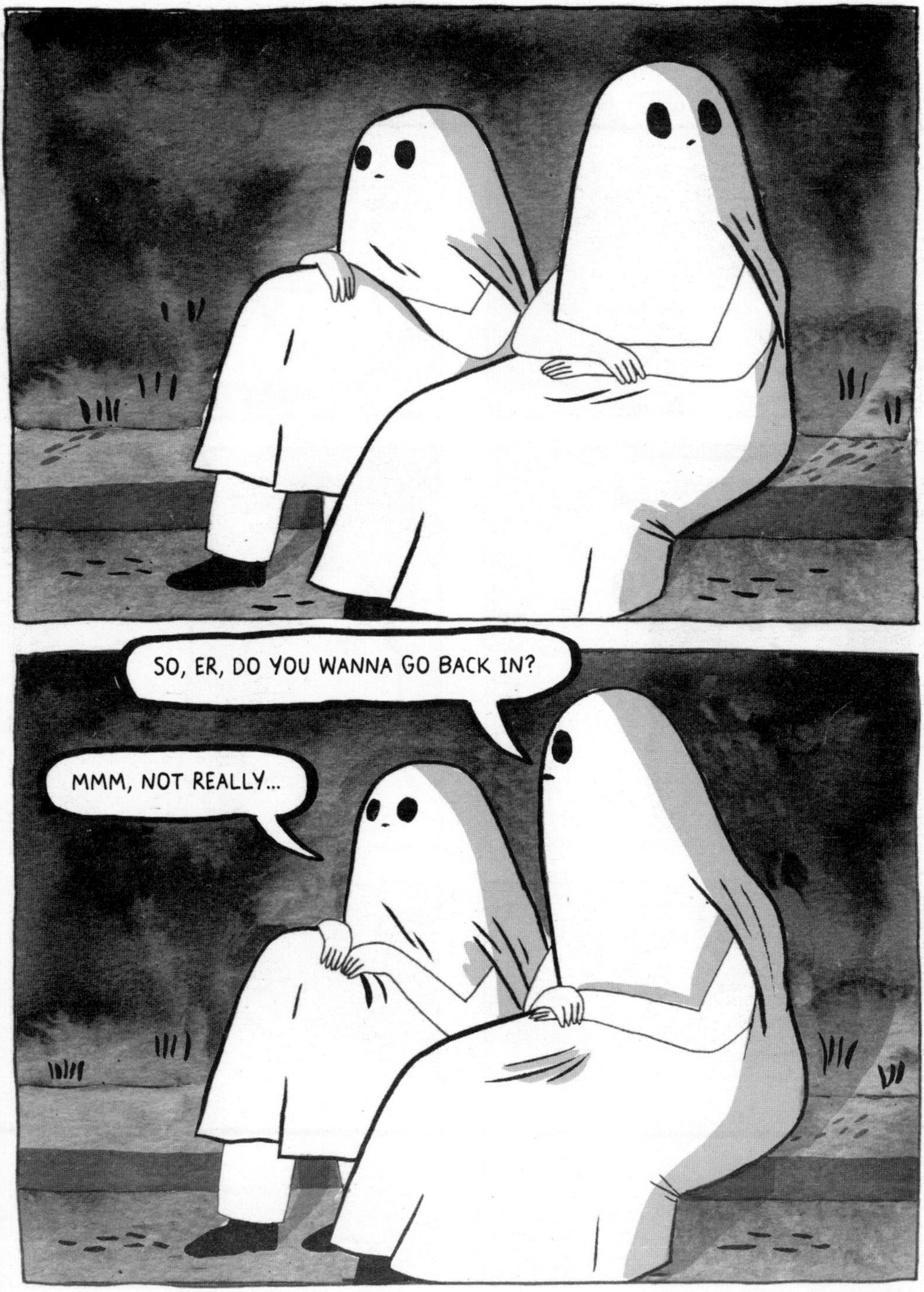
SO, ER, DO YOU WANNA GO BACK IN?
MMM, NOT REALLY...

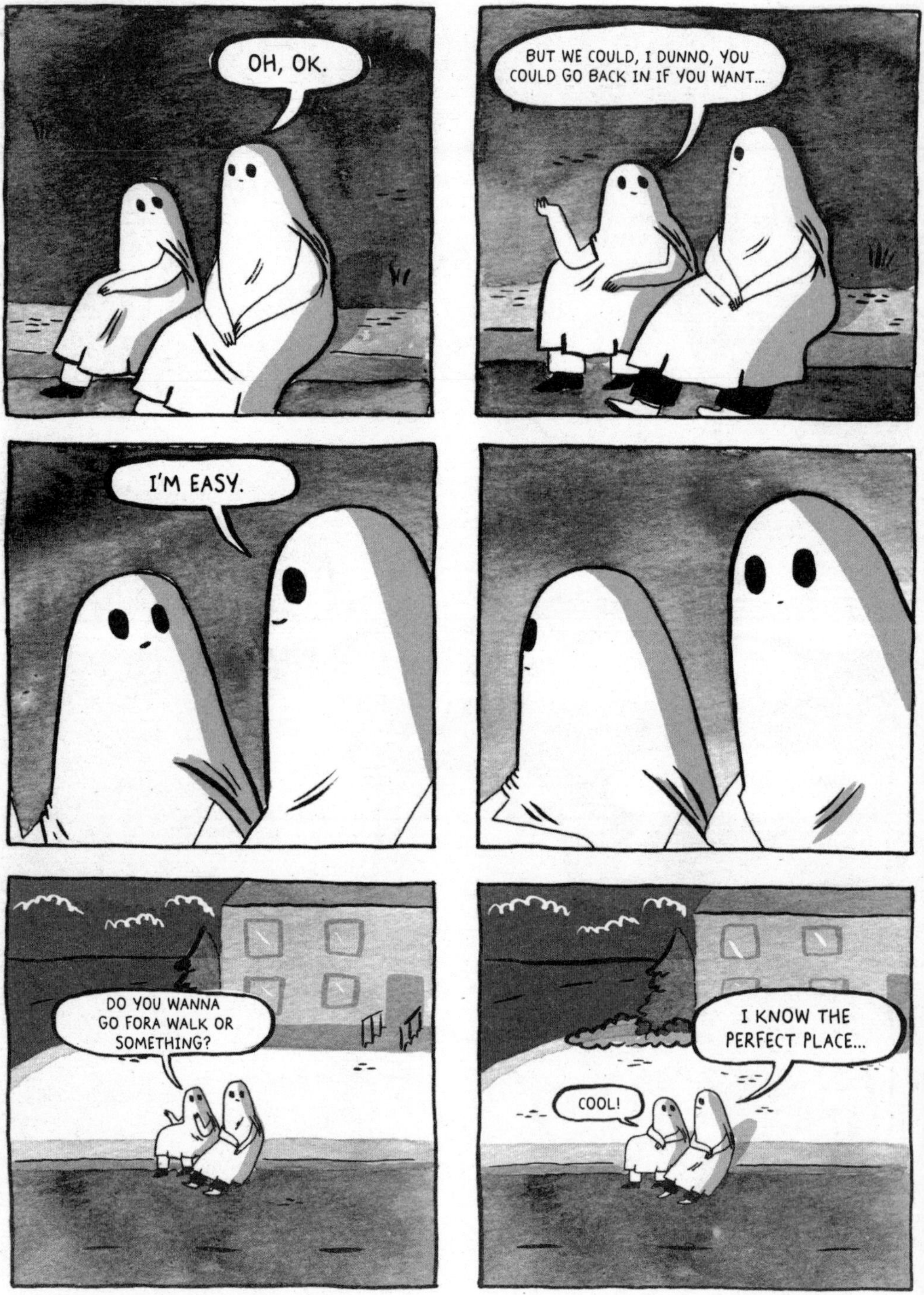
OH, OK.
BUT WE COULD, I DUNNO, YOU COULD GO BACK IN IF YOU WANT...
I'M EASY.
DO YOU WANNA GO FORA WALK OR SOMETHING?
I KNOW THE PERFECT PLACE...
COOL!

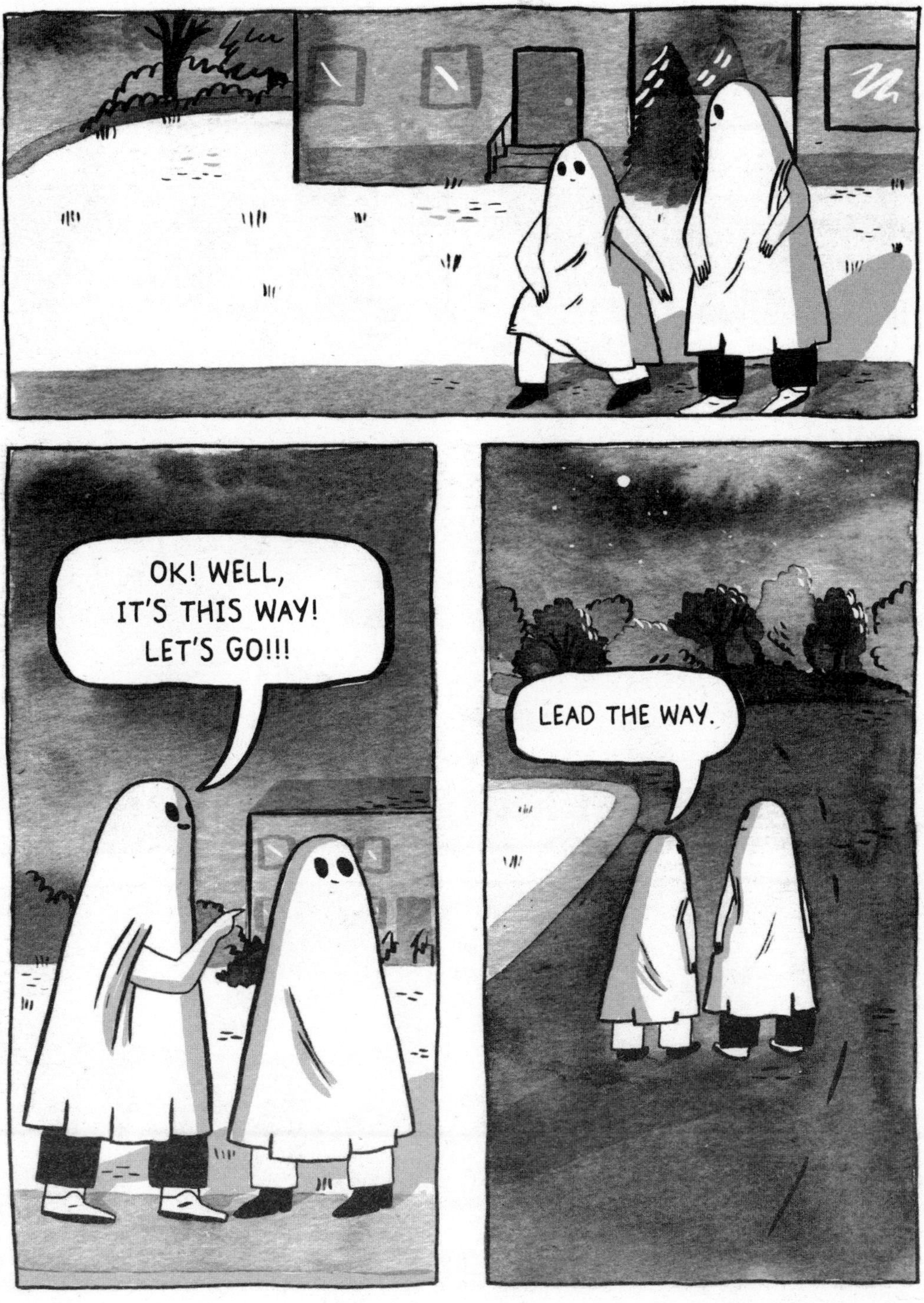
OK! WELL, IT'S THIS WAY! LET'S GO!!!
LEAD THE WAY.

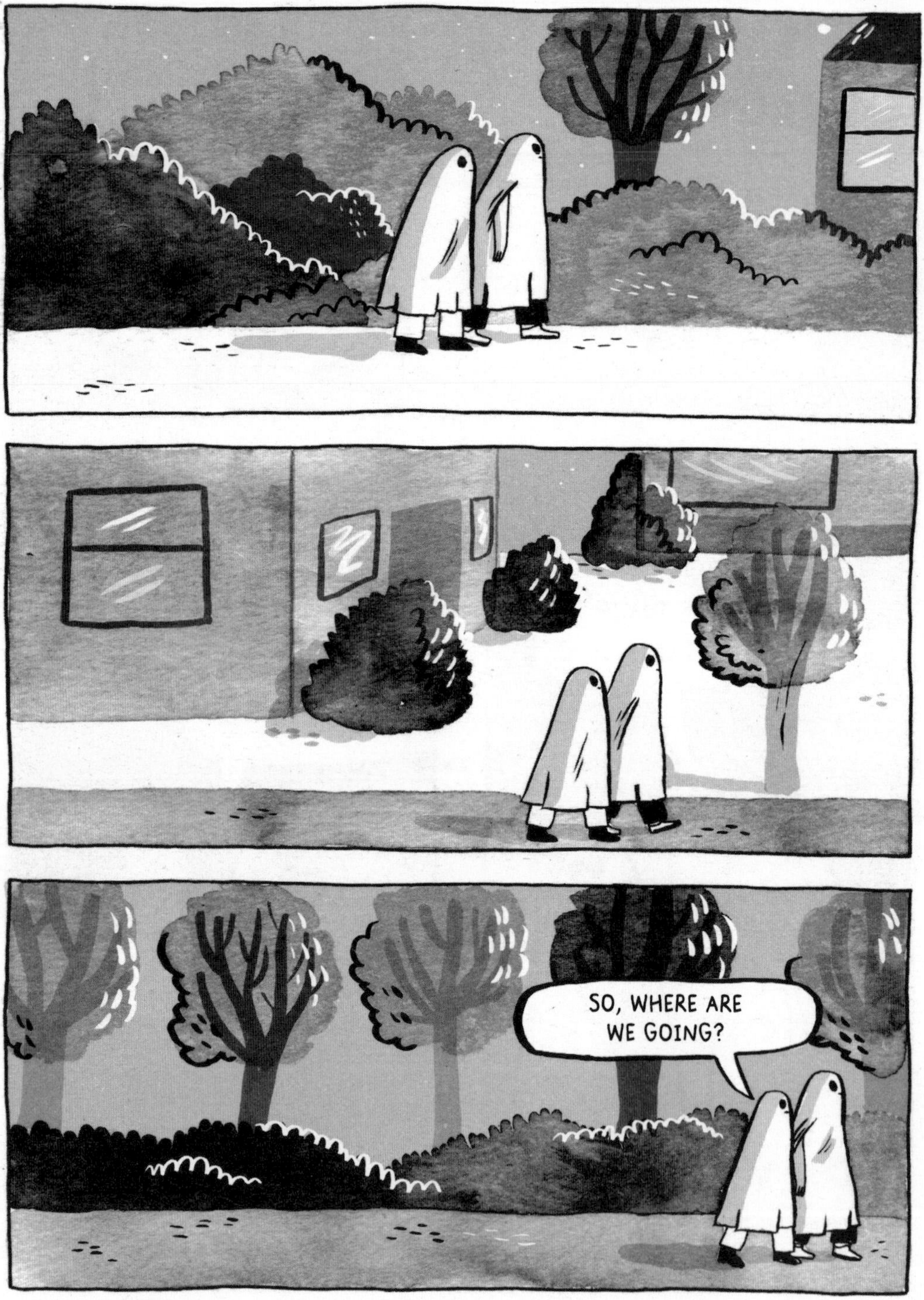
SO, WHERE ARE
WE GOING?

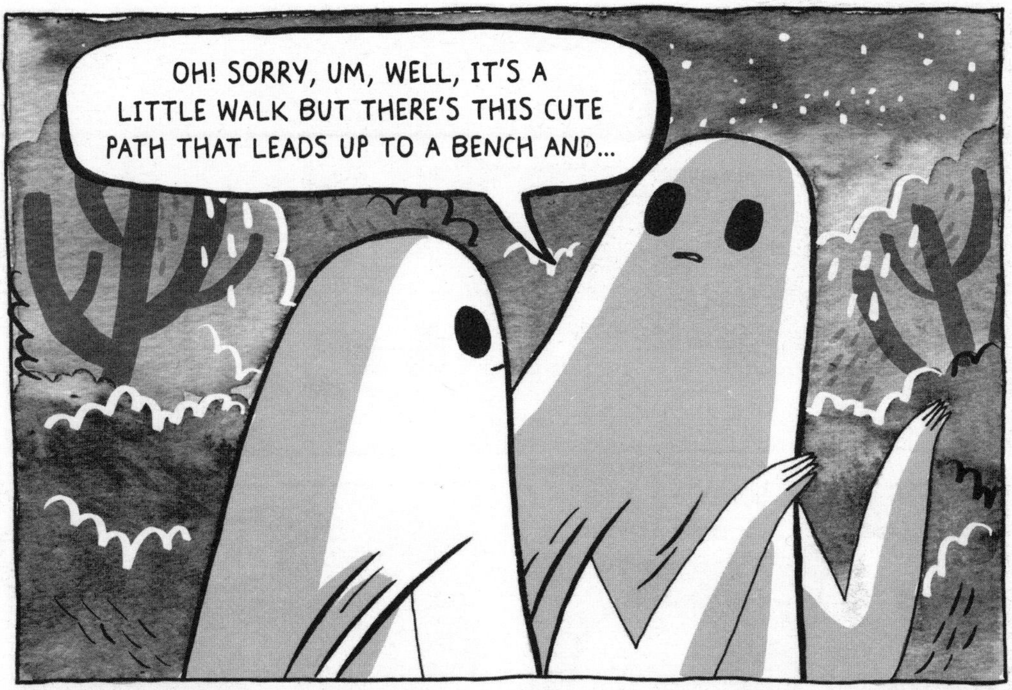
OH! SORRY, UM, WELL, IT'S A LITTLE WALK BUT THERE'S THIS CUTE PATH THAT LEADS UP TO A BENCH AND...

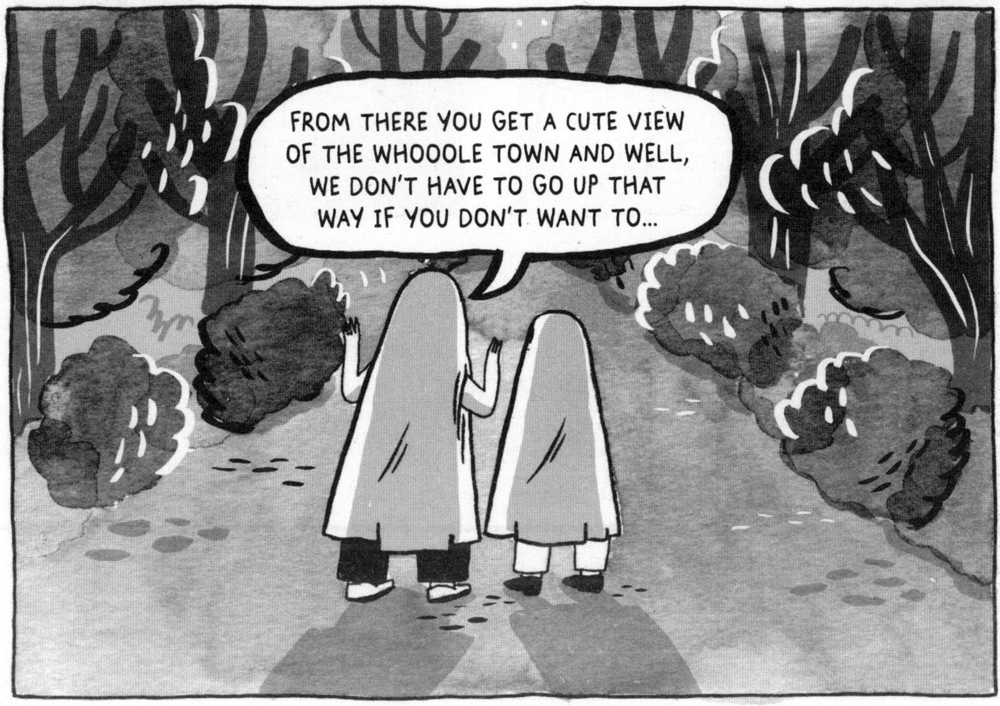
FROM THERE YOU GET A CUTE VIEW OF THE WHOOOLE TOWN AND WELL, WE DON'T HAVE TO GO UP THAT WAY IF YOU DON'T WANT TO...

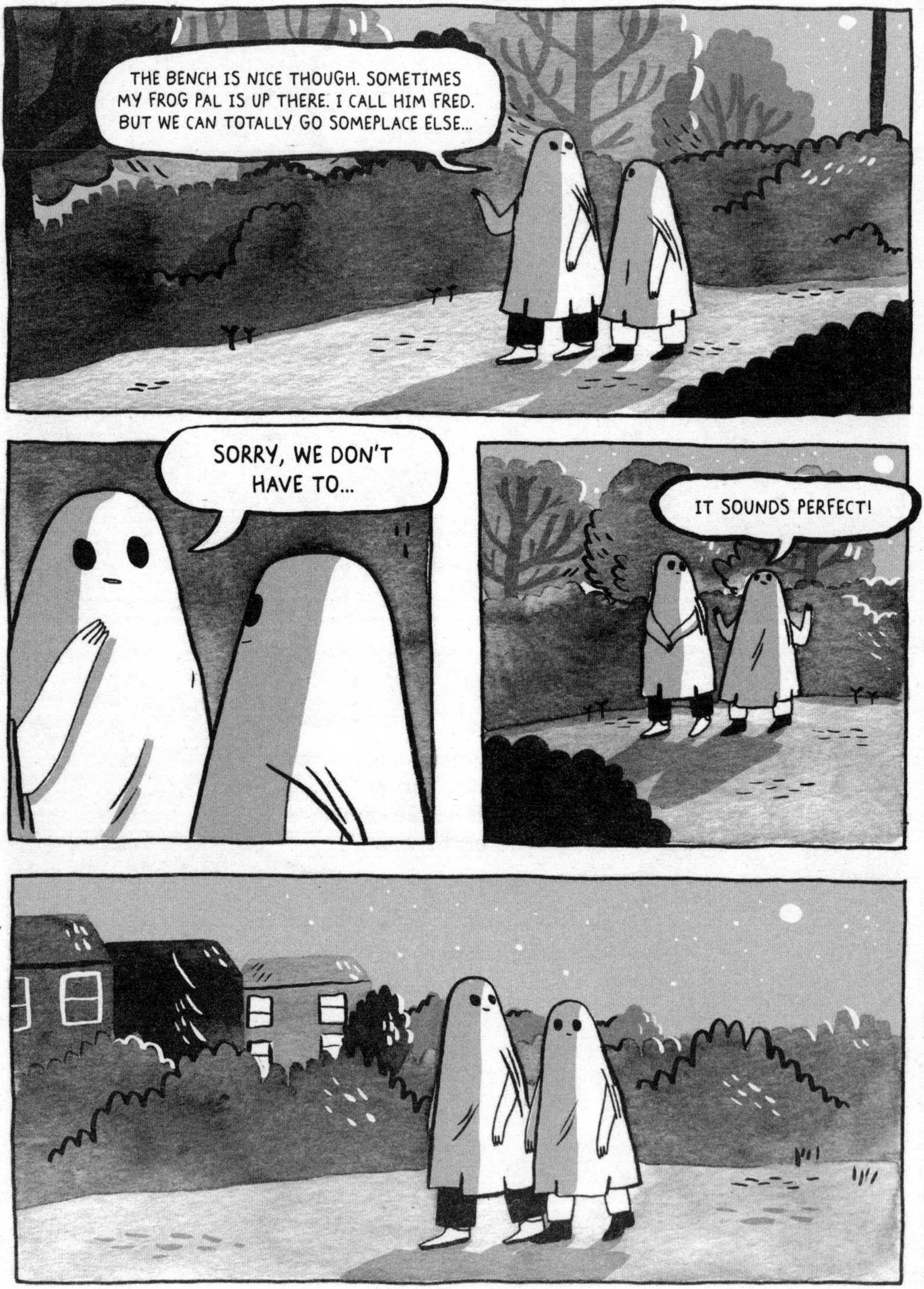
THE BENCH IS NICE THOUGH. SOMETIMES MY FROG PAL IS UP THERE. I CALL HIM FRED. BUT WE CAN TOTALLY GO SOMEPLACE ELSE...
SORRY, WE DON'T HAVE TO...
IT SOUNDS PERFECT!

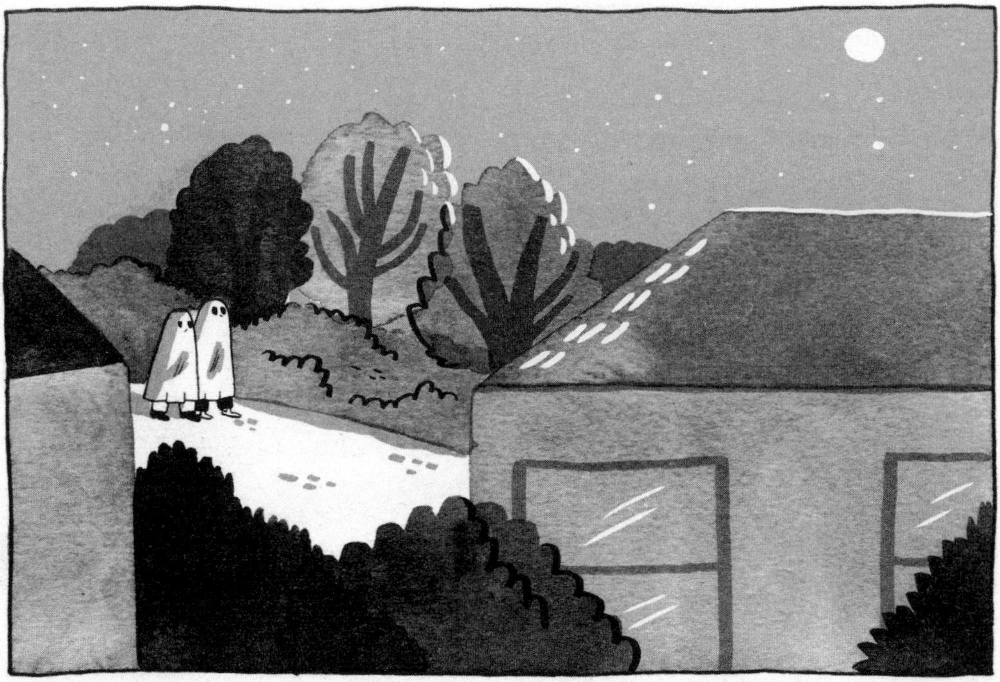

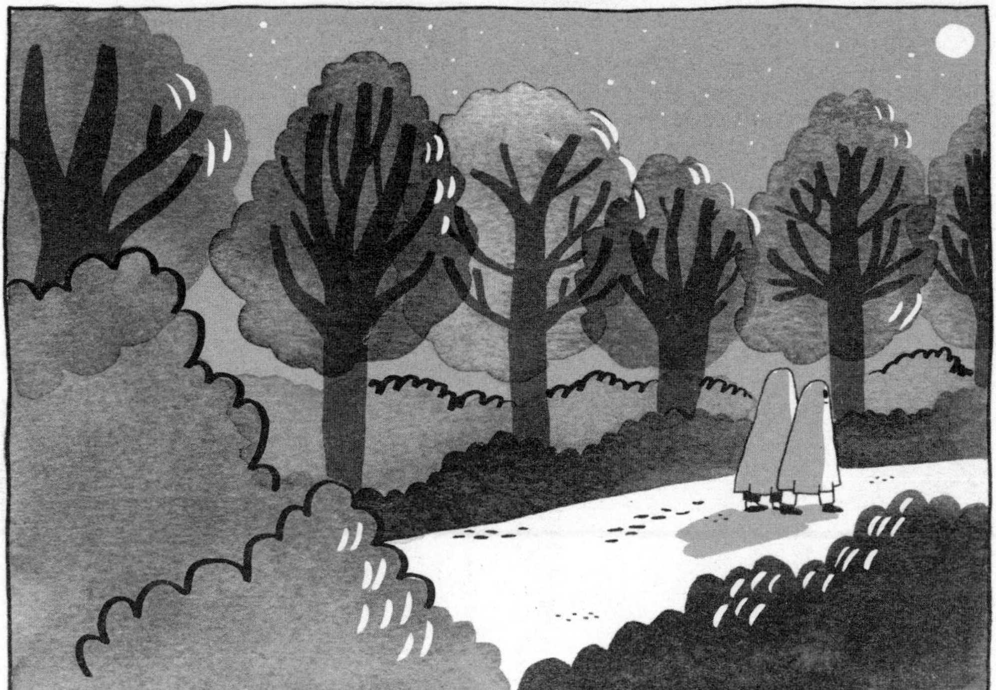

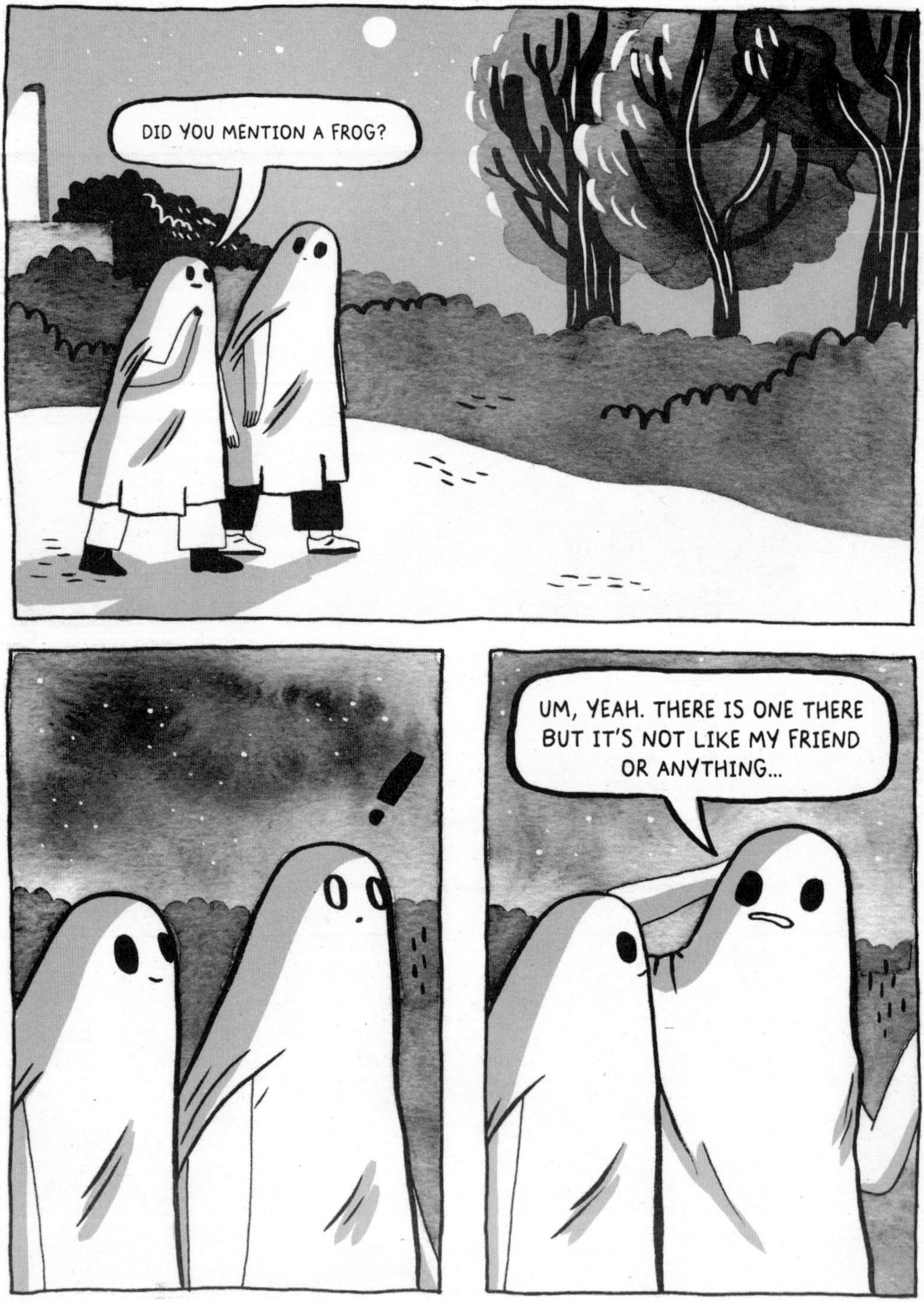
DID YOU MENTION A FROG?
!
UM, YEAH. THERE IS ONE THERE BUT IT'S NOT LIKE MY FRIEND OR ANYTHING...

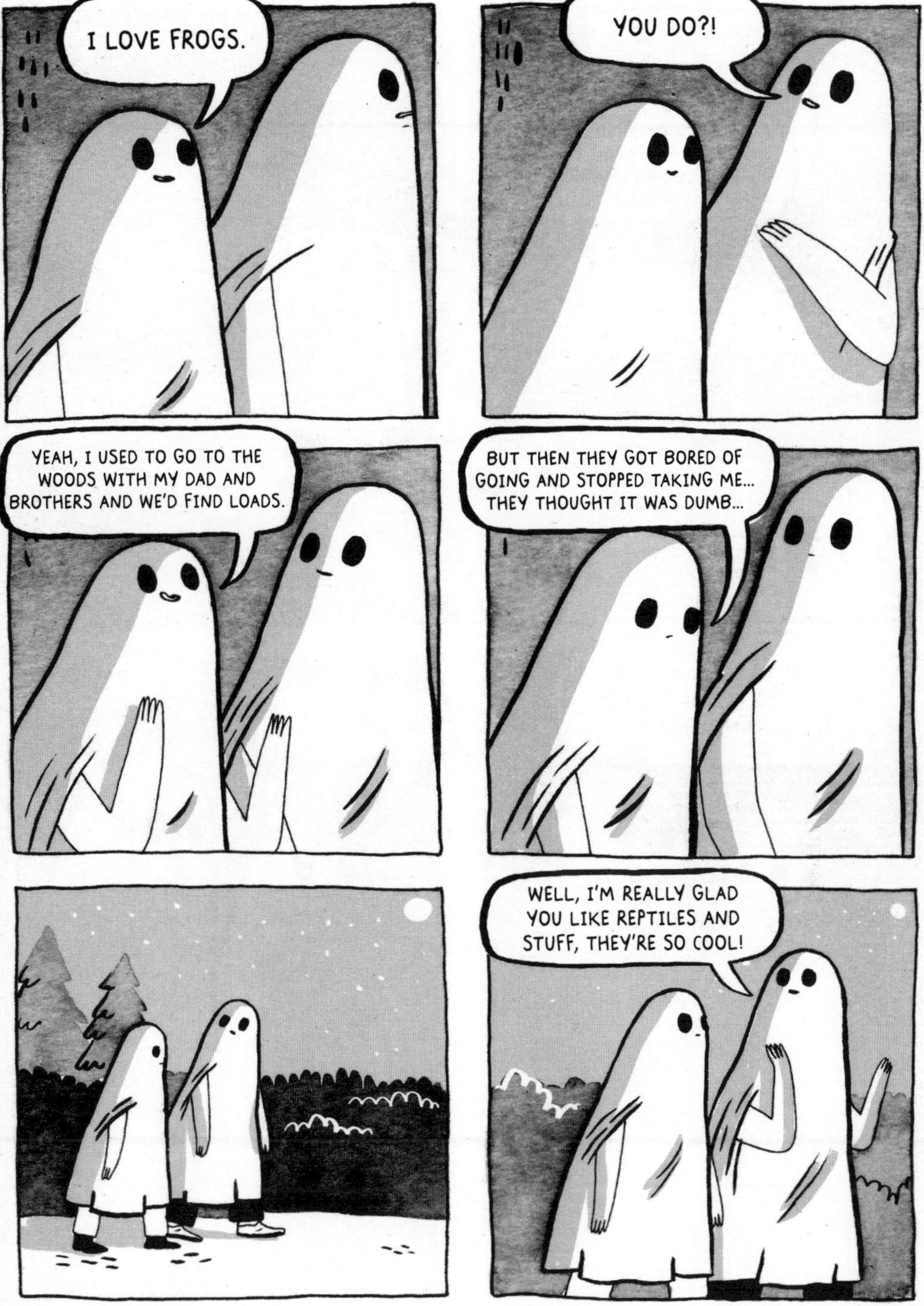
I LOVE FROGS.
YOU DO?!
YEAH, I USED TO GO TO THE WOODS WITH MY DAD AND BROTHERS AND WE'D FIND LOADS.
BUT THEN THEY GOT BORED OF GOING AND STOPPED TAKING ME... THEY THOUGHT IT WAS DUMB...
WELL, I'M REALLY GLAD YOU LIKE REPTILES AND STUFF, THEY'RE SO COOL!

FROGS ARE AMPHIBIANS ACTUALLY BUT YEAH, THEY'RE SUPER COOL AND INTERESTING! LIKE...
DID YOU KNOW THEY CAN JUMP UP TO TWENTY TIMES THEIR OWN LENGTH?
IN ONE LEAP!
THAT'S MAD!

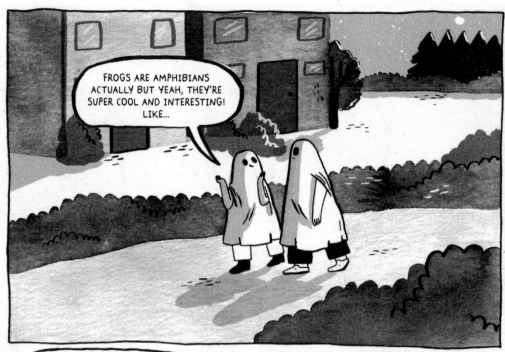

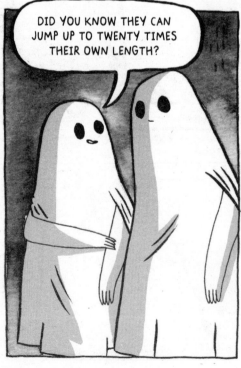

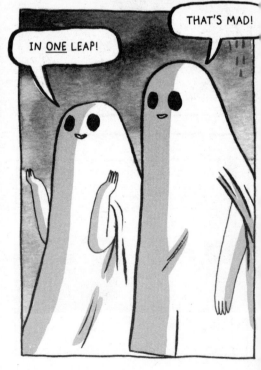

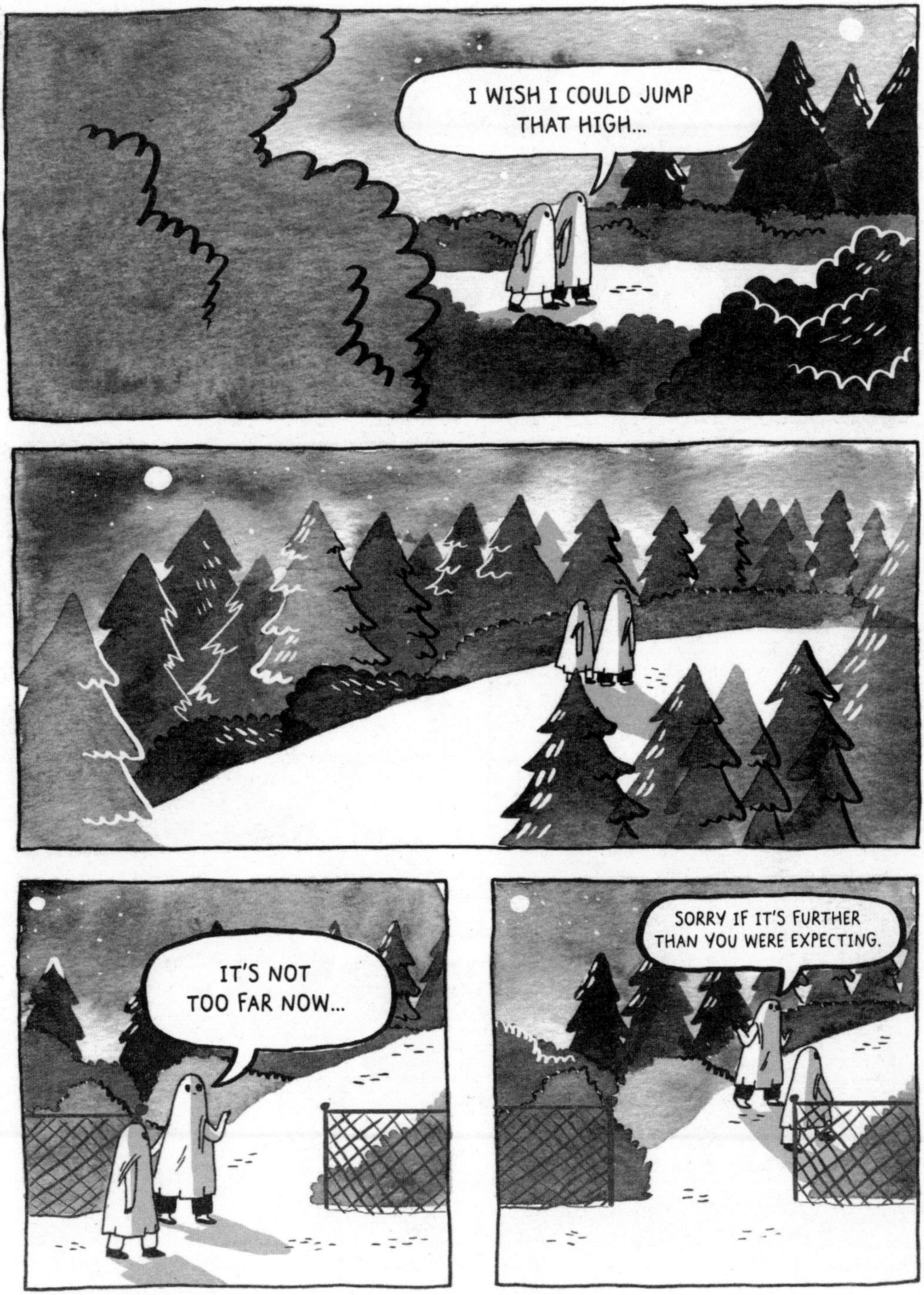
I WISH I COULD JUMP THAT HIGH...
IT'S NOT TOO FAR NOW...
SORRY IF IT'S FURTHER THAN YOU WERE EXPECTING.

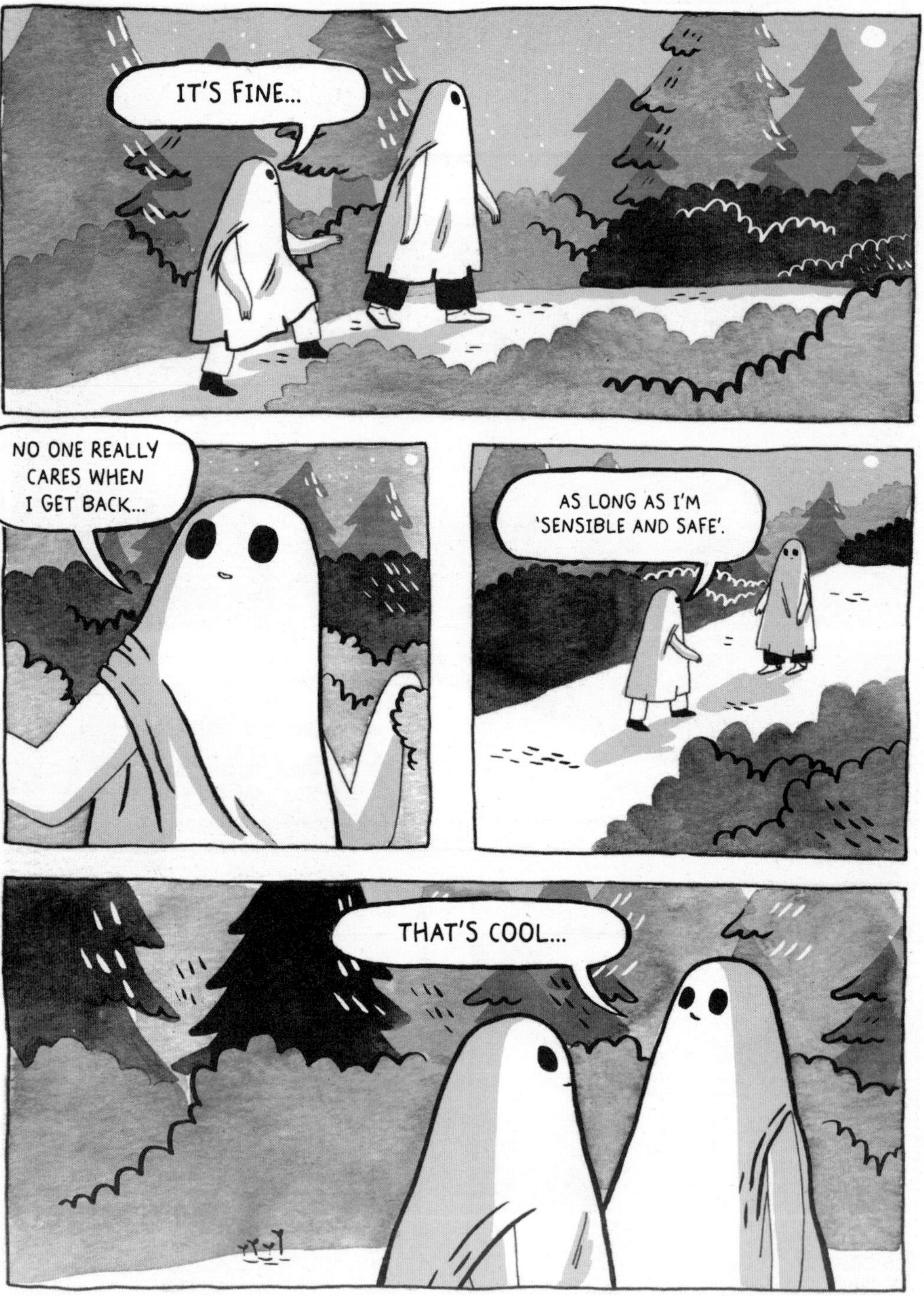
IT'S FINE...
NO ONE REALLY CARES WHEN I GET BACK...
AS LONG AS I'M 'SENSIBLE AND SAFE'.
THAT'S COOL...

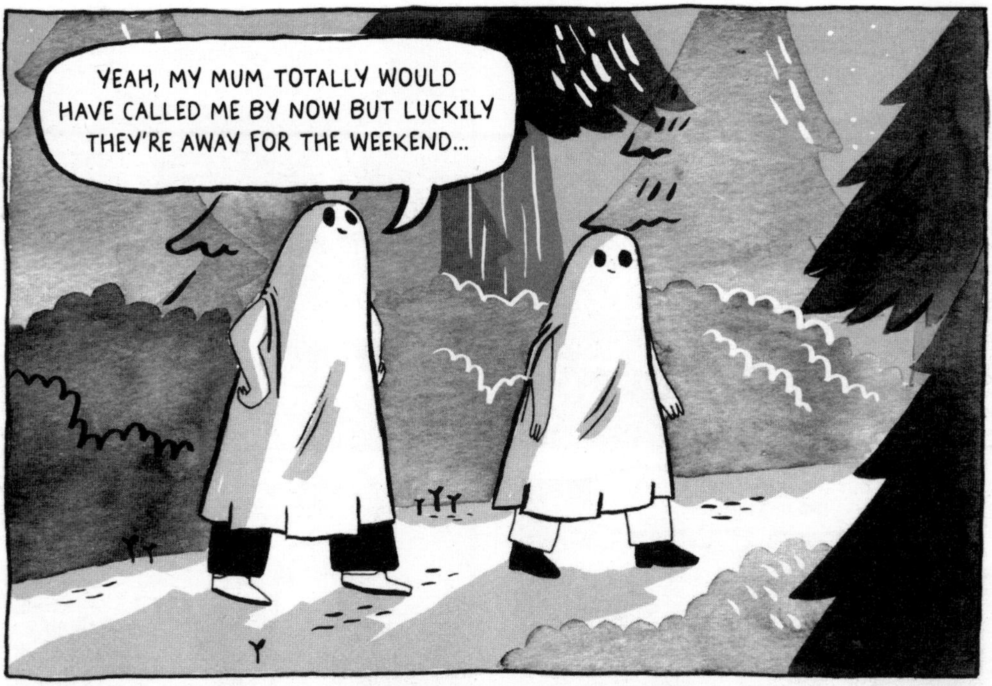
YEAH, MY MUM TOTALLY WOULD HAVE CALLED ME BY NOW BUT LUCKILY THEY'RE AWAY FOR THE WEEKEND...

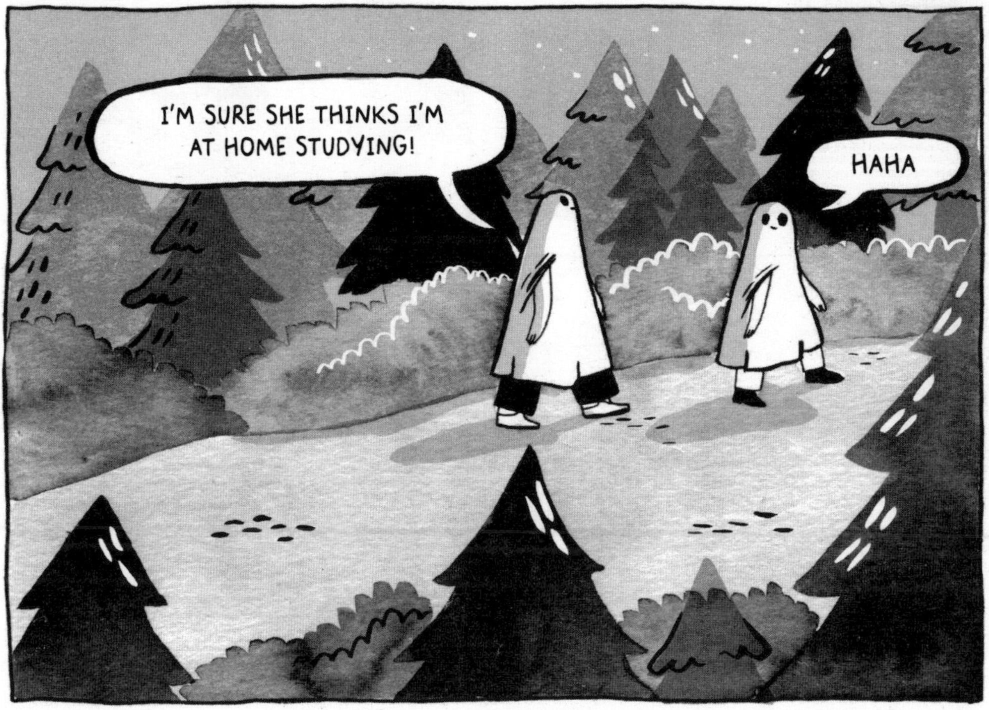
I'M SURE SHE THINKS I'M AT HOME STUDYING!
HAHA

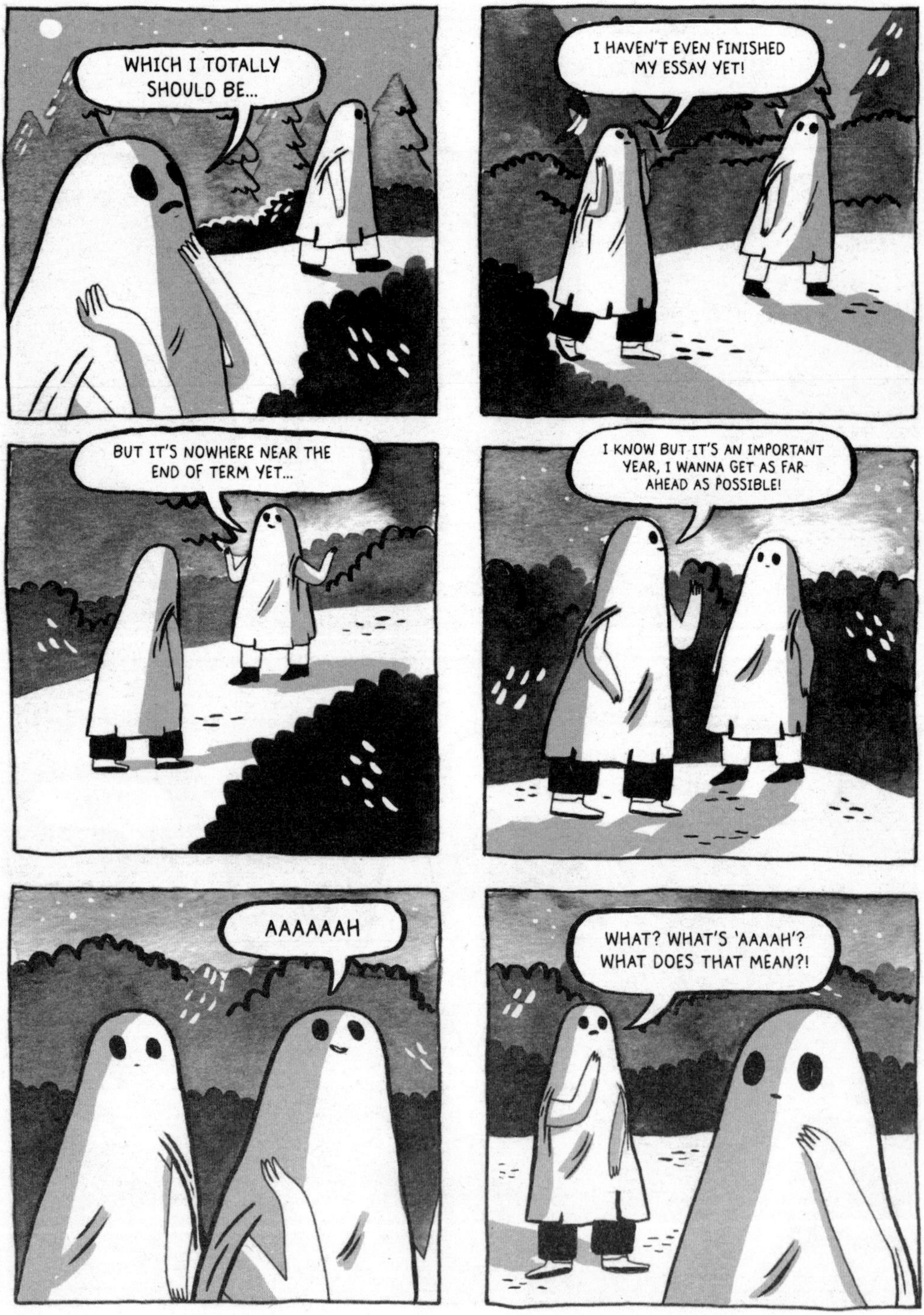
WHICH I TOTALLY SHOULD BE...
I HAVEN'T EVEN FINISHED MY ESSAY YET!
BUT IT'S NOWHERE NEAR THE END OF TERM YET...
I KNOW BUT IT'S AN IMPORTANT YEAR, I WANNA GET AS FAR AHEAD AS POSSIBLE!
AAAAAAH
WHAT? WHAT'S 'AAAAH'? WHAT DOES THAT MEAN?!

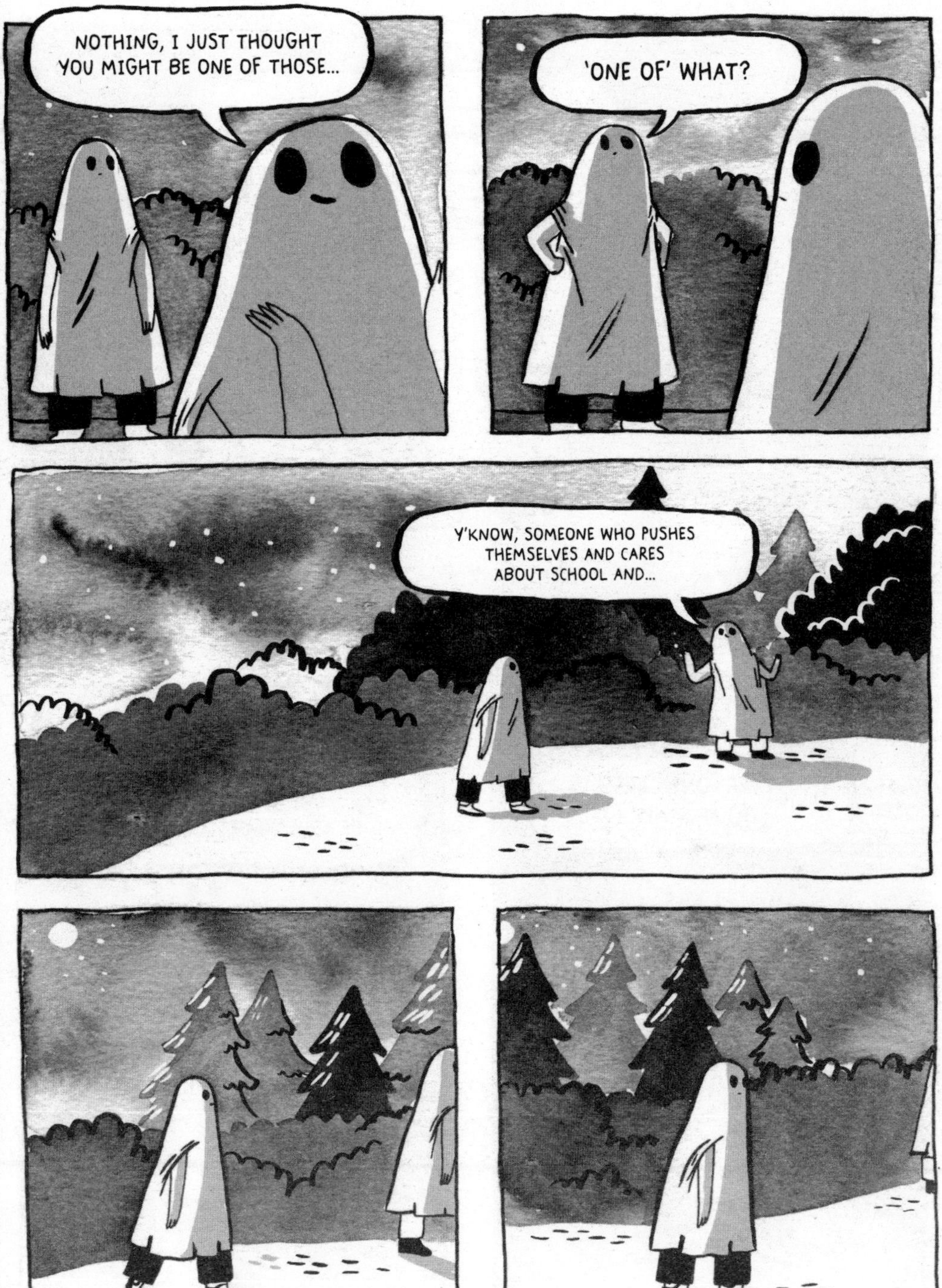
NOTHING, I JUST THOUGHT YOU MIGHT BE ONE OF THOSE...
'ONE OF' WHAT?
Y'KNOW, SOMEONE WHO PUSHES THEMSELVES AND CARES ABOUT SCHOOL AND...

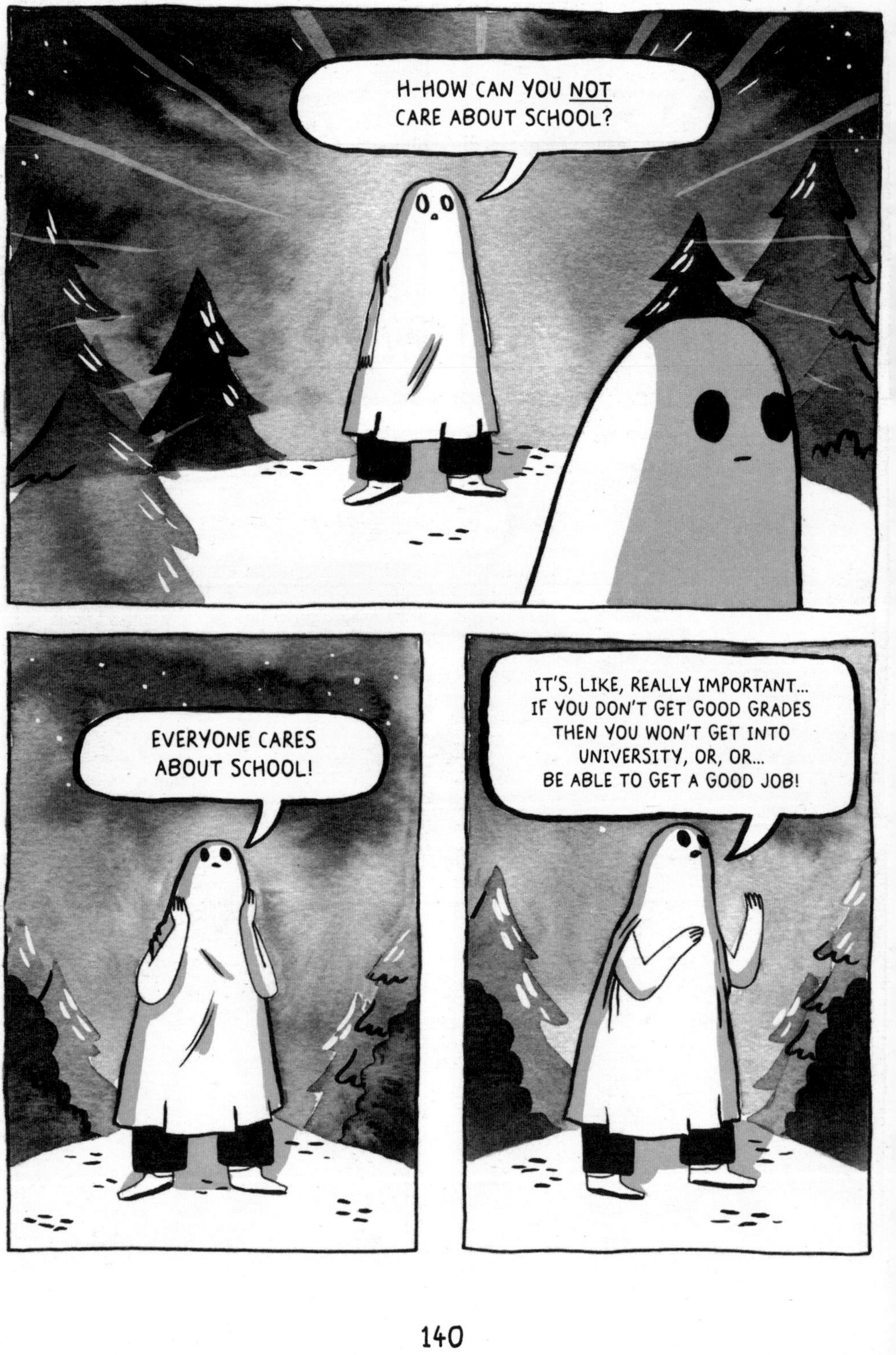
H-HOW CAN YOU NOT CARE ABOUT SCHOOL?
EVERYONE CARES ABOUT SCHOOL!
IT'S, LIKE, REALLY IMPORTANT... IF YOU DON'T GET GOOD GRADES THEN YOU WON'T GET INTO UNIVERSITY, OR, OR... BE ABLE TO GET A GOOD JOB!

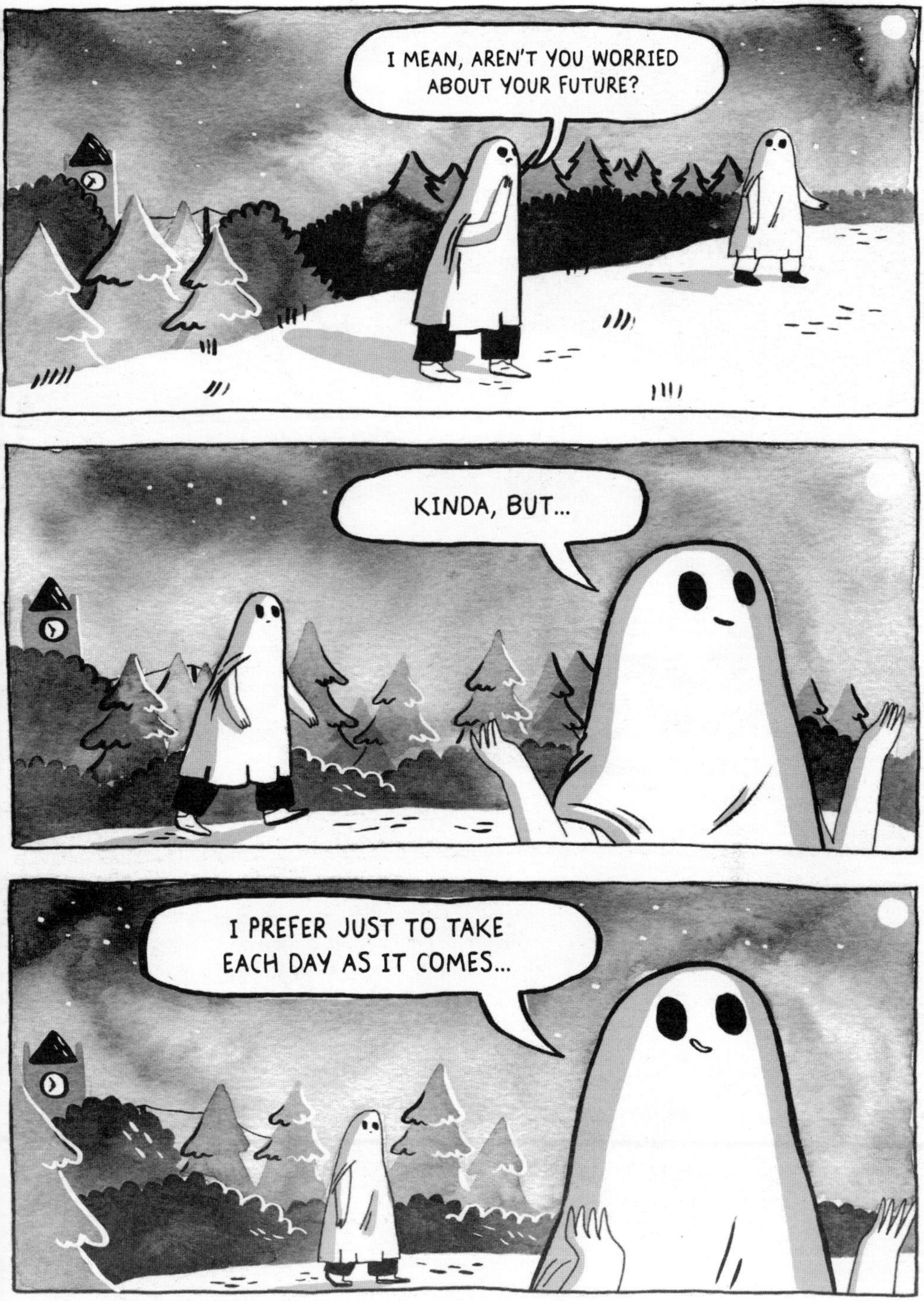
I MEAN, AREN'T YOU WORRIED ABOUT YOUR FUTURE?
KINDA, BUT...
I PREFER JUST TO TAKE EACH DAY AS IT COMES...

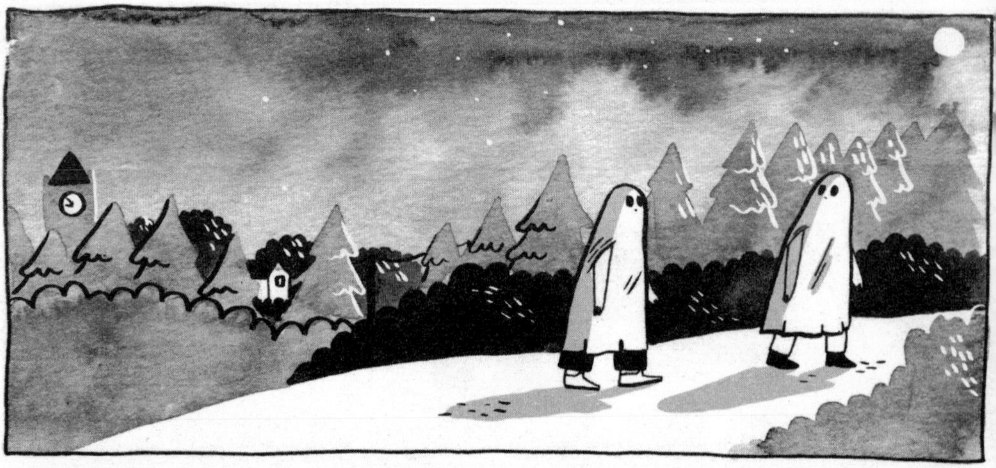

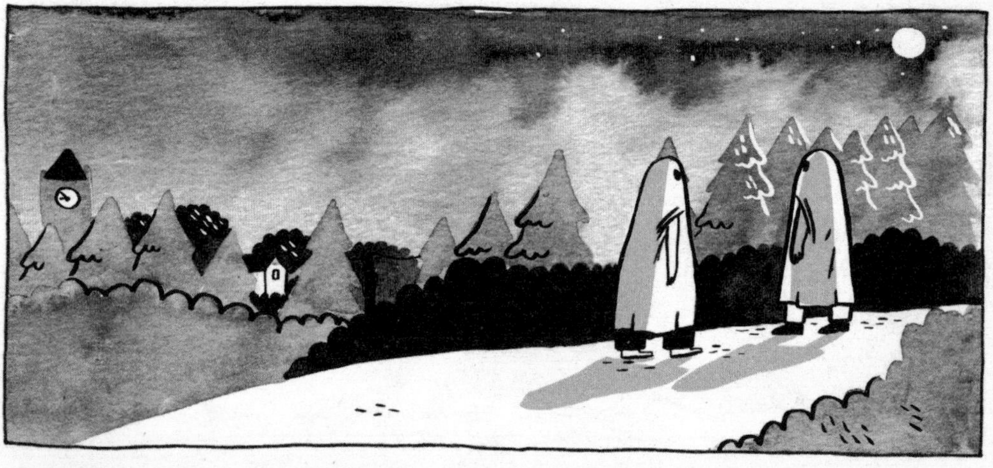

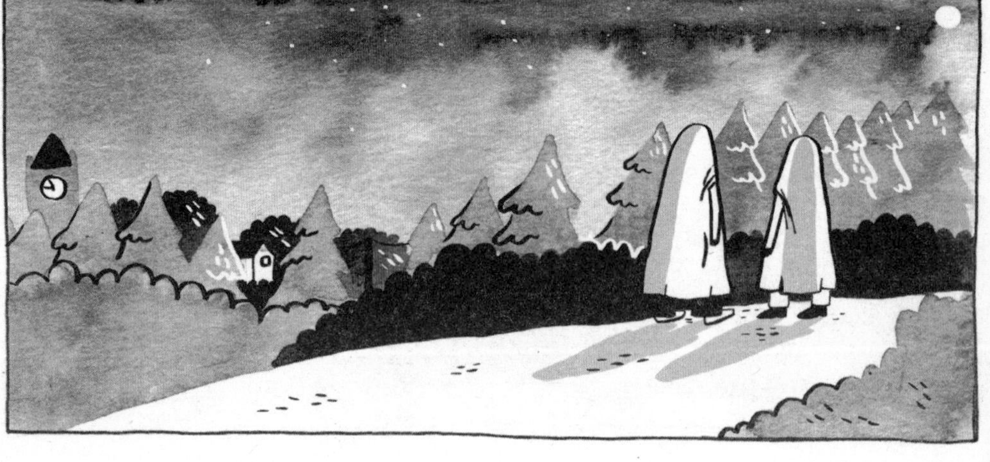

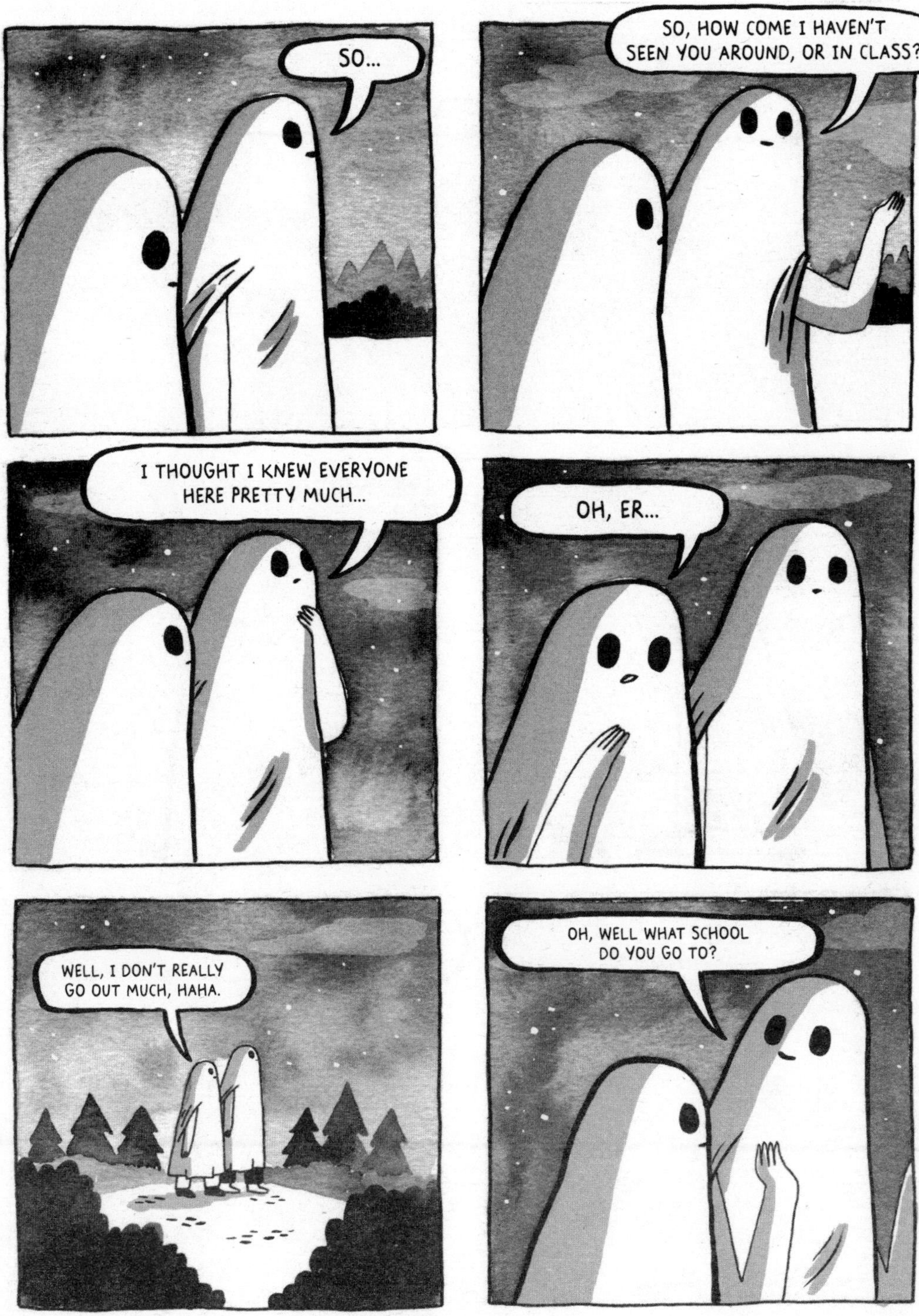
SO...
SO, HOW COME I HAVEN'T SEEN YOU AROUND, OR IN CLASS?
I THOUGHT I KNEW EVERYONE HERE PRETTY MUCH...
OH, ER...
WELL, I DON'T REALLY GO OUT MUCH, HAHA.
OH, WELL WHAT SCHOOL DO YOU GO TO?

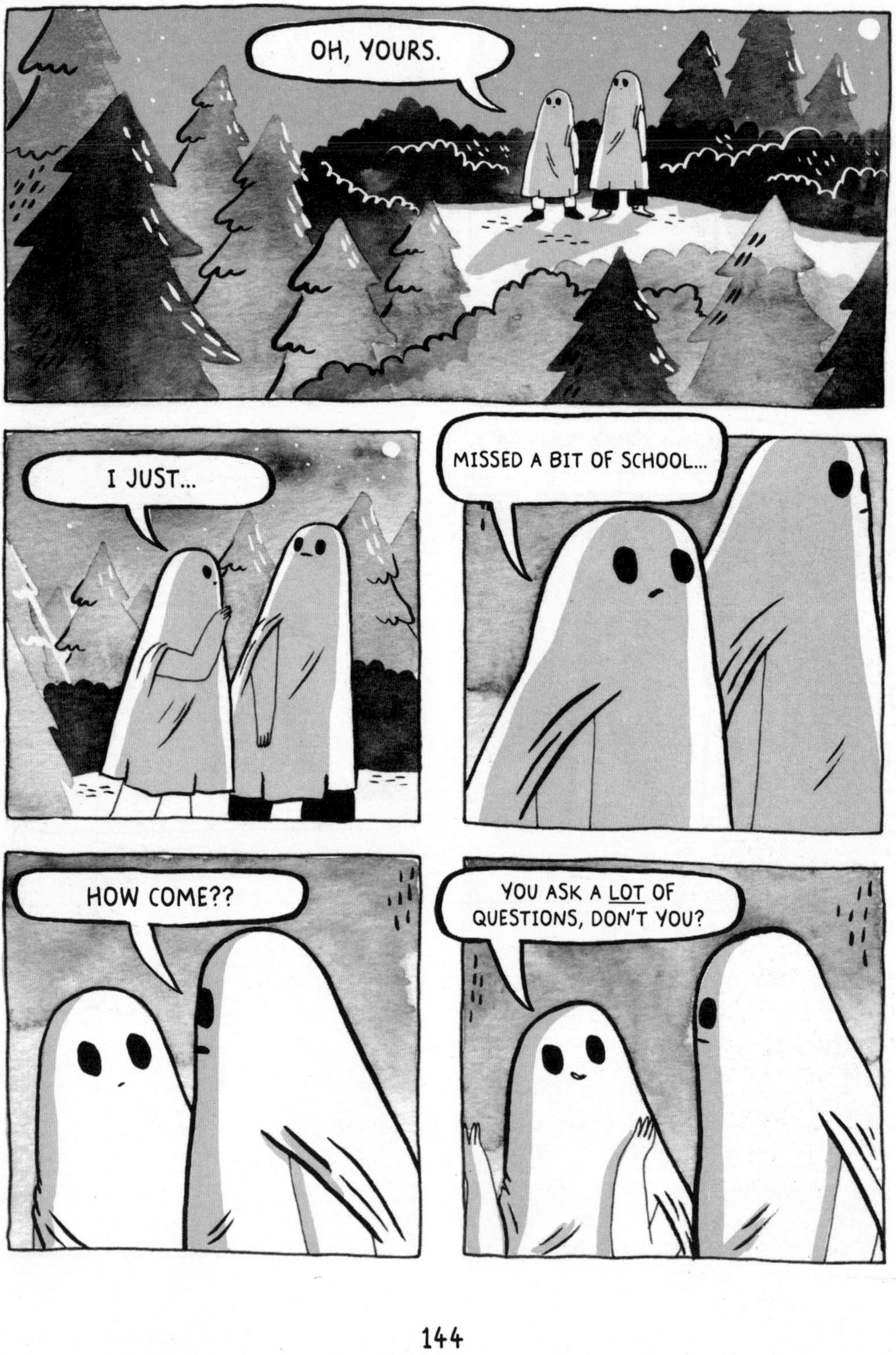
OH, YOURS.
I JUST...
MISSED A BIT OF SCHOOL...
HOW COME??
YOU ASK A LOT OF QUESTIONS, DON'T YOU?

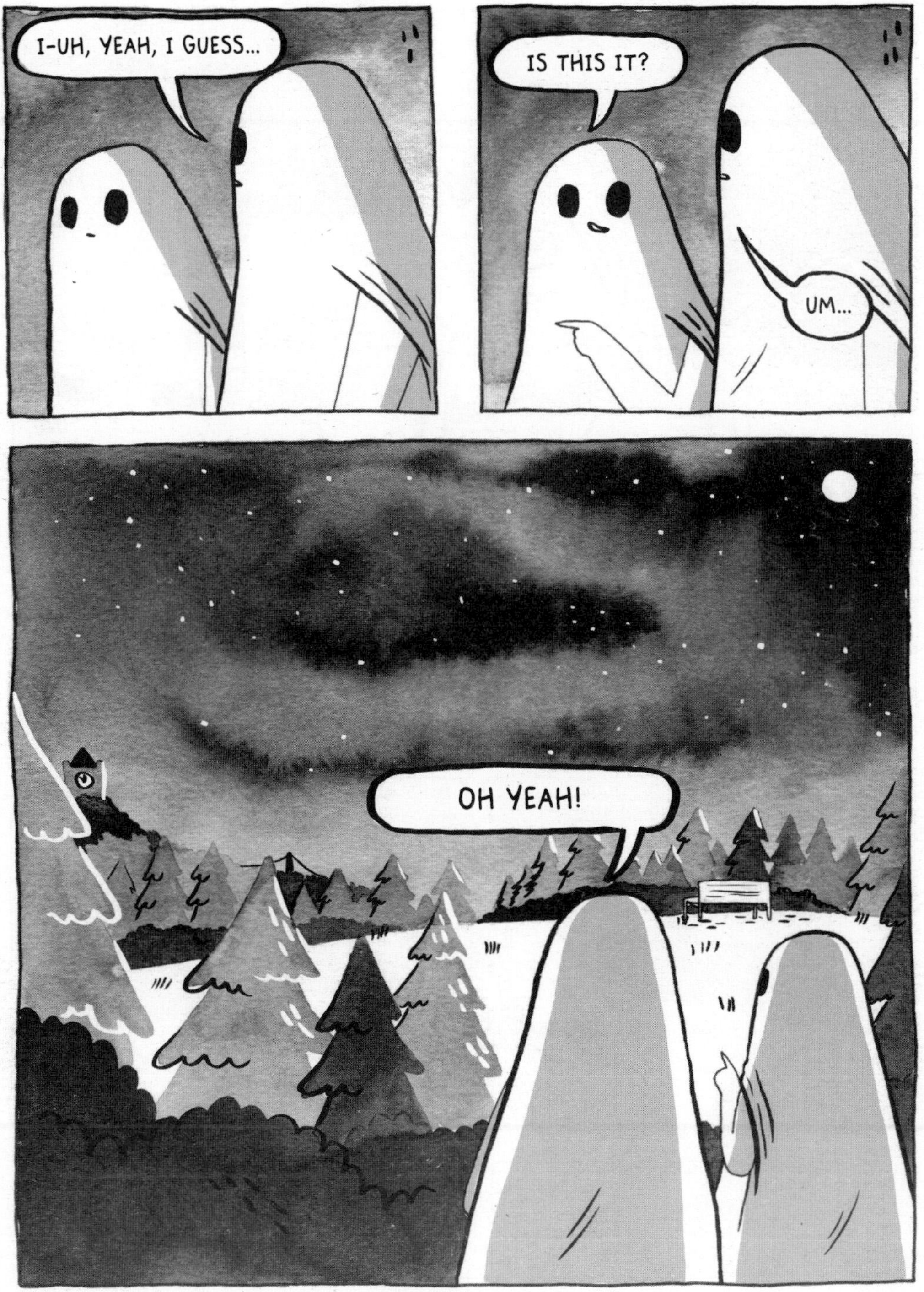
I-UH, YEAH, I GUESS...
IS THIS IT?
UM...
OH YEAH!

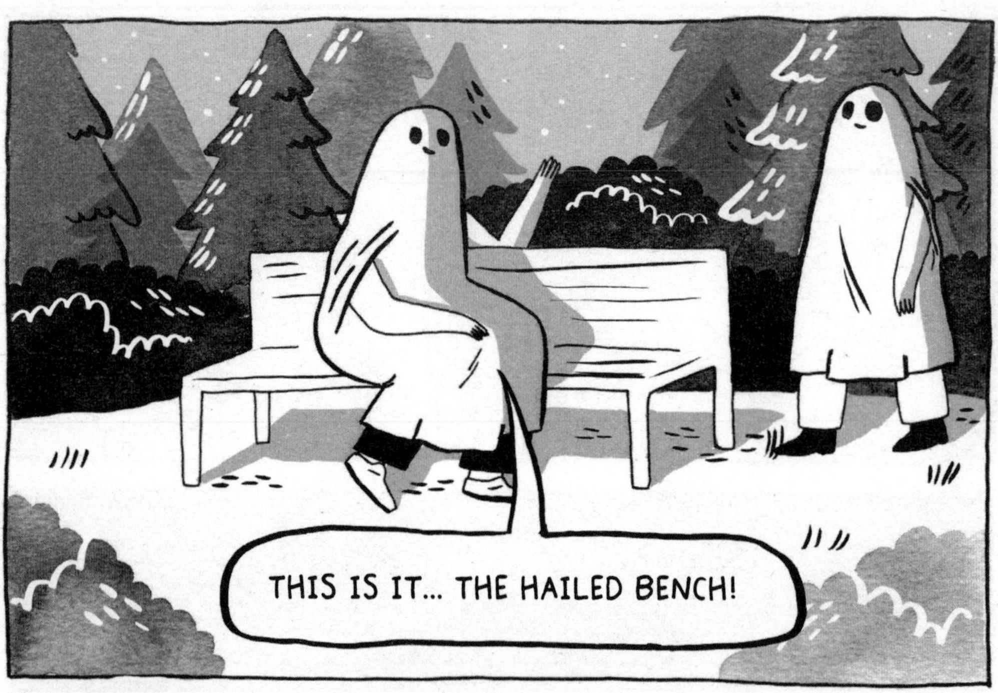
THIS IS IT... THE HAILED BENCH!

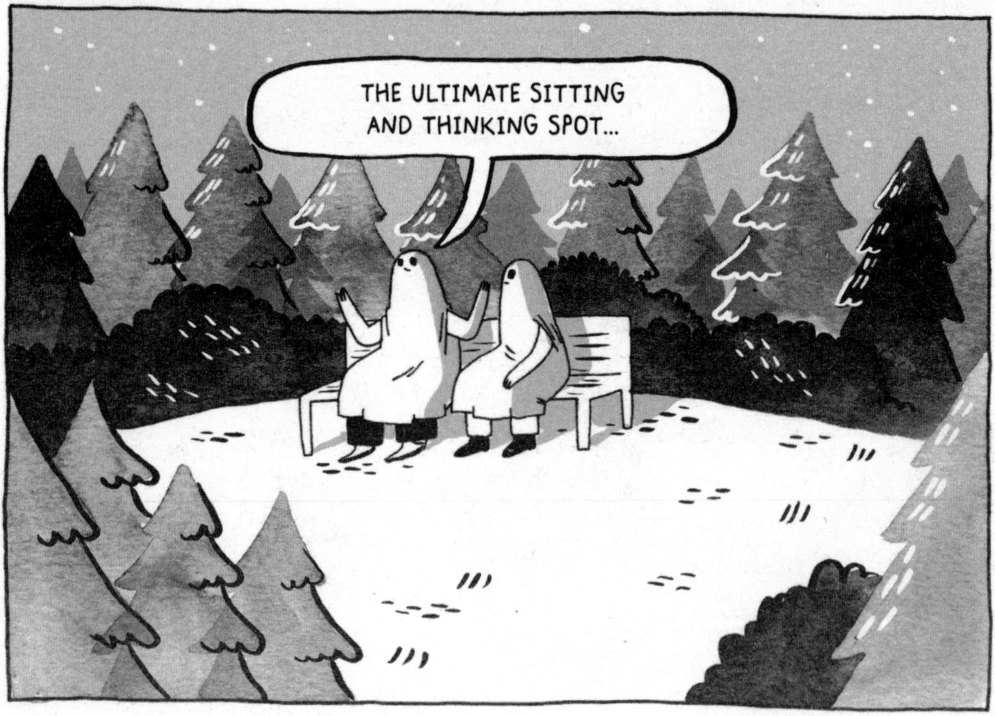
THE ULTIMATE SITTING
AND THINKING SPOT...

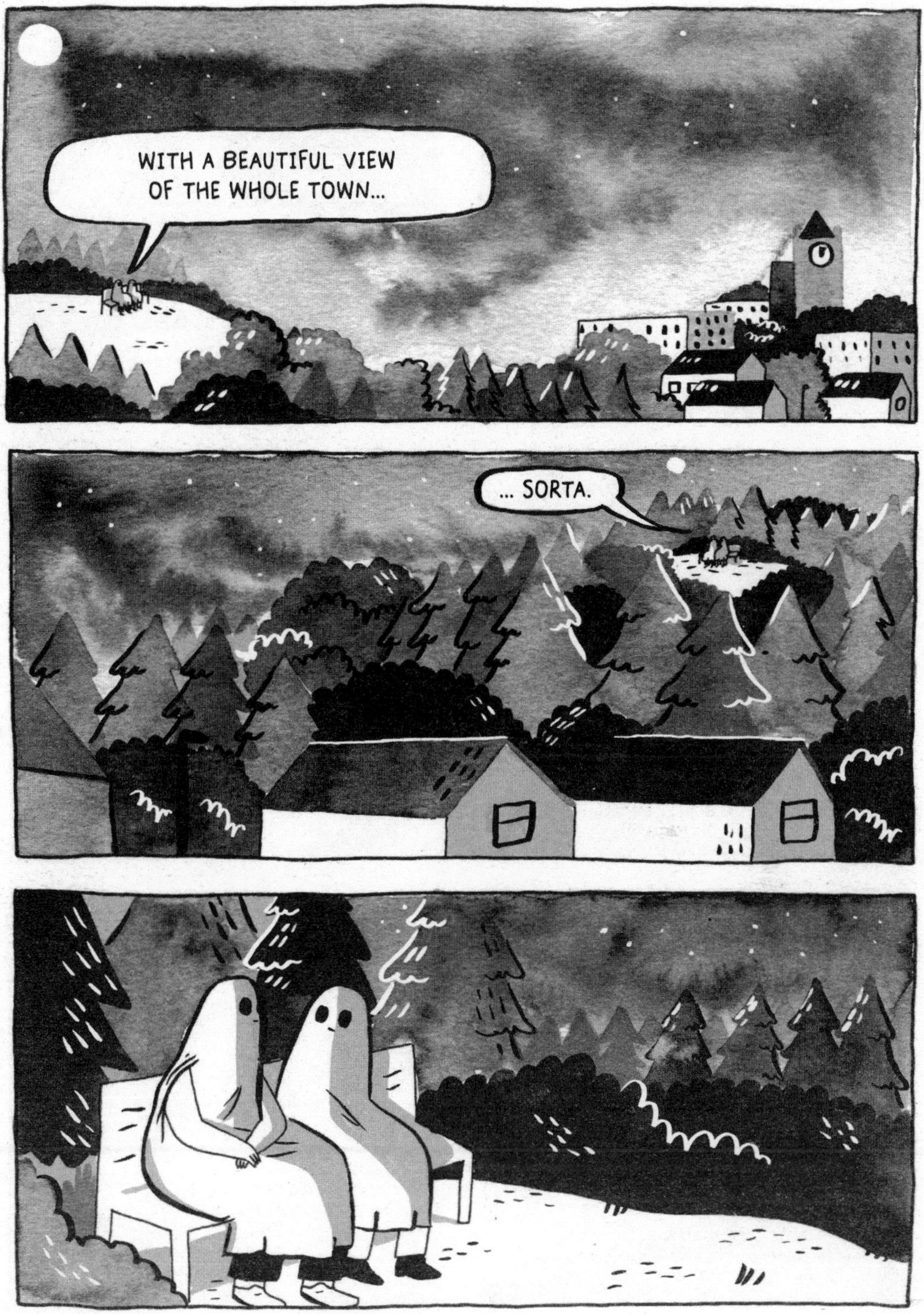
WITH A BEAUTIFUL VIEW
OF THE WHOLE TOWN...
... SORTA.

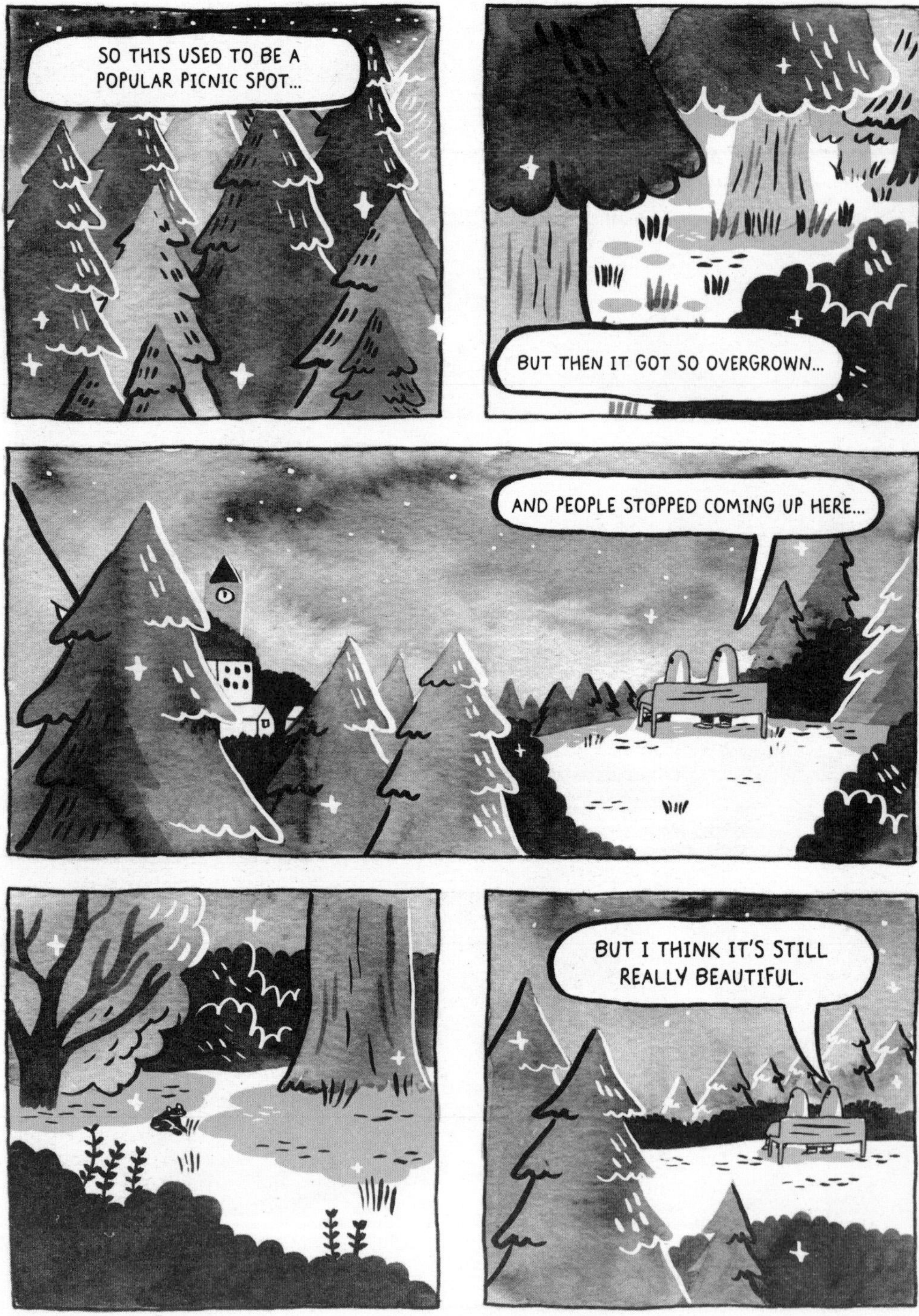
SO THIS USED TO BE A POPULAR PICNIC SPOT...
BUT THEN IT GOT SO OVERGROWN...
AND PEOPLE STOPPED COMING UP HERE...
BUT I THINK IT'S STILL REALLY BEAUTIFUL.

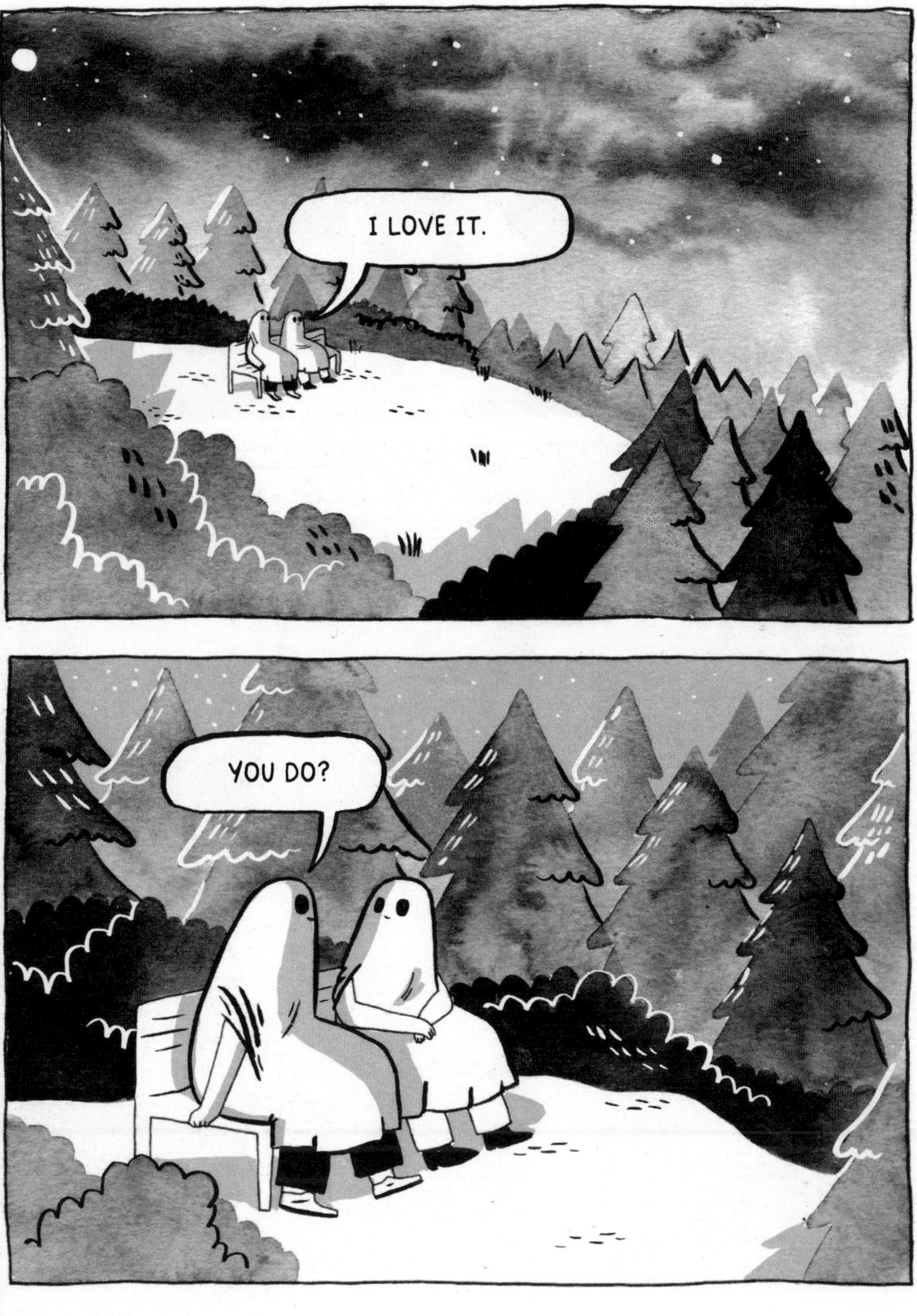
I LOVE IT.
YOU DO?

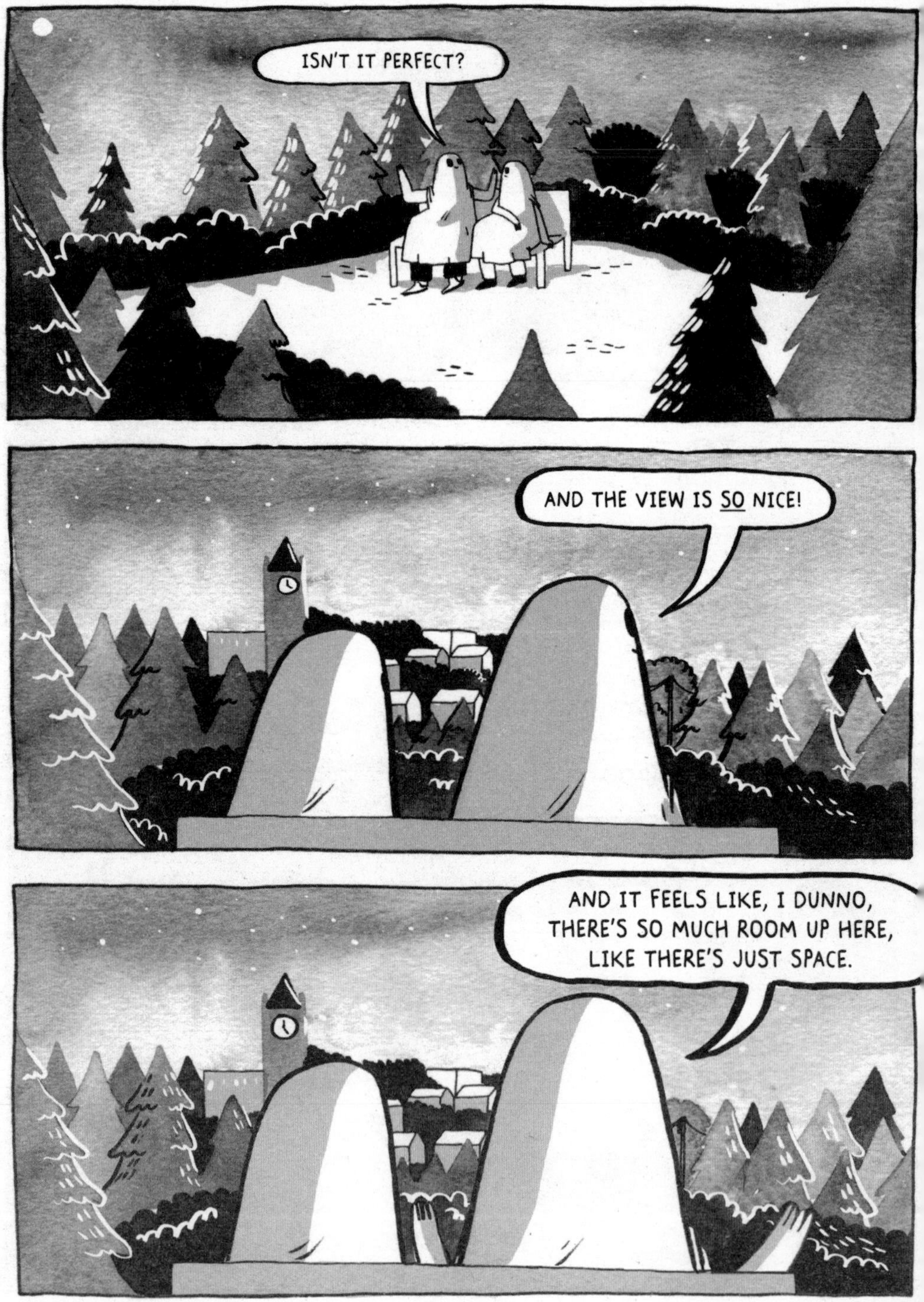
ISN'T IT PERFECT?
AND THE VIEW IS SO NICE!
AND IT FEELS LIKE, I DUNNO, THERE'S SO MUCH ROOM UP HERE, LIKE THERE'S JUST SPACE.

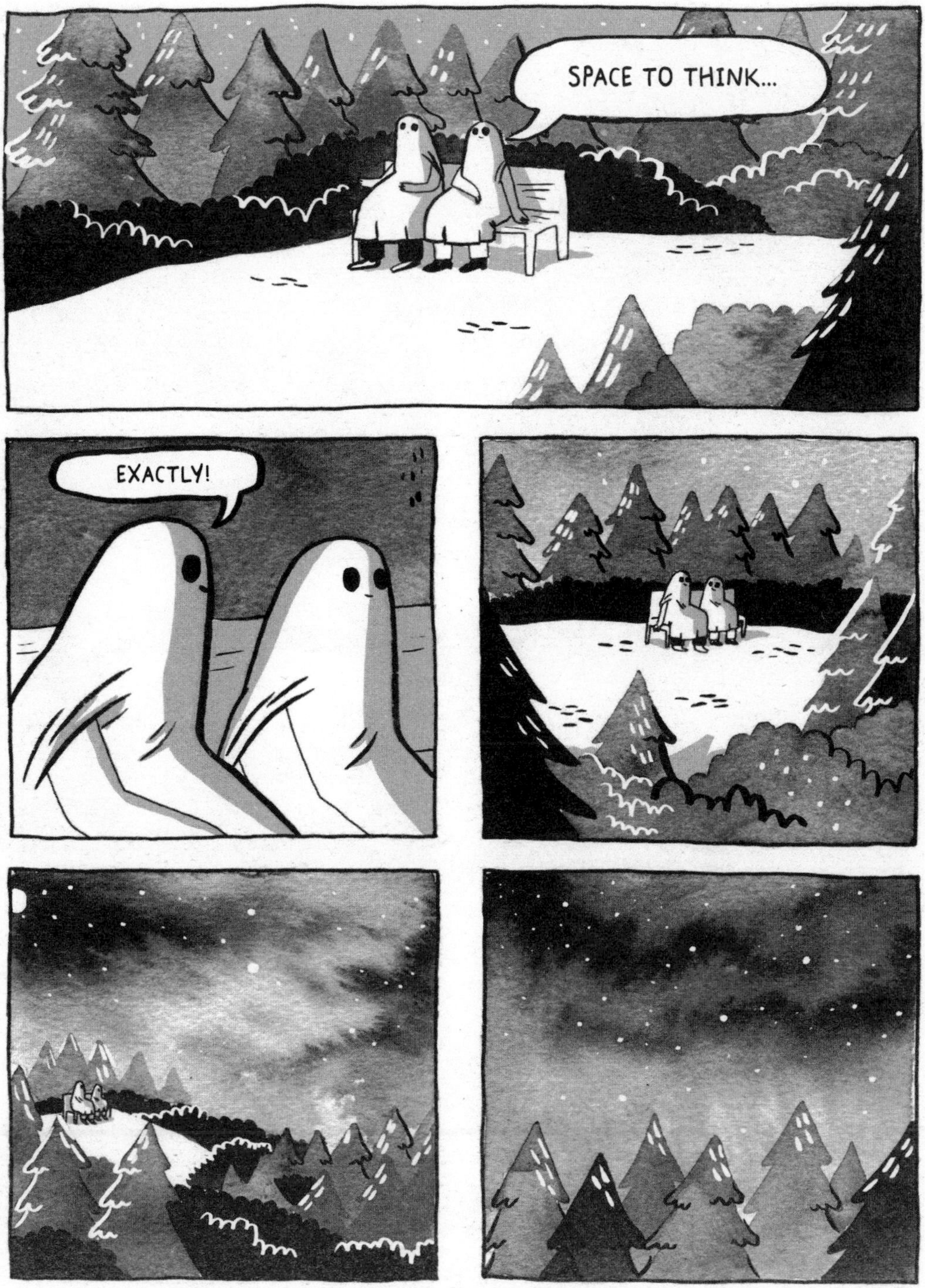
SPACE TO THINK...
EXACTLY!

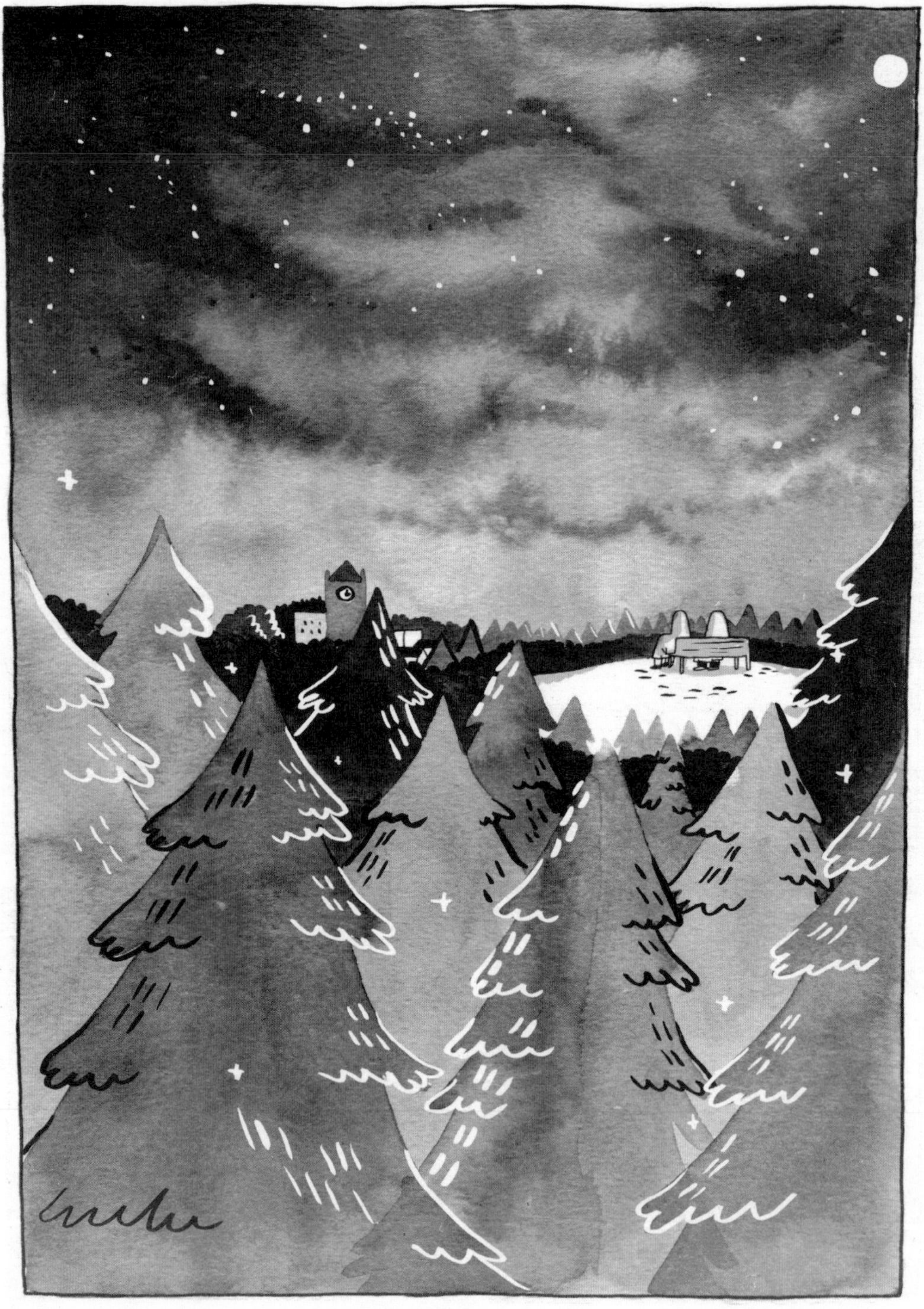

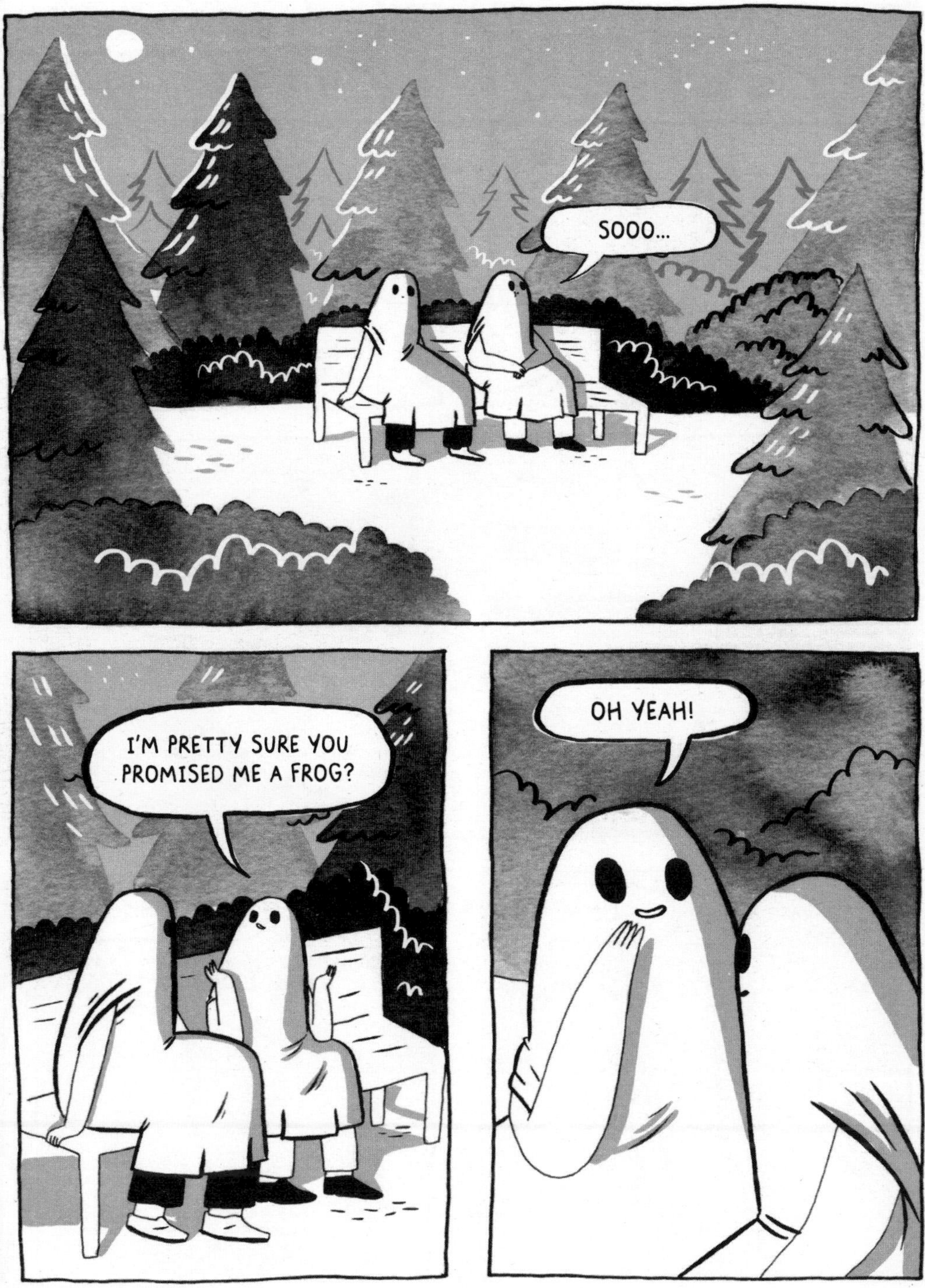
SOOO...
I'M PRETTY SURE YOU PROMISED ME A FROG?
OH YEAH!

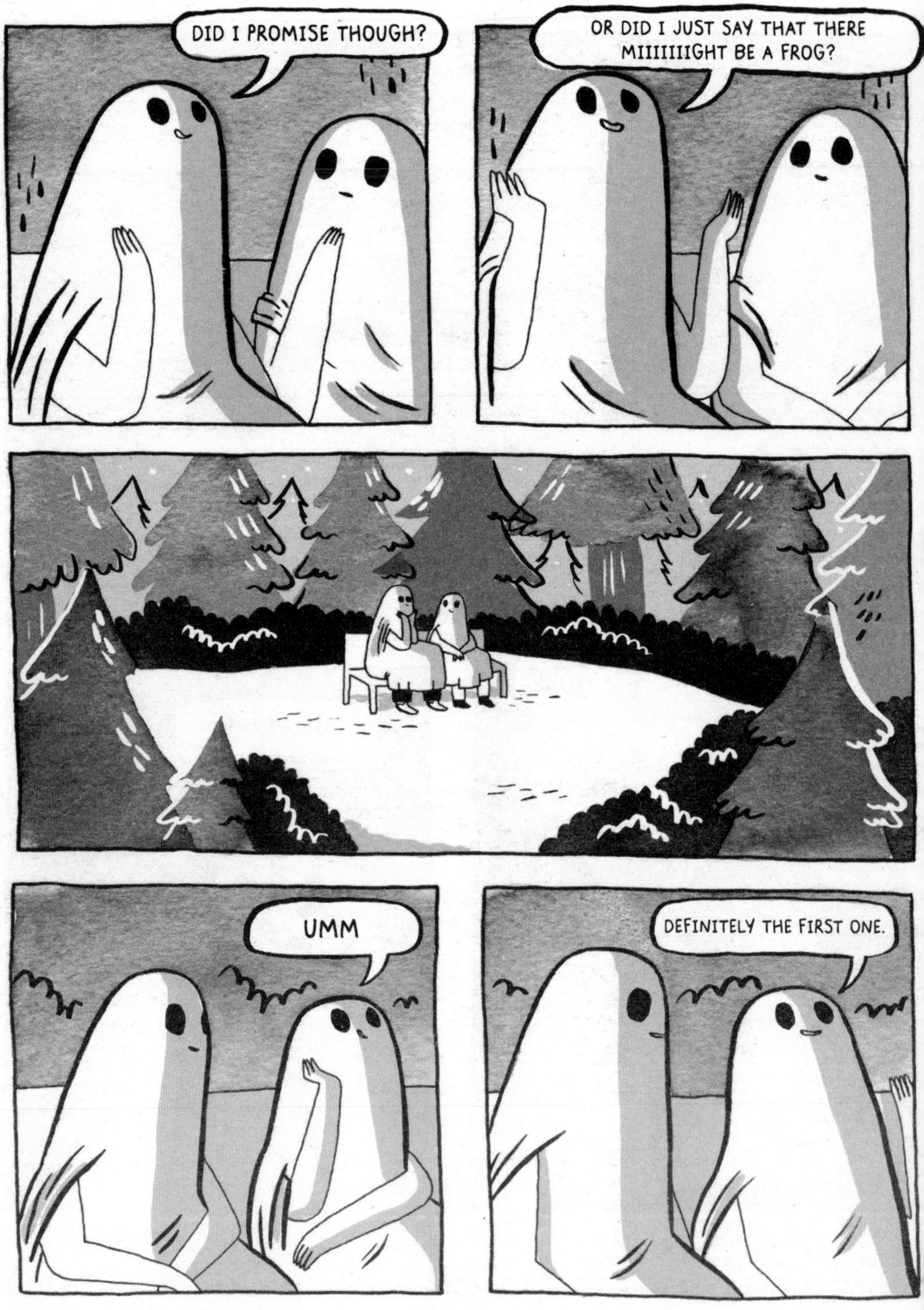
DID I PROMISE THOUGH?
OR DID I JUST SAY THAT THERE MIIIIIIIGHT BE A FROG?
UMM
DEFINITELY THE FIRST ONE.

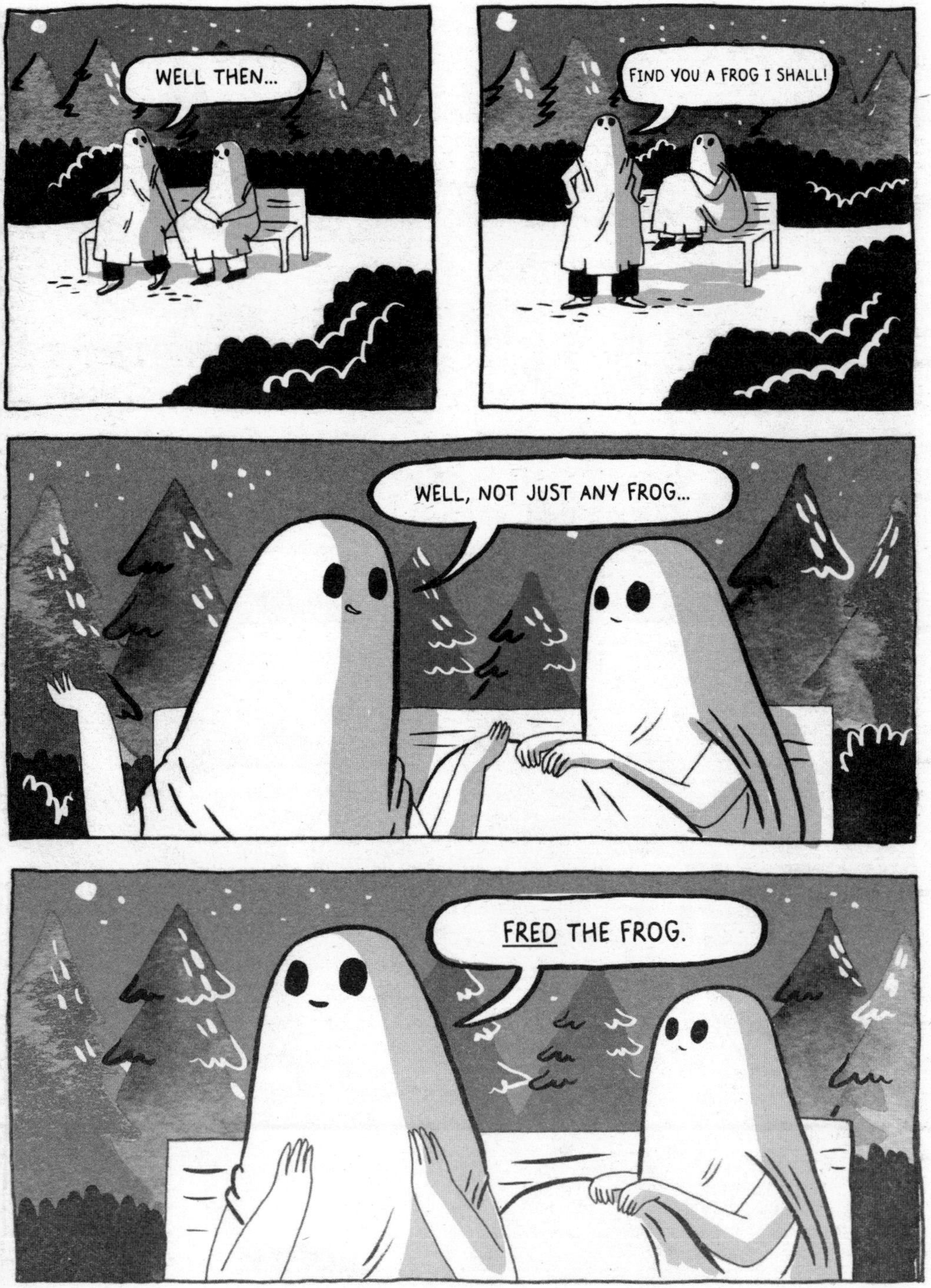
WELL THEN...
FIND YOU A FROG I SHALL!
WELL, NOT JUST ANY FROG...
FRED THE FROG.

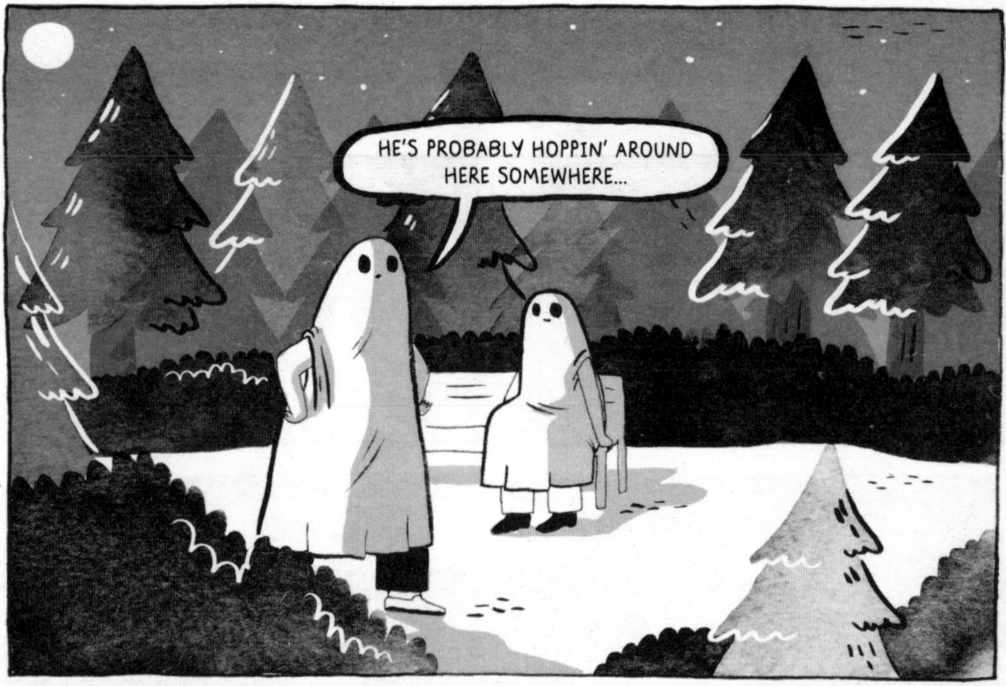
HE'S PROBABLY HOPPIN' AROUND HERE SOMEWHERE...

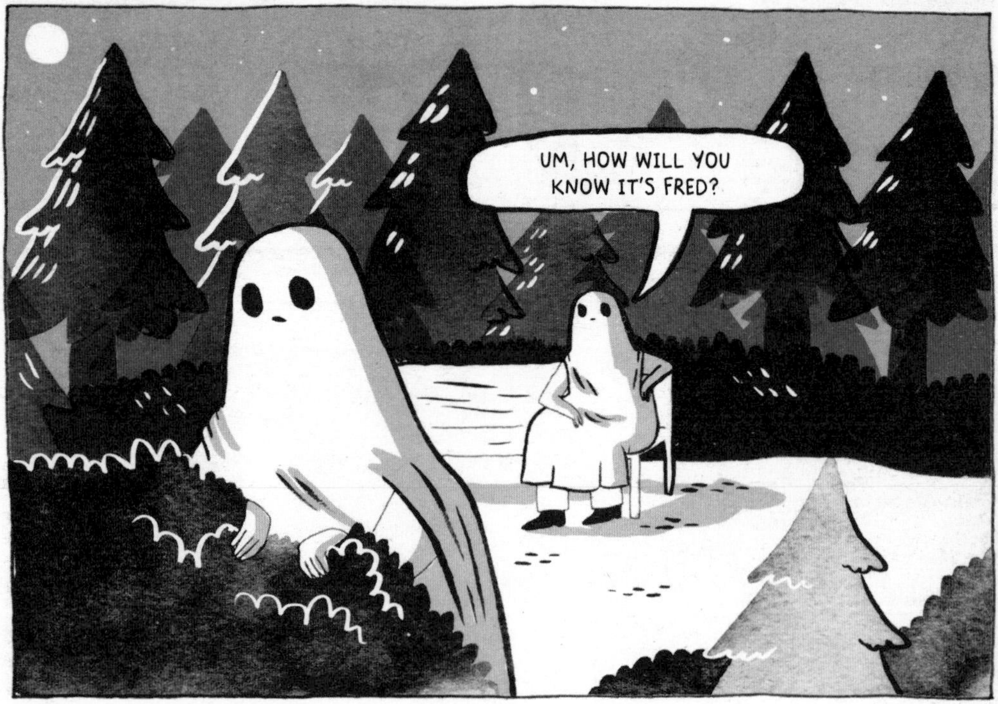
UM, HOW WILL YOU KNOW IT'S FRED?

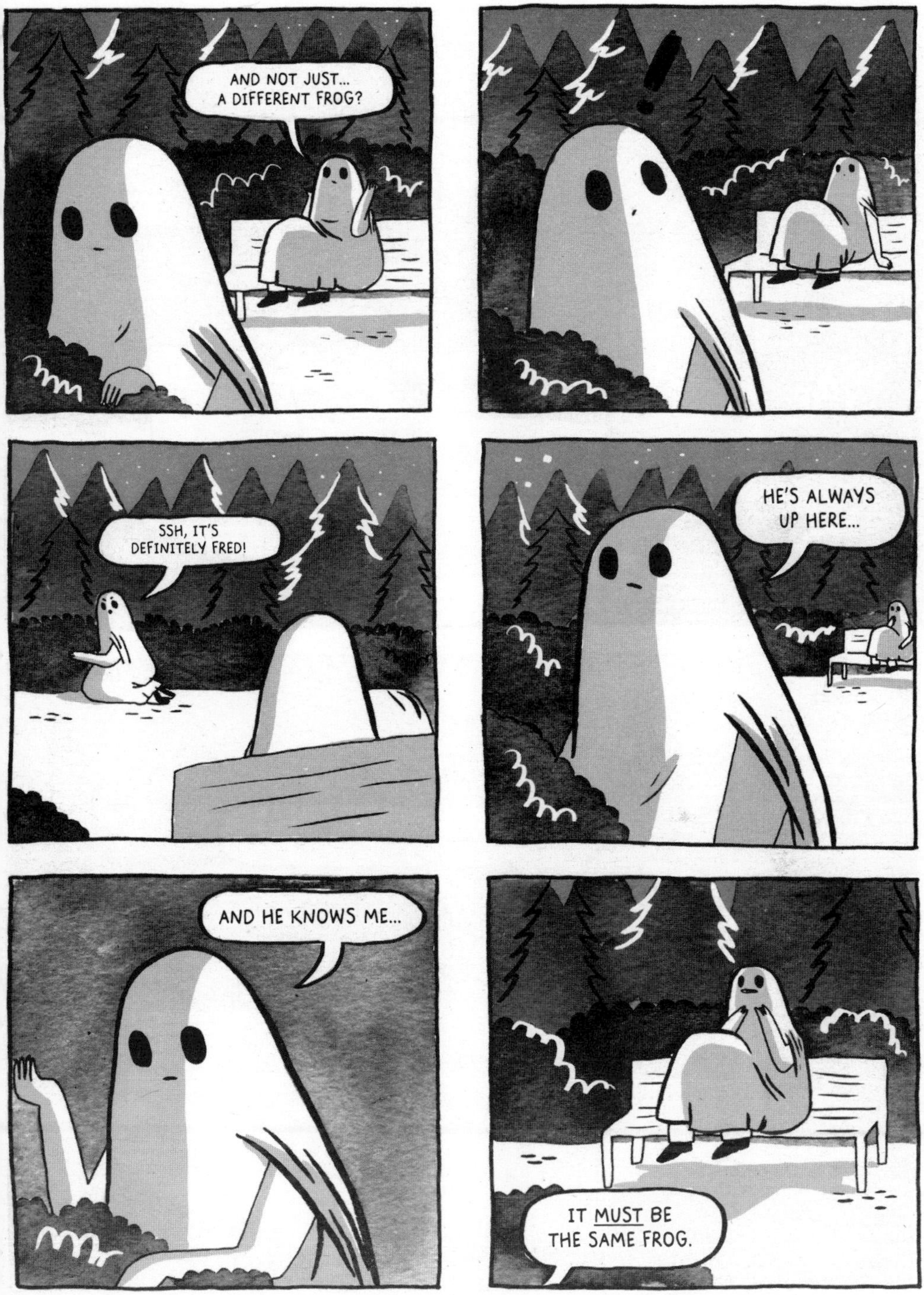
AND NOT JUST...
A DIFFERENT FROG?
SSH, IT'S
DEFINITELY FRED!
HE'S ALWAYS
UP HERE...
AND HE KNOWS ME...
IT MUST BE
THE SAME FROG.

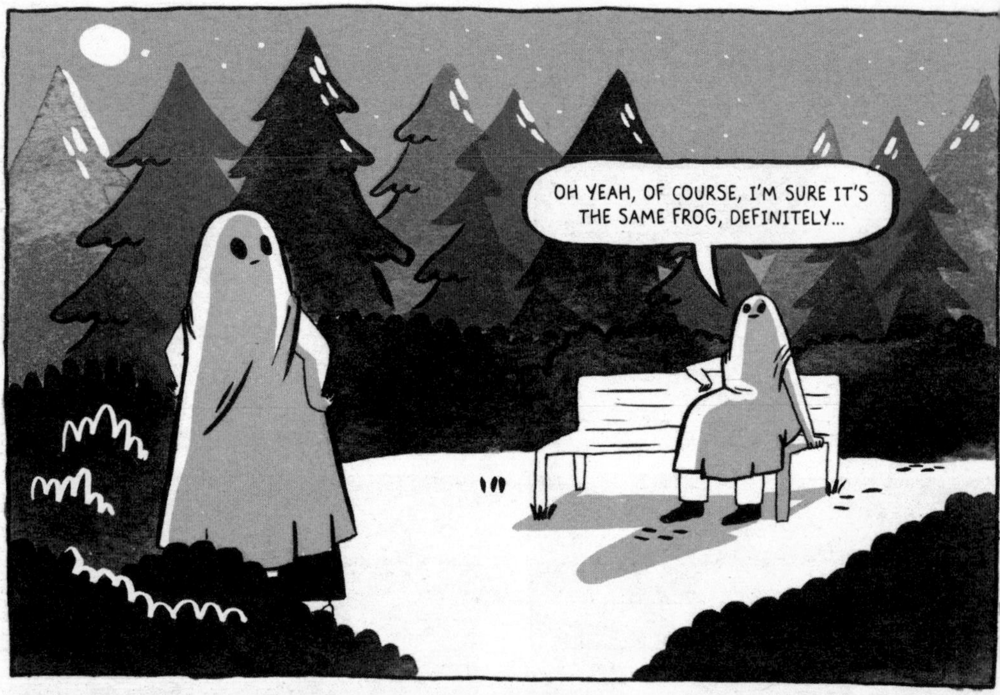
OH YEAH, OF COURSE, I'M SURE IT'S THE SAME FROG, DEFINITELY...

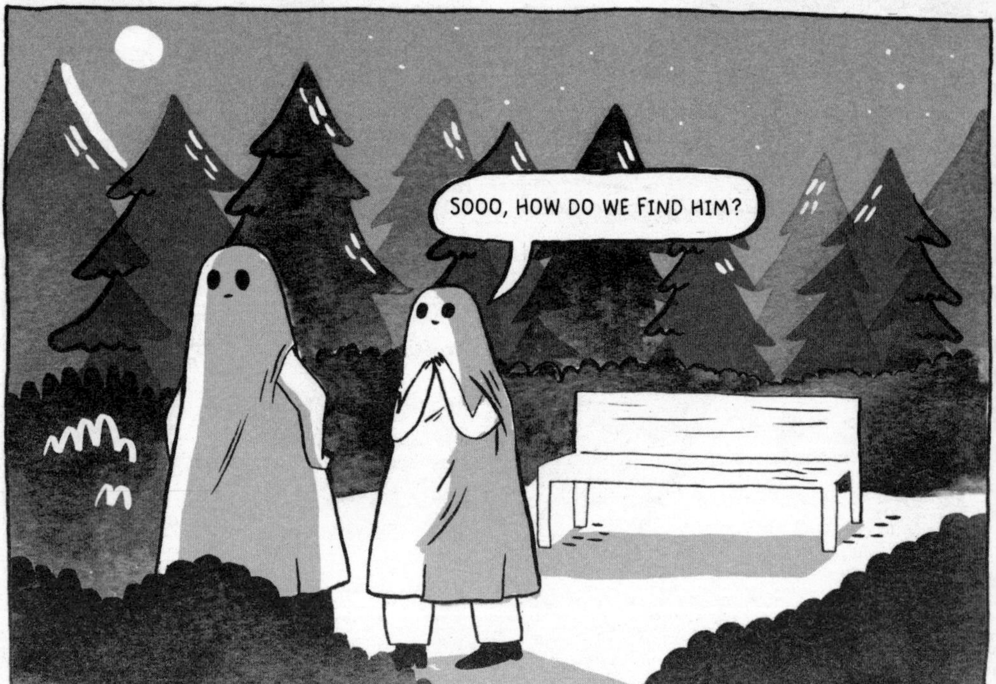
SOOO, HOW DO WE FIND HIM?

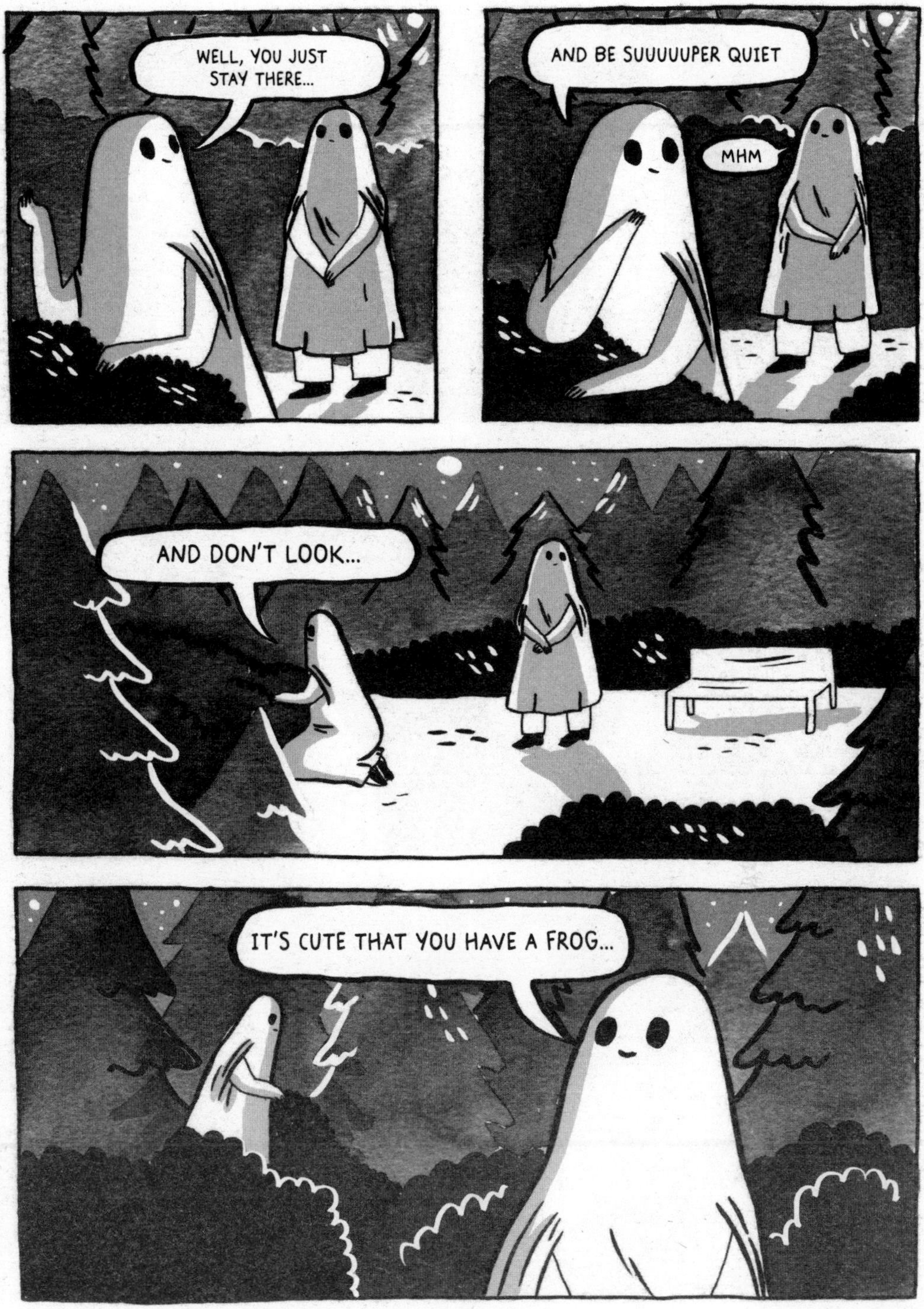
WELL, YOU JUST STAY THERE...
AND BE SUUUUUPER QUIET
MHM
AND DON'T LOOK...
IT'S CUTE THAT YOU HAVE A FROG...

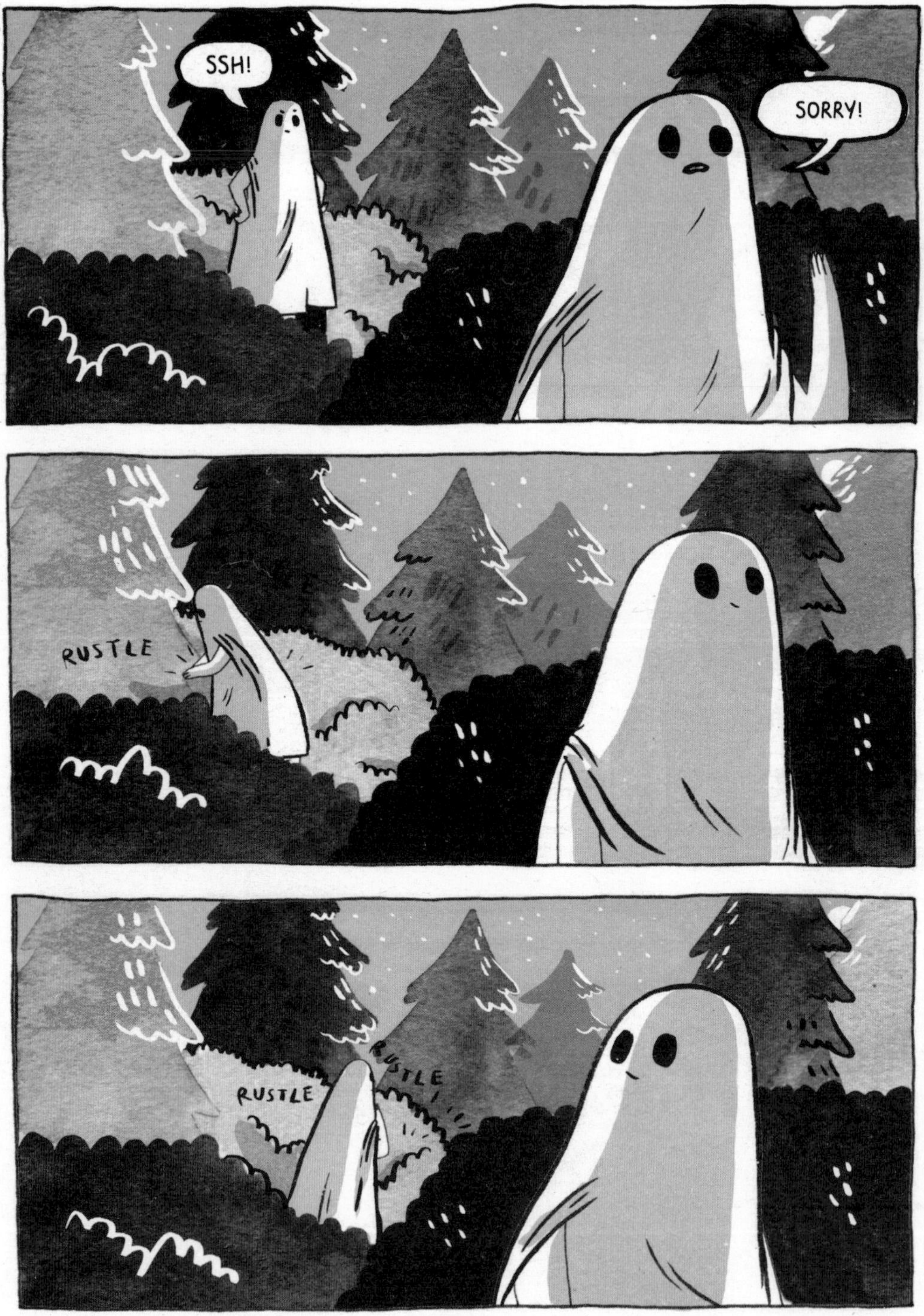
SSH!
SORRY!
RUSTLE
RUSTLE
RUSTLE

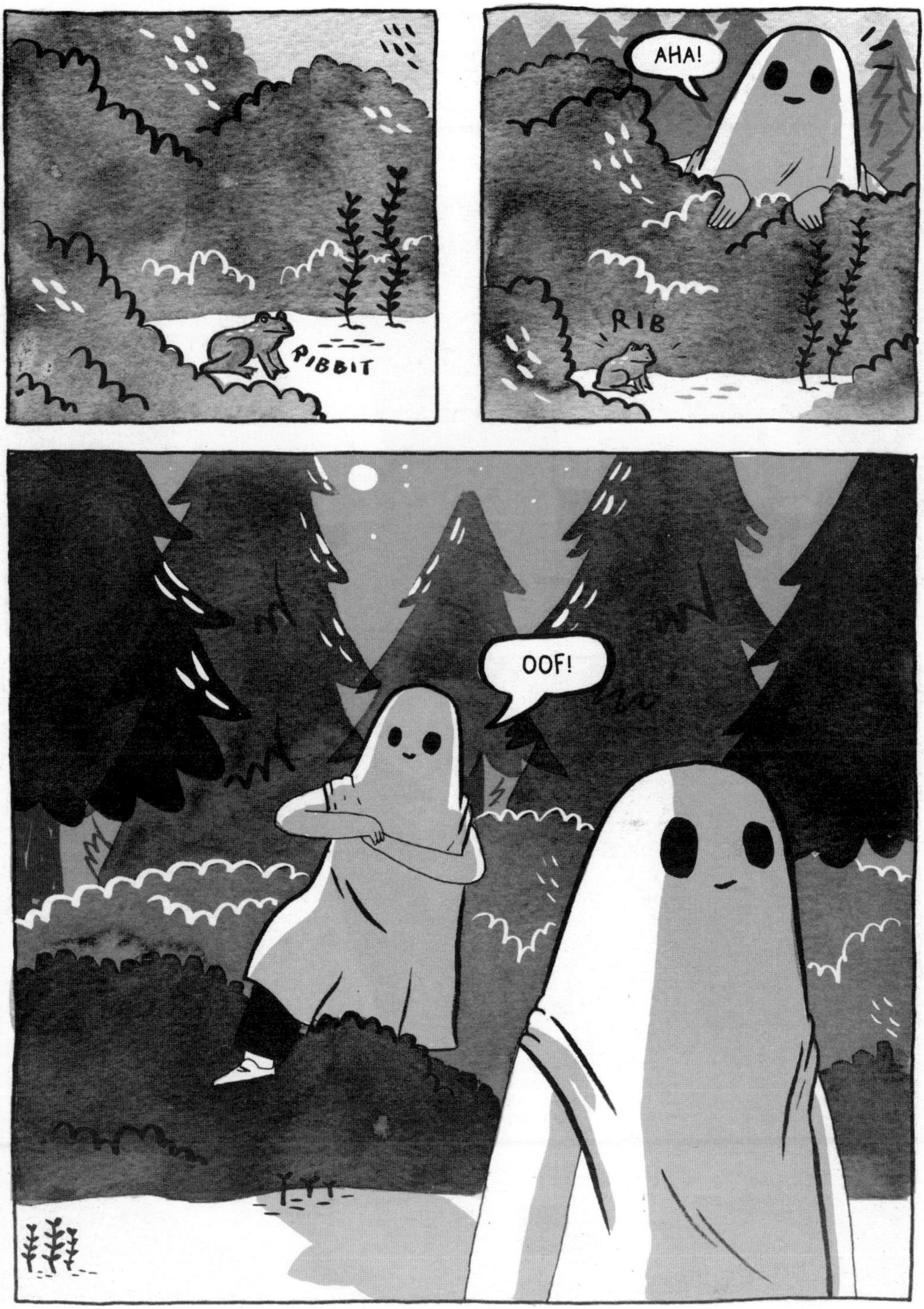
PIBBIT
AHA!
RIB
OOF!

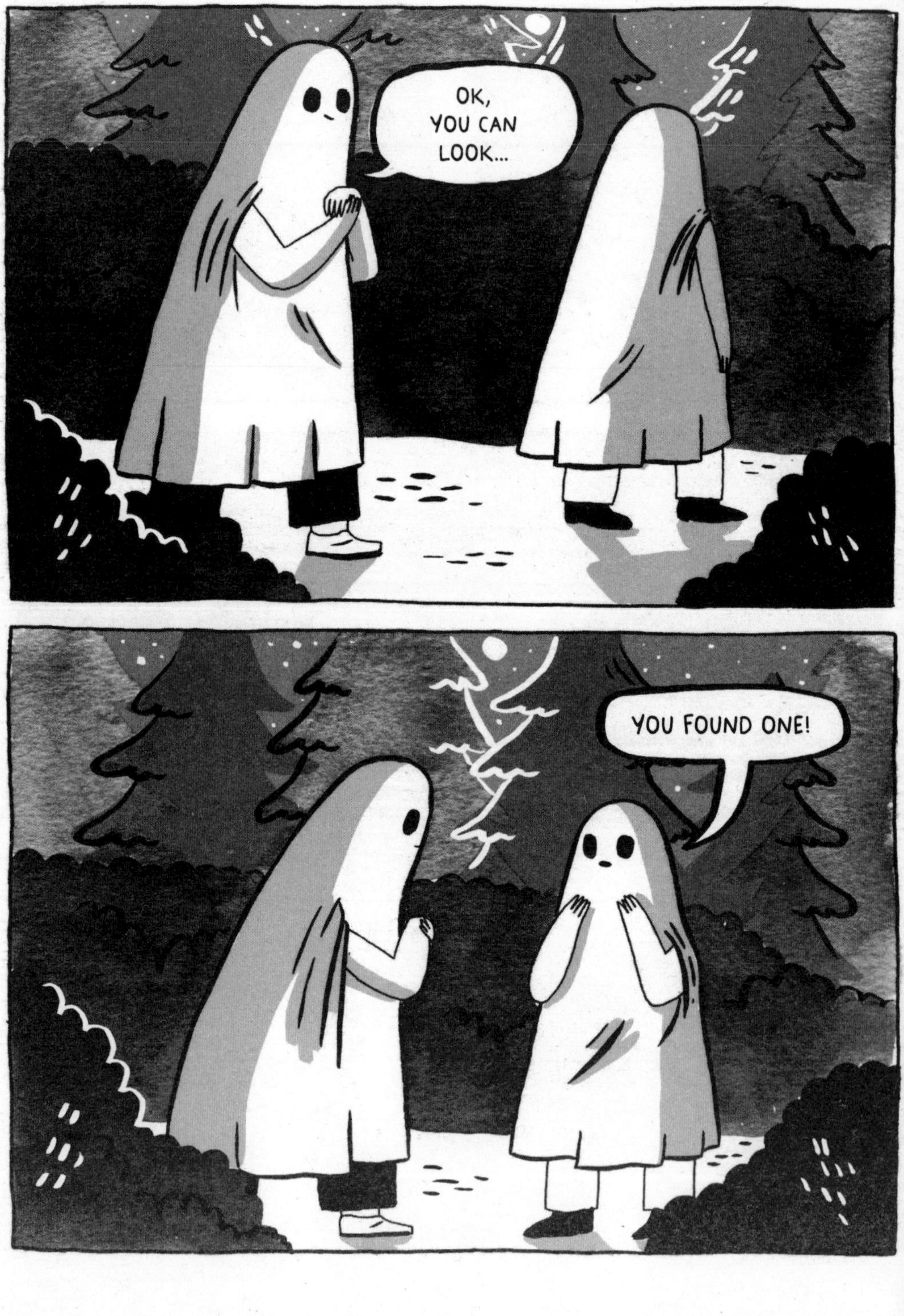
OK, YOU CAN LOOK...
YOU FOUND ONE!

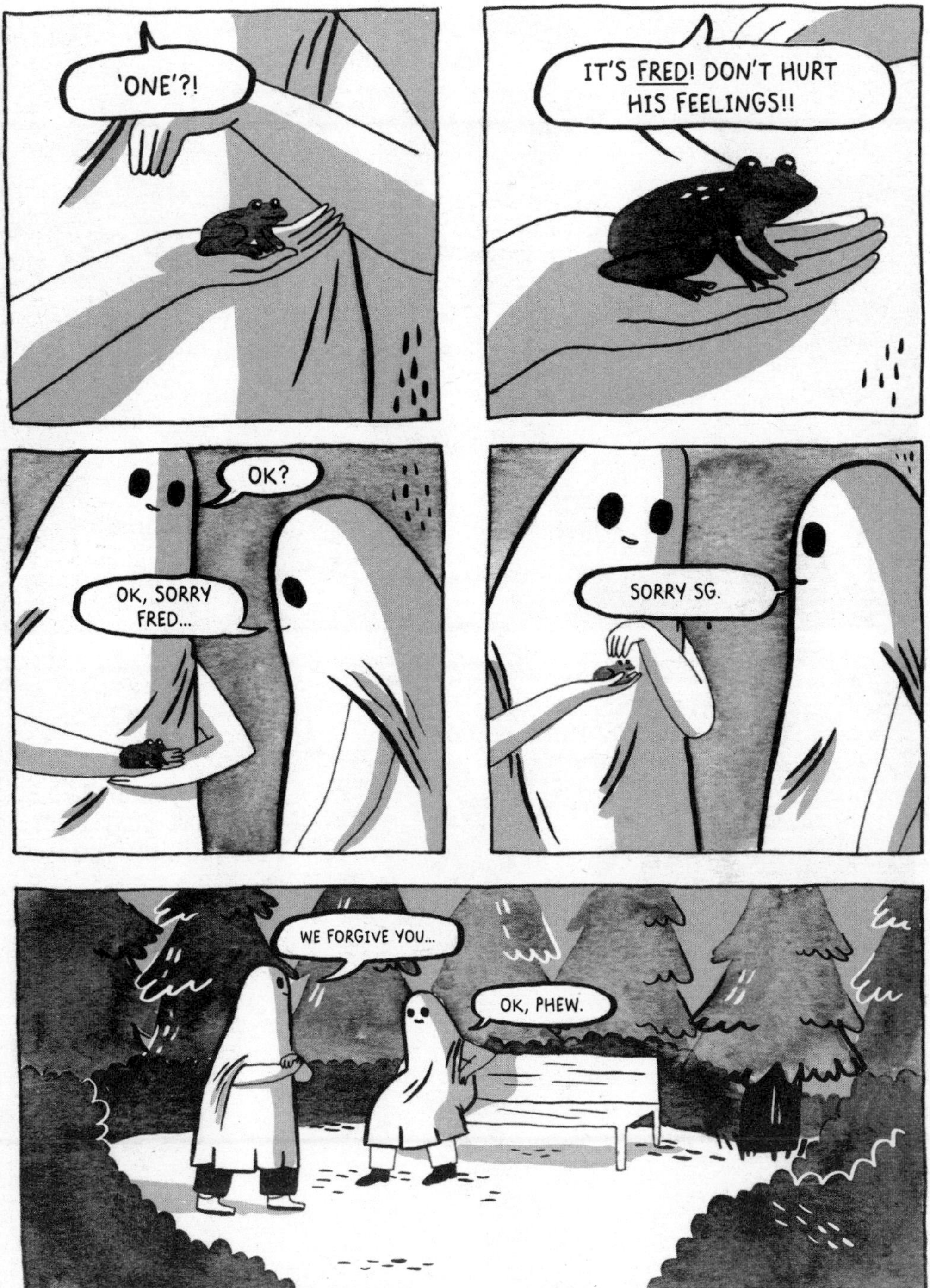
'ONE'?!
IT'S FRED! DON'T HURT HIS FEELINGS!!
OK?
OK, SORRY FRED...
SORRY SG.
WE FORGIVE YOU...
OK, PHEW.

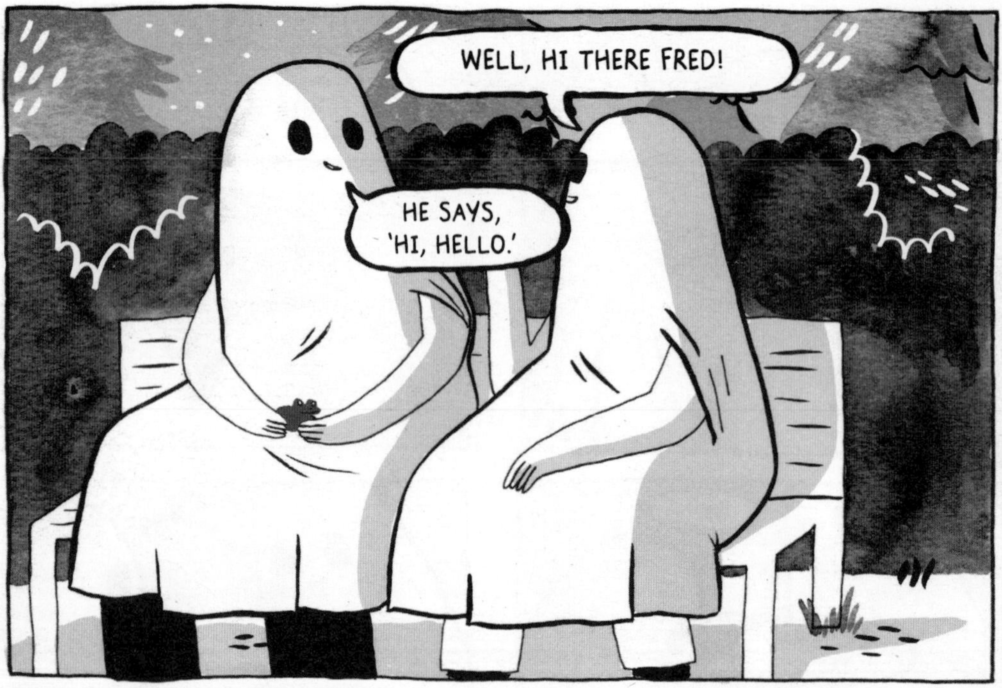
WELL, HI THERE FRED!
HE SAYS, 'HI, HELLO.'

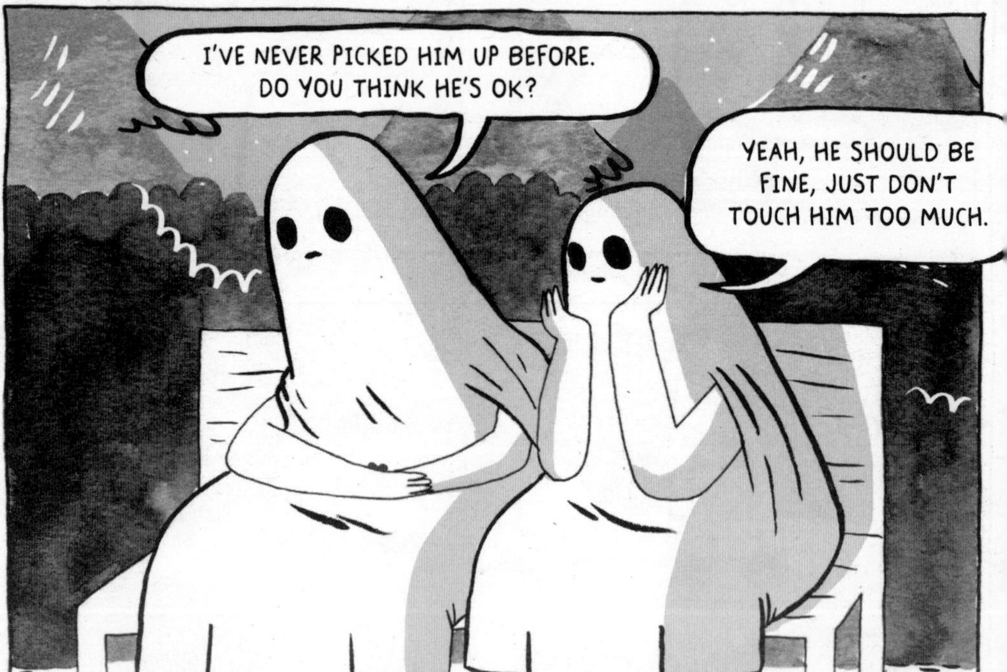
I'VE NEVER PICKED HIM UP BEFORE. DO YOU THINK HE'S OK?
YEAH, HE SHOULD BE FINE, JUST DON'T TOUCH HIM TOO MUCH.

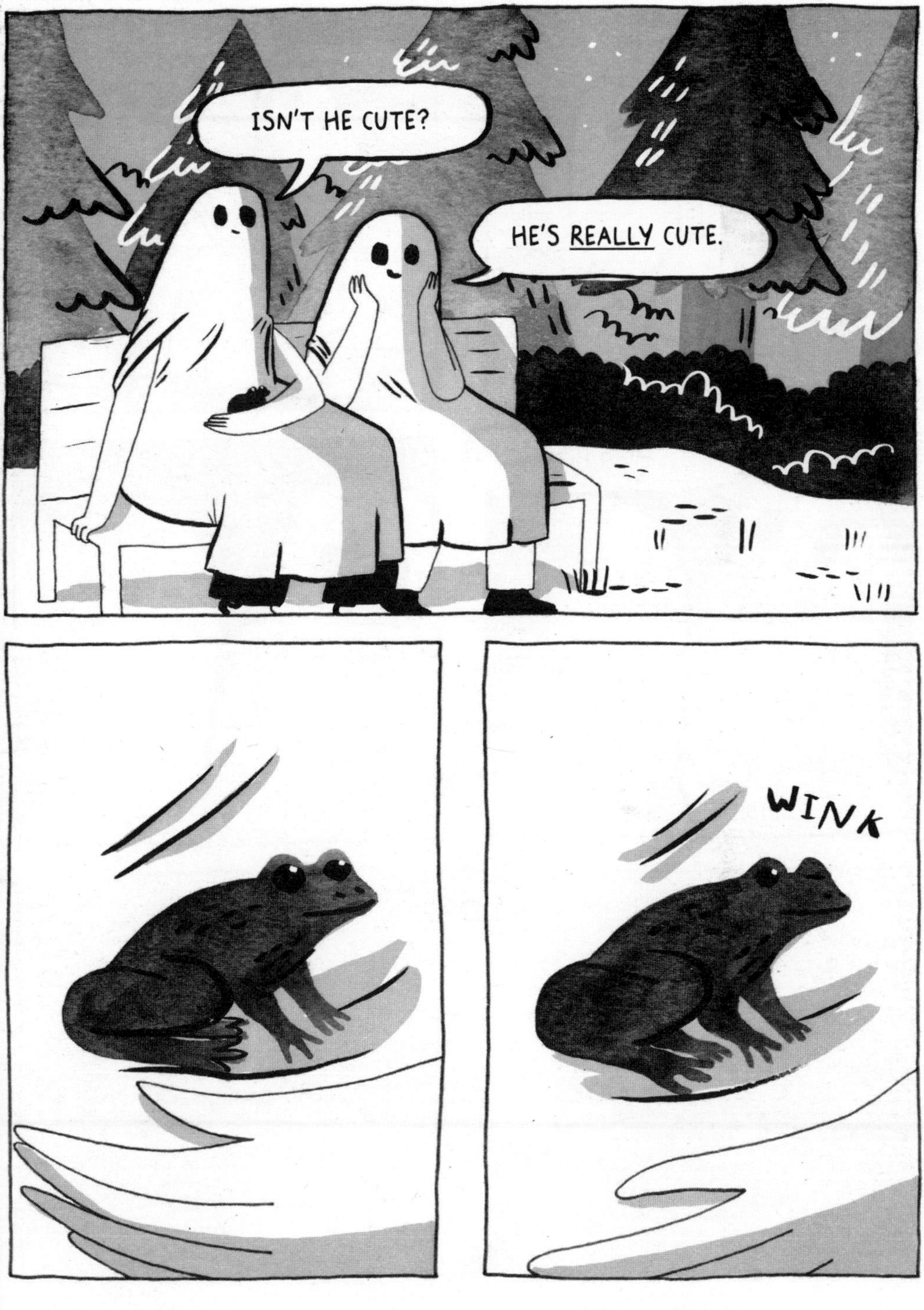
ISN'T HE CUTE?
HE'S REALLY CUTE.
WINK

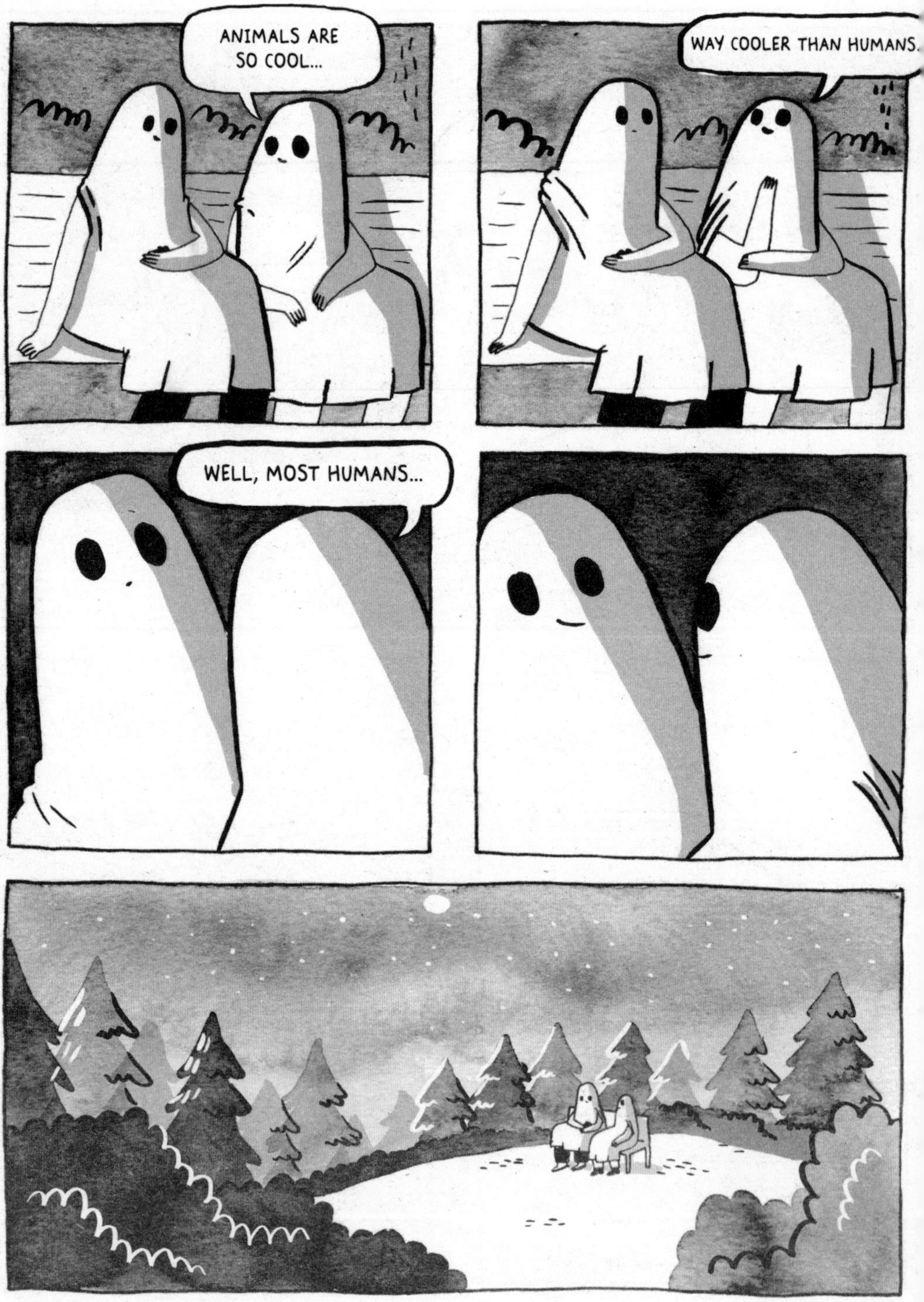
ANIMALS ARE SO COOL...
WAY COOLER THAN HUMANS.
WELL, MOST HUMANS...

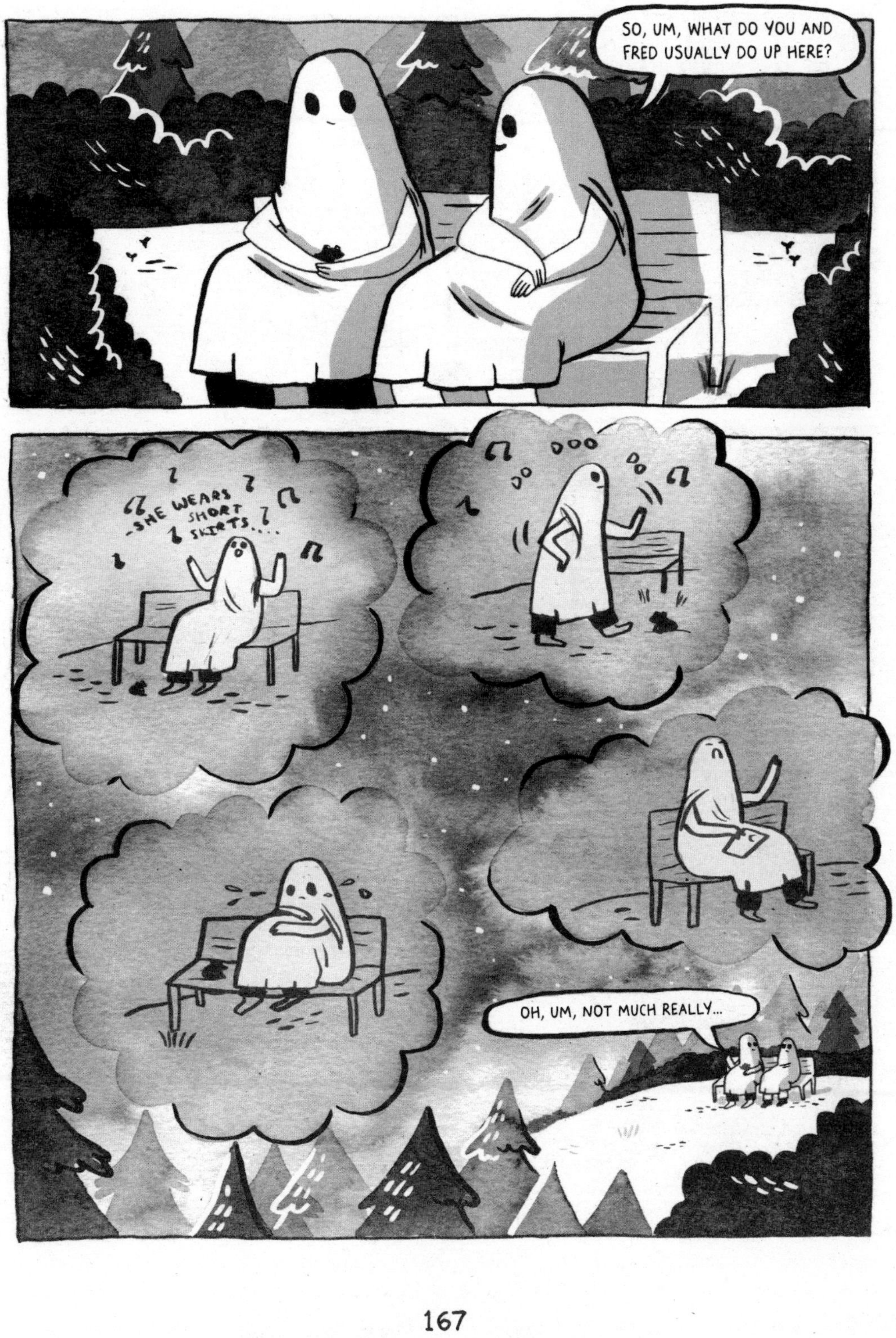
SO, UM, WHAT DO YOU AND FRED USUALLY DO UP HERE?
SHE WEARS SHORT SKIRTS...
DO DOO DO
OH, UM, NOT MUCH REALLY...

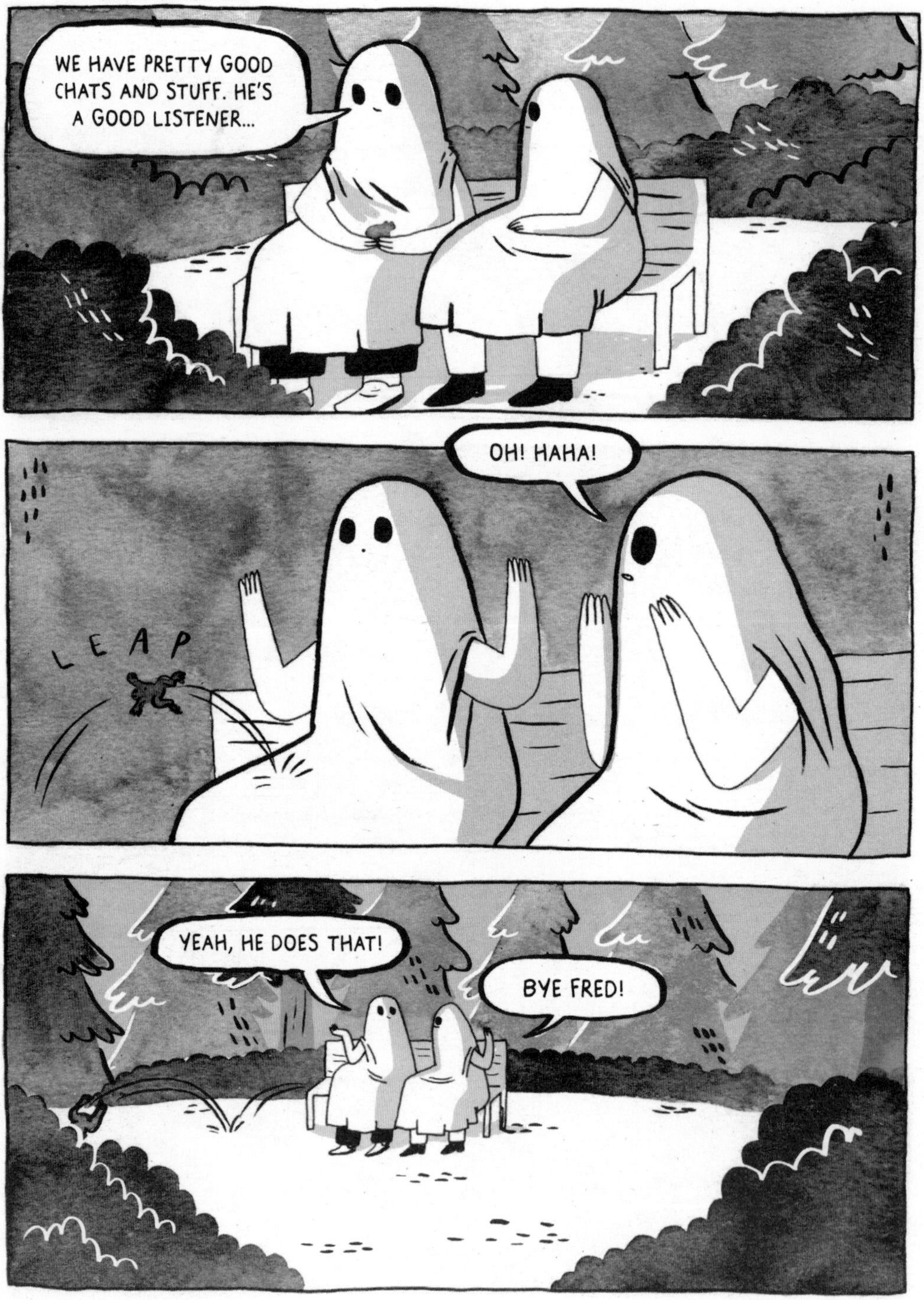
WE HAVE PRETTY GOOD CHATS AND STUFF. HE'S A GOOD LISTENER...
OH! HAHA!
LEAP
YEAH, HE DOES THAT!
BYE FRED!

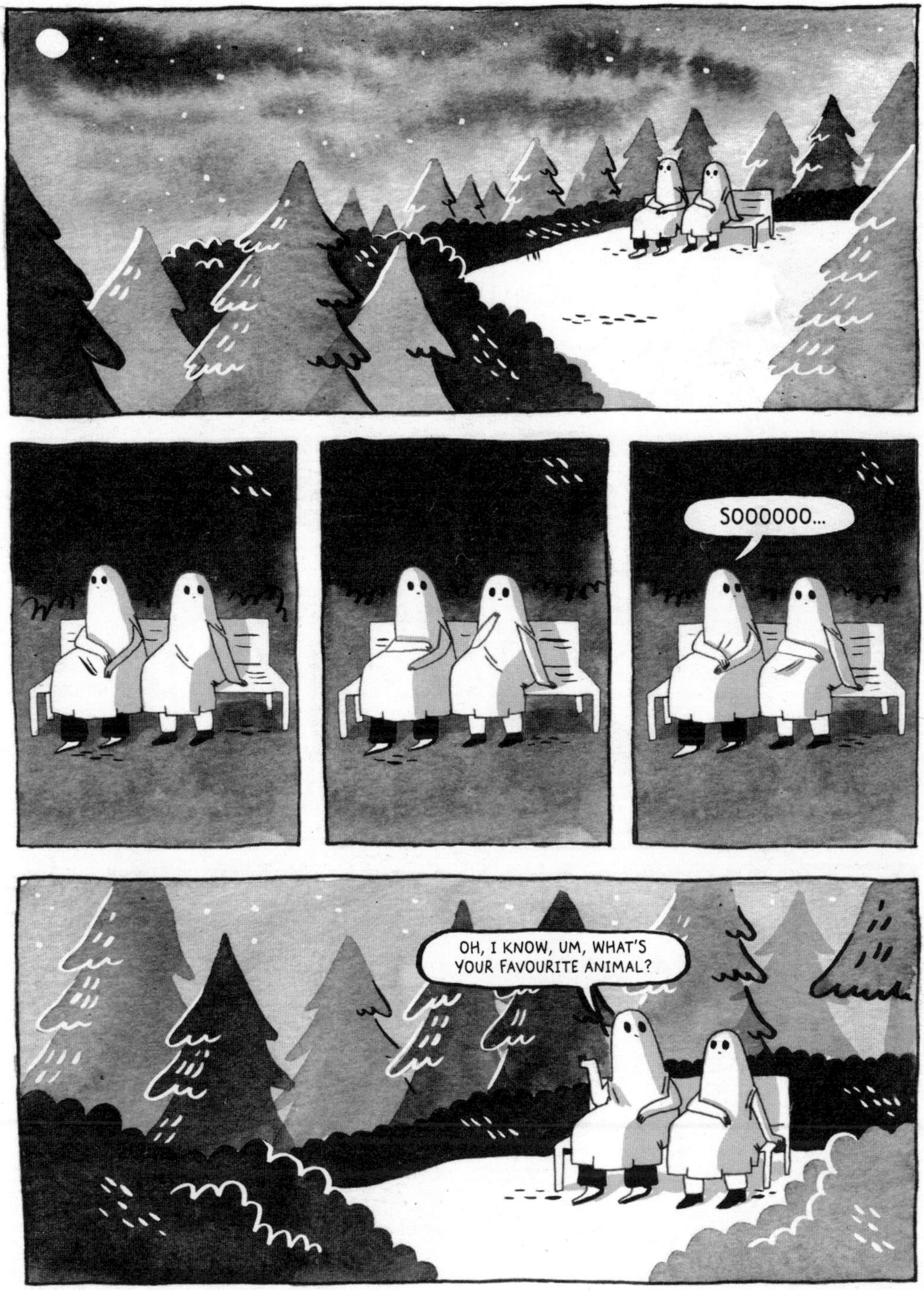
SOOOOOO...
OH, I KNOW, UM, WHAT'S YOUR FAVOURITE ANIMAL?

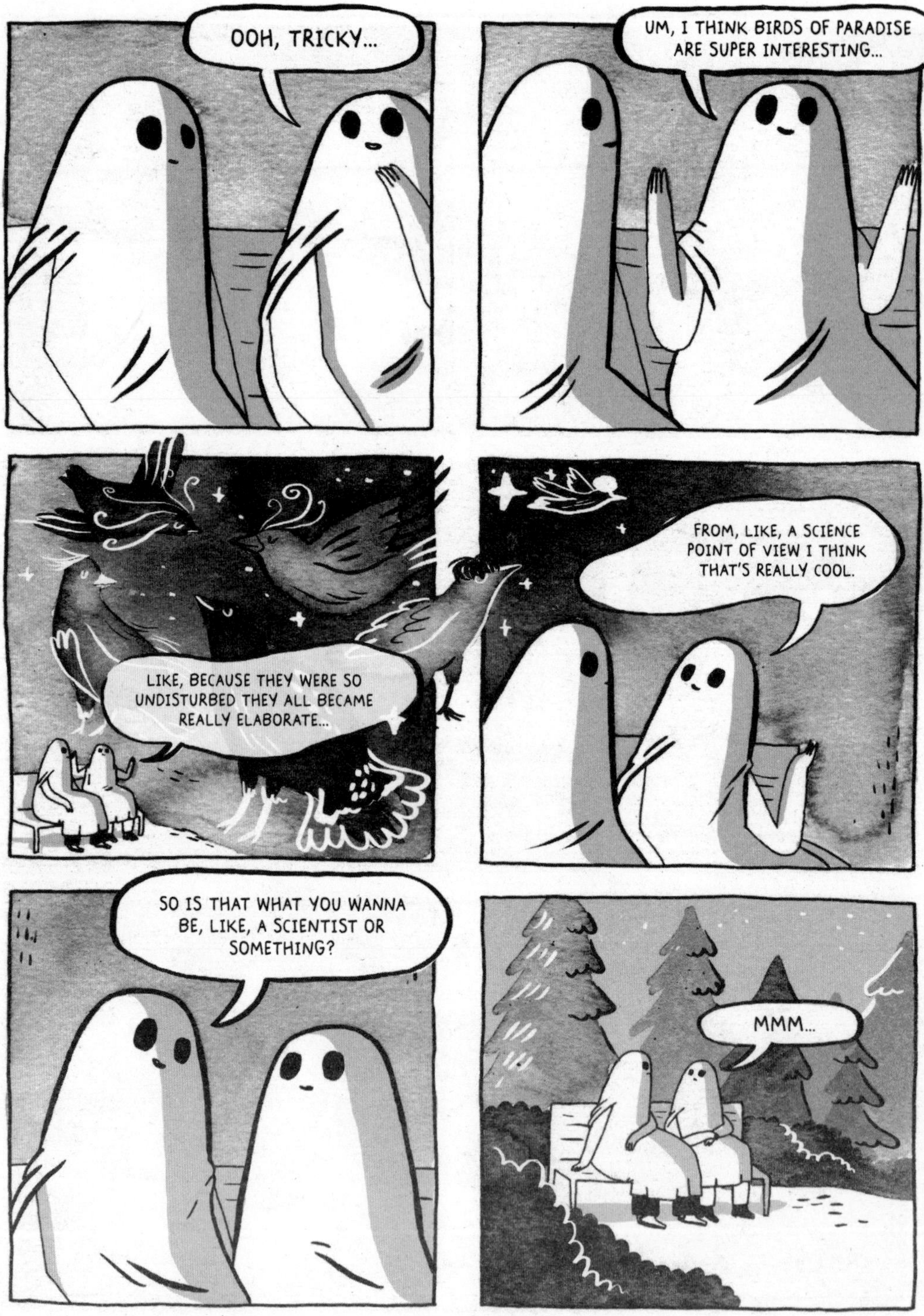
OOH, TRICKY...
UM, I THINK BIRDS OF PARADISE ARE SUPER INTERESTING...
LIKE, BECAUSE THEY WERE SO UNDISTURBED THEY ALL BECAME REALLY ELABORATE...
FROM, LIKE, A SCIENCE POINT OF VIEW I THINK THAT'S REALLY COOL.
SO IS THAT WHAT YOU WANNA BE, LIKE, A SCIENTIST OR SOMETHING?
MMM...

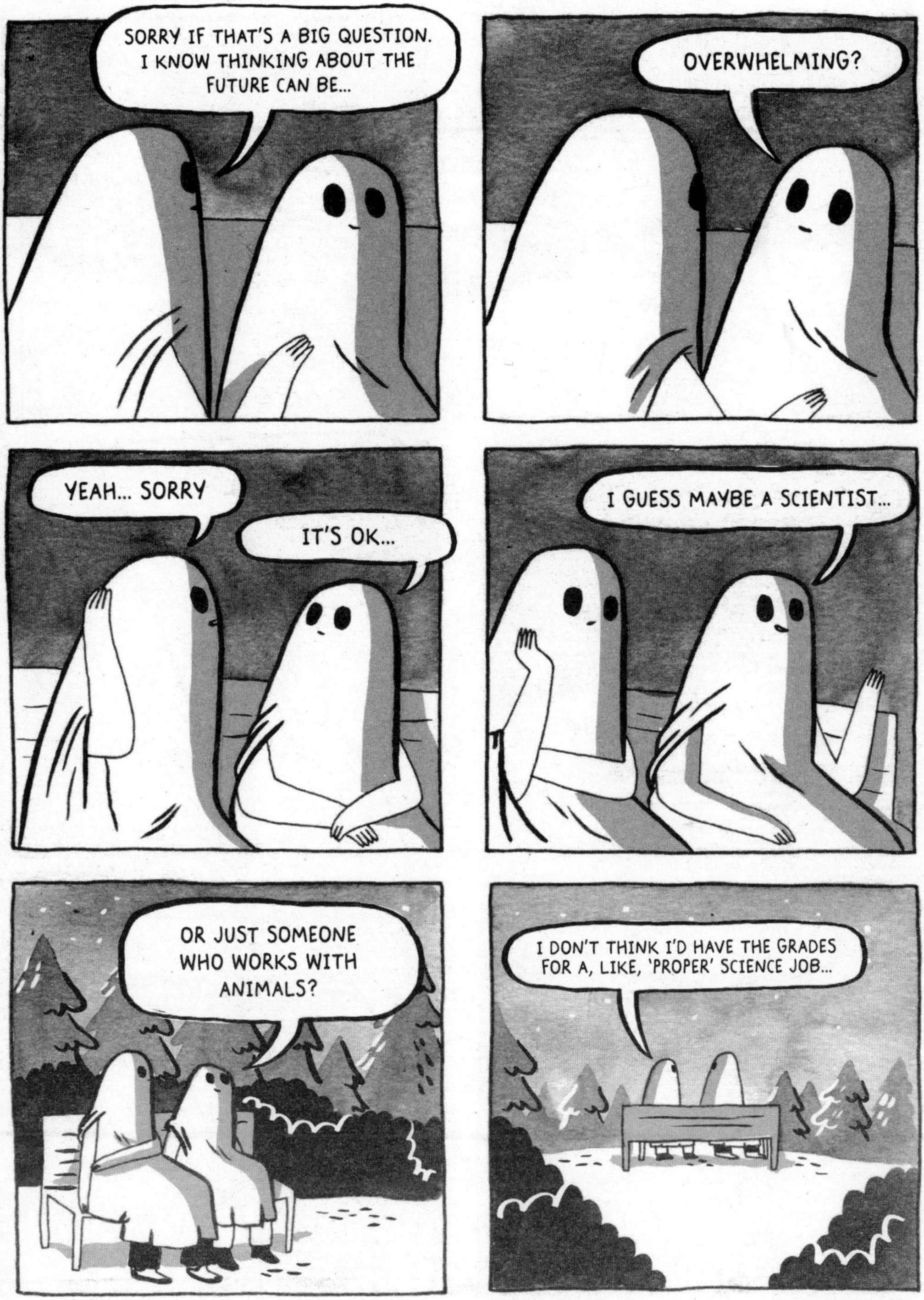
SORRY IF THAT'S A BIG QUESTION. I KNOW THINKING ABOUT THE FUTURE CAN BE...
OVERWHELMING?
YEAH... SORRY
IT'S OK...
I GUESS MAYBE A SCIENTIST...
OR JUST SOMEONE WHO WORKS WITH ANIMALS?
I DON'T THINK I'D HAVE THE GRADES FOR A, LIKE, 'PROPER' SCIENCE JOB...

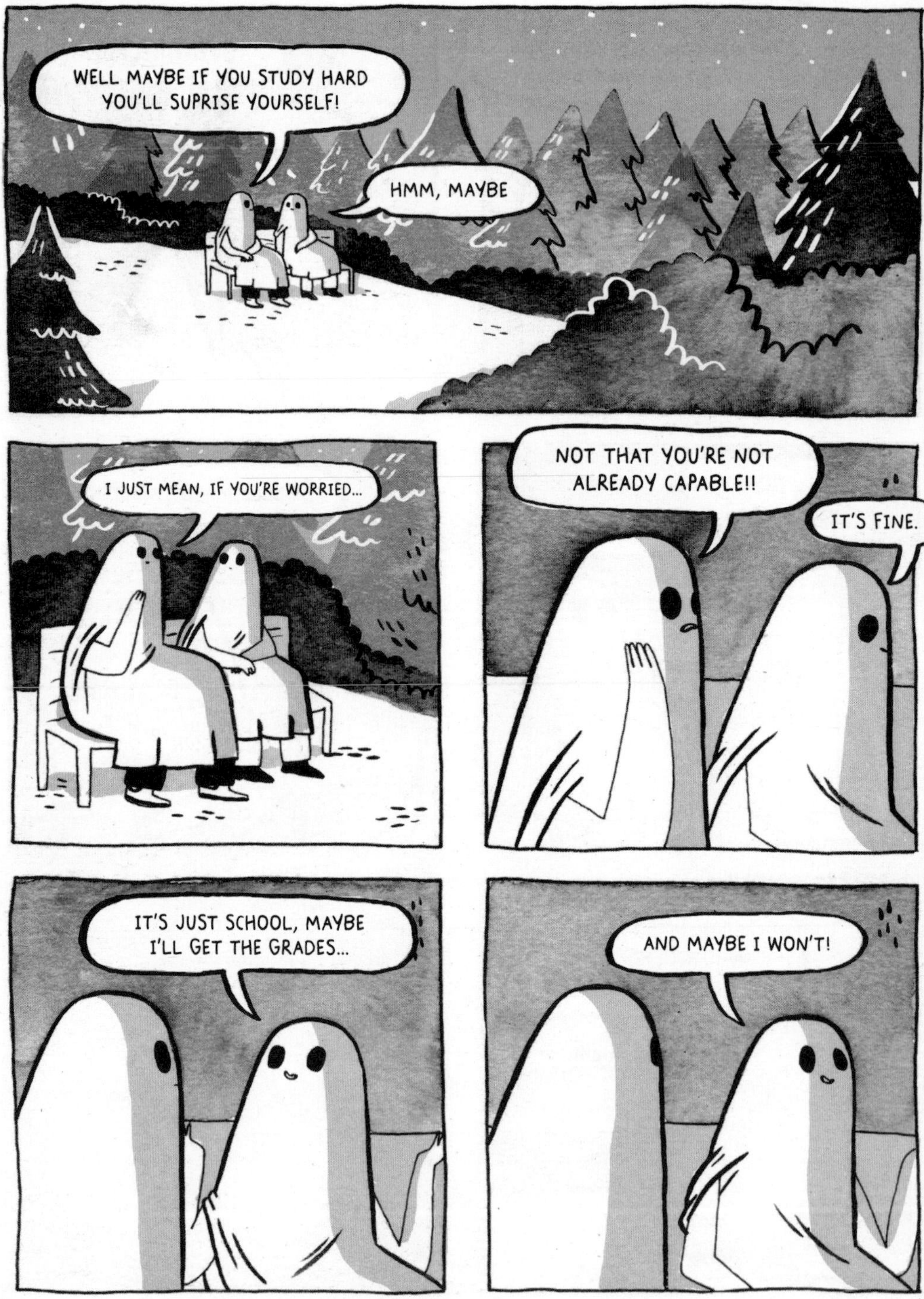
WELL MAYBE IF YOU STUDY HARD YOU'LL SUPRISE YOURSELF!
HMM, MAYBE
I JUST MEAN, IF YOU'RE WORRIED...
NOT THAT YOU'RE NOT ALREADY CAPABLE!!
IT'S FINE.
IT'S JUST SCHOOL, MAYBE I'LL GET THE GRADES...
AND MAYBE I WON'T!

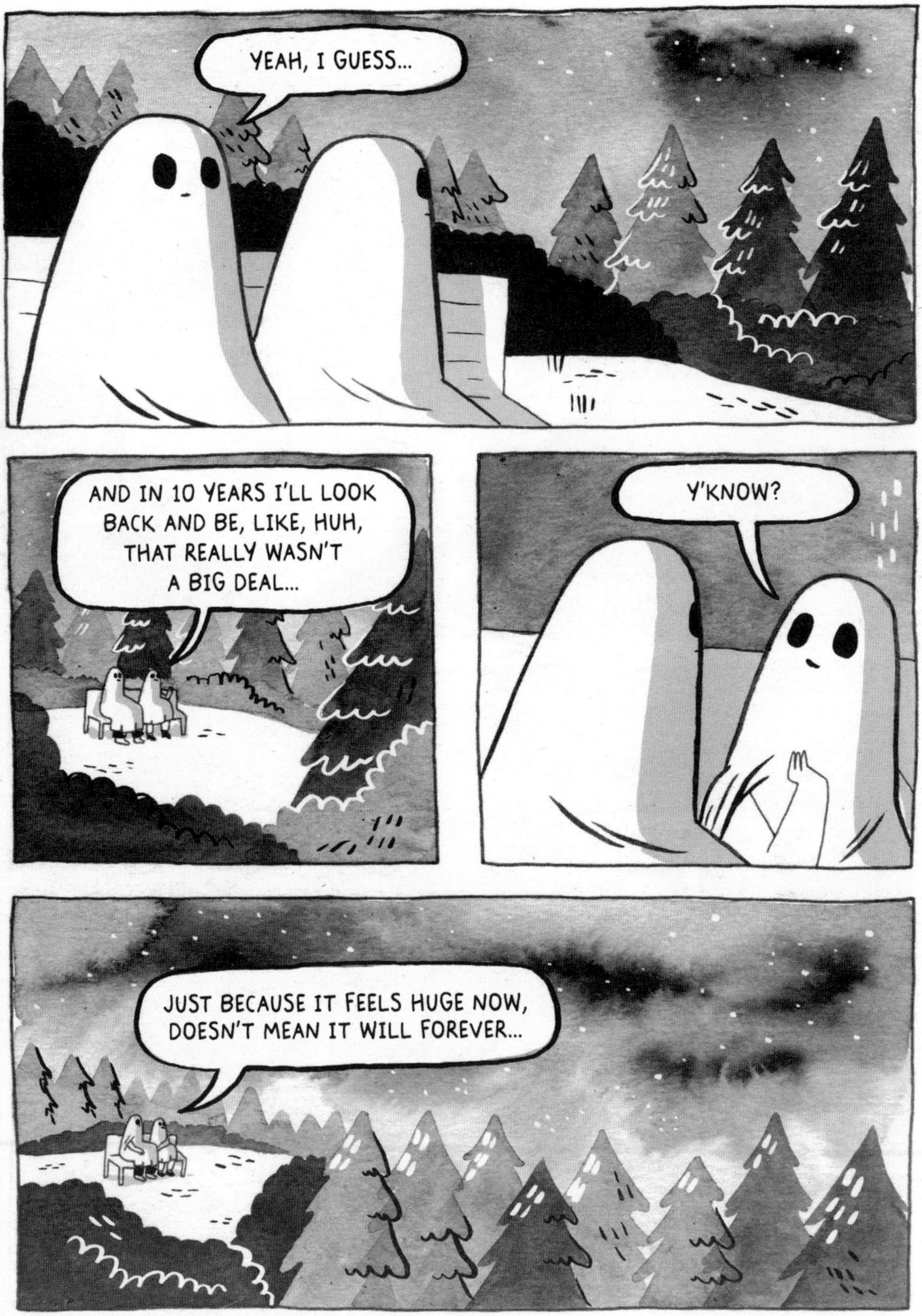
YEAH, I GUESS...
AND IN 10 YEARS I'LL LOOK BACK AND BE, LIKE, HUH, THAT REALLY WASN'T A BIG DEAL...
Y'KNOW?
JUST BECAUSE IT FEELS HUGE NOW, DOESN'T MEAN IT WILL FOREVER...

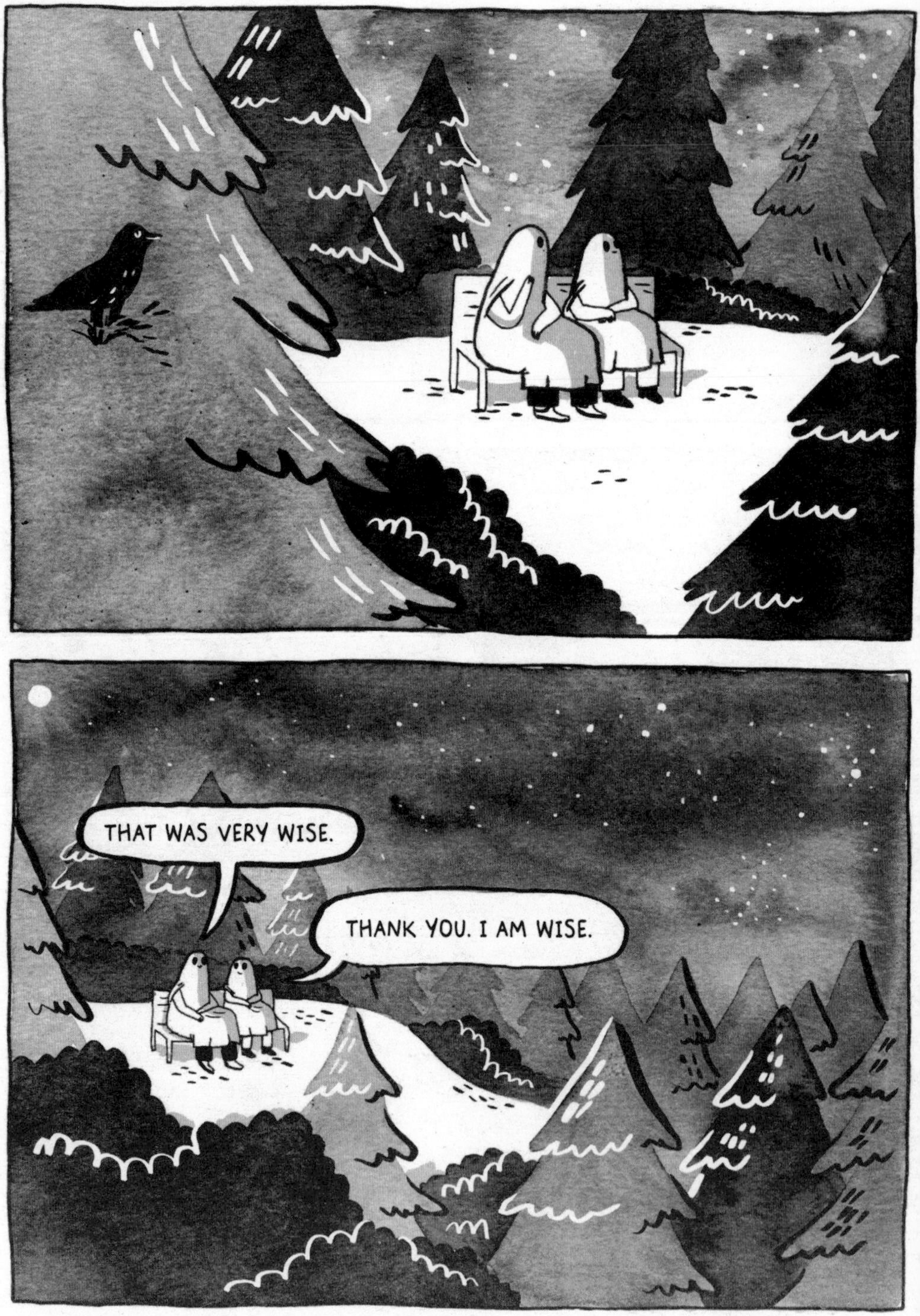
THAT WAS VERY WISE.
THANK YOU. I AM WISE.

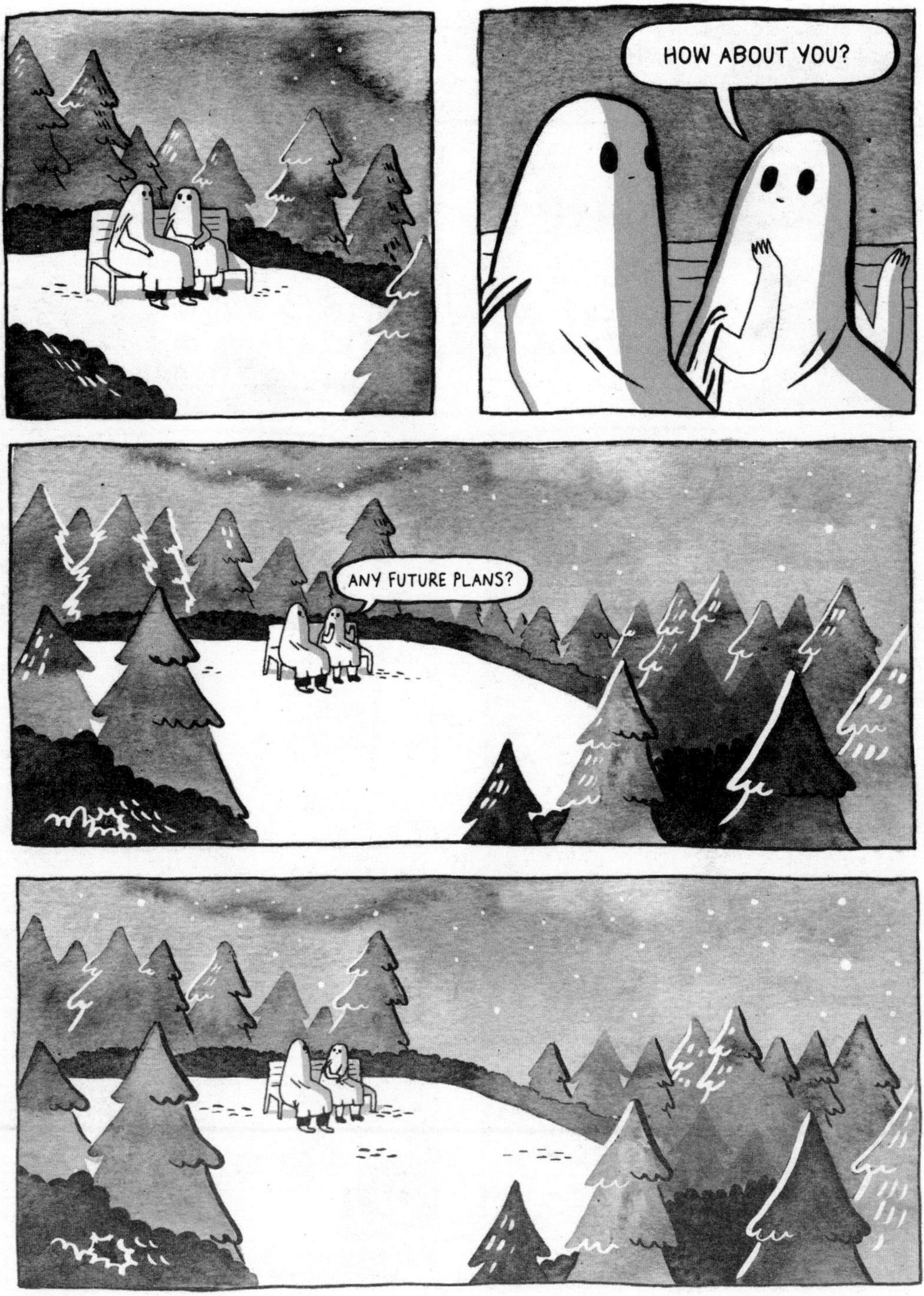
HOW ABOUT YOU?
ANY FUTURE PLANS?

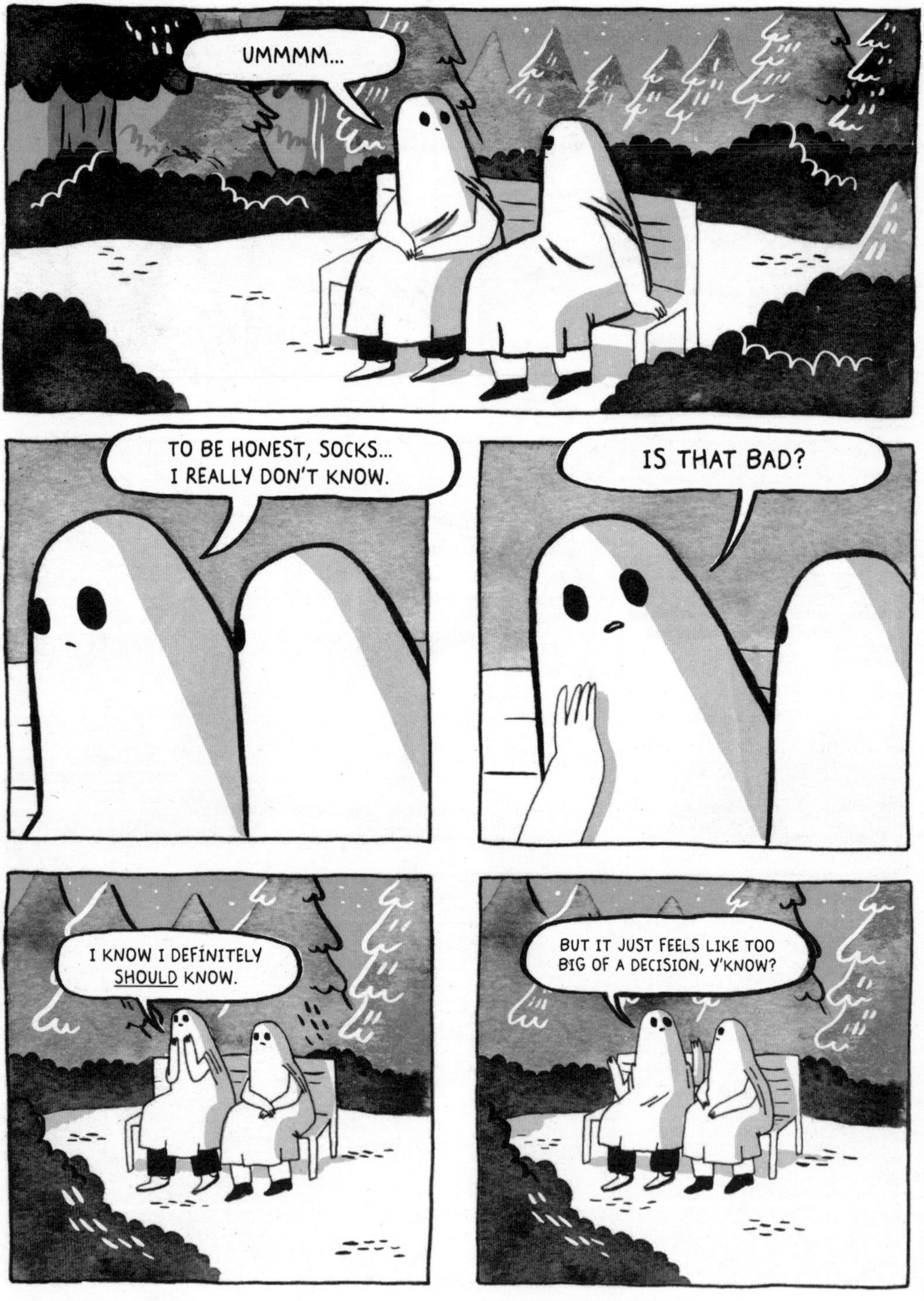
UMMMM...
TO BE HONEST, SOCKS... I REALLY DON'T KNOW.
IS THAT BAD?
I KNOW I DEFINITELY SHOULD KNOW.
BUT IT JUST FEELS LIKE TOO BIG OF A DECISION, Y'KNOW?

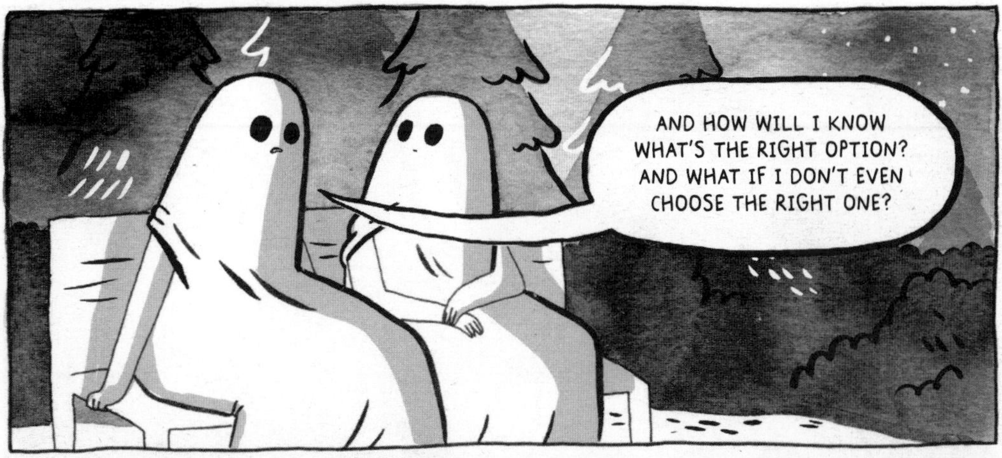
AND HOW WILL I KNOW WHAT'S THE RIGHT OPTION? AND WHAT IF I DON'T EVEN CHOOSE THE RIGHT ONE?

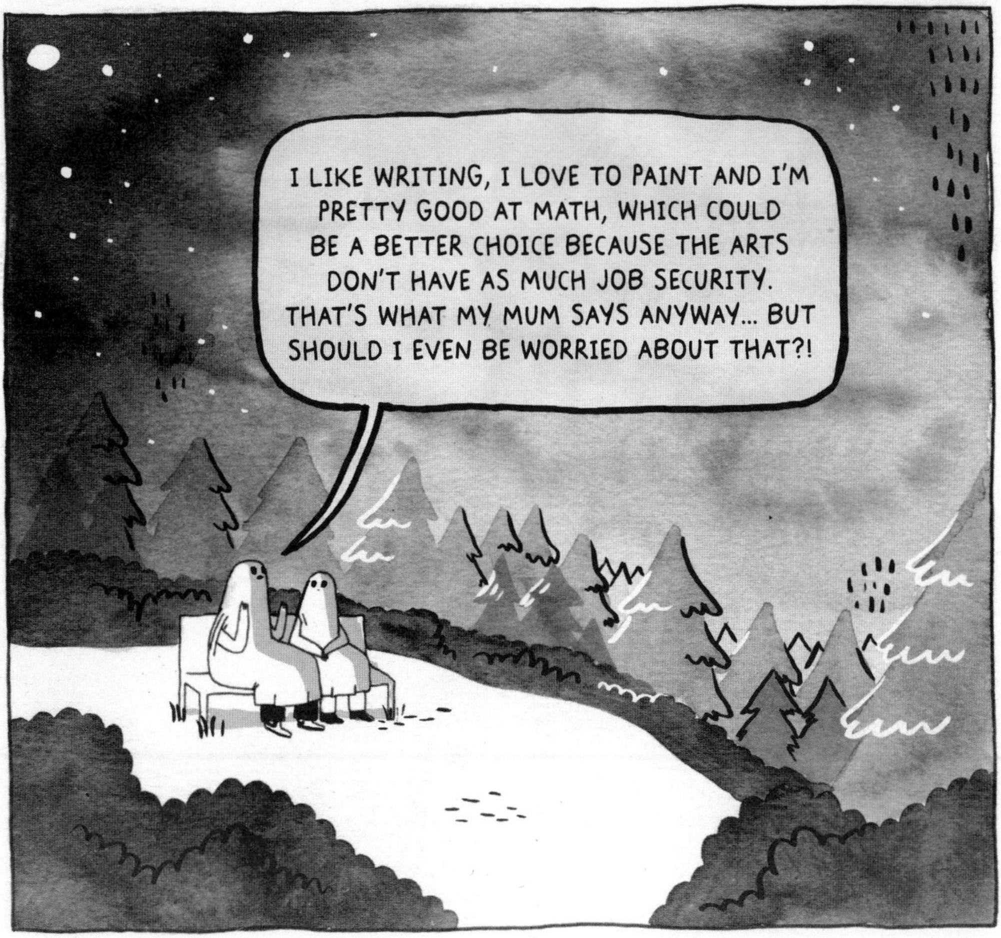
I LIKE WRITING, I LOVE TO PAINT AND I'M PRETTY GOOD AT MATH, WHICH COULD BE A BETTER CHOICE BECAUSE THE ARTS DON'T HAVE AS MUCH JOB SECURITY. THAT'S WHAT MY MUM SAYS ANYWAY... BUT SHOULD I EVEN BE WORRIED ABOUT THAT?!

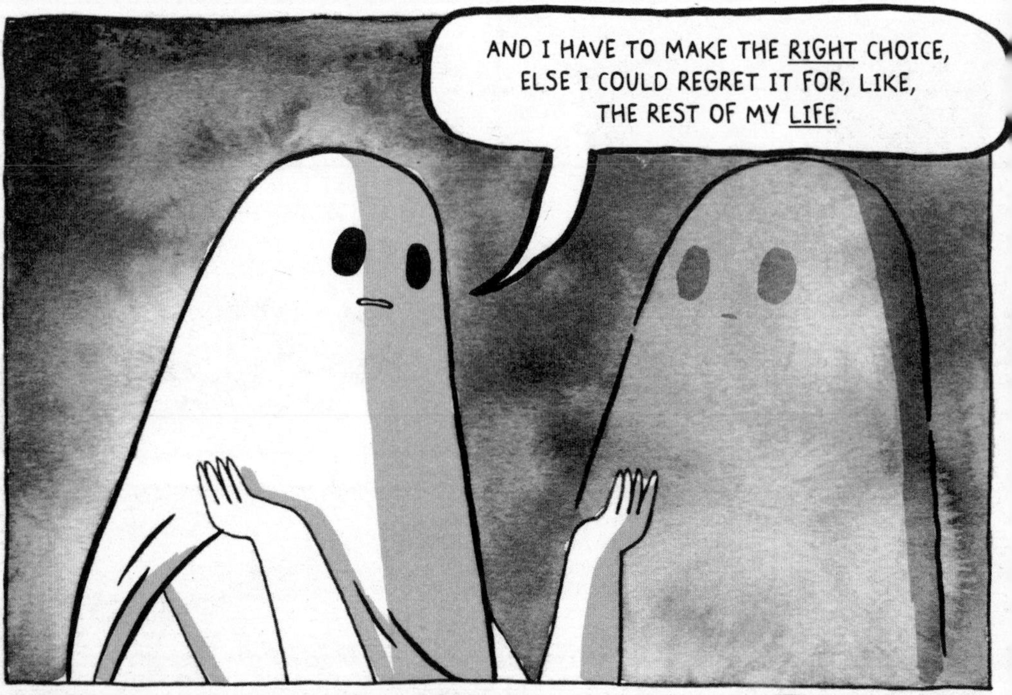
AND I HAVE TO MAKE THE RIGHT CHOICE, ELSE I COULD REGRET IT FOR, LIKE, THE REST OF MY LIFE.

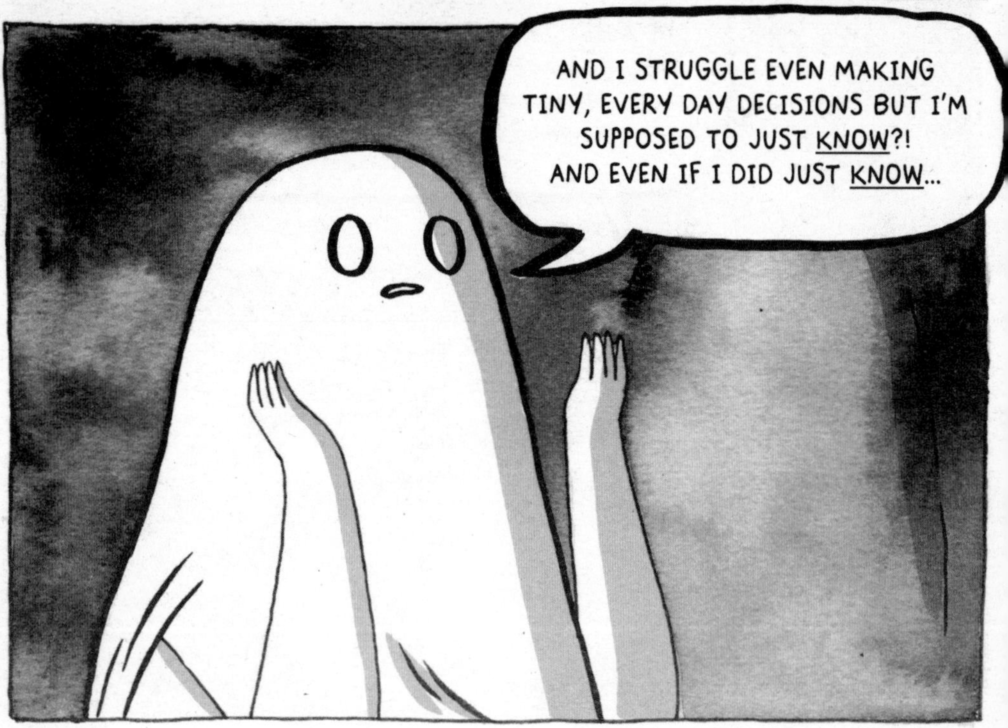
AND I STRUGGLE EVEN MAKING TINY, EVERY DAY DECISIONS BUT I'M SUPPOSED TO JUST KNOW?! AND EVEN IF I DID JUST KNOW...

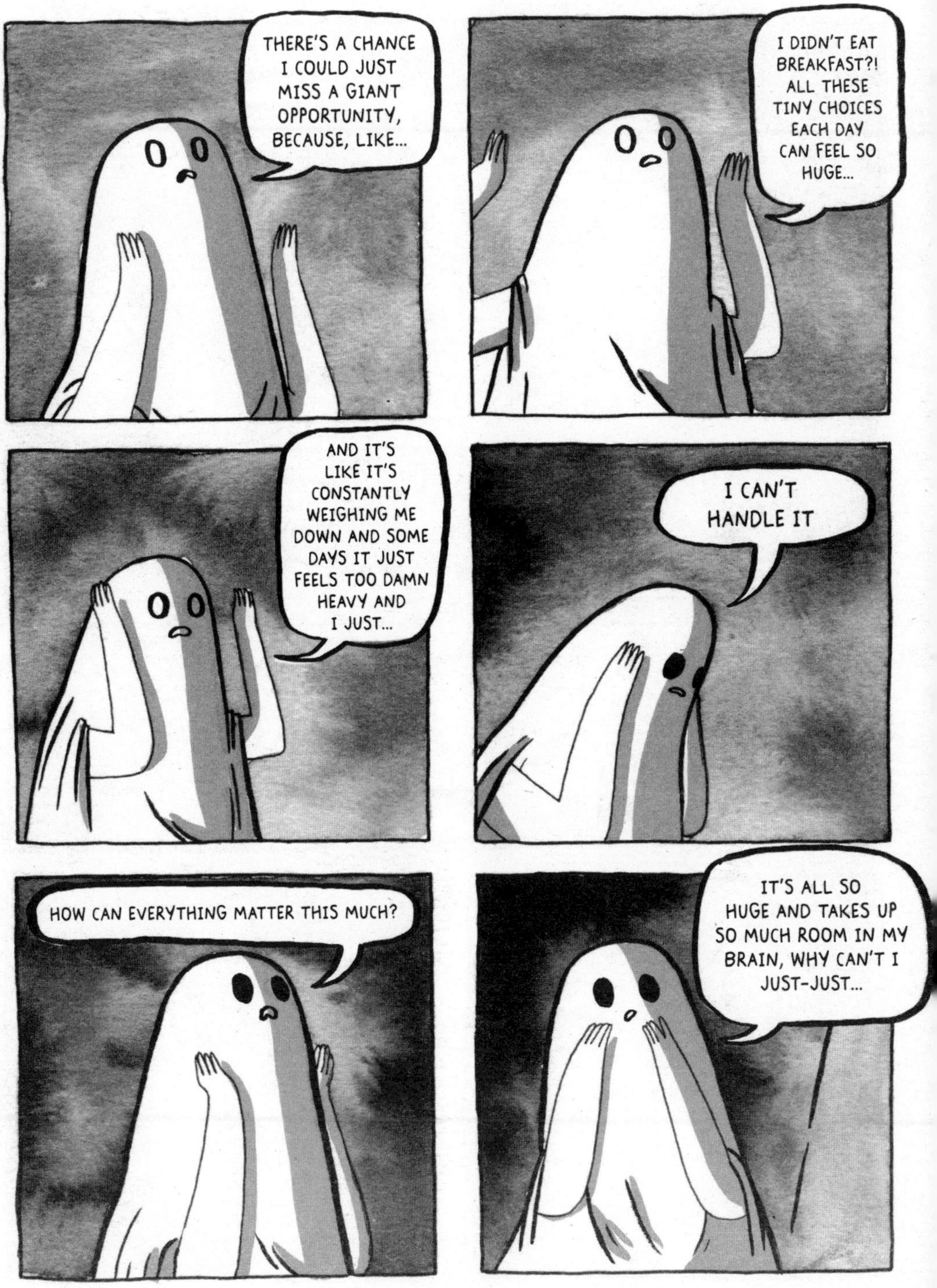
THERE'S A CHANCE I COULD JUST MISS A GIANT OPPORTUNITY, BECAUSE, LIKE...
I DIDN'T EAT BREAKFAST?! ALL THESE TINY CHOICES EACH DAY CAN FEEL SO HUGE...
AND IT'S LIKE IT'S CONSTANTLY WEIGHING ME DOWN AND SOME DAYS IT JUST FEELS TOO DAMN HEAVY AND I JUST...
I CAN'T HANDLE IT
HOW CAN EVERYTHING MATTER THIS MUCH?
IT'S ALL SO HUGE AND TAKES UP SO MUCH ROOM IN MY BRAIN, WHY CAN'T I JUST-JUST...

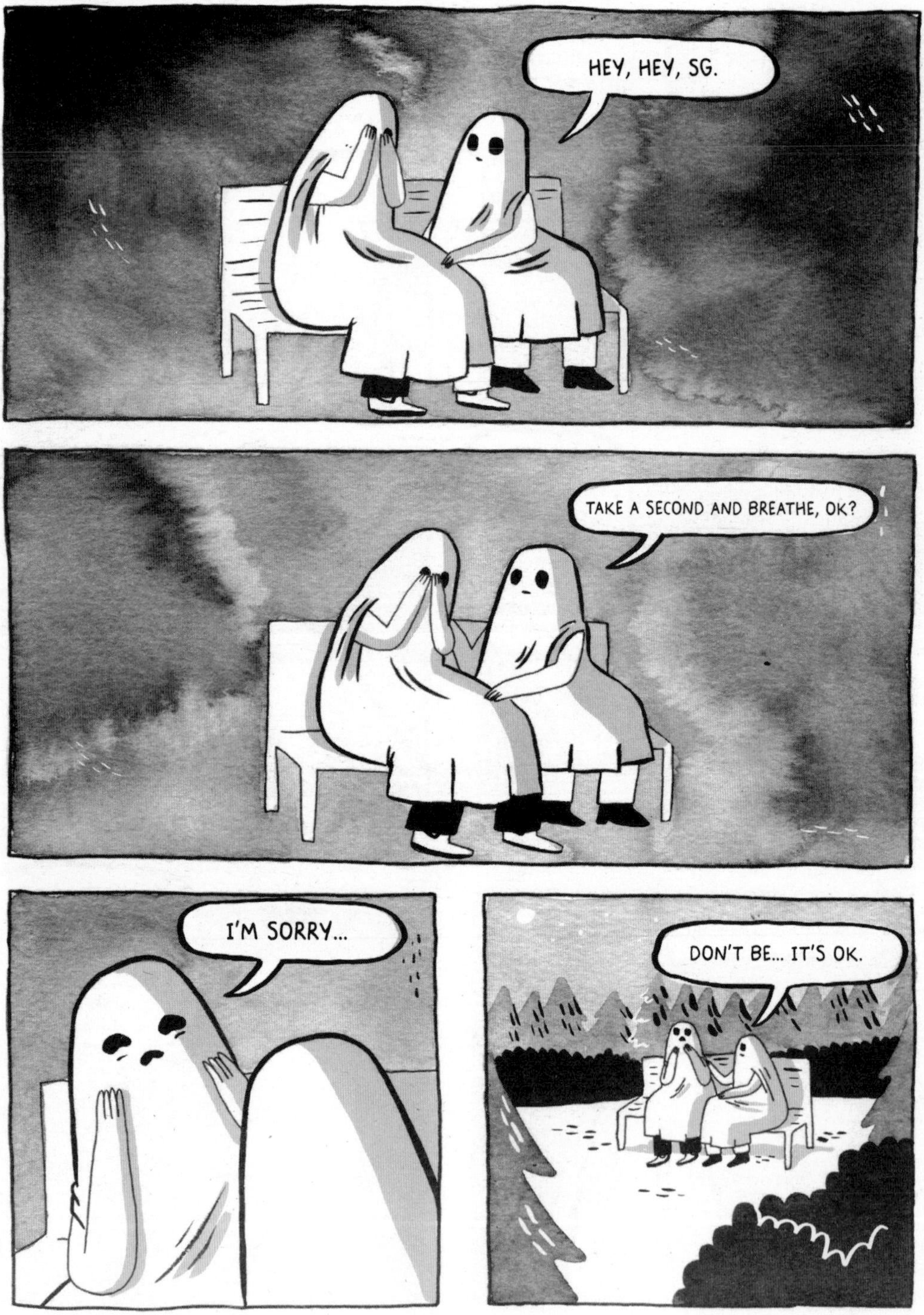
HEY, HEY, SG.
TAKE A SECOND AND BREATHE, OK?
I'M SORRY...
DON'T BE... IT'S OK.

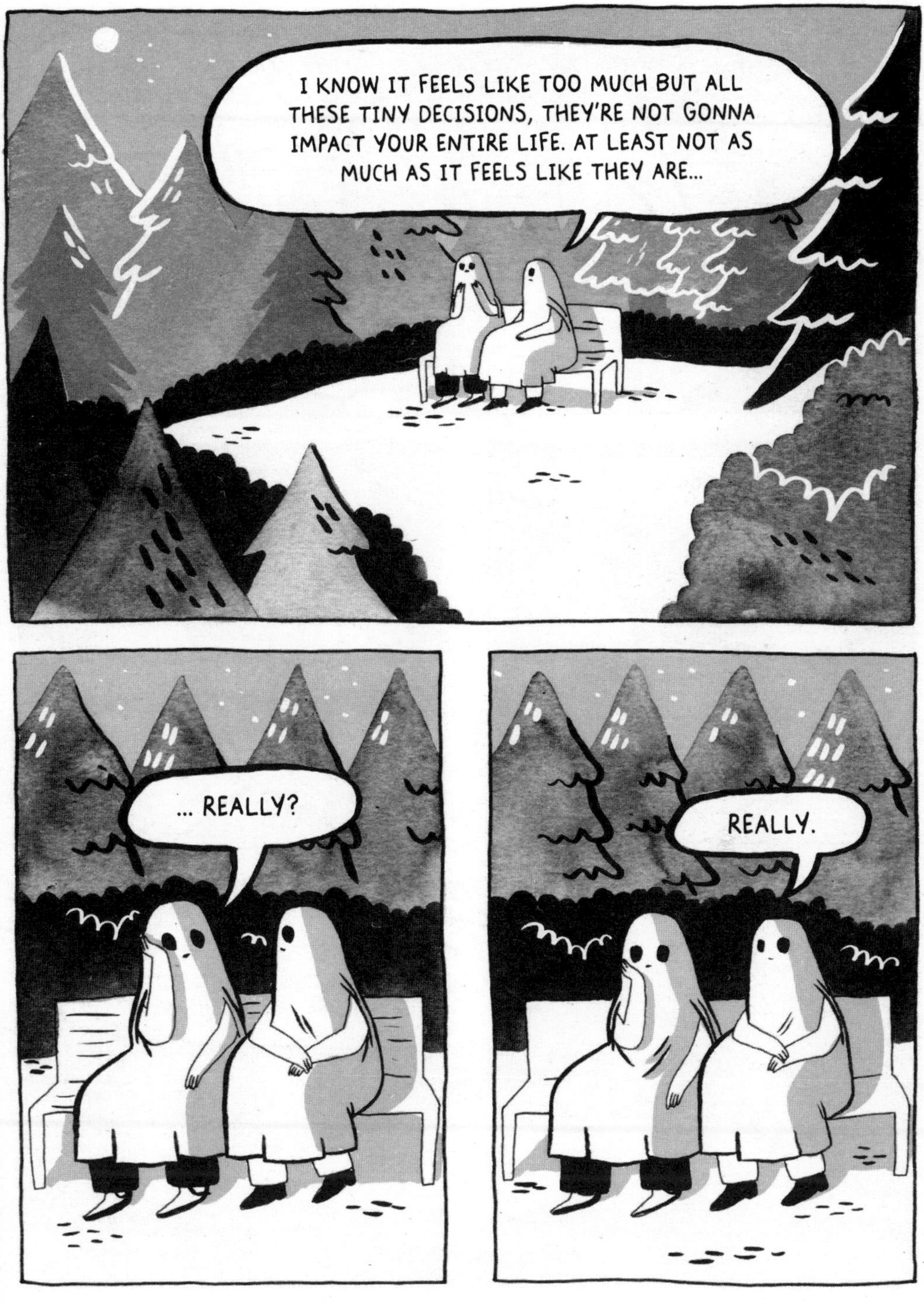
I KNOW IT FEELS LIKE TOO MUCH BUT ALL THESE TINY DECISIONS, THEY'RE NOT GONNA IMPACT YOUR ENTIRE LIFE. AT LEAST NOT AS MUCH AS IT FEELS LIKE THEY ARE...
... REALLY?
REALLY.

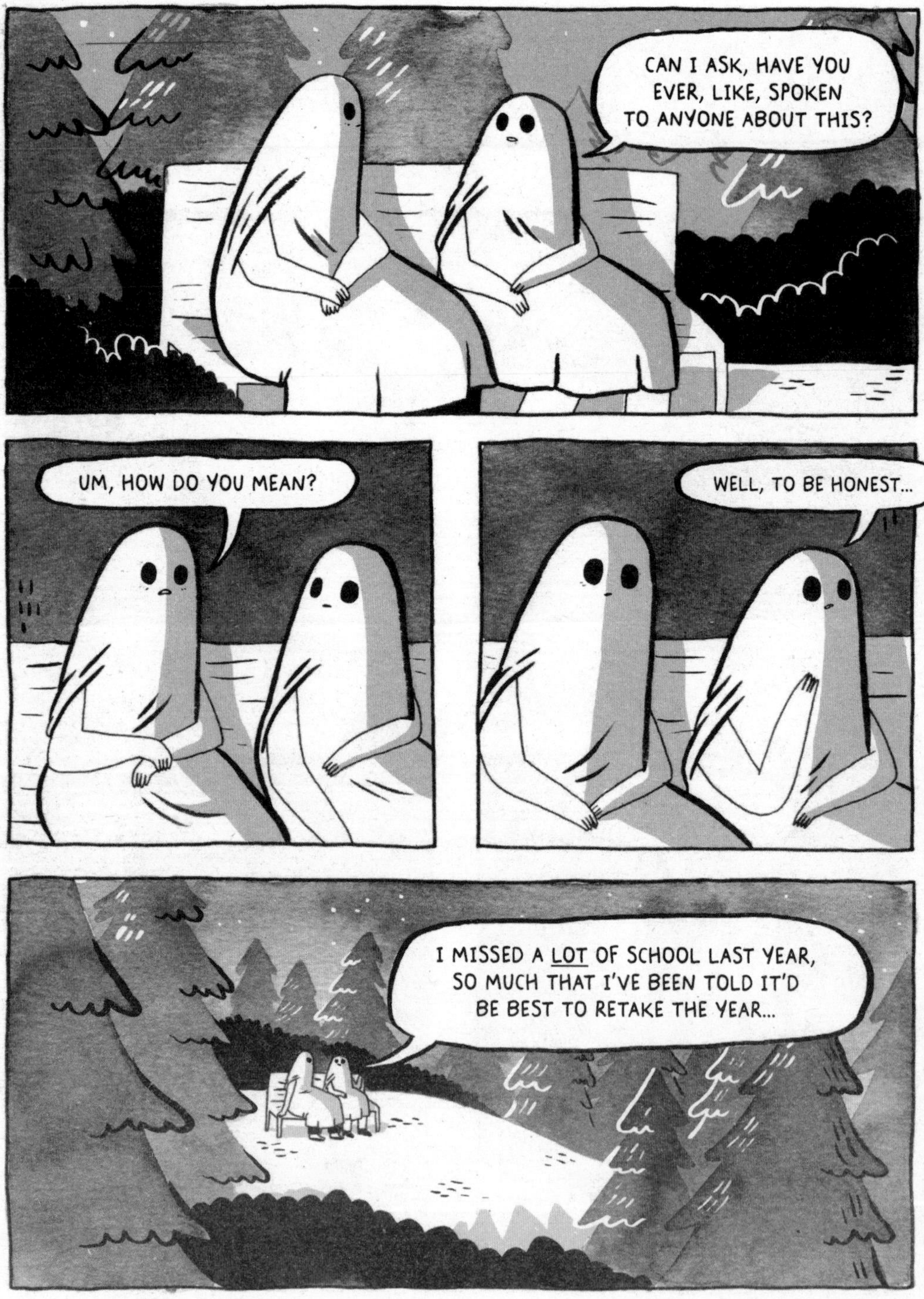
CAN I ASK, HAVE YOU EVER, LIKE, SPOKEN TO ANYONE ABOUT THIS?
UM, HOW DO YOU MEAN?
WELL, TO BE HONEST...
I MISSED A LOT OF SCHOOL LAST YEAR, SO MUCH THAT I'VE BEEN TOLD IT'D BE BEST TO RETAKE THE YEAR...

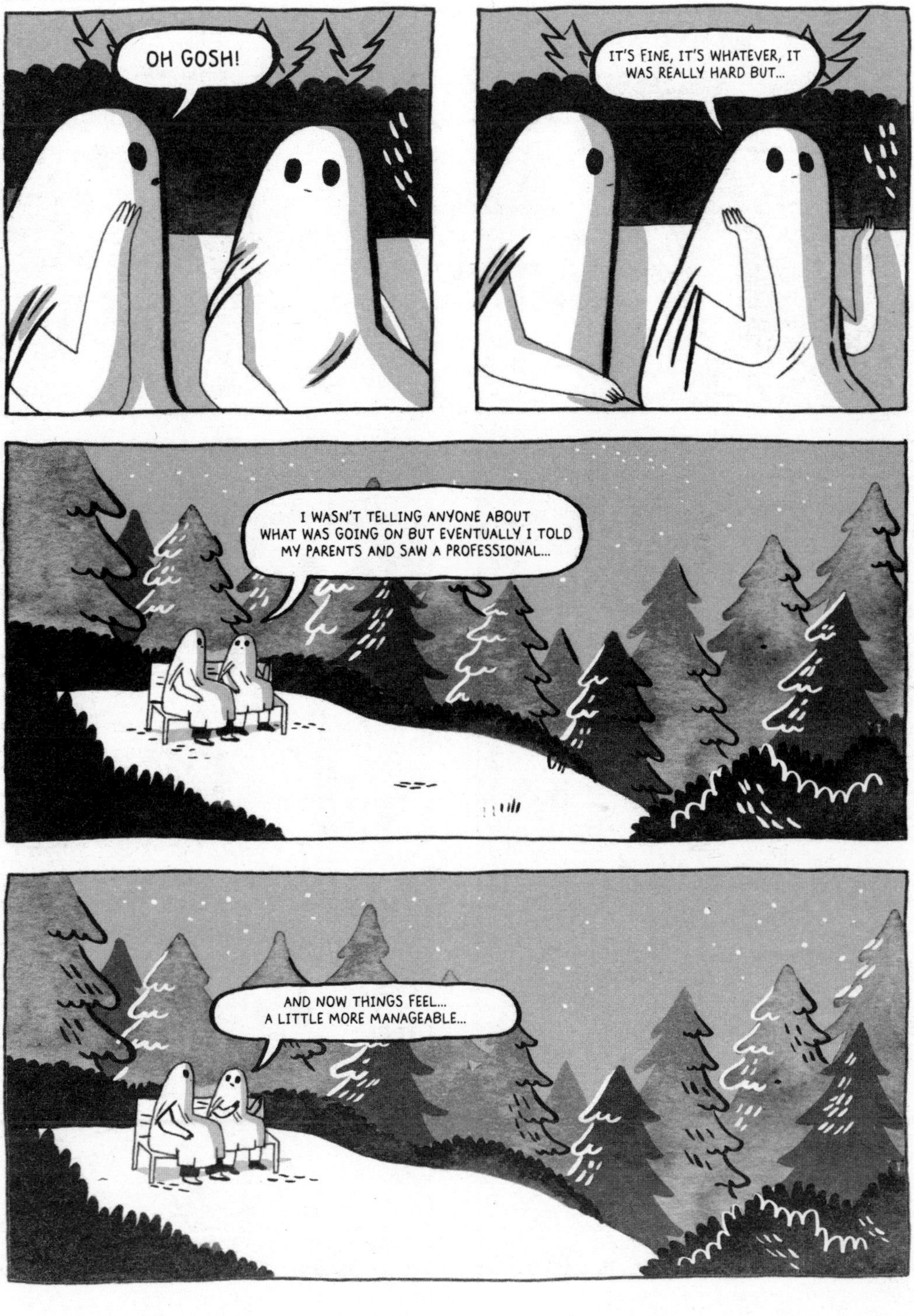
OH GOSH!
IT'S FINE, IT'S WHATEVER, IT WAS REALLY HARD BUT...
I WASN'T TELLING ANYONE ABOUT WHAT WAS GOING ON BUT EVENTUALLY I TOLD MY PARENTS AND SAW A PROFESSIONAL...
AND NOW THINGS FEEL... A LITTLE MORE MANAGEABLE...

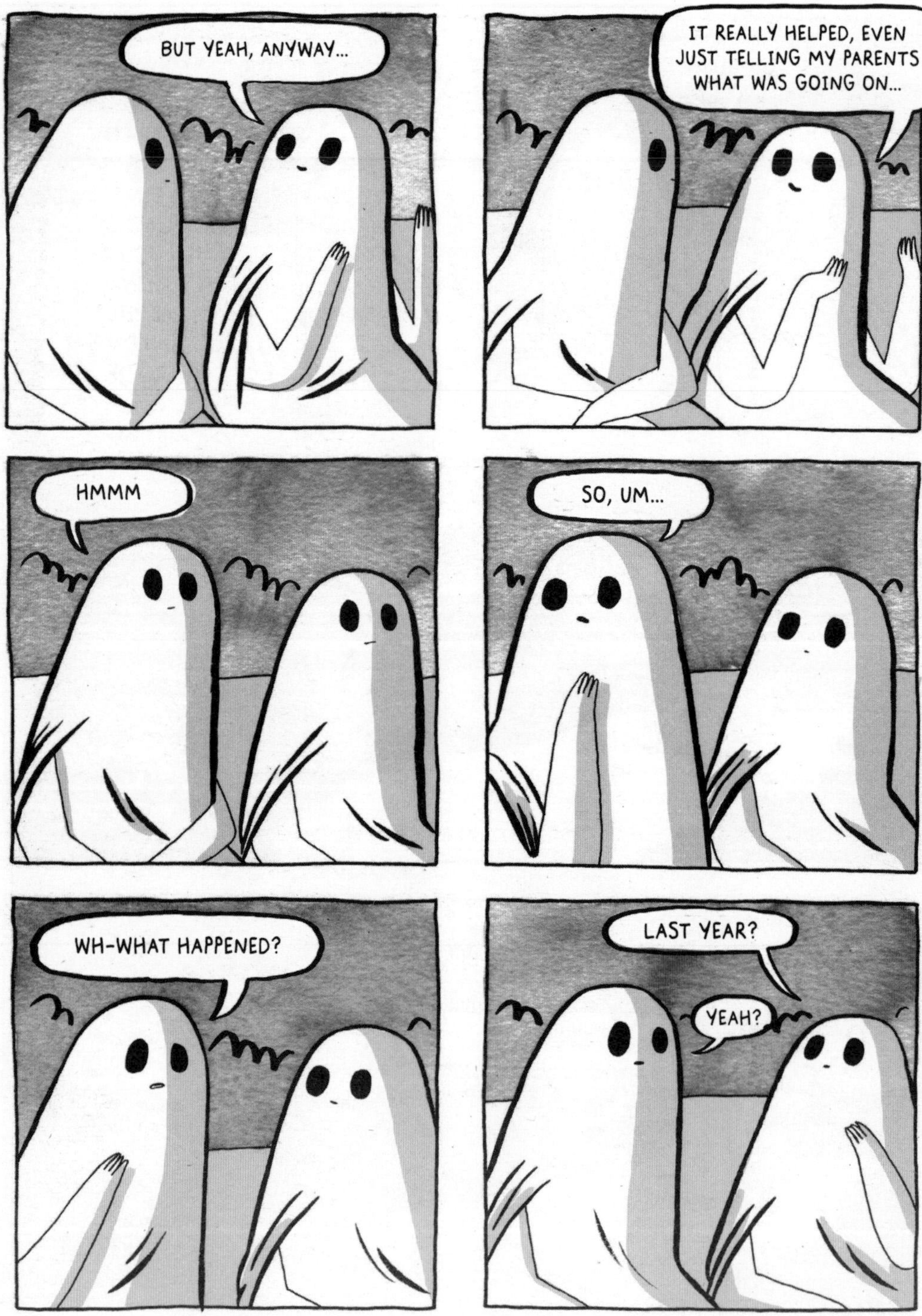
BUT YEAH, ANYWAY...
IT REALLY HELPED, EVEN JUST TELLING MY PARENTS WHAT WAS GOING ON...
HMMM
SO, UM...
WH-WHAT HAPPENED?
LAST YEAR?
YEAH?

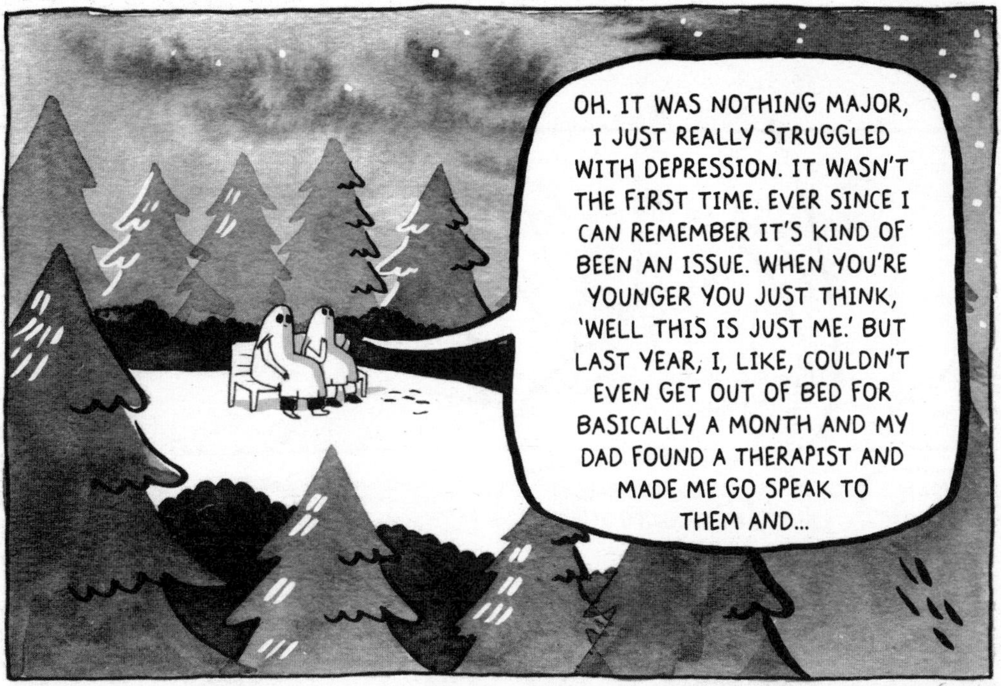
OH. IT WAS NOTHING MAJOR, I JUST REALLY STRUGGLED WITH DEPRESSION. IT WASN'T THE FIRST TIME. EVER SINCE I CAN REMEMBER IT'S KIND OF BEEN AN ISSUE. WHEN YOU'RE YOUNGER YOU JUST THINK, 'WELL THIS IS JUST ME.' BUT LAST YEAR, I, LIKE, COULDN'T EVEN GET OUT OF BED FOR BASICALLY A MONTH AND MY DAD FOUND A THERAPIST AND MADE ME GO SPEAK TO THEM AND...

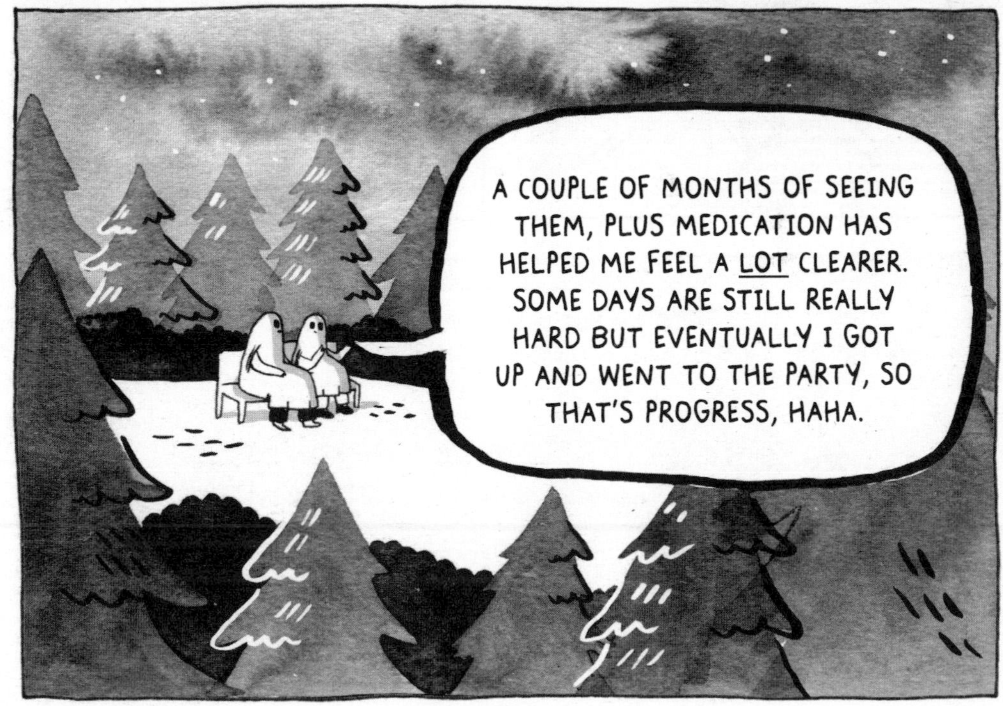
A COUPLE OF MONTHS OF SEEING THEM, PLUS MEDICATION HAS HELPED ME FEEL A LOT CLEARER. SOME DAYS ARE STILL REALLY HARD BUT EVENTUALLY I GOT UP AND WENT TO THE PARTY, SO THAT'S PROGRESS, HAHA.

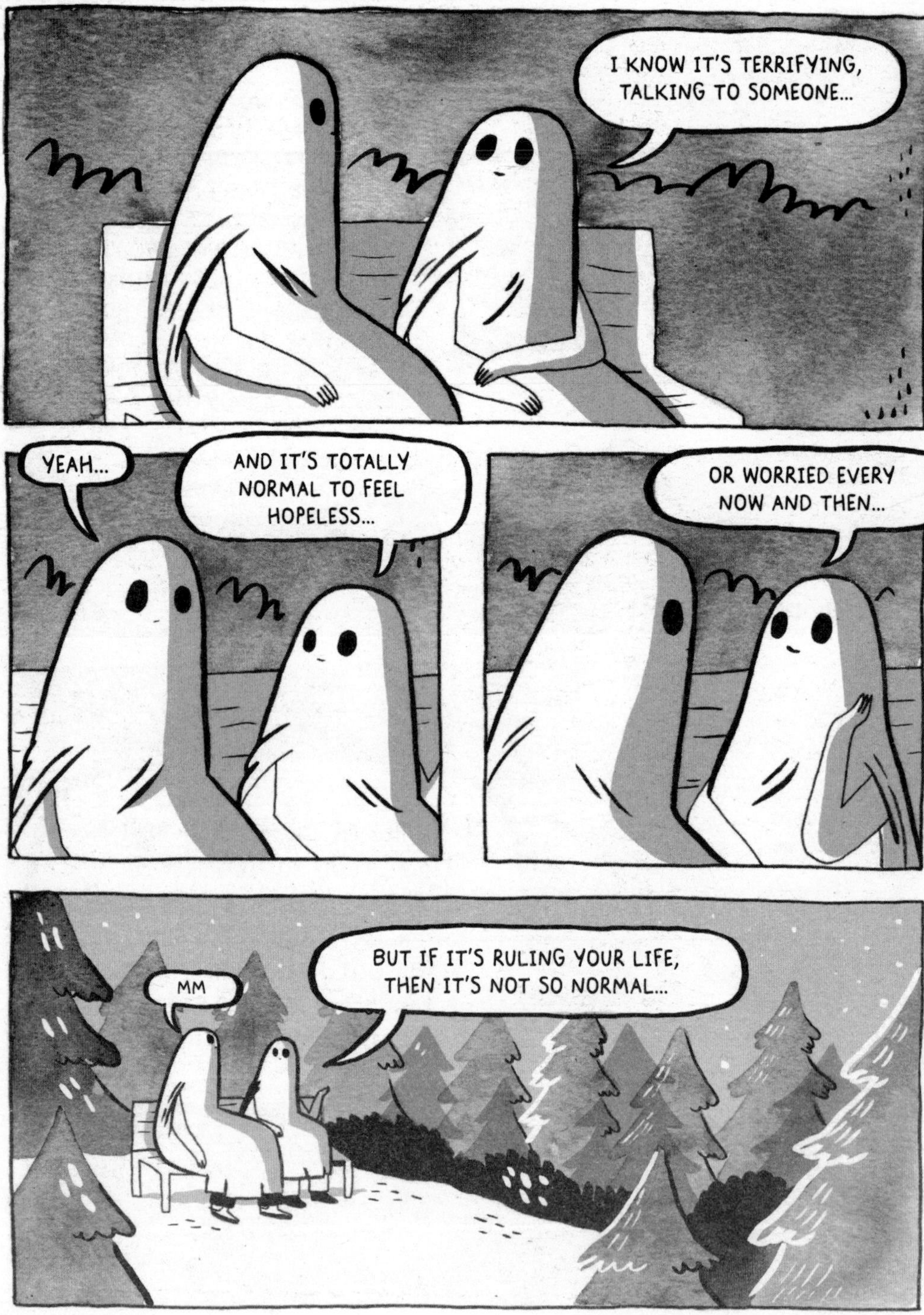
I KNOW IT'S TERRIFYING, TALKING TO SOMEONE...
YEAH...
AND IT'S TOTALLY NORMAL TO FEEL HOPELESS...
OR WORRIED EVERY NOW AND THEN...
MM
BUT IF IT'S RULING YOUR LIFE, THEN IT'S NOT SO NORMAL...

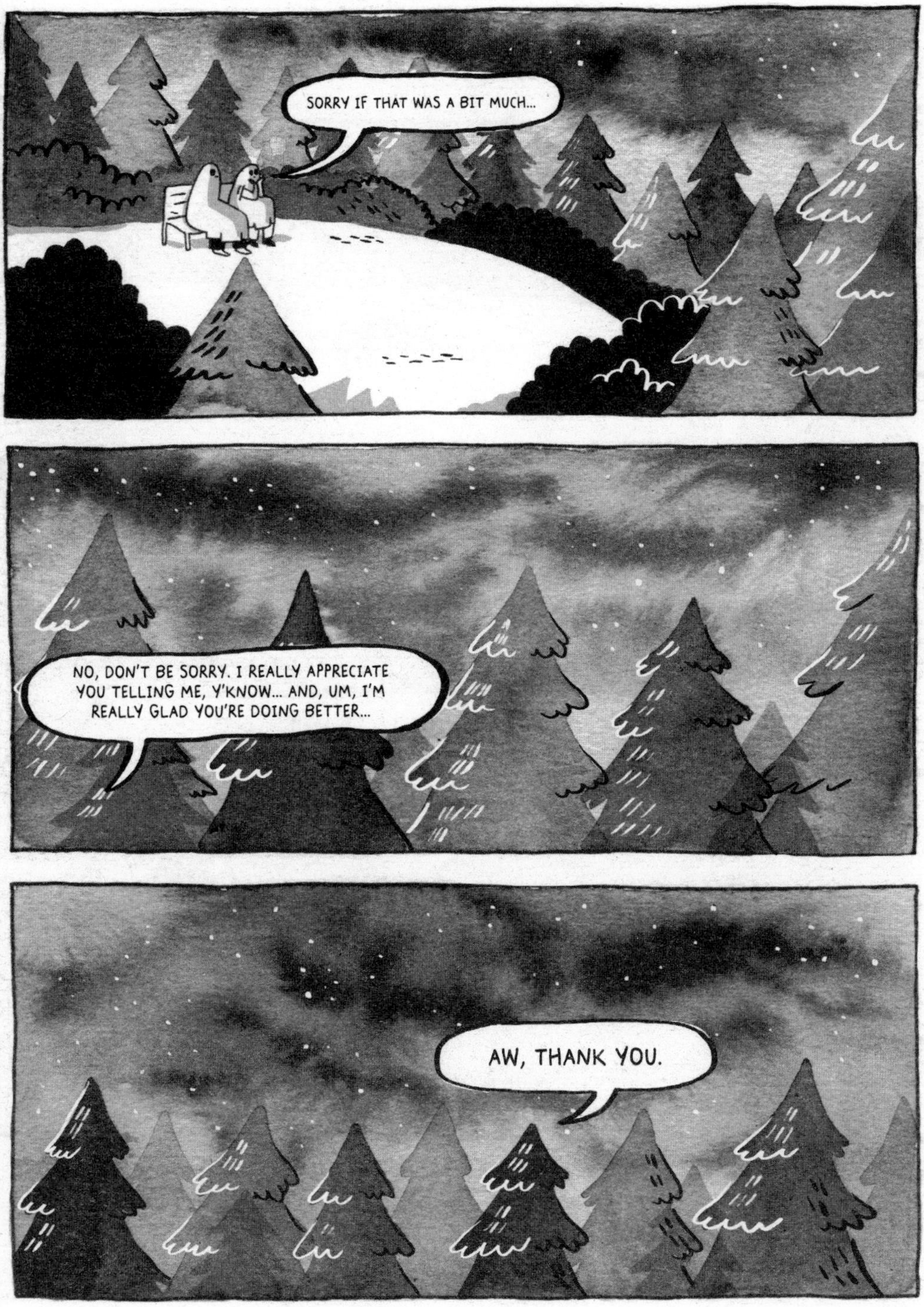
SORRY IF THAT WAS A BIT MUCH...
NO, DON'T BE SORRY. I REALLY APPRECIATE YOU TELLING ME, Y'KNOW... AND, UM, I'M REALLY GLAD YOU'RE DOING BETTER...
AW, THANK YOU.

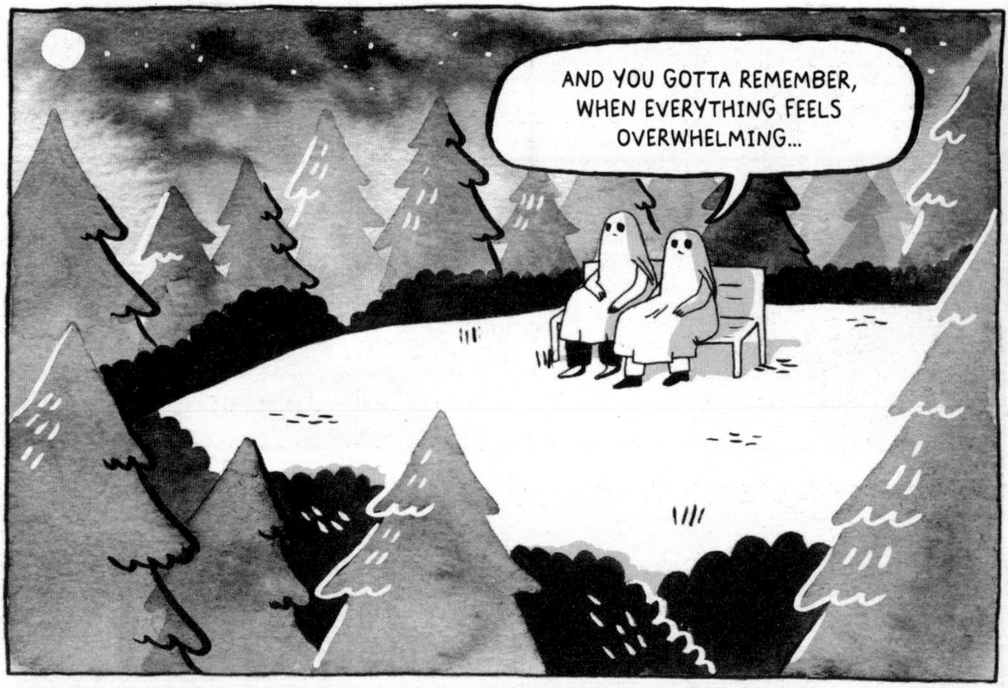
AND YOU GOTTA REMEMBER, WHEN EVERYTHING FEELS OVERWHELMING...

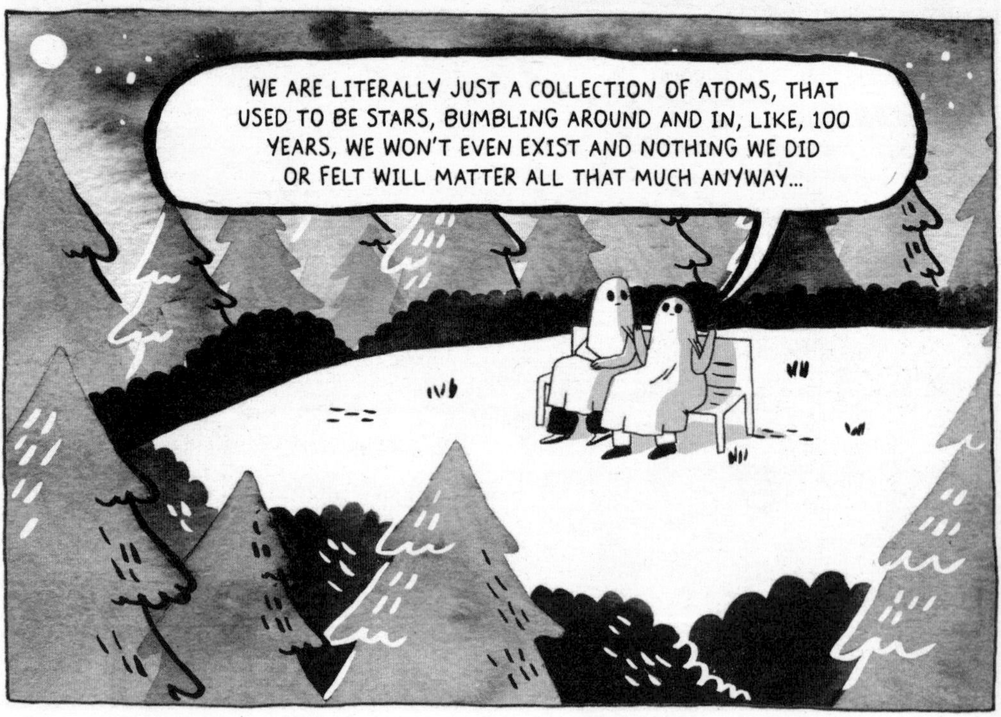
WE ARE LITERALLY JUST A COLLECTION OF ATOMS, THAT USED TO BE STARS, BUMBLING AROUND AND IN, LIKE, 100 YEARS, WE WON'T EVEN EXIST AND NOTHING WE DID OR FELT WILL MATTER ALL THAT MUCH ANYWAY...

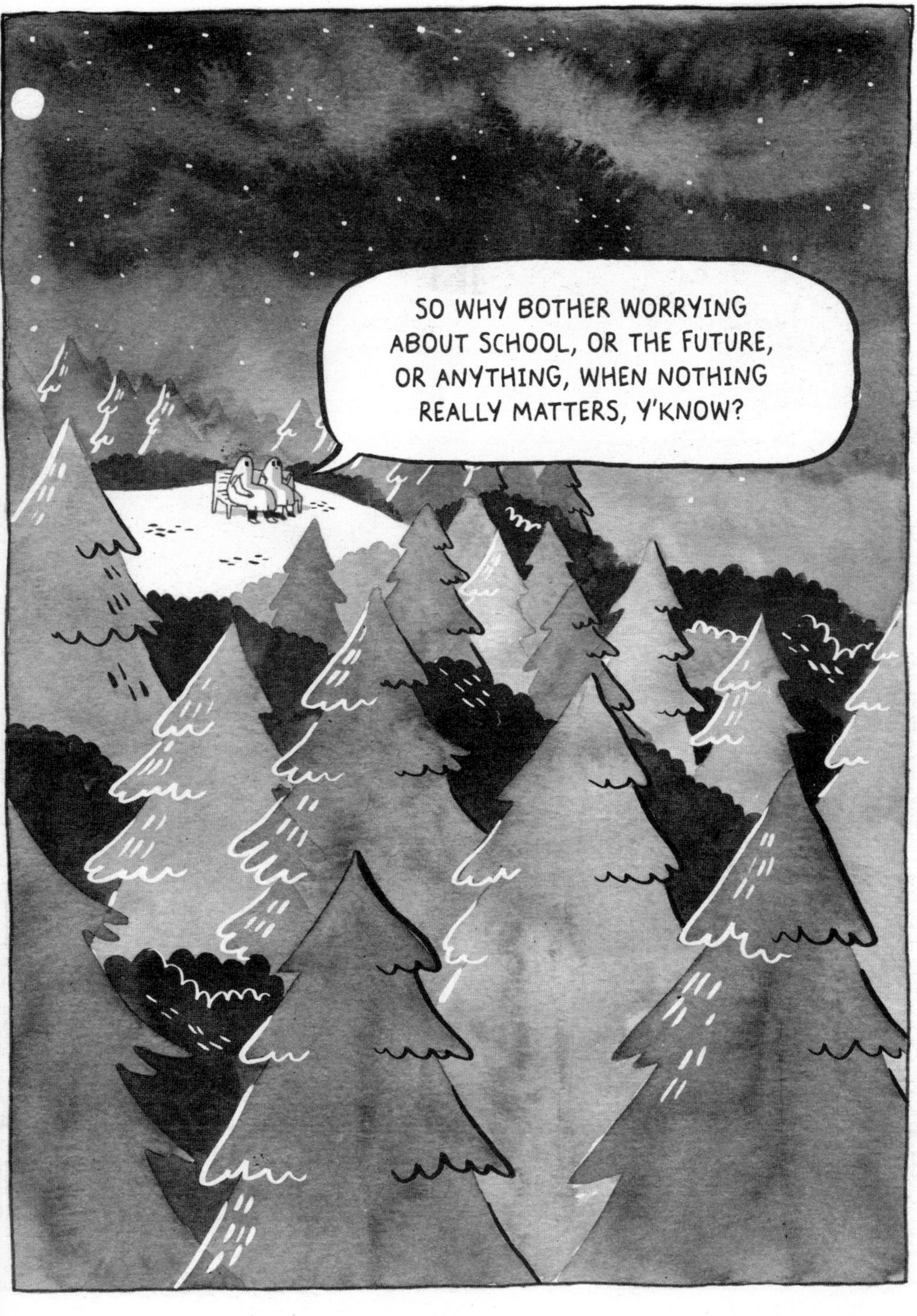
SO WHY BOTHER WORRYING ABOUT SCHOOL, OR THE FUTURE, OR ANYTHING, WHEN NOTHING REALLY MATTERS, Y'KNOW?

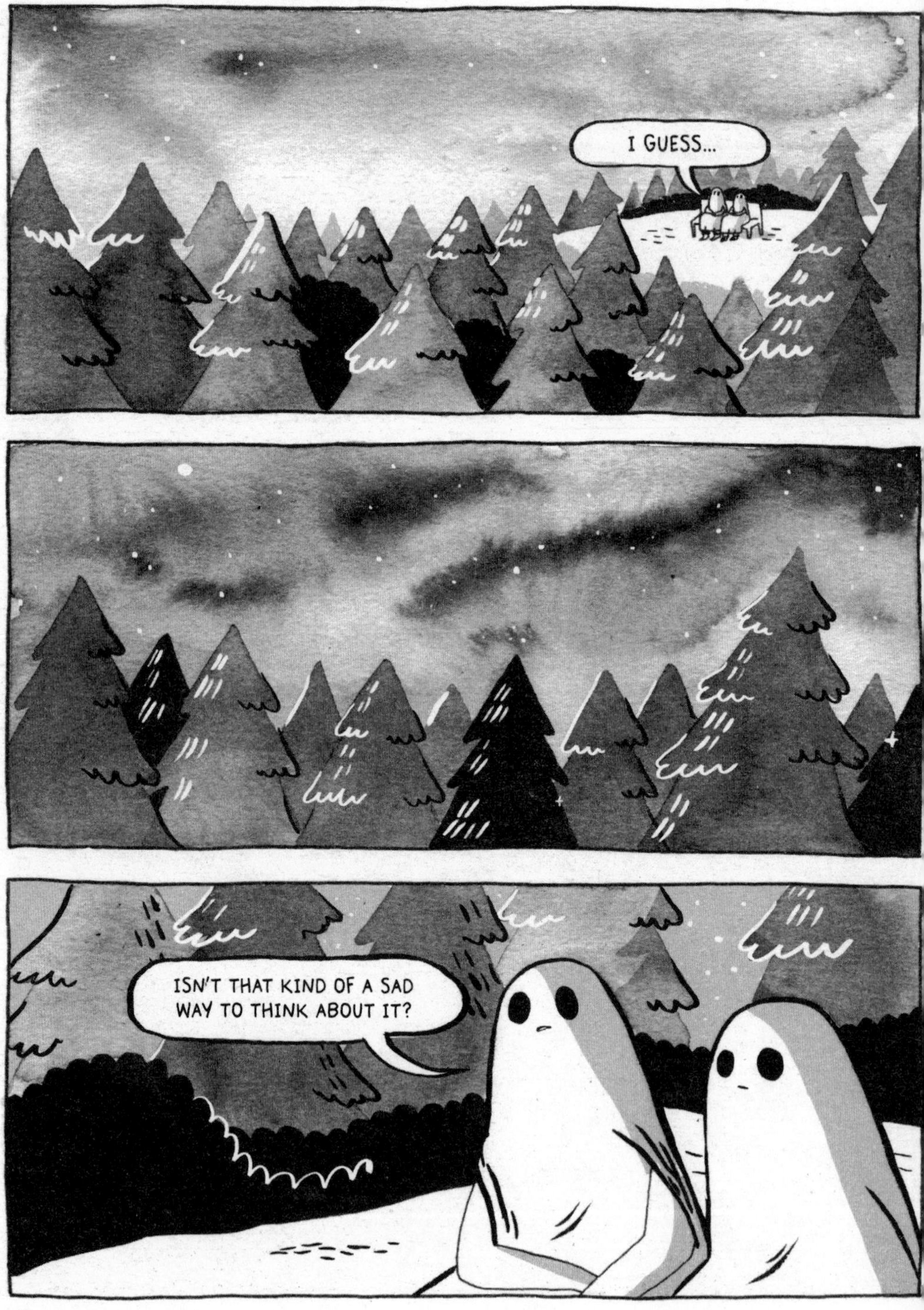
I GUESS...
ISN'T THAT KIND OF A SAD WAY TO THINK ABOUT IT?

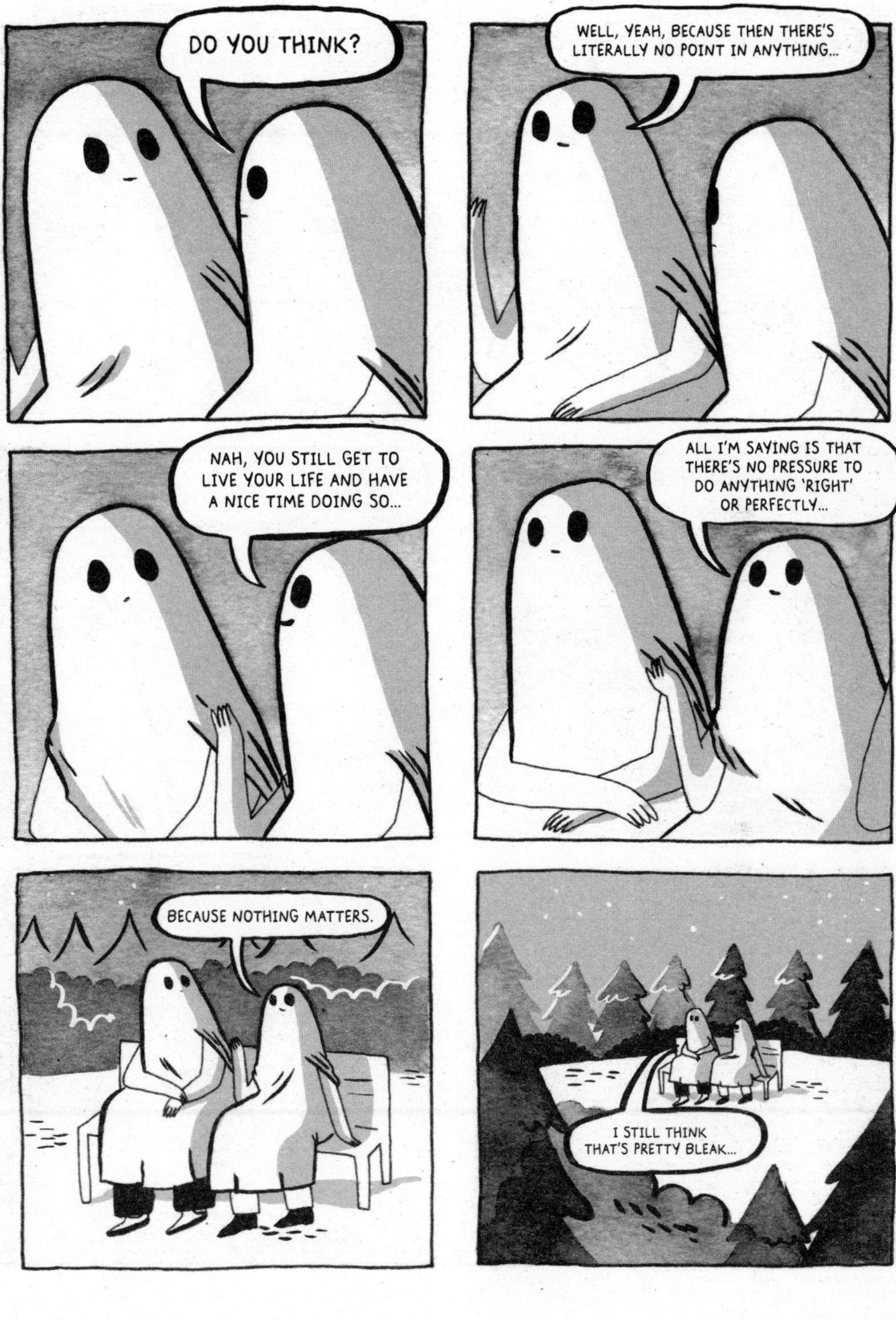
DO YOU THINK?
WELL, YEAH, BECAUSE THEN THERE'S LITERALLY NO POINT IN ANYTHING...
NAH, YOU STILL GET TO LIVE YOUR LIFE AND HAVE A NICE TIME DOING SO...
ALL I'M SAYING IS THAT THERE'S NO PRESSURE TO DO ANYTHING 'RIGHT' OR PERFECTLY...
BECAUSE NOTHING MATTERS.
I STILL THINK THAT'S PRETTY BLEAK...

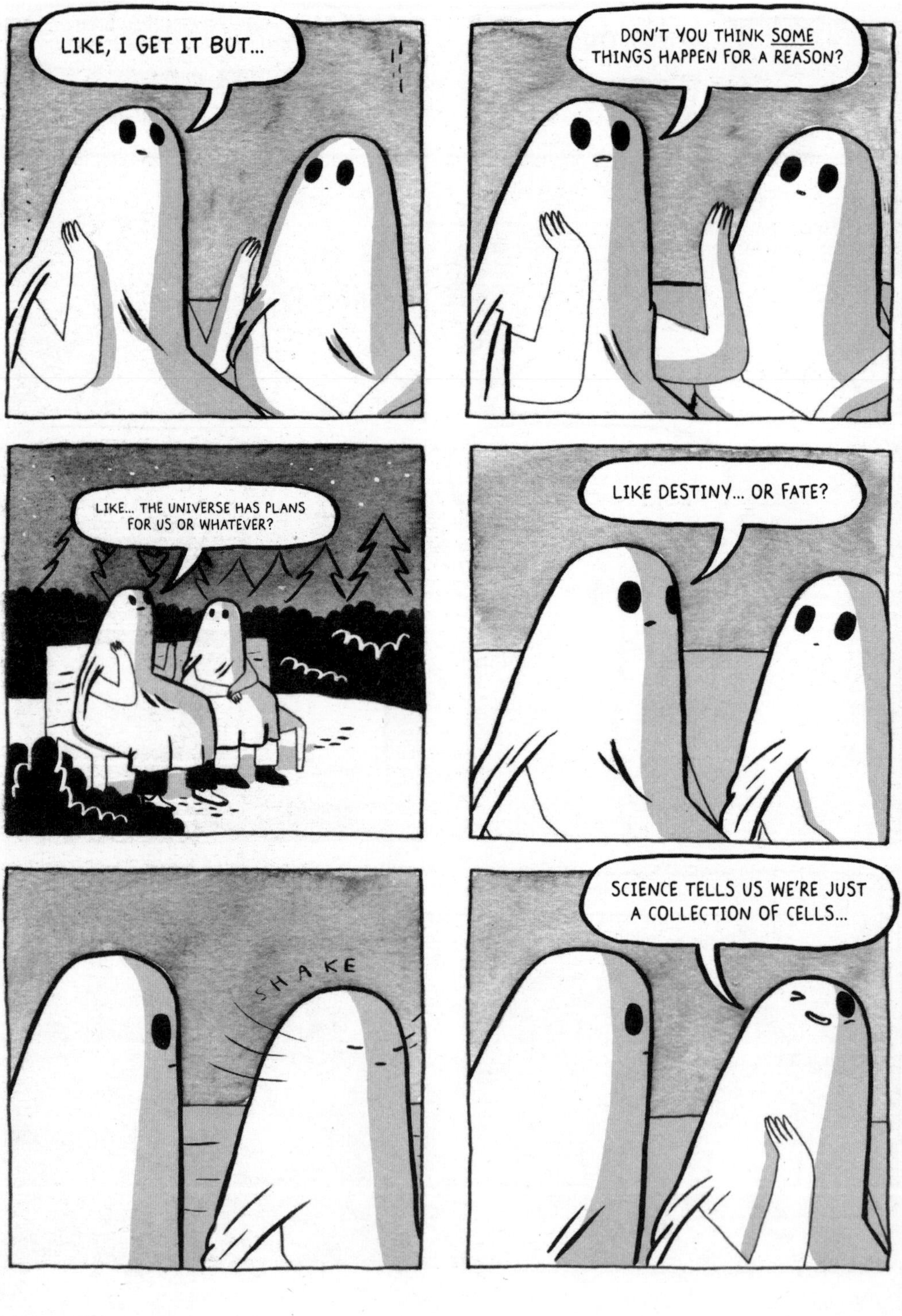
LIKE, I GET IT BUT...
DON'T YOU THINK SOME THINGS HAPPEN FOR A REASON?
LIKE... THE UNIVERSE HAS PLANS FOR US OR WHATEVER?
LIKE DESTINY... OR FATE?
SHAKE
SCIENCE TELLS US WE'RE JUST A COLLECTION OF CELLS...

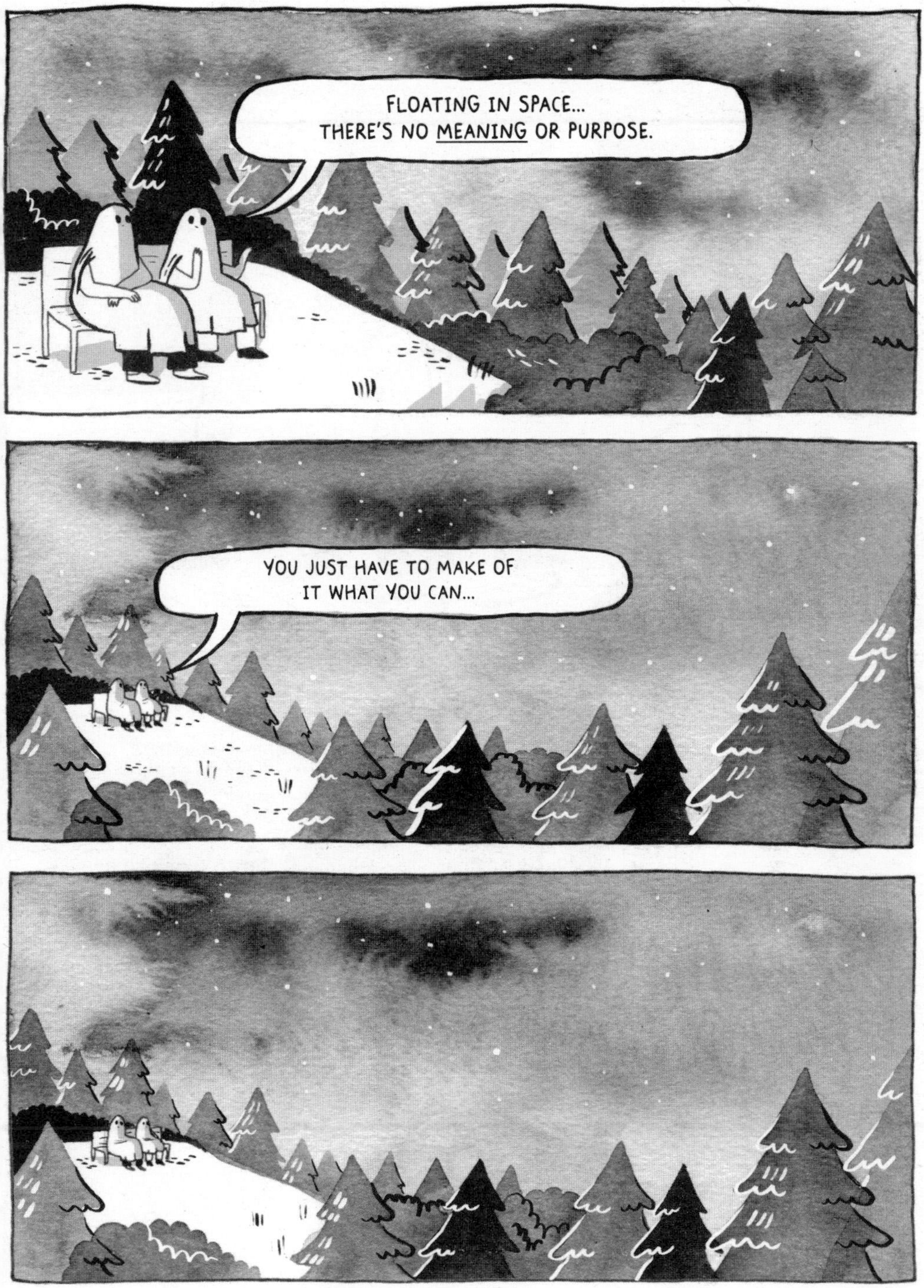
FLOATING IN SPACE...
THERE'S NO MEANING OR PURPOSE.
YOU JUST HAVE TO MAKE OF IT WHAT YOU CAN...

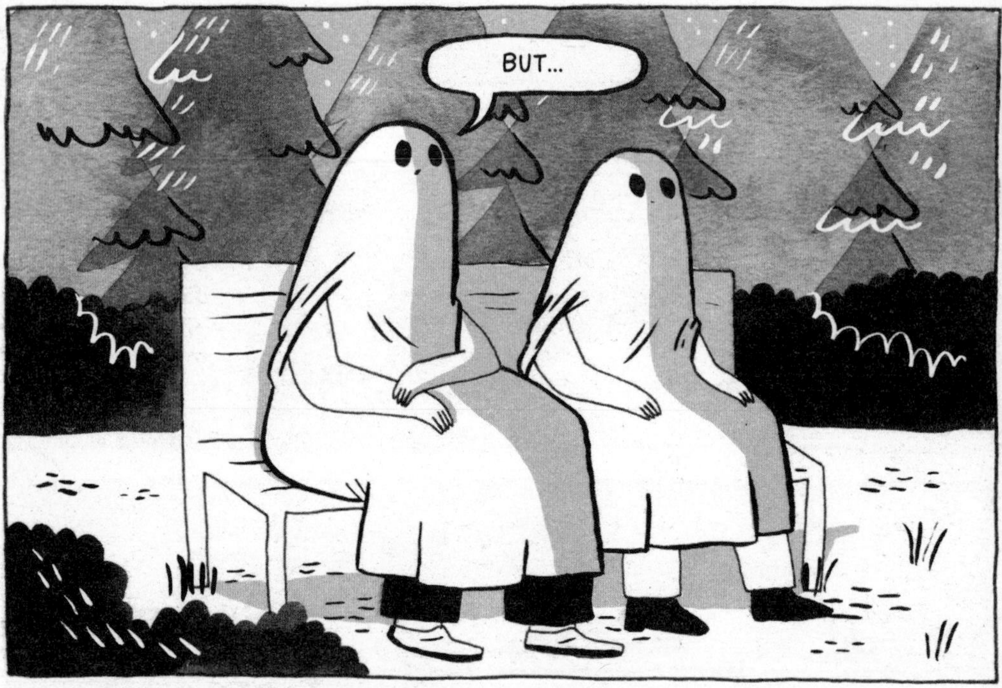
BUT...

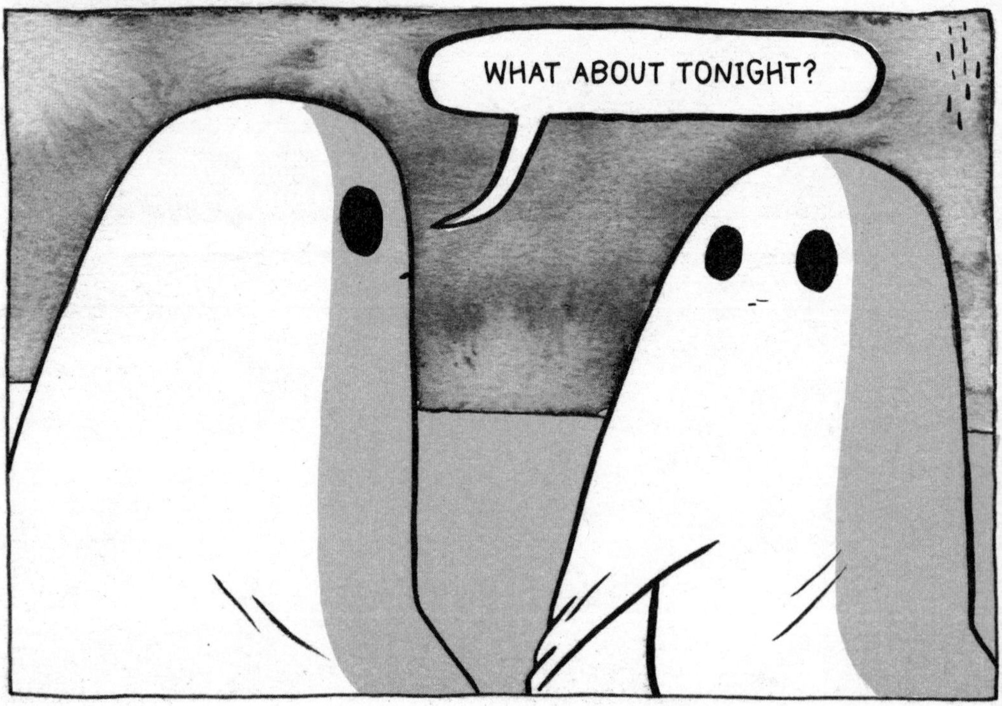
WHAT ABOUT TONIGHT?

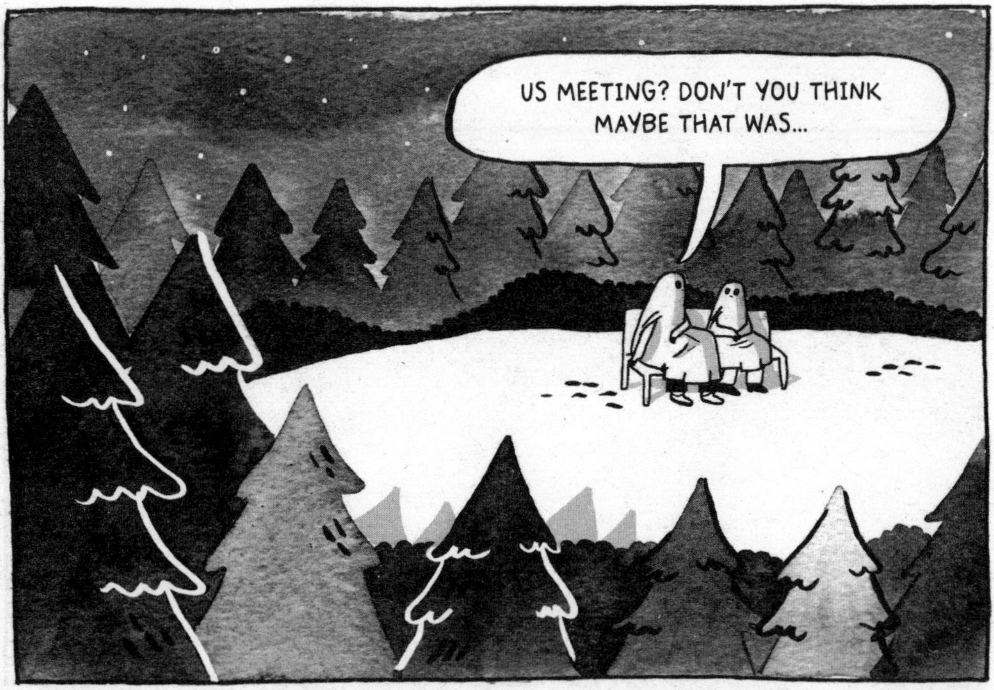
US MEETING? DON'T YOU THINK MAYBE THAT WAS...

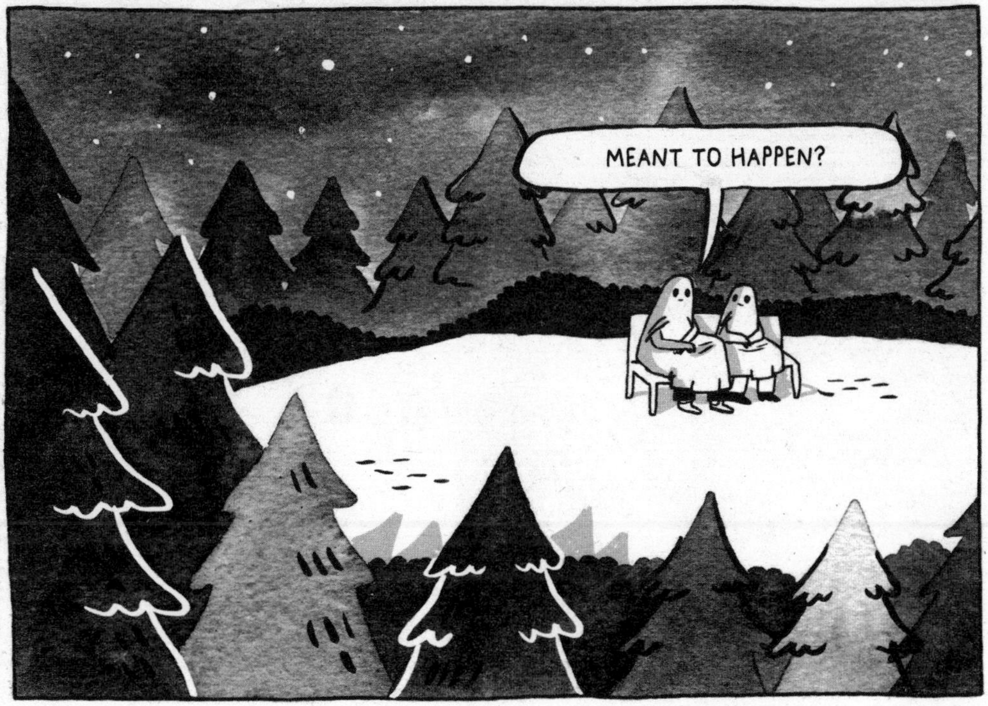
MEANT TO HAPPEN?

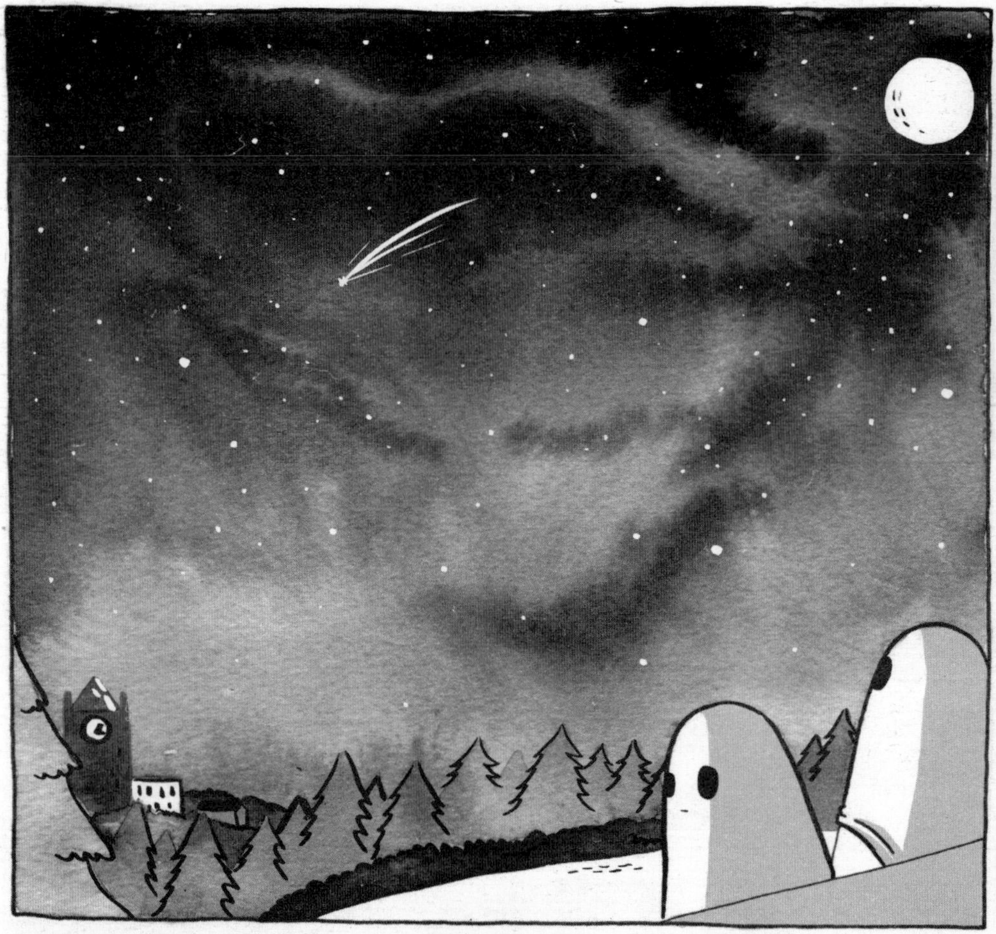

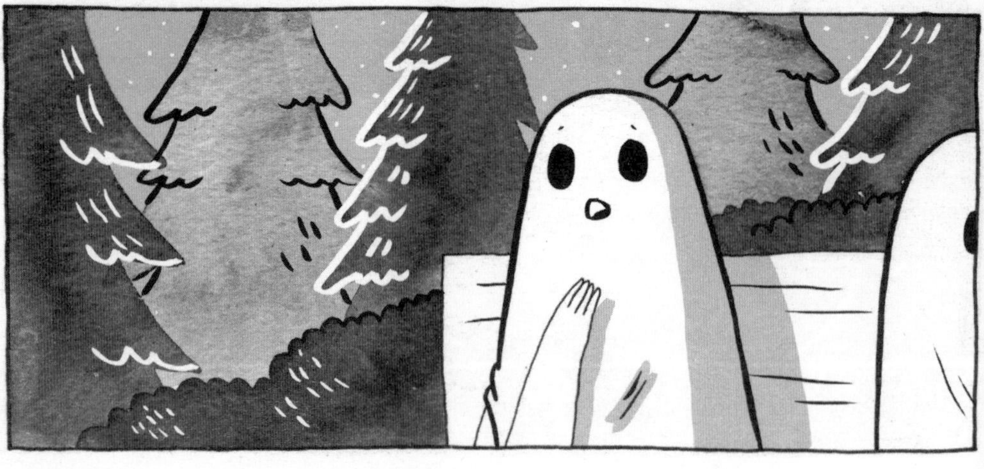

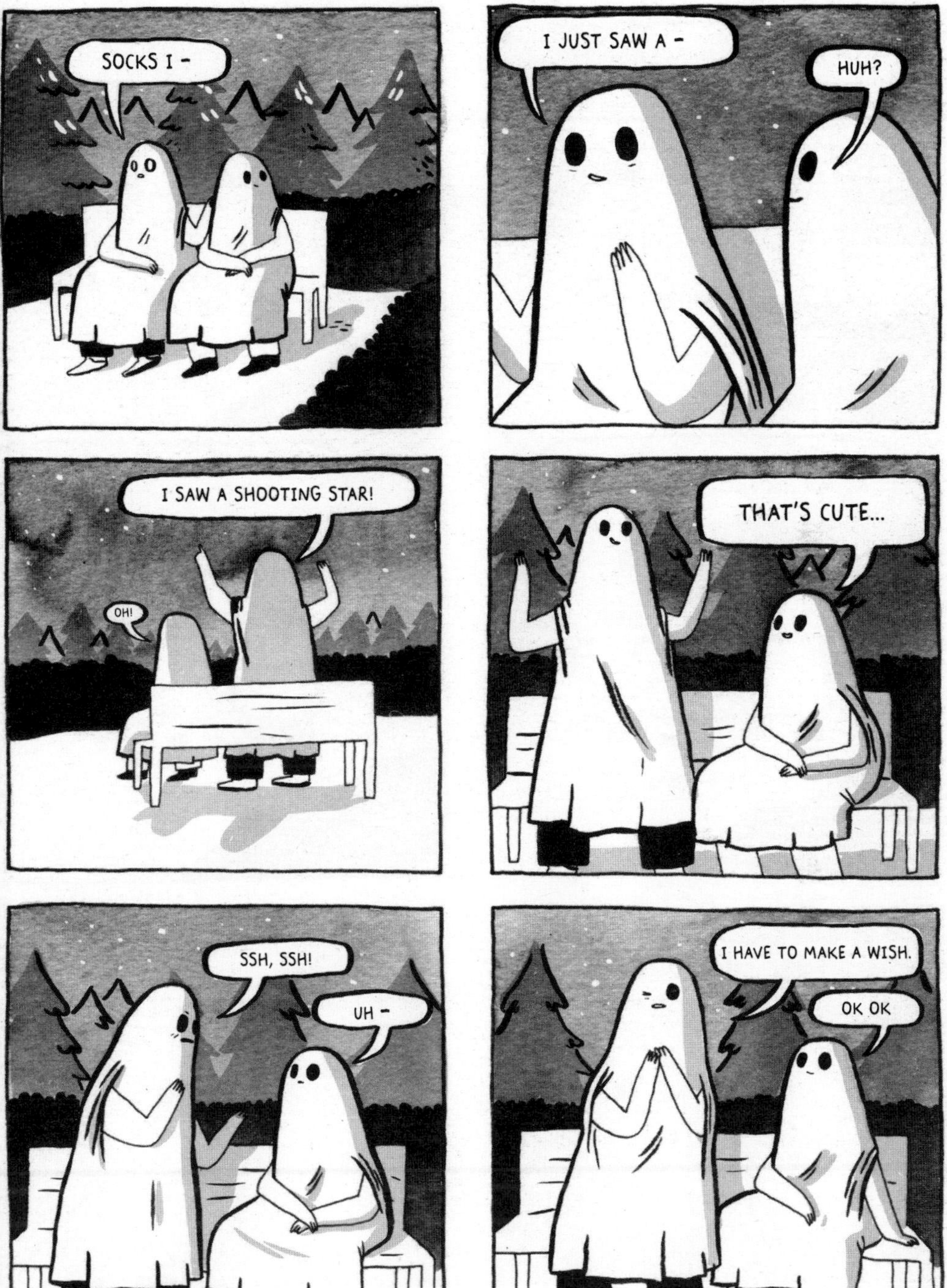
SOCKS I -
I JUST SAW A -
HUH?
I SAW A SHOOTING STAR!
OH!
THAT'S CUTE...
SSH, SSH!
UH -
I HAVE TO MAKE A WISH.
OK OK

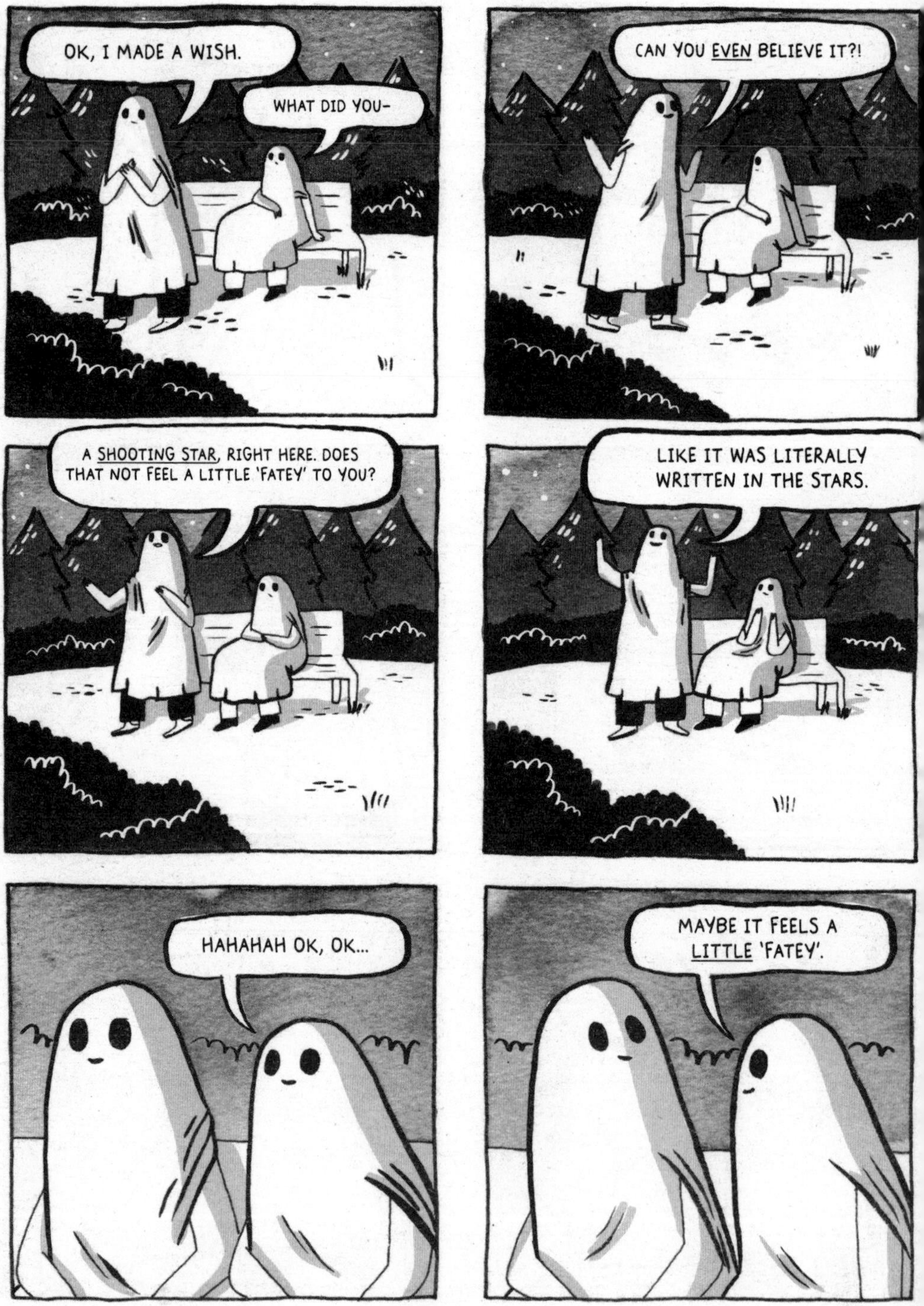
OK, I MADE A WISH.
WHAT DID YOU-
CAN YOU EVEN BELIEVE IT?!
A SHOOTING STAR, RIGHT HERE. DOES THAT NOT FEEL A LITTLE 'FATEY' TO YOU?
LIKE IT WAS LITERALLY WRITTEN IN THE STARS.
HAHAHAH OK, OK...
MAYBE IT FEELS A LITTLE 'FATEY'.

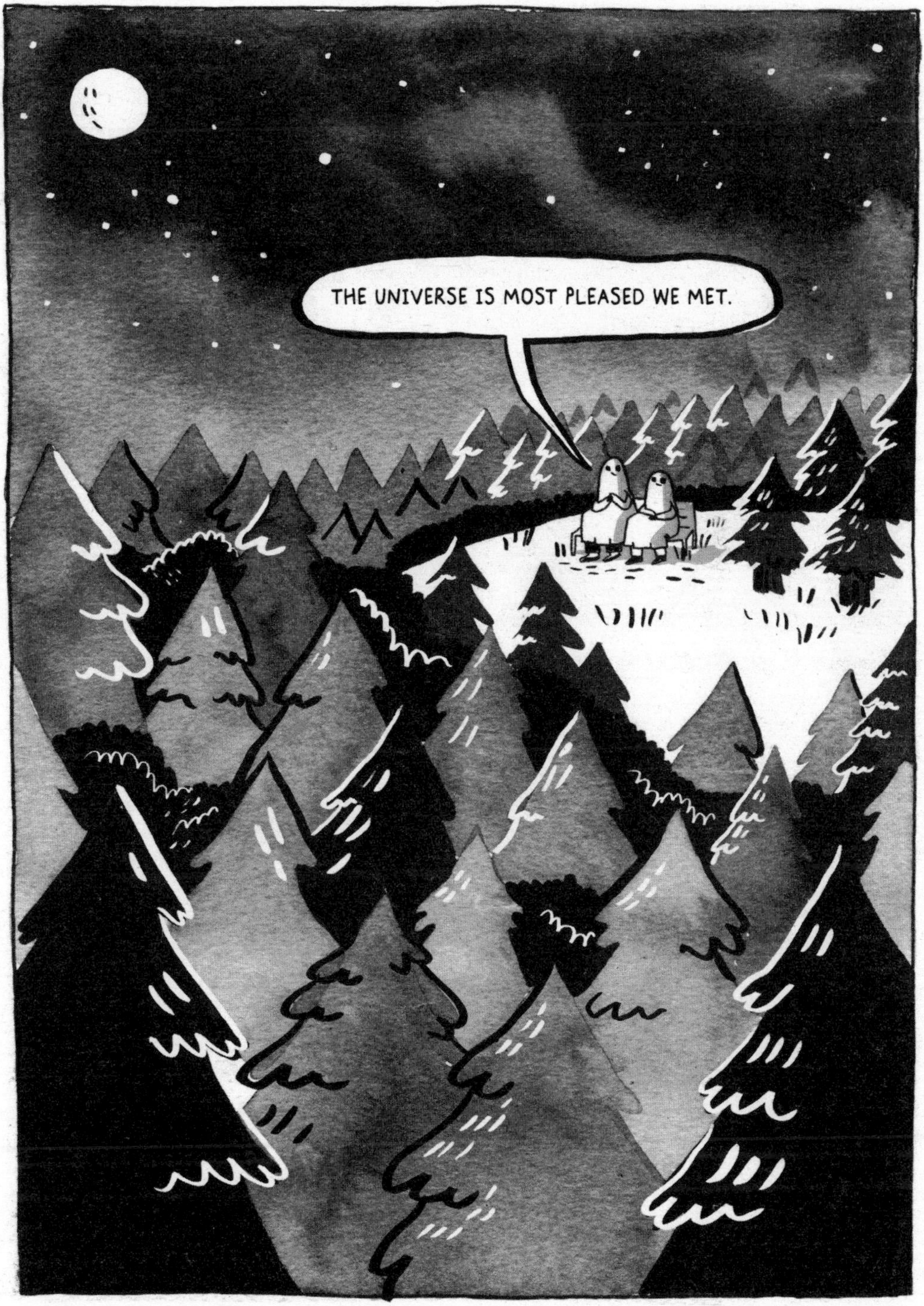
THE UNIVERSE IS MOST PLEASED WE MET.

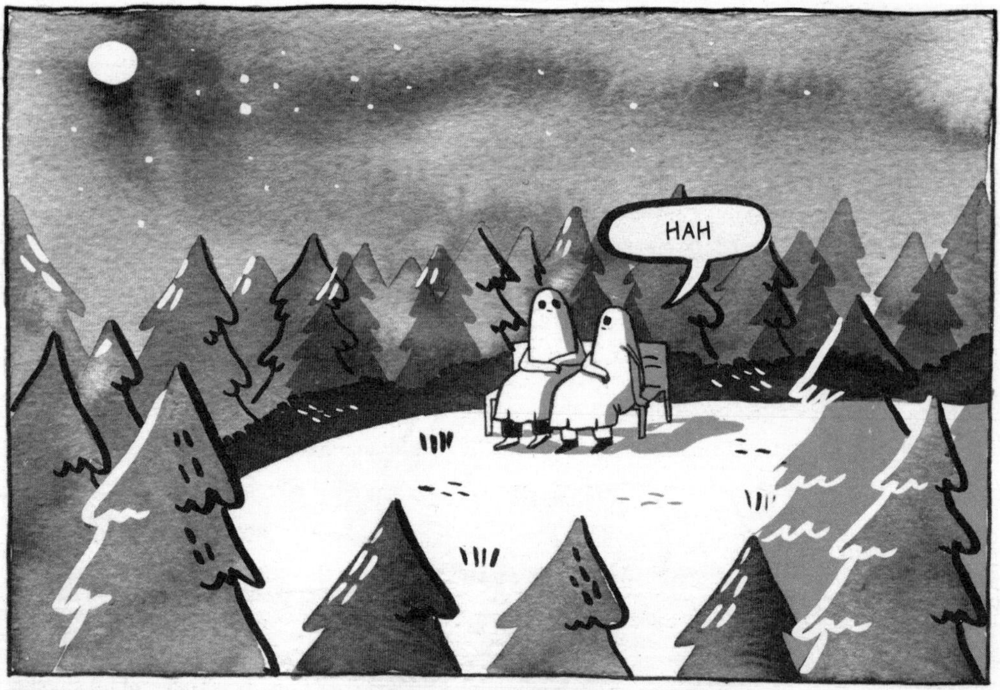
HAH

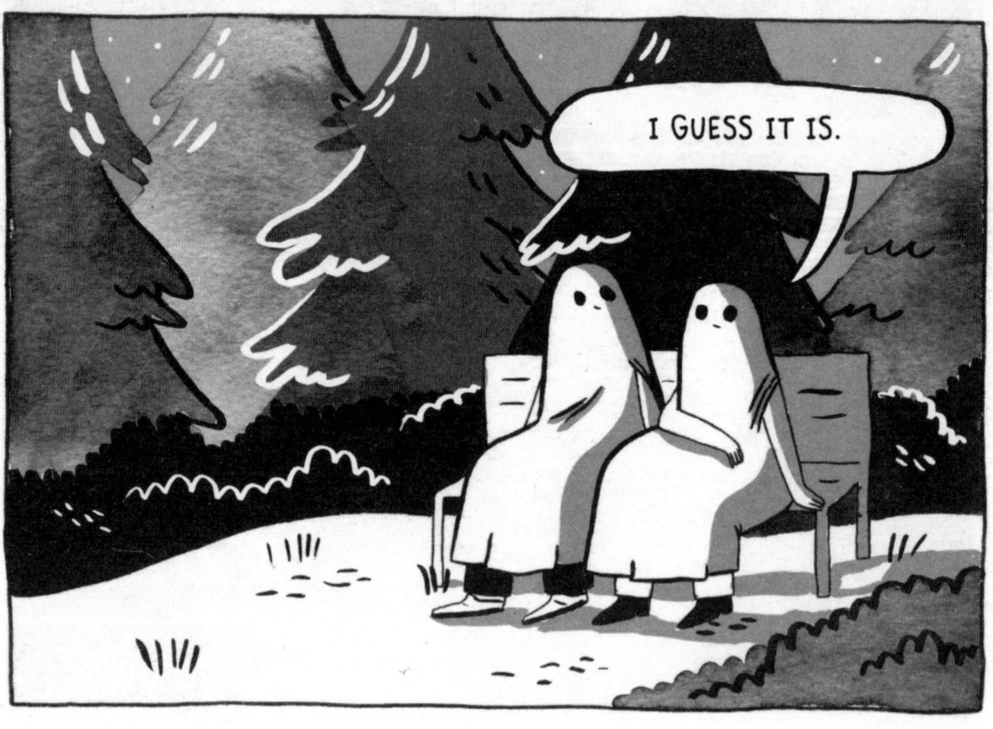
I GUESS IT IS.

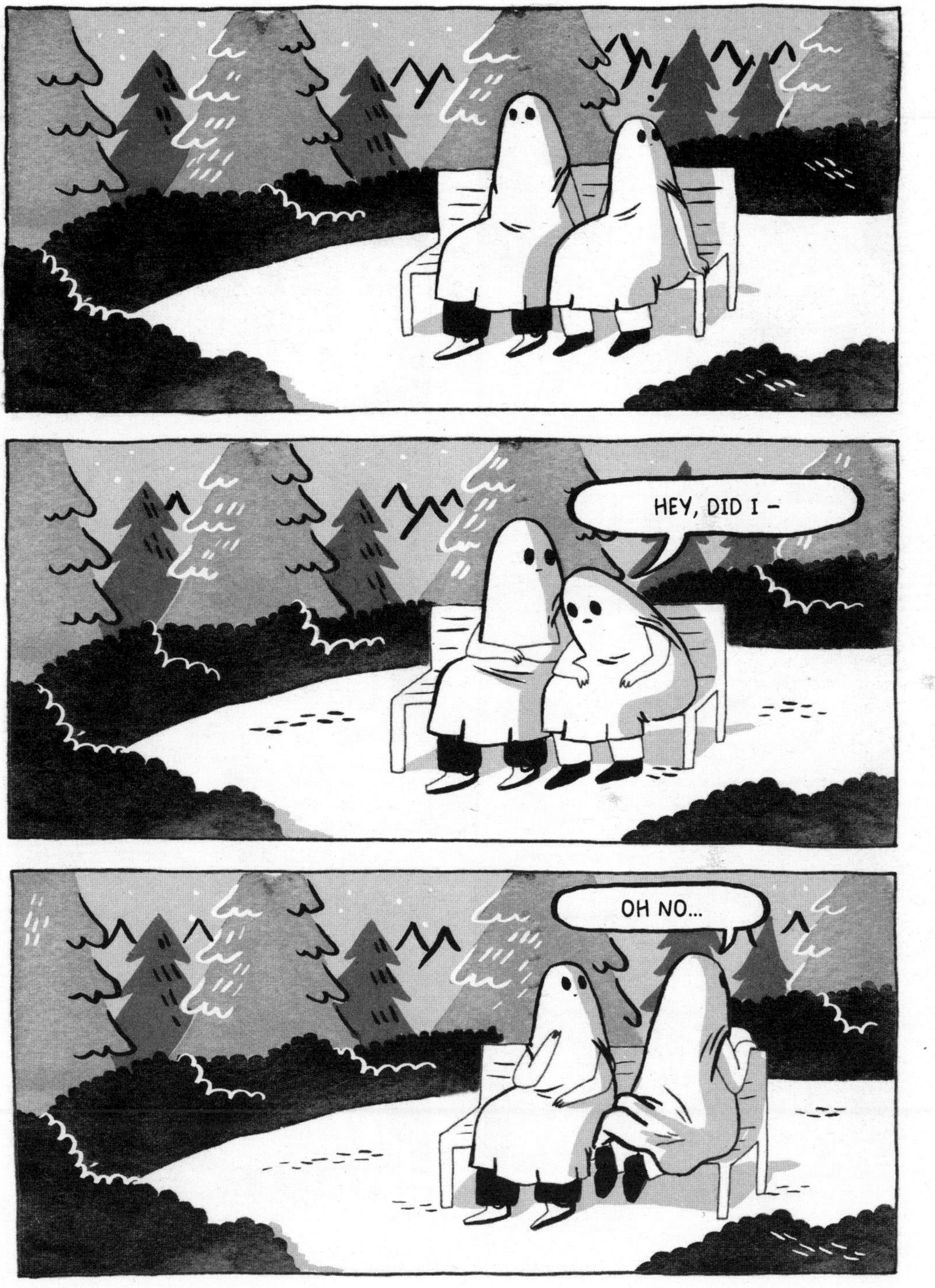
!
HEY, DID I -
OH NO...

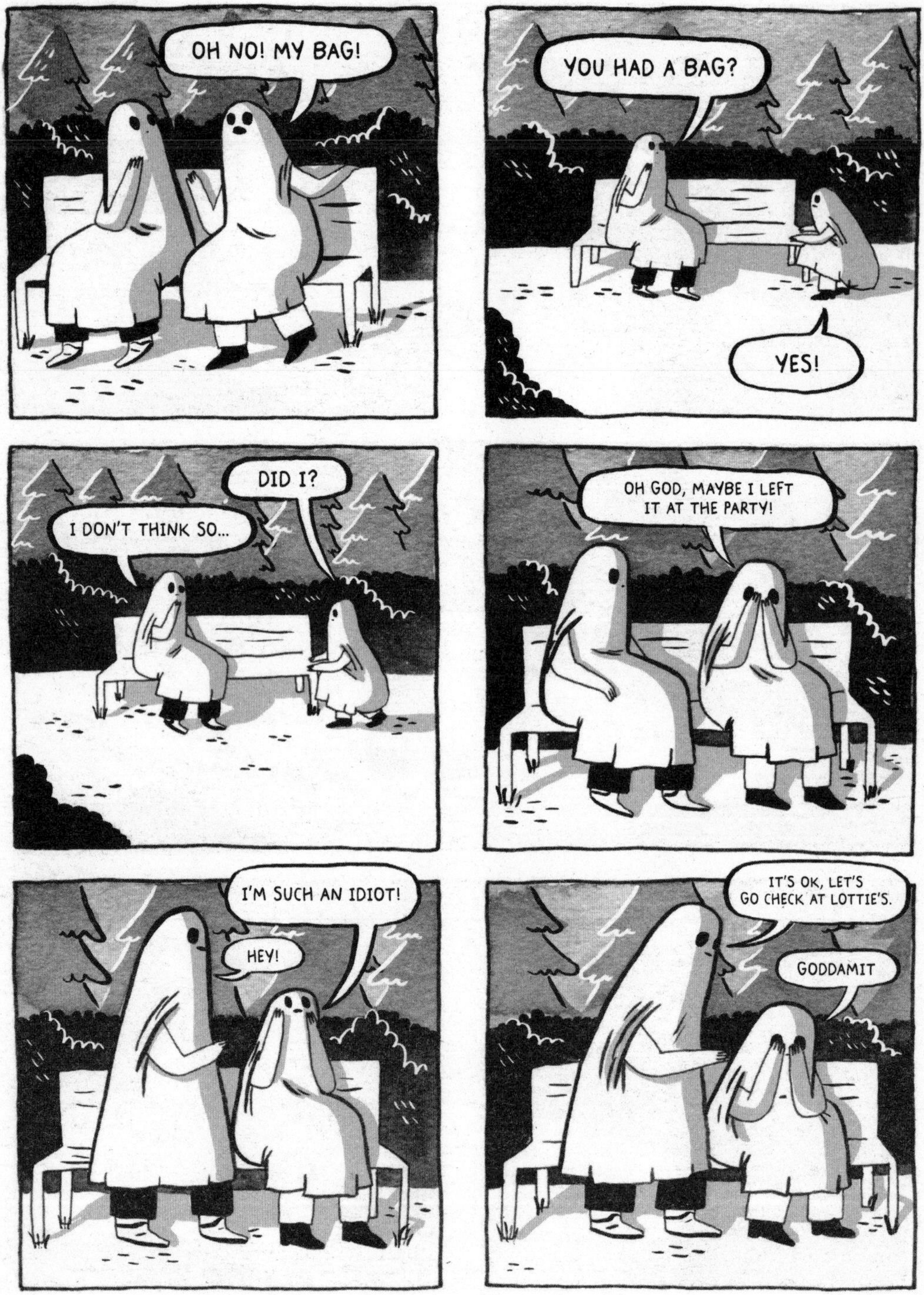
OH NO! MY BAG!
YOU HAD A BAG?
YES!
I DON'T THINK SO...
DID I?
OH GOD, MAYBE I LEFT IT AT THE PARTY!
I'M SUCH AN IDIOT!
HEY!
IT'S OK, LET'S GO CHECK AT LOTTIE'S.
GODDAMIT

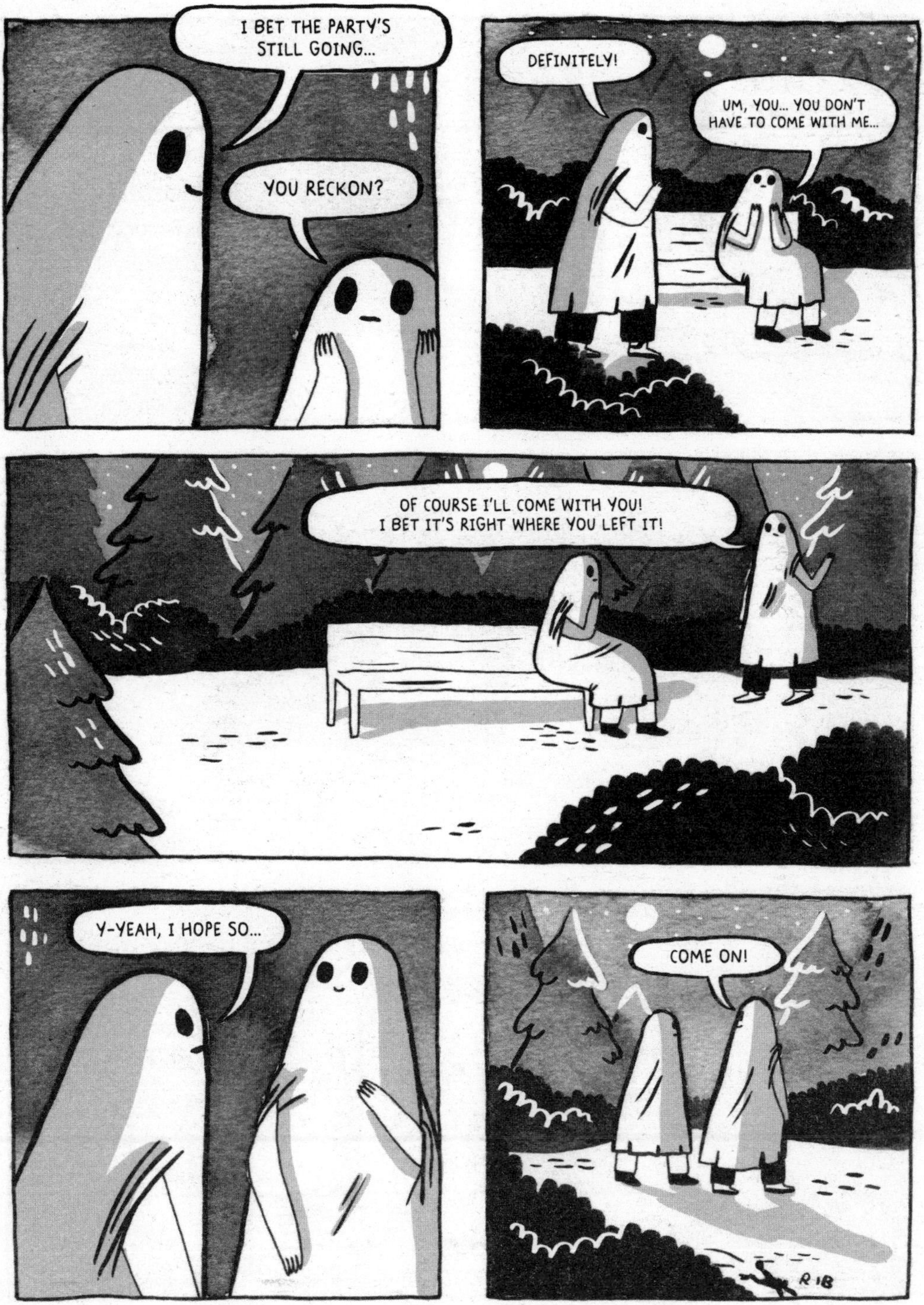
I BET THE PARTY'S STILL GOING...
YOU RECKON?
DEFINITELY!
UM, YOU... YOU DON'T HAVE TO COME WITH ME...
OF COURSE I'LL COME WITH YOU! I BET IT'S RIGHT WHERE YOU LEFT IT!
Y-YEAH, I HOPE SO...
COME ON!
RIB

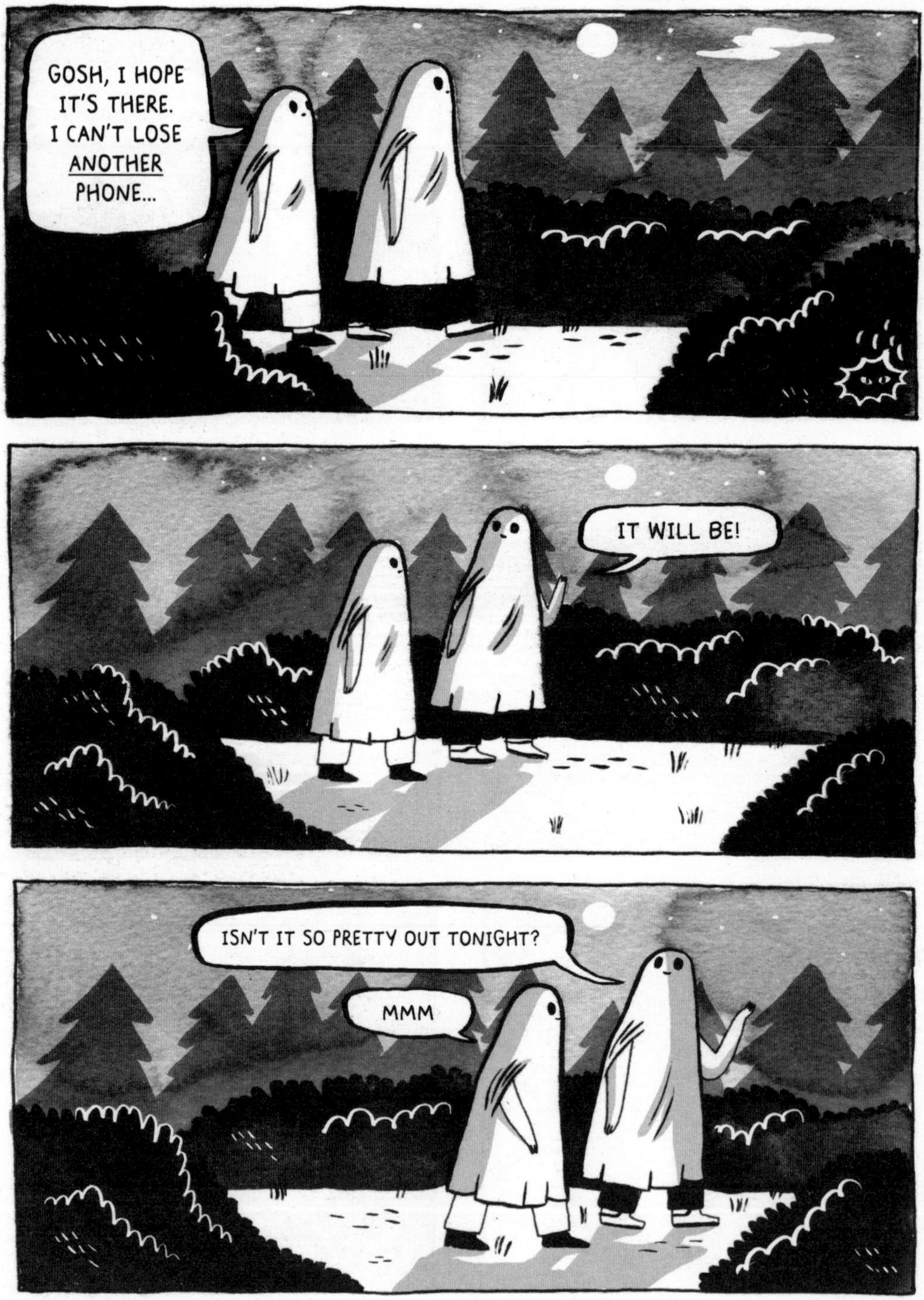
GOSH, I HOPE IT'S THERE. I CAN'T LOSE ANOTHER PHONE...
IT WILL BE!
ISN'T IT SO PRETTY OUT TONIGHT?
MMM

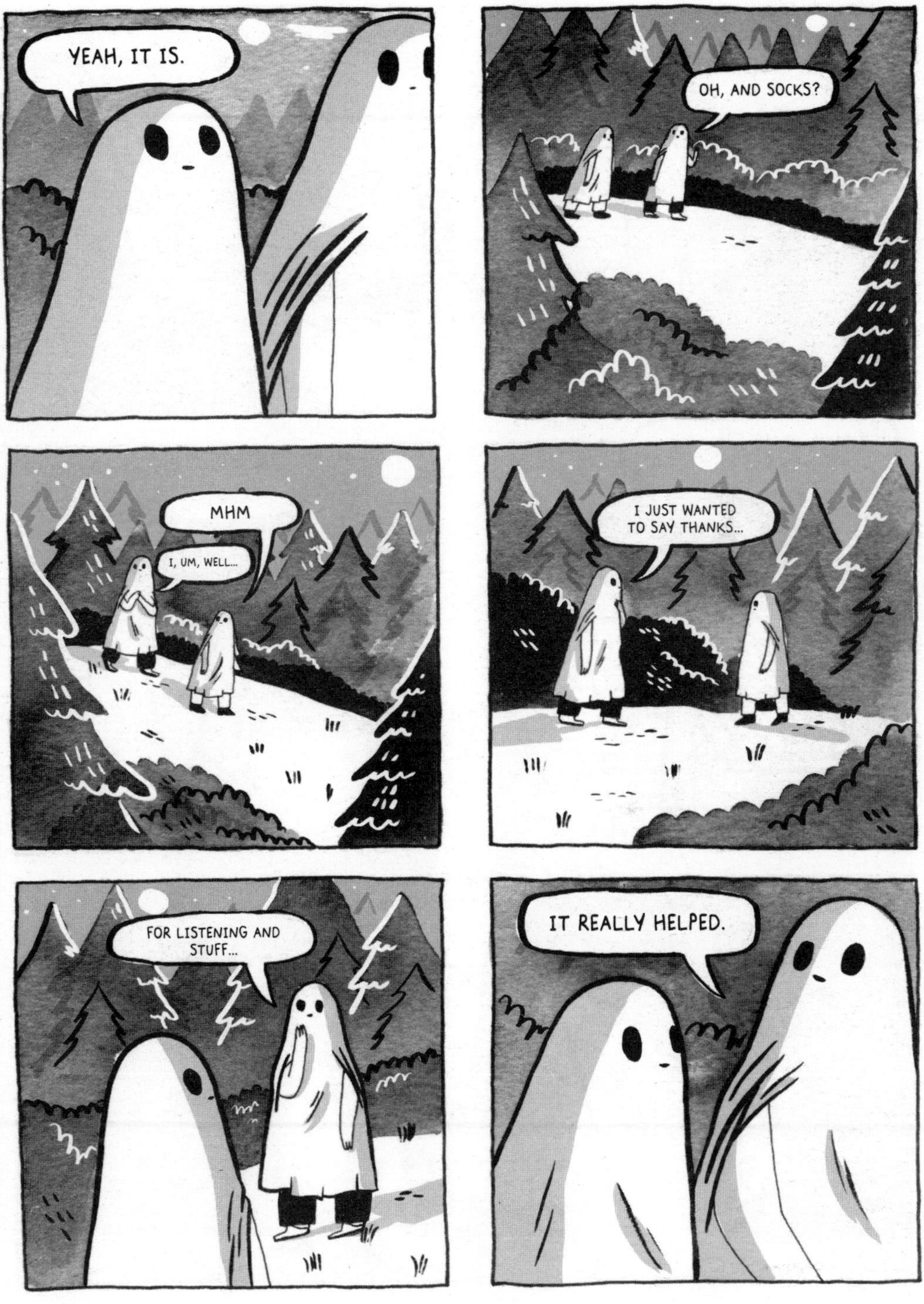
YEAH, IT IS.
OH, AND SOCKS?
MHM
I, UM, WELL...
I JUST WANTED TO SAY THANKS...
FOR LISTENING AND STUFF...
IT REALLY HELPED.

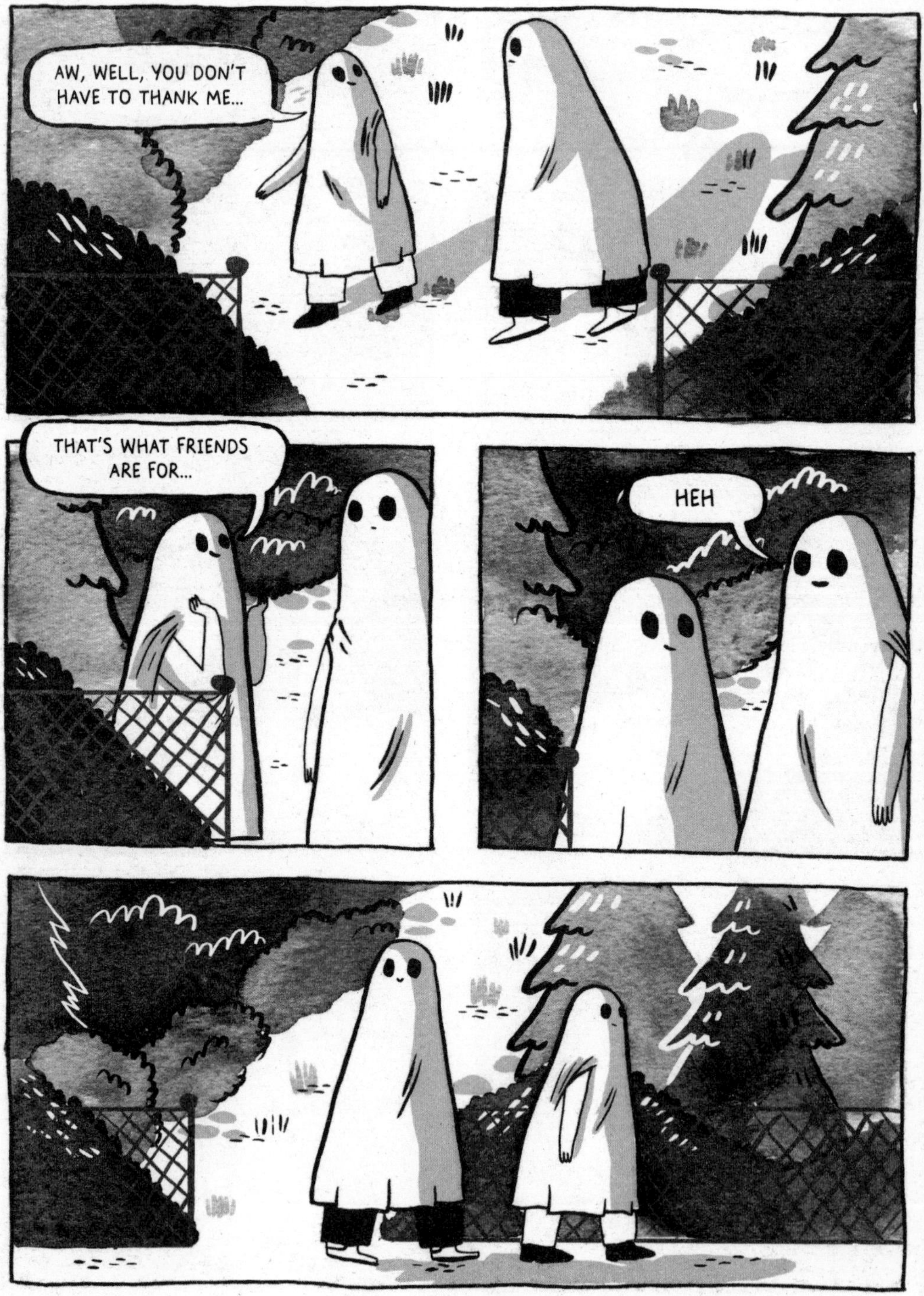
AW, WELL, YOU DON'T HAVE TO THANK ME...
THAT'S WHAT FRIENDS ARE FOR...
HEH

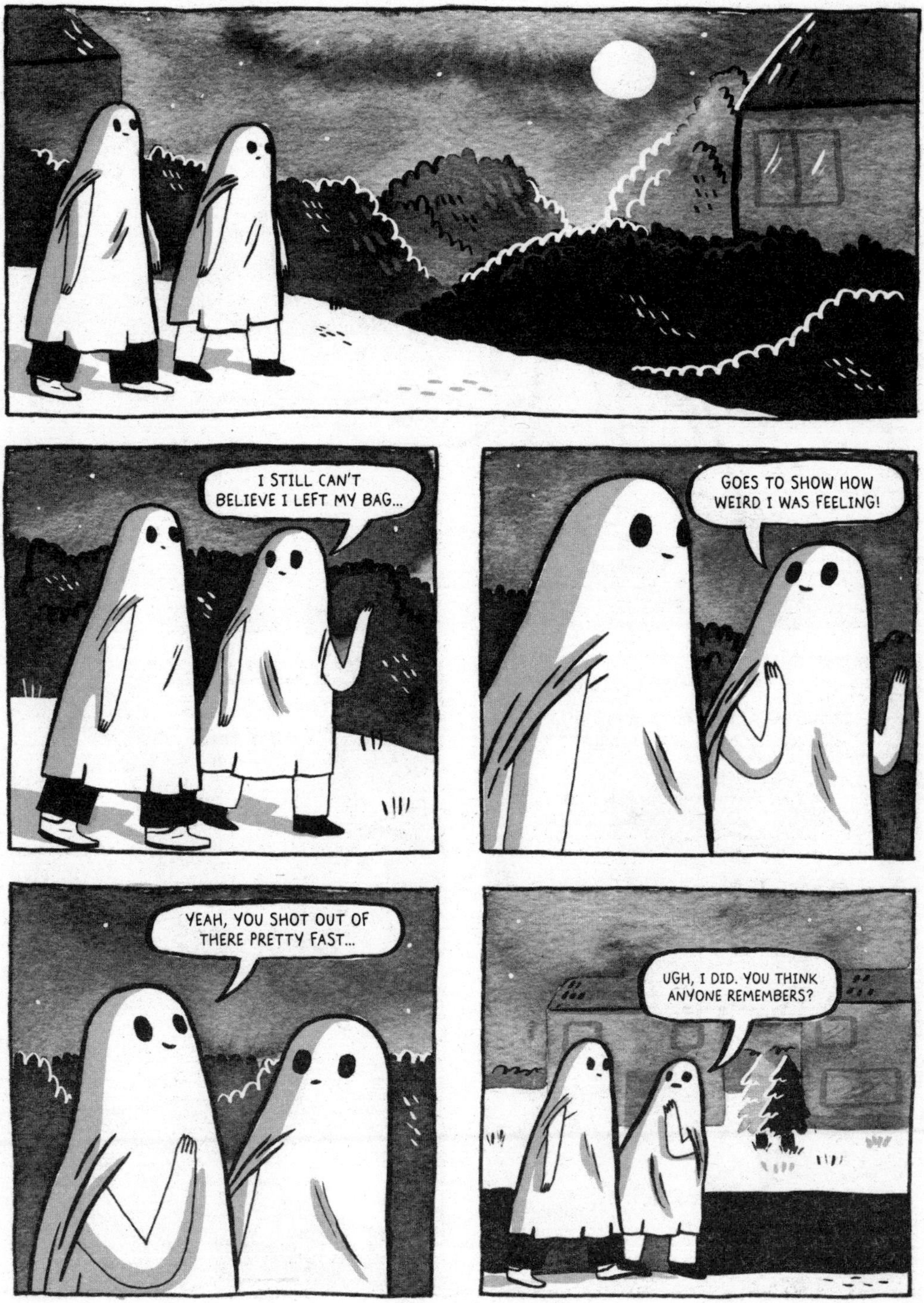
I STILL CAN'T BELIEVE I LEFT MY BAG...
GOES TO SHOW HOW WEIRD I WAS FEELING!
YEAH, YOU SHOT OUT OF THERE PRETTY FAST...
UGH, I DID. YOU THINK ANYONE REMEMBERS?

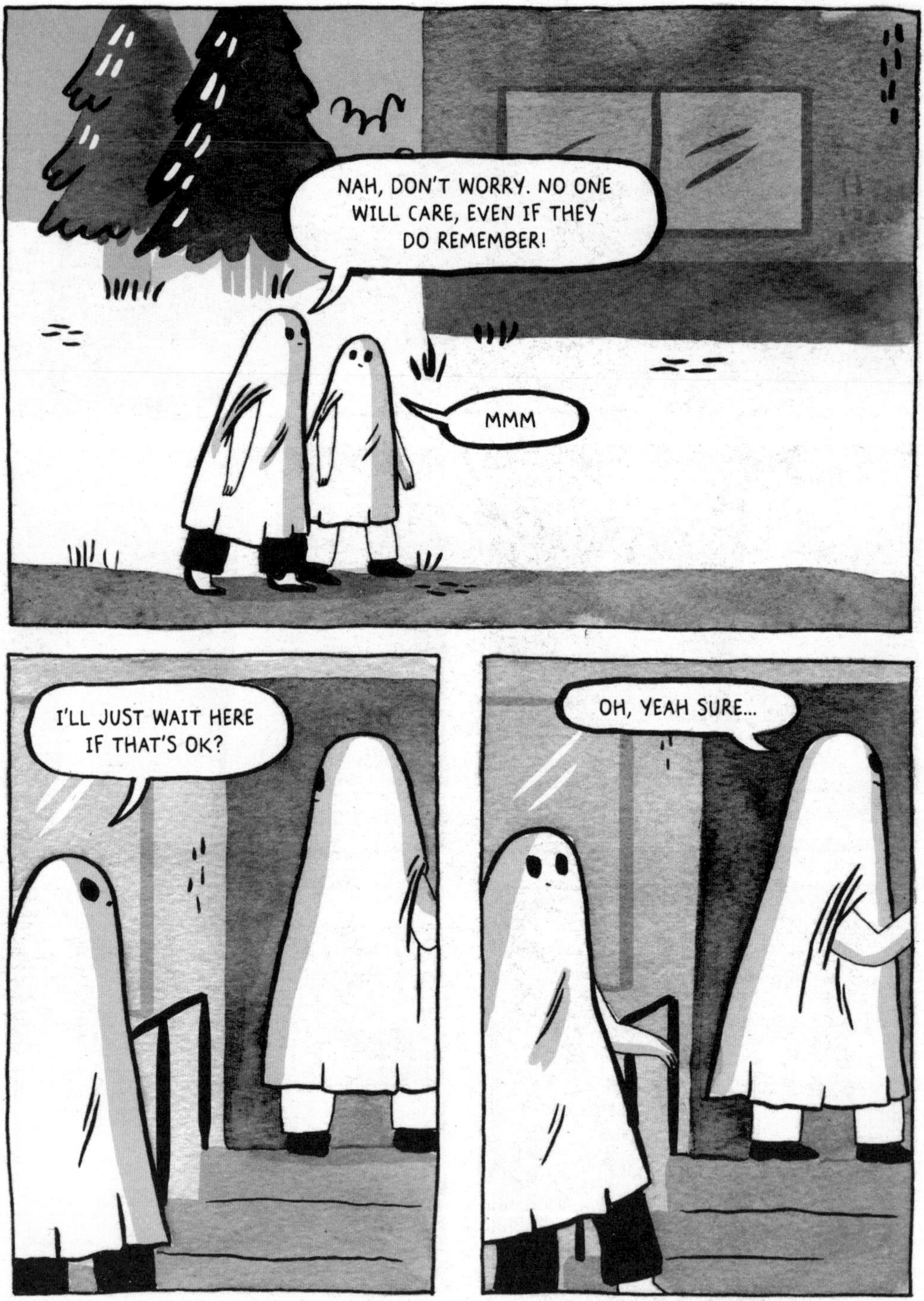
NAH, DON'T WORRY. NO ONE WILL CARE, EVEN IF THEY DO REMEMBER!
MMM
I'LL JUST WAIT HERE IF THAT'S OK?
OH, YEAH SURE...

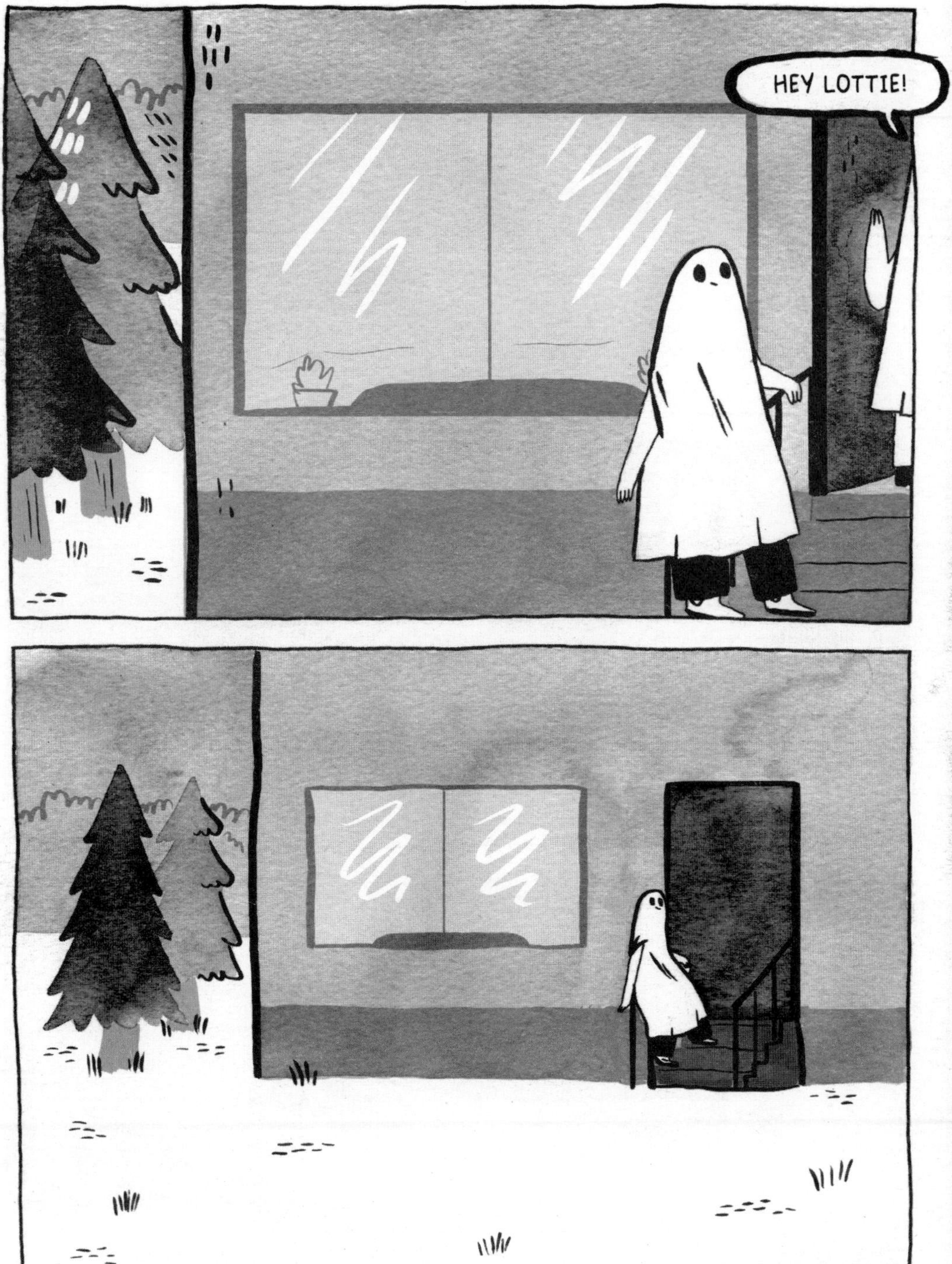
HEY LOTTIE!

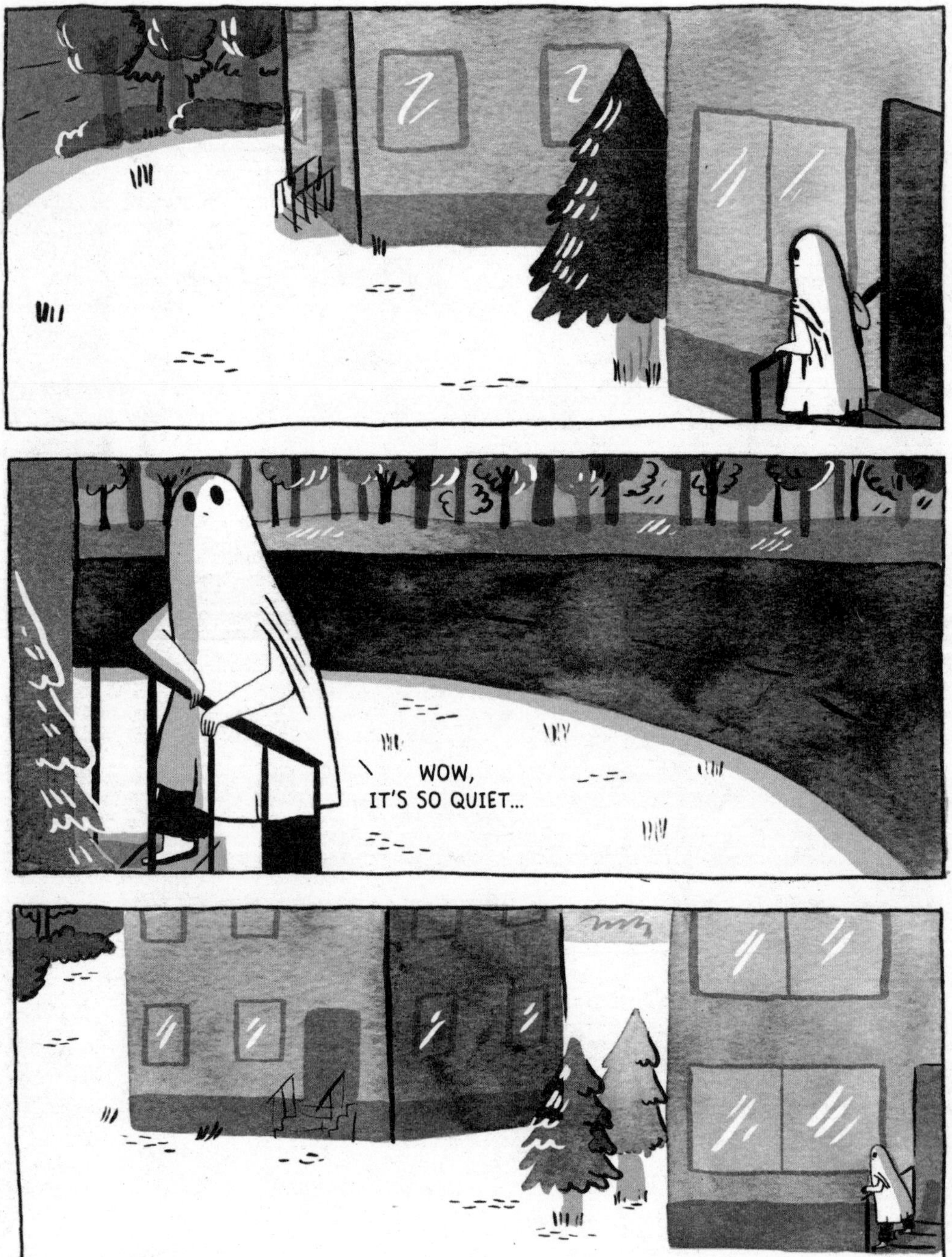
WOW,
IT'S SO QUIET...

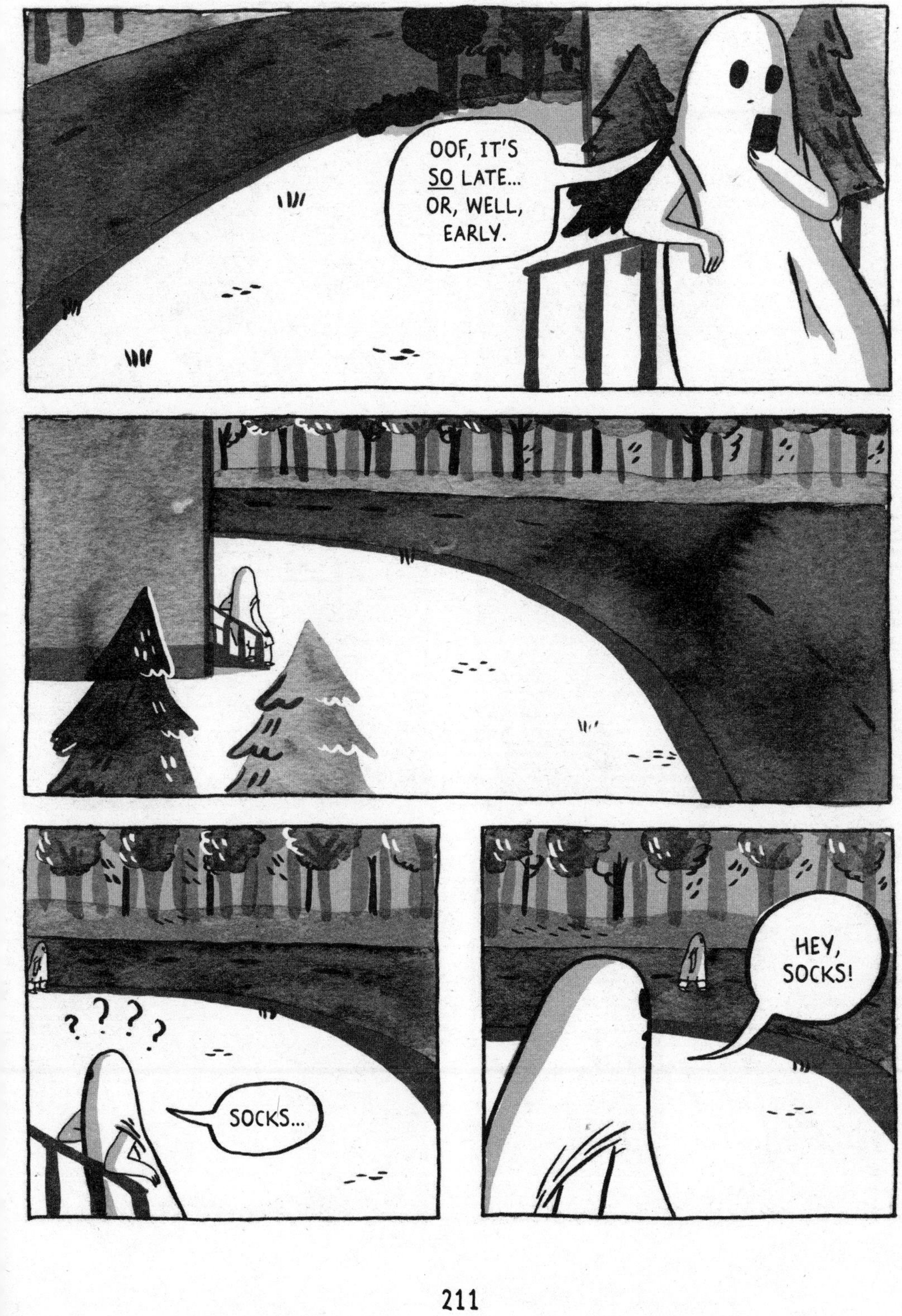
OOF, IT'S SO LATE... OR, WELL, EARLY.
SOCKS...
HEY, SOCKS!

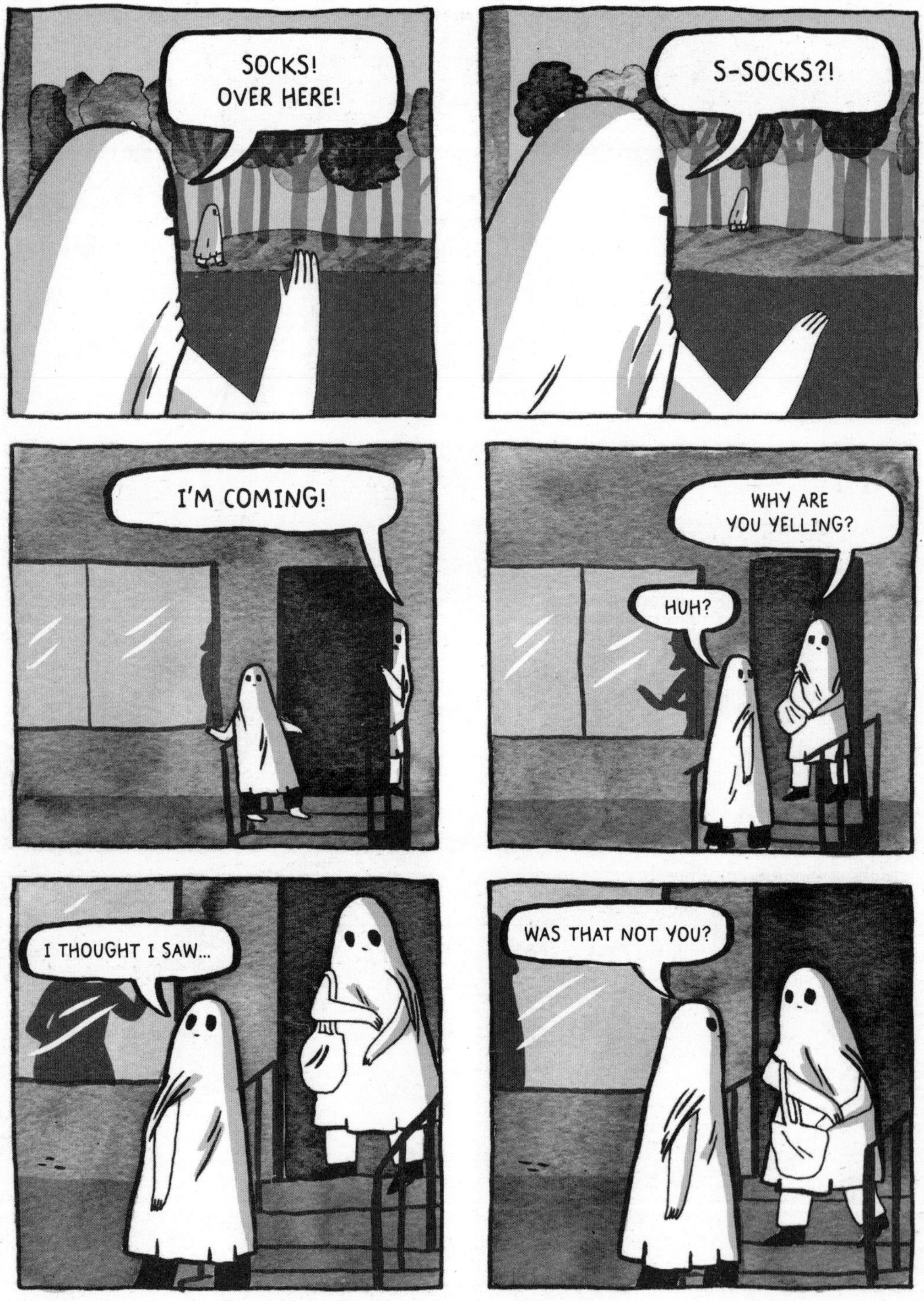
SOCKS! OVER HERE!
S-SOCKS?!
I'M COMING!
WHY ARE YOU YELLING?
HUH?
I THOUGHT I SAW...
WAS THAT NOT YOU?

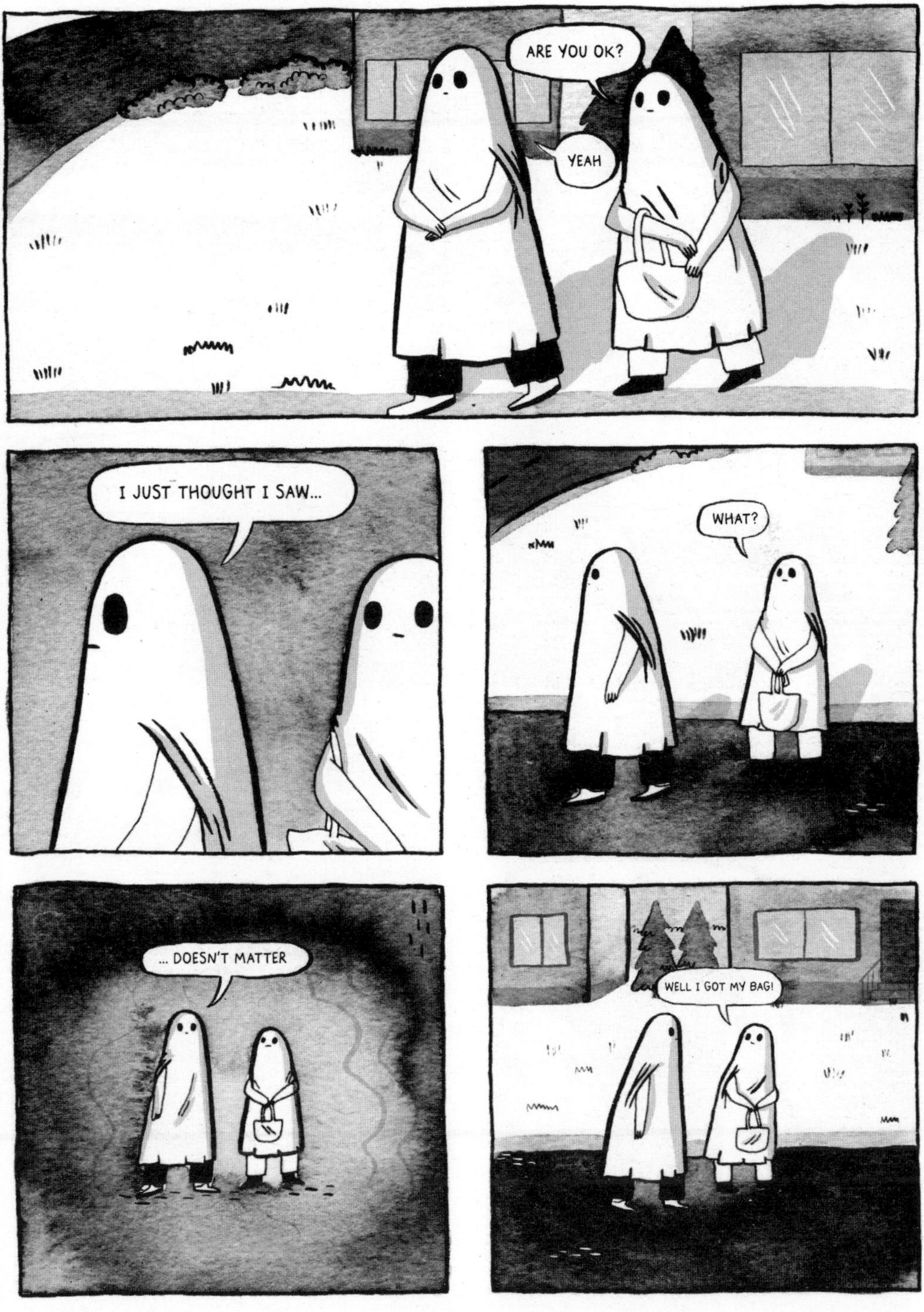
ARE YOU OK?
YEAH
I JUST THOUGHT I SAW...
WHAT?
... DOESN'T MATTER
WELL I GOT MY BAG!

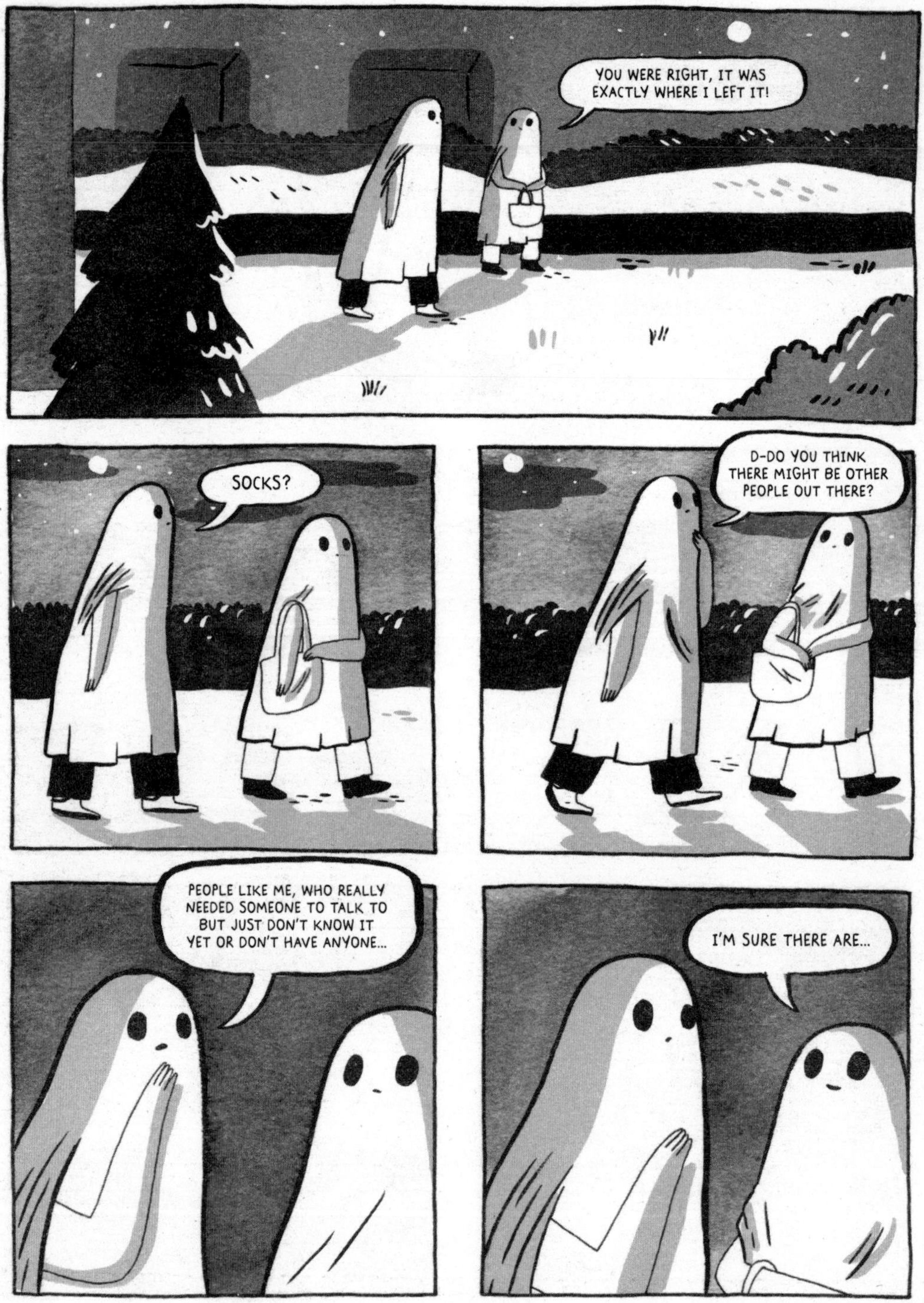
YOU WERE RIGHT, IT WAS EXACTLY WHERE I LEFT IT!
SOCKS?
D-DO YOU THINK THERE MIGHT BE OTHER PEOPLE OUT THERE?
PEOPLE LIKE ME, WHO REALLY NEEDED SOMEONE TO TALK TO BUT JUST DON'T KNOW IT YET OR DON'T HAVE ANYONE...
I'M SURE THERE ARE...

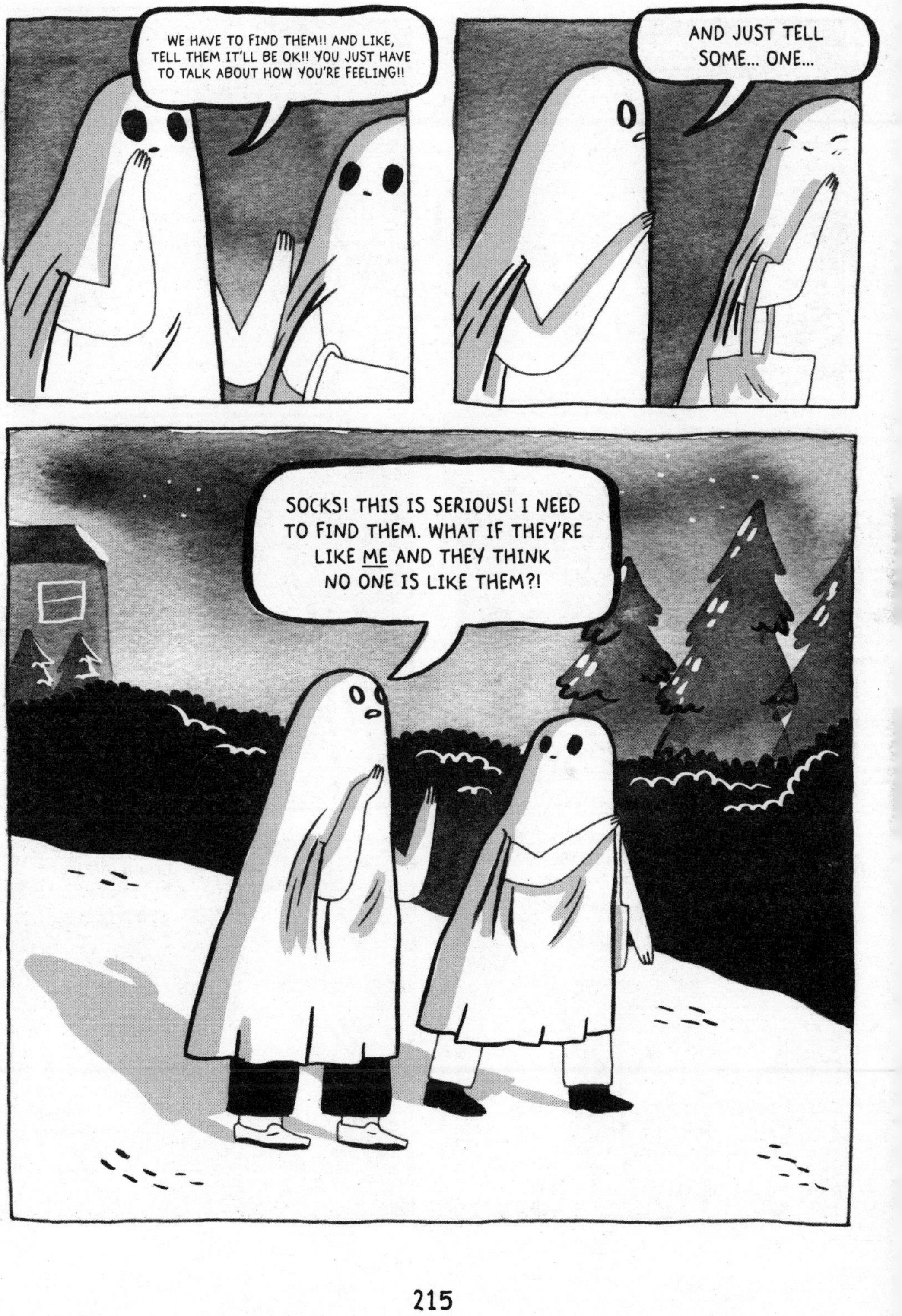
WE HAVE TO FIND THEM!! AND LIKE, TELL THEM IT'LL BE OK!! YOU JUST HAVE TO TALK ABOUT HOW YOU'RE FEELING!!
AND JUST TELL SOME... ONE...
SOCKS! THIS IS SERIOUS! I NEED TO FIND THEM. WHAT IF THEY'RE LIKE ME AND THEY THINK NO ONE IS LIKE THEM?!

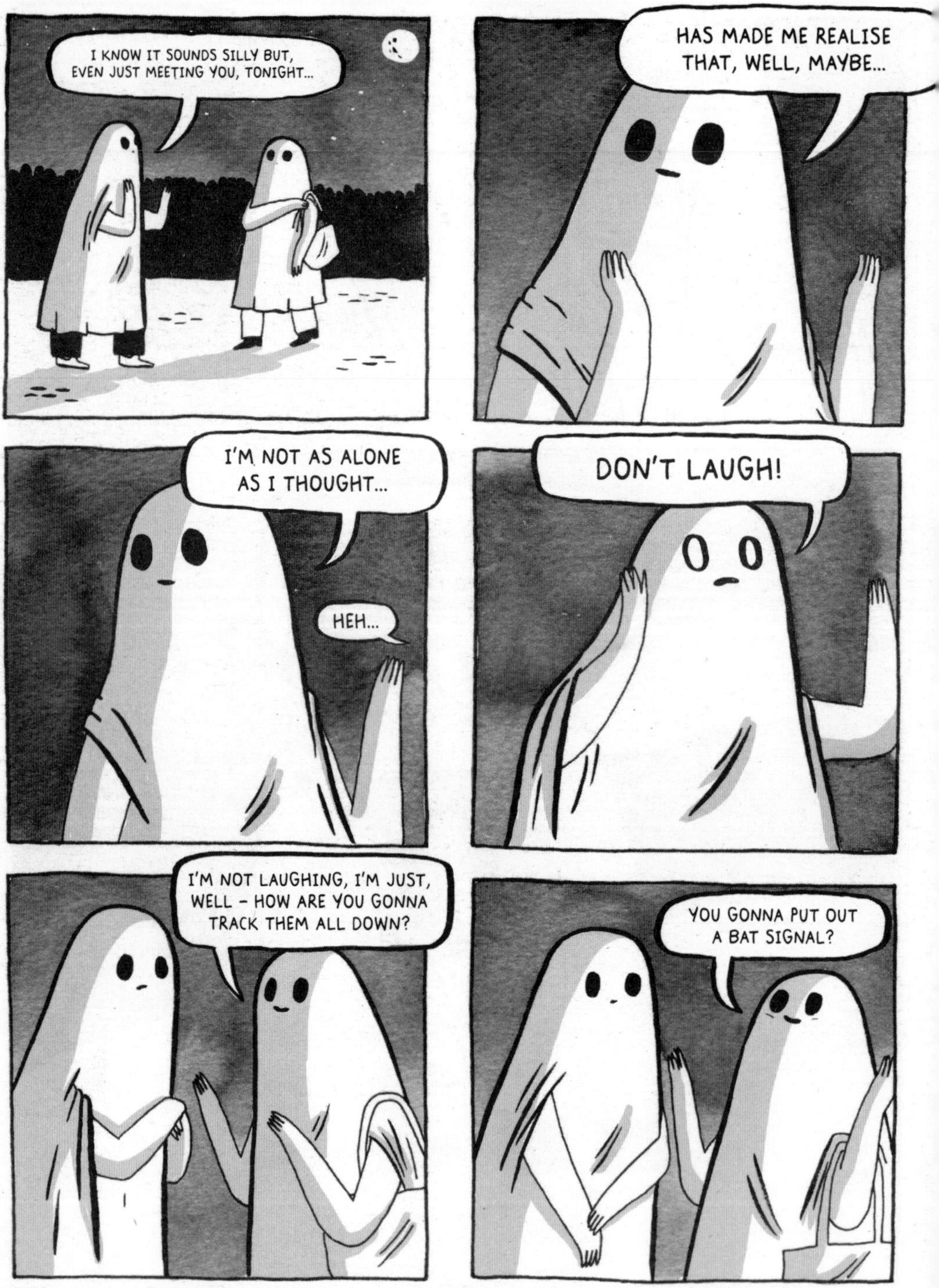

I KNOW IT SOUNDS SILLY BUT, EVEN JUST MEETING YOU, TONIGHT...
HAS MADE ME REALISE THAT, WELL, MAYBE...
I'M NOT AS ALONE AS I THOUGHT...
HEH...
DON'T LAUGH!
I'M NOT LAUGHING, I'M JUST, WELL - HOW ARE YOU GONNA TRACK THEM ALL DOWN?
YOU GONNA PUT OUT A BAT SIGNAL?

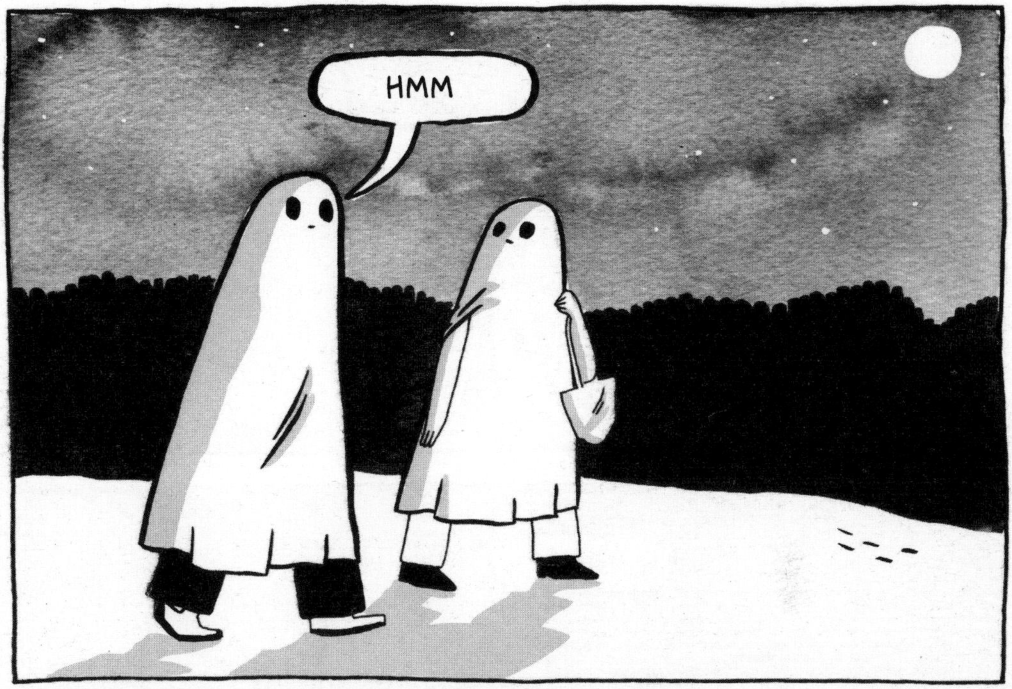
HMM

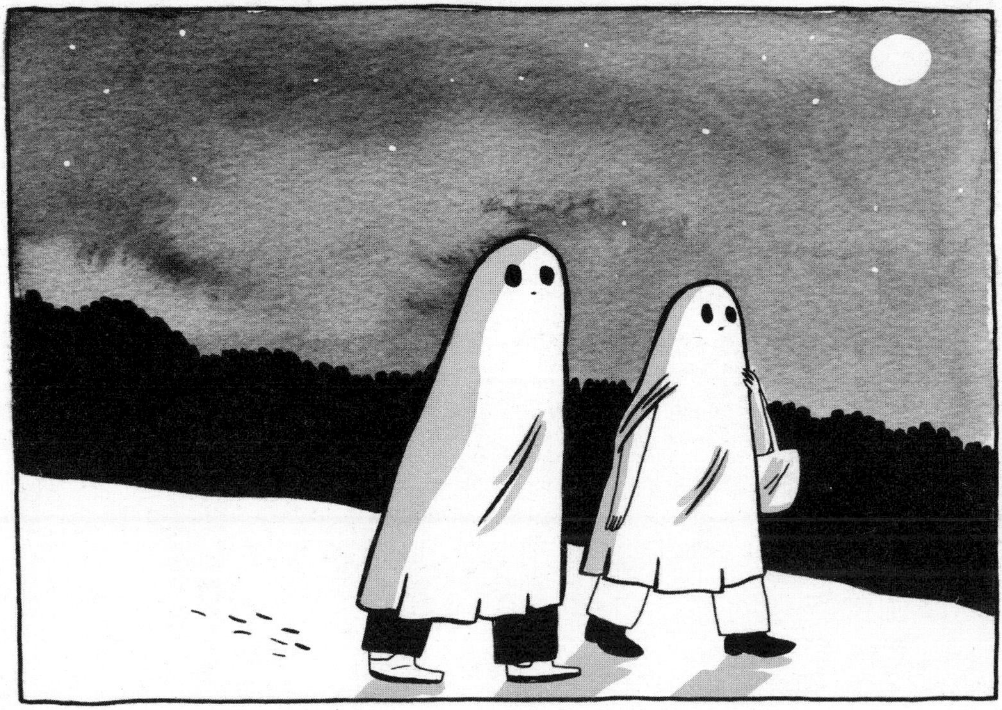

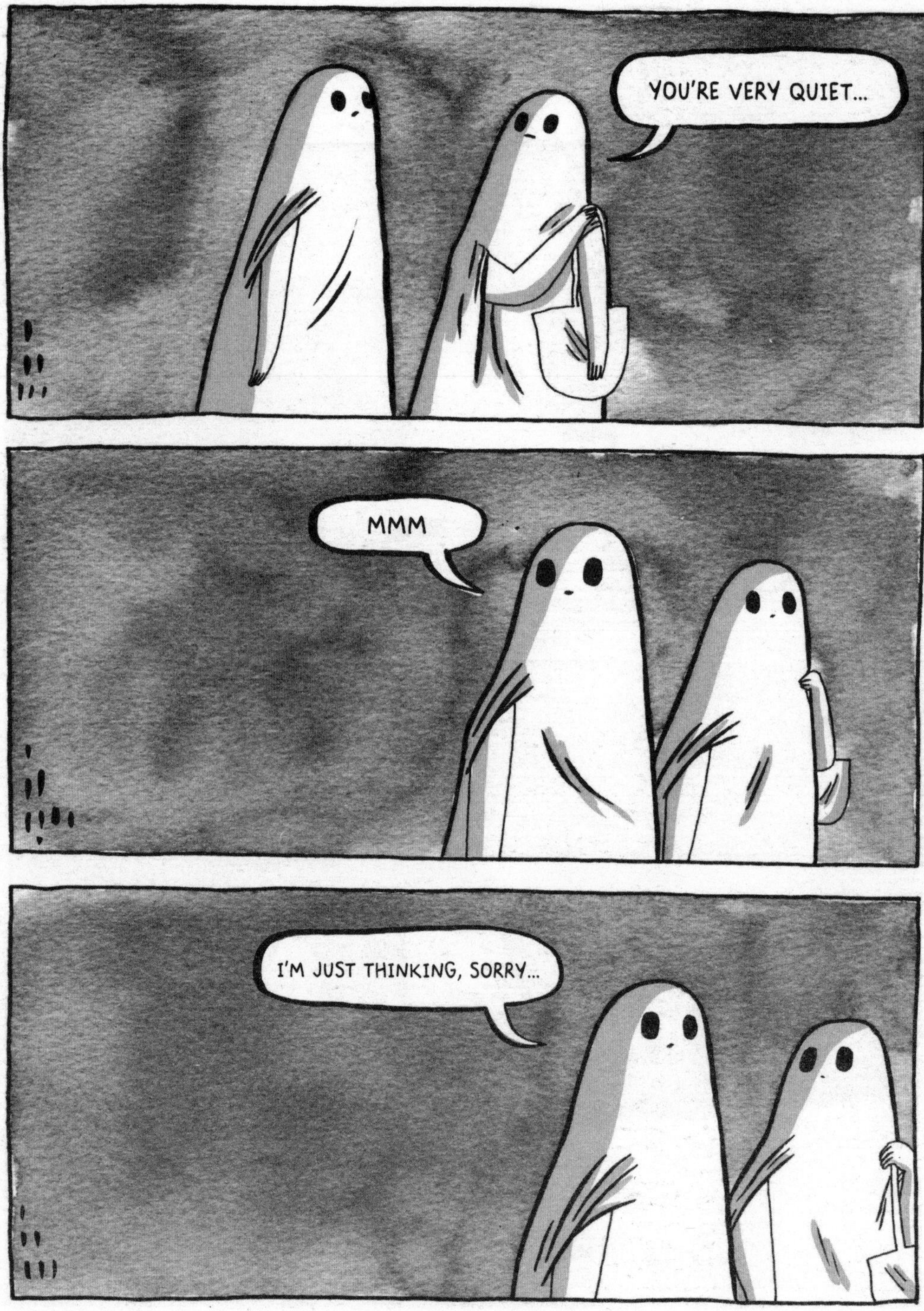
YOU'RE VERY QUIET...
MMM
I'M JUST THINKING, SORRY...

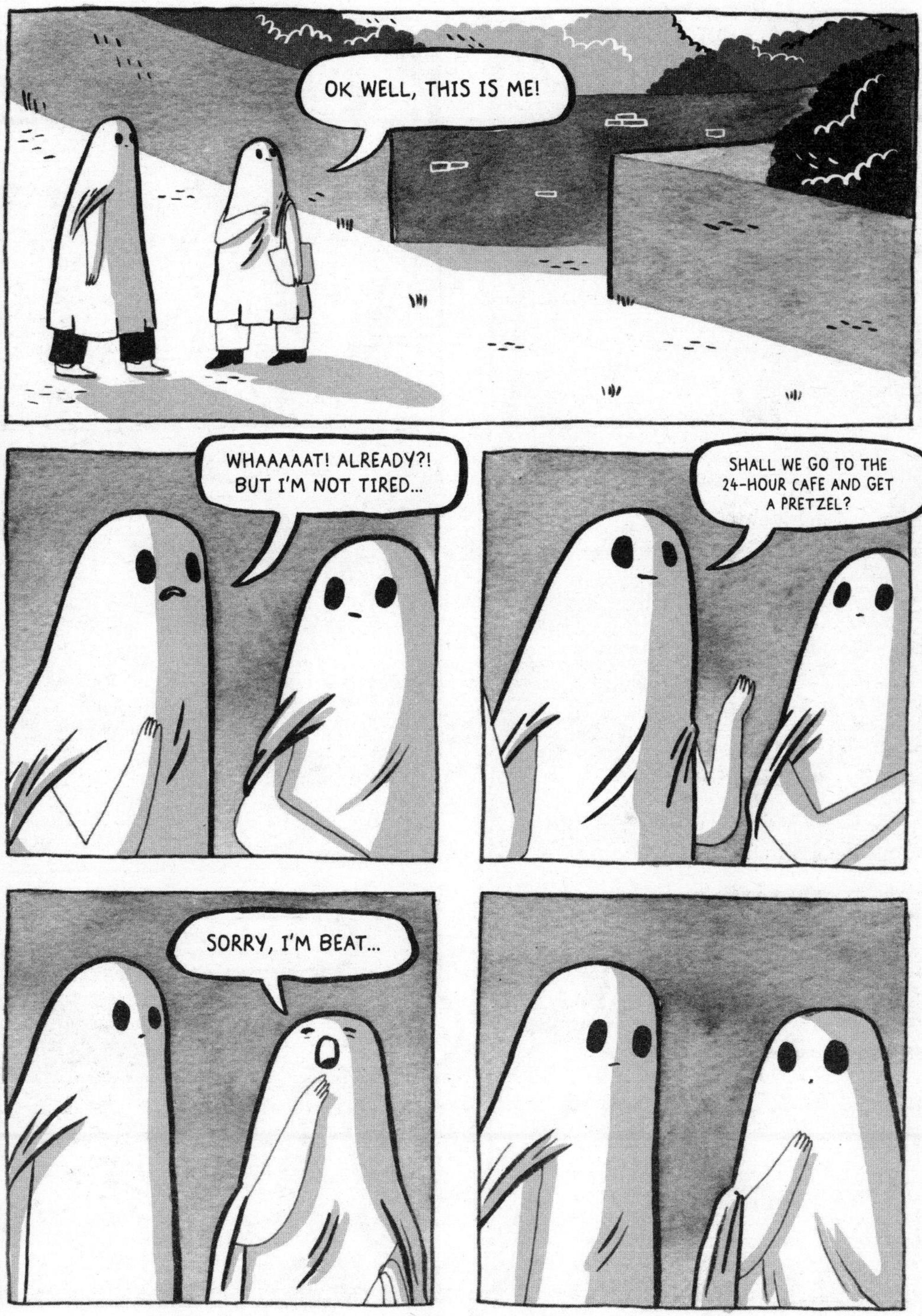
OK WELL, THIS IS ME!
WHAAAAAT! ALREADY?! BUT I'M NOT TIRED...
SHALL WE GO TO THE 24-HOUR CAFE AND GET A PRETZEL?
SORRY, I'M BEAT...

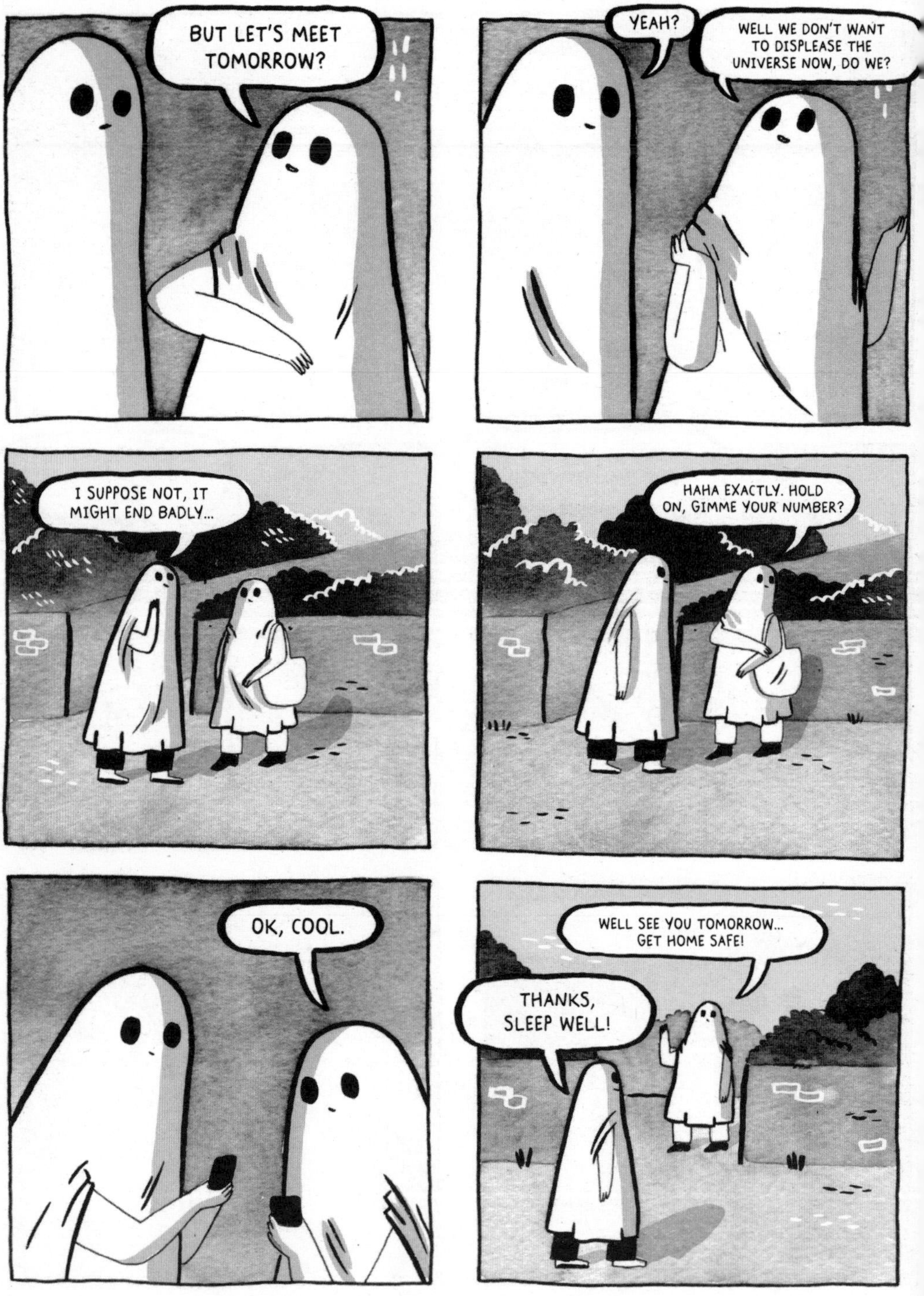
BUT LET'S MEET TOMORROW?
YEAH?
WELL WE DON'T WANT TO DISPLEASE THE UNIVERSE NOW, DO WE?
I SUPPOSE NOT, IT MIGHT END BADLY...
HAHA EXACTLY. HOLD ON, GIMME YOUR NUMBER?
OK, COOL.
WELL SEE YOU TOMORROW... GET HOME SAFE!
THANKS, SLEEP WELL!

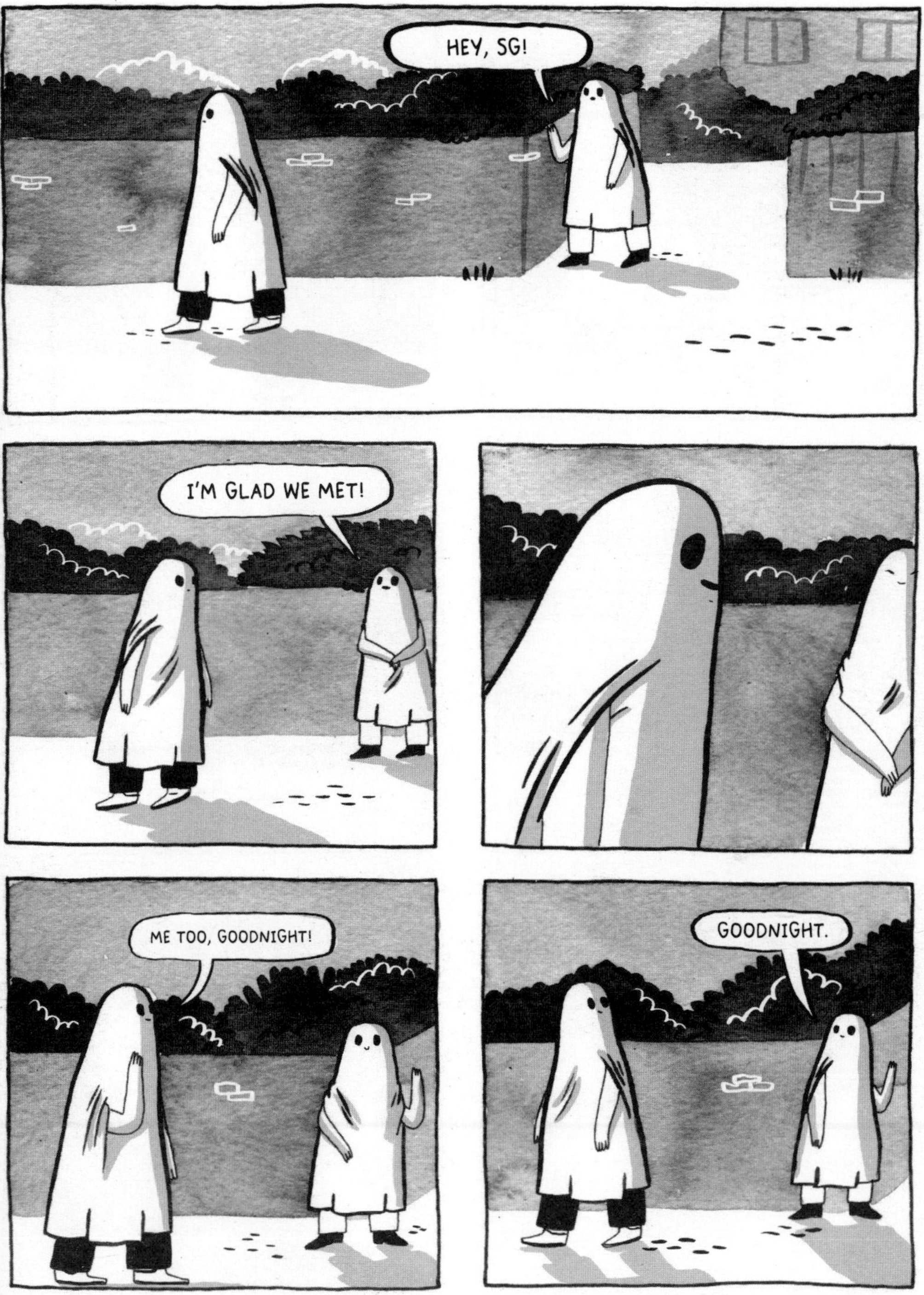
HEY, SG!
I'M GLAD WE MET!
ME TOO, GOODNIGHT!
GOODNIGHT.

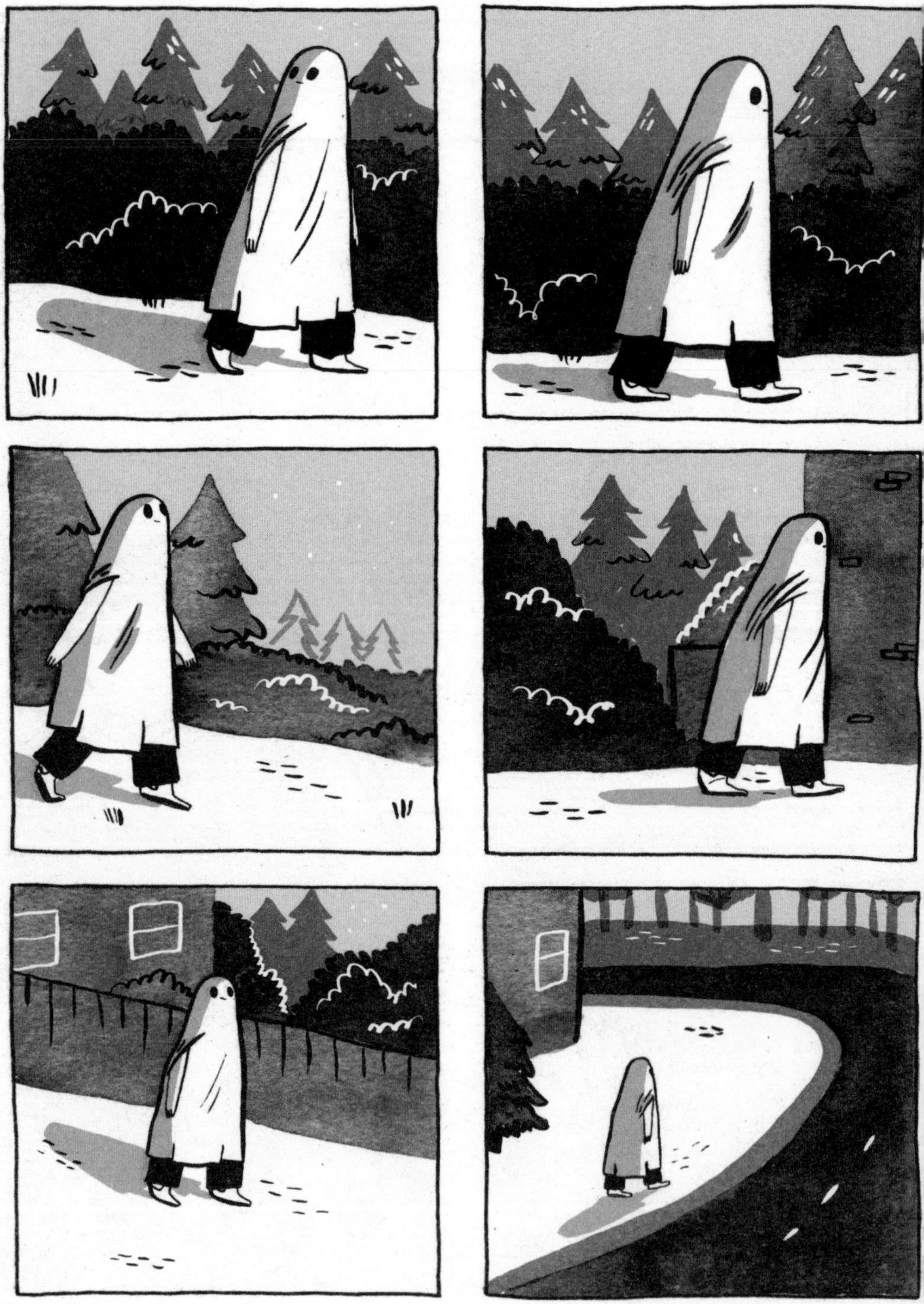

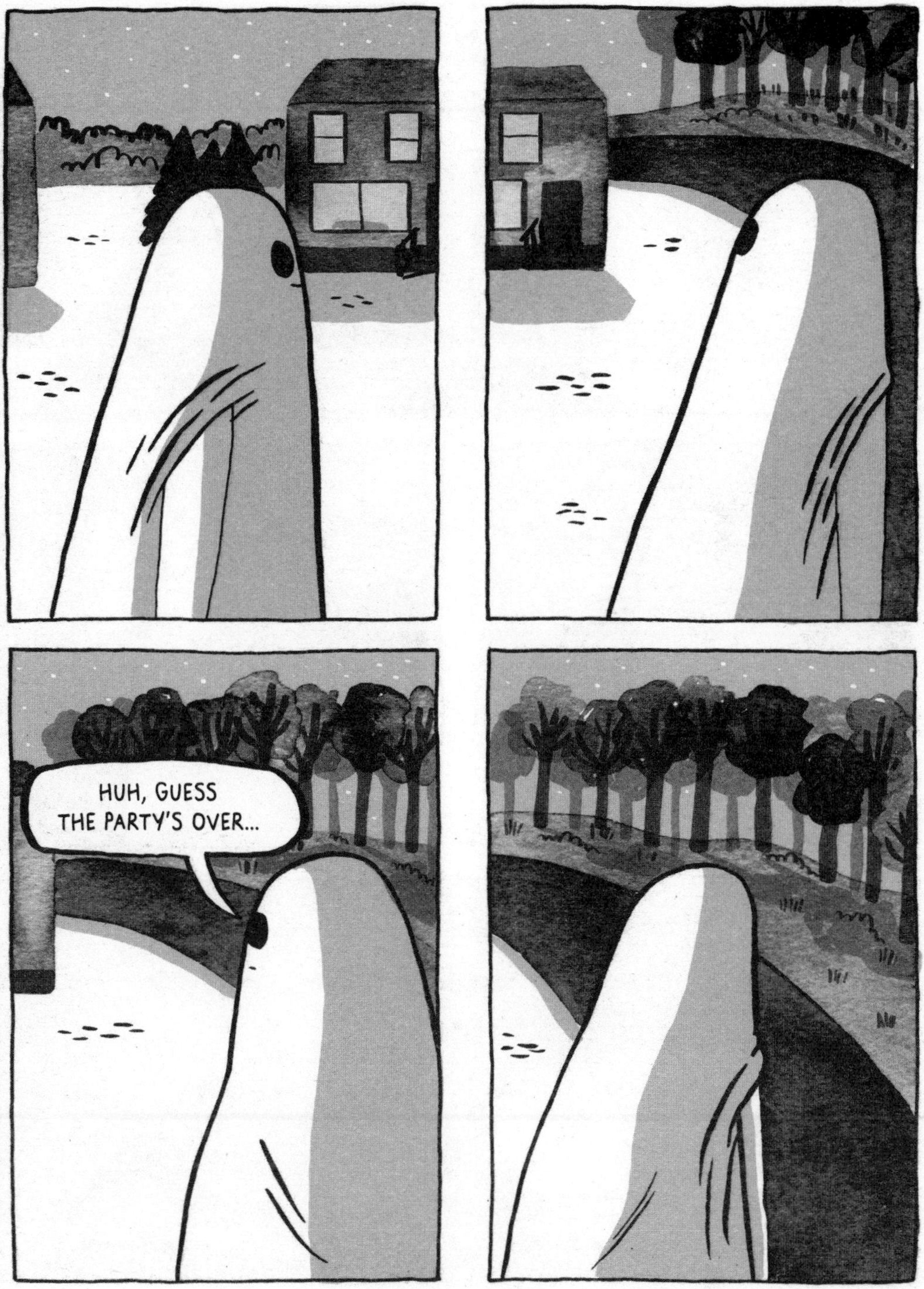
HUH, GUESS THE PARTY'S OVER...

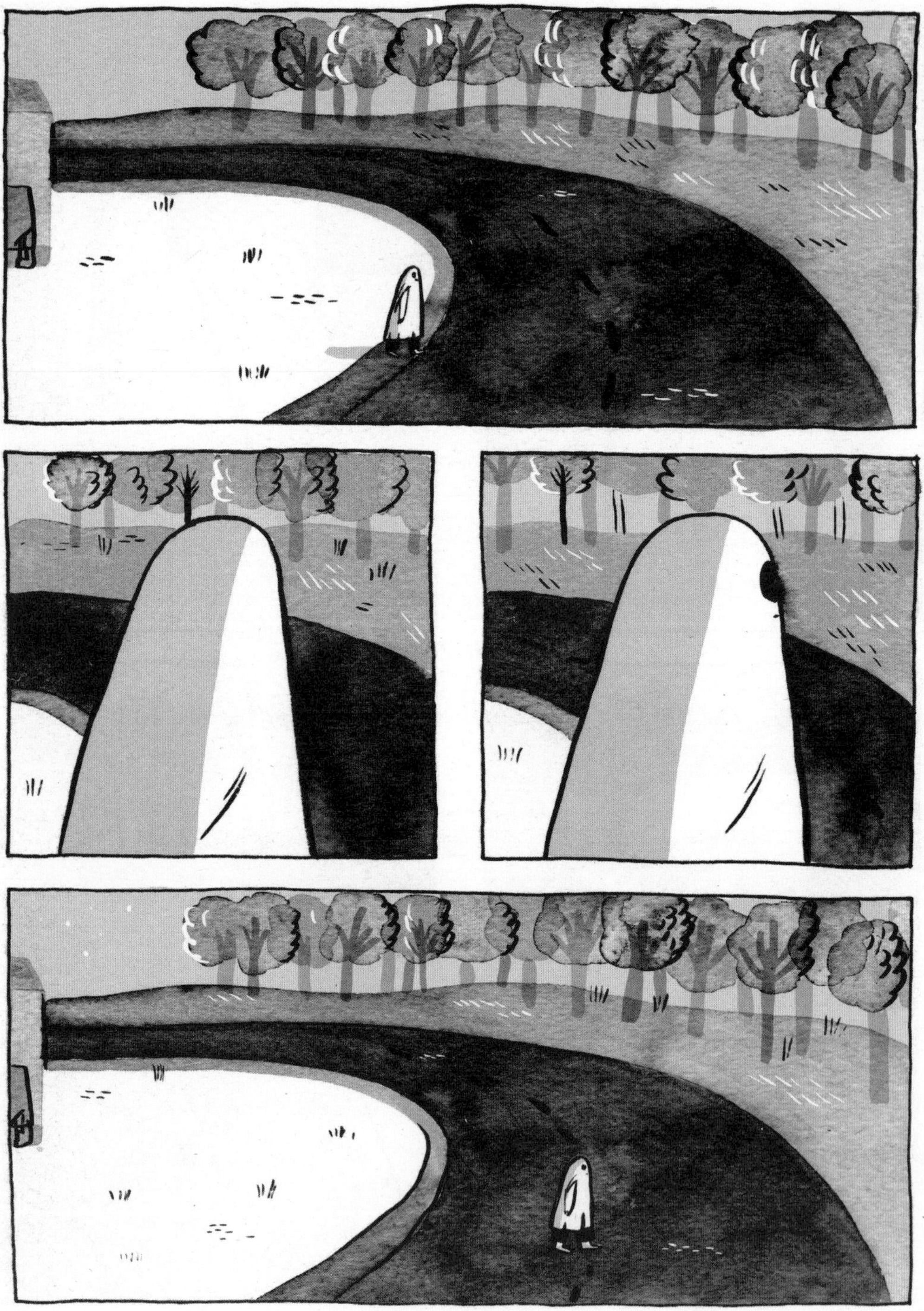

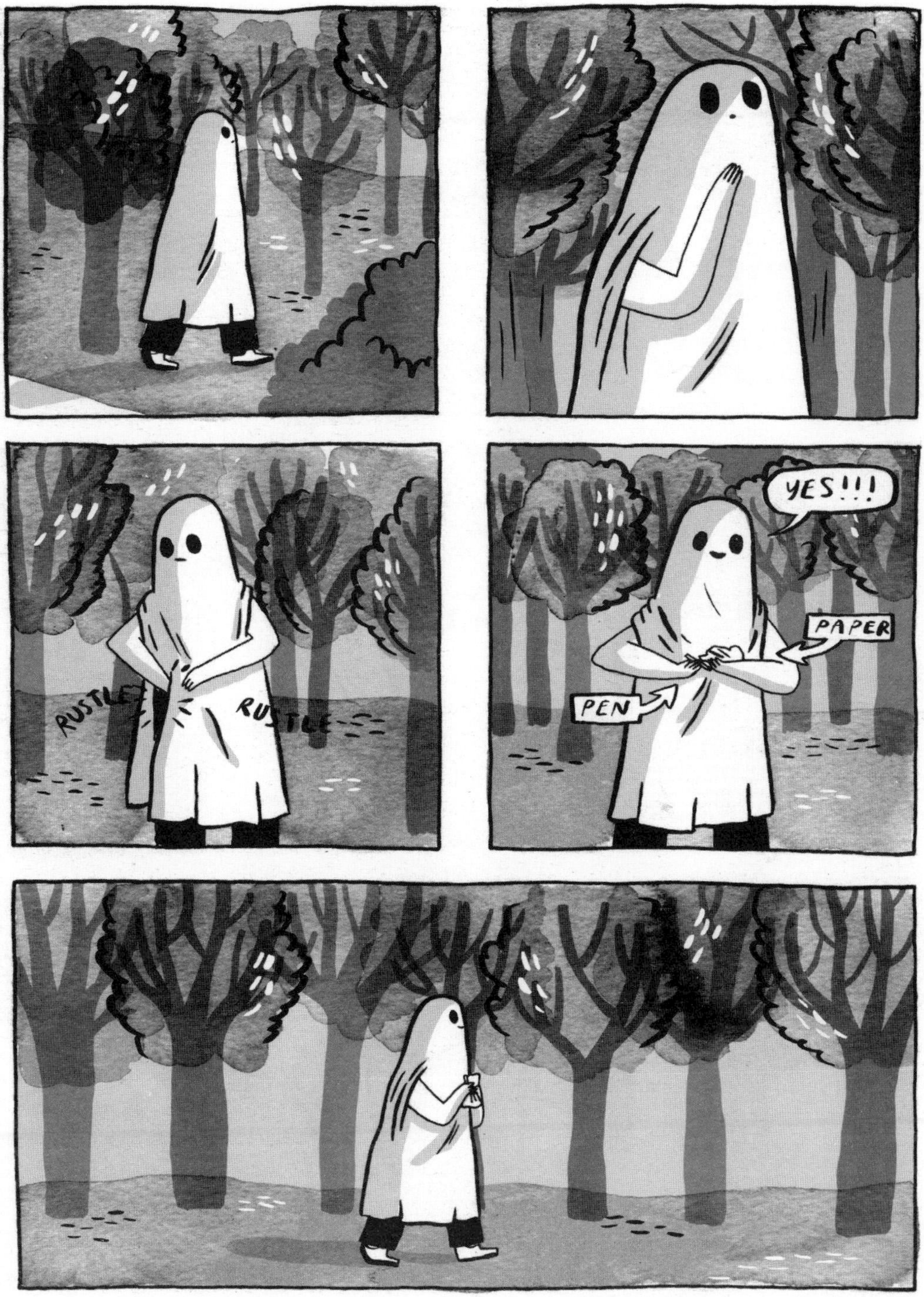
RUSTLE
RUSTLE
YES!!!
PAPER
PEN

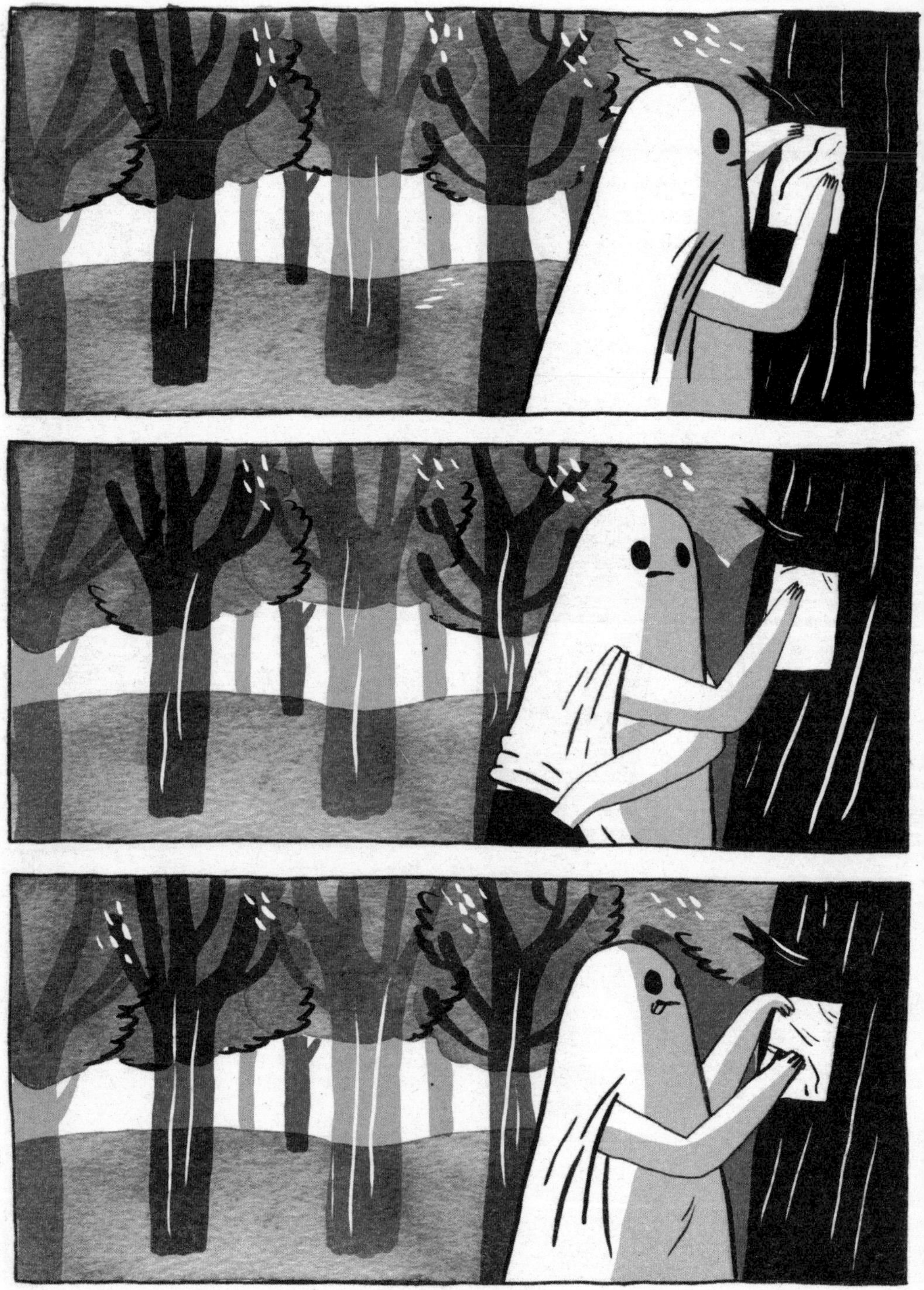

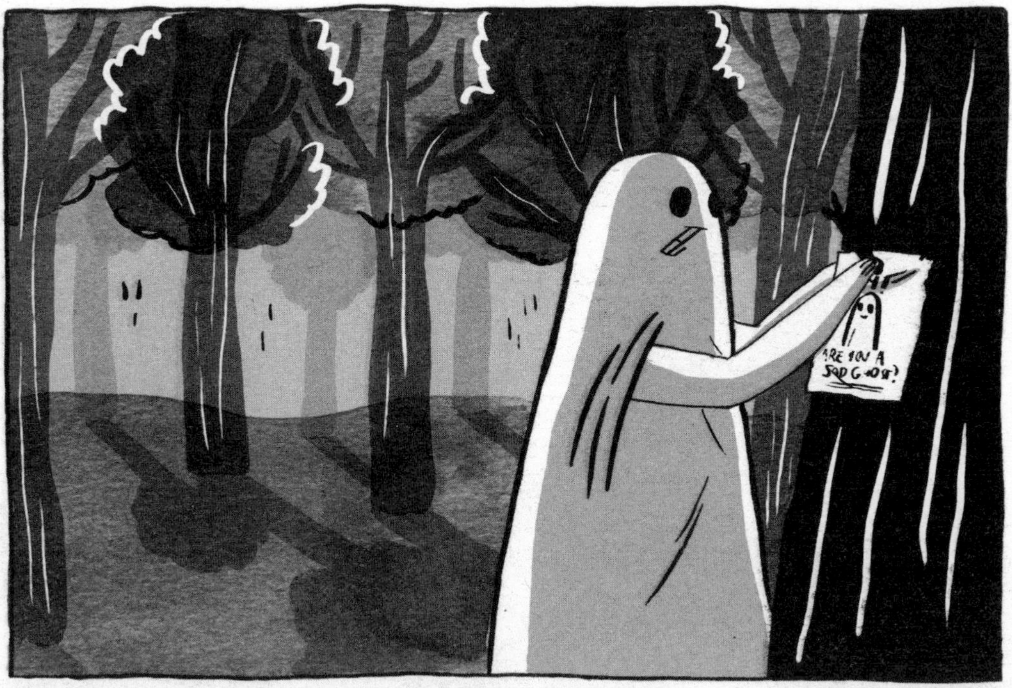
ARE YOU A SAD GHOST?

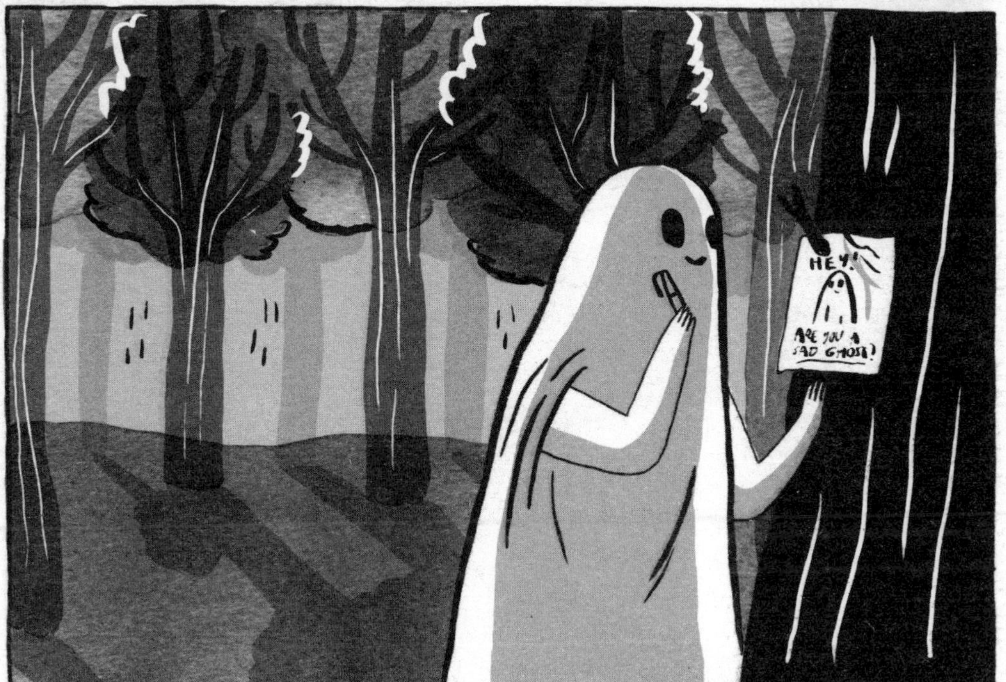
HEY!
ARE YOU A SAD GHOST?

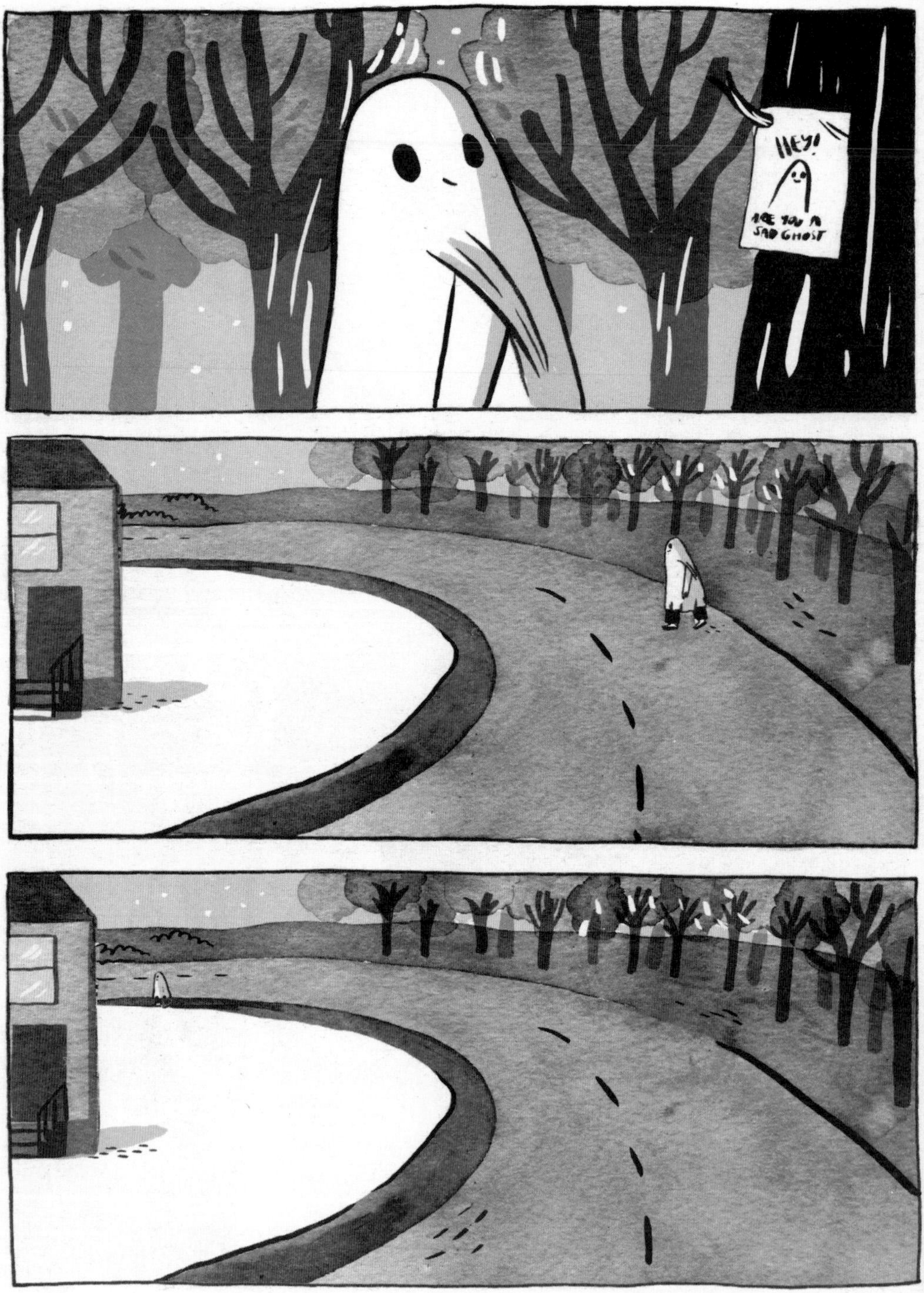
HEY!
ARE YOU A SAD GHOST

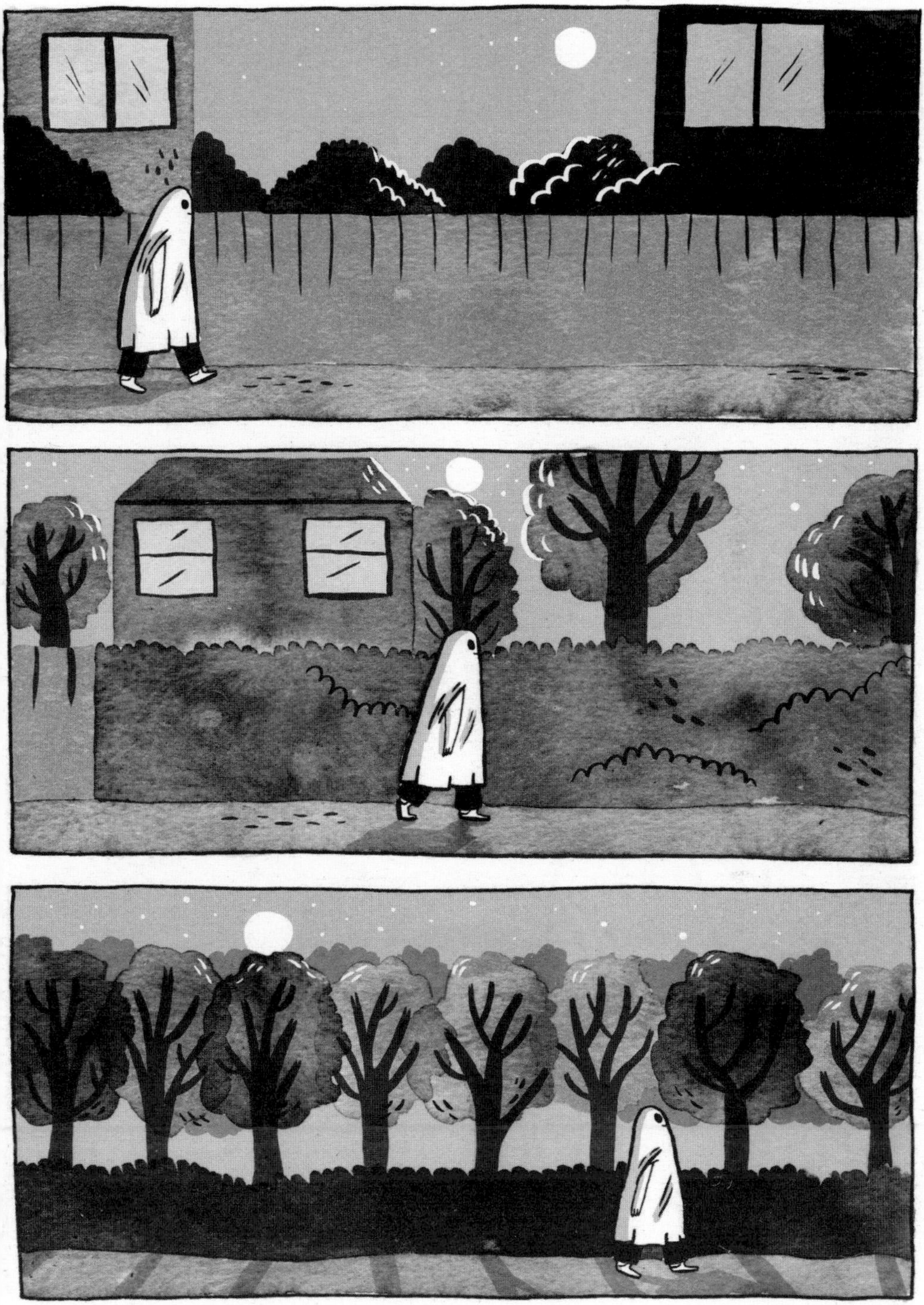

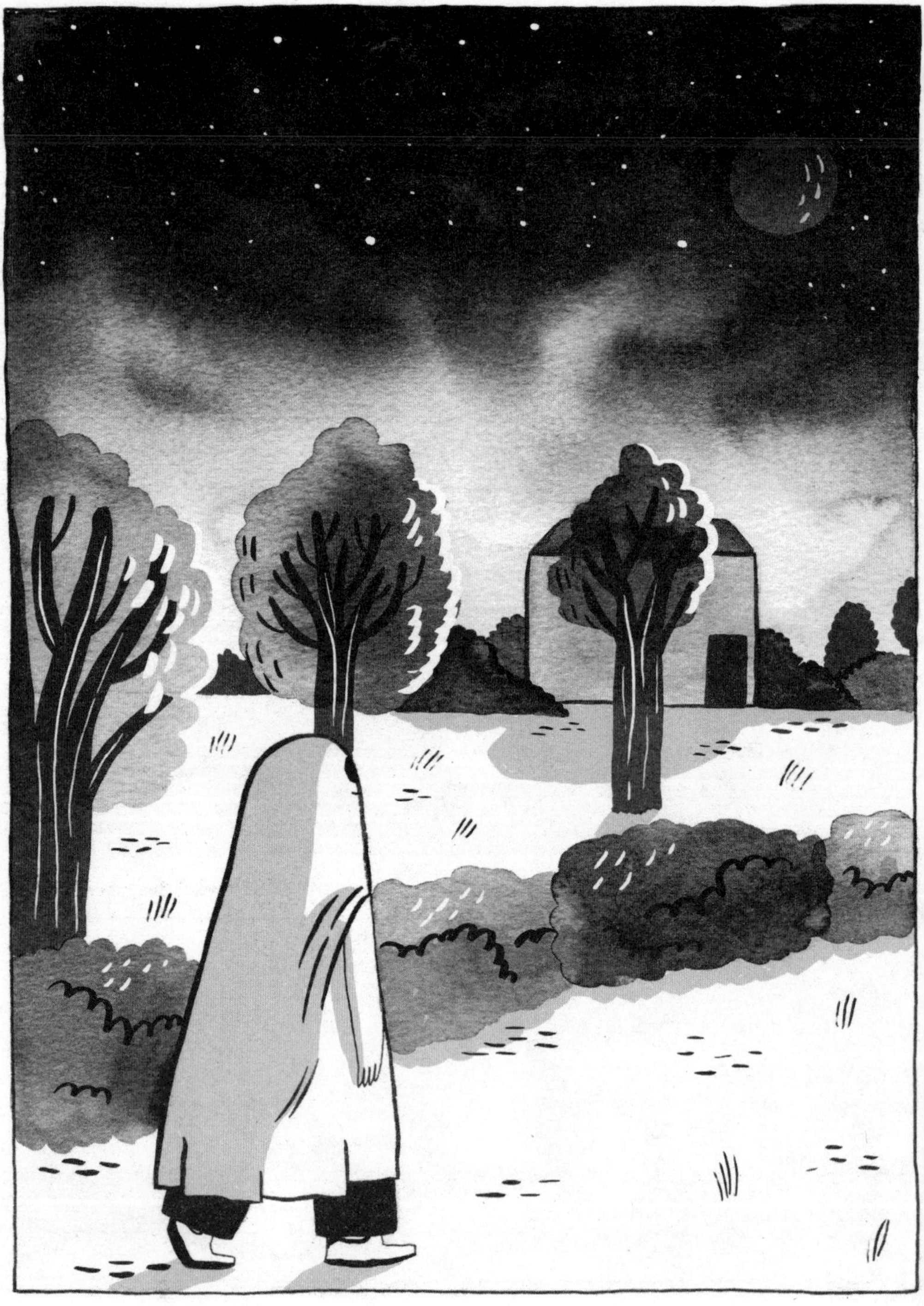

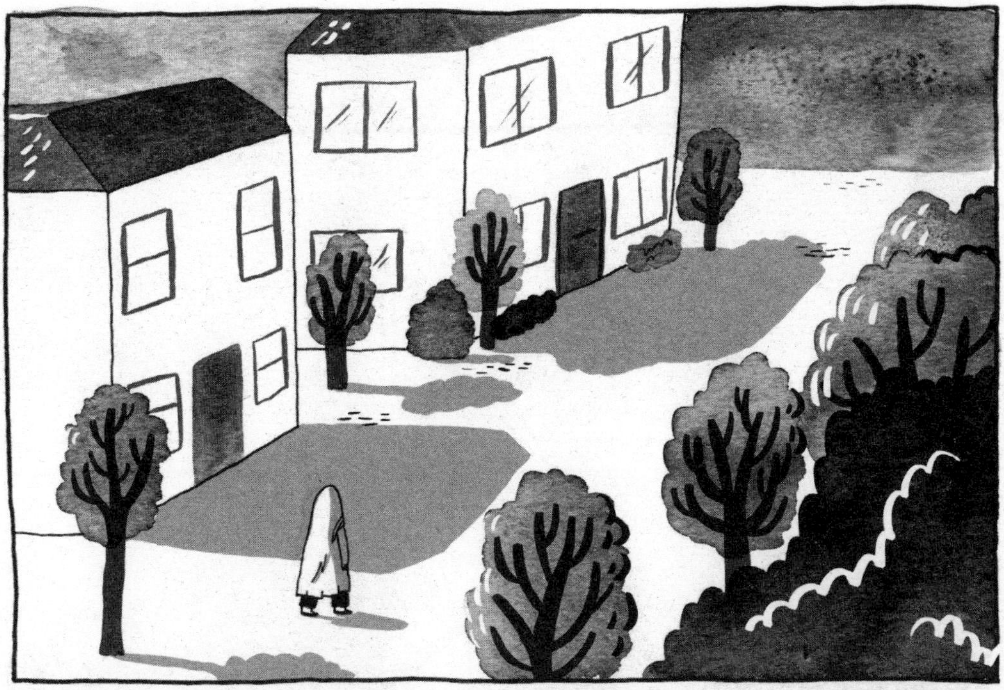

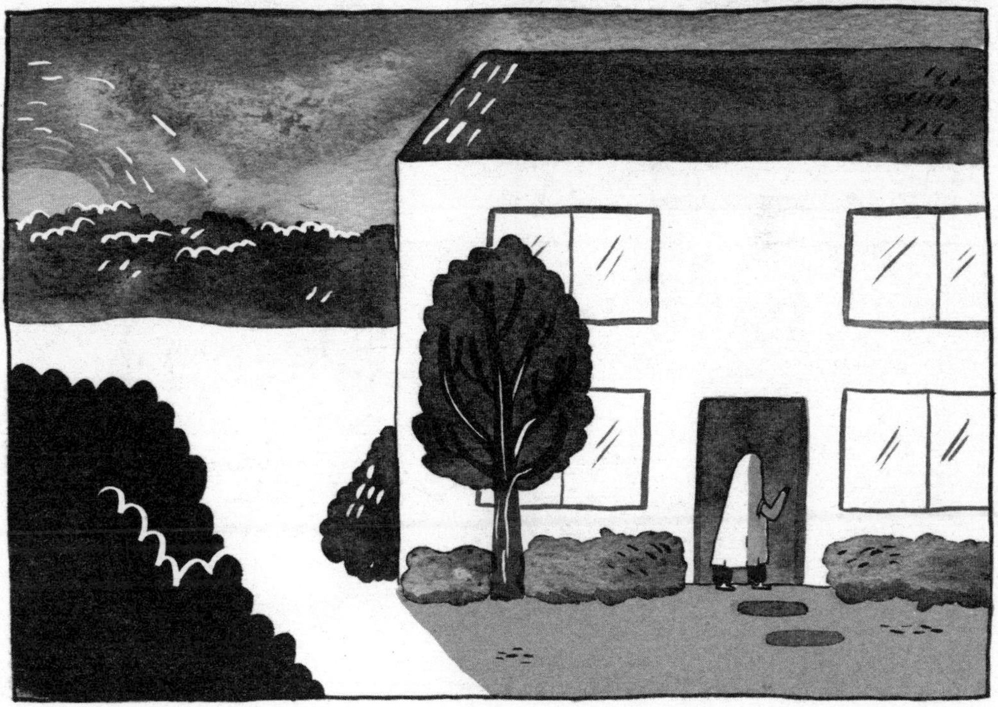

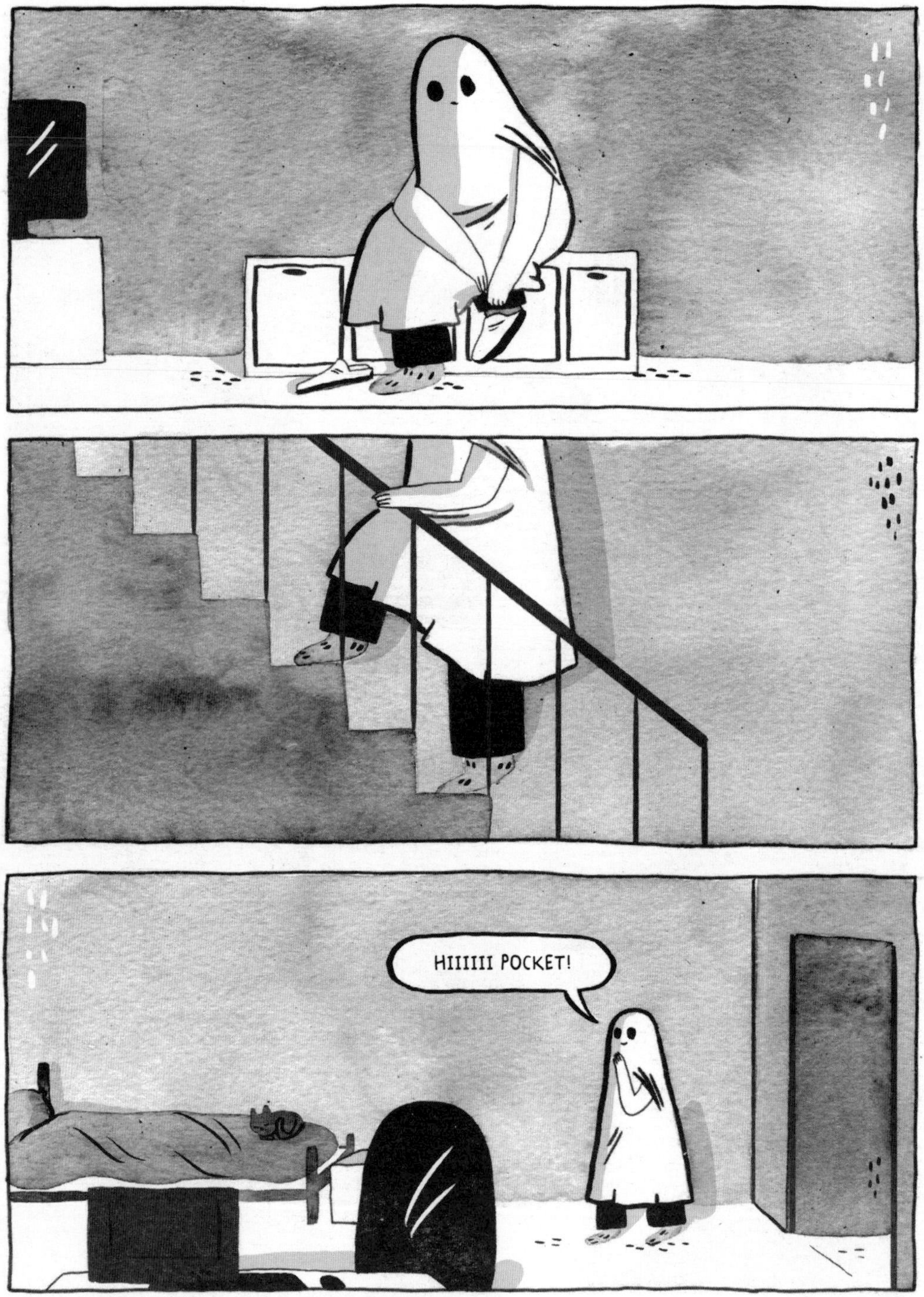
HIIIIII POCKET!

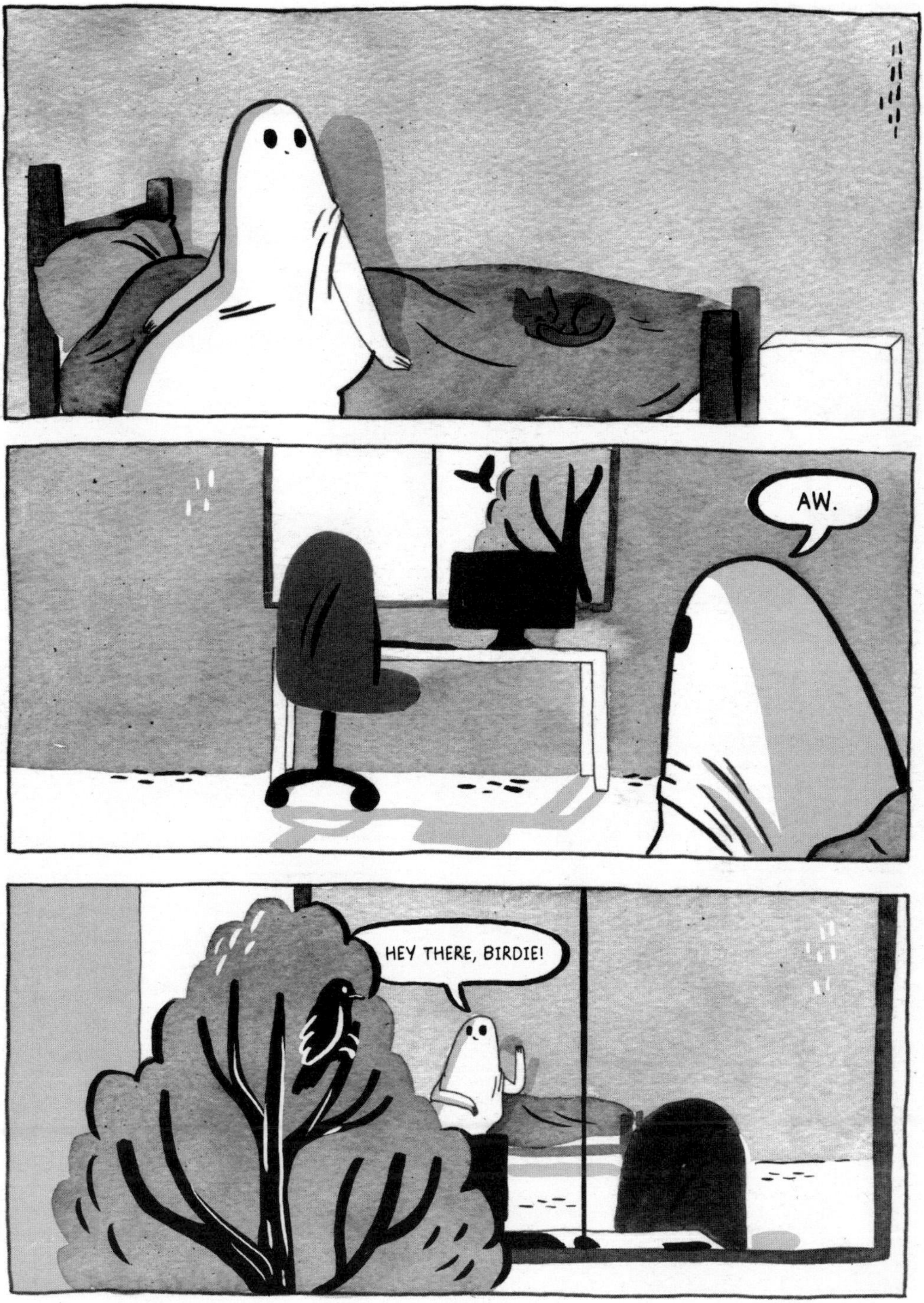
AW.
HEY THERE, BIRDIE!

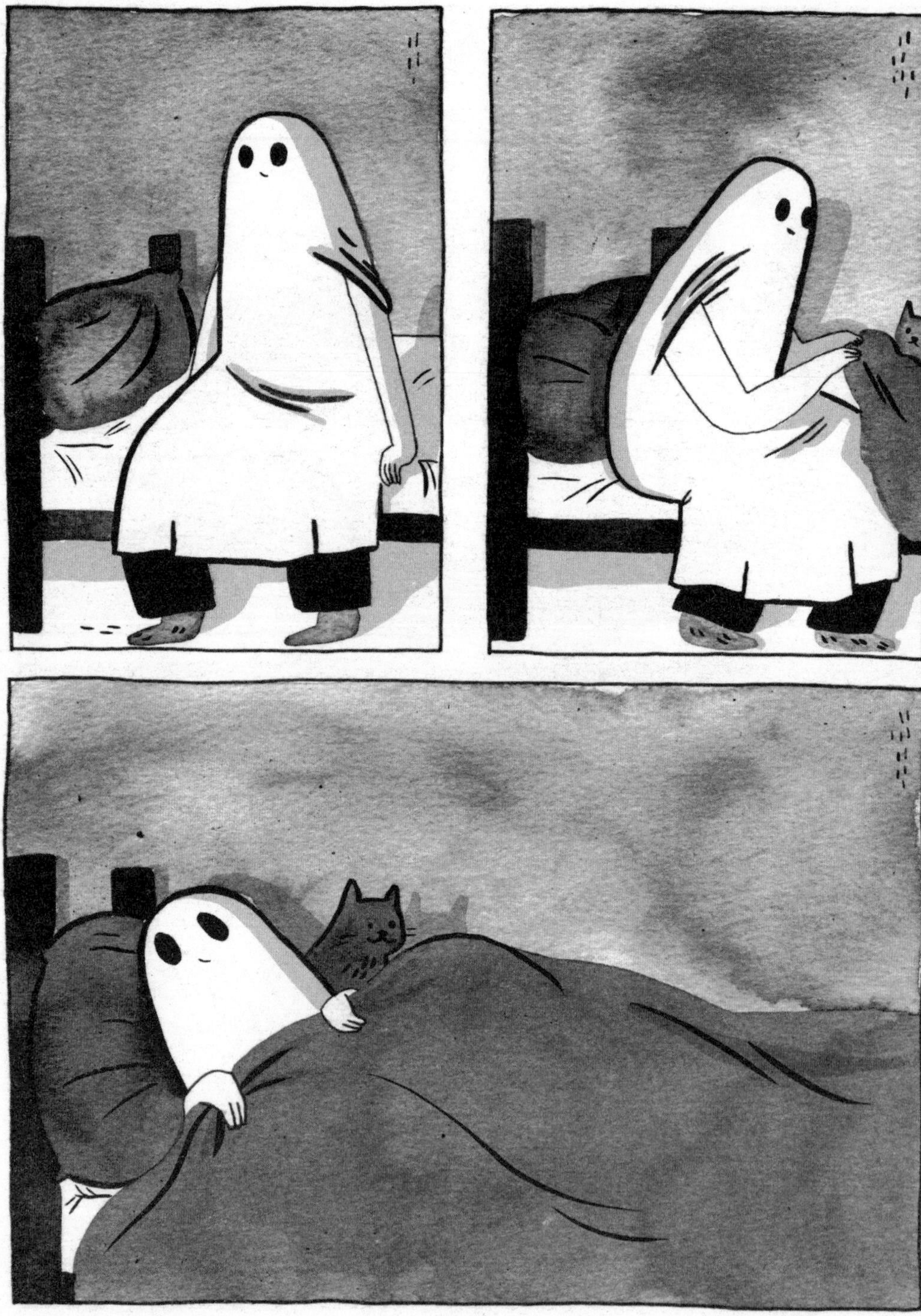

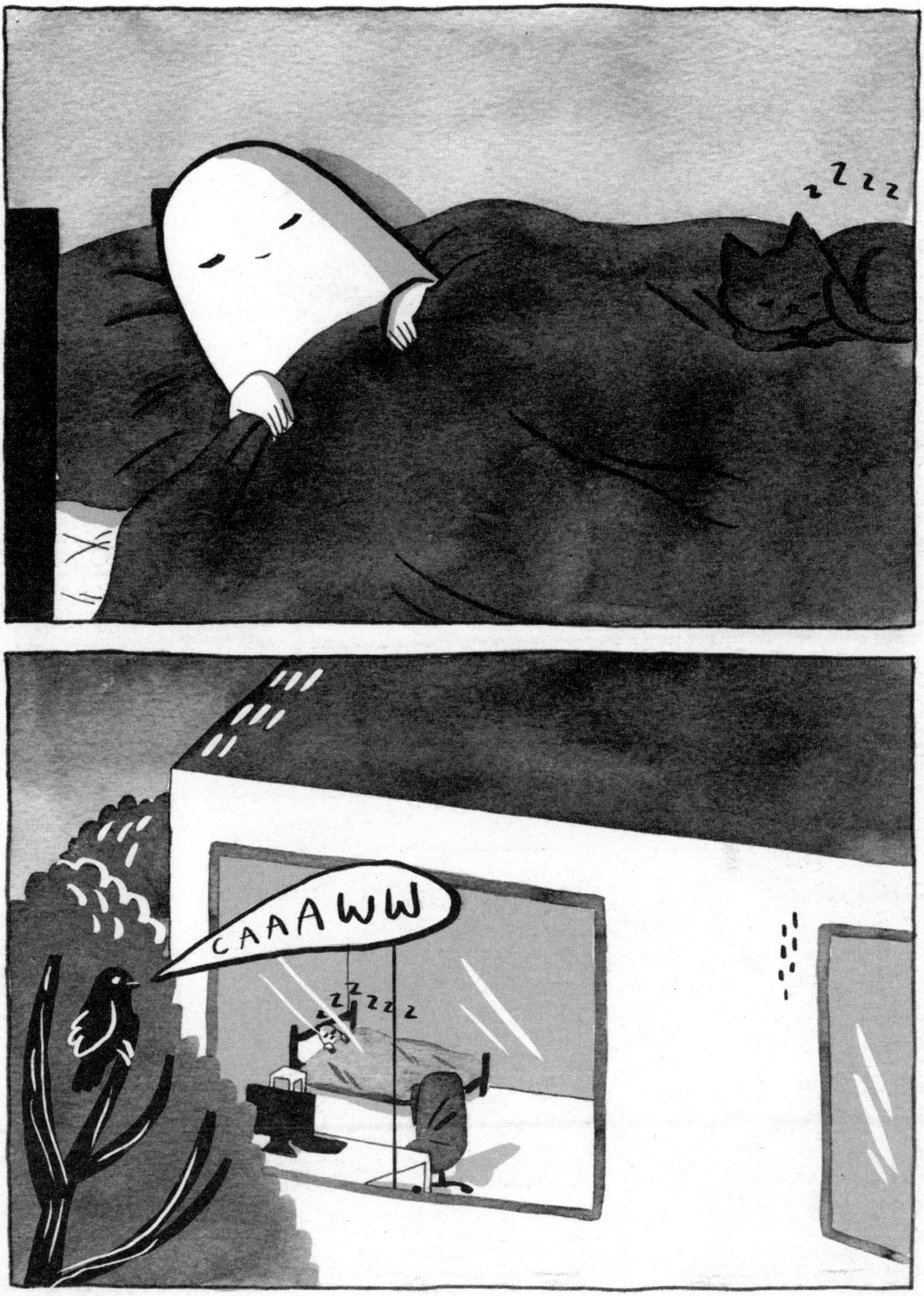
zzzz
CAAAWW
zzzzz

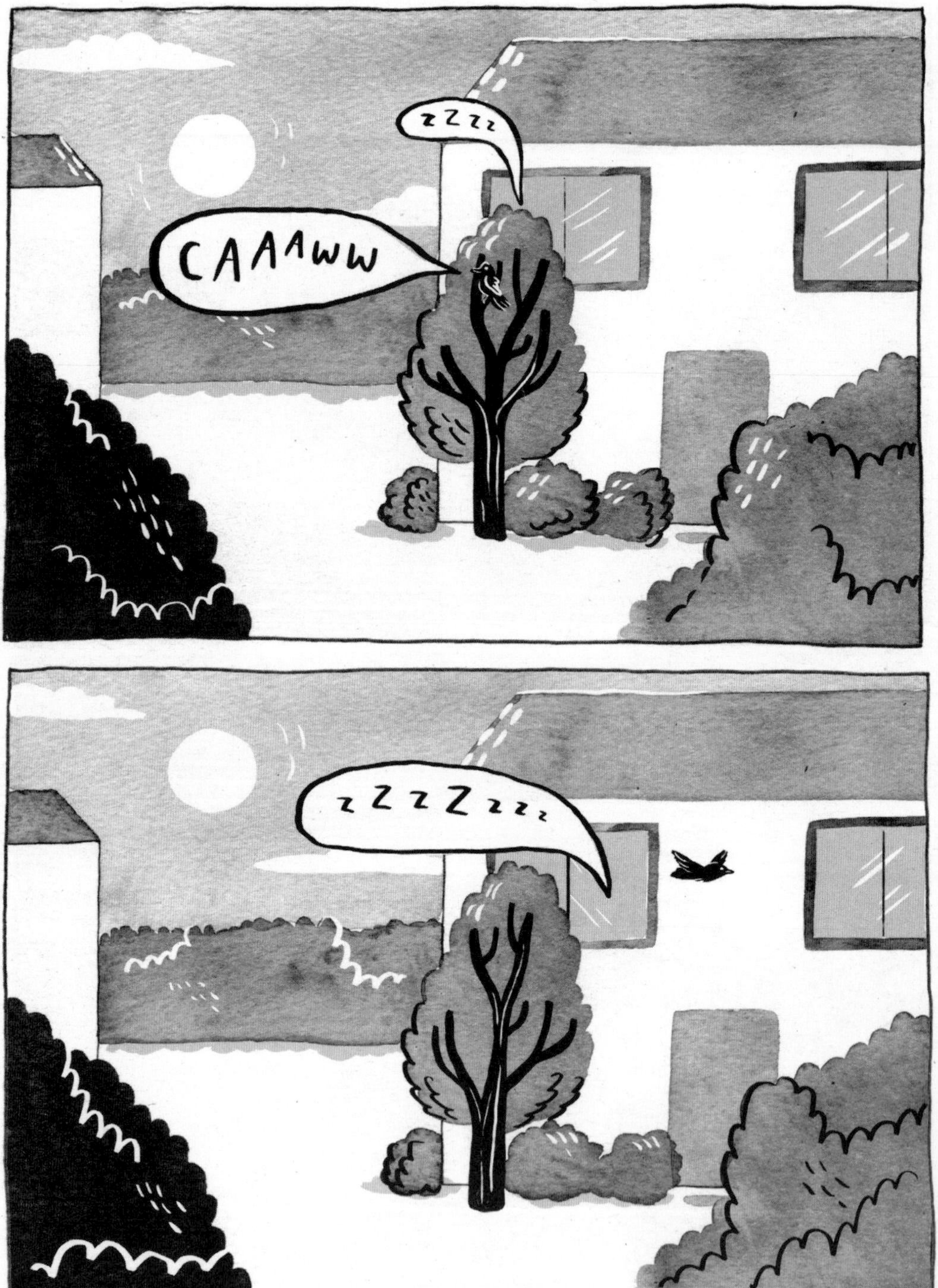
zZzz
CAAAWW
zZzZzzz

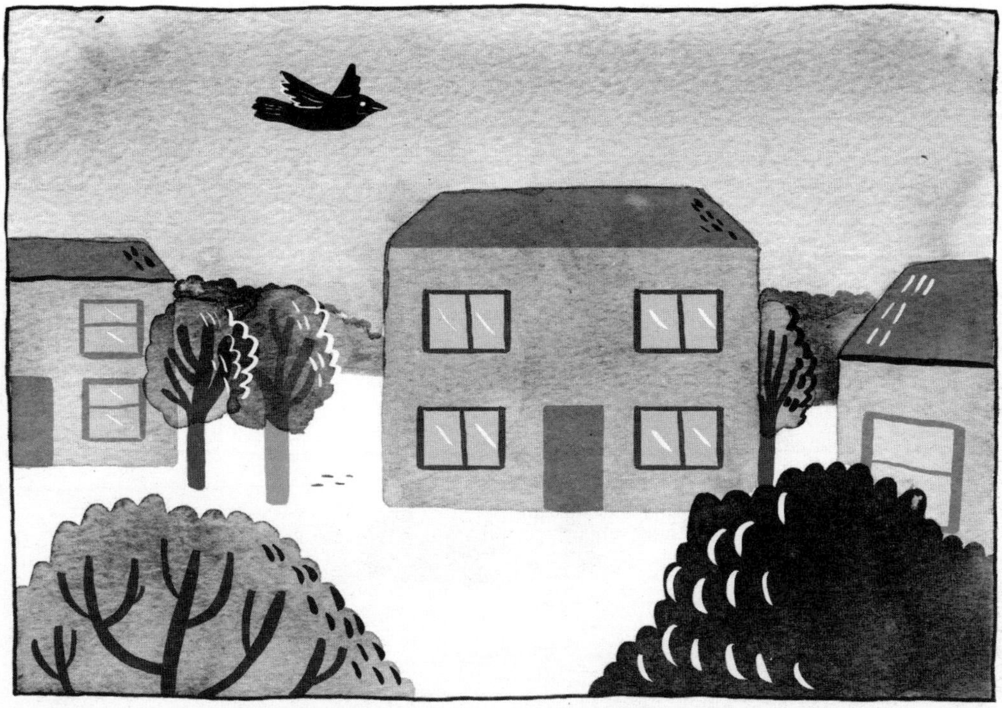

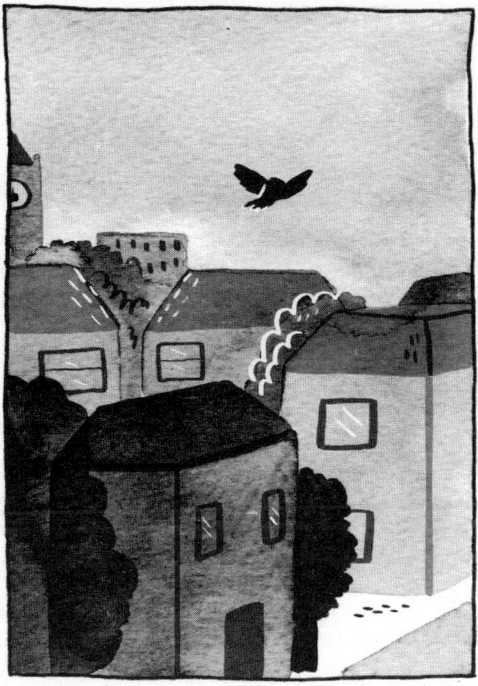

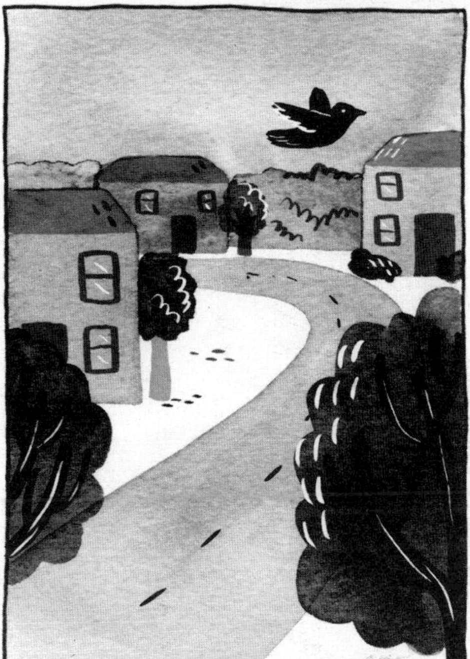

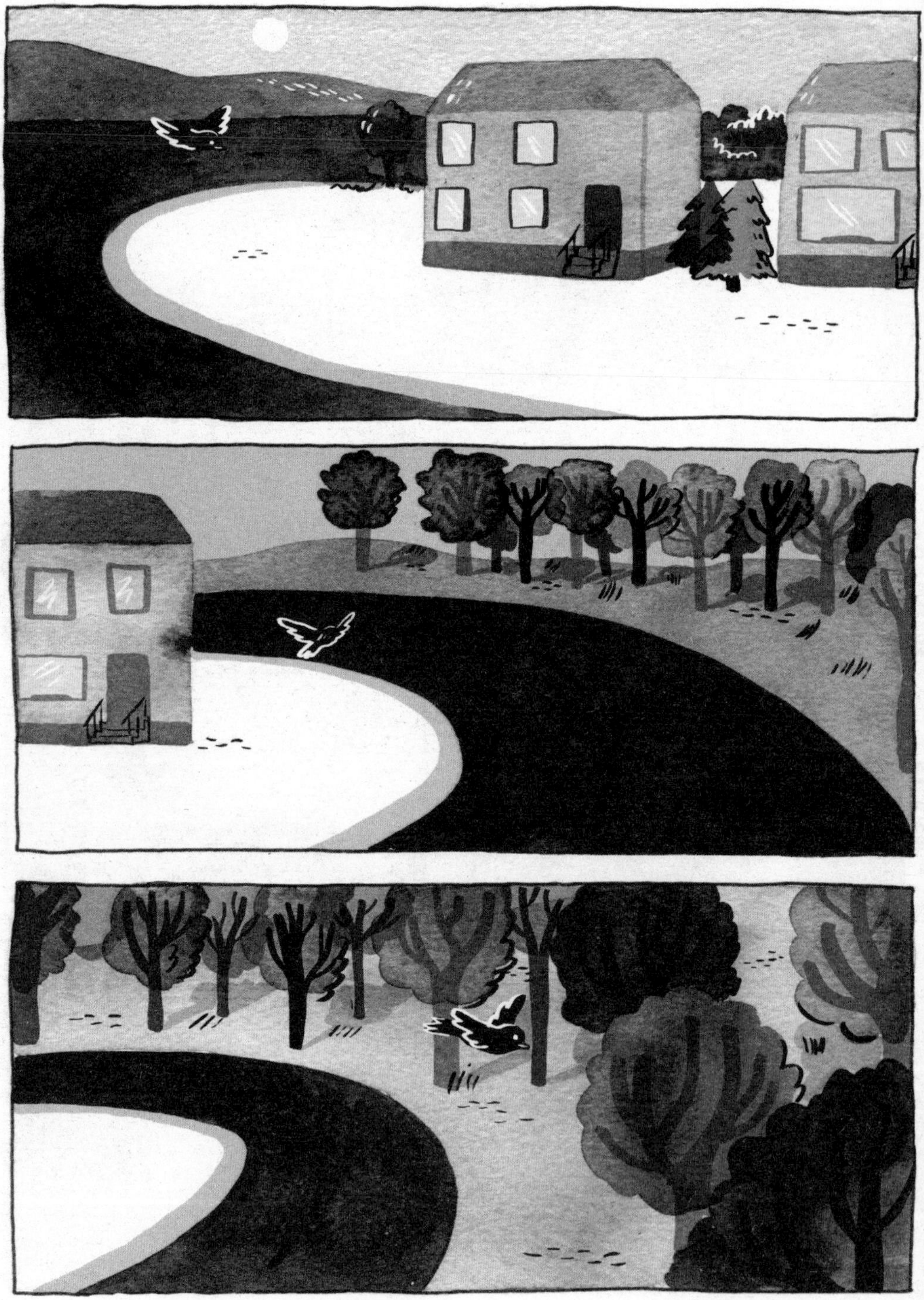

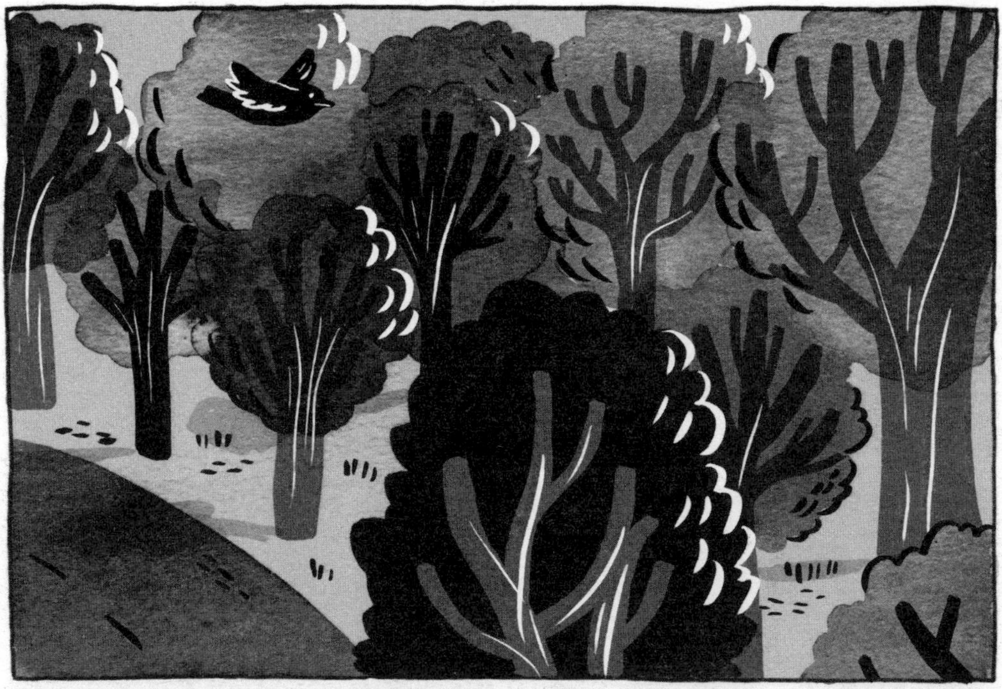

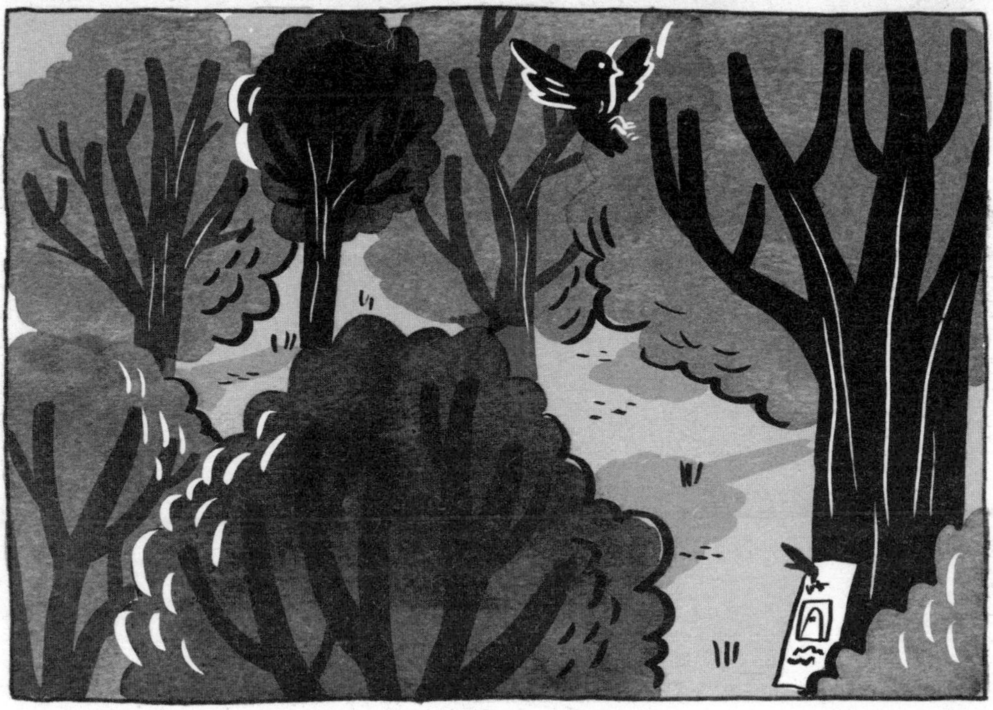

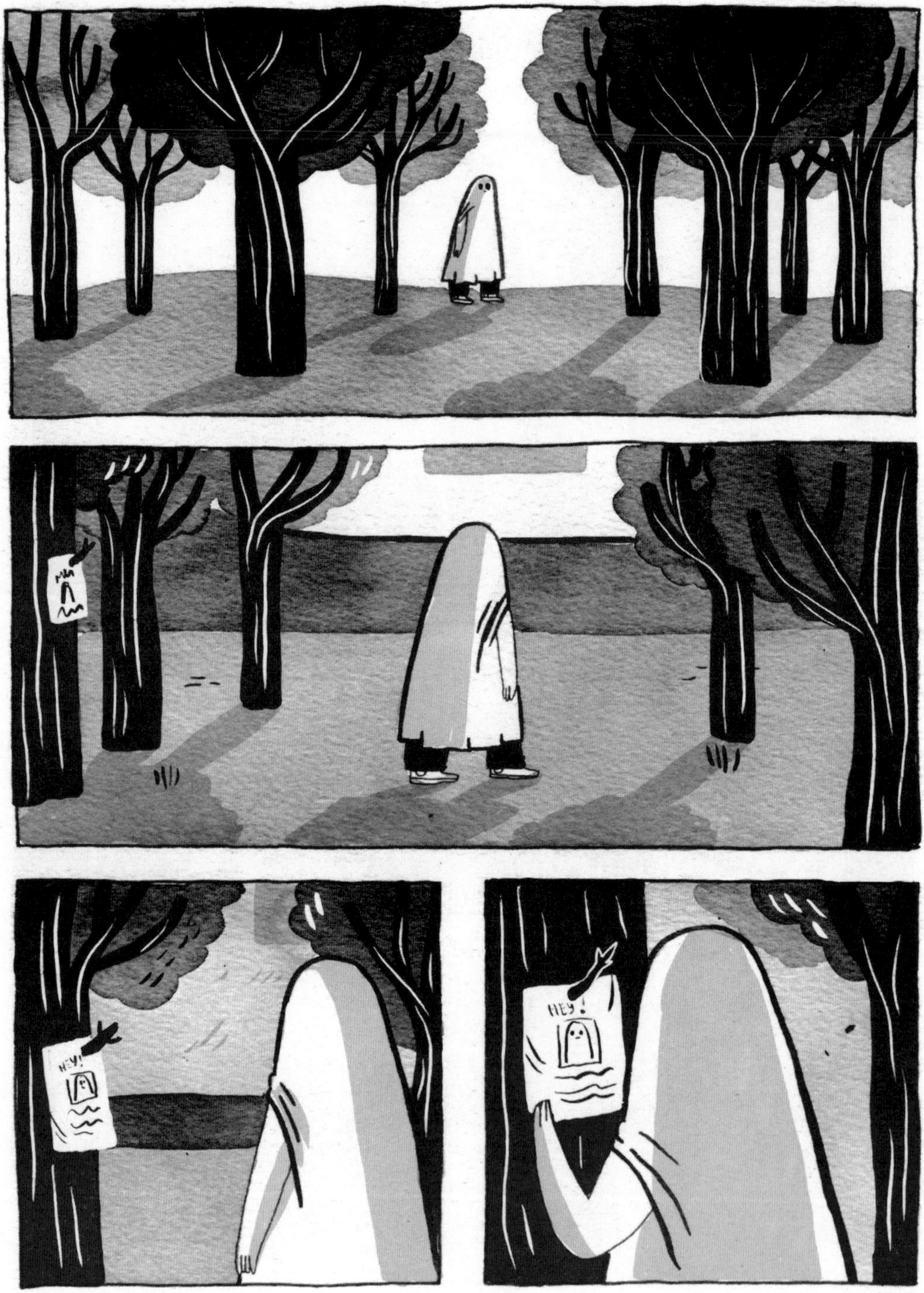
HEY!
HEY!

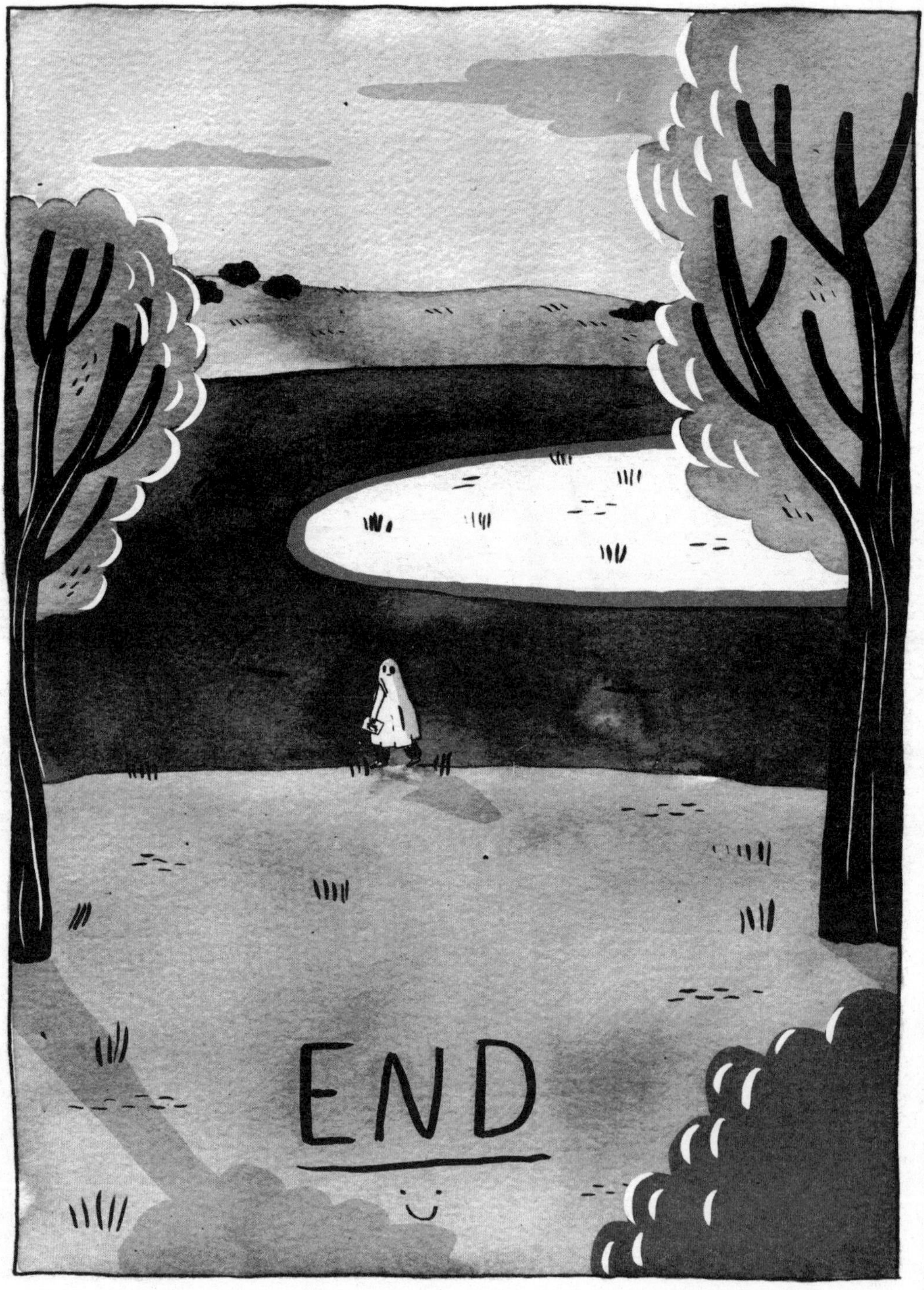
END

HEY!

IS THIS YOU?

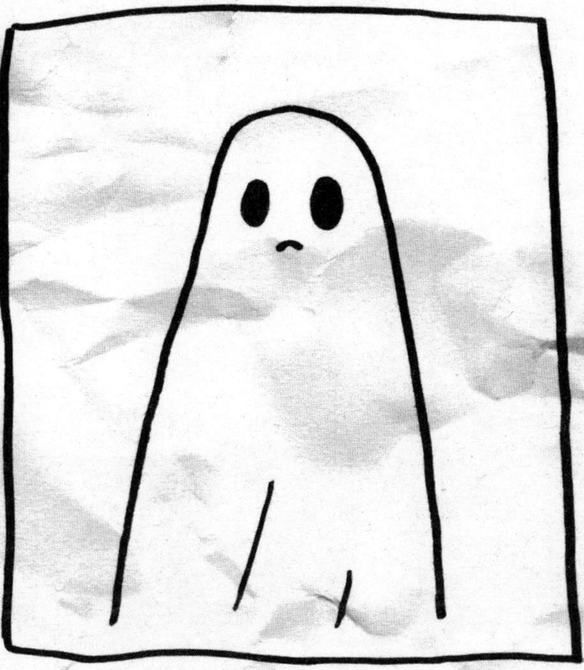

ARE YOU A SAD GHOST?
ME TOO! IF YOU WANT TO -
EMAIL ME
SADGHOSTSSTICKTOGETHER
@GMAIL.COM

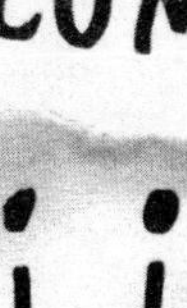

MEANWHILE...

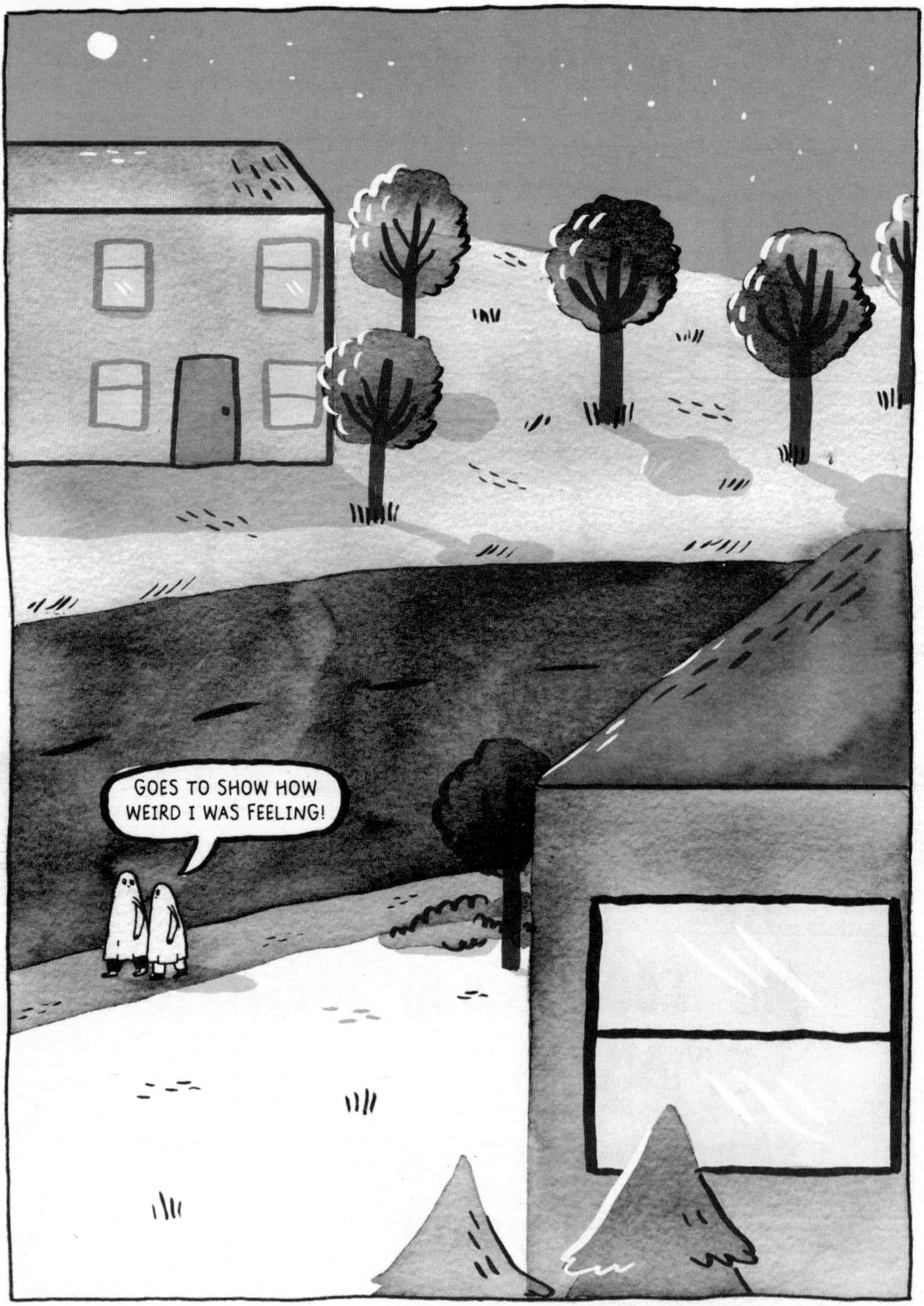
GOES TO SHOW HOW WEIRD I WAS FEELING!

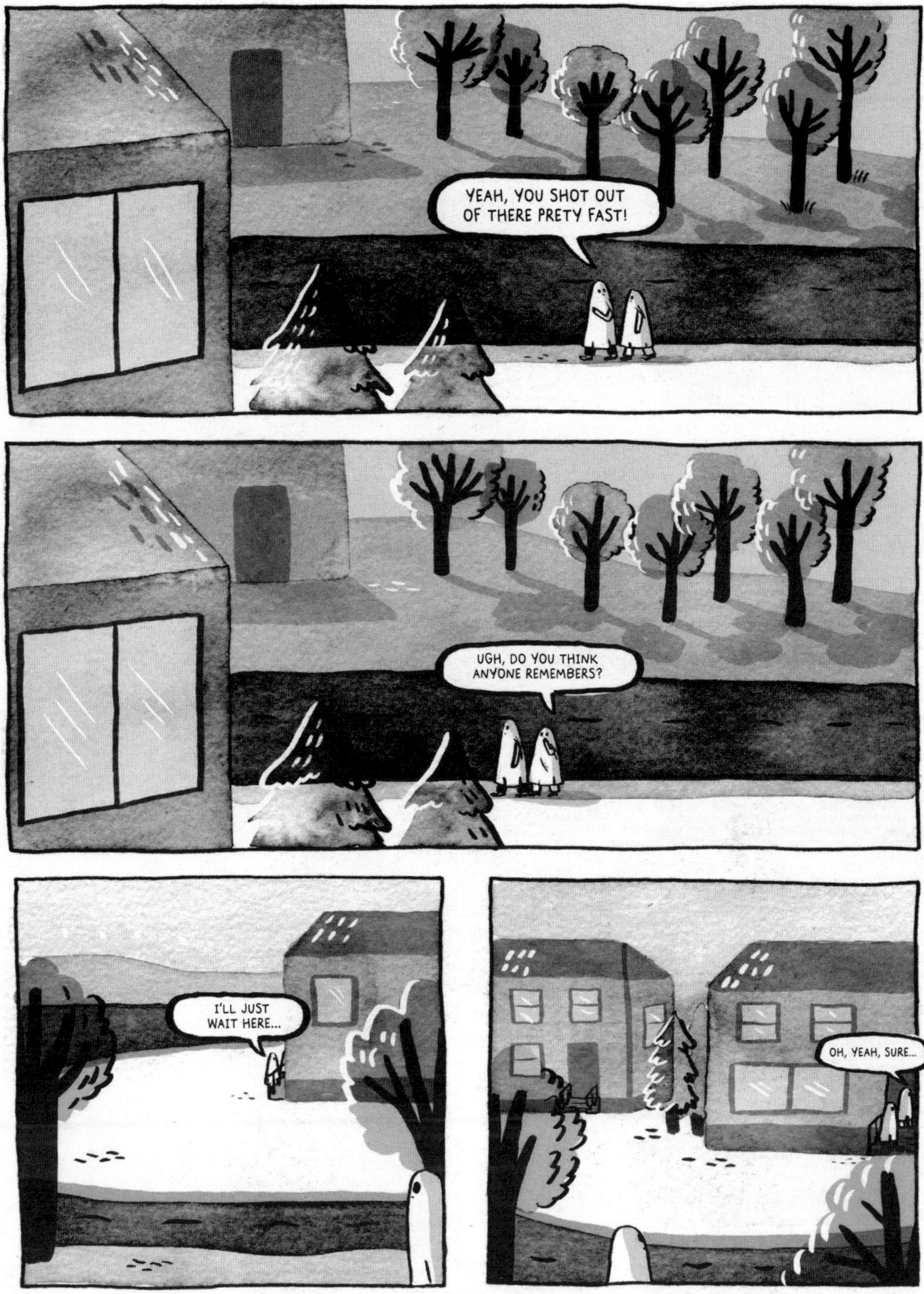
YEAH, YOU SHOT OUT OF THERE PRETY FAST!
UGH, DO YOU THINK ANYONE REMEMBERS?
I'LL JUST WAIT HERE...
OH, YEAH, SURE...

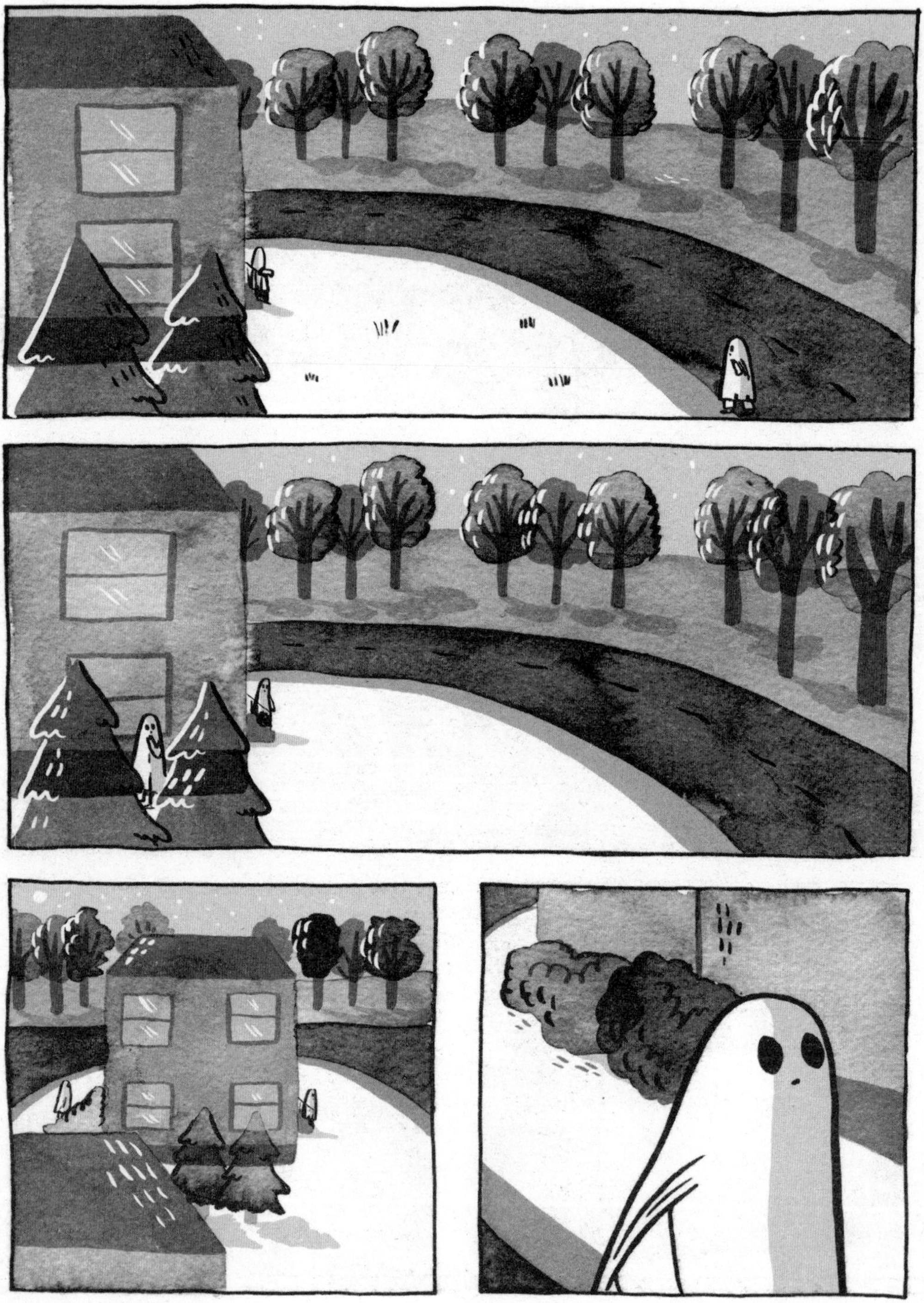

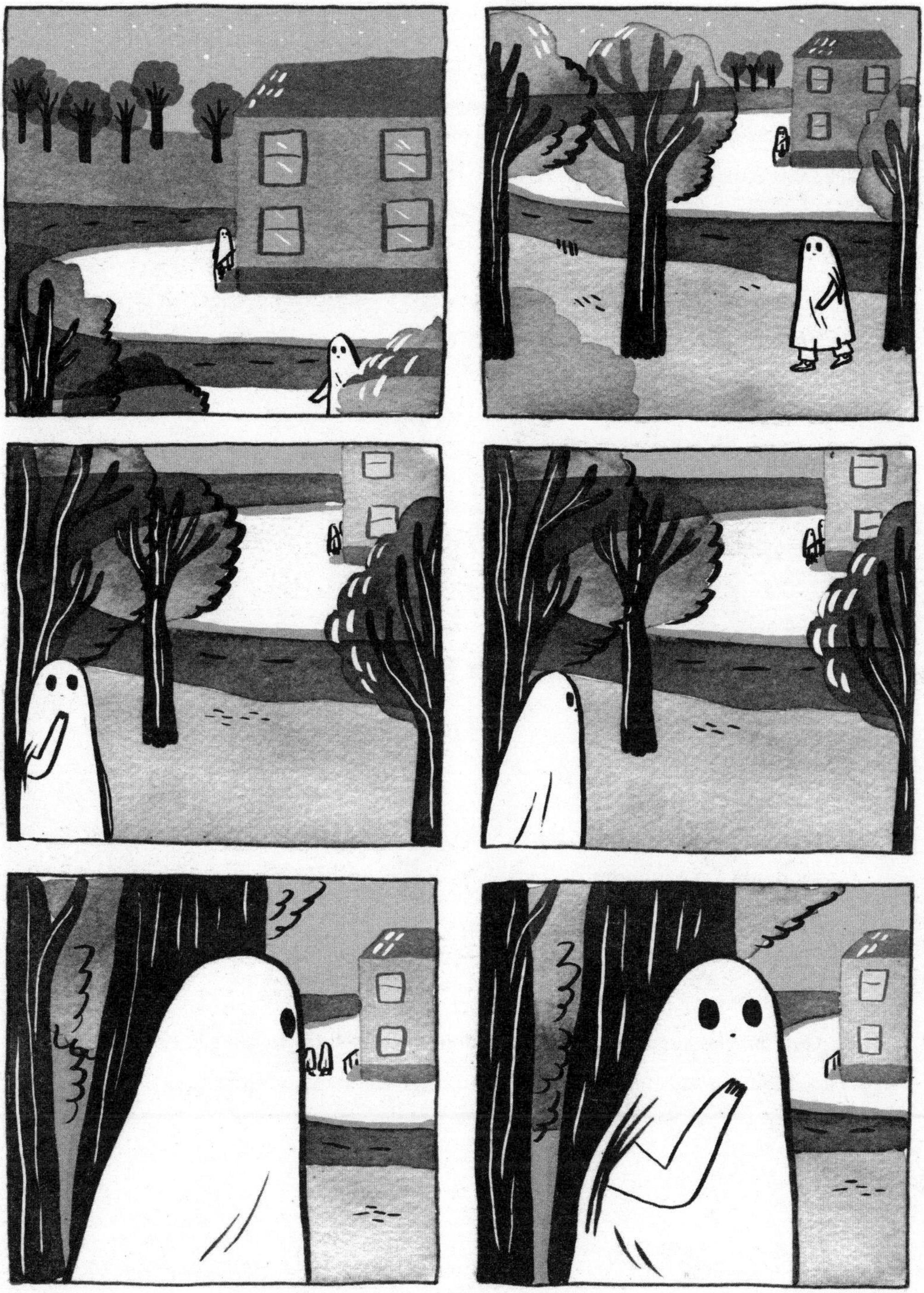

RESOURCES

ANXIETY UK

For those affected by anxiety, stress and anxiety-based depression.

anxietyuk.org.uk

CHILDLINE

A free, private and confidential service to help anyone under 19 in the UK with any issue they're going through.

childline.org.uk

MIND

Advice and support to anyone experiencing a mental health problem.

mind.org.uk

THE MIX.

A support service for young people.

themix.org.uk

NIGHTLINE

A listening, emotional support, information and supplies service, run by students for students.

nightline.ac.uk

PAPYRUS

Confidential support and advice to young people struggling with thoughts of suicide, and anyone worried about a young person.

papyrus-uk.org

SAMARITANS

For anyone who's struggling to cope, who needs someone to listen without judgement or pressure.

samaritans.org

SANEline

A national out-of-hours mental health helpline offering specialist emotional support, guidance and information to anyone affected by mental illness.

sane.org.uk/home

SHOUT 85258

A free, confidential, 24/7 text messaging support service for anyone who is struggling to cope.

giveusashout.org

SWITCHBOARD

A safe space for anyone to discuss anything, including sexuality, gender identity, sexual health and emotional well-being. Phone operators all identify as LGBT+.

switchboard.lgbt

THANK YOU TO EVERY SAD GHOST
OUT THERE, FOR MAKING THIS
GHOSTIE FEEL LESS ALONE.
SAD GHOSTS FOREVER.